***THE NOVEL THAT INSPIRED
THE CBS TELEVISION DRAMA!***

Praise for Stephen King and

UNDER THE DOME

An invisible prison holds an entire town captive in Stephen King's acclaimed #1 *New York Times* bestseller . . . his boldest novel since *The Stand*!

"It has the scope and flavor of literary Americana, even if King's particular patch of American turf is located smack in the middle of the Twilight Zone. . . . Tight and energetic from start to finish. . . . Hard as this thing is to hoist, it's even harder to put down."

—Janet Maslin, *The New York Times*

"Seven words: the best yet from the best ever. America's greatest living novelist delivers his masterpiece."

—Lee Child

"The sort of book for which the phrase 'page-turner' was coined."

—*The Miami Herald*

"A master storyteller having a whole lot of fun."

—*Los Angeles Times*

"Classic King, sure to please any fan."

—*Baltimore Sun*

In Chester's Mill, Maine, the destinies of everyday people will be decided . . . under the dome.

Dale "Barbie" Barbara: The decorated Iraq vet had plans that didn't include being a hero again. But a hero is just what Chester's Mill needs. **Big Jim Rennie, Sr.:** The used-car dealer turned politician intends to turn the isolated town into his personal fiefdom. **Julia Shumway:** The Republican newspaper publisher joins forces with Barbie and finds a strength she didn't know she had. **Joe McClatchey:** The thirteen-year-old "King of the Geeks" is smarter than anyone, and proves it in a crisis unlike any the world has ever witnessed.

"Wildly entertaining."

—*People* (3½ stars)

"One of his most powerful novels ever . . . and our stock of literature in the great American Gothic tradition is brilliantly replenished because of it. . . . Reveals King's greatest qualities as a writer. . . . Never once do we doubt the veracity of this large cast. The psychological insight into these small-town people is pin-sharp, vivid, and utterly convincing."

—*The Washington Post*

"Irresistibly compelling. . . . A nonstop thrill ride as well as a disturbing, moving meditation on our capacity for good and evil."

—*Publishers Weekly*

"Moves so fast and grips the reader so tightly that it's practically incapacitating."

—*New York Newsday*

"One of those works of fiction that successfully capture the national zeitgeist at this particularly strange and breathless period in American history. . . . Stephen King, at his best."

—The Associated Press

"An author whose continued and slightly frenzied commerce with his muse has been one of the more enthralling spectacles in American literature. . . . Writing flat-out seems to magnetize his imagination."

—*The New York Times Book Review*

STEPHEN KING

UNDER THE DOME

PART
ONE

POCKET BOOKS
New York   London   Toronto   Sydney   New Delhi

Pocket Books
A Division of Simon & Schuster, Inc.
1230 Avenue of the Americas
New York, NY 10020

First Pocket Books paperback edition March 2014

POCKET and colophon are registered trademarks of Simon & Schuster, Inc.

For information about special discounts for bulk purchases, please contact Simon & Schuster Special Sales at 1-866-506-1949 or business@simonandschuster.com.

The Simon & Schuster Speakers Bureau can bring authors to your live event. For more information or to book an event, contact the Simon & Schuster Speakers Bureau at 1-866-248-3049 or visit our website at www.simonspeakers.com.

Map by Paul J. Pugliese

Manufactured in the United States of America

10 9 8 7 6 5 4 3 2 1

ISBN: 978-1-4767-6727-7
ISBN: 978-1-4391-6803-5 (ebook)

In memory of Surendra Dahyabhai Patel.

We miss you, my friend.

Who you lookin for
What was his name
you can prob'ly find him
at the football game
it's a small town
you know what I mean
it's a small town, son
and we all support the team

—JAMES MCMURTRY

HEALTH CENTER

HOSPITAL

PRETTY VALLEY ROAD

119

CONGO CHURCH

PEACE BRIDGE

TOWN COMMON

RENNIE'S

117

TOWN HALL

PD

McCLATCHEY'S

MAIN STREET

RADIO STATION WCIK

CHRIST THE HOLY REDEEMER CHURCH

MOVIE THEATER (CLOSED)

BOOKSTORE

DEMOCRAT

SANDERS HOMETOWN DRUG

LITTLE BITCH ROAD

CHESTER'S MILL, MAINE

MOTTON ROAD

SOME (BUT NOT ALL) OF THOSE IN CHESTER'S MILL ON DOME DAY:

TOWN OFFICIALS

Andy Sanders, First Selectman
Jim Rennie, Second Selectman
Andrea Grinnell, Third Selectman

SWEETBRIAR ROSE STAFF

Rose Twitchell, Owner
Dale Barbara, Cook
Anson Wheeler, Dishwasher
Angie McCain, Waitress
Dodee Sanders, Waitress

POLICE DEPARTMENT

Howard "Duke" Perkins, Chief
Peter Randolph, Assistant Chief

Marty Arsenault, Officer
Freddy Denton, Officer
George Frederick, Officer
Rupert Libby, Officer
Toby Whelan, Officer
Jackie Wettington, Officer
Linda Everett, Officer
Stacey Moggin, Officer/Dispatch
Junior Rennie, Special Deputy
Georgia Roux, Special Deputy
Frank DeLesseps, Special Deputy
Melvin Searles, Special Deputy
Carter Thibodeau, Special Deputy

PASTORAL CARE

Reverend Lester Coggins, Christ the Holy Redeemer
   Church
Reverend Piper Libby, First Congregational Church

MEDICAL STAFF

Ron Haskell, Doctor
Rusty Everett, Physician's Assistant
Ginny Tomlinson, Nurse
Dougie Twitchell, Nurse
Gina Buffalino, Volunteer Nurse
Harriet Bigelow, Volunteer Nurse

TOWN KIDS

Little Walter Bushey
"Scarecrow" Joe McClatchey
Norrie Calvert
Benny Drake
Judy and Janelle Everett
Ollie and Rory Dinsmore

TOWNSPEOPLE OF NOTE

Tommy and Willow Anderson, Owner/Operators of
    Dipper's Roadhouse
Stewart and Fernald Bowie, Owner/Operators of
    Bowie Funeral Home
Joe Boxer, Dentist
Romeo Burpee, Owner/Operator of Burpee's
    Department Store
Phil Bushey, Chef of Dubious Repute
Samantha Bushey, His Wife
Jack Cale, Supermarket Manager
Ernie Calvert, Supermarket Manager (ret.)
Johnny Carver, Convenience Store Operator
Alden Dinsmore, Dairy Farmer
Roger Killian, Chicken Farmer
Lissa Jamieson, Town Librarian
Claire McClatchey, Scarecrow Joe's Mom
Alva Drake, Benny's Mom
Stubby Norman, Antique Dealer
Brenda Perkins, Chief Perkins's Wife
Julia Shumway, Owner/Editor of the Local
    Newspaper
Tony Guay, Sports Reporter

Pete Freeman, News Photographer
"Sloppy" Sam Verdreaux, Town Drunk

OUT-OF-TOWNERS

Alice and Aidan Appleton, Dome Orphans
    ("Dorphans")
Thurston Marshall, Literary Man with Medical Skills
Carolyn Sturges, Graduate Student

DOGS OF NOTE

Horace, Julia Shumway's Corgi
Clover, Piper Libby's German Shepherd
Audrey, the Everetts' Golden Retriever

THE AIRPLANE AND
THE WOODCHUCK

1

From two thousand feet, where Claudette Sanders was taking a flying lesson, the town of Chester's Mill gleamed in the morning light like something freshly made and just set down. Cars trundled along Main Street, flashing up winks of sun. The steeple of the Congo Church looked sharp enough to pierce the unblemished sky. The sun raced along the surface of Prestile Stream as the Seneca V overflew it, both plane and water cutting the town on the same diagonal course.

"Chuck, I think I see two boys beside the Peace Bridge! Fishing!" Her very delight made her laugh. The flying lessons were courtesy of her husband, who was the town's First Selectman. Although of the opinion that if God had wanted man to fly, He would have given him wings, Andy was an extremely coaxable man, and eventually Claudette had gotten her way. She had enjoyed the experience from the first. But this wasn't mere enjoyment; it was exhilaration. Today was the first time she had really understood what made flying great. What made it cool.

Chuck Thompson, her instructor, touched the control yoke gently, then pointed at the instrument panel. "I'm sure," he said, "but let's keep the shiny side up, Claudie, okay?"

"Sorry, sorry."

"Not at all." He had been teaching people to do this for years, and he liked students like Claudie, the ones who were eager to learn something new. She might cost Andy Sanders some real money before long; she loved the Seneca, and had expressed a desire to have one just like it, only new. That would run somewhere in the neighborhood of a million dollars. Although not exactly spoiled, Claudie Sanders had undeniably expensive tastes which, lucky man, Andy seemed to have no trouble satisfying.

Chuck also liked days like this: unlimited visibility, no wind, perfect teaching conditions. Nevertheless, the Seneca rocked slightly as she overcorrected.

"You're losing your happy thoughts. Don't do that. Come to one-twenty. Let's go out Route 119. And drop on down to nine hundred."

She did, the Seneca's trim once more perfect. Chuck relaxed.

They passed above Jim Rennie's Used Cars, and then the town was behind them. There were fields on either side of 119, and trees burning with color. The Seneca's cruciform shadow fled up the blacktop, one dark wing briefly brushing over an ant-man with a pack on his back. The ant-man looked up and waved. Chuck waved back, although he knew the guy couldn't see him.

"*Beautiful* goddam day!" Claudie exclaimed. Chuck laughed.

Their lives had another forty seconds to run.

2

The woodchuck came bumbling along the shoulder of Route 119, headed in the direction of Chester's Mill, although the town was still a mile and a half away and even Jim Rennie's Used Cars was only a series of twinkling sunflashes arranged in rows at the place where the highway curved to the left. The chuck planned (so far as a woodchuck can be said to plan anything) to head back into the woods long before he got that far. But for now, the shoulder was fine. He'd come farther from his burrow than he meant to, but the sun had been warm on his back and the smells were crisp in his nose, forming rudimentary images—not quite pictures—in his brain.

He stopped and rose on his back paws for an instant. His eyes weren't as good as they used to be, but good enough to make out a human up there, walking in his direction on the other shoulder.

The chuck decided he'd go a little farther anyway. Humans sometimes left behind good things to eat.

He was an old fellow, and a fat fellow. He had raided many garbage cans in his time, and knew the way to the Chester's Mill landfill as well as he knew the three tunnels of his own burrow; always good things to eat at the landfill. He waddled a complacent old fellow's waddle, watching the human walking on the other side of the road.

The man stopped. The chuck realized he had been spotted. To his right and just ahead was a fallen birch. He would hide under there, wait for the man to go by, then investigate for any tasty—

The chuck got that far in his thoughts—and another three waddling steps—although he had been cut in two. Then he fell apart on the edge of the road. Blood squirted and pumped; guts tumbled into the dirt; his rear legs kicked rapidly twice, then stopped.

His last thought before the darkness that comes to us all, chucks and humans alike: *What happened?*

3

All the needles on the control panel dropped dead.

"What the *hell*?" Claudie Sanders said. She turned to Chuck. Her eyes were wide, but there was no panic in them, only bewilderment. There was no time for panic.

Chuck never saw the control panel. He saw the Seneca's nose crumple toward him. Then he saw both propellers disintegrate.

There was no time to see more. No time for anything. The Seneca exploded over Route 119 and rained fire on the countryside. It also rained body parts. A smoking forearm—Claudette's—landed with a thump beside the neatly divided woodchuck.

It was October twenty-first.

BARBIE

Barbie started feeling better as soon as he passed Food City and left downtown behind. When he saw the sign reading YOU ARE LEAVING THE VILLAGE OF CHESTER'S MILL *COME BACK REAL SOON!*, he felt better still. He was glad to be on his way, and not just because he had taken a pretty good beating in The Mill. It was plain old moving on that had lightened him up. He had been walking around under his own little gray cloud for at least two weeks before getting his shit handed to him in the parking lot of Dipper's.

"Basically, I'm just a ramblin guy," he said, and laughed. "A ramblin guy on his way to the Big Sky." And hell, why not? Montana! Or Wyoming. Fucking Rapid City, South Dakota. Anyplace but here.

He heard an approaching engine, turned around— walking backward now—and stuck out his thumb. What he saw was a lovely combination: a dirty old Ford pickemup with a fresh young blonde behind the wheel. *Ash* blonde, his favorite blonde of all. Barbie offered his most engaging smile. The girl driving the pickemup responded with one of her own, and oh my Lord if she was a ticktock over nineteen, he'd eat his last paycheck from Sweetbriar Rose. Too young for a gentleman of thirty summers, no doubt, but perfectly street-legal, as they'd said back in the days of his cornfed Iowa youth.

The truck slowed, he started toward it . . . and then it sped up again. She gave him one more brief look as she went past. The smile was still on her face, but it had turned regretful. *I had a brain-cramp there for a minute,* the smile said, *but now sanity has reasserted itself.*

And Barbie thought he recognized her a little, although it was impossible to say with certainty; Sunday mornings in Sweetbriar were always a madhouse. But he thought he'd seen her with an older man, probably her dad, both of them with their faces mostly buried in sections of the Sunday *Times.* If he could have spoken to her as she rolled past, Barbie would have said: *If you trusted me to cook your sausage and eggs, surely you can trust me for a few miles in the shotgun seat.*

But of course he didn't get the chance, so he simply raised his hand in a little no-offense-taken salute. The truck's taillights flickered, as if she were reconsidering. Then they went out and the truck sped up.

During the following days, as things in The Mill started going from bad to worse, he would replay this little moment in the warm October sun again and again. It was that second reconsidering flicker of the taillights he thought of . . . as if she had recognized him, after all. *That's the cook from Sweetbriar Rose, I'm almost sure. Maybe I ought to—*

But *maybe* was a gulf better men than him had fallen into. If she *had* reconsidered, everything in his life thereafter would have changed. Because she must have made it out; he never saw the fresh-faced blonde or the dirty old Ford F-150 again. She must have crossed over the Chester's Mill town line minutes (or even seconds) before the border slammed shut. If he'd been with her, he would have been out and safe.

Unless, of course, he'd think later, when sleep wouldn't come, *the stop to pick me up was just long enough to be* too *long. In that case, I probably still wouldn't be here. And neither would she. Because the speed limit out that way on 119 is fifty miles an hour. And at fifty miles an hour . . .*

At this point he would always think of the plane.

2

The plane flew over him just after he passed Jim Rennie's Used Cars, a place for which Barbie had no love. Not that he'd bought a lemon there (he hadn't owned a car in over a year, had sold the last one in Punta Gorda, Florida). It was just that Jim Rennie Jr. had been one of the fellows that night in Dipper's parking lot. A frat boy with something to prove, and what he could not prove alone he would prove as part of a group. That was the way the Jim Juniors of the world did business, in Barbie's experience.

But it was behind him now. Jim Rennie's, Jim Junior, Sweetbriar Rose (Fried Clams Our Specialty! Always *"Whole"* Never *"Strips"*), Angie McCain, Andy Sanders. The whole deal, including Dipper's. (Beatings Administered in the Parking Lot Our Specialty!) All behind him. And ahead of him? Why, the gates of America. Goodbye smalltown Maine, hello Big Sky.

Or maybe, hell, he'd head down south again. No matter how beautiful this particular day, winter was lurking a page or two over on the calendar. The south might be good. He'd never been to Muscle Shoals, and he liked the sound of the name. That was goddam poetry, Muscle Shoals was, and the idea so cheered him that when he heard the little plane approaching, he looked up and gave a big old exuberant wave. He hoped for a wing-waggle in return, but didn't get one, although the plane was slow-poking at low altitude. Barbie's guess was sightseers—this was a day for them, with the trees in full flame—or maybe some young kid on his learner's permit, too worried about screwing up to bother with groundlings like Dale Barbara. But he wished them well. Sightseers or a kid still six weeks from his first solo cruise, Barbie wished them very well. It was a good day, and every step away from Chester's Mill made it better. Too many assholes in The Mill, and besides: travel was good for the soul.

Maybe moving on in October should be a law, he thought. *New national motto: EVERYBODY LEAVES IN OCTOBER. You get your Packing Permit in August, give your required week's notice in mid-September, then—*

He stopped. Not too far ahead of him, on the other side of the blacktop highway, was a woodchuck. A damned fat one. Sleek and sassy, too. Instead of scurrying off into the high grass, it was coming on ahead. There was a fallen birch sticking its top half out onto the shoulder of the road, and Barbie was betting the woodchuck would scurry under there and wait for the big bad Two-Legs to go by. If not, they would pass each other like the ramblin guys they were, the one on four legs headed north, the one on two headed south. Barbie hoped that would happen. It would be cool.

These thoughts went through Barbie's mind in seconds; the shadow of the airplane was still between him and the chuck, a black cross racing along the highway. Then two things happened almost simultaneously.

The first was the woodchuck. It was whole, then it was in two pieces. Both were twitching and bleeding. Barbie stopped, mouth hanging open on the suddenly lax hinge of his lower jaw. It was as if an invisible guillotine blade had dropped. And that was when, directly above the sev-ered woodchuck, the little airplane exploded.

3

Barbie looked up. Falling from the sky was a squashed Bizarro World version of the pretty little airplane that had passed over him seconds before. Twisting orange-red petals of fire hung above it in the air, a flower that was still opening, an American Disaster rose. Smoke billowed from the plummeting plane.

Something clanged to the road and sprayed up clods of asphalt before spinning drunkenly into the high grass to the left. A propeller.

If that had bounced my way—

Barbie had a brief image of being cut in two—like the unfortunate woodchuck—and turned to run. Something thudded down in front of him and he screamed. But it wasn't the other propeller; it was a man's leg dressed in denim. He could see no blood, but the side-seam had been blown wide open, revealing white flesh and wiry black hair.

There was no foot attached.

Barbie ran in what felt like slow motion. He saw one of his own feet, clad in an old scuffed workboot, stride out and clop down. Then it disappeared behind him as his other foot strode out. All slow, slow. Like watching the baseball replay of a guy trying to steal second.

There was a tremendous hollow clang from behind him, followed by the boom of a secondary explosion, followed by a blast of heat that struck him from heels to nape. It shoved him on his way like a warm hand. Then all thoughts blew away and there was nothing but the body's brute need to survive.

Dale Barbara ran for his life.

4

A hundred yards or so down the road, the big warm hand became a ghost hand, although the smell of burning gas—plus a sweeter stench that had to be a mixture of melting plastic and roasting flesh—was strong, carried to him on a light breeze. Barbie ran another sixty yards, then stopped and turned around. He was panting. He didn't think it was the running; he didn't smoke, and he was in good shape (well . . . fair; his ribs on the right side still hurt from the beating in Dipper's parking lot). He thought it was terror and dismay. He could have been killed by falling pieces of airplane—not just the runaway propeller—or burned to death. It was only blind luck that he hadn't been.

Then he saw something that made his rapid breathing stop in mid-gasp. He straightened up, looking back at the site of the accident. The road was littered with debris—it really was a wonder that he hadn't been struck and at least wounded. A twisted wing lay on the right; the other wing was poking out of the uncut timothy grass on the left, not far from where the runaway propeller had come to rest. In addition to the bluejeans-clad leg, he could see a severed hand and arm. The hand seemed to be pointing at a head, as if to say *That's mine.* A woman's head, judging from the hair. The power lines running beside the highway had been severed. They lay crackling and twisting on the shoulder.

Beyond the head and arm was the twisted tube of the airplane's fuselage. Barbie could read **NJ3.** If there was more, it was torn away.

But none of this was what had caught his eye and stopped his breath. The Disaster rose was gone now, but there was still fire in the sky. Burning fuel, certainly. But . . .

But it was running down the air in a thin sheet. Beyond it and through it, Barbie could see the Maine countryside—still peaceful, not yet reacting, but in motion nevertheless. Shimmering like the air over an incinerator or a burning-barrel. It was as if someone had splashed gasoline over a pane of glass and then set it alight.

Almost hypnotized—that was what it felt like, anyway—Barbie started walking back toward the scene of the crash.

5

His first impulse was to cover the body parts, but there were too many. Now he could see another leg (this one in green slacks), and a female torso caught in a clump of juniper. He could pull off his shirt and drape it over the woman's head, but after that? Well, there were two extra shirts in his backpack—

Here came a car from the direction of Motton, the next town to the south. One of the smaller SUVs, and moving fast. Someone had either heard the crash or seen the flash. Help. Thank God for help. Straddling the white line and standing well clear of the fire that was still running down from the sky in that weird water-on-a-windowpane way, Barbie waved his arms over his head, crossing them in big Xs.

The driver honked once in acknowledgment, then slammed on his brakes, laying forty feet of rubber. He was out almost before his little green Toyota had stopped, a big, rangy fellow with long gray hair cascading out from under a Sea Dogs baseball cap. He ran toward the side of the road, meaning to skirt the main firefall.

"What happened?" he cried. "What in the blue fu—"

Then he struck something. Hard. There was nothing there, but Barbie saw the guy's nose snap to the side as it broke. The man rebounded from the nothing, bleeding from the mouth, nose, and forehead. He fell on his back, then struggled to a sitting position. He stared at Barbie with dazed, wondering eyes as blood from his nose and mouth cascaded down the front of his workshirt, and Barbie stared back.

JUNIOR AND ANGIE

1

The two boys fishing near the Peace Bridge didn't look up when the plane flew overhead, but Junior Rennie did. He was a block farther down, on Prestile Street, and he recognized the sound. It was Chuck Thompson's Seneca V. He looked up, saw the plane, then dropped his head fast when the bright sunlight shining through the trees sent a bolt of agony in through his eyes. Another headache. He'd been having a lot of them lately. Sometimes the medication killed them. Sometimes, especially in the last three or four months, it didn't.

Migraines, Dr. Haskell said. All Junior knew was that they hurt like the end of the world, and bright light made them worse, especially when they were hatching. Sometimes he thought of the ants he and Frank DeLesseps had burned up when they were just kids. You used a magnifying glass and focused the sun on them as they crawled in and out of their hill. The result was fricasseed formicants. Only these days, when one of his headaches was hatching, his brain was the anthill and his eyes turned into twin magnifying glasses.

He was twenty-one. Did he have this to look forward to until he was forty-five or so, when Dr. Haskell said they might let up?

Maybe. But this morning a headache wasn't going to

stop him. The sight of Henry McCain's 4Runner or La-Donna McCain's Prius in the driveway might have; in that case he might've turned around, gone back to his own house, taken another Imitrex, and lain down in his bedroom with the shades drawn and a cool washcloth on his forehead. Possibly feeling the pain start to diminish as the headache derailed, but probably not. Once those black spiders really got a foothold—

He looked up again, this time squinting his eyes against the hateful light, but the Seneca was gone, and even the buzz of its engine (also aggravating—all sounds were aggravating when he was getting one of these bitch-kitties) was fading. Chuck Thompson with some flyboy or flygirl wannabe. And although Junior had nothing against Chuck—hardly knew him—he wished with sudden, childish ferocity that Chuck's pupil would fuck up bigtime and crash the plane.

Preferably in the middle of his father's car dealership.

Another sickish throb of pain twisted through his head, but he went up the steps to the McCains' door anyway. This had to be done. This was over-fucking-due. Angie needed a lesson.

But just a little one. Don't let yourself get out of control.

As if summoned, his mother's voice replied. Her maddeningly complacent voice. *Junior was always a bad-tempered boy, but he keeps it under much better control now. Don't you, Junior?*

Well. Gee. He *had*, anyway. Football had helped. But now there was no football. Now there wasn't even college. Instead, there were the headaches. And they made him feel like one mean motherfucker.

Don't let yourself get out of control.

No. But he would talk to her, headache or no head-ache.

And, as the old saying was, he just might have to talk to her by hand. Who knew? Making Angie feel worse might make him feel better.

Junior rang the bell.

2

Angie McCain was just out of the shower. She slipped on a robe, belted it, then wrapped a towel around her wet hair. "Coming!" she called as she not-quite-trotted down the stairs to the first floor. There was a little smile on her face. It was Frankie, she was quite sure it must be Frankie. Things were finally coming rightside up. The bastardly short-order cook (good-looking but still a bastard) had either left town or was leaving, and her parents were out. Combine the two and you got a sign from God that things were coming rightside up. She and Frankie could put all the crap in the rearview and get back together.

She knew exactly how to handle it: open the door and then open her robe. Right there in the Saturday-morning daylight, where anybody passing might see her. She'd make sure it was Frankie first, of course—she had no intention of flashing fat old Mr. Wicker if he'd rung the bell with a package or a registered mail—but it was at least half an hour too early for the mail.

No, it was Frankie. She was sure.

She opened the door, the little smile widening to a welcoming grin—perhaps not fortunate, since her teeth were rather crammed together and the size of jumbo Chiclets. One hand was on the tie of her robe. But she didn't pull it. Because it wasn't Frankie. It was Junior, and he looked so *angry*—

She had seen his black look before—many times, in

fact—but never this black since eighth grade, when Junior broke the Dupree kid's arm. The little fag had dared to swish his bubble-butt onto the town common basketball court and ask to play. And she supposed Junior must have had the same thunderstorm on his face that night in Dipper's parking lot, but of course she hadn't been there, she had only heard about it. Everybody in The Mill had heard about it. She'd been called in to talk to Chief Perkins, that damn Barbie had been there, and eventually that had gotten out, too.

"Junior? Junior, what—"

Then he slapped her, and thinking pretty much ceased.

3

He didn't get much into that first one, because he was still in the doorway and there wasn't much room to swing; he could only draw his arm back to half-cock. He might not have hit her at all (at least not to start with) had she not been flashing a grin—God, those *teeth,* they'd given him the creeps even in grammar school—and if she hadn't called him Junior.

Of course *everyone* in town called him Junior, he thought of *himself* as Junior, but he hadn't realized how much he hated it, how much he hoped-to-die-in-a-maggot-pie *hated* it until he heard it come bolting out from between the spooky tombstone teeth of the bitch who had caused him so much trouble. The sound of it went through his head like the sunglare when he'd looked up to see the plane.

But as slaps from half-cock go, this one wasn't bad. She went stumbling backward against the newel post of the stairway and the towel flew off her hair. Wet brown

snaggles hung around her cheeks, making her look like
Medusa. The smile had been replaced by a look of stunned
surprise, and Junior saw a trickle of blood running from
the corner of her mouth. That was good. That was fine.
The bitch deserved to bleed for what she had done. So
much *trouble,* not just for him but for Frankie and Mel
and Carter, too.

His mother's voice in his head: *Don't let yourself get out of
control, honey.* She was dead and still wouldn't stop giving
advice. *Teach her a lesson, but make it a little one.*

And he really might have managed to do that, but then
her robe came open and she was naked underneath it. He
could see the dark patch of hair over her breeding-farm,
her goddam itchy breeding-farm that was all the fucking
trouble, when you got right down to it those farms were
all the fucking trouble in the *world,* and his head was
throbbing, thudding, whamming, smashing, splitting. It
felt like it was going to go thermonuclear at any moment.
A perfect little mushroom cloud would shoot out of each
ear just before everything exploded above the neck, and
Junior Rennie (who didn't know he had a brain tumor—
wheezy old Dr. Haskell had never even considered the
possibility, not in an otherwise healthy young man hardly
out of his teens) went crazy. It wasn't a lucky morning for
Claudette Sanders or Chuck Thompson; in point of fact,
it wasn't a lucky morning for anyone in Chester's Mill.

But few were as unlucky as the ex-girlfriend of Frank
DeLesseps.

4

She *did* have two more semi-coherent thoughts as she
leaned against the newel post and looked at his bulging

eyes and the way he was biting his tongue—biting it so hard his teeth sunk into it.

He's crazy. I have to call the police before he really hurts me.

She turned to run down the front hall to the kitchen, where she would pull the handset off the wall phone, punch 911, and then just start screaming. She got two steps, then stumbled on the towel she'd wrapped around her hair. She regained her balance quickly—she had been a cheerleader in high school and those skills hadn't left her—but it was still too late. Her head snapped back and her feet flew out in front of her. He had grabbed her by her hair.

He yanked her against his body. He was baking, as if with a high fever. She could feel his heartbeat: quick-quick, running away with itself.

"You lying bitch!" he screamed directly into her ear. It sent a spike of pain deep into her head. She screamed herself, but the sound seemed faint and inconsequential compared to his. Then his arms were wrapped around her waist and she was being propelled down the hall at a manic speed, nothing but her toes touching the carpet. Something went through her mind about being the hood ornament on a runaway car, and then they were in the kitchen, which was filled with brilliant sunshine.

Junior screamed again. This time not with rage but pain.

5

The light was killing him, it was frying his howling brains, but he didn't let it stop him. Too late for that now.

He ran her straight into the Formica-topped kitchen table without slowing. It struck her in the stomach, then slid and slammed into the wall. The sugar bowl and the salt and pepper went flying. Her breath escaped her in a big woofing sound. Holding her around the waist with one hand and by the wet snaggles of her hair with the other, Junior whirled her and threw her against the Cold-spot. She struck it with a bang that knocked off most of the fridge magnets. Her face was dazed and paper-pale. Now she was bleeding from her nose as well as her lower lip. The blood was brilliant against her white skin. He saw her eyes shift toward the butcher block filled with knives on the counter, and when she tried to rise, he brought his knee into the center of her face, hard. There was a muffled crunching sound, as if someone had dropped a big piece of china—a platter, maybe—in another room.

It's what I should have done to Dale Barbara, he thought, and stepped back with the heels of his palms pressed against his throbbing temples. Tears from his watering eyes spilled down his cheeks. He had bitten his tongue badly—blood was streaming down his chin and pattering on the floor—but Junior wasn't aware of it. The pain in his head was too intense.

Angie lay facedown among the fridge magnets. The largest said **WHAT GOES IN YOUR MOUTH TODAY SHOWS UP ON YOUR ASS TOMORROW.** He thought she was out, but all at once she began to shiver all over. Her fingers trembled as if she were preparing to play something complex on the piano. (*Only instrument this bitch ever played is the skinflute,* he thought.) Then her legs began to crash up and down, and her arms followed suit. Now Angie looked like she was trying to swim away from him. She was having a goddam seizure.

"Stop it!" he shouted. Then, as she voided herself: "Stop it! *Stop doing that, you bitch!*"

He dropped on his knees, one on each side of her head,

which was now bobbing up and down. Her forehead repeatedly smacked the tile, like one of those camel jockeys saluting Allah.

"Stop it! *Fucking stop it!*"

She began to make a growling noise. It was surprisingly loud. Christ, what if someone heard her? What if he got caught here? This wouldn't be like explaining to his father why he'd left school (a thing Junior had not as yet been able to bring himself to do). This time it would be worse than having his monthly allowance cut by seventy-five percent because of that goddam fight with the cook—the fight *this* useless bitch had instigated. This time Big Jim Rennie wouldn't be able to talk Chief Perkins and the local fuzznuts around. This could be—

A picture of Shawshank State Prison's brooding green walls suddenly popped into his mind. He couldn't go there, he had his whole life ahead of him. But he would. Even if he shut her up now, he would. Because she'd talk later. And her face—which looked a lot worse than Barbie's had after the fight in the parking lot—would talk for her.

Unless he shut her up completely.

Junior seized her by the hair and helped her wham her head against the tiles. He was hoping it would knock her out so he could finish doing . . . well, whatever . . . but the seizure only intensified. She began beating her feet against the Coldspot, and the rest of the magnets came down in a shower.

He let go of her hair and seized her by the throat. Said, "I'm sorry, Ange, it wasn't supposed to happen like this." But he wasn't sorry. He was only scared and in pain and convinced that her struggles in this horribly bright kitchen would never end. His fingers were already getting tired. Who knew it was so hard to choke a person?

Somewhere, far off to the south, there was a boom. As if someone had fired a very large gun. Junior paid no attention. What Junior did was redouble his grip, and at last Angie's struggles began to weaken. Somewhere much closer by—in the house, on this floor—a low chiming began. He looked up, eyes wide, at first sure it was the doorbell. Someone had heard the ruckus and the cops were here. His head was exploding, it felt like he had sprained all his fingers, and it had all been for nothing. A terrible picture flitted through his mind: Junior Rennie being escorted into the Castle County courthouse for arraignment with some cop's sportcoat over his head.

Then he recognized the sound. It was the same chiming his own computer made when the electricity went out and it had to switch over to battery power.

Bing . . . Bing . . . Bing . . .

Room service, send me up a room, he thought, and went on choking. She was still now but he kept at it for another minute with his head turned to one side, trying to avoid the smell of her shit. How like her to leave such a nasty going-away present! How like them all! Women! Women and their breeding-farms! Nothing but anthills covered with hair! And they said *men* were the problem!

6

He was standing over her bloody, beshitted, and undoubtedly dead body, wondering what to do next, when there was another distant boom from the south. Not a gun; much too big. An explosion. Maybe Chuck Thompson's fancy little airplane had crashed after all. It wasn't impossible; on a day when you set out just to shout at someone—read them the riot act a little, no more than that—and she ended up making you *kill* her, anything was possible.

A police siren started yowling. Junior was sure it was for him. Someone had looked in the window and seen him choking her. It galvanized him into action. He started down the hall to the front door, got as far as the towel he'd knocked off her hair with that first slap, then stopped. They'd come that way, that was just the way they'd come. Pull up out front, those bright new LED flashers sending arrows of pain into the squalling meat of his poor brain—

He turned around and ran back to the kitchen. He looked down before stepping over Angie's body, he couldn't help it. In first grade, he and Frank had sometimes pulled her braids and she would stick her tongue out at them and cross her eyes. Now her eyes bulged from their sockets like ancient marbles and her mouth was full of blood.

Did I do that? Did I really?

Yes. He had. And even that single fleeting look was enough to explain why. Her fucking teeth. Those humungous choppers.

A second siren joined the first, then a third. But they were going away. Thank Christ, they were going away. They were heading south down Main Street, toward those booming sounds.

Nevertheless, Junior did not slow down. He skulked across the McCains' backyard, unaware that he would have screamed guilt about *something* to anyone who happened to be watching (no one was). Beyond LaDonna's tomato plants was a high board fence and a gate. There was a padlock, but it was hanging open on the hasp. In his years of growing up and sometimes hanging out here, Junior had never seen it closed.

He opened the gate. Beyond were scrub woods and a

path leading down to the muted babble of Prestile Stream. Once, when he was thirteen, Junior had spied Frank and Angie standing on that path and kissing, her arms around his neck, his hand cupping her breast, and understood that childhood was almost over.

He leaned down and vomited into the running water. The sun-dapples on the water were malicious, awful. Then his vision cleared enough so he could see the Peace Bridge to his right. The fisherboys were gone, but as he looked, a pair of police cars raced down Town Common Hill.

The town whistle went off. The Town Hall generator had kicked on just as it was supposed to during a power failure, allowing the whistle to broadcast its high-decibel disaster message. Junior moaned and covered his ears.

The Peace Bridge was really just a covered pedestrian walkway, now ramshackle and sagging. Its actual name was the Alvin Chester Pass-Through, but it had become the Peace Bridge in 1969, when some kids (at the time there had been rumors in town about which ones) had painted a big blue peace sign on the side. It was still there, although now faded to a ghost. For the last ten years Peace Bridge had been condemned. Police DO NOT CROSS tape Xed both ends, but of course it was still used. Two or three nights a week, members of Chief Perkins's Fuzznuts Brigade would shine their lights in there, always at one end or the other, never both. They didn't want to bust the kids who were drinking and necking, just scare them away. Every year at town meeting, someone would move that Peace Bridge be demolished and someone else would move that it be renovated, and both motions would be tabled. The town had its own secret will, it seemed, and that secret will wanted the Peace Bridge to stay just as it was.

Today, Junior Rennie was glad of that.

He shambled along the Prestile's northern bank until

he was beneath the bridge—the police sirens now fading, the town whistle yelling as loud as ever—and climbed up to Strout Lane. He looked both ways, then trotted past the sign reading DEAD END, BRIDGE CLOSED. He ducked under the crisscross of yellow tape, into the shadows. The sun shone through the holey roof, dropping dimes of light on the worn wooden boards underfoot, but after the blaze of that kitchen from hell, it was blessedly dark. Pigeons sweettalked in the roofbeams. Beer cans and Allen's Coffee Flavored Brandy bottles were scattered along the wooden sides.

I will never get away with this. I don't know if I left any of me under her nails, can't remember if she got me or not, but my blood's there. And my fingerprints. I only have two choices, really: run or turn myself in.

No, there was a third. He could kill himself.

He had to get home. Had to draw all the curtains in his room and turn it into a cave. Take another Imitrex, lie down, maybe sleep a little. Then he might be able to think. And if they came for him while he was asleep? Why, that would save him the problem of choosing between Door #1, Door #2, or Door #3.

Junior crossed the town common. When someone— some old guy he only vaguely recognized—grabbed his arm and said, "What happened, Junior? What's going on?" Junior only shook his head, brushed the old man's hand away, and kept going.

Behind him, the town whistle whooped like the end of the world.

HIGHWAYS AND BYWAYS

There was a weekly newspaper in Chester's Mill called the *Democrat*. Which was misinformation, since ownership and management—both hats worn by the formidable Julia Shumway—was Republican to the core. The masthead looked like this:

THE CHESTER'S MILL *DEMOCRAT*
Est. 1890
Serving "The Little Town That Looks Like A Boot!"

But the motto was misinformation, too. Chester's Mill didn't look like a boot; it looked like a kid's athletic sock so filthy it was able to stand up on its own. Although touched by the much larger and more prosperous Castle Rock to the southwest (the heel of the sock), The Mill was actually surrounded by four towns larger in area but smaller in population: Motton, to the south and southeast; Harlow to the east and northeast; the unincorporated TR-90 to the north; and Tarker's Mills to the west. Chester's and Tarker's were sometimes known as the Twin Mills, and between them—in the days when central and western Maine textile mills were running full bore—had turned Prestile Stream into a polluted and fishless sump that changed color almost daily and according to location.

In those days you could start out by canoe in Tarker's running on green water, and be on bright yellow by the time you crossed out of Chester's Mill and into Motton. Plus, if your canoe was made of wood, the paint might be gone below the waterline.

But the last of those profitable pollution factories had closed in 1979. The weird colors had left the Prestile and the fish had returned, although whether or not they were fit for human consumption remained a matter of debate. (The *Democrat* voted "Aye!")

The town's population was seasonal. Between Memorial Day and Labor Day, it was close to fifteen thousand. The rest of the year it was just a tad over or under two, depending on the balance of births and deaths at Catherine Russell, which was considered to be the best hospital north of Lewiston.

If you asked the summer people how many roads led in and out of The Mill, most would say there were two: Route 117, which led to Norway–South Paris, and Route 119, which went through downtown Castle Rock on its way to Lewiston.

Residents of ten years or so could have named at least eight more, all twolane blacktop, from the Black Ridge and Deep Cut Roads that went into Harlow, to the Pretty Valley Road (yes, just as pretty as its name) that wound north into TR-90.

Residents of thirty years or more, if given time to mull it over (perhaps in the back room of Brownie's Store, where there was still a woodstove), could have named another dozen, with names both sacred (God Creek Road) and profane (Little Bitch Road, noted on local survey maps with nothing but a number).

The oldest resident of Chester's Mill on what came to be known as Dome Day was Clayton Brassey. He was also the oldest resident of Castle County, and thus holder of the *Boston Post* Cane. Unfortunately, he no longer knew what a *Boston Post* Cane was, or even precisely who *he* was. He sometimes mistook his great-great-granddaughter Nell for his wife, who was forty years dead, and the *Democrat* had stopped doing its yearly "oldest resident" interview with him three years previous. (On the last occasion, when asked for the secret of his longevity, Clayton had responded, "Where's my Christing dinner?") Senility had begun to creep up shortly after his hundredth birthday; on this October twenty-first, he was a hundred and five. He had once been a fine finish carpenter specializing in dressers, banisters, and moldings. His specialties in these latter days included eating Jell-O pudding without getting it up his nose and occasionally making it to the toilet before releasing half a dozen blood-streaked pebbles into the commode.

But in his prime—around the age of eighty-five, say—he could have named almost all the roads leading in and out of Chester's Mill, and the total would have been thirty-four. Most were dirt, many were forgotten, and almost all of the forgotten ones wound through deep tangles of second-growth forest owned by Diamond Match, Continental Paper Company, and American Timber.

And shortly before noon on Dome Day, every one of them snapped closed.

2

On most of these roads, there was nothing so spectacular as the explosion of the Seneca V and the ensuing pulp-truck disaster, but there was trouble. Of course there was. If the equivalent of an invisible stone wall suddenly goes up around an entire town, there is bound to be trouble.

At the exact same moment the woodchuck fell in two pieces, a scarecrow did the same in Eddie Chalmers's pumpkin field, not far from Pretty Valley Road. The scarecrow stood directly on the town line dividing The Mill from TR-90. Its divided stance had always amused Eddie, who called his bird-frightener the Scarecrow Without A Country—Mr. SWAC for short. Half of Mr. SWAC fell in The Mill; the other half fell "on the TR," as the locals would have put it.

Seconds later, a flight of crows bound for Eddie's pumpkins (the crows had never been afraid of Mr. SWAC) struck something where nothing had ever been before. Most broke their necks and fell in black clumps on Pretty Valley Road and the fields on both sides. Birds everywhere, on both sides of the Dome, crashed and fell dead; their bodies would be one of the ways the new barrier was eventually delineated.

On God Creek Road, Bob Roux had been digging potatoes. He came in for lunch (more commonly known as "dinnah" in those parts), sitting astride his old Deere tractor and listening to his brand new iPod, a gift from his wife on what would prove to be his final birthday. His house was only half a mile from the field he'd been digging, but unfortunately for him, the field was in Motton and the house was in Chester's Mill. He struck the barrier at fifteen miles an hour, while listening to James Blunt sing "You're Beautiful." He had the loosest of grips on the tractor's steering wheel, because he could see the road all the way to his house and there was nothing on it. So when his tractor came to a smash-halt, the potato-digger rising up behind and then crashing back down, Bob was flung forward over the engine block and directly into the

Dome. His iPod exploded in the wide front pocket of his
bib overalls, but he never felt it. He broke his neck and
fractured his skull on the nothing he collided with and
died in the dirt shortly thereafter, by one tall wheel of his
tractor, which was still idling. Nothing, you know, runs
like a Deere.

3

At no point did the Motton Road actually run through
Motton; it ran just inside the Chester's Mill town line.
Here were new residential homes, in an area that had
been called Eastchester since 1975 or so. The owners were
thirty- and fortysomethings who commuted to Lewiston-
Auburn, where they worked for good wages, mostly in
white-collar jobs. All of these homes were in The Mill, but
many of their backyards were in Motton. This was the case
with Jack and Myra Evans's home at 379 Motton Road.
Myra had a vegetable garden behind their house, and although most of the goodies had been harvested, there
were still a few fat Blue Hubbard squashes beyond the
remaining (and badly rotted) pumpkins. She was reaching for one of these when the Dome came down, and
although her knees were in Chester's Mill, she happened
to be reaching for a Blue Hubbard that was growing a
foot or so across the Motton line.

She didn't cry out, because there was no pain—not at
first. It was too quick and sharp and clean for that.

Jack Evans was in the kitchen, whipping eggs for
a noontime frittata. LCD Soundsystem was playing—"North American Scum"—and Jack was singing
along when a small voice spoke his name from behind
him. He didn't at first recognize the voice as belonging

to his wife of fourteen years; it sounded like the voice of
a child. But when he turned he saw it was indeed Myra.
She was standing inside the doorway, holding her right
arm across her middle. She had tracked mud onto the
floor, which was very unlike her. Usually she took her
garden shoes off on the stoop. Her left hand, clad in a
filthy gardening glove, was cradling her right hand, and
red stuff was running through the muddy fingers. At first
he thought *Cranberry juice,* but only for a second. It was
blood. Jack dropped the bowl he'd been holding. It shattered on the floor.

Myra said his name again in that same tiny, trembling
childvoice.

"What happened? Myra, what happened to you?"

"I had an accident," she said, and showed him her right
hand. Only there was no muddy right gardening glove to
match the left one, and no right hand. Only a spouting
stump. She gave him a weak smile and said "Whoops."
Her eyes rolled up to whites. The crotch of her gardening
jeans darkened as her urine let go. Then her knees also let
go and she went down. The blood gushing from her raw
wrist—an anatomy lesson cutaway—mixed with the eggy
batter splattered across the floor.

When Jack dropped to his knees beside her, a shard
from the bowl jabbed deep into his knee. He hardly noticed, although he would limp on that leg for the rest
of his life. He seized her arm and squeezed. The terrible
bloodgush from her wrist slowed but didn't stop. He tore
his belt free of its loops and noosed it around her lower
forearm. That did the job, but he couldn't notch the belt
tight; the loop was far beyond the buckle.

"Christ," he told the empty kitchen. "Christ."

It was darker than it had been, he realized. The power
had gone out. He could hear the computer in the study

chiming its distress call. LCD Soundsystem was okay, because the little boombox on the counter was battery-powered. Not that Jack cared any longer; he'd lost his taste for techno.

So much blood. So much.

Questions about how she'd lost her hand left his mind. He had more immediate concerns. He couldn't let go of the belt-tourniquet to get to the phone; she'd start to bleed again, and she might already be close to bleeding out. She would have to go with him. He tried pulling her by her shirt, but first it yanked out of her pants and then the collar started to choke her—he heard her breathing turn harsh. So he wrapped a hand in her long brown hair and hauled her to the phone caveman style.

It was a cell, and it worked. He dialed 911 and 911 was busy.

"It can't be!" he shouted to the empty kitchen where the lights were now out (although from the boombox, the band played on). "911 cannot be fucking *busy*!"

He punched redial.

Busy.

He sat in the kitchen with his back propped up against the counter, holding the tourniquet as tightly as he could, staring at the blood and the batter on the floor, periodically hitting redial on the phone, always getting the same stupid *dah-dah-dah*. Something blew up not too distant, but he barely heard it over the music, which was really cranked (and he never heard the Seneca explosion at all). He wanted to turn the music off, but in order to reach the boombox he would have to lift Myra. Lift her or let go of the belt for two or three seconds. He didn't want to do either one. So he sat there and "North American Scum" gave way to "Someone Great" and "Someone Great" gave way to "All My Friends," and after a few more songs, finally the CD, which was called *Sound of Silver,* ended. When it did, when there was silence except for police sirens in the distance and the endlessly chiming computer closer by, Jack realized that his wife was no longer breathing.

But I was going to make lunch, he thought. *A nice lunch, one you wouldn't be ashamed of inviting Martha Stewart to.*

Sitting against the counter, still holding the belt (opening his fingers again would prove exquisitely painful), the lower right leg of his own pants darkening with blood from his lacerated knee, Jack Evans cradled his wife's head against his chest and began to weep.

4

Not too far away, on an abandoned woods road not even old Clay Brassey would have remembered, a deer was foraging tender shoots at the edge of Prestile Marsh. Her neck happened to be stretched across the Motton town line, and when the Dome dropped, her head tumbled off. It was severed so neatly that the deed might have been done with a guillotine blade.

5

We have toured the sock-shape that is Chester's Mill and arrived back at Route 119. And, thanks to the magic of narration, not an instant has passed since the sixtyish fellow from the Toyota slammed face-first into something invisible but very hard and broke his nose. He's sitting up and staring at Dale Barbara in utter bewilderment. A seagull, probably on its daily commute from the tasty

buffet at the Motton town dump to the only slightly less
tasty one at the Chester's Mill landfill, drops like a stone
and thumps down not three feet from the sixtyish fellow's
Sea Dogs baseball cap, which he picks up, brushes off,
and puts back on.

Both men look up at where the bird came from and see
one more incomprehensible thing in a day that will turn
out to be full of them.

6

Barbie's first thought was that he was looking at an after-
image from the exploding plane—the way you sometimes
see a big blue floating dot after someone triggers a flash
camera close to your face. Only this wasn't a dot, it wasn't
blue, and instead of floating along when he looked in a different direction—in this case, at his new acquaintance—
the smutch hanging in the air stayed exactly where it was.

Sea Dogs was looking up and rubbing his eyes. He
seemed to have forgotten about his broken nose, swelling
lips, and bleeding forehead. He got to his feet, almost losing his balance because he was craning his neck so severely.

"What's that?" he said. "What the hell is that, mister?"

A big black smear—candleflame-shaped, if you really
used your imagination—discolored the blue sky.

"Is it . . . a cloud?" Sea Dogs asked. His doubtful tone
suggested he already knew it wasn't.

Barbie said, "I think . . ." He really didn't want to hear
himself say this. "I think it's where the plane hit."

"Say *what*?" Sea Dogs asked, but before Barbie could
reply, a good-sized grackle swooped fifty feet overhead. It
struck nothing—nothing they could see, at any rate—and
dropped not far from the gull.

Sea Dogs said, "Did you *see* that?"

Barbie nodded, then pointed to the patch of burning hay to his left. It and the two or three patches on the right side of the road were sending up thick columns of black smoke to join the smoke rising from the pieces of the dismembered Seneca, but the fire wasn't going far; there had been heavy rain the day before, and the hay was still damp. Lucky thing, or there would have been grassfires racing away in both directions.

"Do you see *that*?" Barbie asked Sea Dogs.

"I'll be dipped in shit," Sea Dogs said after taking a good long look. The fire had burned a patch of ground about sixty feet square, moving forward until it was almost opposite the place where Barbie and Sea Dogs were facing one another. And there it spread—west to the edge of the highway, east into some small dairy farmer's four acres of grazeland—not raggedly, not the way grassfires normally advance, with the fire a bit ahead in one place and falling a little behind somewhere else—but as if on a straightedge.

Another gull came flying toward them, this one bound for Motton rather than The Mill.

"Look out," Sea Dogs said. "Ware that bird."

"Maybe it'll be okay," Barbie said, looking up and shading his eyes. "Maybe whatever it is only stops them if they're coming from the south."

"Judging by yonder busted plane, I doubt that," Sea Dogs said. He spoke in the musing tones of a man who is deeply perplexed.

The outbound gull struck the barrier and fell directly into the largest chunk of the burning plane.

"Stops em both ways," Sea Dogs said. He spoke in the tone of a man who has gotten confirmation of a strongly held but previously unproved conviction. "It's some kind of force field, like in a *Star Trick* movie."

"*Trek,*" Barbie said.

"Huh?"

"Oh shit," Barbie said. He was looking over Sea Dogs's shoulder.

"Huh?" Sea Dogs looked over his own shoulder. "Blue *fuck*!"

A pulp-truck was coming. A big one, loaded well past the legal weight limit with huge logs. It was also rolling well above the legal limit. Barbie tried to calculate what the stopping-speed on such a behemoth might be and couldn't even guess.

Sea Dogs sprinted for his Toyota, which he'd left parked askew on the highway's broken white line. The guy behind the wheel of the pulper—maybe high on pills, maybe smoked up on meth, maybe just young, in a big hurry, and feeling immortal—saw him and laid on his horn. He wasn't slowing.

"*Fuck me sideways!*" Sea Dogs cried as he threw himself behind the wheel. He keyed the engine and backed the Toyota out of the road with the driver's door flapping. The little SUV thumped into the ditch with its square nose canted up to the sky. Sea Dogs was out the next moment. He stumbled, landed on one knee, and then took off running into the field.

Barbie, thinking of the plane and the birds—thinking of that weird black smutch that might have been the plane's point of impact—also ran into the grazeland, at first sprinting through low, unenthusiastic flames and sending up puffs of black ash. He saw a man's sneaker—it was too big to be a woman's—with the man's foot still in it.

Pilot, he thought. And then: *I have to stop running around like this.*

"*YOU IDIOT, SLOW DOWN!*" Sea Dogs cried at the

pulp-truck in a thin, panicky voice, but it was too late for such instructions. Barbie, looking back over his shoulder (helpless not to), thought the pulp-wrangler might have tried to brake at the last minute. He probably saw the wreckage of the plane. In any case, it wasn't enough. He struck the Motton side of the Dome at sixty or a little more, carrying a log-load of almost forty thousand pounds. The cab disintegrated as it stopped cold. The overloaded carrier, a prisoner of physics, continued forward. The fuel tanks were driven under the logs, shredding and sparking. When they exploded, the load was already airborne, flipping over where the cab—now a green metal accordion—had been. The logs sprayed forward and upward, struck the invisible barrier, and rebounded in all directions. Fire and black smoke boiled upward in a thick plume. There was a terrific thud that rolled across the day like a boulder. Then the logs were raining back down on the Motton side, landing on the road and the surrounding fields like enormous jackstraws. One struck the roof of Sea Dogs's SUV and smashed it flat, spilling the windshield onto the hood in a spray of diamond crumbles. Another landed right in front of Sea Dogs himself.

Barbie stopped running and only stared.

Sea Dogs got to his feet, fell down, grasped the log that had almost smashed out his life, and got up again. He stood swaying and wild-eyed. Barbie started toward him and after twelve steps ran into something that felt like a brick wall. He staggered backward and felt warmth cascade from his nose and over his lips. He wiped away a palmload of blood, looked at it unbelievingly, and then smeared it on his shirt.

Now cars were coming from both directions—Motton and Chester's Mill. Three running figures, as yet still small, were cutting across the grazeland from a farmhouse at the other end. Several of the cars were honking their horns, as if that would somehow solve all problems. The first car to arrive on the Motton side pulled over to the shoulder, well back from the burning truck. Two women got out and gawked at the column of smoke and fire, shading their eyes.

7

"Fuck," Sea Dogs said. He spoke in a small, breathless voice. He approached Barbie through the field, cutting a prudent east-tending diagonal away from the blazing pyre. The trucker might have been overloaded and moving too fast, Barbie thought, but at least he was getting a Viking funeral. "Did you see where that one log landed? I was almost kilt. Squashed like a bug."

"Do you have a cell phone?" Barbie had to raise his voice to be heard over the furiously burning pulper.

"In my truck," Sea Dogs said. "I'll try for it if you want."

"No, wait," Barbie said. He realized with sudden relief that all this could be a dream, the irrational kind where riding your bicycle underwater or talking of your sex life in some language you never studied seems normal.

The first person to arrive on his side of the barrier was a chubby guy driving an old GMC pickup. Barbie recognized him from Sweetbriar Rose: Ernie Calvert, the previous manager of Food City, now retired. Ernie was staring at the burning clutter on the road with wide eyes, but he had his cell phone in his hand and was ratchet-jawing into it. Barbie could hardly hear him over the roar of the burning pulp-truck, but he made out "Looks like a bad one" and figured Ernie was talking to the police. Or the fire department. If it was the FD, Barbie hoped it was the one in Castle Rock. There were two engines in the tidy little Chester's Mill firebarn, but Barbie had an idea that if they showed up here, the most they'd be able to do was douse a grassfire that was going to putter out on its own before much longer. The burning pulp-truck was close, but Barbie didn't think they'd be able to get to it.

It's a dream, he told himself. *If you keep telling yourself that, you'll be able to operate.*

The two women on the Motton side had been joined by half a dozen men, also shading their eyes. Cars were now parked on both shoulders. More people were getting out and joining the crowd. The same thing was happening on Barbie's side. It was as if a couple of dueling flea markets, both full of juicy bargains, had opened up out here: one on the Motton side of the town line, one on the Chester's Mill side.

The trio from the farm arrived—a farmer and his teenaged sons. The boys were running easily, the farmer redfaced and panting.

"Holy shit!" the older boy said, and his father whapped him backside of the head. The boy didn't seem to notice. His eyes were bugging. The younger boy reached out his hand, and when the older boy took it, the younger boy started to cry.

"What happened here?" the farmer asked Barbie, pausing to whoop in a big deep breath between *happened* and *here.*

Barbie ignored him. He advanced slowly toward Sea Dogs with his right hand held out in a *stop* gesture. Without speaking, Sea Dogs did the same. As Barbie approached the place where he knew the barrier to be—he had only to look at that peculiar straight-edge of burnt ground—he slowed down. He had already whammed his face; he didn't want to do it again.

Suddenly he was swept by horripilation. The goosebumps swept up from his ankles all the way to the nape of his neck, where the hairs stirred and tried to lift. His balls tingled like tuning forks, and for a moment there was a sour metallic taste in his mouth.

Five feet away from him—five feet and closing—Sea Dogs's already wide eyes widened some more. "Did you feel that?"

"Yes," Barbie said. "But it's gone now. You?"

"Gone," Sea Dogs agreed.

Their outstretched hands did not quite meet, and Barbie again thought of a pane of glass; putting your inside hand up against the hand of some outside friend, the fingers together but not touching.

He pulled his hand back. It was the one he'd used to wipe his bloody nose, and he saw the red shapes of his own fingers hanging on thin air. As he watched, the blood began to bead. Just as it would on glass.

"Holy God, what does it mean?" Sea Dogs whispered.

Barbie had no answer. Before he could say anything, Ernie Calvert tapped him on the back. "I called the cops," he said. "They're coming, but no one answers at the Fire Department—I got a recording telling me to call Castle Rock."

"Okay, do that," Barbie said. Then another bird dropped about twenty feet away, falling into the farmer's grazeland and disappearing. Seeing it brought a new idea into Barbie's mind, possibly sparked by the time he'd spent toting a gun on the other side of the world. "But first, I think you better call the Air National Guard, up in Bangor."

Ernie gaped at him. "The *Guard*?"

"They're the only ones who can institute a no-fly zone over Chester's Mill," Barbie said. "And I think they better do it right away."

LOTTA DEAD BIRDS

The Mill's Chief of Police heard neither explosion, though he was outside, raking leaves on the lawn of his Morin Street home. The portable radio was sitting on the hood of his wife's Honda, playing sacred music on WCIK (call letters standing for *Christ Is King* and known by the town's younger denizens as Jesus Radio). Also, his hearing wasn't what it once had been. At sixty-seven, was anybody's?

But he heard the first siren when it cut through the day; his ears were attuned to that sound just as a mother's are to the cries of her children. Howard Perkins even knew which car it was, and who was driving. Only Three and Four still had the old warblers, but Johnny Trent had taken Three over to Castle Rock with the FD, to that damned training exercise. A "controlled burn," they called it, although what it really amounted to was grown men having fun. So it was car Four, one of their two remaining Dodges, and Henry Morrison would be driving.

He stopped raking and stood, head cocked. The siren started to fade, and he started raking again. Brenda came out on the stoop. Almost everyone in The Mill called him Duke—the nickname a holdover from his high school days, when he had never missed a John Wayne picture down at the Star—but Brenda had quit that soon after they were married in favor of the other nickname. The one he disliked.

"Howie, the power's out. And there were *bangs*."

Howie. Always Howie. As in *Here's Howie* and *Howie's tricks* and *Howie's life treatin you.* He tried to be a Christian about it—hell, he *was* a Christian about it—but sometimes he wondered if that nickname wasn't at least partially responsible for the little gadget he now carried around in his chest.

"What?"

She rolled her eyes, marched to the radio on the hood of her car, and pushed the power button, cutting off the Norman Luboff Choir in the middle of "What a Friend We Have in Jesus."

"How many times have I told you not to stick this thing on the hood of my car? You'll scratch it and the resale value will go down."

"Sorry, Bren. What did you say?"

"The *power's* out! And something *boomed*. That's probably what Johnny Trent's rolling on."

"It's Henry," he said. "Johnny's over in The Rock with the FD."

"Well, whoever it is—"

Another siren started up, this one of the newer kind that Duke Perkins thought of as Tweety Birds. That would be Two, Jackie Wettington. Had to be Jackie, while Randolph sat minding the store, rocked back in his chair with his feet cocked up on his desk, reading the *Democrat.* Or sitting in the crapper. Peter Randolph was a fair cop, and he could be just as hard as he needed to be, but Duke didn't like him. Partly because he was so clearly Jim Rennie's man, partly because Randolph was sometimes harder than he needed to be, but mostly because he thought Randolph was lazy, and Duke Perkins could not abide a lazy policeman.

Brenda was looking at him with large eyes. She had

been a policeman's wife for forty-three years, and she knew that two booms, two sirens, and a power failure added up to nothing good. If the lawn got raked this weekend—or if Howie got to listen to his beloved Twin Mills Wildcats take on Castle Rock's football team—she would be surprised.

"You better go on in," she said. "Something got knocked down. I just hope no one's dead."

He took his cell phone off his belt. Goddam thing hung there like a leech from morning til night, but he had to admit it was handy. He didn't dial it, just stood looking down at it, waiting for it to ring.

But then another Tweety Bird siren went off: car One. Randolph rolling after all. Which meant something very serious. Duke no longer thought the phone would ring and moved to put it back on his belt, but then it did. It was Stacey Moggin.

"*Stacey?*" He knew he didn't have to bellow into the goddam thing, Brenda had told him so a hundred times, but he couldn't seem to help it. "*What are you doing at the station on Saturday m—*"

"I'm not, I'm at home. Peter called me and said to tell you it's out on 119, and it's bad. He said . . . an airplane and a pulp-truck collided." She sounded dubious. "I don't see how that can be, but—"

A plane. Jesus. Five minutes ago, or maybe a little longer, while he'd been raking leaves and singing along with "How Great Thou Art"—

"Stacey, was it Chuck Thompson? I saw that new Piper of his flying over. Pretty low."

"I don't know, Chief, I've told you everything Peter told me."

Brenda, no dummy, was already moving her car so he could back the forest-green Chief's car down the driveway. She had set the portable radio beside his small pile of raked leaves.

"Okay, Stace. Power out on your side of town, too?"

"Yes, and the landlines. I'm on my cell. It's probably bad, isn't it?"

"I hope not. Can you go in and cover? I bet the place is standing there empty and unlocked."

"I'll be there in five. Reach me on the base unit."

"Roger that."

As Brenda came back up the driveway, the town whistle went off, its rise and fall a sound that never failed to make Duke Perkins feel tight in the gut. Nevertheless, he took time to put an arm around Brenda. She never forgot that he took the time to do that. "Don't let it worry you, Brennie. It's programmed to do that in a general power outage. It'll stop in three minutes. Or four. I forget which."

"I know, but I still hate it. That idiot Andy Sanders blew it on nine-eleven, do you remember? As if they were going to suicide-bomb *us* next."

Duke nodded. Andy Sanders *was* an idiot. Unfortunately, he was also First Selectman, the cheery Mortimer Snerd dummy that sat on Big Jim Rennie's lap.

"Honey, I have to go."

"I know." But she followed him to the car. "What is it? Do you know yet?"

"Stacy said a truck and an airplane collided out on 119."

Brenda smiled tentatively. "That's a joke, right?"

"Not if the plane had engine trouble and was trying to land on the highway," Duke said. Her little smile faded and her fisted right hand came to rest just between her breasts, body language he knew well. He climbed behind the wheel, and although the Chief's cruiser was relatively new, he still settled into the shape of his own butt. Duke Perkins was no lightweight.

"On your day off!" she cried. "Really, it's a shame! And when you could retire on a full P!"

"They'll just have to take me in my Saturday slops," he said, and grinned at her. It was work, that grin. This felt like it was going to be a long day. "Just as I am, Lord, just as I am. Stick me a sandwich or two in the fridge, will you?"

"Just one. You're getting too heavy. Even Dr. Haskell said so and he never scolds *anybody*."

"One, then." He put the shift in reverse . . . then put it back in park. He leaned out the window, and she realized he wanted a kiss. She gave him a good one with the town whistle blowing across the crisp October air, and he caressed the side of her throat while their mouths were together, a thing that always gave her the shivers and he hardly ever did anymore.

His touch there in the sunshine: she never forgot that, either.

As he rolled down the driveway, she called something after him. He caught part of it but not all. He really was going to have to get his ears checked. Let them fit him with a hearing aid if necessary. Although that would probably be the final thing Randolph and Big Jim needed to kick him out on his aging ass.

Duke braked and leaned out again. "Take care of my *what*?"

"*Your pacemaker!*" she practically screamed. Laughing. Exasperated. Still feeling his hand on her throat, stroking skin that had been smooth and firm—so it seemed to her—only yesterday. Or maybe it had been the day before, when they had listened to KC and the Sunshine Band instead of Jesus Radio.

"Oh, you bet!" he called back, and drove away. The next time she saw him, he was dead.

2

Billy and Wanda Debec never heard the double boom because they were on Route 117, and because they were arguing. The fight had started simply enough, with Wanda observing it was a beautiful day and Billy responding he had a headache and didn't know why they had to go to the Saturday flea market in Oxford Hills, anyway; it would just be the usual pawed-over crap.

Wanda said that he wouldn't have a headache if he hadn't sunk a dozen beers the night before.

Billy asked her if she had counted the cans in the recycling bin (no matter how loaded he got, Billy did his drinking at home and always put the cans in the recycling bin—these things, along with his work as an electrician, were his pride).

She said yes she had, you bet she had. Furthermore—

They got as far as Patel's Market in Castle Rock, having progressed through *You drink too much, Billy* and *You nag too much, Wanda* to *My mother told me not to marry you* and *Why do you have to be such a bitch.* This had become a fairly well-worn call-and-response during the last two years of their four-year marriage, but this morning Billy suddenly felt he had reached his limit. He swung into the market's wide hot-topped parking lot without signaling or slowing, and then back out onto 117 without a single glance into his rearview mirror, let alone over his shoulder. On the road behind him, Nora Robichaud honked. Her best friend, Elsa Andrews, tutted. The two women, both retired nurses, exchanged a glance but not a single word.

They had been friends too long for words to be necessary in such situations.

Meanwhile, Wanda asked Billy where he thought he was going.

Billy said back home to take a nap. She could go to the shitfair on her own.

Wanda observed that he had almost hit those two old ladies (said old ladies now dropping behind fast; Nora Robichaud felt that, lacking some damned good reason, speeds over forty miles an hour were the devil's work).

Billy observed that Wanda both looked and sounded like her mother.

Wanda asked him to elucidate just what he meant by that.

Billy said that both mother and daughter had fat asses and tongues that were hung in the middle and ran on both ends.

Wanda told Billy he was hungover.

Billy told Wanda she was ugly.

It was a full and fair exchange of feelings, and by the time they crossed from Castle Rock into Motton, headed for an invisible barrier that had come into being not long after Wanda had opened this spirited discussion by saying it was a beautiful day, Billy was doing better than sixty, which was almost top end for Wanda's little Chevy shitbox.

"What's that smoke?" Wanda asked suddenly, pointing northeast, toward 119.

"I don't know," he said. "Did my mother-in-law fart?" This cracked him up and he started laughing.

Wanda Debec realized she had finally had enough. This clarified the world and her future in a way that was almost magical. She was turning to him, the words *I want a divorce* on the tip of her tongue, when they reached the

Motton–Chester's Mill town line and struck the barrier. The Chevy shitbox was equipped with airbags, but Billy's did not deploy and Wanda's didn't pop out completely. The steering wheel collapsed Billy's chest; the steering column smashed his heart; he died almost instantly.

Wanda's head collided with the dashboard, and the sudden, catastrophic relocation of the Chevy's engine block broke one of her legs (the left) and one of her arms (the right). She was not aware of any pain, only that the horn was blaring, the car was suddenly askew in the middle of the road with its front end smashed almost flat, and her vision had come over all red.

When Nora Robichaud and Elsa Andrews rounded the bend just to the south (they had been animatedly discussing the smoke rising to the northeast for several minutes now, and congratulating themselves on having taken the lesser traveled highway this forenoon), Wanda Debec was dragging herself up the white line on her elbows. Blood gushed down her face, almost obscuring it. She had been half scalped by a piece of the collapsing windshield and a huge flap of skin hung down over her left cheek like a misplaced jowl.

Nora and Elsa looked at each other grimly.

"Shit-my-pajamas," Nora said, and that was all the talk between them there was. Elsa got out the instant the car stopped and ran to the staggering woman. For an elderly lady (Elsa had just turned seventy), she was remarkably fleet.

Nora left the car idling in park and joined her friend. Together they supported Wanda to Norma's old but perfectly maintained Mercedes. Wanda's jacket had gone from brown to a muddy roan color; her hands looked as if she had dipped them in red paint.

"Whe' Billy?" she asked, and Nora saw that most of

the poor woman's teeth had been knocked out. Three of them were stuck to the front of her bloody jacket. "Whe' Billy, he arri'? Wha' happen?"

"Billy's fine and so are you," Nora said, then looked a question at Elsa. Elsa nodded and hurried toward the Chevy, now partly obscured by the steam escaping its ruptured radiator. One look through the gaping passenger door, which hung on one hinge, was enough to tell Elsa, who had been a nurse for almost forty years (final employer: Ron Haskell, MD—the MD standing for Medical Doofus), that Billy was not fine at all. The young woman with half her hair hanging upside down beside her head was now a widow.

Elsa returned to the Mercedes and got into the backseat next to the young woman, who had slipped into semiconsciousness. "He's dead and she will be, too, if you don't get us to Cathy Russell hurry-up-chop-chop," she told Nora.

"Hang on, then," Nora said, and floored it. The Mercedes had a big engine, and it leaped forward. Nora swerved smartly around the Debec Chevrolet and crashed into the invisible barrier while still accelerating. For the first time in twenty years Nora had neglected to fasten her seat belt, and she went out through the windshield, where she broke her neck on the invisible barrier just as Bob Roux had. The young woman shot between the Mercedes's front bucket seats, out through the shattered windshield, and landed facedown on the hood with her bloodspattered legs splayed. Her feet were bare. Her loafers (bought at the last Oxford Hills flea market she had attended) had come off in the first crash.

Elsa Andrews hit the back of the driver's seat, then rebounded, dazed but essentially unhurt. Her door stuck at first, but popped open when she put her shoulder against it and rammed. She got out and looked around at the littered wreckage. The puddles of blood. The smashed-up Chevy shitbox, still gently steaming.

"What happened?" she asked. This had also been Wanda's question, although Elsa didn't remember that. She stood in a strew of chrome and bloody glass, then put the back of her left hand to her forehead, as if checking for a fever. "What happened? What just happened? Nora? Nora-pie? Where are you, dear?"

Then she saw her friend and uttered a scream of grief and horror. A crow watching from high in a pine tree on The Mill side of the barrier cawed once, a cry that sounded like a contemptuous snort of laughter.

Elsa's legs turned rubbery. She backed until her bottom struck the crumpled nose of the Mercedes. "Nora-pie," she said. "Oh, honey." Something tickled the back of her neck. She wasn't sure, but thought it was probably a lock of the wounded girl's hair. Only now, of course, she was the dead girl.

And poor sweet Nora, with whom she'd sometimes shared illicit nips of gin or vodka in the laundry room at Cathy Russell, the two of them giggling like girls away at camp. Nora's eyes were open, staring up at the bright midday sun, and her head was cocked at a nasty angle, as if she had died trying to look back over her shoulder and make sure Elsa was all right.

Elsa, who *was* all right—"just shaken up," as they'd said of certain lucky survivors back in their ER days— began to cry. She slid down the side of the car (ripping her own coat on a jag of metal) and sat on the asphalt of 117. She was still sitting there and still crying when Barbie and his new friend in the Sea Dogs cap came upon her.

3

Sea Dogs turned out to be Paul Gendron, a car salesman from upstate who had retired to his late parents' farm in Motton two years before. Barbie learned this and a great deal more about Gendron between their departure from the crash scene on 119 and their discovery of another one—not quite so spectacular but still pretty horrific—at the place where Route 117 crossed into The Mill. Barbie would have been more than willing to shake Gendron's hand, but such niceties would have to remain on hold until they found the place where the invisible barrier ended.

Ernie Calvert had gotten through to the Air National Guard in Bangor, but had been put on hold before he had a chance to say why he was calling. Meanwhile, approaching sirens heralded the imminent arrival of the local law.

"Just don't expect the Fire Department," said the farmer who'd come running across the field with his sons. His name was Alden Dinsmore, and he was still getting his breath back. "They're over to Castle Rock, burnin down a house for practice. Could have gotten plenty of practice right h—" Then he saw his younger son approaching the place where Barbie's bloody handprint appeared to be drying on nothing more than sunny air. "Rory, get away from there!"

Rory, agog with curiosity, ignored him. He reached out and knocked on the air just to the right of Barbie's handprint. But before he did, Barbie saw goosebumps rash out on the kid's arms below the ragged sleeves of his cut-off Wildcats sweatshirt. There was something there, something that kicked in when you got close. The only place Barbie had ever gotten a similar sensation was close to the big power generator in Avon, Florida, where he'd once taken a girl necking.

The sound of the kid's fist was like knuckles on the side of a Pyrex casserole dish. It silenced the little babbling crowd of spectators, who had been staring at the burning remains of the pulp-truck (and in some cases taking pictures of it with their cell phones).

"I'll be dipped in shit," someone said.

Alden Dinsmore dragged his son away by the ragged collar of his sweatshirt, then whapped him backside of the head as he had the older brother not long before. "Don't you ever!" Dinsmore cried, shaking the boy. "Don't you *ever*, when you don't know what it is!"

"Pa, it's like a glass wall! It's—"

Dinsmore shook him some more. He was still panting, and Barbie feared for his heart. "Don't you *ever*!" he repeated, and pushed the kid at his older brother. "Hang onto this fool, Ollie."

"Yessir," Ollie said, and smirked at his brother.

Barbie looked toward The Mill. He could now see the approaching flashers of a police car, but far ahead of it—as if escorting the cops by virtue of some higher authority—was a large black vehicle that looked like a rolling coffin: Big Jim Rennie's Hummer. Barbie's fading bumps and bruises from the fight in Dipper's parking lot seemed to give a sympathetic throb at the sight.

Rennie Senior hadn't been there, of course, but his son had been the prime instigator, and Big Jim had taken care of Junior. If that meant making life in The Mill tough for a certain itinerant short-order cook—tough enough so the short-order cook in question would decide to just haul stakes and leave town—even better.

Barbie didn't want to be here when Big Jim arrived. Especially not with the cops. Chief Perkins had treated him okay, but the other one—Randolph—had looked at him as if Dale Barbara were a piece of dogshit on a dress shoe.

Barbie turned to Sea Dogs and said: "You interested in taking a little hike? You on your side, me on mine? See how far this thing goes?"

"And get away from here before yonder gasbag arrives?" Gendron had also seen the oncoming Hummer. "My friend, you're on. East or west?"

4

They went west, toward Route 117, and they didn't find the end of the barrier, but they saw the wonders it had created when it came down. Tree branches had been sheared off, creating pathways to the sky where previously there had been none. Stumps had been cut in half. And there were feathered corpses everywhere.

"Lotta dead birds," Gendron said. He resettled his cap on his head with hands that trembled slightly. His face was pale. "Never seen so many."

"Are you all right?" Barbie asked.

"Physically? Yeah, I think so. Mentally, I feel like I've lost my frickin mind. How about you?"

"Same," Barbie said.

Two miles west of 119, they came to God Creek Road and the body of Bob Roux, lying beside his still-idling tractor. Barbie moved instinctively toward the downed man and once again bumped the barrier . . . although this time he remembered at the last second and slowed in time to keep from bloodying his nose again.

Gendron knelt and touched the farmer's grotesquely cocked neck. "Dead."

"What's that littered all around him? Those white scraps?"

Gendron picked up the largest piece. "I think it's one of

those computer-music doohickies. Musta broke when he hit the . . ." He gestured in front of him. "The you-know."

From the direction of town a whooping began, hoarser and louder than the town whistle had been.

Gendron glanced toward it briefly. "Fire siren," he said. "Much good it'll do."

"FD's coming from Castle Rock," Barbie said. "I hear them."

"Yeah? Your ears are better'n mine, then. Tell me your name again, friend."

"Dale Barbara. Barbie to my friends."

"Well, Barbie, what now?"

"Go on, I guess. We can't do anything for this guy."

"Nope, can't even call anyone," Gendron said gloomily. "Not with my cell back there. Guess you don't have one?"

Barbie did, but he had left it behind in his now-vacated apartment, along with some socks, shirts, jeans, and underwear. He'd lit out for the territories with nothing but the clothes on his back, because there was nothing from Chester's Mill he wanted to carry with him. Except a few good memories, and for those he didn't need a suitcase or even a knapsack.

All this was too complicated to explain to a stranger, so he just shook his head.

There was an old blanket draped over the seat of the Deere. Gendron shut the tractor off, took the blanket, and covered the body.

"I hope he was listenin to somethin he liked when it happened," Gendron said.

"Yeah," Barbie said.

"Come on. Let's get to the end of this whatever-it-is. I want to shake your hand. Might even break down and give you a hug."

5

Shortly after discovering Roux's body—they were now very close to the wreck on 117, although neither of them knew it—they came to a little stream. The two men stood there for a moment, each on his own side of the barrier, looking in wonder and silence.

At last Gendron said, "Holy jumped-up God."

"What does it look like from your side?" Barbie asked. All he could see on his was the water rising and spreading into the undergrowth. It was as if the stream had encountered an invisible dam.

"I don't know how to describe it. I never seen anything quite like it." Gendron paused, scratching both cheeks, drawing his already long face down so he looked a little like the screamer in that Edvard Munch painting. "Yes I have. Once. Sorta. When I brought home a couple of goldfish for my daughter's sixth birthday. Or maybe she was seven that year. I brought em home from the pet store in a plastic bag, and that's what this looks like—water in the bottom of a plastic bag. Only flat instead of saggin down. The water piles up against that . . . thing, then trickles off both ways on your side."

"Is none going through at all?"

Gendron bent down, his hands on his knees, and squinted. "Yeah, some appears to go through. But not very much, just a trickle. And none of the crap the water's carrying. You know, sticks and leaves and such."

They pushed on, Gendron on his side and Barbie on his. As yet, neither of them were thinking in terms of inside and outside. It didn't occur to them that the barrier might not have an end.

6

Then they came to Route 117, where there had been another nasty accident—two cars and at least two fatals that Barbie could be sure of. There was another, he thought, slumped behind the wheel of an old Chevrolet that had been mostly demolished. Only this time there was also a survivor, sitting beside a smashed-up Mercedes-Benz with her head lowered. Paul Gendron rushed to her, while Barbie could only stand and watch. The woman saw Gendron and struggled to rise.

"No, ma'am, not at all, you don't want to do that," he said.

"I think I'm fine," she said. "Just . . . you know, shaken up." For some reason this made her laugh, although her face was puffy with tears.

At that moment another car appeared, a slowpoke driven by an old fellow who was leading a parade of three or four other no doubt impatient drivers. He saw the accident and stopped. The cars behind him did, too.

Elsa Andrews was on her feet now, and with-it enough to ask what would become the question of the day: "What did we hit? It wasn't the other car, Nora went around the other car."

Gendron answered with complete honesty. "Dunno, ma'am."

"Ask her if she has a cell phone," Barbie said. Then he called to the gathering spectators. "Hey! Who's got a cell phone?"

"I do, mister," a woman said, but before she could say more, they all heard an approaching *whup-whup-whup* sound. It was a helicopter.

Barbie and Gendron exchanged a stricken glance.

The copter was blue and white, flying low. It was angling toward the pillar of smoke marking the crashed pulp-truck on 119, but the air was perfectly clear, with that almost magnifying effect that the best days in northern New England seem to have, and Barbie could easily read the big blue 13 on its side. And see the CBS eye logo. It was a news chopper, out of Portland. It must already have been in the area, Barbie thought. And it was a perfect day to get some juicy crash footage for the six o'clock news.

"Oh, no," Gendron moaned, shading his eyes. Then he shouted: *"Get back, you fools! Get back!"*

Barbie chimed in. *"No! Stop it! Get away!"*

It was useless, of course. Even more useless, he was waving his arms in big go-away gestures.

Elsa looked from Gendron to Barbie, bewildered.

The chopper dipped to treetop level and hovered.

"I think it's gonna be okay," Gendron breathed. "The people back there must be waving em off, too. Pilot musta seen—"

But then the chopper swung north, meaning to hook in over Alden Dinsmore's grazeland for a different view, and it struck the barrier. Barbie saw one of the rotors break off. The helicopter dipped, dropped, and swerved, all at the same time. Then it exploded, showering fresh fire down on the road and fields on the other side of the barrier.

Gendron's side.

The outside.

7

Junior Rennie crept like a thief into the house where he had grown up. Or a ghost. It was empty, of course; his father would be out at his giant used car lot on Route

119—what Junior's friend Frank sometimes called the Holy Tabernacle of No Money Down—and for the last four years Francine Rennie had been hanging out nonstop at Pleasant Ridge Cemetery. The town whistle had quit and the police sirens had faded off to the south somewhere. The house was blessedly quiet.

He took two Imitrex, then dropped his clothes and got into the shower. When he emerged, he saw there was blood on his shirt and pants. He couldn't deal with it now. He kicked the clothes under his bed, drew the shades, crawled into the rack, and drew the covers up over his head, as he had when he was a child afraid of closet-monsters. He lay there shivering, his head gonging like all the bells of hell.

He was dozing when the fire siren went off, jolting him awake. He began to shiver again, but the headache was better. He'd sleep a little, then think about what to do next. Killing himself still seemed by far the best option. Because they'd catch him. He couldn't even go back and clean up; he wouldn't have time before Henry or LaDonna McCain came back from their Saturday errands. He could run—maybe—but not until his head stopped aching. And of course he'd have to put some clothes on. You couldn't begin life as a fugitive buckytail naked.

On the whole, killing himself would probably be best. Except then the fucking short-order cook would win. And when you really considered the matter, all this was the fucking cook's fault.

At some point the fire whistle quit. Junior slept with the covers over his head. When he woke up, it was nine PM. His headache was gone.

And the house was still empty.

CLUSTERMUG

1

When Big Jim Rennie scrunched to a stop in his H3 Alpha Hummer (color: Black Pearl; accessories: you name it), he was a full three minutes ahead of the town cops, which was just the way he liked it. Keep ahead of the competish, that was Rennie's motto.

Ernie Calvert was still on the phone, but he raised a hand in a half-assed salute. His hair was in disarray and he looked nearly insane with excitement. "Yo, Big Jim, I got through to em!"

"Through to who?" Rennie asked, not paying much attention. He was looking at the still-burning pyre of the pulp-truck, and at the wreckage of what was clearly a plane. This was a mess, one that could mean a black eye for the town, especially with the two newest firewagons over in The Rock. A training exercise he had approved of . . . but Andy Sanders's signature was the one on the approval form, because Andy was First Selectman. That was good. Rennie was a great believer in what he called the Protectability Quotient, and being Second Selectman was a prime example of the Quotient in action; you got all of the power (at least when the First was a nit like Sanders), but rarely had to take the blame when things went wrong.

And this was what Rennie—who had given his heart to

Jesus at age sixteen and did not use foul language—called "a clustermug." Steps would have to be taken. Control would have to be imposed. And he couldn't count on that elderly ass Howard Perkins to do the job. Perkins might have been a perfectly adequate police chief twenty years ago, but this was a new century.

Rennie's frown deepened as he surveyed the scene. Too many spectators. Of course there were always too many at things such as this; people loved blood and destruction. And some of these appeared to be playing a bizarre sort of game: seeing how far they could lean over, or something.

Bizarre.

"You people get back from there!" he shouted. He had a good voice for giving orders, big and confident. "That's an accident site!"

Ernie Calvert—another idiot, the town was full of them, Rennie supposed any town was—tugged at his sleeve. He looked more excited than ever. "Got through to the ANG, Big Jim, and—"

"The who? The *what*? What are you talking about?"

"The Air National Guard!"

Worse and worse. People playing games, and this fool calling the—

"Ernie, why would you call them, for gosh sakes?"

"Because he said . . . the guy said . . ." But Ernie couldn't remember exactly what Barbie had said, so he moved on. "Well anyway, the colonel at the ANG listened to what I was telling him, then connected me with Homeland Security in their Portland office. Put me right through!"

Rennie slapped his hands to his cheeks, a thing he did often when he was exasperated. It made him look like a cold-eyed Jack Benny. Like Benny, Big Jim did indeed tell jokes from time to time (always clean ones). He joked because he sold cars, and because he knew politicians were *supposed* to joke, especially when election time came around. So he kept a small rotating stock of what he called "funnies" (as in "Do you boys want to hear a funny?"). He memorized these much as a tourist in a foreign land will pick up the phrases for stuff like *Where is the bathroom* or *Is there a hotel with Internet in this village?*

But he didn't joke now. "Homeland Security! What in the cotton-picking devil *for?*" *Cotton-picking* was by far Rennie's favorite epithet.

"Because the young guy said there's somethin across the road. And there is, Jim! Somethin you can't see! People can lean on it! See? They're doin it now. Or . . . if you throw a stone against it, it bounces back! Look!" Ernie picked up a stone and threw it. Rennie did not trouble looking to see where it went; he reckoned if it had struck one of the rubberneckers, the fellow would have given a yell. "The truck crashed into it . . . into the whatever-it-is . . . and the plane did, too! And so the guy told me to—"

"Slow down. What guy exactly are we talking about?"

"He's a young guy," Rory Dinsmore said. "He cooks at Sweetbriar Rose. If you ask for a hamburg medium, that's how you get it. My dad says you can hardly ever get medium, because nobody knows how to cook it, but this guy does." His face broke into a smile of extraordinary sweetness. "I know his name."

"Shut up, Roar," his brother warned. Mr. Rennie's face had darkened. In Ollie Dinsmore's experience, this was the way teachers looked just before they slapped you with a week's worth of detention.

Rory, however, paid no mind. "It's a girl's name! It's *Baaarbara.*"

Just when I think I've seen the last of him, that cotton-picker pops up again, Rennie thought. *That darned useless no-account.*

He turned to Ernie Calvert. The police were almost here, but Rennie thought he had time to put a stop to this latest bit of Barbara-induced lunacy. Not that Rennie saw him around. Nor expected to, not really. How like Barbara to stir up the stew, make a mess, then flee.

"Ernie," he said, "you've been misinformed."

Alden Dinsmore stepped forward. "Mr. Rennie, I don't see how you can say that, when you don't know what the information is."

Rennie smiled at him. Pulled his lips back, anyway. "I know Dale Barbara, Alden; I have *that* much information." He turned back to Ernie Calvert. "Now, if you'll just—"

"Hush," Calvert said, holding up a hand. "I got someone."

Big Jim Rennie did not like to be hushed, especially by a retired grocery store manager. He plucked the phone from Ernie's hand as though Ernie were an assistant who had been holding it for just that purpose.

A voice from the cell phone said, "To whom am I speaking?" Less than half a dozen words, but they were enough to tell Rennie that he was dealing with a bureaucratic son-of-a-buck. The Lord knew he'd dealt with enough of them in his three decades as a town official, and the Feds were the worst.

"This is James Rennie, Second Selectman of Chester's Mill. Who are you, sir?"

"Donald Wozniak, Homeland Security. I understand you have some sort of problem out there on Highway 119. An interdiction of some kind."

Interdiction? *Interdiction?* What kind of Fedspeak was that?

"You have been misinformed, sir," Rennie said. "What

we have is an airplane—a *civilian* plane, a *local* plane—
that tried to land on the road and hit a truck. The situation is completely under control. We do not require the
aid of Homeland Security."

"Mister Rennie," the farmer said, "that is *not* what
happened."

Rennie flapped a hand at him and began walking toward the first police cruiser. Hank Morrison was getting
out. Big, six-five or so, but basically useless. And behind
him, the gal with the big old tiddies. Wettington, her
name was, and she was worse than useless: a smart mouth
run by a dumb head. But behind *her,* Peter Randolph
was pulling up. Randolph was the Assistant Chief, and a
man after Rennie's own heart. A man who could get 'er
done. If Randolph had been the duty officer on the night
Junior got in trouble at that stupid devilpit of a bar, Big
Jim doubted if Mr. Dale Barbara would still have been in
town to cause trouble today. In fact, Mr. Barbara might
have been behind bars over in The Rock. Which would
have suited Rennie fine.

Meanwhile, the man from Homeland Security—did
they have the nerve to call themselves agents?—was still
jabbering away.

Rennie interrupted him. "Thank you for your interest,
Mr. Wozner, but we've got this handled." He pushed the
END button without saying goodbye. Then he tossed the
phone back to Ernie Calvert.

"Jim, I don't think that was wise."

Rennie ignored him and watched Randolph stop behind the Wettington gal's cruiser, bubblegum bars flashing. He thought about walking down to meet Randolph,
and rejected the idea before it was fully formed in his
mind. Let Randolph come to him. That was how it was
supposed to work. And how it *would* work, by God.

2

"Big Jim," Randolph said. "What's happened here?"

"I believe that's obvious," Big Jim said. "Chuck Thompson's airplane got into a little argument with a pulp-truck. Looks like they fought it to a draw." Now he could hear sirens coming from Castle Rock. Almost certainly FD responders (Rennie hoped their own two new—and horribly expensive—firewagons were among them; it would play better if no one actually realized the new trucks had been out of town when this clustermug happened). Ambulances and police would be close behind.

"That ain't what happened," Alden Dinsmore said stubbornly. "I was out in the side garden, and I saw the plane just—"

"Better move those people back, don't you think?" Rennie asked Randolph, pointing to the lookie-loos. There were quite a few on the pulp-truck side, standing prudently away from the blazing remains, and even more on The Mill side. It was starting to look like a convention.

Randolph addressed Morrison and Wettington. "Hank," he said, and pointed at the spectators from The Mill. Some had begun prospecting among the scattered pieces of Thompson's plane. There were cries of horror as more body parts were discovered.

"Yo," Morrison said, and got moving.

Randolph turned Wettington toward the spectators on the pulp-truck side. "Jackie, you take . . ." But there Randolph trailed off.

The disaster-groupies on the south side of the accident were standing in the cow pasture on one side of the road and knee-deep in scrubby bushes on the other. Their mouths hung open, giving them a look of stupid interest Rennie was very familiar with; he saw it on individual faces every day, and en masse every March, at town meeting. Only these people weren't looking at the burning truck. And now Peter Randolph, certainly no dummy (not brilliant, not by a long shot, but at least he knew which side his bread was buttered on), was looking at the same place as the rest of them, and with that same expression of slack-jawed amazement. So was Jackie Wettington.

It was the smoke the rest were looking at. The smoke rising from the burning pulper.

It was dark and oily. The people downwind should have been darned near choking on it, especially with a light breeze out of the south, but they weren't. And Rennie saw the reason why. It was hard to believe, but he saw it, all right. The smoke *did* blow north, at least at first, but then it took an elbow-bend—almost a right angle—and rose straight up in a plume, as if in a chimney. And it left a dark brown residue behind. A long smudge that just seemed to float on the air.

Jim Rennie shook his head to clear the image away, but it was still there when he stopped.

"What is it?" Randolph asked. His voice was soft with wonder.

Dinsmore, the farmer, placed himself in front of Randolph. "*That* guy"—pointing at Ernie Calvert—"had Homeland Security on the phone, and *this* guy"—pointing at Rennie in a theatrical courtroom gesture Rennie didn't care for in the least—"took the phone out of his hand and hung up! He shun't'a done that, Pete. Because that was no collision. The plane wasn't anywhere near the ground. I seen it. I was covering plants in case of frost, and I *seen* it."

"I did, too—" Rory began, and this time it was his brother Ollie who went up the backside of Rory's head. Rory began to whine.

Alden Dinsmore said, "It *hit* something. Same thing the truck hit. It's there, you can touch it. That young fella—the cook—said there oughta be a no-fly zone out here, and he was right. But Mr. Rennie"—again pointing at Rennie like he thought he was a gosh-darn Perry Mason instead of a fellow who earned his daily bread attaching suction cups to cows' tiddies—"wouldn't even *talk*. Just hung up."

Rennie did not stoop to rebuttal. "You're wasting time," he told Randolph. Moving a little closer and speaking just above a whisper, he added: "The Chief's coming. My advice would be to look sharp and control this scene before he gets here." He cast a cold momentary eye on the farmer. "You can interview the witnesses later."

But—maddeningly—it was Alden Dinsmore who got the last word. "That fella Barber was right. He was right and Rennie was wrong."

Rennie marked Alden Dinsmore for later action. Sooner or later, farmers always came to the Selectmen with their hats in their hands—wanting an easement, a zoning exception, something—and when Mr. Dinsmore next showed up, he would find little comfort, if Rennie had anything to say about it. And he usually did.

"Control this scene!" he told Randolph.

"Jackie, move those people back," the Assistant Chief said, pointing toward the lookie-loos on the pulp-truck side of the accident. "Establish a perimeter."

"Sir, I think those folks are actually in Motton—"

"I don't care, move them back." Randolph glanced over his shoulder to where Duke Perkins was working his way out of the green Chief's car—a car Randolph longed to see in his own driveway. And would, with Big Jim Rennie's help. In another three years at the very latest. "Castle Rock PD'll thank you when they get here, believe me."

"What about . . ." She pointed at the smoke-smudge, which was still spreading. Seen through it, the October-colorful trees looked a uniform dark gray, and the sky was an unhealthy shade of yellowy-blue.

"Stay clear of it," Randolph said, then went to help Hank Morrison establish the perimeter on the Chester's Mill side. But first he needed to bring Perk up to speed.

Jackie approached the people on the pulp-truck side. The crowd over there was growing all the time as the early arrivers worked their cell phones. Some had stamped out little fires in the bushes, which was good, but now they were just standing around, gawking. She used the same shooing gestures Hank was employing on The Mill side, and chanted the same mantra.

"Get back, folks, it's all over, nothing to see you haven't seen already, clear the road for the firetrucks and the police, get back, clear the area, go home, get ba—"

She hit something. Rennie had no idea what it was, but he could see the result. The brim of her hat collided with it first. It bent, and the hat tumbled off behind her. An instant later those insolent tiddies of hers—a couple of cotton-picking gunshells was what they were—flattened. Then her nose squashed and gave up a jet of blood that splattered against something . . . and began to run down in long drips, like paint on a wall. She went on her well-padded ass with an expression of shock on her face.

The goddarn farmer stuck his oar in then: "See? What'd I tell you?"

Randolph and Morrison hadn't seen. Neither had Perkins; the three of them were conferring together by the hood of the Chief's car. Rennie briefly considered going to Wettington, but others were doing that, and besides—she was still a little too close to whatever it was she'd run into. He hurried toward the men instead, set face and big hard belly projecting get-'er-done authority. He spared a glare for Farmer Dinsmore on his way by.

"Chief," he said, butting in between Morrison and Randolph.

"Big Jim," Perkins said, nodding. "You didn't waste any time, I see."

This was perhaps a gibe, but Rennie, a sly old fish, did not rise to the bait. "I'm afraid there's more going on here than meets the eye. I think someone had better get in touch with Homeland Security." He paused, looking suitably grave. "I don't want to say there's terrorism involved . . . but I won't say there isn't."

3

Duke Perkins looked past Big Jim. Jackie was being helped to her feet by Ernie Calvert and Johnny Carver, who ran Mill Gas & Grocery. She was dazed and her nose was bleeding, but she appeared all right otherwise. Nevertheless, this whole situation was hinky. Of course, any accident where there were fatalities felt that way to some extent, but there was more wrong here.

For one thing, the plane hadn't been trying to land. There were too many pieces, and they were too widely scattered, for him to believe that. And the spectators. They weren't right, either. Randolph hadn't noticed, but Duke Perkins did. They should have formed into one big spreading clump. It was what they always did, as if for comfort in the face of death. Only these had formed *two* clumps, and the one on the Motton side of the town line marker was awfully close to the still-burning truck. Not in any danger, he judged . . . but why didn't they move over here?

The first firetrucks swept around the curve to the

south. Three of them. Duke was glad to see that the second one in line had CHESTER'S MILL FIRE DEPARTMENT PUMPER NO. 2 printed in gold on the side. The crowd shuffled back farther into the scrubby bushes, giving them room. Duke returned his attention to Rennie. "What happened here? Do you know?"

Rennie opened his mouth to reply, but before he could, Ernie Calvert spoke up. "There's a barrier across the road. You can't see it, but it's there, Chief. The truck hit it. The plane, too."

"Damn right!" Dinsmore exclaimed.

"Officer Wettington hit it, too," Johnny Carver said. "Lucky for her she was goin slower." He had placed an arm around Jackie, who looked dazed. Duke observed her blood on the sleeve of Carver's I GOT GASSED AT MILL DISCOUNT jacket.

On the Motton side, another FD truck had arrived. The first two had blocked the road in a V. Firemen were already spilling out and unrolling hoses. Duke could hear the warble of an ambulance from the direction of Castle Rock. *Where's ours?* he wondered. Had it also gone to that stupid damn training exercise? He didn't like to think so. Who in their right mind would order an ambulance to an empty burning house?

"There seems to be an invisible barrier—" Rennie began.

"Yeah, I got that," Duke said. "I don't know what it means, but I got it." He left Rennie and went to his bleeding officer, not seeing the dark red color that suffused the Second Selectman's cheeks at this snub.

"Jackie?" Duke asked, taking her gently by the shoulder. "All right?"

"Yeah." She touched her nose, where the blood-flow was slowing. "Does it look broken? It doesn't *feel* broken."

"It's not broken, but it's going to swell. Think you'll look all right by the time the Harvest Ball comes around, though."

She offered a weak smile.

"Chief," Rennie said, "I really think we ought to call someone on this. If not Homeland Security—on more mature reflection that seems a little radical—then perhaps the State Police—"

Duke moved him aside. It was gentle but unequivocal. Almost a push. Rennie balled his hands into fists, then unrolled them again. He had built a life in which he was a pusher rather than a pushee, but that didn't alter the fact that fists were for idiots. Witness his own son. All the same, slights needed to be noted and addressed. Usually at some later date . . . but sometimes later was better.

Sweeter.

"Peter!" Duke called to Randolph. "Give the Health Center a shout and ask where the hell our ambulance is! I want it out here!"

"Morrison can do that," Randolph said. He had grabbed the camera from his car and was turning to snap pictures of the scene.

"*You* can do it, and right now."

"Chief, I don't think Jackie's too banged up, and no one else—"

"When I want your opinion I'll ask for it, Peter."

Randolph started to give him a look, then saw the expression on Duke's face. He tossed the camera back onto the front seat of his shop and grabbed his cell phone.

"What was it, Jackie?" Duke asked.

"I don't know. First there was a buzzy feeling like you get if you accidentally touch the prongs of a plug when you're sticking it into the wall. It passed, but then I hit . . . jeez, I don't know what I hit."

An *ahhh* sound went up from the spectators. The firemen had trained their hoses on the burning pulp-truck, but beyond it, some of the spray was rebounding. Striking something and splattering back, creating rainbows in the air. Duke had never seen anything like it in his life . . . except maybe when you were in a car wash, watching the high-pressure jets hit your windshield.

Then he saw a rainbow on the Mill side as well: a small one. One of the spectators—Lissa Jamieson, the town librarian—walked toward it.

"Lissa, get away from there!" Duke shouted.

She ignored him. It was as if she were hypnotized. She stood inches from where a jet of high-pressure water was striking thin air and splashing back, her hands spread. He could see drops of mist sparkling on her hair, which was pulled away from her face and bunned at the back. The little rainbow broke up, then re-formed behind her.

"Nothing but mist!" she called, sounding rapturous. "All that water over there and nothing but mist over here! Like from a humidifier."

Peter Randolph held up his cell phone and shook his head. "I get a signal, but I'm not getting through. My guess is that all these spectators"—he swept his arm in a big arc—"have got everything jammed up."

Duke didn't know if that were possible, but it was true that almost everyone he could see was either yakking or taking pictures. Except for Lissa, that was, who was still doing her wood-nymph imitation.

"Go get her," Duke told Randolph. "Pull her back before she decides to haul out her crystals or something."

Randolph's face suggested that such errands were far below his pay grade, but he went. Duke uttered a laugh. It was short but genuine.

"What in the goodness sakes do you see that's worth

laughing about?" Rennie asked. More Castle County cops were pulling up on the Motton side. If Perkins didn't look out, The Rock would end up taking control of this thing. And getting the gosh-darn credit.

Duke stopped laughing, but he was still smiling. Unabashed. "It's a clustermug," he said. "Isn't that your word, Big Jim? And in my experience, sometimes laughing is the only way to deal with a clustermug."

"I have no idea what you're talking about!" Rennie almost shouted. The Dinsmore boys stepped back from him and stood beside their father.

"I know." Duke spoke gently. "And that's okay. All you need to understand right now is that I'm the chief law enforcement officer on the scene, at least until the County Sheriff gets here, and you're a town selectman. You have no official standing, so I'd like you to move back."

Duke raised his voice and pointed to where Officer Henry Morrison was stringing yellow tape, stepping around two largeish pieces of airplane fuselage to do it. "I'd like *everyone* to move back and let us do our job! Follow Selectman Rennie. He's going to lead you behind the yellow tape."

"I don't appreciate this, Duke," Rennie said.

"God bless you, but I don't give a shit," Duke said. "Get off my scene, Big Jim. And be sure to go around the tape. No need for Henry to have to string it twice."

"Chief Perkins, I want you to remember how you spoke to me today. Because I will."

Rennie stalked toward the tape. The other spectators followed, most looking over their shoulders to watch the water spray off the diesel-smudged barrier and form a line of wetness on the road. A couple of the sharper ones (Ernie Calvert, for instance) had already noticed that this line exactly mimicked the border between Motton and The Mill.

Rennie felt a childish temptation to snap Hank Morrison's carefully strung tape with his chest, but restrained himself. He would not, however, go around and get his Land's End slacks snagged in a mess of burdocks. They had cost him sixty dollars. He shuffled under, holding up the tape with one hand. His belly made serious ducking impossible.

Behind him, Duke walked slowly toward the place where Jackie had suffered her collision. He held one hand outstretched before him like a blind man prospecting his way across an unfamiliar room.

Here was where she had fallen down . . . and *here* . . .

He felt the buzzing she had described, but instead of passing, it deepened to searing pain in the hollow of his left shoulder. He had just enough time to remember the last thing Brenda had said—*Take care of your pacemaker*—and then it exploded in his chest with enough force to blow open his Wildcats sweatshirt, which he'd donned that morning in honor of this afternoon's game. Blood, scraps of cotton, and bits of flesh struck the barrier.

The crowd *aaah*ed.

Duke tried to speak his wife's name and failed, but he saw her face clearly in his mind. She was smiling.

Then, darkness.

4

The kid was Benny Drake, fourteen, and a Razor. The Razors were a small but dedicated skateboarding club, frowned on by the local constabulary but not actually outlawed, in spite of calls from Selectmen Rennie and Sanders for such action (at last March's town meeting, this same dynamic duo had succeeded in tabling a budget item that would have funded a safe-skateboarding area on the town common behind the bandstand).

The adult was Eric "Rusty" Everett, thirty-seven, a physician's assistant working with Dr. Ron Haskell, whom Rusty often thought of as The Wonderful Wizard of Oz. *Because,* Rusty would have explained (if he'd anyone other than his wife he could trust with such disloyalty), *he so often remains behind the curtain while I do the work.*

Now he checked the state of young Master Drake's last tetanus shot. Fall of 2009, very good. Especially considering that young Master Drake had done a Wilson while cement-shooting and torn up his calf pretty good. Not a total jake, but a lot worse than simple roadrash.

"Power's back on, dude," young Master Drake offered.

"Generator, dude," Rusty said. "Handles the hospital *and* the Health Center. Radical, huh?"

"Old-school," young Master Drake agreed.

For a moment the adult and the adolescent regarded the six-inch gash in Benny Drake's calf without speaking. Cleaned of dirt and blood, it looked ragged but no longer downright awful. The town whistle had quit, but far in the distance, they could hear sirens. Then the fire whistle went off, making them both jump.

Ambulance is gonna roll, Rusty thought. *Sure as shit. Twitch and Everett ride again. Better hurry this up.*

Except the kid's face was pretty white, and Rusty thought there were tears standing in his eyes.

"Scared?" Rusty asked.

"A little," Benny Drake said. "Ma's gonna ground me."

"Is that what you're scared of?" Because he guessed that Benny Drake had been grounded a few times before. Like often, dude.

"Well . . . how much is it gonna hurt?"

Rusty had been hiding the syringe. Now he injected

three cc's of Xylocaine and epinephrine—a deadening compound he still called Novocain. He took his time infiltrating the wound, so as not to hurt the kid any more than he had to. "About that much."

"Whoa," Benny said. "Stat, baby. Code blue."

Rusty laughed. "Did you full-pipe before you Wilsoned?" As a long-retired boarder, he was honestly curious.

"Only half, but it was toxic!" Benny said, brightening. "How many stitches, do you think? Norrie Calvert took twelve when she ledged out in Oxford last summer."

"Not that many," Rusty said. He knew Norrie, a minigoth whose chief aspiration seemed to be killing herself on a skateboard before bearing her first woods colt. He pressed near the wound with the needle end of the syringe. "Feel that?"

"Yeah, dude, totally. Did you hear, like, a bang out there?" Benny pointed vaguely south as he sat on the examining table in his undershorts, bleeding onto the paper cover.

"Nope," Rusty said. He had actually heard two: not bangs but, he was afraid, explosions. Had to make this fast. And where was The Wizard? Doing rounds, according to Ginny. Which probably meant snoozing in the Cathy Russell doctors' lounge. It was where The Wonderful Wiz did most of his rounds these days.

"Feel it now?" Rusty poked again with the needle. "Don't look, looking is cheating."

"No, man, nothin. You're goofin wit me."

"I'm not. You're numb." *In more ways than one,* Rusty thought. "Okay, here we go. Lie back, relax, and enjoy flying Cathy Russell Airlines." He scrubbed the wound with sterile saline, debrided, then trimmed with his trusty no. 10 scalpel. "Six stitches with my very best four-oh nylon."

"Awesome," the kid said. Then: "I think I may hurl."

Rusty handed him an emesis basin, in these circumstances known as a puke pan. "Hurl in this. Faint and you're on your own."

Benny didn't faint. He didn't hurl, either. Rusty was placing a sterile gauze sponge on the wound when there was a perfunctory knock at the door, followed by Ginny Tomlinson's head. "Can I speak to you for a minute?"

"Don't worry about me," Benny said. "I'm like, freely radical." Cheeky little bugger.

"In the hall, Rusty?" Ginny said. She didn't give the kid a glance.

"I'll be right back, Benny. Sit there and take it easy."

"Chillaxin'. No prob."

Rusty followed Ginny out into the hall. "Ambulance time?" he asked. Beyond Ginny, in the sunny waiting room, Benny's mother was looking grimly down at a paperback with a sweet-savage cover.

Ginny nodded. "119, at the Tarker's town line. There's another accident on the *other* town line—Motton—but I'm hearing everyone involved in that one is DATS." Dead at the scene. "Truck-plane collision. The plane was trying to land."

"Are you *shitting* me?"

Alva Drake looked around, frowning, then went back to her paperback. Or at least to looking at it while she tried to decide if her husband would support her in grounding Benny until he was eighteen.

"This is an authentic no-shit situation," Ginny said. "I'm getting reports of other crashes, too—"

"Weird."

"—but the guy out on the Tarker's town line is still alive. Rolled a delivery truck, I believe. Buzz, cuz. Twitch is waiting."

"You'll finish the kid?"

"Yes. Go on, go."

"Dr. Rayburn?"

"Had patients in Stephens Memorial." This was the Norway–South Paris hospital. "He's on his way, Rusty. Go."

He paused on his way out to tell Mrs. Drake that Benny was fine. Alva did not seem overjoyed at the news, but thanked him. Dougie Twitchell—Twitch—was sitting on the bumper of the out-of-date ambulance Jim Rennie and his fellow selectmen kept not replacing, smoking a cigarette and taking some sun. He was holding a portable CB, and it was lively with talk: voices popping like corn and jumping all over each other.

"Put out that cancer-stick and let's get rolling," Rusty said. "You know where we're going, right?"

Twitch flipped the butt away. Despite his nickname, he was the calmest nurse Rusty had ever encountered, and that was saying a lot. "I know what Gin-Gin told you—Tarker's-Chester's town line, right?"

"Yes. Overturned truck."

"Yeah, well, plans have changed. We gotta go the other way." He pointed to the southern horizon, where a thick black pillar of smoke was rising. "Ever had a desire to see a crashed plane?"

"I have," Rusty said. "In the service. Two guys. You could have spread what was left on bread. That was plenty for me, pilgrim. Ginny says they're all dead out there, so why—"

"Maybe so, maybe no," Twitch said, "but now Perkins is down, and he might not be."

"*Chief* Perkins?"

"The very same. I'm thinking the prognosis ain't good if the pacemaker blew right out of his chest—which is what Peter Randolph is claiming—but he *is* the Chief of Police. Fearless Leader."

"Twitch. Buddy. A pacemaker can't blow like that. It's perfectly unpossible."

"Then maybe he *is* still alive, and we can do some good," Twitch said. Halfway around the hood of the ambo, he took out his cigarettes.

"You're not smoking in the ambulance," Rusty said.

Twitch looked at him sadly.

"Unless you share, that is."

Twitch sighed and handed him the pack.

"Ah, Marlboros," Rusty said. "My very favorite OPs."

"You slay me," Twitch said.

5

They blew through the stoplight where Route 117 **T**'d into 119 at the center of town, siren blaring, both of them smoking like fiends (with the windows open, which was SOP), listening to the chatter from the radio. Rusty understood little of it, but he was clear on one thing: he was going to be working long past four o'clock.

"Man, I don't know what happened," Twitch said, "but there's this: we're gonna see a genuine aircraft crash site. Post-crash, true, but beggars cannot be choosers."

"Twitch, you're one sick canine."

There was a lot of traffic, mostly headed south. A few of these folks might have legitimate errands, but Rusty thought most were human flies being drawn to the smell of blood. Twitch passed a line of four with no problem; the northbound lane of 119 was oddly empty.

"Look!" Twitch said, pointing. "News chopper! We're

gonna be on the six o'clock news, Big Rusty! Heroic para-
medics fight to—"

But that was where Dougie Twitchell's flight of fancy
ended. Ahead of them—at the accident site, Rusty pre-
sumed—the helicopter did a buttonhook. For a moment
he could read the number **13** on its side and see the CBS
eye. Then it exploded, raining down fire from the cloudless early afternoon sky.

Twitch cried out: *"Jesus, I'm sorry! I didn't mean it!"* And
then, childishly, hurting Rusty's heart even in his shock:
"I take it back!"

6

"I gotta go back," Gendron said. He took off his Sea Dogs
cap and wiped his bloody, grimy, pallid face with it. His nose
had swollen until it looked like a giant's thumb. His eyes
peered out of dark circles. "I'm sorry, but my schnozz is
hurting like hell, and . . . well, I ain't as young as I used to be.
Also . . ." He raised his arms and dropped them. They were
facing each other, and Barbie would have taken the guy in
his arms and given him a pat on the back, if it were possible.

"Shock to the system, isn't it?" he asked Gendron.

Gendron gave a bark of laughter. "That copter was
the final touch." And they both looked toward the fresh
column of smoke.

Barbie and Gendron had gone on from the accident
site on 117 after making sure that the witnesses were getting help for Elsa Andrews, the sole survivor. At least she
didn't seem badly hurt, although she was clearly heartbroken over the loss of her friend.

"Go on back, then. Slow. Take your time. Rest when
you need to."

"Pushing on?"

"Yes."

"Still think you're gonna find the end of it?"

Barbie was silent for a moment. At first he'd been sure, but now—

"I hope so," he said.

"Well, good luck." Gendron tipped his cap to Barbie before putting it back on. "I hope to shake your hand before the day's out."

"Me, too," Barbie said. He paused. He had been thinking. "Can you do something for me, if you can get to your cell phone?"

"Sure."

"Call the Army base at Fort Benning. Ask for the liaison officer and tell them you need to get in touch with Colonel James O. Cox. Tell them it's urgent, that you're calling for Captain Dale Barbara. Can you remember that?"

"Dale Barbara. That's you. James Cox, that's him. Got it."

"If you reach him . . . I'm not sure you will, but *if* . . . tell him what's going on here. Tell him if no one's gotten in touch with Homeland Security, he's the man. Can you do that?"

Gendron nodded. "If I can, I will. Good luck, soldier."

Barbie could have done without ever having been called that again, but he touched a finger to his forehead. Then he went on, looking for what he no longer thought he would find.

7

He found a woods road that roughly paralleled the barrier. It was overgrown and disused, but much better than pushing through the puckerbrush. Every now and then he diverted to the west, feeling for the wall between Chester's Mill and the outside world. It was always there.

When Barbie came to where 119 crossed into The Mill's sister town of Tarker's Mills, he stopped. The driver of the overturned delivery truck had been taken away by some good Samaritan on the other side of the barrier, but the truck itself lay blocking the road like a big dead animal. The back doors had sprung open on impact. The tar was littered with Devil Dogs, Ho Hos, Ring Dings, Twinkies, and peanut butter crackers. A young man in a George Strait tee-shirt sat on a stump, eating one of the latter. He had a cell phone in hand. He looked up at Barbie. "Yo. Did you come from . . ." He pointed vaguely behind Barbie. He looked tired and scared and disillusioned.

"From the other side of town," Barbie said. "Right."

"Invisible wall the whole way? Border closed?"

"Yes."

The young man nodded and hit a button on his cell. "Dusty? You there yet?" He listened some more, then said: "Okay." He ended the call. "My friend Dusty and I started east of here. Split up. He went south. We've been staying in touch by phone. When we can get through, that is. He's where the copter crashed now. Says it's getting crowded there."

Barbie bet it was. "No break in this thing anywhere on your side?"

The young man shook his head. He didn't say more, and didn't need to. They could have missed breaks, Barbie knew that was possible—holes the size of windows or doors—but he doubted it.

He thought they were cut off.

WE ALL SUPPORT
THE TEAM

1

Barbie walked back down Route 119 into the center of town, a distance of about three miles. By the time he got there, it was six o'clock. Main Street was almost deserted, but alive with the roar of generators; dozens of them, by the sound. The traffic light at the intersection of 119 and 117 was dark, but Sweetbriar Rose was lit and loaded. Looking through the big front window, Barbie saw that every table was taken. But when he walked in the door, he heard none of the usual big talk: politics, the Red Sox, the local economy, the Patriots, newly acquired cars and pickemups, the Celtics, the price of gas, the Bruins, newly acquired power tools, the Twin Mills Wildcats. None of the usual laughter, either.

There was a TV over the counter, and everyone was watching it. Barbie observed, with that sense of disbelief and dislocation everyone who actually finds him- or herself at the site of a major disaster must feel, that CNN's Anderson Cooper was standing out on Route 119 with the still-smoldering hulk of the wrecked pulp-truck in the background.

Rose herself was waiting table, occasionally darting back to the counter to take an order. Wispy locks of hair were escaping her net and hanging around her face. She looked tired and harried. The counter was supposed to be Angie McCain's territory from four until closing, but Barbie saw no sign of her tonight. Perhaps she'd been out of town when the barrier slammed down. If that were the case, she might not be back behind the counter for a good long while.

Anson Wheeler—whom Rosie usually just called "the kid," although the guy had to be at least twenty-five—was cooking, and Barbie dreaded to think what Anse might do to anything more complicated than beans and franks, the traditional Saturday-night special at Sweetbriar Rose. Woe to the fellow or gal who ordered breakfast-for-dinner and had to face Anson's nuclear fried eggs. Still, it was good he was here, because in addition to the missing Angie, there was also no sign of Dodee Sanders. Although *that* particular drip didn't need a disaster to keep her away from work. She wasn't lazy, exactly, but she was easily distracted. And when it came to brainpower . . . jeez, what could you say? Her father—Andy Sanders, The Mill's First Selectman—would never be a Mensa candidate, but Dodee made him look like Albert Einstein.

On the TV, helicopters were landing behind Anderson Cooper, blowing his groovy white hair around and nearly drowning his voice. The copters looked like Pave Lows. Barbie had ridden in his share during his time in Iraq. Now an Army officer walked into the picture, covered Cooper's mike with one gloved hand, and spoke in the reporter's ear.

The assembled diners in Sweetbriar Rose murmured among themselves. Barbie understood their disquiet. He felt it himself. When a man in a uniform covered a famous TV reporter's mike without so much as a by-your-leave, it was surely the End of Days.

The Army guy—a Colonel but not *his* Colonel, seeing Cox would have completed Barbie's sense of mental dislocation—finished what he had to say. His glove made a windy *whroop* sound when he took it off the mike. He walked out of the shot, his face a stolid blank. Barbie recognized the look: Army pod-person.

Cooper was saying, "The press is being told we have to fall back half a mile, to a place called Raymond's Roadside Store." The patrons murmured again at this. They all knew Raymond's Roadside in Motton, where the sign in the window said COLD BEER HOT SANDWICHES FRESH BAIT. "This area, less than a hundred yards from what we're calling the barrier—for want of a better term—has been declared a national security site. We'll resume our coverage as soon as we can, but right now I'm sending it back to you in Washington, Wolf."

The headline on the red band beneath the location shot read **BREAKING NEWS MAINE TOWN CUT OFF MYSTERY DEEPENS.** And in the upper righthand corner, in red, the word **SEVERE** was blinking like a neon tavern sign. *Drink Severe Beer,* Barbie thought, and nearly chuckled.

Wolf Blitzer took Anderson Cooper's place. Rose had a crush on Blitzer and would not allow the TV to be tuned to anything but *The Situation Room* on weekday afternoons; she called him "my Wolfie." This evening Wolfie was wearing a tie, but it was badly knotted and Barbie thought the rest of his clothes looked suspiciously like Saturday grubs.

"Recapping our story," Rose's Wolfie said, "this afternoon at roughly one o'clock—"

"'Twas earlier than that, and by quite a patch," someone said.

"Is it true about Myra Evans?" someone else asked. "Is she really dead?"

"Yes," Fernald Bowie said. The town's only undertaker,

Stewart Bowie, was Fern's older brother. Fern sometimes helped him out when he was sober, and he looked sober tonight. Shocked sober. "Now shutcha quack so I can hear this."

Barbie wanted to hear it, too, because Wolfie was even now addressing the question Barbie cared most about, and saying what Barbie wanted to hear: that the airspace over Chester's Mill had been declared a no-fly zone. In fact, all of western Maine and eastern New Hampshire, from Lewiston-Auburn to North Conway, was a no-fly zone. The President was being briefed. And for the first time in nine years, the color of the National Threat Advisory had exceeded orange.

Julia Shumway, owner and editor of the *Democrat,* shot Barbie a glance as he passed her table. Then the pinched and secretive little smile that was her specialty—almost her trademark—flickered on her face. "It seems that Chester's Mill doesn't want to let you go, Mr. Barbara."

"So it seems," Barbie agreed. That she knew he had been leaving—and why—didn't surprise him. He'd spent enough time in The Mill to know Julia Shumway knew everything worth knowing.

Rose saw him as she was serving beans and franks (plus a smoking relic that might once have been a pork chop) to a party of six crammed around a table for four. She froze with a plate in each hand and two more on her arm, eyes wide. Then she smiled. It was one full of undisguised happiness and relief, and it lifted his heart.

This is what home feels like, he thought. *Goddamned if it isn't.*

"Good gravy, I never expected to see *you* again, Dale Barbara!"

"You still got my apron?" Barbie asked. A little shyly. Rose had taken him in, after all—just a drifter with a few scribbled references in his backpack—and given him work. She'd told him she completely understood why he felt he had to blow town, Junior Rennie's dad wasn't a fellow you wanted for an enemy, but Barbie still felt as if he'd left her in the lurch.

Rose put down her load of plates anywhere there was room for them and hurried to Barbie. She was a plump little woman, and she had to stand on tiptoe to hug him, but she managed.

"I'm so goddam glad to see you!" she whispered. Barbie hugged her back and kissed the top of her head.

"Big Jim and Junior won't be," he said. But at least neither Rennie was here; there was that to be grateful for. Barbie was aware that, for the time being, at least, he had become even more interesting to the assembled Millites than their very own town on national TV.

"Big Jim Rennie can blow me!" she said. Barbie laughed, delighted by her fierceness but glad for her discretion—she was still whispering. "I thought you were gone!"

"I almost was, but I got a late start."

"Did you see . . . it?"

"Yes. Tell you later." He released her, held her at arm's length, and thought: *If you were ten years younger, Rose . . . or even five . . .*

"So I can have my apron back?"

She wiped the corners of her eyes and nodded. "*Please* take it back. Get Anson out of there before he kills us all."

Barbie gave her a salute, then hooked around the counter into the kitchen and sent Anson Wheeler to the counter, telling him to take care of orders and cleanup there before helping Rose in the main room. Anson stepped back from the grill with a sigh of relief. Before going to the counter, he shook Barbie's right hand in both of his. "Thank God, man—I never seen such a rush. I was lost."

"Don't worry. We're gonna feed the five thousand."

Anson, no Biblical scholar, looked blank. "Huh?"

"Never mind."

The bell sitting in the corner of the pass-through binged. "Order up!" Rose called.

Barbie grabbed a spatula before taking the slip—the grill was a mess, it always was when Anson was engaged in those cataclysmic heat-induced changes he called cooking—then slipped his apron over his head, tied it in back, and checked the cabinet over the sink. It was full of baseball caps, which served Sweetbriar Rose grill-monkeys as chef's toques. He selected a Sea Dogs cap in honor of Paul Gendron (now in the bosom of his nearest and dearest, Barbie hoped), yanked it on backward, and cracked his knuckles.

Then he grabbed the first slip and went to work.

2

By nine fifteen, more than an hour after their usual Saturday night closing time, Rose ushered the final patrons out. Barbie locked the door and turned the sign from OPEN to CLOSED. He watched those last four or five cross the street to the town common, where there were as many as fifty people gathered and talking among themselves. They were facing south, where a great white light formed a bubble over 119. Not TV lights, Barbie judged; that was the U.S. Army, creating and securing a perimeter. And how did you secure a perimeter at night? Why, by posting sentries and lighting the dead zone, of course.

Dead zone. He didn't like the sound of that.

Main Street, on the other hand, was unnaturally dark. There were electric lights shining in some of the buildings—where there were gennies at work—and battery-powered emergency lights shining in Burpee's Department Store, the Gas & Grocery, Mill New & Used Books, Food City at the foot of Main Street Hill, and half a dozen others, but the streetlights were dark and there were candles shining in most of Main Street's second-floor windows, where there were apartments.

Rose sat at a table in the middle of the room, smoking a cigarette (illegal in public buildings, but Barbie would never tell). She pulled the net off her head and gave Barbie a wan smile as he sat down across from her. Behind them Anson was swabbing the counter, his own shoulder-length hair now liberated from its Red Sox cap.

"I thought Fourth of July was bad, but this was worse," Rose said. "If you hadn't turned up, I'd be curled in the corner, screaming for my mommy."

"There was a blonde in an F-150," Barbie said, smiling at the memory. "She almost gave me a ride. If she had, I might've been out. On the other hand, what happened to Chuck Thompson and the woman in that airplane with him might have happened to me." Thompson's name had been part of CNN's coverage; the woman hadn't been identified.

But Rose knew. "It was Claudette Sanders. I'm almost sure it was. Dodee told me yesterday that her mom had a lesson today."

There was a plate of french fries between them on the table. Barbie had been reaching for one. Now he stopped. All at once he didn't want any more fries. Any more of anything. And the red puddle on the side of the plate looked more like blood than ketchup.

"So that's why Dodee didn't come in."

Rose shrugged. "Maybe. I can't say for sure. I haven't heard from her. Didn't really expect to, with the phones out."

Barbie assumed she meant the landlines, but even from the kitchen he'd heard people complaining about trouble getting through on their cells. Most assumed it was because everyone was trying to use them at the same time, jamming the band. Some thought the influx of TV people—probably hundreds by this time, toting Nokias, Motorolas, iPhones, and BlackBerries—was causing the problem. Barbie had darker suspicions; this was a national security situation, after all, in a time when the whole country was paranoid about terrorism. Some calls were getting through, but fewer and fewer as the evening went on.

"Of course," Rose said, "Dodes might also have taken it into that air head of hers to blow off work and go to the Auburn Mall."

"Does Mr. Sanders know it was Claudette in the plane?"

"I can't say for sure, but I'd be awfully surprised if he doesn't by now." And she sang, in a small but tuneful voice: "It's a small town, you know what I mean?"

Barbie smiled a little and sang the next line back to her: "Just a small town, baby, and we all support the team." It was from an old James McMurtry song that had the previous summer gained a new and mysterious two-month vogue on a couple of western Maine c&w stations. Not WCIK, of course; James McMurtry was not the sort of artist Jesus Radio supported.

Rose pointed to the french fries. "You going to eat any more of those?"

"Nope. Lost my appetite."

Barbie had no great love for either the endlessly grinning Andy Sanders or for Dodee the Dim, who had almost certainly helped her good friend Angie spread the rumor that had caused Barbie's trouble at Dipper's, but the idea that those body parts (it was the green-clad leg his mind's eye kept trying to look at) had belonged to Dodee's *mother* . . . the First Selectman's *wife* . . .

"Me too," Rose said, and put her cigarette out in the ketchup. It made a *pfisss* sound, and for one awful moment Barbie thought he was going to throw up. He turned his head and gazed out the window onto Main Street, although there was nothing to see from in here. From in here it was all dark.

"President's gonna speak at midnight," Anson announced from the counter. From behind him came the low, constant groan of the dishwasher. It occurred to Barbie that the big old Hobart might be doing its last chore, at least for a while. He would have to convince Rosie of that. She'd be reluctant, but she'd see sense. She was a bright and practical woman.

Dodee Sanders's mother. Jesus. What are the odds?

He realized that the odds were actually not that bad. If it hadn't been Mrs. Sanders, it might well have been someone else he knew. *It's a small town, baby, and we all support the team.*

"No President for me tonight," Rose said. "He'll have to God-bless-America on his own. Five o'clock comes early." Sweetbriar Rose didn't open until seven on Sunday mornings, but there was prep. Always prep. And on Sundays, that included cinnamon rolls. "You boys stay up and watch if you want to. Just make sure we're locked up tight when you leave. Front *and* back." She started to rise.

"Rose, we need to talk about tomorrow," Barbie said.

"Fiddle-dee-dee, tomorrow's another day. Let it go for now, Barbie. All in good time." But she must have seen something on his face, because she sat back down. "All right, why the grim look?"

"When's the last time you got propane?"

"Last week. We're almost full. Is that all you're worried about?"

It wasn't, but it was where his worries started. Barbie calculated. Sweetbriar Rose had two tanks hooked together. Each tank had a capacity of either three hundred and twenty-five or three hundred and fifty gallons, he couldn't remember which. He'd check in the morning, but if Rose was right, she had over six hundred gallons on hand. That was good. A bit of luck on a day that had been spectacularly unlucky for the town as a whole. But there was no way of knowing how much bad luck could still be ahead. And six hundred gallons of propane wouldn't last forever.

"What's the burn rate?" he asked her. "Any idea?"

"Why does that matter?"

"Because right now your generator is running this place. Lights, stoves, fridges, pumps. The furnace, too, if it gets cold enough to kick on tonight. And the gennie is eating propane to do it."

They were quiet for a moment, listening to the steady roar of the almost-new Honda behind the restaurant.

Anson Wheeler came over and sat down. "The gennie sucks two gallons of propane an hour at sixty percent utilization," he said.

"How do you know that?" Barbie asked.

"Read it on the tag. Running everything, like we have since around noon, when the power went out, it probably ate three an hour. Maybe a little more."

Rose's response was immediate. "Anse, kill all the lights but the ones in the kitchen. Right now. And turn the furnace thermostat down to fifty." She considered. "No, turn it off."

Barbie smiled and gave her a thumbs-up. She got it. Not everyone in The Mill would. Not everyone in The Mill would *want* to.

"Okay." But Anson looked doubtful. "You don't think by tomorrow morning . . . tomorrow afternoon at the latest . . . ?"

"The President of the United States is going to make a TV speech," Barbie said. "At midnight. What do *you* think, Anse?"

"I think I better turn off the lights," he said.

"And the thermostat, don't forget that," Rose said. As he hurried away, she said to Barbie: "I'll do the same in my place when I go up." A widow for ten years or more, she lived over her restaurant.

Barbie nodded. He had turned over one of the paper placemats ("Have You Visited These 20 Maine Landmarks?") and was figuring on the back. Twenty-seven to thirty gallons of propane burned since the barrier went up. That left five hundred and seventy. If Rose could cut her use back to twenty-five gallons a day, she could theoretically keep going for three weeks. Cut back to twenty gallons a day—which she could probably do by closing between breakfast and lunch and again between lunch and dinner—and she could press on for nearly a month.

Which is fine enough, he thought. *Because if this town isn't open again after a month, there won't be anything here to cook, anyway.*

"What are you thinking?" Rose asked. "And what's up with those numbers? I have no idea what they mean."

"Because you're looking at them upside down," Barbie said, and realized everyone in town was apt to do the same. These were figures no one would want to look at rightside up.

Rose turned Barbie's makeshift scratchpad toward her.

She ran the numbers for herself. Then she raised her head and looked at Barbie, shocked. At that moment Anson turned most of the lights out, and the two of them were staring at each other in a gloom that was—to Barbie, at least—horribly persuasive. They could be in real trouble here.

"Twenty-eight days?" she asked. "You think we need to plan for *four weeks?*"

"I don't know if we do or not, but when I was in Iraq, someone gave me a copy of Chairman Mao's *Little Red Book.* I carried it around in my pocket, read it cover to cover. Most of it makes more sense than our politicians do on their sanest days. One thing that stuck with me was this: *Wish for sunshine, but build dykes.* I think that's what we—you, I mean—"

"We," she said, and touched his hand. He turned his over and clasped it.

"Okay, we. I think that's what we have to plan for. Which means closing between meals, cutting back on the ovens—no cinnamon rolls, even though I love em as much as anybody—and no dishwasher. It's old and energy inefficient. I know Dodee and Anson won't love the idea of washing dishes by hand . . ."

"I don't think we can count on Dodee coming back soon, maybe not at all. Not with her mother dead." Rose sighed. "I almost hope she *did* go to the Auburn Mall. Although I suppose it'll be in the papers tomorrow."

"Maybe." Barbie had no idea how much information was going to come out of or into Chester's Mill if this situation didn't resolve quickly, and with some rational explanation. Probably not much. He thought Maxwell Smart's fabled Cone of Silence would descend soon, if it hadn't already.

Anson came back to the table where Barbie and Rose

were sitting. He had his jacket on. "Is it okay for me to go now, Rose?"

"Sure," she said. "Six tomorrow?"

"Isn't that a little late?" He grinned and added, "Not that I'm complaining."

"We're going to open late." She hesitated. "And close between meals."

"Really? Cool." His gaze shifted to Barbie. "You got a place to stay tonight? Because you can stay with me. Sada went to Derry to visit her folks." Sada was Anson's wife.

Barbie in fact did have a place to go, almost directly across the street.

"Thanks, but I'll go back to my apartment. I'm paid up until the end of the month, so why not? I dropped off the keys with Petra Searles in the drugstore before I left this morning, but I still have a dupe on my key ring."

"Okay. See you in the morning, Rose. Will you be here, Barbie?"

"Wouldn't miss it."

Anson's grin widened. "Excellent."

When he was gone, Rose rubbed her eyes, then looked at Barbie grimly. "How long is this going to go on? Best guess."

"I don't *have* a best guess, because I don't know what happened. Or when it will *stop* happening."

Very low, Rose said: "Barbie, you're scaring me."

"I'm scaring myself. We both need to go to bed. Things will look better in the morning."

"After this discussion, I'll probably need an Ambien to get to sleep," she said, "tired as I am. But thank God you came back."

Barbie remembered what he'd been thinking about supplies.

"One other thing. If Food City opens tomorrow—"

"It's always open on Sundays. Ten to six."

"*If* it opens tomorrow, you need to go shopping."

"But Sysco delivers on—" She broke off and stared at him dismally. "On Tuesdays, but we can't count on that, can we? Of course not."

"No," he said. "Even if what's wrong suddenly becomes right, the Army's apt to quarantine this burg, at least for a while."

"What should I buy?"

"Everything, but especially meat. Meat, meat, meat. If the store opens. I'm not sure it will. Jim Rennie may persuade whoever manages it now—"

"Jack Cale. He took over when Ernie Calvert retired last year."

"Well, Rennie may persuade him to close until further notice. Or get Chief Perkins to *order* the place closed."

"You don't know?" Rose asked, and at his blank look: "You don't. Duke Perkins is dead, Barbie. He died out there." She gestured south.

Barbie stared at her, stunned. Anson had neglected to turn off the television, and behind them, Rose's Wolfie was again telling the world that an unexplained force had cut off a small town in western Maine, the area had been isolated by the armed forces, the Joint Chiefs were meeting in Washington, the President would address the nation at midnight, but in the meantime he was asking the American people to unite their prayers for the people of Chester's Mill with his own.

3

"Dad? *Dad*?"

Junior Rennie stood at the top of the stairs, head cocked, listening. There was no response, and the TV was silent. His dad was *always* home from work and in front of the TV by now. On Saturday nights he forwent CNN and FOX News for either Animal Planet or The History Channel. Not tonight, though. Junior listened to his watch to make sure it was still ticking. It was, and what it said sort of made sense, because it was dark outside.

A terrible thought occurred to him: Big Jim might be with Chief Perkins. The two of them could at this minute be discussing how to arrest Junior with the least possible fuss. And why had they waited so long? So they could spirit him out of town under cover of darkness. Take him to the county jail over in Castle Rock. Then a trial. And then?

Then Shawshank. After a few years there, he'd probably just call it The Shank, like the rest of the murderers, robbers, and sodomites.

"That's stupid," he whispered, but was it? He'd awakened thinking that killing Angie had just been a dream, must have been, because he would never kill anyone. Beat them up, maybe, but *kill*? Ridiculous. He was . . . was . . . well . . . *a regular person*!

Then he'd looked at the clothes under the bed, seen the blood on them, and it all came back. The towel falling off her hair. Her pussypatch, somehow goading him. The complicated crunching sound from behind her face when he'd gotten her with his knee. The rain of fridge magnets and the way she had thrashed.

But that wasn't me. That was . . .

"It was the headache." Yes. True. But who'd believe that? He'd have better luck if he said the butler did it.

"Dad?"

Nothing. Not here. And not at the police station, conspiring against him, either. Not his dad. He wouldn't. His dad always said family came first.

But *did* family come first? Of course he *said* that—he was a Christian, after all, and half-owner of WCIK—but Junior had an idea that for his dad, Jim Rennie's Used Cars might come before family, and that being the town's First Selectman might come before the Holy Tabernacle of No Money Down.

Junior could be—it was possible—third in line.

He realized (for the first time in his life; it was a genuine flash of insight) that he was only guessing. That he might not really know his father at all.

He went back to his room and turned on the overhead. It cast an odd unsteady light, waxing bright and then dim. For a moment Junior thought something was wrong with his eyes. Then he realized he could hear their generator running out back. And not just theirs, either. The town's power was out. He felt a surge of relief. A big power outage explained everything. It meant his father was likely in the Town Hall conference room, discussing matters with those other two idiots, Sanders and Grinnell. Maybe sticking pins in the big map of the town, making like George Patton. Yelling at Western Maine Power and calling them a bunch of lazy cotton-pickers.

Junior got his bloody clothes, raked the shit out of his jeans—wallet, change, keys, comb, an extra headache pill—and redistributed it in the pockets of his clean pants. He hurried downstairs, stuck the incriminating garments in the washer, set it for hot, then reconsidered, remembering something his mother had told him when he was no more than ten: cold water for bloodstains. As he moved the dial to COLD WASH/COLD RINSE, Junior wondered idly if his dad had started his hobby of secretary-fucking way back then, or if he was still keeping his cotton-picking penis at home.

He started the washer going and thought about what

to do next. With the headache gone, he found that he *could* think.

He decided he should go back to Angie's house after all. He didn't want to—God almighty, it was the *last* thing he wanted to do—but he probably should scope out the scene. Walk past and see how many police cars were there. Also whether or not the Castle County forensics van was there. Forensics was key. He knew that from watching *CSI*. He'd seen the big blue-and-white van before, while visiting the county courthouse with his dad. And if it was at the McCains' . . .

I'll run.

Yes. As fast and far as he could. But before he did, he'd come back here and visit the safe in his dad's study. His dad didn't think Junior knew the combo to that safe, but Junior did. Just as he knew the password to his dad's computer, and thus about his dad's penchant for watching what Junior and Frank DeLesseps called Oreo sex: two black chicks, one white guy. There was plenty of money in that safe. Thousands of dollars.

What if you see the van and come back and he's here?

The money first, then. The money right now.

He went into the study and for a moment thought he saw his father sitting in the high-backed chair where he watched the news and nature programs. He'd fallen asleep, or . . . what if he'd had a heart attack? Big Jim had had heart problems off and on for the last three years; mostly arrhythmia. He usually went up to Cathy Russell and either Doc Haskell or Doc Rayburn buzzed him with something, got him back to normal. Haskell would have been content to keep on doing that forever, but Rayburn (whom his father called "an overeducated cotton-picker") had finally insisted that Big Jim see a cardiologist at CMG in Lewiston. The cardiologist said he needed a procedure to knock out that irregular heartbeat once and for all. Big Jim (who was terrified of hospitals) said he needed to talk to God more, and you called that a *prayer* procedure. Meantime, he took his pills, and for the last few months he'd seemed fine, but now . . . maybe . . .

"Dad?"

No answer. Junior flipped the light switch. The overhead gave that same unsteady glow, but it dispelled the shadow Junior had taken for the back of his father's head. He wouldn't be exactly heartbroken if his dad vapor-locked, but on the whole he was glad it hadn't happened tonight. There was such a thing as too many complications.

Still, he walked to the wall where the safe was with big soft steps of cartoon caution, watching for the splash of headlights across the window that would herald his father's return. He set aside the picture that covered the safe (Jesus giving the Sermon on the Mount), and ran the combination. He had to do it twice before the handle would turn, because his hands were shaking.

The safe was stuffed with cash and stacks of parchment-like sheets with the words **BEARER BONDS** stamped on them. Junior gave a low whistle. The last time he'd opened this—to filch fifty for last year's Fryeburg Fair—there had been plenty of cash, but nowhere near this much. And no **BEARER BONDS.** He thought of the plaque on his father's desk at the car store: WOULD JESUS APPROVE OF THIS DEAL? Even in his distress and fear, Junior found time to wonder if Jesus would approve of whatever deal his dad had going on the side these days.

"Never mind his business, I gotta run mine," he said in a low voice. He took five hundred in fifties and twenties, started to close the safe, reconsidered, and took some of the hundreds as well. Given the obscene glut of cash in there, his dad might not even miss it. If he did, it was possible he'd understand why Junior had taken it. And might approve. As Big Jim always said, "The Lord helps those who help themselves."

In that spirit, Junior helped himself to another four hundred. Then he closed the safe, spun the combo, and hung Jesus back on the wall. He grabbed a jacket from the front hall closet and went out while the generator roared and the Maytag sudsed Angie's blood from his clothes.

4

There was no one at the McCains' house.

Fucking *no one*.

Junior lurked on the other side of the street, in a moderate shower of maple leaves, wondering if he could trust what he was seeing: the house dark, Henry McCain's 4Runner and LaDonna's Prius still not in evidence. It seemed too good to be true, far too good.

Maybe they were on the town common. A lot of people were tonight. Possibly they were discussing the power failure, although Junior couldn't remember any such gatherings before when the lights went out; people mostly went home and went to bed, sure that that—unless there'd been a whopper of a storm—the lights would be back on when they got up for breakfast.

Maybe this power failure had been caused by some spectacular accident, the kind of thing the TV news broke into regular coverage to report. Junior had a vague memory of some geezer asking him what was going on not long after Angie had her own accident. In any case, Junior had taken care to speak to nobody on his way over here. He had walked along Main Street with his head down and his collar turned up (he had, in fact, almost bumped into Anson Wheeler as Anse left Sweetbriar Rose). The streetlights were out, and that helped preserve his anonymity. Another gift from the gods.

And now this. A third gift. A *gigantic* one. Was it really possible that Angie's body hadn't been discovered yet? Or was he looking at a trap?

Junior could picture the Castle County Sheriff or a state police detective saying, *We only have to keep out of sight and wait, boys. The killer always revisits the scene of his crime. It's a well-known fact.*

TV bullshit. Still, as he crossed the street (drawn, it seemed, by a force outside himself), Junior kept expecting spotlights to go on, pinning him like a butterfly on a piece of cardboard; kept expecting someone to shout—probably through a bullhorn: *"Stop where you are and get those hands in the air!"*

Nothing happened.

When he reached the foot of the McCain driveway, heart skittering in his chest and blood thumping in his temples (still no headache, though, and that was good, a good sign), the house remained dark and silent. Not even a generator roaring, although there was one at the Grinnells' next door.

Junior looked over his shoulder and saw a vast white bubble of light rising above the trees. Something at the south end of town, or perhaps over in Motton. The source of the accident that had killed the power? Probably.

He went to the back door. The front door would still be unlocked if no one had returned since Angie's accident, but he didn't want to go in the front. He would if he had to, but maybe he wouldn't. He was, after all, on a roll.

The doorknob turned.

Junior stuck his head into the kitchen and smelled the blood at once—an odor a little like spray starch, only gone stale. He said, "Hi? Hello? Anybody home?" Almost positive there wasn't, but if someone was, if by some crazy chance Henry or LaDonna had parked over by the common and returned on foot (somehow missing their daughter lying dead on the kitchen floor), he would scream. Yes! Scream and "discover the body." That wouldn't do anything about the dreaded forensics van, but it would buy him a little time.

"Hello? Mr. McCain? Mrs. McCain?" And then, in a flash of inspiration: "Angie? Are you home?"

Would he call her like that if he'd killed her? Of course not! But then a terrible thought lanced through him: What if she answered? Answered from where she was lying on the floor? Answered through a throatful of blood?

"Get a grip," he muttered. Yes, he had to, but it was hard. Especially in the dark. Besides, in the Bible stuff like that happened all the time. In the Bible, people sometimes returned to life like the zombies in *Night of the Living Dead*.

"Anybody home?"

Zip. *Nada*.

His eyes had adjusted to the gloom, but not enough. He needed a light. He should've brought a flashlight from the house, but it was easy to forget stuff like that when you were used to just flipping a switch. Junior crossed the kitchen, stepping over Angie's body, and opened the first of two doors on the far side. It was a pantry. He could just make out the shelves of bottled and canned goods. He tried the other door and had better luck. It was the laundry. And unless he was mistaken about the shape of the thing standing on the shelf just to his right, he was still on a roll.

He wasn't mistaken. It was a flashlight, a nice bright

one. He'd have to be careful about shining it around the kitchen—easing down the shades would be an excellent idea—but in the laundry room he could shine it around to his heart's content. In here he was fine.

Soap powder. Bleach. Fabric softener. A bucket and a Swiffer. Good. With no generator there'd only be cold water, but there would probably be enough to fill one bucket from the taps, and then, of course, there were the various toilet tanks. And cold was what he wanted. Cold for blood.

He would clean like the demon housekeeper his mother had once been, mindful of her husband's exhortation: "Clean house, clean hands, clean heart." He would clean up the blood. Then he'd wipe everything he could remember touching and everything he might have touched without remembering. But first . . .

The body. He had to do something with the body.

Junior decided the pantry would do for the time being. He dragged her in by the arms, then let them go: *flump*. After that he set to work. He sang under his breath as he first replaced the fridge magnets, then drew the shades. He had filled the bucket almost to the top before the faucet started spitting. Another bonus.

He was still scrubbing, the work well begun but nowhere near done, when the knock came at the front door.

Junior looked up, eyes wide, lips drawn back in a humorless grin of horror.

"Angie?" It was a girl, and she was sobbing. "Angie, are you there?" More knocking, and then the door opened. His roll, it seemed, was over. "Angie, *please* be here. I saw your car in the garage . . ."

Shit. The garage! He never checked the fucking garage!

"Angie?" Sobbing again. Someone he knew. Oh God,

was it that idiot Dodee Sanders? It was. "Angie, she said my mom's dead! Mrs. Shumway said that she *died*!"

Junior hoped she'd go upstairs first, check Angie's room. But she came down the hall toward the kitchen instead, moving slowly and tentatively in the dark.

"Angie? Are you in the kitchen? I thought I saw a light."

Junior's head was starting to ache again, and it was this interfering dope-smoking cunt's fault. Whatever happened next . . . that would be her fault, too.

5

Dodee Sanders was still a little stoned and a little drunk; she was hungover; her mother was dead; she was fumbling up the hall of her best friend's house in the dark; she stepped on something that slid away under her foot and almost went ass over teapot. She grabbed at the stair railing, bent two of her fingers painfully back, and cried out. She sort of understood all this was happening to her, but at the same time it was impossible to believe. She felt as if she'd wandered into some parallel dimension, like in a science fiction movie.

She bent to see what had nearly spilled her. It looked like a towel. Some fool had left a towel on the front hall floor. Then she thought she heard someone moving in the darkness up ahead. In the kitchen.

"Angie? Is that you?"

Nothing. She still felt someone was there, but maybe not.

"Angie?" She shuffled forward again, holding her throbbing right hand—her fingers were going to swell, she thought they were swelling already—against her side.

She held her left hand out before her, feeling the dark air. "Angie, *please* be there! My mother's dead, it's not a joke, Mrs. Shumway told me and she doesn't joke, I *need* you!"

The day had started so well. She'd been up early (well . . . ten; early for her) and she'd had no intention of blowing off work. Then Samantha Bushey had called to say she'd gotten some new Bratz on eBay and to ask if Dodee wanted to come over and help torture them. Bratz-torture was something they'd gotten into in high school—buy them at yard sales, then hang them, pound nails into their stupid little heads, douse them with lighter fluid and set them on fire—and Dodee knew they should have grown out of it, they were adults now, or almost. It was kid-stuff. Also a little creepy, when you really thought about it. But the thing was, Sammy had her own place out on the Motton Road—just a trailer, but all hers since her husband had taken off in the spring—and Little Walter slept practically all day. Plus Sammy usually had bitchin weed. Dodee guessed she got it from the guys she partied with. Her trailer was a popular place on the weekends. But the thing was, Dodee had sworn off weed. Never again, not since all that trouble with the cook. Never again had lasted over a week on the day Sammy called.

"You can have Jade and Yasmin," Sammy coaxed. "Also, I've got some great you-know." She always said that, as if someone listening in wouldn't know what she was talking about. "Also, we can you-know."

Dodee knew what *that* you-know was, too, and she felt a little tingle Down There (in her you-know), even though that was *also* kid-stuff, and they should have left it behind long ago.

"I don't think so, Sam. I have to be at work at two, and—"

"Yasmin awaits," Sammy said. "And you know you hate dat bitch."

Well, that was true. Yasmin was the bitchiest of the Bratz, in Dodee's opinion. And it was almost four hours until two o'clock. Further *and,* if she was a little late, so what? Was Rose going to fire her? Who else would work that shit job?

"Okay. But just for a little while. And only because I hate Yasmin."

Sammy giggled.

"But I don't you-know anymore. *Either* you-know."

"Not a problem," Sammy said. "Come quick."

So Dodee had driven out, and of course she discovered Bratz-torture was no fun if you weren't a little high, so she got a little high and so did Sammy. They collaborated on giving Yasmin some drain-cleaner plastic surgery, which was pretty hilarious. Then Sammy wanted to show her this sweet new camisole she'd gotten at Deb, and although Sam was getting a little bit of a potbelly, she still looked good to Dodee, perhaps because they were a little bit stoned—wrecked, in fact—and since Little Walter was still asleep (his father had insisted on naming the kid after some old bluesman, and all that *sleeping,* yow, Dodee had an idea Little Walter was retarded, which would be no surprise given the amount of rope Sam had smoked while carrying him), they ended up getting into Sammy's bed and doing a little of the old you-know. Afterward they'd fallen asleep, and when Dodee woke up Little Walter was blatting—holy shit, call NewsCenter 6—and it was past five. Really too late to go in to work, and besides, Sam had produced a bottle of Johnnie Walker Black, and they had one-shot two-shot three-shot-four, and Sammy decided she wanted to see what happened to a Baby Bratz in the microwave, only the power was out.

Dodee had crept back to town at roughly sixteen miles an hour, still high and paranoid as hell, constantly checking the rearview mirror for cops, knowing if she did get stopped it would be by that redhaired bitch Jackie Wettington. Or her father would be taking a break from the store and he'd smell the booze on her breath. Or her mother would be home, so tired out from her stupid flying lesson that she had decided to stay home from the Eastern Star Bingo.

Please, God, she prayed. *Please get me through this and I'll never you-know again.* Either *you-know. Never in this life.*

God heard her prayer. Nobody was home. The power was out here too, but in her altered state, Dodee hardly noticed. She crept upstairs to her room, shucked out of her pants and shirt, and laid down on her bed. Just for a few minutes, she told herself. Then she'd put her clothes, which smelled of *ganja,* in the washer, and put herself in the shower. She smelled of Sammy's perfume, which she must buy a gallon at a time down at Burpee's.

Only she couldn't set the alarm with the power out and when the knocking at the door woke her up it was dark. She grabbed her robe and went downstairs, suddenly sure that it would be the redheaded cop with the big boobs, ready to put her under arrest for driving under the influence. Maybe for crack-snacking, too. Dodee didn't think that particular you-know was against the law, but she wasn't entirely sure.

It wasn't Jackie Wettington. It was Julia Shumway, the editor-publisher of the *Democrat.* She had a flashlight in one hand. She shined it in Dodee's face—which was probably puffed with sleep, her eyes surely still red and her hair a haystack—and then lowered it again. Enough light kicked up to show Julia's own face, and Dodee saw a sympathy there that made her feel confused and afraid.

"Poor kid," Julia said. "You don't know, do you?"

"Don't know what?" Dodee had asked. It was around

then that the parallel universe feeling had started. "Don't know *what*?"

And Julia Shumway had told her.

6

"Angie? Angie, *please*!"

Fumbling her way up the hall. Hand throbbing. *Head* throbbing. She could have looked for her father—Mrs. Shumway had offered to take her, starting at Bowie Funeral Home—but her blood ran cold at the thought of that place. Besides, it was Angie that she wanted. Angie who would hug her tight with no interest in the you-know. Angie who was her best friend.

A shadow came out of the kitchen and moved swiftly toward her.

"There you are, thank God!" She began to sob harder, and hurried toward the figure with her arms outstretched. "Oh, it's awful! I'm being punished for being a bad girl, I know I am!"

The dark figure stretched out its own arms, but they did not enfold Dodee in a hug. Instead, the hands at the end of those arms closed around her throat.

THE GOOD OF
THE TOWN, THE GOOD
OF THE PEOPLE

1

Andy Sanders was indeed at the Bowie Funeral Home. He had walked there, toting a heavy load: bewilderment, grief, a broken heart.

He was sitting in Remembrance Parlor I, his only company in the coffin at the front of the room. Gertrude Evans, eighty-seven (or maybe eighty-eight), had died of congestive heart failure two days before. Andy had sent a condolence note, although God knew who'd eventually receive it; Gert's husband had died a decade ago. It didn't matter. He always sent condolences when one of his constituents died, handwritten on a sheet of cream stationery reading FROM THE DESK OF THE FIRST SELECTMAN. He felt it was part of his duty.

Big Jim couldn't be bothered with such things. Big Jim was too busy running what he called "our business," by which he meant Chester's Mill. Ran it like his own private railroad, in point of fact, but Andy had never resented this; he understood that Big Jim was *smart*. Andy understood something else, as well: without Andrew De-Lois Sanders, Big Jim probably couldn't have been elected dogcatcher. Big Jim could sell used cars by promising eye-watering deals, low-low financing, and premiums like cheap Korean vacuum cleaners, but when he'd tried to get the Toyota dealership that time, the company had settled on Will Freeman instead. Given his sales figures and location out on 119, Big Jim hadn't been able to understand how Toyota could be so stupid.

Andy could. He maybe wasn't the brightest bear in the woods, but he knew Big Jim had no warmth. He was a hard man (some—those who'd come a cropper on all that low-low financing, for instance—would have said hardhearted), and he was persuasive, but he was also chilly. Andy, on the other hand, had warmth to spare. When he went around town at election time, Andy told folks that he and Big Jim were like the Doublemint Twins, or Click and Clack, or peanut butter and jelly, and Chester's Mill wouldn't be the same without both of them in harness (along with whichever third happened to be currently along for the ride—right now Rose Twitchell's sister, Andrea Grinnell). Andy had always enjoyed his partnership with Big Jim. Financially, yes, especially during the last two or three years, but also in his heart. Big Jim knew how to get things done, and why they *should* be done. *We're in this for the long haul,* he'd say. *We're doing it for the town. For the people. For their own good.* And that was good. Doing good was good.

But now . . . tonight . . .

"I hated those flying lessons from the first," he said, and began to cry again. Soon he was sobbing noisily, but that was all right, because Brenda Perkins had left in silent tears after viewing the remains of her husband and the Bowie brothers were downstairs. They had a lot of work to do (Andy understood, in a vague way, that something very bad had happened). Fern Bowie had gone out for a bite at Sweetbriar Rose, and when he came back, Andy was sure Fern would kick him out, but Fern passed down the hall without even looking in at where Andy sat with his hands between his knees and his tie loosened and his hair in disarray.

Fern had descended to what he and his brother Stewart called "the workroom." (Horrible; horrible!) Duke Perkins was down there. Also that damned old Chuck Thompson, who maybe hadn't talked his wife into those flying lessons but sure hadn't talked her out of them, either. Maybe others were down there, too.

Claudette for sure.

Andy voiced a watery groan and clasped his hands together more tightly. He couldn't live without her; no way could he live without her. And not just because he'd loved her more than his own life. It was Claudette (along with regular, unreported, and ever larger cash infusions from Jim Rennie) who kept the drugstore going; on his own, Andy would have run it into bankruptcy before the turn of the century. His specialty was people, not accounts and ledgers. His wife was the numbers specialist. Or had been.

As the past perfect clanged in his mind, Andy groaned again.

Claudette and Big Jim had even collaborated on fixing up the town's books that time when the state audited them. It was supposed to be a surprise audit, but Big Jim had gotten advance word. Not much; just enough for them to go to work with the computer program Claudette called MR. CLEAN. They called it that because it always produced clean numbers. They'd come out of that audit shiny side up instead of going to jail (which wouldn't have been fair, since most of what they were doing—almost all, in fact—was for the town's own good).

The truth about Claudette Sanders was this: she'd been a prettier Jim Rennie, a *kinder* Jim Rennie, one he could sleep with and tell his secrets to, and life without her was unthinkable.

Andy started to tear up again, and that was when Big Jim himself put a hand on his shoulder and squeezed.

Andy hadn't heard him come in, but he didn't jump. He had almost expected the hand, because its owner always seemed to turn up when Andy needed him the most.

"I thought I'd find you here," Big Jim said. "Andy—pal—I'm just so, so sorry."

Andy lurched to his feet, groped his arms around Big Jim's bulk, and began to sob against Big Jim's jacket. *"I told her those lessons were dangerous! I told her Chuck Thompson was a jackass, just like his father!"*

Big Jim rubbed his back with a soothing palm. "I know. But she's in a better place now, Andy—she had dinner with Jesus Christ tonight—roast beef, fresh peas, mashed with gravy! How's that for an awesome thought? You hang onto that. Think we should pray?"

"Yes!" Andy sobbed. "Yes, Big Jim! Pray with me!"

They got on their knees and Big Jim prayed long and hard for the soul of Claudette Sanders. (Below them, in the workroom, Stewart Bowie heard, looked up at the ceiling, and observed: "That man shits from both ends.")

After four or five minutes of *we see through a glass darkly* and *when I was a child I spake as a child* (Andy didn't quite see the relevance of that one, but didn't care; it was comforting just to be kneebound with Big Jim), Rennie finished up—"ForJesussakeamen"—and helped Andy to his feet.

Face-to-face and bosom to bosom, Big Jim grasped Andy by the upper arms and looked into his eyes. "So, partner," he said. He always called Andy partner when the situation was serious. "Are you ready to go to work?"

Andy stared at him dumbly.

Big Jim nodded as if Andy had made a reasonable (under the circumstances) protest. "I know it's hard. Not fair. Inappropriate time to ask you. And you'd be within your rights—God knows you would—if you were to bust me one right in the cotton-picking chops. But sometimes we have to put the welfare of others first—isn't that true?"

"The good of the town," Andy said. For the first time since getting the news about Claudie, he saw a sliver of light.

Big Jim nodded. His face was solemn, but his eyes were shining. Andy had a strange thought: *He looks ten years younger.* "Right you are. We're custodians, partner. Custodians of the common good. Not always easy, but never unnecessary. I sent the Wettington woman to hunt up Andrea. Told her to bring Andrea to the conference room. In handcuffs, if that's what it takes." Big Jim laughed. "She'll be there. And Pete Randolph's making a list of all the available town cops. Aren't enough. We've got to address that, partner. If this situation goes on, authority's going to be key. So what do you say? Can you suit up for me?"

Andy nodded. He thought it might take his mind off this. Even if it didn't, he needed to make like a bee and buzz. Looking at Gert Evans's coffin was beginning to give him the willies. The silent tears of the Chief's widow had given him the willies, too. And it wouldn't be hard. All he really needed to do was sit there at the conference table and raise his hand when Big Jim raised his. Andrea Grinnell, who never seemed entirely awake, would do the same. If emergency measures of some sort needed to be implemented, Big Jim would see that they were. Big Jim would take care of everything.

"Let's go," Andy replied.

Big Jim clapped him on the back, slung an arm over Andy's thin shoulders, and led him out of the Remembrance Parlor. It was a heavy arm. Meaty. But it felt good.

He never even thought of his daughter. In his grief, Andy Sanders had forgotten her entirely.

2

Julia Shumway walked slowly down Commonwealth Street, home of the town's wealthiest residents, toward Main Street. Happily divorced for ten years, she lived over the offices of the *Democrat* with Horace, her elderly Welsh Corgi. She had named him after the great Mr. Greeley, who was remembered for a single bon mot—"Go West, young man, go West"—but whose real claim to fame, in Julia's mind, was his work as a newspaper editor. If Julia could do work half as good as Greeley's on the New York *Trib,* she would consider herself a success.

Of course, *her* Horace always considered her a success, which made him the nicest dog on earth, in Julia's book. She would walk him as soon as she got home, then enhance herself further in his eyes by scattering a few pieces of last night's steak on top of his kibble. That would make them both feel good, and she wanted to feel good—about something, anything—because she was troubled.

This was not a new state for her. She had lived in The Mill for all of her forty-three years, and in the last ten she liked what she saw in her hometown less and less. She worried about the inexplicable decay of the town's sewer system and waste treatment plant in spite of all the money that had been poured into them, she worried about the impending closure of Cloud Top, the town's ski resort, she worried that James Rennie was stealing even more from the town till than she suspected (and she suspected he had been stealing a great deal for decades). And of course she was worried about this new thing, which seemed to her almost too big to comprehend. Every time she tried to get a handle on it, her mind would fix on some part that was small but concrete: her increasing inability to place calls on her cell phone, for instance. And she hadn't *received* a

single one, which was very troubling. Never mind concerned friends and relatives outside of town trying to get
in touch; she should have been jammed up with calls from
other papers: the Lewiston *Sun,* the Portland *Press Herald,*
perhaps even the *New York Times.*

Was everyone else in The Mill having the same problems?

She should go out to the Motton town line and see
for herself. If she couldn't use her phone to buzz Pete
Freeman, her best photographer, she could take some pix
herself with what she called her Emergency Nikon. She
had heard there was now some sort of quarantine zone
in place on the Motton and Tarker's Mills sides of the
barrier—probably the other towns, as well—but surely
she could get close on this side. They could warn her off,
but if the barrier was as impermeable as she was hearing,
warning would be the extent of it.

"Sticks and stones will break my bones, but words will
never hurt me," she said. Absolutely true. If words *could*
hurt her, Jim Rennie would have had her in ICU after the
story she'd written about that joke audit the state had
pulled three years ago. Certainly he'd blabbed aplenty-o
about suing the paper, but blabbing was all it had been;
she had even briefly considered an editorial on the subject,
mostly because she had a terrific headline: SUPPOSED
SUIT SLIPS FROM SIGHT.

So, yes, she had worries. They came with the job. What
she wasn't used to worrying about was her own behavior,
and now, standing on the corner of Main and Comm, she
was. Instead of turning left on Main, she looked back the
way she had come. And spoke in the low murmur she
usually reserved for Horace. "I shouldn't have left that
girl alone."

Julia would not have done, if she'd come in her car.

But she'd come on foot, and besides—Dodee had been so *insistent*. There had been a smell about her, too. Pot? Maybe. Not that Julia had any strong objections to that. She had smoked her own share over the years. And maybe it would calm the girl. Take the edge off her grief while it was sharpest and most likely to cut.

"Don't worry about me," Dodee had said, "I'll find my dad. But first I have to dress." And indicated the robe she was wearing.

"I'll wait," Julia had replied . . . although she didn't *want* to wait. She had a long night ahead of her, beginning with her duty to her dog. Horace must be close to bursting by now, having missed his five o'clock walk, and he'd be hungry. When those things were taken care of, she really had to go out to what people were calling the barrier. See it for herself. Photograph whatever there was to be photographed.

Even that wouldn't be the end. She'd have to see about putting out some sort of extra edition of the *Democrat*. It was important to her and she thought it might be important to the town. Of course, all this might be over tomorrow, but Julia had a feeling—partly in her head, partly in her heart—that it wouldn't be.

And yet. Dodee Sanders should not have been left alone. She'd seemed to be holding herself together, but that might only have been shock and denial masquerading as calm. And the dope, of course. But she *had* been coherent.

"You don't need to wait. I don't want you to wait."

"I don't know if being alone right now is wise, dear."

"I'll go to Angie's," Dodee said, and seemed to brighten a little at the thought even as the tears continued to roll down her cheeks. "She'll go with me to find Daddy." She nodded. "Angie's the one I want."

In Julia's opinion, the McCain girl had only marginally more sense than this one, who had inherited her mother's looks but—unfortunately—her father's brains. Angie was a friend, though, and if ever there was a friend in need who needed a friend indeed, it was Dodee Sanders tonight.

"I could go with you. . . ." Not wanting to. Knowing that, even in her current state of fresh bereavement, the girl could probably see that.

"No. It's only a few blocks."

"Well . . ."

"Ms. Shumway . . . are you *sure?* Are you sure my mother—?"

Very reluctantly, Julia had nodded. She'd gotten confirmation of the airplane's tail number from Ernie Calvert. She'd gotten something else from him as well, a thing that should more properly have gone to the police. Julia might have insisted that Ernie take it to them, but for the dismaying news that Duke Perkins was dead and that incompetent weasel Randolph was in charge.

What Ernie gave her was Claudette's bloodstained driver's license. It had been in Julia's pocket as she stood on the Sanders stoop, and in her pocket it had stayed. She'd give it either to Andy or to this pale, mussy-haired girl when the right time came . . . but this was not the time.

"Thank you," Dodee had said in a sadly formal tone of voice. "Now please go away. I don't mean to be crappy about it, but—" She never finished the thought, only closed the door on it.

And what had Julia Shumway done? Obeyed the command of a grief-stricken twenty-year-old girl who might be too stoned to be fully responsible for herself. But there were other responsibilities tonight, hard as that was. Horace, for one. And the newspaper. People might make fun of Pete Freeman's grainy black-and-white photos and the *Democrat*'s exhaustive coverage of such local fetes as Mill Middle School's Enchanted Night dance; they might claim its only practical use was as a cat-box liner—but they needed it, especially when something bad happened. Julia meant to see that they had it tomorrow, even if she had to stay up all night. Which, with both of her regular reporters out of town for the weekend, she probably would.

Julia found herself actually looking forward to this challenge, and Dodee Sanders's woeful face began to slip from her mind.

3

Horace looked at her reproachfully when she came in, but there were no damp patches on the carpet and no little brown package under the chair in the hall—a magic spot he seemed to believe invisible to human eyes. She snapped his leash on, took him out, and waited patiently while he pissed by his favorite sewer, tottering as he did it; Horace was fifteen, old for a Corgi. While he went, she stared at the white bubble of light on the southern horizon. It looked to her like an image out of a Steven Spielberg science fiction movie. It was bigger than ever, and she could hear the *whupapa-whuppa-whuppa* of helicopters, faint but constant. She even saw one in silhouette, speeding across that tall arc of brilliance. How many Christing spotlights had they set up out there, anyway? It was as if North Motton had become an LZ in Iraq.

Horace was now walking in lazy circles, sniffing out the perfect place to finish tonight's ritual of elimination, doing that ever-popular doggie dance, the Poop Walk.

Julia took the opportunity to try her cell phone again. As had been the case all too often tonight, she got the normal series of peeping tones . . . and then nothing but silence.

I'll have to Xerox the paper. Which means seven hundred and fifty copies, max.

The *Democrat* hadn't printed its own paper for twenty years. Until 2002, Julia had taken each week's dummy over to View Printing in Castle Rock, and now she didn't even have to do that. She e-mailed the pages on Tuesday nights, and the finished papers, neatly bound in plastic, were delivered by View Printing before seven o'clock the next morning. To Julia, who'd grown up dealing with penciled corrections and typewritten copy that was "nailed" when it was finished, this seemed like magic. And, like all magic, slightly untrustworthy.

Tonight, the mistrust was justified. She might still be able to e-mail comps to View Printing, but no one would be able to deliver the finished papers in the morning. She guessed that by the morning, nobody would be able to get within five miles of The Mill's borders. *Any* of its borders. Luckily for her, there was a nice big generator in the former print room, her photocopying machine was a monster, and she had over five hundred reams of paper stacked out back. If she could get Pete Freeman to help her . . . or Tony Guay, who covered sports . . .

Horace, meanwhile, had finally assumed the position. When he was done, she swung into action with a small green bag labeled Doggie Doo, wondering to herself what Horace Greeley would have thought of a world where picking up dogshit from the gutter was not just socially expected but a legal responsibility. She thought he might have shot himself.

Once the bag was filled and tied off, she tried her phone again.

Nothing.

She took Horace back inside and fed him.

4

Her cell rang while she was buttoning her coat to drive out to the barrier. She had her camera over her shoulder and almost dropped it, scrabbling in her pocket. She looked at the number and saw the words PRIVATE CALLER.

"Hello?" she said, and there must have been something in her voice, because Horace—waiting by the door, more than ready for a nighttime expedition now that he was cleaned out and fed—pricked up his ears and looked around at her.

"Mrs. Shumway?" A man's voice. Clipped. Official-sounding.

"*Ms.* Shumway. To whom am I speaking?"

"Colonel James Cox, Ms. Shumway. United States Army."

"And to what do I owe the honor of this call?" She heard the sarcasm in her voice and didn't like it—it wasn't professional—but she was afraid, and sarcasm had ever been her response to fear.

"I need to get in touch with a man named Dale Barbara. Do you know this man?"

Of course she did. And had been surprised to see him at Sweetbriar earlier tonight. He was crazy to still be in town, and hadn't Rose herself said just yesterday that he had given notice? Dale Barbara's story was one of hundreds Julia knew but hadn't written. When you published a smalltown newspaper, you left the lids on a great many cans of worms. You had to pick your fights. The way she was sure Junior Rennie and his friends picked theirs. And she doubted very much if the rumors about Barbara and

Dodee's good friend Angie were true, anyway. For one thing, she thought Barbara had more taste.

"Ms. Shumway?" Crisp. Official. An on-the-outside voice. She could resent the owner of the voice just for that. "Still with me?"

"Still with you. Yes, I know Dale Barbara. He cooks at the restaurant on Main Street. Why?"

"He has no cell phone, it seems, the restaurant doesn't answer—"

"It's closed—"

"—and the landlines don't work, of course."

"Nothing in this town seems to work very well tonight, Colonel Cox. Cell phones included. But I notice you didn't have any trouble getting through to me, which makes me wonder if you fellows might not be responsible for that." Her fury—like her sarcasm, born of fear—surprised her. "What did you *do*? What did you people *do*?"

"Nothing. So far as I know now, nothing."

She was so surprised she could think of no follow-up. Which was very unlike the Julia Shumway longtime Mill residents knew.

"The cell phones, yes," he said. "Calls in and out of Chester's Mill are pretty well shut down now. In the interests of national security. And with all due respect, ma'am, you would have done the same, in our position."

"I doubt that."

"Do you?" he sounded interested, not angry. "In a situation that's unprecedented in the history of the world, and suggestive of technology far beyond what we or anyone else can even understand?"

Once more she found herself stuck for a reply.

"It's quite important that I speak to Captain Barbara," he said, returning to his original scripture. In a way, Julia was surprised he'd wandered as far off-message as he had.

"*Captain* Barbara?"

"Retired. Can you find him? Take your cell phone. I'll give you a number to call. It'll go through."

"Why me, Colonel Cox? Why didn't you call the police station? Or one of the town selectmen? I believe all three of them are here."

"I didn't even try. I grew up in a small town, Ms. Shumway—"

"Bully for you."

"—and in my experience, town politicians know a little, the town cops know a lot, and the local newspaper editor knows everything."

That made her laugh in spite of herself.

"Why bother with a call when you two can meet face-to-face? With me as your chaperone, of course. I'm going out to my side of the barrier—was leaving when you called, in fact. I'll hunt Barbie up—"

"Still calling himself that, is he?" Cox sounded bemused.

"I'll hunt him up and bring him with me. We can have a mini press conference."

"I'm not in Maine. I'm in D.C. With the Joint Chiefs."

"Is that supposed to impress me?" Although it did, a little.

"Ms. Shumway, I'm busy, and probably you are, too. So, in the interests of resolving this thing—"

"Is that possible, do you think?"

"Quit it," he said. "You were undoubtedly a reporter before you were an editor, and I'm sure asking questions comes naturally to you, but time is a factor here. Can you do as I ask?"

"I can. But if you want him, you get me, too. We'll come out 119 and call you from there."

"No," he said.

"That's fine," she said pleasantly. "It's been very nice talking to you, Colonel C—"

"Let me finish. Your side of 119 is totally FUBAR. That means—"

"I know the expression, Colonel, I used to be a Tom Clancy reader. What exactly do you mean by it in regard to Route 119?"

"I mean it looks like, pardon the vulgarity, opening night at a free whorehouse out there. Half your town has parked their cars and pickups on both sides of the road and in some dairy farmer's field."

She put her camera on the floor, took a notepad from her coat pocket, and scrawled *Col. James Cox* and *Like open night at free w'house.* Then she added *Dinsmore farm?* Yes, he was probably talking about Alden Dinsmore's place.

"All right," she said, "what do you suggest?"

"Well, I can't stop you from coming, you're absolutely right about that." He sighed, the sound seeming to suggest it was an unfair world. "And I can't stop what you print in your paper, although I don't think it matters, since no one outside of Chester's Mill is going to see it."

She stopped smiling. "Would you mind explaining that?"

"I would, actually, and you'll work it out for yourself. My suggestion is that, if you want to see the barrier—although you can't actually *see* it, as I'm sure you've been told—you bring Captain Barbara out to where it cuts Town Road Number Three. Do you know Town Road Number Three?"

For a moment she didn't. Then she realized what he was talking about, and laughed.

"Something amusing, Ms. Shumway?"

"In The Mill, folks call that one Little Bitch Road. Because in mud season, it's one little bitch."

"Very colorful."

"No crowds out on Little Bitch, I take it?"

"No one at all right now."

"All right." She put the pad in her pocket and picked up the camera. Horace continued waiting patiently by the door.

"Good. When may I expect your call? Or rather, Barbie's call on your cell?"

She looked at her watch and saw it had just gone ten. How in God's name had it gotten that late so early? "We'll be out there by ten thirty, assuming I can find him. And I think I can."

"That's fine. Tell him Ken says hello. That's a—"

"A joke, yes, I get it. Will someone meet us?"

There was a pause. When he spoke again, she sensed reluctance. "There will be lights, and sentries, and soldiers manning a roadblock, but they have been instructed not to speak to the residents."

"Not to—*why*? In God's name, *why*?"

"If this situation doesn't resolve, Ms. Shumway, all these things will become clear to you. Most you really will figure out on your own—you sound like a very bright lady."

"Well fuck you very much, Colonel!" she cried, stung. At the door, Horace pricked up his ears.

Cox laughed, a big unoffended laugh. "Yes, ma'am, receiving you five-by-five. Ten thirty?"

She was tempted to tell him no, but of course there was no way she could do that.

"Ten thirty. Assuming I can hunt him up. And I call you?"

"Either you or him, but it's him I need to speak with. I'll be waiting with one hand on the phone."

"Then give me the magic number." She crooked the phone against her ear and fumbled the pad out again. Of course you always wanted your pad again after you'd put it away; that was a fact of life when you were a reporter, which she now was. Again. The number he gave her to call somehow scared her more than anything else he'd said. The area code was 000.

"One more thing, Ms. Shumway: do you have a pace-maker implant? Hearing-aid implants? Anything of that nature?"

"No. Why?"

She thought he might again decline to answer, but he didn't. "Once you're close to the Dome, there's some kind of interference. It's not harmful to most people, they feel it as nothing more than a low-level electric shock which goes away a second or two after it comes, but it plays hell with electronic devices. Shuts some down—most cell phones, for instance, if they come closer than five feet or so—and explodes others. If you bring a tape recorder out, it'll shut down. Bring an iPod or something sophisticated like a BlackBerry, it's apt to explode."

"Did Chief Perkins's pacemaker explode? Is that what killed him?"

"Ten thirty. Bring Barbie, and be sure to tell him Ken says hello."

He broke the connection, leaving Julia standing in si-lence beside her dog. She tried calling her sister in Lewis-ton. The numbers peeped . . . then nothing. Blank silence, as before.

The Dome, she thought. *He didn't call it the barrier there at the end; he called it the Dome.*

5

Barbie had taken off his shirt and was sitting on his bed to untie his sneakers when the knock came at the door, which one reached by climbing an outside flight of stairs on the side of Sanders Hometown Drug. The knock wasn't welcome. He had walked most of the day, then put on an apron and cooked for most of the evening. He was beat.

And suppose it was Junior and a few of his friends, ready to throw him a welcome-back party? You could say it was unlikely, even paranoid, but the day had been a festival of unlikely. Besides, Junior and Frank DeLesseps and the rest of their little band were among the few people he hadn't seen at Sweetbriar tonight. He supposed they might be out on 119 or 117, rubbernecking, but maybe somebody had told them he was back in town and they'd been making plans for later tonight. Later like now.

The knock came again. Barbie stood up and put a hand on the portable TV. Not much of a weapon, but it would do some damage if thrown at the first one who tried to cram through the door. There was a wooden closet rod, but all three rooms were small and it was too long to swing effectively. There was also his Swiss Army Knife, but he wasn't going to do any cutting. Not unless he had t—

"Mr. Barbara?" It was a woman's voice. "Barbie? Are you in there?"

He took his hand off the TV and crossed the kitchenette. "Who is it?" But even as he asked, he recognized the voice.

"Julia Shumway. I have a message from someone who wants to speak to you. He told me to tell you that Ken says hello."

Barbie opened the door and let her in.

6

In the pine-paneled basement conference room of the Chester's Mill Town Hall, the roar of the generator out back (an elderly Kelvinator) was no more than a dim drone. The table in the center of the room was handsome red maple, polished to a high gleam, twelve feet long. Most of the chairs surrounding it were empty that night. The four attendees of what Big Jim was calling the Emergency Assessment Meeting were clustered at one end. Big Jim himself, although only the Second Selectman, sat at the head of the table. Behind him was a map showing the athletic-sock shape of the town.

Those present were the selectmen and Peter Randolph, the acting Chief of Police. The only one who seemed entirely with it was Rennie. Randolph looked shocked and scared. Andy Sanders was, of course, dazed with grief. And Andrea Grinnell—an overweight, graying version of her younger sister, Rose—just seemed dazed. This was not new.

Four or five years previous, Andrea had slipped in her icy driveway while going to the mailbox one January morning. She had fallen hard enough to crack two discs in her back (being eighty or ninety pounds overweight probably hadn't helped). Dr. Haskell had prescribed that new wonder-drug, OxyContin, to ease what had been no doubt excruciating pain. And had been giving it to her ever since. Thanks to his good friend Andy, who ran the local drugstore, Big Jim knew that Andrea had begun at forty milligrams a day and had worked her way up to a giddy four hundred. This was useful information.

Big Jim said, "Due to Andy's great loss, I'm going to chair this meeting, if no one objects. We're all very sorry, Andy."

"You bet, sir," Randolph said.

"Thank you," Andy said, and when Andrea briefly covered his hand with her own, he began to ooze at the eyes again.

"Now, we all have an idea of what's happened here," Big Jim said, "although no one in town understands it yet—"

"I bet no one out of town does, either," Andrea said.

Big Jim ignored her. "—and the military presence hasn't seen fit to communicate with the town's elected officials."

"Problems with the phones, sir," Randolph said. He was on a first-name basis with all of these people—in fact considered Big Jim a friend—but in this room he felt it wise to stick to sir or ma'am. Perkins had done the same, and on that, at least, the old man had probably been right.

Big Jim waved a hand as if swatting at a troublesome fly. "Someone could have come to the Motton or Tarker's side and sent for me—us—and no one has seen fit to do so."

"Sir, the situation is still very . . . uh, fluid."

"I'm sure, I'm sure. And it's very possible that's why no one has put us in the picture just yet. Could be, oh yes, and I pray that's the answer. I hope you've all been praying."

They nodded dutifully.

"But right now . . ." Big Jim looked around gravely. He *felt* grave. But he also felt excited. And *ready.* He thought it not impossible that his picture would be on the cover of *Time* magazine before the year was out. Disaster— especially the sort triggered by terrorists—was not always a completely bad thing. Look what it had done for Rudy Giuliani. "*Right now,* lady and gentlemen, I think we have to face the very real possibility that we are on our own."

Andrea put a hand to her mouth. Her eyes shone either with fear or too much dope. Possibly both. "Surely not, Jim!"

"Hope for the best, prepare for the worst, that's what Claudette always says." Andy spoke in tones of deep meditation. "Said, I mean. She made me a nice breakfast this morning. Scrambled eggs and leftover taco cheese. Gosh!"

The tears, which had slowed, began to ooze again. Andrea once more covered his hand. This time Andy gripped it. *Andy and Andrea,* Big Jim thought, and a thin smile creased the lower half of his fleshy face. *The Dumbsey Twins.*

"Hope for the best, plan for the worst," he said. "What good advice that is. The worst in this case could entail days cut off from the outside world. Or a week. Possibly even a month." He didn't actually believe that, but they'd be quicker to do what he wanted if they were frightened.

Andrea repeated: "Surely not!"

"We just don't know," Big Jim said. This, at least, was the unvarnished truth. "How can we?"

"Maybe we ought to close Food City," Randolph said. "At least for the time being. If we don't, it's apt to fill up like before a blizzard."

Rennie was annoyed. He had an agenda, and this was on it, but it wasn't *first* on it.

"Or maybe that's not a good idea," Randolph said, reading the Second Selectman's face.

"Actually, Pete, I *don't* think it's a good idea," Big Jim said. "Same principle as never declaring a bank holiday when currency is tight. You only provoke a run."

"Are we talking about closing the banks, too?" Andy asked. "What'll we do about the ATMs? There's one at Brownie's Store . . . Mill Gas and Grocery . . . my drugstore, of course . . ." He looked vague, then brightened. "I think I even saw one at the Health Center, although I'm not entirely sure about that one . . ."

Rennie wondered briefly if Andrea had been loaning the man some of her pills. "I was only making a metaphor, Andy." Keeping his voice low and kind. This was exactly the kind of thing you could expect when people wandered off the agenda. "In a situation like this, food *is* money, in a manner of speaking. What I'm saying is it should be business as usual. It'll keep people calm."

"Ah," Randolph said. This he understood. "Gotcha."

"But you'll need to talk to the supermarket manager—what's his name, Cade?"

"Cale," Randolph said. "Jack Cale."

"Also Johnny Carver at the Gas and Grocery, and . . . who in the heck runs Brownie's since Dil Brown died?"

"Velma Winter," Andrea said. "She's from Away, but she's very nice."

Rennie was pleased to see Randolph writing the names down in his pocket notebook. "Tell those three people that beer and liquor sales are off until further notice." His face cramped in a rather frightening expression of pleasure. "And Dipper's is *closed*."

"A lot of people aren't going to like a booze shutdown," Randolph said. "People like Sam Verdreaux." Verdreaux was the town's most notorious tosspot, a perfect example—in Big Jim's opinion—of why the Volstead Act should never have been repealed.

"Sam and the others like him will just have to suffer once their current supplies of beer and coffee brandy are gone. We can't have half the town getting drunk like it was New Year's Eve."

"Why not?" Andrea asked. "They'll use up the supplies and that'll be the end of it."

"And if they riot in the meantime?"

Andrea was silent. She couldn't see what people would have to riot *about*—not if they had food—but arguing with Jim Rennie, she had found, was usually unproductive and always wearying.

"I'll send a couple of the guys out to talk to them," Randolph said.

"Talk to Tommy and Willow Anderson *personally*." The Andersons ran Dipper's. "They can be troublesome." He lowered his voice. "Wingnuts."

Randolph nodded. "*Left*-wingnuts. Got a picture of Uncle Barack over the bar."

"That's it exactly." *And,* he didn't need to say, *Duke Perkins let those two hippy cotton-pickers get a foothold with their dancing and loud rock and roll and drinking until one in the morning. Protected them. And look at the trouble it led to for my son and his friends.* He turned to Andy Sanders. "Also, you've got to put all the prescription drugs under lock and key. Oh, not Nasonex or Lyrica, that sort of thing. You know the stuff I mean."

"Anything people might use to get high," Andy said, "is already under lock and key." He seemed uneasy at this turn of the conversation. Rennie knew why, but he wasn't concerned about their various sales endeavors just now; they had more pressing business.

"Better take extra precautions, just the same."

Andrea was looking alarmed. Andy patted her hand. "Don't worry," he said, "we always have enough to take care of those in real need."

Andrea smiled at him.

"Bottom line is, this town is going to stay sober until the crisis ends," Big Jim said. "Are we in agreement? Show of hands."

The hands went up.

"Now," Rennie said, "may I go back to where I wanted to start?" He looked at Randolph, who spread his hands in a gesture that simultaneously conveyed *go ahead* and *sorry.*

"We need to recognize that people are apt to be scared. And when people are scared, they can get up to dickens, booze or no booze."

Andrea looked at the console to Big Jim's right: switches that controlled the TV, the AM/FM radio, and the built-in taping system, an innovation Big Jim hated. "Shouldn't that be on?"

"I see no need."

The darned taping system (shades of Richard Nixon) had been the idea of a meddling medico named Eric Everett, a thirtysomething pain in the buttinsky who was known around town as Rusty. Everett had sprung the taping system idiocy at town meeting two years before, presenting it as a great leap forward. The proposal came as an unwelcome surprise to Rennie, who was seldom surprised, especially by political outsiders.

Big Jim had objected that the cost would be prohibitive. This tactic usually worked with thrifty Yankees, but not that time; Everett had presented figures, possibly supplied by Duke Perkins, showing that the federal government would pay eighty percent. Some Disaster Assistance Whatever; a leftover from the free-spending Clinton years. Rennie had found himself outflanked.

It wasn't a thing that happened often, and he didn't like it, but he had been in politics for many more years than Eric "Rusty" Everett had been tickling prostates, and he knew there was a big difference between losing a battle and losing the war.

"Or at least someone should take notes?" Andrea asked timidly.

"I think it might be best to keep this informal, for the time being," Big Jim said. "Just among the four of us."

"Well . . . if you think so . . ."

"Two can keep a secret if one of them is dead," Andy said dreamily.

"That's right, pal," Rennie said, just as if that made sense. Then he turned back to Randolph. "I'd say our prime concern—our prime responsibility to the town—is maintaining order for the duration of this crisis. Which means police."

"Damn straight!" Randolph said smartly.

"Now, I'm sure Chief Perkins is looking down on us from Above—"

"With my wife," Andy said. "With Claudie." He produced a snot-clogged honk that Big Jim could have done without. Nonetheless, he patted Andy's free hand.

"That's right, Andy, the two of them together, bathed in Jesus's glory. But for us here on earth . . . Pete, what kind of force can you muster?"

Big Jim knew the answer. He knew the answers to most of his own questions. Life was easier that way. There were eighteen officers on the Chester's Mill police payroll, twelve full-timers and six part-timers (the latter all past sixty, which made their services entrancingly cheap). Of those eighteen, he was quite sure five of the full-timers were out of town; they had either gone to that day's high school football game with their wives and families or to the controlled burn in Castle Rock. A sixth, Chief Perkins, was dead. And while Rennie would never speak ill of the dead, he was sure the town was better off with Perkins in heaven rather than down here, trying to manage a clustermug that was far beyond his limited abilities.

"I'll tell you what, folks," Randolph said, "it's not that good. There's Henry Morrison and Jackie Wettington, both of whom responded with me to the initial Code Three. There's also Rupe Libby, Fred Denton, and George Frederick—although his asthma's so bad I don't know how much use he'll be. He was planning to take early retirement at the end of this year."

"Poor old George," Andy said. "He just about lives on Advair."

"And as you know, Marty Arsenault and Toby Whelan aren't up to much these days. The only part-timer I'd call really able-bodied is Linda Everett. Between that damned firefighting exercise and the football game, this couldn't have happened at a worse time."

"Linda Everett?" Andrea asked, a little interested. "Rusty's wife?"

"Pshaw!" Big Jim often said *pshaw* when he was irritated. "She's just a jumped-up crossing guard."

"Yes, sir," Randolph said, "but she qualified on the county range over in The Rock last year and she has a sidearm. No reason she can't carry it and go on duty. Maybe not full-time, the Everetts have got a couple of kids, but she can pull her weight. After all, it *is* a crisis."

"No doubt, no doubt." But Rennie was damned if he was going to have Everetts popping up like darned old jack-in-the-boxes every time he turned around. Bottom line: he didn't want that cotton-picker's wife on his first team. For one thing, she was still quite young, no more than thirty, and pretty as the devil. He was sure she'd be a bad influence on the other men. Pretty women always were. Wettington and her gunshell tiddies were bad enough.

"So," Randolph said, "that's only eight out of eighteen."

"You forgot to count yourself," Andrea said.

Randolph hit his forehead with the heel of his hand, as if trying to knock his brains back into gear. "Oh. Yeah. Right. Nine."

"Not enough," Rennie said. "We need to beef up the

force. Just temporarily, you know; until this situation works itself out."

"Who were you thinking about, sir?" Randolph asked.

"My boy, to begin with."

"Junior?" Andrea raised her eyebrows. "He's not even old enough to vote . . . is he?"

Big Jim briefly visualized Andrea's brain: fifteen percent favorite online shopping sites, eighty percent dope receptors, two percent memory, and three percent actual thought process. Still, it was what he had to work with. *And,* he reminded himself, *the stupidity of one's colleagues makes life simpler.*

"He's twenty-one, actually. Twenty-two in November. And either by luck or the grace of God, he's home from school this weekend."

Peter Randolph knew that Junior Rennie was home from school *permanently*—he'd seen it written on the phone pad in the late Chief's office earlier in the week, although he had no idea how Duke had gotten the information or why he'd thought it important enough to write down. Something else had been written there, too: *Behavioral issues?*

This was probably not the time to share such information with Big Jim, however.

Rennie was continuing, now in the enthusiastic tones of a game-show host announcing a particularly juicy prize in the Bonus Round. "*And,* Junior has three friends who would also be suitable: Frank DeLesseps, Melvin Searles, and Carter Thibodeau."

Andrea was once more looking uneasy. "Um . . . weren't those the boys . . . the young men . . . involved in that altercation at Dipper's . . . ?"

Big Jim turned a smile of such genial ferocity on her that Andrea shrank back in her seat.

"That business was overblown. *And* sparked by alcohol, as most such trouble is. Plus, the instigator was that fellow Barbara. Which is why no charges were filed. It was a wash. Or am I wrong, Peter?"

"Absolutely not," Randolph said, although he too looked uneasy.

"These fellows are all at least twenty-one, and I believe Carter Thibodeau might be twenty-three."

Thibodeau was indeed twenty-three, and had lately been working as a part-time mechanic at Mill Gas & Grocery. He'd been fired from two previous jobs—temper issues, Randolph had heard—but he seemed to have settled down at the Gas & Grocery. Johnny said he'd never had anyone so good with exhaust and electrical systems.

"They've all hunted together, they're good shots—"

"Please God we don't have to put *that* to the test," Andrea said.

"No one's going to get shot, Andrea, and no one's suggesting we make these young fellows full-time police. What I'm saying is that we need to fill out an extremely depleted roster, and *fast*. So how about it, Chief? They can serve until the crisis is over, and we'll pay them out of the contingency fund."

Randolph didn't like the idea of Junior toting a gun on the streets of Chester's Mill—Junior with his possible *behavioral issues*—but he also didn't like the idea of bucking Big Jim. And it really might be a good idea to have a few extra widebodies on hand. Even if they were young. He didn't anticipate problems in town, but they could be put on crowd control out where the main roads hit the barrier. If the barrier was still there. And if it wasn't? Problems solved.

He put on a team-player smile. "You know, I think that's a great idea, sir. You send em around to the station tomorrow around ten—"

"Nine might be better, Pete."

"Nine's fine," Andy said in his dreamy voice.

"Further discussion?" Rennie asked.

There was none. Andrea looked as if she might have had something to say but couldn't remember what it was.

"Then I call the question," Rennie said. "Will the board ask acting Chief Randolph to take on Junior, Frank De-Lesseps, Melvin Searles, and Carter Thibodeau as deputies at base salary? Their period of service to last until this darn crazy business is sorted out? Those in favor signify in the usual manner."

They all raised their hands.

"The measure is approv—"

He was interrupted by two reports that sounded like gunfire. They all jumped. Then a third came, and Rennie, who had worked with motors for most of his life, realized what it was.

"Relax, folks. Just a backfire. Generator clearing its throa—"

The elderly gennie backfired a fourth time, then died. The lights went out, leaving them for a moment in stygian blackness. Andrea shrieked.

On his left, Andy Sanders said: "Oh my gosh, Jim, the propane—"

Rennie reached out with his free hand and grabbed Andy's arm. Andy shut up. As Rennie was relaxing his grip, light crept back into the long pine-paneled room. Not the bright overheads but the emergency box-lights mounted in the four corners. In their weak glow, the faces clustered at the conference table's north end looked yellow and years older. They looked frightened. Even Big Jim Rennie looked frightened.

"No problem," Randolph said with a cheeriness that

sounded manufactured rather than organic. "Tank just ran dry, that's all. Plenty more in the town supply barn."

Andy shot Big Jim a look. It was no more than a shifting of the eyes, but Rennie had an idea Andrea saw it. What she might eventually make of it was another question.

She'll forget it after her next dose of Oxy, he told himself. *By morning for sure.*

And in the meantime, the town's supplies of propane—or lack thereof—didn't concern him much. He would take care of that situation when it became necessary.

"Okay, folks, I know you're as anxious to get out of here as I am, so let's move on to our next order of business. I think we should officially confirm Pete here as our Chief of Police pro tem."

"Yes, why not?" Andy asked. He sounded tired.

"If there's no discussion," Big Jim said, "I'll call the question."

They voted as he wanted them to vote.

They always did.

7

Junior was sitting on the front step of the big Rennie home on Mill Street when the lights of his father's Hummer splashed up the driveway. Junior was at peace. The headache had not returned. Angie and Dodee were stored in the McCain pantry, where they would be fine—at least for a while. The money he'd taken was back in his father's safe. There was a gun in his pocket—the pearl-grip .38 his father had given him for his eighteenth birthday. Now he and his father would speak. Junior would listen very closely to what the King of No Money Down had to say. If he sensed his father knew what he, Junior, had done—he didn't see how that was possible, but his father knew so much—then Junior would kill him. After that he would turn the gun on himself. Because there would be no running away, not tonight. Probably not tomorrow, either. On his way back, he had stopped on the town common and listened to the conversations going on there. What they were saying was insane, but the large bubble of light to the south—and the smaller one to the southwest, where 117 ran toward Castle Rock—suggested that tonight, insanity just happened to be the truth.

The door of the Hummer opened, chunked closed. His father walked toward him, his briefcase banging one thigh. He didn't look suspicious, wary, or angry. He sat down beside Junior on the step without a word. Then, in a gesture that took Junior completely by surprise, he put a hand on the younger man's neck and squeezed gently.

"You heard?" he asked.

"Some," Junior said. "I don't understand it, though."

"None of us do. I think there are going to be some hard days ahead while this gets sorted out. So I have to ask you something."

"What's that?" Junior's hand closed around the butt of the pistol.

"Will you play your part? You and your friends? Frankie? Carter and the Searles boy?"

Junior was silent, waiting. What was *this* shit?

"Peter Randolph's acting chief now. He's going to need some men to fill out the police roster. Good men. Are you willing to serve as a deputy until this damn clustermug is over?"

Junior felt a wild urge to scream with laughter. Or triumph. Or both. Big Jim's hand was still on the nape of his neck. Not squeezing. Not pinching. Almost . . . caressing.

Junior took his hand off the gun in his pocket. It occurred to him that he was *still* on a roll—the roll of all rolls.

Today he had killed two girls he'd known since childhood.

Tomorrow he was going to be a town-cop.

"Sure, Dad," he said. "If you need us, we are *there*." And for the first time in maybe four years (it could have been longer), he kissed his father's cheek.

PRAYERS

Barbie and Julia Shumway didn't talk much; there wasn't much to say. Theirs was, as far as Barbie could see, the only car on the road, but lights streamed from most of the farmhouse windows once they cleared town. Out here, where there were always chores to be done and no one fully trusted Western Maine Power, almost everyone had a gennie. When they passed the WCIK radio tower, the two red lights at the top were flashing as they always did. The electric cross in front of the little studio building was also lit, a gleaming white beacon in the dark. Above it, the stars spilled across the sky in their usual extravagant profusion, a never-ending cataract of energy that needed no generator to power it.

"Used to come fishing out this way," Barbie said. "It's peaceful."

"Any luck?"

"Plenty, but sometimes the air smells like the dirty underwear of the gods. Fertilizer, or something. I never dared to eat what I caught."

"Not fertilizer—bullshit. Also known as the smell of self-righteousness."

"I beg your pardon?"

She pointed at a dark steeple-shape blocking out the stars. "Christ the Holy Redeemer Church," she said. "They own WCIK just back the road. Sometimes known as Jesus Radio?"

He shrugged. "I guess maybe I have seen the steeple. And I know the station. Can't very well miss it if you live around here and own a radio. Fundamentalist?"

"They make the hardshell Baptists look soft. I go to the Congo, myself. Can't stand Lester Coggins, hate all the ha-ha-you're-going-to-hell-and-we're-not stuff. Different strokes for different folks, I guess. Although I *have* often wondered how they afford a fifty-thousand-watt radio station."

"Love offerings?"

She snorted. "Maybe I ought to ask Jim Rennie. He's a deacon."

Julia drove a trim Prius Hybrid, a car Barbie would not have expected of a staunch Republican newspaper owner (although he supposed it did fit a worshipper at the First Congregational). But it was quiet, and the radio worked. The only problem was that out here on the western side of town, CIK's signal was so powerful it wiped out everything on the FM band. And tonight it was broadcasting some holy accordion shit that hurt Barbie's head. It sounded like polka music played by an orchestra dying of bubonic plague.

"Try the AM band, why don't you?" she said.

He did, and got only nighttime gabble until he hit a sports station near the bottom of the dial. Here he heard that before the Red Sox–Mariners playoff game at Fenway Park, there had been a moment of silence for the victims of what the announcer called "the western Maine event."

"Event," Julia said. "A sports-radio term if ever I heard one. Might as well turn it off."

A mile or so past the church, they began to see a glow through the trees. They came around a curve and into the glare of lights almost the size of Hollywood premiere kliegs. Two pointed in their direction; two more were tilted straight up. Every pothole in the road stood out in stark relief. The trunks of the birches looked like narrow ghosts. Barbie felt as if they were driving into a noir movie from the late nineteen forties.

"Stop, stop, stop," he said. "This is as close as you want to go. Looks like there's nothing there, but take my word for it, there is. It would likely blow the electronics in your little car, if nothing else."

She stopped and they got out. For a moment they just stood in front of the car, squinting into the bright light. Julia raised one hand to shield her eyes.

Parked beyond the lights, nose to nose, were two brown canvasback military trucks. Sawhorses had been placed on the road for good measure, their feet braced with sandbags. Motors roared steadily in the darkness— not one generator but several. Barbie saw thick electrical cables snaking away from the spotlights and into the woods, where other lights glared through the trees.

"They're going to light the perimeter," he said, and twirled one finger in the air, like an ump signaling a home run. "Lights around the whole town, shining in and shining up."

"Why up?"

"The up ones to warn away air traffic. If any gets through, that is. I'd guess it's mostly tonight they're worried about. By tomorrow they'll have the airspace over The Mill sewn up like one of Uncle Scrooge's moneybags."

On the dark side of the spotlights, but visible in their backsplash, were half a dozen armed soldiers, standing at parade rest with their backs turned. They must have heard the approach of the car, quiet as it was, but not one of them so much as looked around.

Julia called, "Hello, fellas!"

No one turned. Barbie didn't expect it—on their way out, Julia had told Barbie what Cox had told her—but he had to try. And because he could read their insignia, he knew *what* to try. The Army might be running this show—Cox's involvement suggested that—but these fellows weren't Army.

"Yo, Marines!" he called.

Nothing. Barbie stepped closer. He saw a dark horizontal line hanging on the air above the road, but ignored it for the time being. He was more interested in the men guarding the barrier. Or the Dome. Shumway had said Cox called it the Dome.

"I'm surprised to see you Force Recon boys stateside," he said, walking a little closer. "That little Afghanistan problem over, is it?"

Nothing. He walked closer. The grit of the hardpan under his shoes seemed very loud.

"A remarkably high number of pussies in Force Recon, or so I've heard. I'm relieved, actually. If this situation was really bad, they would have sent in the Rangers."

"Pogeybait," one of them muttered.

It wasn't much, but Barbie was encouraged. "Stand easy, fellas; stand easy and let's talk this over."

More nothing. And he was as close to the barrier (or the Dome) as he wanted to go. His skin didn't rash out in goosebumps and the hair on his neck didn't try to stand up, but he knew the thing was there. He sensed it.

And could see it: that stripe hanging on the air. He didn't know what color it would be in daylight, but he was guessing red, the color of danger. It was spray paint, and he would have bet the entire contents of his bank account (currently just over five thousand dollars) that it went all the way around the barrier.

Like a stripe on a shirtsleeve, he thought.

He balled a fist and rapped on his side of the stripe, once more producing that knuckles-on-glass sound. One of the Marines jumped.

Julia began: "I'm not sure that's a good—"

Barbie ignored her. He was starting to be angry. Part of him had been waiting to be angry all day, and here was his chance. He knew it would do no good to go off on these guys—they were only spear-carriers—but it was hard to bite back. "Yo, Marines! Help a brother out."

"Quit it, pal." Although the speaker didn't turn around, Barbie knew it was the CO of this happy little band. He recognized the tone, had used it himself. Many times. "We've got our orders, so *you* help a brother out. Another time, another place, I'd be happy to buy you a beer or kick your ass. But not here, not tonight. So what do you say?"

"I say okay," Barbie said. "But seeing as how we're all on the same side, I don't have to like it." He turned to Julia. "Got your phone?"

She held it up. "You should get one. They're the coming thing."

"I have one," Barbie said. "A disposable Best Buy special. Hardly ever use it. Left it in a drawer when I tried to blow town. Saw no reason not to leave it there tonight."

She handed him hers. "You'll have to punch the number, I'm afraid. I've got work to do." She raised her voice so the soldiers standing beyond the glaring lights could hear her. "I'm the editor of the local newspaper, after all, and I want to get some pix." She raised her voice a little more. "Especially a few of soldiers standing with their backs turned on a town that's in trouble."

"Ma'am, I kind of wish you wouldn't do that," the CO said. He was a blocky fellow with a broad back.

"Stop me," she invited.

"I think you know we can't do that," he said. "As far as our backs being turned, those are our orders."

"Marine," she said, "you take your orders, roll em tight, bend over, and stick em where the air quality is questionable." In the brilliant light, Barbie saw a remarkable thing: her mouth set in a harsh, unforgiving line and her eyes streaming tears.

While Barbie dialed the number with the weird area code, she got her camera and began snapping. The flash wasn't very bright compared to the big generator-driven spotlights, but Barbie saw the soldiers flinch every time it went off. *Probably hoping their fucking insignia doesn't show,* he thought.

2

United States Army Colonel James O. Cox had said he'd be sitting with a hand on the phone at ten thirty. Barbie and Julia Shumway had run a little late and Barbie didn't place the call until twenty of eleven, but Cox's hand must have stayed right there, because the phone only managed half a ring before Barbie's old boss said, "Hello, this is Ken."

Barbie was still mad, but laughed just the same. "Yes sir. And I continue to be the bitch who gets all the good shit."

Cox also laughed, no doubt thinking they were off to a good start. "How are you, Captain Barbara?"

"Sir, I'm fine, sir. But with respect, it's just Dale Barbara now. The only things I captain these days are the grills and Fry-O-Lators in the local restaurant, and I'm in no mood for small talk. I am perplexed, sir, and since

I'm looking at the backs of a bunch of pogeybait Marines who won't turn around and look me in the eye, I'm also pretty goddam pissed off."

"Understood. And *you* need to understand something from my end. If there was anything at all those men could do to aid or end this situation, you would be looking at their faces instead of their asses. Do you believe that?"

"I'm hearing you, sir." Which wasn't exactly an answer.

Julia was still snapping. Barbie shifted to the edge of the road. From his new position he could see a bivouac tent beyond the trucks. Also what might have been a small mess tent, plus a parking area filled with more trucks. The Marines were building a camp here, and probably bigger ones where Routes 119 and 117 left town. That suggested permanence. His heart sank.

"Is the newspaper woman there?" Cox asked.

"She's here. Taking pictures. And sir, full disclosure, whatever you tell me, I tell her. I'm on this side now."

Julia stopped what she was doing long enough to flash Barbie a smile.

"Understood, Captain."

"Sir, calling me that earns you no points."

"All right, just Barbie. Is that better?"

"Yes, sir."

"As to how much the lady decides to publish . . . for the sake of the people in that little town of yours, I hope she's got sense enough to pick and choose."

"My guess is she does."

"And if she e-mails pictures to anyone on the outside—one of the newsmagazines or the *New York Times,* for instance—you may find your Internet goes the way of your landlines."

"Sir, that's some dirty sh—"

"The decision would be made above my pay grade. I'm just saying."

Barbie sighed. "I'll tell her."

"Tell me what?" Julia asked.

"That if you try to transmit those pictures, they may take it out on the town by shutting down Internet access."

Julia made a hand gesture Barbie did not ordinarily associate with pretty Republican ladies. He returned his attention to the phone.

"How much can you tell me?"

"Everything I know," Cox said.

"Thank you, sir." Although Barbie doubted Cox would actually spill everything. The Army never told everything it knew. Or thought it knew.

"We're calling it the Dome," Cox said, "but it's not a Dome. At least, we don't think it is. We think it's a capsule whose edges conform exactly to the borders of the town. And I do mean exactly."

"Do you know how high it goes?"

"It appears to top out at forty-seven thousand and change. We don't know if the top is flat or rounded. At least not yet."

Barbie said nothing. He was flabbergasted.

"As to how deep . . . who knows. All we can say now is more than a hundred feet. That's the current depth of an excavation we're making on the border between Chester's Mill and the unincorporated township to the north."

"TR-90." To Barbie's ears, his voice sounded dull and listless.

"Whatever. We started in a gravel pit that was already dug down to forty feet or so. I've seen spectrographic images that blow my mind. Long sheets of metamorphic rock that have been sheared in two. There's no gap, but you can see a shift where the northern part of the sheet dropped a little. We've checked seismographic reports from the Portland meteorological station, and bingo. There was a bump at eleven forty-four AM. Two point one on the Richter. So that's when it happened."

"Great," Barbie said. He supposed he was being sarcastic, but he was too amazed and perplexed to be sure.

"None of this is conclusive, but it's persuasive. Of course the exploring has just started, but right now it does look as if the thing is down as well as up. And if it goes *up* five miles . . ."

"How do you know that? Radar?"

"Negative, this thing doesn't show on radar. There's no way of telling it's there until you hit it, or until you're so close you can't stop. The human toll when the thing went up was remarkably low, but you've got one hell of a bird-kill around the edges. Inside *and* outside."

"I know. I've seen them." Julia was done with her pictures now. She was standing next to him, listening to Barbie's end of the conversation. "So how do you know how high it is? Lasers?"

"No, they also shoot right through. We've been using missiles with dummy warheads. We've been flying F-15A sorties out of Bangor since four this afternoon. Surprised you didn't hear them."

"I might have heard something," Barbie said. "But my mind was occupied with other things." Like the airplane. And the pulp-truck. The dead people out on Route 117. Part of the remarkably low human toll.

"They kept bouncing off . . . and then, at forty-seven thousand plus, just zippity-zoom, up up and away. Between you and me, I'm surprised we didn't lose any of those fighter-jocks."

"Have you actually overflown it yet?"

"Less than two hours ago. Mission successful."

"Who did it, Colonel?"

"We don't know."

"Was it us? Is this an experiment that went wrong? Or, God help us, some kind of test? You owe me the truth. You owe this town the truth. These people are goddam terrified."

"Understood. But it wasn't us."

"Would you know if it was?"

Cox hesitated. When he next spoke, his voice was lower. "We have good sources in my department. When they fart in the NSA, we hear it. The same is true about Group Nine at Langley and a couple of other little deals you never heard of."

It was possible that Cox was telling the truth. And it was possible he wasn't. He was a creature of his calling, after all; if he had been drawing sentry duty out here in the chilly autumn dark with the rest of the pogeybait Marines, Cox too would have been standing with his back turned. He wouldn't have liked it, but orders were orders.

"Any chance it's some sort of natural phenomenon?" Barbie asked.

"One that conforms exactly to the man-made borders of a whole town? Every nook and fucking cranny? What do you think?"

"I had to ask. Is it permeable? Do you know?"

"Water goes through," Cox said. "A little, anyway."

"How is that possible?" Although he'd seen for himself the weird way water behaved; both he and Gendron had seen it.

"We don't know, how could we?" Cox sounded exasperated. "We've been working on this less than twelve hours. People here are slapping themselves on the back just for figuring out how high it goes. We may figure it out, but for now we just don't know."

"Air?"

"Air goes through to a greater degree. We've set up a monitoring station where your town borders on . . . mmm . . ." Faintly, Barbie heard paper rustle. "Harlow. They've done what they call 'puff tests.' I guess that must measure outgoing air pressure against what bounces back. Anyway, air goes through, and a lot more freely than water does, but the scientists say still not completely. This is going to severely fuck up your weather, pal, but nobody can say how much or how bad. Hell, maybe it'll turn Chester's Mill into Palm Springs." He laughed, rather feebly.

"Particulates?" Barbie thought he knew the answer to that one.

"Nope," Cox said. "Particulate matter doesn't go through. At least we don't think so. And you want to be aware that works both ways. If particulate matter doesn't get in, it won't get out. That means auto emissions—"

"Nobody's got that far to drive. Chester's Mill is maybe four miles across at its widest. Along a diagonal—" He looked at Julia.

"Seven, tops," she said.

Cox said, "We don't think oil-heat pollutants are going to be a big deal, either. I'm sure everybody in town has a nice expensive oil furnace—in Saudi Arabia they have bumper stickers on their cars these days saying I Heart New England—but modern oil furnaces need electricity to provide a constant spark. Your oil reserves are probably good, considering the home-heating season hasn't started yet, but we don't think it's going to be very useful to you. In the long run, that may be a good thing, from the pollution standpoint."

"You think so? Come on up here when it's thirty below zero and the wind's blowing at—" He stopped for a moment. "*Will* the wind blow?"

"We don't know," Cox said. "Ask me tomorrow and I may at least have a theory."

"We can burn wood," Julia said. "Tell him that."

"Ms. Shumway says we can burn wood."

"People have to be careful about that, Captain Barbara—Barbie. Sure, you've got plenty of wood up there and you don't need electricity to ignite it and keep it going, but wood produces ash. Hell, it produces carcinogens."

"Heating season here starts . . ." Barbie looked at Julia.

"November fifteenth," she said. "Or thereabouts."

"Ms. Shumway says mid-November. So tell me you're going to have this worked out by then."

"All I can say is that we intend to try like hell. Which brings me to the point of this conversation. The smart boys—the ones we've been able to convene so far—all agree that we're dealing with a force field—"

"Just like on *Star Trick*," Barbie said. "Beam me up, Snotty."

"Beg your pardon?"

"Doesn't matter. Go on, sir."

"They all agree that a force field doesn't just happen. Something either close to the field of effect or in the center of it has to generate it. Our guys think the center is most likely. 'Like the handle of an umbrella,' one of them said."

"You think this is an inside job?"

"We think it's a *possibility*. And we just happen to have a decorated soldier in town—"

Ex-soldier, Barbie thought. *And the decorations went into the Gulf of Mexico eighteen months ago.* But he had an idea his term of service had just been extended, like it or not. Held over by popular demand, as the saying went.

"—whose specialty in Iraq was hunting down Al Qaeda bomb factories. Hunting them down and shutting them down."

So. Basically just another gennie. He thought of all those he and Julia Shumway had passed on the way out here, roaring away in the dark, providing heat and light. Eating propane to do it. He realized that propane and storage batteries, even more than food, had become the new gold standard in Chester's Mill. One thing he knew: people *would* burn wood. If it got cold and the propane was gone, they'd burn plenty. Hardwood, softwood, trashwood. And fuck the carcinogens.

"It won't be like the generators working away in your part of the world tonight," Cox said. "A thing that could do this . . . we don't know *what* it would be like, or who could build such a thing."

"But Uncle Sammy wants it," Barbie said. He was gripping the phone almost tightly enough to crack it. "That's actually the priority, isn't it? Sir? Because a thing like that could change the world. The people of this town are strictly secondary. Collateral damage, in fact."

"Oh, let's not be melodramatic," Cox said. "In this matter our interests coincide. Find the generator, if it's there to be found. Find it the way you found those bomb factories, and then shut it down. Problem solved."

"If it's there."

"If it's there, roger that. Will you try?"

"Do I have a choice?"

"Not that I can see, but I'm career military. For us, free will isn't an option."

"Ken, this is one fucked-up fire drill."

Cox was slow to reply. Although there was silence on the line (except for a faint high hum that might mean the proceedings were being recorded), Barbie could almost hear him reflecting. Then he said: "That's true, but you still get all the good shit, you bitch."

Barbie laughed. He couldn't help it.

3

On the way back, passing the dark shape that was Christ the Holy Redeemer Church, he turned to Julia. In the glow of the dashboard lights, her face looked tired and solemn.

"I won't tell you to keep quiet about any of this," he said, "but I think you should hold one thing back."

"The generator that may or may not be in town." She took a hand off the wheel, reached back, and stroked Horace's head, as if for comfort and reassurance.

"Yes."

"Because if there's a generator spinning the field—creating your Colonel's Dome—then somebody must be running it. Somebody here."

"Cox didn't say that, but I'm sure it's what he thinks."

"I'll withhold that. And I won't e-mail any pictures."

"Good."

"They should run first in the *Democrat* anyway, dammit." Julia continued stroking the dog. People who drove one-handed usually made Barbie nervous, but not tonight. They had both Little Bitch and 119 to themselves. "Also, I understand that sometimes the greater good is more important than a great story. Unlike the *New York Times*."

"Zing," Barbie said.

"And if you find the generator, I won't have to spend too many days shopping at Food City. I hate that place." She looked startled. "Do you think it'll even be open tomorrow?"

"I'd say yes. People can be slow to catch up with the new deal when the old deal changes."

"I think I better do a little Sunday shopping," she said thoughtfully.

"When you do, say hello to Rose Twitchell. She'll probably have the faithful Anson Wheeler with her." Remembering his earlier advice to Rose, he laughed and said, "Meat, meat, meat."

"Beg your pardon?"

"If you have a generator at your house—"

"Of course I do, I live over the newspaper. Not a house; a very nice apartment. The generator was a tax deduction." She said this proudly.

"Then buy meat. Meat and canned goods, canned goods and meat."

She thought about it. Downtown was just ahead now. There were far fewer lights than usual, but still plenty. *For how long?* Barbie wondered. Then Julia asked, "Did your Colonel give you any ideas about how to find this generator?"

"Nope," Barbie said. "Finding shit used to be my job. He knows that." He paused, then asked: "Do you think there might be a Geiger counter in town?"

"I know there is. In the basement of the Town Hall. Actually the subbasement, I guess you'd say. There's a fallout shelter there."

"You're shittin me!"

She laughed. "No shit, Sherlock. I did a feature story on it three years ago. Pete Freeman took the pictures. In the basement there's a big conference room and a little kitchen. The shelter's half a flight of stairs down from the kitchen. Pretty good-sized. It was built in the fifties, when the smart money was on us blowing ourselves to hell."

"*On the Beach,*" Barbie said.

"Yep, see you that and raise you *Alas, Babylon.* It's a pretty depressing place. Pete's pictures reminded me of the *Führerbunker,* just before the end. There's a kind of pantry—shelves and shelves of canned goods—and half a dozen cots. Also some equipment supplied by the government. Including a Geiger counter."

"The canned stuff must be extremely tasty after fifty years."

"Actually, they rotate in new goods every so often. There's even a small generator that went in after nine-eleven. Check the Town Report and you'll see an appropriation item for the shelter every four years or so. Used to be three hundred dollars. Now it's six hundred. You've got your Geiger counter." She shifted her eyes to him briefly. "Of course, James Rennie sees all things Town Hall, from the attic to the fallout shelter, as his personal property, so he'll want to know why you want it."

"Big Jim Rennie isn't going to know," he said.

She accepted this without comment. "Would you like to come back to the office with me? Watch the President's speech while I start comping the paper? It'll be a quick and dirty job, I can tell you that. One story, half a dozen pictures for local consumption, no Burpee's Autumn Sales Days circular."

Barbie considered it. He was going to be busy tomorrow, not just cooking but asking questions. Starting the old job all over again, in the old way. On the other hand, if he went back to his place over the drugstore, would he be able to sleep?

"Okay. And I probably shouldn't be telling you this, but I have excellent office-boy skills. I also make a mean cup of coffee."

"Mister, you are on." She raised her right hand off the wheel and Barbie slapped her five.

"Can I ask you one more question? Strictly not for publication?"

"Sure," he said.

"This sci-fi generator. Do you think you'll find it?"

Barbie thought it over as she pulled in beside the storefront that housed the *Democrat*'s offices.

"No," he said at last. "That would be too easy."

She sighed and nodded. Then she grasped his fingers. "Would it help, do you think, if I prayed for your success?"

"Couldn't hurt," Barbie said.

4

There were only two churches in Chester's Mill on Dome Day; both purveyed the Protestant brand of goods (although in very different ways). Catholics went to Our Lady of Serene Waters in Motton, and the town's dozen or so Jews attended Congregation Beth Shalom in Castle Rock when they felt in need of spiritual consolation. Once there had been a Unitarian church, but it had died of neglect in the late eighties. Everyone agreed it had been sort of hippy-dippy, anyway. The building now housed Mill New & Used Books.

Both Chester's Mill pastors were what Big Jim Rennie liked to call "kneebound" that night, but their modes of address, states of mind, and expectations were very different.

The Reverend Piper Libby, who ministered to her flock from the pulpit of the First Congregational Church, no longer believed in God, although this was a fact she had not shared with her congregants. Lester Coggins, on the other hand, believed to the point of martyrdom or madness (both words for the same thing, perhaps).

The Rev. Libby, still wearing her Saturday grubs—and still pretty enough, even at forty-five, to look good in them—knelt in front of the altar in almost total darkness (the Congo had no generator), with Clover, her German shepherd, lying behind her with his nose on his paws and his eyes at half-mast.

"Hello, Not-There," Piper said. Not-There was her private name for God just lately. Earlier in the fall it had been The Great Maybe. During the summer, it had been The Omnipotent Could-Be. She'd liked that one; it had a certain ring. "You know the situation I've been in—You should, I've bent Your ear about it enough—but that's not what I'm here to talk about tonight. Which is probably a relief to You."

She sighed.

"We're in a mess here, my Friend. I hope You understand it, because I sure don't. But we both know this place is going to be full of people tomorrow, looking for heavenly disaster assistance."

It was quiet inside the church, and quiet outside. "Too quiet," as they said in the old movies. Had she ever heard The Mill this quiet on a Saturday night? There was no traffic, and the bass thump of whatever weekend band happened to be playing at Dipper's (always advertised as being **DIRECT FROM BOSTON!**) was absent.

"I'm not going to ask that You show me Your will, because I'm no longer convinced You actually *have* a will. But on the off chance that You are there after all—always a possibility, I'm more than happy to admit that—please help me to say something helpful. Hope not in heaven, but right here on earth. Because . . ." She was not surprised to find that she had started to cry. She bawled so often now, although always in private. New Englanders strongly disapproved of public tears from ministers and politicians.

Clover, sensing her distress, whined. Piper told him to hush, then turned back to the altar. She often thought of the cross there as the religious version of the Chevrolet

Bowtie, a logo that had come into being for no other reason than because some guy saw it on the wallpaper of a Paris hotel room a hundred years ago and liked it. If you saw such symbols as divine, you were probably a lunatic.

Nevertheless, she persevered.

"Because, as I'm sure You know, Earth is what we have. What we're sure of. I want to help my people. That's my job, and I still want to do it. Assuming You're there, and that You care—shaky assumptions, I admit—then please help me. Amen."

She stood up. She had no flashlight, but anticipated no trouble finding her way outside with unbarked shins. She knew this place step for step and obstacle for obstacle. Loved it, too. She didn't fool herself about either her lack of faith or her stubborn love of the idea itself.

"Come on, Clove," she said. "President in half an hour. The other Great Not-There. We can listen on the car radio."

Clover followed placidly, untroubled by questions of faith.

5

Out on Little Bitch Road (always referred to as Number Three by Holy Redeemer worshippers), a far more dynamic scene was taking place, and under bright electric lights. Lester Coggins's house of worship possessed a generator new enough for the shipping tags still to be pasted on its bright orange side. It had its own shed, also painted orange, next to the storage barn behind the church.

Lester was a man of fifty so well maintained—by genetics as well as his own strenuous efforts to take care of the temple of his body—that he looked no more than thirty-five (judicious applications of Just For Men helped in this regard). He wore nothing tonight but a pair of gym shorts with ORAL ROBERTS GOLDEN EAGLES printed on the right leg, and almost every muscle on his body stood out.

During services (of which there were five each week), Lester prayed in an ecstatic televangelist tremolo, turning the Big Fellow's name into something that sounded as if it could have come from an overamped wah-wah pedal: not *God* but *GUH-UH-UH-ODD!* In his private prayers, he sometimes fell into these same cadences without realizing it. But when he was deeply troubled, when he really needed to take counsel with the God of Moses and Abraham, He who traveled as a pillar of smoke by day and a pillar of fire by night, Lester held up his end of the conversation in a deep growl that made him sound like a dog on the verge of attacking an intruder. He wasn't aware of this because there was no one in his life to hear him pray. Piper Libby was a widow who had lost her husband and both young sons in an accident three years before; Lester Coggins was a lifelong bachelor who as an adolescent had suffered nightmares of masturbating and looking up to see Mary Magdalene standing in his bedroom doorway.

The church was almost as new as the generator, and constructed of expensive red maple. It was also plain to the point of starkness. Behind Lester's bare back stretched a triple rank of pews beneath a beamed ceiling. Ahead of him was the pulpit: nothing but a lectern with a Bible on it and a large redwood cross hanging on a drape of royal purple. The choir loft was above and to the right, with musical instruments—including the Stratocaster Lester himself sometimes played—clustered at one end.

"God hear my prayer," Lester said in his growly I'm-really-praying voice. In one hand he held a heavy length of rope that had been knotted twelve times, one knot for each disciple. The ninth knot—the one signifying Judas—had been painted black. "God hear my prayer, I ask it in the name of the crucified and risen Jesus."

He began to whip himself across the back with the rope, first over the left shoulder and then over the right, his arm rising and flexing smoothly. His not inconsiderable biceps and delts began to pop a sweat. When it struck his already well-scarred skin, the knotted rope made a carpet-beater sound. He had done this many times before, but never with such force.

"God hear my *prayer*! God hear *my* prayer! God *hear* my prayer! *God* hear my prayer!"

Whack and *whack* and *whack* and *whack*. The sting like fire, like nettles. Sinking in along the turnpikes and by-roads of his miserable human nerves. Both terrible and terribly satisfying.

"Lord, we have sinned in this town, and I am chief among sinners. I listened to Jim Rennie and believed his lies. Yea, I believed, and here is the price, and it is now as it was of old. It's not just the one that pays for the sin of one, but the many. You are slow to anger, but when it comes, Your anger is like the storms that sweep a field of wheat, laying low not just one stalk or a score but every one. I have sowed the wind and reaped the whirlwind, not just for one but for many."

There were other sins and other sinners in The Mill—he knew that, he was not naïve, they swore and danced and sexed and took drugs he knew far too much about—and they no doubt deserved to be punished, to be *scourged*, but that was true of *every* town, surely, and this was the only one that had been singled out for this terrible act of God.

And yet . . . and yet . . . was it possible that this strange curse was not because of *his* sin? Yes. Possible. Although not likely.

"Lord, I need to know what to do. I'm at the crossroads. If it's Your will that I should stand in this pulpit tomorrow morning and confess to what that man talked me into—the sins we participated in together, the sins I have participated in alone—then I will do so. But that would mean the end of my ministry, and it's hard for me to believe that's Your will at such a crucial time. If it's Your will that I should wait . . . wait and see what happens next . . . wait and pray with my flock that this burden should be lifted . . . then I'll do that. Your will be done, Lord. Now and always."

He paused in his scourging (he could feel warm and comforting trickles running down his bare back; several of the rope knots had begun to turn red) and turned his tearstained face up toward the beamed roof.

"Because these folks need me, Lord. You *know* they do, now more than ever. So . . . if it's Your will that this cup should be removed from my lips . . . please give me a sign."

He waited. And behold, the Lord God said unto Lester Coggins, "I will shew you a sign. Goest thou to thy Bible, even as you did as a child after those nasty dreams of yours."

"This minute," Lester said. "This *second*."

He hung the knotted rope around his neck, where it printed a blood horseshoe on his chest and shoulders, then mounted to the pulpit with more blood trickling down the hollow of his spine and dampening the elastic waistband of his shorts.

He stood at the pulpit as if to preach (although never in his worst nightmares had he dreamed of preaching in such scant garb), closed the Bible lying open there, then shut his eyes. "Lord, Thy will be done—I ask in the name of Your Son, crucified in shame and risen in glory."

And the Lord said, "Open My Book, and see what you see."

Lester did as instructed (taking care not to open the big Bible too close to the middle—this was an Old Testament job if ever there.had been one). He plunged his finger down to the unseen page, then opened his eyes and bent to look. It was the second chapter of Deuteronomy, the twenty-eighth verse. He read:

"The Lord shalt smite thee with madness and blindness and astonishment of the heart."

Astonishment of the heart was probably good, but on the whole this wasn't encouraging. Or clear. Then the Lord spake again, saying: "Don't stop there, Lester."

He read the twenty-ninth verse.

"And thou shalt grope at noonday—"

"Yes, Lord, yes," he breathed, and read on.

"—as the blind gropeth in darkness, and thou shalt not prosper in thy ways: and thou shalt be only oppressed and spoiled evermore, and no man shall save thee."

"Will I be struck blind?" Lester asked, his growly prayer-voice rising slightly. "Oh God, please don't do that—although, if it is Thy will—"

The Lord spake unto him again, saying, "Did you get up on the stupid side of the bed today, Lester?"

His eyes flew wide. God's voice, but one of his mother's favorite sayings. A true miracle. "No, Lord, no."

"Then look again. What am I shewing you?"

"It's something about madness. Or blindness."

"Which of the two dost thou thinkest most likely?"

Lester scored the verses. The only word repeated was *blind.*

"Is that . . . Lord, is that my sign?"

The Lord answered, saying, "Yea, verily, but not thine own blindness; for now thine eyes see more clearly. Lookest thou for the blinded one who has gone mad. When you see him, you must tell your congregation what Rennie has been up to out here, and your part in it. You both must tell. We'll talk about this more, but for now, Lester, go to bed. You're dripping on the floor."

Lester did, but first he cleaned up the little splatters of blood on the hardwood behind the pulpit. He did it on his knees. He didn't pray as he worked, but he meditated on the verses. He felt much better.

For the time being, he would speak only generally of the sins which might have brought this unknown barrier down between The Mill and the outside world; but he would look for the sign. For a blind man or woman who had gone crazy, yea, verily.

6

Brenda Perkins listened to WCIK because her husband liked it (*had* liked it), but she would never have set foot inside the Holy Redeemer Church. She was Congo to the core, and she made sure her husband went with her.

Had made sure. Howie would only be in the Congo church once more. Would lie there, unknowing, while Piper Libby preached his eulogy.

This realization—so stark and immutable—struck home. For the first time since she'd gotten the news, Brenda let loose and wailed. Perhaps because now she could. Now she was alone.

On the television, the President—looking solemn and frighteningly old—was saying, "My fellow Americans, you want answers. And I pledge to give them to you as soon as I have them. There will be no secrecy on this issue. My window on events will be your window. That is my solemn promise—"

"Yeah, and you've got a bridge you want to sell me," Brenda said, and that made her cry harder, because it was one of Howie's faves. She snapped off the TV, then dropped the remote on the floor. She felt like stepping on it and breaking it but didn't, mostly because she could see Howie shaking his head and telling her not to be silly.

She went into his little study instead, wanting to touch him somehow while his presence here was still fresh. *Needing* to touch him. Out back, their generator purred. *Fat n happy,* Howie would have said. She'd hated the expense of that thing when Howie ordered it after nine-eleven (*Just to be on the safe side,* he'd told her), but now she regretted every sniping word she'd said about it. Missing him in the dark would have been even more terrible, more lonely.

His desk was bare except for his laptop, which was standing open. His screen saver was a picture from a long-ago Little League game. Both Howie and Chip, then eleven or twelve, were wearing the green jerseys of the Sanders Hometown Drug Monarchs; the picture had been taken the year Howie and Rusty Everett had taken the Sanders team to the state finals. Chip had his arms around his father and Brenda had her arms around both of them. A good day. But fragile. As fragile as a crystal goblet. Who knew such things at the time, when it still might be possible to hold on a little?

She hadn't been able to get hold of Chip yet, and the thought of that call—supposing she could make it—undid her completely. Sobbing, she got down on her knees beside her husband's desk. She didn't fold her hands but put them together palm to palm, as she had as a child, kneeling in flannel pajamas beside her bed and reciting the mantra of *God bless Mom, God bless Dad, God bless my goldfish who doesn't have a name yet.*

"God, this is Brenda. I don't want him back . . . well, I do, but I know You can't do that. Only give me the strength to bear this, okay? And I wonder if maybe . . . I don't know if this is blasphemy or not, probably it is, but I wonder if You could let him talk to me one more time. Maybe let him touch me one more time, like he did this morning."

At the thought of it—his fingers on her skin in the sunshine—she cried even harder.

"I know You don't deal in ghosts—except of course for the Holy one—but maybe in a dream? I know it's a lot to ask, but . . . oh God, there's such a hole in me tonight. I didn't know there could *be* such holes in a person, and I'm afraid I'll fall in. If You do this for me, I'll do something for You. All You have to do is ask. Please, God, just a touch. Or a word. Even if it's in a dream." She took a deep, wet breath. "Thank you. Thy will be done, of course. Whether I like it or not." She laughed weakly. "Amen."

She opened her eyes and got up, holding the desk for support. One hand nudged the computer, and the screen brightened at once. He was always forgetting to turn it off, but at least he kept it plugged in so the battery wouldn't run down. And he kept his electronic desktop far neater than she did; hers was always cluttered with downloads and electronic sticky-notes. On Howie's desktop, always just three files stacked neatly below the hard-disc icon: CURRENT, where he kept reports of ongoing investigations; COURT, where he kept a list of who (including himself) was down to testify, and where, and why. The third file was MORIN ST. MANSE, where he kept everything having to do with the house. It occurred to her that if she opened that one she might find something about the generator, and she needed to know about that so she could keep it running as long as possible. Henry Morrison from the PD would probably be happy to change the current propane canister, but what if there were no spares? If that were the case, she should buy more at Burpee's or the Gas & Grocery before they were all gone.

She put her fingertip on the mousepad, then paused. There was a fourth file on the screen, lurking way down in the lefthand corner. She had never seen it before. Brenda tried to remember the last time she'd happened to look at the desktop of this computer, and couldn't.

VADER, the filename read.

Well, there was only one person in town Howie referred to as Vader, as in Darth: Big Jim Rennie.

Curious, she moved the cursor to the file and double-clicked it, wondering if it was password protected.

It was. She tried WILDCATS, which opened his CURRENT file (he hadn't bothered to protect COURT), and it worked. In the file were two documents. One was labeled ONGOING INVESTIGATION. The other was a PDF doc titled LETTER FROM SMAG. In Howie-speak, that stood for State of Maine Attorney General. She clicked on it.

Brenda scanned the AG's letter with growing amazement as the tears dried on her cheeks. The first thing her eye happened on was the salutation: not *Dear Chief Perkins* but *Dear Duke*.

Although the letter was couched in lawyer-speak rather than Howie-speak, certain phrases leaped out at her as if in boldface type. **Misappropriation of town goods and services** was the first. **Selectman Sanders's involvement seems all but certain** was the next. Then **This malfeasance is wider and deeper than we could have imagined three months ago.**

And near the bottom, seeming not just in boldface but in capital letters: **MANUFACTURE AND SALE OF ILLEGAL DRUGS.**

It appeared that her prayer had been answered, and in a completely unexpected way. Brenda sat down in Howie's chair, clicked ONGOING INVESTIGATION in the VADER file, and let her late husband talk to her.

7

The President's speech—long on comfort, short on information—wrapped up at 12:21 AM. Rusty Everett watched it in the third-floor lounge of the hospital, made a final check of the charts, and went home. He had ended days more tired than this during his medical career, but he had never been more disheartened or worried about the future.

The house was dark. He and Linda had discussed buying a generator last year (and the year before), because Chester's Mill always lost its power four or five days each winter, and usually a couple of times in the summer as well; Western Maine Power was not the most reliable of service providers. The bottom line had been that they just couldn't afford it. Perhaps if Lin went full-time with the cops, but neither of them wanted that with the girls still small.

At least we've got a good stove and a helluva woodpile. If we need it.

There was a flashlight in the glove compartment, but when he turned it on it emitted a weak beam for five seconds and then died. Rusty muttered an obscenity and reminded himself to stock up on batteries tomorrow— later today, now. Assuming the stores were open.

If I can't find my way around here after twelve years, I'm a monkey.

Yes, well. He *felt* a little like a monkey tonight—one fresh-caught and slammed into a zoo cage. And he definitely smelled like one. Maybe a shower before bed—

But nope. No power, no shower.

It was a clear night, and although there was no moon, there were a billion stars above the house, and they looked the same as ever. Maybe the barrier didn't exist overhead. The President hadn't spoken to that issue, so perhaps the people in charge of investigating didn't know yet. If The Mill were at the bottom of a newly created well instead of caught underneath some weird bell jar, then things might still work out. The government could airdrop supplies. Surely if the country could spend hundreds of billions for corporate bailouts, then it could afford to parachute in extra Pop-Tarts and a few lousy generators.

He mounted the porch steps, taking out his housekey, but when he got to the door, he saw something hanging over the lockplate. He bent closer, squinting, and smiled. It was a mini-flashlight. At Burpee's End of Summer Blowout Sale, Linda had bought six for five bucks. At the time he'd thought it a foolish expenditure, even remembered thinking, *Women buy stuff at sales for the same reason men climb mountains—because they're there.*

A small metal loop stuck out on the bottom of the light. Threaded through it was a lace from one of his old tennis shoes. A note had been taped to the lace. He took it off and trained the light on it.

Hello sweet man. Hope you're OK. The 2 Js are finally down for the night. Both worried & upset, but finally corked off. I have the duty all day tomorrow & I do mean <u>all day</u>, from 7 to 7, Peter Randolph says (our *new Chief—GROAN). Marta Edmunds said she'd take the girls, so God bless Marta. Try not to wake me. (Altho I may not be asleep.) We are in for hard days I fear, but we'll get thru this. Plenty to eat in pantry, thank God.*

Sweetie, I know you're tired, but will you walk Audrey? She's still doing that weird Whining Thing of hers. Is it possible she knew this was coming? They say dogs can sense earthquakes, so maybe . . . ?

Judy & Jannie say they love their Daddy. So do I.

We'll find time to talk tomorrow, won't we? Talk and take stock.

I'm a little scared.

Lin

He was scared, too, and not crazy about his wife working a twelve tomorrow when he was likely to be working a sixteen or even longer. Also not crazy about Judy and Janelle spending a whole day with Marta when *they* were undoubtedly scared, too.

But the thing he was least crazy about was having to walk their golden retriever at nearly one in the morning. He thought it was possible she *had* sensed the advent of the barrier; he knew that dogs were sensitive to many impending phenomena, not just earthquakes. Only if that were the case, what he and Linda called the Whining Thing should have stopped, right? The rest of the dogs in town had been grave-quiet on his way back tonight. No barking, no howling. Nor had he heard other reports of dogs doing the Whining Thing.

Maybe she'll be asleep on her bed beside the stove, he thought as he unlocked the kitchen door.

Audrey wasn't asleep. She came to him at once, not bounding joyfully as she usually did—*You're home! You're home! Oh thank God, you're home!*—but sidling, almost *slinking,* with her tail tucked down over her withers, as if expecting a blow (which she had never received) instead of a pat on the head. And yes, she was once more doing the Whining Thing. It had actually been going on since before the barrier. She'd stop for a couple of weeks, and Rusty would begin to hope it was over, and then it would start again, sometimes soft, sometimes loud. Tonight it was loud—or maybe it only seemed that way in the dark kitchen where the digital readouts on the stove and the microwave were out and the usual light Linda left on for him over the sink was dark.

"Stop it, girl," he said. "You'll wake the house."

But Audrey wouldn't. She butted her head softly against his knee and looked up at him in the bright, narrow beam of light he held in his right hand. He would have sworn that was a pleading look.

"All right," he said. "All right, all right. Walkies."

Her leash dangled from a peg beside the pantry door. As he went to get it (dropping the light around his neck to hang by the shoelace as he did), she skittered in front of him, more like a cat than a dog. If not for the flashlight, she might have tripped him up. That would have finished this whore of a day in grand fashion.

"Just a minute, just a minute, hold on."

But she barked at him and backed away.

"Hush! Audrey, hush!"

Instead of hushing she barked again, the sound shockingly loud in the sleeping house. He jerked in surprise. Audrey darted forward and seized the leg of his pants in her teeth and began to back toward the hall, trying to pull him along.

Now intrigued, Rusty allowed himself to be led. When she saw he was coming, Audry let go and ran to the stairs. She went up two, looked back, and barked again.

A light went on upstairs, in their bedroom. "Rusty?" It was Lin, her voice muzzy.

"Yeah, it's me," he called, keeping it as low as he could. "Actually it's Audrey."

He followed the dog up the stairs. Instead of taking them at her usual all-out lope, Audrey kept pausing to look back. To dog-people, their animals' expressions are often perfectly readable, and what Rusty was seeing now was anxiety. Audrey's ears were laid flat, her tail still tucked. If this was the Whining Thing, it had been raised to a new level. Rusty suddenly wondered if there was a prowler in the house. The kitchen door had been locked, Lin was usually good about locking all the doors when she was alone with the girls, but—

Linda came to the head of the stairs, belting a white terry-cloth robe. Audrey saw her and barked again. A get-out-of-my-way bark.

"Audi, *stop* that!" she said, but Audrey ran past her, striking against Lin's right leg hard enough to knock her back against the wall. Then the golden ran down the hall toward the girls' room, where all was still quiet.

Lin fished her own mini-flashlight from a pocket of her robe. "What in the name of *heaven*—"

"I think you better go back to the bedroom," Rusty said.

"Like hell I will!" She ran down the hall ahead of him, the bright beam of the little light bouncing.

The girls were seven and five, and had recently entered what Lin called "the feminine privacy phase." Audrey reached their door, rose up, and began scratching on it with her front paws.

Rusty caught up with Lin just as she opened the door. Audrey bounded in, not even giving Judy's bed a look. Their five-year-old was fast asleep, anyway.

Janelle wasn't asleep. Nor was she awake. Rusty understood everything the moment the two flashlight beams converged on her, and cursed himself for not realizing earlier what was happening, what must have been happening since August or maybe even July. Because the behavior Audrey had been exhibiting—the Whining Thing—was well documented. He just hadn't seen the truth when it was staring him in the face.

Janelle, eyes open but showing only whites, wasn't convulsing—thank God for that—but she was trembling all over. She had pushed the covers down with her feet, probably at onset, and in the double flashlight beams he could see a damp patch on her pajama bottoms. Her fingertips wiggled, as if she were loosening up to play the piano.

Audrey sat by the bed, looking up at her little mistress with rapt attention.

"What's happening to her?" Linda screamed.

In the other bed Judy stirred and spoke. "Mumma? Is it brefkus? Did I miss the bus?"

"She's having a seizure," Rusty said.

"Well help her!" Linda cried. *"Do something! Is she dying?"*

"No," Rusty said. The part of his brain that remained analytical knew this was almost certainly just petit mal—as the others must have been, or they would have known about this already. But it was different when it was one of your own.

Judy sat bolt upright in bed, spilling stuffed animals everywhere. Her eyes were wide and terrified, nor was she much comforted when Linda tore the child out of bed and clasped her in her arms.

"Make her stop! Make her stop, Rusty!"

If it was petit mal, it would stop on its own.

Please God let it stop on its own, he thought.

He placed his palms on the sides of Jan's trembling,

thrumming head and tried to rotate it upward, wanting to make sure her airway remained clear. At first he wasn't able to—the goddam foam pillow was fighting him. He tossed it on the floor. It struck Audrey on the way down, but she didn't so much as flinch, only maintained her rapt gaze.

Rusty was now able to cock Jannie's head back a little, and he could hear her breathing. It wasn't rapid; there was no harsh tearing for oxygen, either.

"Mommy, what's the matter with Jan-Jan?" Judy asked, beginning to cry. "Is she mad? Is she sick?"

"Not mad and only a little sick," Rusty was astounded at how calm he sounded. "Why don't you let Mommy take you down to our—"

"No!" they cried together, in perfect two-part harmony.

"Okay," he said, "but you have to be quiet. Don't scare her when she wakes up, because she's apt to be scared already.

"A *little* scared," he amended. "Audi, good girl. That's a very *very* good girl."

Such compliments usually sent Audrey into paroxysms of joy, but not tonight. She didn't even wag her tail. Then, suddenly, the golden gave a small woof and lay down, dropping her muzzle onto one paw. Seconds later, Jan's trembling ceased and her eyes closed.

"I'll be damned," Rusty said.

"What?" Linda was now sitting on the edge of Judy's bed with Judy on her lap. *"What?"*

"It's over," Rusty said.

But it wasn't. Not quite. When Jannie opened her eyes again, they were back where they belonged, but they weren't seeing him.

"The Great Pumpkin!" Janelle cried. "It's the Great Pumpkin's fault! You have to stop the Great Pumpkin!"

Rusty gave her a gentle shake. "You were having a

dream, Jannie. A bad one, I guess. But it's over and you're all right."

For a moment she still wasn't completely there, although her eyes shifted and he knew she was seeing and hearing him now. "Stop Halloween, Daddy! You have to stop Halloween!"

"Okay, honey, I will. Halloween's off. Completely."

She blinked, then raised one hand to brush her clumped and sweaty hair off her forehead. "What? *Why?* I was going to be Princess Leia! Does everything have to go wrong with my life?" She began to cry.

Linda came over—Judy scurrying behind and holding onto the skirt of her mother's robe—and took Janelle in her arms. "You can still be Princess Leia, honeylove, I promise."

Jan was looking at her parents with puzzlement, suspicion, and growing fright. "What are you *doing* in here? And why is *she* up?" Pointing to Judy.

"You peed in your bed," Judy said smugly, and when Jan realized—realized and started to cry harder—Rusty felt like smacking Judy a good one. He usually felt like a pretty enlightened parent (especially compared to those he sometimes saw creeping into the Health Center with their arm-broke or eye-blackened children), but not tonight.

"It doesn't matter," Rusty said, hugging Jan close. "It wasn't your fault. You had a little problem, but it's over now."

"Does she have to go to the hospital?" Linda asked.

"Only to the Health Center, and not tonight. Tomorrow morning. I'll get her fixed up with the right medicine then."

"*NO SHOTS!*" Jannie screamed, and began to cry harder than ever. Rusty loved the sound of it. It was a healthy sound. Strong.

"No shots, sweetheart. Pills."

"Are you sure?" Lin asked.

Rusty looked at their dog, now lying peacefully with her snout on her paw, oblivious of all the drama.

"*Audrey's* sure," he said. "But she ought to sleep in here with the girls for tonight."

"Yay!" Judy cried. She fell to her knees and hugged Audi extravagantly.

Rusty put an arm around his wife. She laid her head on his shoulder as if too weary to hold it up any longer.

"Why now?" she asked. "Why *now?*"

"I don't know. Just be grateful it was only petit mal."

On that score, his prayer had been answered.

MADNESS, BLINDNESS, ASTONISHMENT OF THE HEART

Scarecrow Joe wasn't up early; he was up late. All night, in fact.

This would be Joseph McClatchey, age thirteen, also known as King of the Geeks and Skeletor, residing at 19 Mill Street. Standing six-two and weighing one-fifty, he was indeed skeletal. And he was a bona fide brain. Joe remained in the eighth grade only because his parents were adamantly opposed to the practice of "skipping forward."

Joe didn't mind. His friends (he had a surprising number for a scrawny thirteen-year-old genius) were there. Also, the work was a tit and there were plenty of computers to goof with; in Maine, every middle school kid got one. Some of the better websites were blocked, of course, but it hadn't taken Joe long to conquer such minor annoyances. He was happy to share the information with his homies, two of whom were those dauntless board-benders Norrie Calvert and Benny Drake. (Benny particularly enjoyed surfing the Blondes in White Panties site during his daily library period.) This sharing no doubt explained some of Joe's popularity, but not all; kids just thought he was cool. The bumper sticker plastered on his backpack probably came closest to explaining why. It read **FIGHT THE POWERS THAT BE.**

Joe was a straight-A student, a dependable and sometimes brilliant basketball center on the middle school team (varsity as a seventh-grader!), and a foxy-good soccer player. He could tickle the piano keys, and two years previous had won second prize in the annual Town Christmas Talent Competition with a hilariously laid-back dance routine to Gretchen Wilson's "Redneck Woman." It had the adults in attendance applauding and screaming with laughter. Lissa Jamieson, the town's head librarian, said he could make a living doing that if he wanted to, but growing up to be Napoleon Dynamite was not Joe's ambition.

"The fix was in," Sam McClatchey had said, gloomily fingering his son's second-place medal. It was probably true; the winner that year had been Dougie Twitchell, who happened to be the Third Selectman's brother. Twitch had juggled half a dozen Indian clubs while singing "Moon River."

Joe didn't care if the fix was in or not. He had lost interest in dancing the way he lost interest in most things once he had to some degree mastered them. Even his love of basketball, which as a fifth-grader he had assumed to be eternal, was fading.

Only his passion for the Internet, that electronic galaxy of endless possibilities, did not seem to pall for him.

His ambition, unexpressed even to his parents, was to become President of the United States. *Maybe,* he sometimes thought, *I'll do the* Napoleon Dynamite *thing at my inaugural. That shit would be on YouTube for eternity.*

Joe spent the entire first night the Dome was in place on the Internet. The McClatcheys had no generator, but Joe's laptop was juiced and ready to go. Also, he had half a dozen spare batteries. He had urged the other seven or eight kids in his informal computer club to also keep spares on hand, and he knew where there were more if they were needed. They might not be; the school had a kickass generator, and he thought he could recharge there with no trouble. Even if Mill Middle went into lockdown, Mr. Allnut, the janitor, would no doubt hook him up; Mr. Allnut was also a fan of blondesinwhitepanties.com. Not to mention country music downloads, which Scarecrow Joe saw he got for free.

Joe all but wore out his Wi-Fi connection that first night, going from blog to blog with the jitter-jive agility of a toad hopping on hot rocks. Each blog was more dire than the last. The facts were thin, the conspiracy theories lush. Joe agreed with his dad and mom, who called the weirder conspiracy theorists who lived on (and for) the Internet "the tinfoil-hat folks," but he was also a believer in the idea that, if you were seeing a lot of horseshit, there had to be a pony in the vicinity.

As Dome Day became Day Two, all the blogs were suggesting the same thing: the pony in this case was not terrorists, invaders from space, or Great Cthulhu, but the good old military-industrial complex. The specifics varied from site to site, but three basic theories ran through all of them. One was that the Dome was some sort of heartless experiment, with the people of Chester's Mill serving as guinea pigs. Another was that it was an experiment that had gone wrong and out of control ("Exactly like in that movie *The Mist*," one blogger wrote). A third was that it wasn't an experiment at all, but a coldly created pretext to justify war with America's stated enemies. "And WE'LL WIN!" ToldjaSo87 wrote. "Because with this new weapon, WHO CAN STAND AGAINST US? My friends, WE HAVE BECOME THE NEW ENGLAND PATRIOTS OF NATIONS!!!!"

Joe didn't know which if any of these theories was

the truth. He didn't really care. What he cared about was the expressed common denominator, which was the government.

It was time for a demonstration, which he of course would lead. Not in town, either, but out on Route 119, where they could stick it directly to The Man. It might only be Joe's guys at first, but it would grow. He had no doubt of that. The Man was probably still keeping the press corps away, but even at thirteen, Joe was wise enough to know that didn't necessarily matter. Because there were *people* inside those uniforms, and thinking brains behind at least some of those expressionless faces. The military presence as a whole might constitute The Man, but there would be individuals hiding in the whole, and some of them would be secret bloggers. They'd get the word out, and some would probably accompany their reports with camera-phone pictures: Joe McClatchey and his friends carrying signs reading END THE SECRECY, STOP THE EXPERIMENT, FREE CHESTER'S MILL, etc., etc.

"Need to post signs around town, too," he murmured. But that would be no problem. All of his guys had printers. And bikes.

Scarecrow Joe began sending e-mails by the dawn's early light. Soon he'd make the rounds on his own bike, and enlist Benny Drake to help him. Maybe Norrie Calvert, too. Ordinarily the members of Joe's posse were late weekend risers, but Joe thought everyone in town would be up early this morning. No doubt The Man would shut down the Internet soon, as He had the phones, but for now it was Joe's weapon, the weapon of the people.

It was time to fight the power.

2

"Fellas, raise your hands," Peter Randolph said. He was tired and baggy-eyed as he stood in front of his new recruits, but he also felt a certain grim happiness. The green Chief's car was parked in the motor pool parking lot, freshly gassed and ready to go. It was his now.

The new recruits—Randolph intended to call them Special Deputies in his formal report to the Selectmen— obediently raised their hands. There were actually five of them, and one was not a fella but a stocky young woman named Georgia Roux. She was an unemployed hairdresser and Carter Thibodeau's girlfriend. Junior had suggested to his father that they probably ought to add a female just to keep everybody happy, and Big Jim had concurred at once. Randolph initially resisted the idea, but when Big Jim favored the new Chief with his fiercest smile, Randolph had given in.

And, he had to admit as he administered the oath (with some of his regular force looking on), they certainly looked tough enough. Junior had lost some pounds over the previous summer and was nowhere near his weight as a high school offensive lineman, but he still had to go one-ninety, and the others, even the girl, were authentic bruisers.

They stood repeating the words after him, phrase for phrase: Junior on the far left, next to his friend Frankie DeLesseps; then Thibodeau and the Roux girl; Melvin Searles on the end. Searles was wearing a vacant going-to-the-county-fair grin. Randolph would have wiped *that* shit off his face in a hurry if he'd had three weeks to train these kids (hell, even one), but he didn't.

The only thing on which he *hadn't* caved to Big Jim was the issue of sidearms. Rennie had argued for them, insisting that these were "levelheaded, Godfearing young people," and saying he'd be glad to provide them himself, if necessary.

Randolph had shaken his head. "The situation's too volatile. Let's see how they do first."

"If one of them gets hurt while you're seeing how they do—"

"Nobody's gonna get hurt, Big Jim," Randolph said, hoping he was right. "This is Chester's Mill. If it was New York City, things might be different."

3

Now Randolph said, " 'And I will, to the best of my ability, protect and serve the people of this town.' "

They gave it back as sweetly as a Sunday School class on Parents' Day. Even the vacantly grinning Searles got it right. And they looked good. No guns—yet—but at least they had walkie-talkies. Nightsticks, too. Stacey Moggin (who would be pulling a street shift herself) had found uniform shirts for everyone but Carter Thibodeau. They had nothing to fit him because he was too broad in the shoulders, but the plain blue workshirt he'd fetched from home looked okay. Not reg, but it was clean. And the silver badge pinned over the left pocket sent the message that needed sending.

Maybe this was going to work.

"So help me God," Randolph said.

"So help me God," they repeated.

From the corner of his eye, Randolph saw the door open. It was Big Jim. He joined Henry Morrison, wheezy George Frederick, Fred Denton, and a dubious-looking Jackie Wettington at the back of the room. Rennie was here to see his son sworn in, Randolph knew. And because he was still uneasy about refusing the new men sidearms (refusing Big Jim anything ran counter to Randolph's politically attuned nature), the new Chief now extemporized, mostly for the Second Selectman's benefit.

"And I will take no shit from anybody."

"And I will take no shit from anybody!" they repeated. With enthusiasm. All smiling now. Eager. Ready to hit the streets.

Big Jim was nodding and giving him a thumbs-up in spite of the cussword. Randolph felt himself expand, unaware the words would come back to haunt him: *I will take no shit from anybody.*

4

When Julia Shumway came into Sweetbriar Rose that morning, most of the breakfast crowd had departed either for church or impromptu forums on the common. It was nine o'clock. Barbie was on his own; neither Dodee Sanders nor Angie McCain had shown up, which surprised no one. Rose had gone to Food City. Anson went with her. Hopefully they'd come back loaded with groceries, but Barbie wouldn't let himself believe it until he actually saw the goodies.

"We're closed until lunch," he said, "but there's coffee."

"And a cinnamon roll?" Julia asked hopefully.

Barbie shook his head. "Rose didn't make them. Trying to conserve the gennie as much as possible."

"Makes sense," she said. "Just coffee, then."

He had carried the pot with him, and poured. "You look tired."

"Barbie, *everyone* looks tired this morning. And scared to death."

"How's that paper coming?"

"I was hoping to have it out by ten, but it's looking more like three this afternoon. The first *Democrat* extra since the Prestile flooded in oh-three."

"Production problems?"

"Not as long as my generator stays online. I just want to go down to the grocery store and see if a mob shows up. Get that part of the story, if one does. Pete Freeman's already there to take pictures."

Barbie didn't like that word *mob*. "Christ, I hope they behave."

"They will; this is The Mill, after all, not New York City."

Barbie wasn't sure there was that much difference between city mice and country mice when they were under stress, but he kept his mouth shut. She knew the locals better than he did.

And Julia, as if reading his mind: "Of course I could be wrong. That's why I sent Pete." She looked around. There were still a few people at the counter up front, finishing eggs and coffee, and of course the big table at the back—the "bullshit table" in Yankee parlance—was full of old men chewing over what had happened and discussing what might happen next. The center of the restaurant, however, she and Barbie had to themselves.

"Couple of things to tell you," she said in a lower voice. "Stop hovering like Willie the Waiter and sit down."

Barbie did so, and poured his own cup of coffee. It was the bottom of the pot and tasted like diesel . . . but of course the bottom of the pot was where the caffeine motherlode was.

Julia reached into the pocket of her dress, brought out her cell, and slid it across to him. "Your man Cox called again at seven this morning. Guess he didn't get much sleep last night, either. Asked me to give you this. Doesn't know you have one of your own."

Barbie let the phone stay where it was. "If he expects a report already, he's seriously overestimated my abilities."

"He didn't say that. He said that if he needed to talk to you, he wanted to be able to reach out."

That decided Barbie. He pushed the cell phone back to her. She took it, not looking surprised. "He also said that if you didn't hear from him by five this afternoon, you should call him. He'll have an update. Want the number with the funny area code?"

He sighed. "Sure."

She wrote it on a napkin: small neat numbers. "I think they're going to try something."

"What?"

"He didn't say; it was just a sense I got that a number of options are on the table."

"I'll bet there are. What else is on your mind?"

"Who says there's anything?"

"It's just a sense I get," he said, grinning.

"Okay, the Geiger counter."

"I was thinking I'd speak to Al Timmons about that." Al was the Town Hall janitor, and a regular at Sweetbriar Rose. Barbie got on well with him.

Julia shook her head.

"No? Why no?"

"Want to guess who gave Al a personal no-interest loan to send Al's youngest son to Heritage Christian in Alabama?"

"Would that be Jim Rennie?"

"Right. Now let's go on to Double Jeopardy, where the scores can really change. Guess who holds the paper on Al's Fisher plow."

"I'm thinking that would also be Jim Rennie."

"Correct. And since you're the dogshit Selectman Rennie can't quite scrape off his shoe, reaching out to people who owe him might not be a good idea." She leaned forward. "But it so happens that I know who had a complete set of the keys to the kingdom: Town Hall, hospital, Health Center, schools, you name it."

"Who?"

"Our late police chief. And I happen to know his wife—widow—very well. She has no love for James Rennie. Plus, she can keep a secret if someone convinces her it needs keeping."

"Julia, her husband isn't even cold yet."

Julia thought of the grim little Bowie funeral parlor and made a grimace of sorrow and distaste. "Maybe not, but he's probably down to room temperature. I take your point, though, and applaud your compassion. But . . ." She grasped his hand. This surprised Barbie but didn't displease him. "These aren't ordinary circumstances. And no matter how brokenhearted she is, Brenda Perkins will know that. You have a job to do. I can convince her of that. You're the inside man."

"The inside man," Barbie said, and was suddenly visited by a pair of unwelcome memories: a gymnasium in Fallujah and a weeping Iraqi man, naked save for his unraveling *keffiyeh*. After that day and that gym, he had stopped wanting to be an inside man. And yet here he was.

"So shall I—"

It was a warm morning for October, and although the door was now locked (people could leave but not reenter), the windows were open. Through those facing Main Street, there now came a hollow metallic bang and a yelp of pain. It was followed by cries of protest.

Barbie and Julia looked at each other across their coffee

cups with identical expressions of surprise and apprehension.

It begins right now, Barbie thought. He knew that wasn't true—it had begun yesterday, when the Dome came down—but at the same time he felt sure it *was* true.

The people at the counter were running to the door. Barbie got up to join them, and Julia followed.

Down the street, at the north end of the town common, the bell in the steeple of the First Congregational Church began to ring, summoning the faithful to worship.

5

Junior Rennie felt great. He had not so much as a shadow of a headache this morning, and breakfast was sitting easy in his stomach. He thought he might even be able to eat lunch. That was good. He hadn't had much use for food lately; half the time just looking at it made him feel throw-uppy. Not this morning, though. Flapjacks and bacon, baby.

If this is the apocalypse, he thought, *it should have come sooner.*

Each Special Deputy had been partnered with a regular full-time officer. Junior drew Freddy Denton, and that was also good. Denton, balding but still trim at fifty, was known as a serious hardass . . . but there were exceptions. He had been president of the Wildcat Boosters Club during Junior's high school football years, and it was rumored he had never given a varsity football player a ticket. Junior couldn't speak for all of them, but he knew that Frankie DeLesseps had been let off by Freddy once, and Junior himself had been given the old "I'm not going to write you up this time but slow down" routine twice.

Junior could have been partnered with Wettington, who probably thought a first down was finally letting some guy into her pants. She had a great rack, but can you say *loser?* Nor had he cared for the cold-eyed look she gave him after the swearing-in, as he and Freddy passed her on their way to the street.

Got a little leftover pantry space for you, if you fuck with me, Jackie, he thought, and laughed. God, the heat and light on his face felt good! How long since it had felt so good?

Freddy looked over. "Something funny, Junes?"

"Nothing in particular," Junior said. "I'm just on a roll, that's all."

Their job—this morning, at least—was to foot-patrol Main Street ("To announce our presence," Randolph had said), first up one side and down the other. Pleasant enough duty in the warm October sunshine.

They were passing Mill Gas & Grocery when they heard raised voices from inside. One belonged to Johnny Carver, the manager and part owner. The other was too slurry for Junior to make out, but Freddy Denton rolled his eyes.

"Sloppy Sam Verdreaux, as I live and breathe," he said. "Shit! And not even nine-thirty."

"Who's Sam Verdreaux?" Junior asked.

Freddy's mouth tightened down to a white line Junior recognized from his football days. It was Freddy's *Ah fuck, we're behind* look. Also his *Ah fuck, that was a bad call* look. "You've been missing the better class of Mill society, Junes. But you're about to get introduced."

Carver was saying, "I *know* it's past nine, Sammy, and I see you've got money, but I still can't sell you any wine. Not this morning, not this afternoon, not tonight. Probably not tomorrow either, unless this mess clears itself up. That's from Randolph himself. He's the new Chief."

"Like fuck he is!" the other voice responded, but it was so slurry it came to Junior's ears sounding as *Li-fuh hizz.* "Pete Randolph ain't but shitlint on Duke Perkins' asshole."

"Duke's dead and Randolph says no booze sales. I'm sorry, Sam."

"Just one bottle of T-Bird," Sam whined. *Juz one barf T-Burr.* "I need it. *Annd,* I can pay for it. Come on. How long I been tradin here?"

"Well shit." Although he sounded disgusted with himself, Johnny was turning to look at the wall-long case of beer and vino as Junior and Freddy came up the aisle. He had probably decided a single bottle of Bird would be a small price to get the old rumpot out of his store, especially since a number of shoppers were watching and avidly awaiting further developments.

The hand-printed sign on the case said absolutely NO ALCOHOL SALES UNTIL FURTHER NOTICE, but the wussy was reaching for the booze just the same, the stuff in the middle. That was where the cheapass popskull lived. Junior had been on the force less than two hours, but he knew *that* was a bad idea. If Carver caved in to the straggle-haired wino, other, less disgusting customers would demand the same privilege.

Freddy Denton apparently agreed. "Don't do that," he told Johnny Carver. And to Verdreaux, who was looking at him with the red eyes of a mole caught in a brushfire: "I don't know if you have enough working brain cells left to read the sign, but I know you heard the man: no alcohol today. So get in the breeze. Quit smelling up the place."

"You can't do that, Officer," Sam said, drawing himself up to his full five and a half feet. He was wearing filthy chinos, a Led Zeppelin tee-shirt, and old slippers with busted backs. His hair looked as if it had last been cut while Bush II was riding high in the polls. "I got my rights. Free country. Says so right in the Constitution of Independence."

"The Constitution's been canceled in The Mill," Junior said, with absolutely no idea that he was speaking prophecy. "So put an egg in your shoe and beat it." God, how fine he felt! In barely a day he had gone from doom and gloom to boom and zoom!

"But . . ."

Sam stood there for a moment with his lower lip trembling, trying to muster more arguments. Junior observed with disgust and fascination that the old fuck's eyes were getting wet. Sam held out his hands, which were trembling far worse than his loose mouth. He only had one more argument to make, but it was a hard one to bring out in front of an audience. Because he had to, he did.

"I really need it, Johnny. No joke. Just a little, to stop the shakes. I'll make it last. And I won't get up to no dickens. Swear on my mother's name. I'll just go home." Home for Sloppy Sam was a shack sitting in a gruesomely bald dooryard dotted with old auto parts.

"Maybe I ought to—" Johnny Carver began.

Freddy ignored him. "Sloppy, you never made a bottle last in your life."

"Don't you call me that!" Sam Verdreaux cried. The tears overspilled his eyes and slid down his cheeks.

"Your fly's unzipped, oldtimer," Junior said, and when Sam looked down at the crotch of his grimy chinos, Junior stroked a finger up the flabby underside of the old man's chin and then tweaked his beak. A grammar school trick, sure, but it hadn't lost its charm. Junior even said what they'd said back then: "Dirty clothes, gotcha nose!"

Freddy Denton laughed. So did a couple of other people. Even Johnny Carver smiled, although he didn't look as if he really wanted to.

"Get outta here, Sloppy," Freddy said. "It's a nice day. You don't want to spend it in a cell."

But something—maybe being called Sloppy, maybe having his nose tweaked, maybe both—had relit some of the rage that had awed and frightened Sam's mates when he'd been a lumber-jockey on the Canadian side of the Merimachee forty years before. The tremble disappeared from his lips and hands, at least temporarily. His eyes lighted on Junior, and he made a phlegmy but undeniably contemptuous throat-clearing sound. When he spoke, the slur had left his voice.

"Fuck you, kid. You ain't no cop, and you was never much of a football player. Couldn't even make the college B-team is what I heard."

His gaze switched to Officer Denton.

"And you, Deputy Dawg. Sunday sales legal after nine o'clock. Has been since the seventies, and that's the end of *that* tale."

Now it was Johnny Carver he was looking at. Johnny's smile was gone, and the watching customers had grown very silent. One woman had a hand to her throat.

"I got money, coin of the realm, and I'm takin what's mine."

He started around the counter. Junior grabbed him by the back of the shirt and the seat of the pants, whirled him around, and ran him toward the front of the store.

"Hey!" Sam shouted as his feet bicycled above the old oiled boards. *"Take your hands off me! Take your fucking hands—"*

Out through the door and down the steps, Junior holding the old man out in front of him. He was light as a bag of feathers. And Christ, he was *farting*! Pow-pow-pow, like a damn machine gun!

Stubby Norman's panel truck was parked at the curb, the one with FURNITURE BOUGHT & SOLD and TOP PRICES FOR ANTIQUES on the side. Stubby himself stood beside it with his mouth open. Junior didn't hesitate. He ran the blabbering old drunk headfirst into the side of the truck. The thin metal gave out a mellow *BONNG!*

It didn't occur to Junior that he might have killed the smelly fuck until Sloppy Sam dropped like a rock, half on the sidewalk and half in the gutter. But it took more than a smack against the side of an old truck to kill Sam Verdreaux. Or silence him. He cried out, then just began to cry. He got to his knees. Scarlet was pouring down his face from his scalp, where the skin had split. He wiped some away, looked at it with disbelief, then held out his dripping fingers.

Foot traffic on the sidewalk had halted so completely that someone might have called a game of Statues. Pedestrians stared with wide eyes at the kneeling man holding out a palmful of blood.

"I'll sue this whole fuckin town for police brutality!" Sam bawled. *"AND I'LL WIN!"*

Freddy came down the store's steps and stood beside Junior.

"Go ahead, say it," Junior told him.

"Say what?"

"I overreacted."

"The fuck you did. You heard what Pete said: Take no shit from anybody. Partner, that deal starts here and now."

Partner! Junior's heart lifted at the word.

"You can't throw me out when I got money!" Sam raved.

"You can't beat me up! I'm an American citizen! I'll see you in court!"

"Good luck on that one," Freddy said. "The courthouse is in Castle Rock, and from what I hear, the road going there is closed."

He hauled the old man to his feet. Sam's nose was also bleeding, and the flow had turned his shirt into a red bib. Freddy reached around to the small of his back for a set of his plastic cuffs (*Gotta get me some of those,* Junior thought admiringly). A moment later they were on Sam's wrists.

Freddy looked around at the witnesses—those on the street, those crowding the doorway of the Gas & Grocery. "This man is being arrested for public disturbance, interfering with police officers, and attempted assault!" he said in a bugling voice Junior remembered well from his days on the football field. Hectoring from the sidelines, it had never failed to irritate him. Now it sounded delightful.

Guess I'm growing up, Junior thought.

"He is also being arrested for violating the new no-alcohol rule, instituted by Chief Randolph. Take a good look!" Freddy shook Sam. Blood flew from Sam's face and filthy hair. "We've got a crisis situation here, folks, but there's a new sheriff in town, and he intends to handle it. Get used to it, deal with it, learn to love it. That's my advice. Follow it, and I'm sure we'll get through this situation just fine. Go against it, and . . ." He pointed to Sam's hands, plasticuffed behind him.

A couple of people actually applauded. For Junior Rennie, the sound was like cold water on a hot day. Then, as Freddy began to frog-march the bleeding old man up the street, Junior felt eyes on him. The sensation so clear it might have been fingers poking the nape of his neck. He turned, and there was Dale Barbara. Standing with the newspaper editor and looking at him with flat eyes.

Barbara, who had beaten him up pretty good that night in the parking lot. Who'd marked all three of them, before sheer weight of numbers had finally begun to turn things around.

Junior's good feelings began to depart. He could almost feel them flying up through the top of his head like birds. Or bats from a belfry.

"What are *you* doing here?" he asked Barbara.

"I've a better question," Julia Shumway said. She was wearing her tight little smile. "What are *you* doing, brutalizing a man who's a quarter your weight and three times your age?"

Junior could think of nothing to say. He felt blood rush into his face and fan out on his cheeks. He suddenly saw the newspaper bitch in the McCain pantry, keeping Angie and Dodee company. Barbara, too. Maybe lying on top of the newspaper bitch, as if he were enjoying a little of the old sumpin-sumpin.

Freddy came to Junior's rescue. He spoke calmly. He wore the stolid policeman's face known the world over. "Any questions about police policy should go to the new Chief, ma'am. In the meantime, you'd do well to remember that, for the time being, we're on our own. Sometimes when people are on their own, examples have to be made."

"Sometimes when people are on their own, they do things they regret later," Julia replied. "Usually when the investigations start."

The corners of Freddy's mouth turned down. Then he hauled Sam down the sidewalk.

Junior looked at Barbie a moment longer, then said: "You want to watch your mouth around me. And your step." He touched a thumb deliberately to his shiny new badge. "Perkins is dead and I'm the law."

"Junior," Barbie said, "you don't look so good. Are you sick?"

Junior looked at him from eyes that were a little too wide. Then he turned and went after his new partner. His fists were clenched.

6

In times of crisis, folks are apt to fall back on the familiar for comfort. That is as true for the religious as it is for the heathen. There were no surprises for the faithful in Chester's Mill that morning; Piper Libby preached hope at the Congo, and Lester Coggins preached hellfire at Christ the Holy Redeemer. Both churches were packed.

Piper's scripture was from the book of John: *A new commandment I give unto you, That ye love one another, as I have loved you, that ye also love one another.* She told those who filled the pews of the Congo church that prayer was important in times of crisis—the comfort of prayer, the power of prayer—but it was also important to help one another, depend on one another, and love one another.

"God tests us with things we don't understand," she said. "Sometimes it's sickness. Sometimes it's the unexpected death of a loved one." She looked sympathetically at Brenda Perkins, who sat with her head bowed and her hands clasped in the lap of a black dress. "And now it's some inexplicable barrier that has cut us off from the outside world. We don't understand it, but we don't understand sickness or pain or the unexpected deaths of good people, either. We ask God why, and in the Old Testament, the answer is the one He gave to Job: 'Were you there when I made the world?' In the New—and more enlightened—Testament, it's the answer Jesus gave to his disciples: 'Love one another, as I have loved you.' That's what we have to do today and every day until this thing is over: love one another. Help one another. And wait for the test to end, as God's tests always do."

Lester Coggins's scripture came from Numbers (a section of the Bible not known for optimism): *Behold, ye have sinned against the LORD, and be sure your sin will find you out.*

Like Piper, Lester mentioned the testing concept—an ecclesiastical hit during all the great clustermugs of history—but his major theme had to do with the infection of sin, and how God dealt with such infections, which seemed to be squeezing them with His Fingers the way a man might squeeze a troublesome pimple until the pus squirted out like holy Colgate.

And because, even in the clear light of a beautiful October morning, he was still more than half convinced that the sin for which the town was being punished was his own, Lester was particularly eloquent. There were tears in many eyes, and cries of *"Yes, Lord!"* rang from one amen corner to the other. When he was this inspired, great new ideas sometimes occurred to Lester even as he was preaching. One occurred to him this day, and he articulated it at once, without so much as a pause for thought. It needed no thought. Some things are just too bright, too glowing, not to be right.

"This afternoon I'm going out to where Route 119 strikes God's mysterious Gate," he said.

"Yes, Jesus!" a weeping woman cried. Others clapped their hands or raised them in testimony.

"I reckon two o'clock. I'm going to get on my knees out there in that dairy field, *yea,* and I'm going to pray to God to lift this affliction."

This time the cries of *Yes Lord* and *Yes Jesus* and *God knows it* were louder.

"But first—" Lester raised the hand with which he had whipped his bare back in the dark of night. "First, I'm going to pray about the *SIN* that has caused this *PAIN* and this *SORROW* and this *AFFLICTION*! If I am alone, God may not hear me. If I am with two or three or even five, God *STILL* may not hear me, can you say amen."

They could. They did. All of them were holding up their hands now, and swaying from side to side, caught up in that good-God fever.

"*But if YOU ALL* were to come out—if we were to pray in a circle right there in God's grass, under God's blue sky . . . within sight of the soldiers they say are guarding the work of God's righteous Hand . . . if *YOU ALL* were to come out, if *WE ALL* were to pray together, then we might be able to get to the bottom of this sin, and drag it out into the light to die, and work a God-almighty *miracle! WILL YOU COME? WILL YOU GET KNEEBOUND WITH ME?*"

Of course they would come. Of course they would get kneebound. People enjoy an honest-to-God prayer meeting in good times and bad. And when the band swung into "Whate'er My God Ordains is Right" (key of G, Lester on lead guitar), they sang fit to raise the roof.

Jim Rennie was there, of course; it was Big Jim who made the car-pool arrangements.

7

END THE SECRECY!
FREE CHESTER'S MILL!
DEMONSTRATE!!!!

WHERE? The Dinsmore Dairy Farm on Route 119 (Just look for the WRECKED TRUCK and the MILITARY AGENTS OF OPPRESSION)!

WHEN? 2 PM, EOT (Eastern Oppression Time)!

WHO? YOU, and every Friend you can bring! Tell them WE WANT TO TELL OUR STORY TO THE MEDIA! Tell them WE WANT TO KNOW WHO DID THIS TO US!
                      AND WHY!
Most of all, tell them WE WANT OUT!!!

This is OUR TOWN! We need to fight for it!
        WE NEED TO TAKE IT BACK!!!

Some signs available, but be sure & bring your own (and remember that Profanity is counterproductive).

FIGHT THE POWER!
STICK IT TO THE MAN!

The Committee to Free Chester's Mill

8

If there was one man in town who could take that old Nietzschean saying "Whatever does not kill me makes me stronger" as his personal motto, that man was Romeo Burpee, a hustler with a daddy-cool Elvis pomp and pointed boots with elastic sides. He owed his first name to a romantic Franco-American mother; his last to a hard-ass Yankee father who was practical to his dry pinch-penny core. Romeo had survived a childhood of merciless taunts—plus the occasional beating—to become the richest man in town. (Well . . . no. Big Jim was the richest man in town, but much of his wealth was of necessity hidden.) Rommie owned the largest and most profitable indie department store in the entire state. Back in the eighties, his potential backers in the venture had told him he was mad to go with such a frankly ugly name as Burpee's. Rommie's response had been that if the name hadn't hurt Burpee Seeds, it wouldn't hurt him. And now their biggest summer sellers were tee-shirts reading MEET ME FOR SLURPEES AT BURPEES. Take *that*, you imagination-challenged bankers!

He had succeeded, in large measure, by recognizing the main chance and pursuing it ruthlessly. Around ten that Sunday morning—not long after he'd watched Sloppy Sam hauled off to the cop-shop—another main chance rolled around. As they always did, if you watched for them.

Romeo observed children putting up posters. Computer-generated and very professional-looking. The kids—most on bikes, a couple on skateboards—were doing a good job of covering Main Street. A protest demonstration out on 119. Romeo wondered whose idea *that* had been.

He caught up with one and asked.

"It was my idea," Joe McClatchey said.

"No shit?"

"No shit whatsoever," Joe said.

Rommie tipped the kid five, ignoring his protests and tucking it deep into his back pocket. Information was worth paying for. Rommie thought people would go to the kid's demonstration. They were crazy to express their fear, frustration, and righteous anger.

Shortly after sending Scarecrow Joe on his way, Romeo began to hear people talking about an afternoon prayer meeting, to be held by Pastor Coggins. Same by-God time, same by-God place.

Surely a sign. One reading SALES OPPORTUNITY HERE.

Romeo went into his store, where business was lackadaisical. The people Sunday-shopping today were either doing it at Food City or Mill Gas & Grocery. And they were the minority. Most were either at church or at home watching the news. Toby Manning was behind the cash register, watching CNN on a little battery-powered TV.

"Shut off that quack and close down your register," Romeo said.

"Really, Mr. Burpee?"

"Yes. Drag the big tent out of storage. Get Lily to help you."

"The Summer Blowout Sale tent?"

"That's the baby," Romeo said. "We're gonna pitch it in that cowgrass where Chuck Thompson's plane crashed."

"Alden Dinsmore's field? What if he wants money to use it?"

"Then we'll pay him." Romeo was calculating. The store sold everything, including discount grocery items, and he currently had roughly a thousand packs of discount Happy Boy franks in the industrial freezer behind the store. He'd bought them from Happy Boy HQ in Rhode Island (company now defunct, little microbe problem, thank God not *E. coli*), expecting to sell them to tourists and locals planning Fourth of July cookouts. Hadn't done as well as he'd expected, thanks to the goddam recession, but had held onto them anyway, as stubbornly as a monkey holding onto a nut. And now maybe . . .

Serve them on those little garden-sticks from Taiwan, he thought. *I've still got a billion of those bastards. Call them something cute, like Frank-A-Ma-Bobs.* Plus they had maybe a hundred cartons of Yummy Tummy Lemonade and Limeade powder, another discount item on which he'd expected to take a loss.

"We're going to want to pack up all the Blue Rhino, too." Now his mind was clicking away like an adding machine, which was just the way Romeo liked it to click.

Toby was starting to look excited. "Whatcha got in mind, Mr. Burpee?"

Rommie went on inventorying stuff he'd expected to record on his books as a dead loss. Those cheapshit pin-wheels . . . leftover Fourth of July sparklers . . . the stale candy he'd been saving for Halloween . . .

"Toby," he said, "we're going to throw the biggest damn cookout and field day this town has ever seen. Get moving. We've got a lot to do."

9

Rusty was making hospital rounds with Dr. Haskell when the walkie-talkie Linda had insisted he carry buzzed in his pocket.

Her voice was tinny but clear. "Rusty, I have to go in after all. Randolph says it looks like half the town is going to be out at the barrier on 119 this afternoon—some for a prayer meeting, some for a demonstration. Romeo Burpee is going to pitch a tent and sell hotdogs, so expect an influx of gastroenteritis patients this evening."

Rusty groaned.

"I'll have to leave the girls with Marta after all." Linda sounded defensive and worried, a woman who knew there was suddenly not enough of her to go around. "I'll fill her in on Jannie's problem."

"Okay." He knew if he told her to stay home, she would . . . and all he'd accomplish would be to worry her just when her worries were starting to settle a bit. And if a crowd *did* show up out there, she'd be needed.

"Thank you," she said. "Thank you for understanding."

"Just remember to send the dog to Marta's with the girls," Rusty said. "You know what Haskell said."

Dr. Ron Haskell—The Wiz—had come up big for the Everett family this morning. Had come up big ever since the onset of the crisis, really. Rusty never would have expected it, but he appreciated it. And he could see by the old guy's pouched eyes and drooping mouth that Haskell was paying the price. The Wiz was too old for medical crises; snoozing in the third-floor lounge was more his speed these days. But, other than Ginny Tomlinson and Twitch, it was now just Rusty and The Wiz holding the fort. It was bad luck all around that the Dome had crashed down on a beautiful weekend morning when anyone who could get out of town had done so.

Haskell, although pushing seventy, had stayed at the hospital with Rusty last night until eleven, when Rusty had literally forced him out the door, and he'd been back by seven this morning, when Rusty and Linda arrived with daughters in tow. Also with Audrey, who seemed to take the new environment of Cathy Russell calmly enough. Judy and Janelle had walked on either side of the big golden, touching her for comfort. Janelle had looked scared to death.

"What's with the dog?" Haskell asked, and when Rusty filled him in, Haskell had nodded and said to Janelle: "Let's check you out, hon."

"Will it hurt?" Janelle had asked apprehensively.

"Not unless getting a piece of candy after I look in your eyes hurts."

When the exam was over, the adults left the two girls and the dog in the examining room and went into the hall. Haskell's shoulders were slumped. His hair seemed to have whitened overnight.

"What's your diagnosis, Rusty?" Haskell had asked.

"Petit mal. I'd think brought on by excitement and worry, but Audi's been doing that Whining Thing of hers for months."

"Right. We'll start her on Zarontin. You agree?"

"Yes." Rusty had been touched to be asked. He was beginning to regret some of the mean things he'd said and thought about Haskell.

"And keep the dog with her, yes?"

"Absolutely."

"Will she be all right, Ron?" Linda asked. She'd had no plans to work then; her plan then had been to spend the day in quiet activities with the girls.

"She *is* all right," Haskell said. "Many children suffer petit mal seizures. Most have only one or two. Others have more, over a course of years, and then stop. There's rarely any lasting damage."

Linda looked relieved. Rusty hoped she would never have to know what Haskell wasn't telling her: that instead of finding their way out of the neurological thicket, some unlucky kids went in deeper, progressing to grand mal. And grand mal seizures *could* do damage. They could kill.

Now, after finishing morning rounds (only half a dozen patients, one a new mom with no complications) and hoping for a cup of coffee before jetting over to the Health Center, this call from Linda.

"I'm sure Marta will be fine with having Audi," she said.

"Good. You'll have your cop walkie while you're on duty, right?"

"Yes. Of course."

"Then give your personal walkie to Marta. Agree on a com channel. If something should go wrong with Janelle, I'll come on the run."

"All right. Thanks, honeybunch. Is there any chance you could get out there this afternoon?"

As Rusty considered that, he saw Dougie Twitchell coming down the hall. He had a cigarette tucked behind his ear and was walking in his usual don't-give-a-shit amble, but Rusty saw concern on his face.

"I might be able to play hookey for an hour. No promises."

"I understand, but it would be so great to see you."

"You too. Be careful out there. And tell folks not to eat the hotdogs. Burpee's probably had them in cold storage for ten thousand years."

"Those are his mastodon steaks," Linda said. "Over and out, sweet man. I'll look for you."

Rusty stuck the walkie in the pocket of his white coat and turned to Twitch. "What's up? And get that cigarette out from behind your ear. This is a hospital."

Twitch plucked the cigarette from its resting place and looked at it. "I was going to smoke it out by the storage shed."

"Not a good idea," Rusty said. "That's where the extra propane's stored."

"That's what I came to tell you. Most of the tanks are gone."

"Bullshit. Those things are *huge*. I can't remember if they hold three thousand gallons each or five thousand."

"So what are you saying? I forgot to look behind the door?"

Rusty began to rub his temples. "If it takes them—whoever *they* are—more than three or four days to short out that force field, we're going to need mucho LP."

"Tell me something I don't know," Twitch said. "According to the inventory card on the door, there's supposed to be seven of those puppies, but there are only two." He stowed the cigarette in the pocket of his own white coat. "I checked the other shed just to make sure, thought somebody might have moved the tanks—"

"Why would anyone do that?"

"I dunno, O Great One. Anyway, the other shed's for the really important hospital supplies: gardening and landscaping shit. In that one the tools are present and accounted for, but the fucking fertilizer's gone."

Rusty didn't care about the fertilizer; he cared about the propane. "Well—if push comes to shove, we'll get some from the town supplies."

"You'll get a fight from Rennie."

"When Cathy Russell might be his only option if that ticker of his vapor-locks? I doubt it. You think there's any chance I can get away for a while this afternoon?"

"That'd be up to The Wiz. He now appears to be the ranking officer."

"Where is he?"

"Sleeping in the lounge. Snores like a mad bastard, too. You want to wake him up?"

"No," Rusty said. "Let him sleep. And I'm not going to call him The Wiz anymore. Given how hard he's worked since this shit came down, I think he deserves better."

"Ah so, sensei. You have reached a new level of enlightenment."

"Blow me, grasshopper," Rusty said.

10

Now see this; see it very well.

It's two forty PM on another eye-bustingly gorgeous autumn day in Chester's Mill. If the press were not being kept away they'd be in photo-op heaven—and not just because the trees are in full flame. The imprisoned people of the town have migrated to Alden Dinsmore's dairy field en masse. Alden has struck a use-fee deal with Romeo Burpee: six hundred dollars. Both men are happy, the farmer because he jacked the businessman up considerable from Burpee's starting offer of two hundred, Romeo because he would have gone to a thousand, if pressed.

From the protestors and Jesus-shouters Alden collected not a single crying dime. That doesn't mean he isn't charging them, however; Farmer Dinsmore was born at night, but not last night. When this opportunity came along, he marked out a large parking area just north of the place where the fragments of Chuck Thompson's plane came to rest the day before, and there he has stationed his wife (Shelley), his older son (Ollie; you remember Ollie), and his hired man (Manuel Ortega, a no-greencard Yankee who can ayuh with the best of them). Alden's knocking down five dollars a car, a fortune for a shirttail dairyman who for the last two years has been keeping his farm out of Keyhole Bank's hands by the skin of his teeth. There are complaints about the fee, but not many; they charge more to park at the Fryeburg Fair, and unless folks want to park by the side of the road—which has already been lined on both sides by early arrivals—and then walk half a mile to where all the excitement is, they have no choice.

And what a strange and varied scene! A three-ring circus for sure, with the ordinary citizens of The Mill in all the starring roles. When Barbie arrives with Rose and

Anse Wheeler (the restaurant is closed again, will reopen for supper—just cold sandwiches, no grill orders), they stare in openmouthed silence. Both Julia Shumway and Pete Freeman are taking pictures. Julia stops long enough to give Barbie her attractive but somehow inward-turning smile.

"Some show, wouldn't you say?"

Barbie grins. "Yessum."

In the first ring of this circus, we have the townsfolk who have responded to the posters put up by Scarecrow Joe and his cadre. The protest turnout has been quite satisfying, almost two hundred, and the sixty signs the kids made (the most popular: **LET US OUT, DAMN IT!!**) were gone in no time. Luckily, many people *did* bring their own signs. Joe's favorite is the one with prison bars inked over a map of The Mill. Lissa Jamieson is not just holding it but pumping it aggressively up and down. Jack Evans is there, looking pale and grim. His sign is a collage of photographs featuring the woman who bled to death the day before. **WHO KILLED MY WIFE?** it screams. Scarecrow Joe feels sorry for him . . . but what an awesome sign! If the press could see that one, they'd fill their collective pants with joyshit.

Joe organized the protestors into a big circle that rotates just in front of the Dome, which is marked by a line of dead birds on the Chester's Mill side (those on the Motton side have been removed by the military personnel). The circle gives all of Joe's people—for so he thinks of them—a chance to wave their signs at the posted guards, who stand with their backs resolutely (and maddeningly) turned. Joe also gave out printed "chant-sheets." He wrote these with Benny Drake's skateboarding idol, Norrie Calvert. Besides being balls-to-the-wall on her Blitz deck, Norrie's rhymes are simple but tight, yo? One chant goes, *Ha-ha-ha! Hee-hee-hee! Chester's Mill must be set free!* Another: *You did it! You did it! Come on out and just admit it!* Joe has—with real reluctance—vetoed another Norrie masterpiece that goes *Take off the gags! Take off the gags! Let us talk to the press, you fags!* "We have to be politically correct about this," he told her. What he's wondering just now is if Norrie Calvert is too young to kiss. And if she would slip him any tongue if he did. He has never kissed a girl, but if they're all going to die like starving bugs trapped under a Tupperware bowl, he probably should kiss this one while there's still time.

In the second ring is Pastor Coggins's prayer circle. They are really getting God-sent. And, in a fine show of ecclesiastical détente, the Holy Redeemer choir has been joined by a dozen men and women from the Congo church choir. They're singing "A Mighty Fortress Is Our God," and a good number of unaffiliated townsfolk who know the words have joined in. Their voices rise to the blameless blue sky, with Lester's shrill exhortations and the prayer circle's supporting cries of *amen* and *hallelujah* weaving in and out of the singing in perfect counterpoint (although not harmony—that would be going too far). The prayer circle keeps growing as other townsfolk drop to their knees and join in, laying their signs temporarily aside so they can raise their clasped hands in supplication. The soldiers have turned their backs; perhaps God has not.

But the center ring of this circus is the biggest and most bodacious. Romeo Burpee pitched the End of Summer Blowout Sale tent well back from the Dome and sixty yards east of the prayer circle, calculating the location by testing the faint gasp of breeze that's blowing. He wants to make sure that the smoke from his rank of Hibachis reaches both those praying and those protesting. His only

concession to the afternoon's religious aspect is to make
Toby Manning turn off his boombox, which was blaring
that James McMurtry song about living in a small town; it
didn't mix well with "How Great Thou Art" and "Won't
You Come to Jesus." Business is good and will only get
better. Of this Romeo is sure. The hotdogs—thawing even
as they cook—may gripe some bellies later, but they smell
perfect in the warm afternoon sun; like a county fair instead
of chowtime in prison. Kids race around waving pinwheels
and threatening to set Dinsmore's grass on fire with leftover Fourth of July sparklers. Empty paper cups that held
either citrus-powder drinks (foul) or hastily brewed coffee
(fouler still) are littered everywhere. Later on, Romeo will
have Toby Manning pay some kid, maybe Dinsmore's, ten
bucks to pick up the litter. Community relations, always
important. Right now, though, Romeo's totally focused
on his jackleg cash register, a carton that once contained
Charmin toilet paper. He takes in long green and returns
short silver: it's the way America does business, honeybunch. He's charging four bucks per dog, and he's goddamned if people aren't paying it. He expects to clear at
least 3K by sundown, maybe a lot more.

And look! Here's Rusty Everett! He got away after all!
Good for him! He almost wishes he'd stopped to get the
girls—they would surely enjoy this, and it might allay
their fears to see so many people having a good time—but
it might be a little too much excitement for Jannie.

He spots Linda at the same time she spots him and
starts waving frantically, practically jumping up and
down. With her hair done in the stubby Fearless Police
Girl braids she almost always wears when she's working,
Lin looks like a junior high school cheerleader. She's standing with Twitch's sister Rose and the young man who
short-orders at the restaurant. Rusty's a little surprised;

he thought Barbara had left town. Got on Big Jim Rennie's bad side. A bar fight is what Rusty heard, although he wasn't on duty when the participants came in to get patched up. Fine by Rusty. He's patched up his share of Dipper's customers.

He hugs his wife, kisses her mouth, then plants a kiss on Rose's cheek. Shakes hands with the cook, and gets reintroduced.

"Look at those hotdogs," Rusty mourns. "Oh dear."

"Better line up the bedpans, Doc," Barbie says, and they all laugh. It's amazing to be laughing under these circumstances, but they aren't the only ones . . . and good God, why not? If you can't laugh when things go bad—laugh and put on a little carnival—then you're either dead or wishing you were.

"This is fun," Rose says, unaware of how soon the fun is going to end. A Frisbee floats past. She plucks it out of the air and wings it back to Benny Drake, who leaps to catch it and then spins to throw it on to Norrie Calvert, who catches it behind her back—show-off! The prayer circle prays. The mixed choir, really finding its voice now, has moved on to that all-time chart topper "Onward, Christian Soldiers." A child no more than Judy's age bops past, skirt flapping around her chubby knees, a sparkler clutched in one hand and a cup of the awful limeade in the other. The protestors turn and turn in a widening gyre, chanting *Ha-ha-ha! Hee-hee-hee! Chester's Mill must be set free!* Overhead, puffy clouds with shady bottoms float northward from Motton . . . and then divide as they near the soldiers, skirting around the Dome. The sky directly overhead is a cloudless, flawless blue. There are those in Dinsmore's field who study those clouds and wonder about the future of rain in Chester's Mill, but nobody speaks of this aloud.

"I wonder if we'll still be having fun next Sunday," Barbie says.

Linda Everett looks at him. It's not a friendly look. "Surely you think before then—"

Rose interrupts her. "Look over there. That kid shouldn't be driving that damn rig so fast—he'll tip it over. I *hate* those ATVs."

They all look at the little vehicle with the fat balloon tires, and watch as it cuts a diagonal through the October-white hay. Not toward them, exactly, but certainly toward the Dome. It's going too fast. A couple of the soldiers hear the approaching engine and finally turn around.

"Oh Christ, don't let him crash," Linda Everett moans.

Rory Dinsmore doesn't crash. It would have been better if he had.

11

An idea is like a cold germ: sooner or later someone always catches it. The Joint Chiefs had already caught this one; it had been kicked around at several of the meetings attended by Barbie's old boss, Colonel James O. Cox. Sooner or later someone in The Mill was bound to be infected by the same idea, and it wasn't entirely surprising that the someone should turn out to be Rory Dinsmore, who was by far the sharpest tool in the Dinsmore family box ("I don't know *where* he gets it from," Shelley Dinsmore said when Rory brought home his first all-As rank card . . . and she said it in a voice more worried than proud). If he'd lived in town—and if he'd had a computer, which he did not—Rory would undoubtedly have been a part of Scarecrow Joe McClatchey's posse.

Rory had been forbidden to attend the carnival/prayer

meeting/demonstration; instead of eating weird hotdogs and helping with the car-park operation, he was ordered by his father to stay at home and feed the cows. When that was done, he was to grease their udders with Bag Balm, a job he hated. "And once you got those teats nice and shiny," his father said, "you can sweep the barns and bust up some haybales."

He was being punished for approaching the Dome yesterday after his father had expressly forbidden it. And actually *knocking* on it, for God's sake. Appealing to his mother, which often worked, did no good this time. "You could have been killed," Shelley said. "Also, your dad says you mouthed off."

"Just told em the cook's name!" Rory protested, and for that his father once more had gone upside his head while Ollie looked on with smug and silent approval.

"You're too smart for your own good," Alden said.

Safely behind his father's back, Ollie had stuck out his tongue. Shelley saw, however . . . and went upside *Ollie*'s head. She did not, however, forbid him the pleasures and excitements of that afternoon's makeshift fair.

"And you leave that goddam go-cart alone," Alden said, pointing to the ATV parked in the shade between dairy barns 1 and 2. "You need to move hay, you carry it. It'll build you up a little." Shortly thereafter, the dim Dinsmores went off together, walking across the field toward Romeo's tent. The bright one was left behind with a hayfork and a jar of Bag Balm as big as a flowerpot.

Rory went about his chores glumly but thoroughly; his racing mind sometimes got him in trouble, but he was a good son for all that, and the idea of ditching punishment-chores never crossed his mind. At first *nothing* crossed his mind. He was in that mostly empty-headed state of grace which is sometimes such fertile soil; it's the ground from which our brightest dreams and biggest ideas (both the good and the spectacularly bad) suddenly burst forth, often full-blown. Yet there is always a chain of association.

As Rory began sweeping barn 1's main aisle (he would save the hateful udder-greasing for last, he reckoned), he heard a rapid *pop-pow-pam* that could only be a string of firecrackers. They sounded a little like gunshots. This made him think of his father's .30-.30 rifle, which was propped in the front closet. The boys were forbidden to touch it except under strict supervision—while shooting at targets, or in hunting season—but it wasn't locked up and the ammo was on the shelf above it.

And the idea came. Rory thought: *I could blow a hole in that thing. Maybe pop it.* He had an image, bright and clear, of touching a match to the side of a balloon.

He dropped the broom and ran for the house. Like many bright people (especially bright children), inspiration rather than consideration was his strong suit. If his older brother had had such an idea (unlikely), Ollie would have thought: *If a plane couldn't bust through it, or a pulp-truck going full tilt, what chance does a bullet have?* He might also have reasoned: *I'm in dutch already for disobeying, and this is disobedience raised to the ninth power.*

Well . . . no, Ollie probably wouldn't have thought that. Ollie's mathematical abilities had topped out at simple multiplication.

Rory, however, was already taking college-track algebra, and knocking it dead. If asked how a bullet could accomplish what a truck or an airplane hadn't, he would have said the impact effect of a Winchester Elite XP³ would be far greater than either. It stood to reason. For one thing, the velocity would be greater. For another, the impact itself would be concentrated upon the point of a

180-grain bullet. He was sure it would work. It had the unquestionable elegance of an algebraic equation.

Rory saw his smiling (but of course modest) face on the front page of *USA Today*; being interviewed on *Nightly News with Brian Williams*; sitting on a flower-bedecked float in a parade in his honor, with Prom Queen–type girls surrounding him (probably in strapless gowns, but possibly in bathing suits) as he waved to the crowd and confetti floated down in drifts. He would be THE BOY WHO SAVED CHESTER'S MILL!

He snatched the rifle from the closet, got the step stool, and pawed a box of XP^{3}s down from the shelf. He stuffed two cartridges into the breech (one for a backup), then raced back outside with the rifle held above his head like a conquering *rebelista* (but—give him this—he engaged the safety without even thinking about it). The key to the Yamaha ATV he had been forbidden to ride was hanging on the pegboard in barn 1. He held the key fob between his teeth while he strapped the rifle to the back of the ATV with a couple of bungee cords. He wondered if there would be a sound when the Dome popped. He probably should have taken the shooter's plugs from the top shelf of the closet, but going back for them was unthinkable; he had to do this *now*.

That's how it is with big ideas.

He drove the ATV around barn 2, pausing just long enough to size up the crowd in the field. Excited as he was, he knew better than to head for where the Dome crossed the road (and where the smudges of yesterday's collisions still hung like dirt on an unwashed windowpane). Someone might stop him before he could pop the Dome. Then, instead of being THE BOY WHO SAVED CHESTER'S MILL, he'd likely wind up as THE BOY WHO GREASED COW TITS FOR A YEAR. Yes, and for the first week he'd be doing it in a crouch, his ass too sore to sit down. Someone else would end up getting the credit for *his* big idea.

So he drove on a diagonal that would bring him to the Dome five hundred yards or so from the tent, marking the place to stop by the crushed spots in the hay. Those, he knew, had been made by falling birds. He saw the soldiers stationed in that area turn toward the oncoming blat of the ATV. He heard shouts of alarm from the fair-and-prayer folks. The hymn-singing came to a discordant halt.

Worst of all, he saw his father waving his dirty John Deere cap at him and bawling, *"RORY OH GODDAM-MIT YOU STOP!"*

Rory was in too deep to stop, and—good son or not—he didn't *want* to stop. The ATV struck a hummock and he bounced clear of the seat, holding on with his hands and laughing like a loon. His own Deere cap was spun around backward and he didn't even remember doing it. The ATV tilted, then decided to stay up. Almost there, now, and one of the fatigues-clad soldiers was also shouting at him to stop.

Rory did, and so suddenly he almost somersaulted over the Yamaha's handlebars. He forgot to put the darned thing in neutral and it lurched forward, actually striking the Dome before stalling out. Rory heard the crimp of metal and the tinkle of the headlight as it shattered.

The soldiers, afraid of being hit by the ATV (the eye which sees nothing to block an oncoming object triggers powerful instincts), fell off to either side, leaving a nice big hole and sparing Rory the need of telling them to move away from a possible explosive blowout. He wanted to be a hero, but didn't want to hurt or kill anybody to do it.

He had to hurry. The people closest to his stopping point were the ones in the parking lot and clustered around the Summer Blowout Sale tent, and they were running like hell. His father and brother were among them, both screaming at him to not do whatever he was planning to do.

Rory yanked the rifle free of the bungee cords, socked the butt plate into his shoulder, and aimed at the invisible barrier five feet above a trio of dead sparrows.

"No, kid, bad idea!" one of the soldiers shouted.

Rory paid him no mind, because it was a *good* idea. The people from the tent and the parking lot were close, now. Someone—it was Lester Coggins, who ran a lot better than he played guitar—shouted: *"In the name of God, son, don't do that!"*

Rory pulled the trigger. No; only tried to. The safety was still on. He looked over his shoulder and saw the tall, thin preacher from the holy-roller church blow past his puffing, red-faced father. Lester's shirttail was out and flying. His eyes were wide. The cook from Sweetbriar Rose was right behind him. They were no more than sixty yards away now, and the Reverend looked like he was just getting into fourth gear.

Rory thumbed off the safety.

"No, kid, no!" the soldier cried again, simultaneously crouching on his side of the Dome and holding out his splayed hands.

Rory paid no attention. It's that way with big ideas. He fired.

It was, unfortunately for Rory, a perfect shot. The hi-impact slug struck the Dome dead on, ricocheted, and came back like a rubber ball on a string. Rory felt no immediate pain, but a vast sheet of white light filled his head as the smaller of the slug's two fragments thumbed out his left eye and lodged in his brain. Blood flew in a spray, then ran through his fingers as he dropped to his knees, clutching his face.

12

"I'm blind! I'm blind!" the boy was screaming, and Lester immediately thought of the scripture upon which his finger had landed: *Madness and blindness and astonishment of the heart.*

"I'm blind! I'm blind!"

Lester pried away the boy's hands and saw the red, welling socket. The remains of the eye itself were dangling on Rory's cheek. As he turned his head up to Lester, the splattered remains plopped into the grass.

Lester had a moment to cradle the child in his arms before the father arrived and tore him away. That was all right. That was as it should be. Lester had sinned and begged guidance from the Lord. Guidance had been given, an answer provided. He knew now what he was to do about the sins he'd been led into by James Rennie.

A blind child had shown him the way.

THIS IS *NOT* AS BAD AS IT GETS

What Rusty Everett would recall later was confusion. The only image that stuck out with complete clarity was Pastor Coggins's naked upper body: fishbelly-white skin and stacked ribs.

Barbie, however—perhaps because he'd been tasked by Colonel Cox to put on his investigator's hat again— saw everything. And his clearest memory wasn't of Coggins with his shirt off; it was of Melvin Searles pointing a finger at him and then tilting his head slightly—sign language any man recognizes as meaning *We ain't done yet, Sunshine.*

What everyone else remembered—what brought the town's situation home to them as perhaps nothing else could—were the father's cries as he held his wretched, bleeding boy in his arms, and the mother screaming *"Is he all right, Alden? IS HE ALL RIGHT?"* as she labored her sixty-pounds-overweight bulk toward the scene.

Barbie saw Rusty Everett push through the circle gathering around the boy and join the two kneeling men— Alden and Lester. Alden was cradling his son in his arms as Pastor Coggins stared with his mouth sagging like a gate with a busted hinge. Rusty's wife was right behind him. Rusty fell on his knees between Alden and Lester and tried to pull the boy's hands away from his face. Alden—not surprisingly, in Barbie's opinion—promptly socked him one. Rusty's nose started to bleed.

"No! Let him help!" the PA's wife yelled.

Linda, Barbie thought. *Her name is Linda, and she's a cop.*

"No, Alden! No!" Linda put her hand on the farmer's shoulder and he turned, apparently ready to sock *her.* All sense had departed his face; he was an animal protecting a cub. Barbie moved forward to catch his fist if the farmer let it fly, then had a better idea.

"Medic here!" he shouted, bending into Alden's face and trying to block Linda from his field of vision. "Medic! Medic, med—"

Barbie was yanked backward by the collar of his shirt and spun around. He had just time enough to register Mel Searles—one of Junior's buddies—and to realize that Searles was wearing a blue uniform shirt and a badge. *This is as bad as it gets,* Barbie thought, but as if to prove him wrong, Searles socked *him* in the face, just as he had that night in Dipper's parking lot. He missed Barbie's nose, which had probably been his target, but mashed Barbie's lips back against his teeth.

Searles drew back his fist to do it again, but Jackie Wettington—Mel's unwilling partner that day—grabbed his arm before he could. "Don't do it!" she shouted. "Officer, *don't do it*!"

For a moment the issue was in doubt. Then Ollie Dinsmore, closely followed by his sobbing, gasping mother, passed between them, knocking Searles back a step.

Searles lowered his fist. "Okay," he said. "But you're on a crime scene, asshole. Police investigation scene. Whatever."

Barbie wiped his bleeding mouth with the heel of his hand and thought, *This is* not *as bad as it gets. That's the hell of it—it's not.*

2

The only part of this Rusty heard was Barbie shouting *medic*. Now he said it himself. "Medic, Mr. Dinsmore. Rusty Everett. You know me. Let me look at your boy."

"Let him, Alden!" Shelley cried. "Let him take care of Rory!"

Alden relaxed his grip on the kid, who was swaying back and forth on his knees, his bluejeans soaked with blood. Rory had covered his face with his hands again. Rusty took hold of them—gently, gently does it—and pulled them down. He had hoped it wouldn't be as bad as he feared, but the socket was raw and empty, pouring blood. And the brain behind that socket was hurt plenty. The news was in how the remaining eye cocked senselessly skyward, bulging at nothing.

Rusty started to pull his shirt off, but the preacher was already holding out his own. Coggins's upper body, thin and white in front, striped with crisscrossing red welts in back, was running with sweat. He held the shirt out.

"No," Rusty said. "Rip it, rip it."

For a moment Lester didn't get it. Then he tore the shirt down the middle. The rest of the police contingent was arriving now, and some of the regular cops—Henry Morrison, George Frederick, Jackie Wettington, Freddy Denton—were yelling at the new Special Deputies to help move the crowd back, make some space. The new hires did so, and enthusiastically. Some of the rubberneckers were knocked down, including that famous Bratz-torturer Samantha Bushey. Sammy had Little Walter in a Papoose carrier, and when she went on her ass, both of them began to squall. Junior Rennie stepped over her without so much as a look and grabbed Rory's mom, almost pulling the wounded boy's mother off her feet before Freddy Denton stopped him.

"No, Junior, no! It's the kid's mother! Let her loose!"

"Police brutality!" Sammy Bushey yelled from where she lay in the grass. *"Police brutal—"*

Georgia Roux, the newest hire in what had become Peter Randolph's police department, arrived with Carter Thibodeau (holding his hand, actually). Georgia pressed her boot against one of Sammy's breasts—it wasn't quite a kick—and said, "Yo, dyke, shut up."

Junior let go of Rory's mother and went to stand with Mel, Carter, and Georgia. They were staring at Barbie. Junior added his eyes to theirs, thinking that the cook was like a bad goddamned penny that kept turning up. He thought *Baarbie* would look awfully good in a cell right next to Sloppy Sam's. Junior also thought that being a cop had been his destiny all along; it had certainly helped with his headaches.

Rusty took half of Lester's torn shirt and ripped it again. He folded a piece, started to put it over the gaping wound in the boy's face, then changed his mind and gave it to the father. "Hold it to the—"

The words barely came out; his throat was full of blood from his mashed nose. Rusty hawked it back, turned his head, spat a half-clotted loogie into the grass, and tried again. "Hold it to the wound, Dad. Apply pressure. Hand to the back of his neck and *squeeze.*"

Dazed but willing, Alden Dinsmore did as he was told. The makeshift pad immediately turned red, but the man seemed calmer nonetheless. Having something to do helped. It usually did.

Rusty flung the remaining piece of shirt at Lester. "More!" he said, and Lester began ripping the shirt into smaller pieces. Rusty lifted Dinsmore's hand and removed the first pad, which was now soaked and useless. Shelley Dinsmore shrieked when she saw the empty socket. "Oh, my boy! *My boy!*"

Peter Randolph arrived at a jog, huffing and puffing. Still, he was far ahead of Big Jim, who—mindful of his substandard ticker—was plodding down the slope of the field on grass the rest of the crowd had trampled into a broad path. He was thinking of what a clustermug this had turned out to be. Town gatherings would have to be by permit only in the future. And if he had anything to do with it (he would; he always did), permits would be hard to come by.

"Move these people back further!" Randolph snarled at Officer Morrison. And, as Henry turned to do so: *"Move it back, folks! Give em some air!"*

Morrison bawled: *"Officers, form a line! Push em back! Anyone who resists, put em in cuffs!"*

The crowd began a slow reverse shuffle. Barbie lingered. "Mr. Everett . . . Rusty . . . do you need any help? Are you okay?"

"Fine," Rusty said, and his face told Barbie everything he needed to know: the PA was all right, just a bloody nose. The kid wasn't and never would be again, even if he lived. Rusty applied a fresh pad to the kid's bleeding eyesocket and put the father's hand over it again. "Nape of the neck," he said. "Press hard. *Hard.*"

Barbie started to step back, but then the kid spoke.

3

"It's Halloween. You can't . . . *we* can't . . ."

Rusty froze in the act of folding another piece of shirt into a compression pad. Suddenly he was back in his daughters' bedroom, listening to Janelle scream, *It's the Great Pumpkin's fault!*

He looked up at Linda. She had heard, too. Her eyes were big, the color fleeing her previously flushed cheeks.

"Linda!" Rusty snapped at her. "Get on your walkie! Call the hospital! Tell Twitch to get the ambulance—"

"The fire!" Rory Dinsmore screamed in a high, trembling voice. Lester was staring at him as Moses might have stared at the burning bush. *"The fire! The bus is in the fire! Everyone's screaming! Watch out for Halloween!"*

The crowd was silent now, listening to the child rant. Even Jim Rennie heard as he reached the back of the mob and began to elbow his way through.

"Linda!" Rusty shouted. "Get on your walkie! *We need the ambulance!"*

She started visibly, as if someone had just clapped his hands in front of her face. She pulled the walkie-talkie off her belt.

Rory tumbled forward into the flattened grass and began to seize.

"What's happening?" That was the father.

"Oh dear-to-Jesus, he's dying!" That was the mother.

Rusty turned the trembling, bucking child over (trying not to think of Jannie as he did it, but that, of course, was impossible) and tilting his chin up to create an airway.

"Come on, Dad," he told Alden. "Don't quit on me now. Squeeze the neck. Compression on the wound. Let's stop the bleeding."

Compression might drive the fragment that had taken the kid's eye deeper in, but Rusty would worry about that later. If, that was, the kid didn't die right out here on the grass.

From nearby—but oh so far—one of the soldiers finally spoke up. Barely out of his teens, he looked terrified and sorry. "We tried to stop him. Boy didn't listen. There wasn't nothing we could do."

Pete Freeman, his Nikon dangling by his knee on its strap, favored this young warrior with a smile of singular bitterness. "I think we know that. If we didn't before, we sure do now."

4

Before Barbie could melt into the crowd, Mel Searles grabbed him by the arm.

"Take your hand off me," Barbie said mildly.

Searles showed his teeth in his version of a grin. "In your dreams, Fucko." Then he raised his voice. "Chief! Hey, Chief!"

Peter Randolph turned toward him impatiently, frowning.

"This guy interfered with me while I was trying to secure the scene. Can I arrest him?"

Randolph opened his mouth, possibly to say *Don't waste my time.* Then he looked around. Jim Rennie had finally joined the little group watching Everett work on the boy. Rennie gave Barbie the flat stare of a reptile on a rock, then looked back at Randolph and nodded slightly.

Mel saw it. His grin widened. "Jackie? Officer Wettington, I mean? Can I borrow a pair of your cuffs?"

Junior and the rest of his crew were also grinning. This was better than watching some bleeding kid, and a *lot* better than policing a bunch of holy rollers and dumbbells with signs. "Payback's a bitch, *Baaaar*-bie," Junior said.

Jackie looked dubious. "Pete—Chief, I mean—I think the guy was only trying to h—"

"Cuff him up," Randolph said. "We'll sort out what he was or wasn't trying to do later. In the meantime, I want this mess shut down." He raised his voice. "It's over, folks! You've had your fun, and see what it's come to! *Now go home!*"

Jackie was removing a set of plasticuffs from her belt (she had no intention of handing them to Mel Searles, would put them on herself) when Julia Shumway spoke up. She was standing just behind Randolph and Big Jim (in fact, Big Jim had elbowed her aside on his way to where the action was).

"I wouldn't do that, Chief Randolph, unless you want the PD embarrassed on the front page of the *Democrat*." She was smiling her Mona Lisa smile. "With you so new to the job and all."

"What are you talking about?" Randolph asked. His frown was deeper now, turning his face into a series of unlovely crevices.

Julia held up her camera—a slightly older version of Pete Freeman's. "I have quite a few pictures of Mr. Barbara assisting Rusty Everett with that wounded child, a couple of Officer Searles hauling Mr. Barbara off for no discernible reason . . . and one of Officer Searles punching Mr. Barbara in the mouth. Also for no discernible reason. I'm not much of a photographer, but that one is really quite good. Would you like to see it, Chief Randolph? You can; the camera's digital."

Barbie's admiration for her deepened, because he thought she was running a bluff. If she'd been taking pictures, why was she holding the lenscap in her left hand, as if she'd just taken it off?

"It's a lie, Chief," Mel said. "He tried to take a swing at me. Ask Junior."

"I think my pictures will show that young Mr. Rennie

was involved in crowd control and had his back turned when the punch landed," Julia said.

Randolph was glowering at her. "I could take your camera away," he said. "Evidence."

"You certainly could," she agreed cheerily, "and Pete Freeman would take a picture of you doing it. Then you could take *Pete's* camera . . . but everyone here would see you do it."

"Whose side are you on here, Julia?" Big Jim asked. He was smiling his fierce smile—the smile of a shark about to take a bite out of some plump swimmer's ass.

Julia turned her own smile on him, the eyes above it as innocent and enquiring as a child's. "*Are* there sides, James? Other than over there"—she pointed at the watching soldiers—"and in here?"

Big Jim considered her, his lips now bending the other way, a smile in reverse. Then he flapped one disgusted hand at Randolph.

"I guess we'll let it slide, Mr. Barbara," Randolph said. "Heat of the moment."

"Thanks," Barbie said.

Jackie took her glowering young partner's arm. "Come on, Officer Searles. This part's over. Let's move these people back."

Searles went with her, but not before turning to Barbie and making the gesture: finger pointing, head cocked slightly. *We ain't done yet, Sunshine.*

Rommie's assistant Toby Manning and Jack Evans appeared, carrying a makeshift stretcher made out of canvas and tent poles. Rommie opened his mouth to ask what the hell they thought they were doing, then closed it again. The field day had been canceled anyway, so what the hell.

5

Those with cars got into them. Then they all tried to drive away at the same time.

Predictable, Joe McClatchey thought. *Totally predictable.*

Most of the cops worked to unclog the resulting traffic jam, although even a bunch of kids (Joe was standing with Benny Drake and Norrie Calvert) could tell that the new and improved Five-O had no idea what it was doing. The sound of po-po curses came clear on the summery air (*"Can't you back that sonofawhore UP!"*). In spite of the mess, nobody seemed to be laying on their horns. Most folks were probably too bummed to beep.

Benny said, "Look at those idiots. How many gallons of gas do you think they're blowing out their tailpipes? Like they think the supply's endless."

"Word," Norrie said. She was a tough kid, a small-town riot grrl with a modified Tennessee Tophat mullet 'do, but now she only looked pale and sad and scared. She took Benny's hand. Scarecrow Joe's heart broke, then remended itself in an instant when she took his as well.

"There goes the guy who almost got arrested," Benny said, pointing with his free hand. Barbie and the newspaper lady were trudging across the field toward the make-shift parking lot with sixty or eighty other people, some dragging their protest signs dispiritedly behind them.

"Nancy Newspaper wasn't taking pictures at all, y'know," Scarecrow Joe said. "I was standing right behind her. Pretty foxy."

"Yeah," Benny said, "but I still wouldn't want to be him. Until this shit ends, the cops can do pretty much what they want."

That was true, Joe reflected. And the new cops weren't particularly nice guys. Junior Rennie, for example. The story of Sloppy Sam's arrest was already making the rounds.

"What are you saying?" Norrie asked Benny.

"Nothing right now. It's still cool right now." He considered. "*Fairly* cool. But if this goes on . . . remember *Lord of the Flies*?" They had read it for honors English.

Benny intoned: " 'Kill the pig. Cut her throat. Bash her in.' People call cops pigs, but I'll tell you what *I* think, I think cops *find* pigs when the shit gets deep. Maybe because they get scared, too."

Norrie Calvert burst into tears. Scarecrow Joe put an arm around her. He did it carefully, as if he thought doing such a thing might cause them both to explode, but she turned her face against his shirt and hugged him. It was a one-armed hug, because she was still holding onto Benny with her other hand. Joe thought he had felt nothing in his whole life as weirdly thrilling as her tears dampening his shirt. Over the top of her head, he looked at Benny reproachfully.

"Sorry, dude," Benny said, and patted her back. "No fear."

"His eye was gone!" she cried. The words were muffled against Joe's chest. Then she let go of him. "This isn't fun anymore. This is *not* fun."

"No." Joe spoke as if discovering a great truth. "It isn't."

"Look," Benny said. It was the ambulance. Twitch was bumping across Dinsmore's field with the red roof lights flashing. His sister, the woman who owned Sweetbriar Rose, was walking ahead of him, guiding him around the worst potholes. An ambulance in a hayfield, under a bright afternoon sky in October: it was the final touch.

Suddenly, Scarecrow Joe no longer wanted to protest. Nor did he exactly want to go home.

At that moment, the only thing in the world he wanted was to get out of town.

6

Julia slid behind the wheel of her car but didn't start it; they were going to be here awhile, and there was no sense in wasting gas. She leaned past Barbie, opened the glove compartment, and brought out an old pack of American Spirits. "Emergency supplies," she told him apologetically. "Do you want one?"

He shook his head.

"Do you mind? Because I can wait."

He shook his head again. She lit up, then blew smoke out her open window. It was still warm—a real Indian summer day for sure—but it wouldn't stay that way. Another week or so and the weather would turn wrong, as the oldtimers said. *Or maybe not,* she thought. *Who in the hell knows?* If the Dome stayed in place, she had no doubt that plenty of meteorologists would weigh in on the subject of the weather inside, but so what? The Weather Channel Yodas couldn't even predict which way a snowstorm would turn, and in Julia's opinion they deserved no more credence than the political geniuses who blabbed their days away at the Sweetbriar Rose bullshit table.

"Thanks for speaking up back there," he said. "You saved my bacon."

"Here's a newsflash, honey—your bacon's still hanging in the smokehouse. What are you going to do next time? Have your friend Cox call the ACLU? They might be interested, but I don't think anyone from the Portland office is going to be visiting Chester's Mill soon."

"Don't be so pessimistic. The Dome might blow out to sea tonight. Or just dissipate. We don't know."

"Fat chance. This is a government job—*some* government's—and I'll bet your Colonel Cox knows it."

Barbie was silent. He had believed Cox when Cox said the U.S. hadn't been responsible for the Dome. Not because Cox was necessarily trustworthy, but because Barbie just didn't think America had the technology. Or any other country, for that matter. But what did he know? His last service job had been threatening scared Iraqis. Sometimes with a gun to their heads.

Junior's friend Frankie DeLesseps was out on Route 119, helping to direct traffic. He was wearing a blue uniform shirt over jeans—there probably hadn't been any uniform pants in his size at the station. He was a tall sonofabitch. And, Julia saw with misgivings, he was wearing a gun on his hip. Smaller than the Glocks the regular Mill police carried, probably his own property, but it was a gun, all right.

"What will you do if the Hitler Youth comes after you?" she asked, lifting her chin in Frankie's direction. "Good luck hollering police brutality if they jug you and decide to finish what they started. There's only two lawyers in town. One's senile and the other drives a Boxster Jim Rennie got him at discount. Or so I've heard."

"I can take care of myself."

"Oooh, macho."

"What's up with your paper? It looked ready when I left last night."

"Technically speaking, you left this morning. And yes, it's ready. Pete and I and a few friends will make sure it gets distributed. I just didn't see any point in starting while the town was three-quarters empty. Want to be a volunteer newsboy?"

"I would, but I've got a zillion sandwiches to make. Strictly cold food at the restaurant tonight."

"Maybe I'll drop by." She tossed her cigarette, only half-smoked, from the window. Then, after a moment's consideration, she got out and stepped on it. Starting a grassfire out here would not be cool, not with the town's new firetrucks stranded in Castle Rock.

"I swung by Chief Perkins's house earlier," she said as she got back behind the wheel. "Except of course it's just Brenda's now."

"How is she?"

"Terrible. But when I said you wanted to see her, and that it was important—although I didn't say what it was about—she agreed. After dark might be best. I suppose your friend will be impatient—"

"Stop calling Cox my friend. He's not my friend."

They watched silently as the wounded boy was loaded into the back of the ambulance. The soldiers were still watching, too. Probably against orders, and that made Julia feel a little better about them. The ambulance began to buck its way back across the field, lights flashing.

"This is terrible," she said in a thin voice.

Barbie put an arm around her shoulders. She tensed for a moment, then relaxed. Looking straight ahead—at the ambulance, which was now turning into a cleared lane in the middle of Route 119—she said: "What if they shut me down, my friend? What if Rennie and his pet police decide to shut my little newspaper down?"

"That's not going to happen," Barbie said. But he wondered. If this went on long enough, he supposed every day in Chester's Mill would become Anything Can Happen Day.

"She had something else on her mind," Julia Shumway said.

"Mrs. Perkins?"

"Yes. It was in many ways a very strange conversation."

"She's grieving for her husband," Barbie said. "Grief makes people strange. I said hello to Jack Evans—his wife died yesterday when the Dome came down—and he looked at me as if he didn't know me, although I've been serving him my famous Wednesday meatloaf since last spring."

"I've known Brenda Perkins since she was Brenda Morse," Julia said. "Almost forty years. I thought she might tell me what was troubling her . . . but she didn't."

Barbie pointed at the road. "I think you can go now."

As Julia started the engine, her cell phone trilled. She almost dropped her bag in her hurry to dig it out. She listened, then handed it to Barbie with her ironic smile. "It's for you, boss."

It was Cox, and Cox had something to say. Quite a lot, actually. Barbie interrupted long enough to tell Cox what had happened to the boy now headed to Cathy Russell, but Cox either didn't relate Rory Dinsmore's story to what he was saying, or didn't want to. He listened politely enough, then went on. When he finished, he asked Barbie a question that would have been an order, had Barbie still been in uniform and under his command.

"Sir, I understand what you're asking, but you don't understand the . . . I guess you'd call it the political situation here. And my little part in it. I had some trouble before this Dome thing, and—"

"We know all about that," Cox said. "An altercation with the Second Selectman's son and some of his friends. You were almost arrested, according to what I've got in my folder."

A folder. Now he's got a folder. God help me.

"That's fine intel as far as it goes," Barbie said, "but

let me give you a little more. One, the Police Chief who *kept* me from being arrested died out on 119, not far from where I'm talking to you, in fact—"

Faintly, in a world he could not now visit, Barbie heard paper rattle. He suddenly felt he would like to kill Colonel James O. Cox with his bare hands, simply because Colonel James O. Cox could go out for Mickey-D's any time he wanted, and he, Dale Barbara, could not.

"We know about that, too," Cox said. "A pacemaker problem."

"Two," Barbie went on, "the new Chief, who is asshole buddies with the only powerful member of this town's Board of Selectmen, has hired some new deputies. They're the guys who tried to beat my head off my shoulders in the parking lot of the local nightclub."

"You'll have to rise above that, won't you? Colonel?"

"Why are you calling me Colonel? *You're* the Colonel."

"Congratulations," Cox said. "Not only have you re-enlisted in your country's service, you've gotten an abso-lutely *dizzying* promotion."

"No!" Barbie shouted. Julia was looking at him with concern, but he was hardly aware of it. "No, I don't want it!"

"Yeah, but you've got it," Cox said calmly. "I'm going to e-mail a copy of the essential paperwork to your editor friend before we shut down your unfortunate little town's Internet capacity."

"Shut it *down*? You can't shut it down!"

"The paperwork is signed by the President himself. Are you going to say no to him? I understand he can be a tad grumpy when he's crossed."

Barbie didn't reply. His mind was whirling.

"You need to visit the Selectmen and the Police Chief," Cox said. "You need to tell them the President has invoked martial law in Chester's Mill, and you're the officer in charge. I'm sure you'll encounter some initial resistance, but the information I've just given you should help establish you as the town's conduit to the outside world. And I know your powers of persuasion. Saw them firsthand in Iraq."

"Sir," he said. "You have *so* misread the situation here," He ran a hand through his hair. His ear was throbbing from the goddamned cell phone. "It's as if you can comprehend the idea of the Dome, but not what's happening in this town as a result of it. And it's been less than thirty hours."

"Help me understand, then."

"You say the President wants me to do this. Suppose I were to call him up and tell him he can kiss my rosy red ass?"

Julia was looking at him, horrified, and this actually inspired him.

"Suppose, in fact, I said I was a sleeper Al Qaeda agent, and I was planning to kill him—pow, one to the head. How about that?"

"Lieutenant Barbara—*Colonel* Barbara, I mean—you've said enough."

Barbie did not feel this was so. "Could he send the FBI to come and grab me? The Secret Service? The goddam Red Army? No, sir. He could not."

"We have plans to change that, as I have just explained." Cox no longer sounded loose and good-humored, jest one ole grunt talkin to another.

"And if it works, feel free to have the federal agency of your choice come and arrest me. But if we stay cut off, who in here's going to listen to me? Get it through your head: *this town has seceded.* Not just from America but from the whole world. There's nothing we can do about it, and nothing you can do about it either."

Quietly, Cox said: "We're trying to help you guys."

"You say that and I almost believe you. Will anybody else around here? When they look to see what kind of help their taxes are buying them, they see soldiers standing guard with their backs turned. That sends a hell of a message."

"You're talking a whole lot for someone who's saying no."

"I'm *not* saying no. But I'm only about nine feet from being arrested, and proclaiming myself the commandant pro tem won't help."

"Suppose I were to call the First Selectman . . . what's his name . . . Sanders . . . and tell him . . ."

"That's what I mean about how little you know. It's like Iraq all over again, only this time you're in Washington instead of boots on the ground, and you seem as clueless as the rest of the desk soldiers. Read my lips, sir: *some* intelligence is worse than no intelligence at all."

"A little learning is a dangerous thing," Julia said dreamily.

"If not Sanders, then who?"

"James Rennie. The *Second* Selectman. He's the Boss Hog around here."

There was a pause. Then Cox said, "Maybe we can give you the Internet. Some of us are of the opinion that cutting it off's just a knee-jerk reaction, anyway."

"Why would you think that?" Barbie asked. "Don't you guys know that if you let us stay on the Net, Aunt Sarah's cranberry bread recipe is sure to get out sooner or later?"

Julia sat up straight and mouthed, *They're trying to cut the Internet?* Barbie raised one finger toward her—*Wait.*

"Just hear me out, Barbie. Suppose we call this Rennie and tell him the Internet's got to go, so sorry, crisis situation, extreme measures, et cetera, et cetera. Then you can convince him of your usefulness by changing our minds."

Barbie considered. It might work. For a while, anyway. Or it might not.

"Plus," Cox said brightly, "you'll be giving them this other information. Maybe saving some lives, but saving people the scare of their lives, for sure."

Barbie said, "Phones stay up as well as Internet."

"That's hard. I might be able to keep the Net for you, but . . . listen, man. There are at least five Curtis LeMay types sitting on the committee presiding over this mess, and as far as they're concerned, everyone in Chester's Mill is a terrorist until proved otherwise."

"What can these hypothetical terrorists do to harm America? Suicide-bomb the Congo Church?"

"Barbie, you're preaching to the choir."

Of course that was probably the truth.

"Will you do it?"

"I'll have to get back to you on that. Wait for my call before you do anything. I have to talk to the late Police Chief's widow first."

Cox persisted. "Will you keep the horse-trading part of this conversation to yourself?"

Again, Barbie was struck by how little even Cox—a freethinker, by military standards—understood about the changes the Dome had already wrought. In here, the Cox brand of secrecy no longer mattered.

Us against them, Barbie thought. *Now it's us against them. Unless their crazy idea works, that is.*

"Sir, I really will have to get back to you on that; this phone is suffering a bad case of low battery." A lie he told with no remorse. "And you need to wait to hear from me before you talk to anybody else."

"Just remember, the big bang's scheduled for thirteen

hundred tomorrow. If you want to maintain viability on this, you better stay out front."

Maintain viability. Another meaningless phrase under the Dome. Unless it applied to keeping your gennie supplied with propane.

"We'll talk," Barbie said. He closed the phone before Cox could say more. 119 was almost clear now, although DeLesseps was still there, leaning against his vintage muscle car with his arms folded. As Julia drove past the Nova, Barbie noted a sticker reading ASS, GAS, OR GRASS—NOBODY RIDES FOR FREE. Also a police bubblegum light on the dash. He thought the contrast summed up everything that was now wrong in Chester's Mill.

As they rode, Barbie told her everything Cox had said.

"What they're planning is really no different than what that kid just tried," she said, sounding appalled.

"Well, a *little* different," Barbie said. "The kid tried it with a rifle. They've got a Cruise missile lined up. Call it the Big Bang theory."

She smiled. It wasn't her usual one; wan and bewildered, it made her look sixty instead of forty-three. "I think I'm going to be putting out another paper sooner than I thought."

Barbie nodded. "Extra, extra, read all about it."

7

"Hello, Sammy," someone said. "How are you?"

Samantha Bushey didn't recognize the voice and turned toward it warily, hitching up the Papoose carrier as she did. Little Walter was asleep and he weighed a ton. Her butt hurt from falling on it, and her feelings were hurt, too—that damn Georgia Roux, calling her a dyke.

Georgia Roux, who had come whining around Sammy's trailer more than once, looking to score an eightball for her and the musclebound freak she went around with.

It was Dodee's father. Sammy had spoken with him thousands of times, but she hadn't recognized his voice; she hardly recognized *him*. He looked old and sad—broken, somehow. He didn't even scope out her boobs, which was a first.

"Hi, Mr. Sanders. Gee, I didn't even see you at the—" She flapped her hand back toward the flattened-down field and the big tent, now half collapsed and looking forlorn. Although not as forlorn as Mr. Sanders.

"I was sitting in the shade." That same hesitant voice, coming through an apologetic, hurting smile that was hard to look at. "I had something to drink, though. Wasn't it warm for October? Golly, yes. I thought it was a good afternoon—a real *town* afternoon—until that boy . . ."

Oh crispy crackers, he was crying.

"I'm awful sorry about your wife, Mr. Sanders."

"Thank you, Sammy. That's very kind. Can I carry your baby back to your car for you? I think you can go now—the road's almost clear."

That was an offer Sammy couldn't refuse even if he *was* crying. She scooped Little Walter out of the Papoose—it was like picking up a big clump of warm bread dough—and handed him over. Little Walter opened his eyes, smiled glassily, belched, then went back to sleep.

"I think he might have a package in his diaper," Mr. Sanders said.

"Yeah, he's a regular shit machine. Good old Little Walter."

"Walter's a very nice old-fashioned name."

"Thanks." Telling him that her baby's first name was

actually Little didn't seem worth the trouble . . . and she was sure she'd had that conversation with him before, anyway. He just didn't remember. Walking with him like this—even though he was carrying the baby—was the perfect bummer end to a perfect bummer afternoon. At least he was right about the traffic; the automotive mosh pit had finally cleared out. Sammy wondered how long it would be before the whole town was riding bicycles again.

"I never liked the idea of her in that plane," Mr. Sanders said. He seemed to be picking up the thread of some interior conversation. "Sometimes I even wondered if Claudie was sleeping with that guy."

Dodee's mom sleeping with Chuck Thompson? Sammy was both shocked and intrigued.

"Probably not," he said, and sighed. "In any case, it doesn't matter now. Have you seen Dodee? She didn't come home last night."

Sammy almost said *Sure, yesterday afternoon*. But if the Dodester hadn't slept at home last night, saying that would only worry the Dodester's dadster. And let Sammy in for a long conversation with a guy who had tears streaming down his face and a snotrunner hanging from one nostril. That would not be cool.

They had reached her car, an old Chevrolet with cancer of the rocker panels. She took Little Walter and grimaced at the smell. That wasn't just mail in his diaper, that was UPS and Federal Express combined.

"No, Mr. Sanders, haven't seen her."

He nodded, then wiped his nose with the back of his hand. The snotrunner disappeared, or at least went somewhere else. That was a relief. "She probably went to the mall with Angie McCain, then to her aunt Peg's in Sabattus when she couldn't get back into town."

"Yeah, that's probably it." And when Dodee turned

up right here in The Mill, he'd have a pleasant surprise. God knew he deserved one. Sammy opened the car door and laid Little Walter on the passenger side. She'd given up on the child-restraint seat months ago. Too much of a pain in the ass. And besides, she was a very safe driver.

"Good to see you, Sammy." A pause. "Will you pray for my wife?"

"Uhhh . . . sure, Mr. Sanders, no prob."

She started to get in the car, then remembered two things: that Georgia Roux had shoved her tit with her goddam motorcycle boot—probably hard enough to leave a bruise—and that Andy Sanders, brokenhearted or not, was the town's First Selectman.

"Mr. Sanders?"

"Yes, Sammy?"

"Some of those cops were kinda rough out there. You might want to do something about that. Before it, you know, gets out of hand."

His unhappy smile didn't change. "Well, Sammy, I understand how you young people feel about police—I was young myself once—but we've got a pretty bad situation here. And the quicker we establish a little authority, the better off everyone will be. You understand that, don't you?"

"Sure," Sammy said. What she understood was that grief, no matter how genuine, did not seem to impede a politician's flow of bullshit. "Well, I'll see you."

"They're a good team," Andy said vaguely. "Pete Randolph will see they all pull together. Wear the same hat. Do . . . uh . . . the same dance. Protect and serve, you know."

"Sure," Samantha said. The protect-and-serve dance, with the occasional tit-kick thrown in. She pulled away with Little Walter once more snoring on the seat. The smell of babyshit was terrific. She unrolled the windows, then looked in the rearview mirror. Mr. Sanders was still standing in the makeshift parking lot, which was now almost entirely deserted. He raised a hand to her.

Sammy raised her own in turn, wondering just where Dodee *had* stayed last night if she hadn't gone home. Then she dismissed it—it was really none of her concern—and flipped on the radio. The only thing she could get clearly was Jesus Radio, and she turned it off again.

When she looked up, Frankie DeLesseps was standing in the road in front of her with his hand up, just like a real cop. She had to stomp the brake to keep from hitting him, then put her hand on the baby to keep him from falling. Little Walter awoke and began to blat.

"Look what you did!" she yelled at Frankie (with whom she'd once had a two-day fling back in high school, when Angie was at band camp). "The baby almost went on the floor!"

"Where's his seat?" Frankie leaned in her window, biceps bulging. Big muscles, little dick, that was Frankie DeLesseps. As far as Sammy was concerned, Angie could have him.

"None of your beeswax."

A real cop might have written her up—for the lip as much as the child-restraint law—but Frankie only smirked. "You seen Angie?"

"No." This time it was the truth. "She probably got caught out of town." Although it seemed to Sammy that the ones *in* town were the ones who'd gotten caught.

"What about Dodee?"

Sammy once again said no. She practically had to, because Frankie might talk to Mr. Sanders.

"Angie's car is at her house," Frankie said. "I looked in the garage."

"Big whoop. They probably went off somewhere in Dodee's Kia."

He seemed to consider this. They were almost alone now. The traffic jam was just a memory. Then he said, "Did Georgia hurt your booby, baby?" And before she could answer, he reached in and grabbed it. Not gently, either. "Want me to kiss it all better?"

She slapped his hand. On her right, Little Walter blatted and blatted. Sometimes she wondered why God had made men in the first place, she really did. Always blatting or grabbing, grabbing or blatting.

Frankie wasn't smiling now. "You want to watch that shit," he said. "Things are different now."

"What are you going to do? Arrest me?"

"I'd think of something better than that," he said. "Go on, get out of here. And if you *do* see Angie, tell her I want to see her."

She drove away, mad and—she didn't like to admit this to herself, but it was true—a little frightened. Half a mile down the road she pulled over and changed Little Walter's diaper. There was a used diaper bag in back, but she was too mad to bother. She threw the shitty Pamper onto the shoulder of the road instead, not far from the big sign reading:

JIM RENNIE'S USED CARS
FOREIGN & DOMESTIC
A$K U$ 4 CREDIT!
YOU'LL BE WHEELIN'
BECAUSE BIG JIM IS DEALIN'!

She passed some kids on bikes and wondered again how long it would be before everyone was riding them. Except it wouldn't come to that. Someone would figure things out before it did, just like in one of those disaster movies she enjoyed watching on TV while she was stoned: volcanoes erupting in LA, zombies in New York. And when things went back to normal, Frankie and Carter Thibodeau would revert to what they'd been before: smalltown losers with little or no jingle in their pockets. In the meantime, though, she might do well to keep a low profile.

All in all, she was glad she'd kept her mouth shut about Dodee.

8

Rusty listened to the blood-pressure monitor begin its urgent beeping and knew they were losing the boy. Actually they'd been losing him ever since the ambulance—hell, from the moment the ricochet struck him—but the sound of the monitor turned the truth into a headline. Rory should have been Life-Flighted to CMG immediately, right from where he'd been so grievously wounded. Instead he was in an underequipped operating room that was too warm (the air-conditioning had been turned off to conserve the generator), being operated on by a doctor who should have retired years ago, a physician's assistant who had never assisted in a neurosurgery case, and a single exhausted nurse who spoke up now.

"V-fib, Dr. Haskell."

The heart monitor had joined in. Now it was a chorus.

"I know, Ginny. I'm not death." He paused. "*Deaf,* I mean. Christ."

For a moment he and Rusty looked at each other over the boy's sheet-swaddled form. Haskell's eyes were clear and with-it—this was not the same stethoscope-equipped time-server who had been plodding through the rooms and corridors of Cathy Russell for the last couple of years like a dull ghost—but he looked terribly old and frail.

"We tried," Rusty said.

In truth, Haskell had done more than try; he'd reminded Rusty of one of those sports novels he'd loved as a kid, where the aging pitcher comes out of the bullpen for one more shot at glory in the seventh game of the World Series. But only Rusty and Ginny Tomlinson had been in the stands for this performance, and this time there would be no happy ending for the old warhorse.

Rusty had started the saline drip, adding mannitol to reduce brain swelling. Haskell had left the OR at an actual run to do the bloodwork in the lab down the hall, a complete CBC. It had to be Haskell; Rusty was unqualified and there were no lab techs. Catherine Russell was now hideously understaffed. Rusty thought the Dinsmore boy might be only a down payment on the price the town would eventually have to pay for that lack of personnel.

It got worse. The boy was A-negative, and they had none in their small blood supply. They did, however, have O-negative—the universal donor—and had given Rory four units, which left exactly nine more in supply. Giving it to the boy had probably been tantamount to pouring it down the scrub-room drain, but none of them had said so. While the blood ran into him, Haskell sent Ginny down to the closet-sized cubicle that served as the hospital's library. She came back with a tattered copy of *On Neurosurgery: A Brief Overview.* Haskell operated with the book beside him, an otiscope laid across the pages to hold them down. Rusty thought he would never forget the whine of the saw, the smell of the bone dust in the unnaturally warm air, or the clot of jellied blood that oozed out after Haskell removed the bone plug.

For a few minutes, Rusty had actually allowed himself to hope. With the pressure of the hematoma relieved by the burr-hole, Rory's vital signs had stabilized—or tried to. Then, while Haskell was attempting to determine if the bullet fragment was within his reach, everything had started going downhill again, and fast.

Rusty thought of the parents, waiting and hoping against hope. Now, instead of wheeling Rory to the left outside the OR—toward Cathy Russell's ICU, where his folks might be allowed to creep in and see him—it looked like Rory would be taking a right, toward the morgue.

"If this were an ordinary situation, I'd maintain life support and ask the parents about organ donation," Haskell said. "But of course, if this were an ordinary situation, he wouldn't be here. And even if he was, I wouldn't be trying to operate on him using a . . . a goddam *Toyota* manual." He picked up the otiscope and threw it across the OR. It struck the green tiles, chipped one, and fell to the floor.

"Do you want to administer epi, Doctor?" Ginny asked. Calm, cool, and collected . . . but she looked tired enough to drop in her tracks.

"Was I not clear? I won't prolong this boy's agony." Haskell reached toward the red switch on the back of the respirator. Some wit—Twitch, perhaps—had put a small sticker there that read BOOYA! "Do you want to express a contrary opinion, Rusty?"

Rusty considered the question, then slowly shook his head. The Babinski test had been positive, indicating major brain damage, but the main thing was that there was just no chance. Never had been, really.

Haskell flipped the switch. Rory Dinsmore took one labored breath on his own, appeared to try for a second one, and then gave up.

"I make it . . ." Haskell looked at the big clock on the wall. "Five fifteen PM. Will you note that as the TOD, Ginny?"

"Yes, Doctor."

Haskell pulled down his mask, and Rusty noted with concern that the old man's lips were blue. "Let's get out of here," he said. "The heat is killing me."

But it wasn't the heat; his heart was doing that. He collapsed halfway down the corridor, on his way to give Alden and Shelley Dinsmore the bad news. Rusty got to administer epi after all, but it did no good. Neither did closed-chest massage. Or the paddles.

Time of death, five forty-nine PM. Ron Haskell outlived his last patient by exactly thirty-four minutes. Rusty sat down on the floor, his back against the wall. Ginny had given Rory's parents the news; from where he sat with his face in his hands, Rusty could hear the mother's shrieks of grief and sorrow. They carried well in the nearly empty hospital. She sounded as if she would never stop.

9

Barbie thought that the Chief's widow must once have been an extremely beautiful woman. Even now, with dark circles under her eyes and an indifferent choice of clothes (faded jeans and what he was pretty sure was a pajama top), Brenda Perkins was striking. He thought maybe smart people rarely lost their good looks—if they had good ones to begin with, that was—and he saw the clear light of intelligence in her eyes. Something else, too. She might be in mourning, but it hadn't killed her curiosity. And right now, the object of her curiosity was him.

She looked over his shoulder at Julia's car, backing

down the driveway, and raised her hands to it: *Where you going?*

Julia leaned out the window and called, "I have to make sure the paper gets out! I also have to go by Sweetbriar Rose and give Anson Wheeler the bad news—he's on sandwich detail tonight! Don't worry, Bren, Barbie's safe!" And before Brenda could reply or remonstrate, Julia was off down Morin Street, a woman on a mission. Barbie wished he were with her, his only objective the creation of forty ham-and-cheese and forty tuna sandwiches.

With Julia gone, Brenda resumed her inspection. They were on opposite sides of the screen door. Barbie felt like a job applicant facing a tough interview.

"Are you?" Brenda asked.

"Beg your pardon, ma'am?"

"Are you safe?"

Barbie considered it. Two days ago he would have said yes, of course he was, but on this afternoon he felt more like the soldier of Fallujah than the cook of Chester's Mill. He settled for saying he was housebroken, which made her smile.

"Well, I'll have to make my own judgment on that," she said. "Even though right now my judgment isn't the best. I've suffered a loss."

"I know, ma'am. I'm very sorry."

"Thank you. He's being buried tomorrow. Out of that cheesy little Bowie Funeral Home that continues to stagger along somehow, even though almost everyone in town uses Crosman's in Castle Rock. Folks call Stewart Bowie's establishment Bowie's Buryin Barn. Stewart's an idiot and his brother Fernald's worse, but now they're all we have. All *I* have." She sighed like a woman confronting some vast chore. *And why not?* Barbie thought. *The death of a loved one may be many things, but work is certainly one of them.*

She surprised him by stepping out onto the stoop with him. "Walk around back with me, Mr. Barbara. I may invite you in later on, but not until I'm sure of you. Ordinarily I'd take a character reference from Julia like a shot, but these are not ordinary times." She was leading him along the side of the house, over nicely clipped grass raked clear of autumn leaves. On the right was a board fence separating the Perkins home from its next-door neighbor; on the left were nicely kept flowerbeds.

"The flowers were my husband's bailiwick. I suppose you think that's a strange hobby for a law enforcement officer."

"Actually, I don't."

"I never did, either. Which makes us in the minority. Small towns harbor small imaginations. Grace Metalious and Sherwood Anderson were right about that.

"Also," she said as they rounded the rear corner of the house and entered a commodious backyard, "it will stay light out here longer. I have a generator, but it died this morning. Out of fuel, I believe. There's a spare tank, but I don't know how to change it. I used to nag Howie about the generator. He wanted to teach me how to maintain it. I refused to learn. Mostly out of spite." A tear overspilled one eye and trickled down her cheek. She wiped it away absently. "I'd apologize to him now if I could. Admit he was right. But I can't do that, can I?"

Barbie knew a rhetorical question when he heard one. "If it's just the canister," he said, "I can change it out."

"Thank you," she said, leading him to a patio table with an Igloo cooler sitting beside it. "I was going to ask Henry Morrison to do it, and I was going to get more canisters at Burpee's, too, but by the time I got down to the high street this afternoon, Burpee's was closed and Henry was out at Dinsmore's field, along with everyone else. Do you think I'll be able to get extra canisters tomorrow?"

"Maybe," Barbie said. In truth, he doubted it.

"I heard about the little boy," she said. "Gina Buffalino from next door came over and told me. I'm terribly sorry. Will he live?"

"I don't know." And, because intuition told him honesty would be the most direct route to this woman's trust (provisional though that might be), he added, "I don't think so."

"No." She sighed and wiped at her eyes again. "No, it sounded very bad." She opened the Igloo. "I have water and Diet Coke. That was the only soft drink I allowed Howie to have. Which do you prefer?"

"Water, ma'am."

She opened two bottles of Poland Spring and they drank. She looked at him with her sadly curious eyes. "Julia told me you want a key to the Town Hall. I understand why you want it. I also understand why you don't want Jim Rennie to know—"

"He may have to. The situation's changed. You see—"

She held up her hand and shook her head. Barbie ceased.

"Before you tell me that, I want you to tell me about the trouble you had with Junior and his friends."

"Ma'am, didn't your husband—?"

"Howie rarely talked about his cases, but this one he *did* talk about. It troubled him, I think. I want to see if your story matches his. If it does, we can talk about other matters. If it doesn't, I'll invite you to leave, although you may take your bottle of water with you."

Barbie pointed to the little red shed by the left corner of the house. "That your gennie?"

"Yes."

"If I change out the canister while we talk, will you be able to hear me?"

"Yes."

"And you want the whole deal, right?"

"Yes indeed. And if you call me ma'am again, I may have to brain you."

The door of the little generator shed was held shut with a hook-and-eye of shiny brass. The man who had lived here until yesterday had taken care of his things . . . although it was a shame about that lone canister. Barbie decided that, no matter how this conversation went, he would take it upon himself to try and get her a few more tomorrow.

In the meantime, he told himself, *tell her everything she wants to know about that night.* But it would be easier to tell with his back turned; he didn't like saying the trouble had happened because Angie McCain had seen him as a slightly overage boy-toy.

Sunshine Rule, he reminded himself, and told his tale.

10

What he remembered most clearly about last summer was the James McMurtry song that seemed to be playing everywhere—"Talkin' at the Texaco," it was called. And the line he remembered most clearly was the one about how in a small town "we all must know our place." When Angie started standing too close to him while he was cooking, or pressing a breast against his arm while she reached for something he could have gotten for her, the line recurred. He knew who her boyfriend was, and he knew that Frankie DeLesseps was part of the town's power structure, if only by virtue of his friendship with

Big Jim Rennie's son. Dale Barbara, on the other hand, was little more than a drifter. In the Chester's Mill scheme of things, he *had* no place.

One evening she had reached around his hip and given his crotch a light squeeze. He reacted, and he saw by her mischievous grin that she'd felt him react.

"You can have one back, if you want," she said. They'd been in the kitchen, and she'd twitched the hem of her skirt, a short one, up a little, giving him a quick glimpse of frilly pink underwear. "Fair's fair."

"I'll pass," he said, and she stuck her tongue out at him.

He'd seen similar hijinks in half a dozen restaurant kitchens, had even played along from time to time. It might have amounted to no more than a young girl's passing letch for an older and moderately good-looking co-worker. But then Angie and Frankie broke up, and one night when Barbie was dumping the swill in the Dumpster out back after closing, she'd put a serious move on him.

He turned around and she was there, slipping her arms around his shoulders and kissing him. At first he kissed her back. Angie unlocked one arm long enough to take his hand and put it on her left breast. That woke his brain up. It was good breast, young and firm. It was also trouble. *She* was trouble. He tried to pull back, and when she hung on one-handed (her nails now biting into the nape of his neck) and tried to thrust her hips against him, he pushed her away with a little more force than he had intended. She stumbled against the Dumpster, glared at him, touched the seat of her jeans, and glared harder.

"Thanks! Now I've got crap all over my pants!"

"You should know when to let go," he said mildly.

"You liked it!"

"Maybe," he said, "but I don't like you." And when

he saw the hurt and anger deepen on her face, he added: "I mean I do, just not that way." But of course people have a way of saying what they really mean when they're shaken up.

Four nights later, in Dipper's, someone poured a glass of beer down the back of his shirt. He turned and saw Frankie DeLesseps.

"Did you like that, *Baaarbie*? If you did, I can do it again—it's two-buck pitcher night. Of course, if you didn't, we can take it outside."

"I don't know what she told you, but it's wrong," Barbie said. The jukebox had been playing—not the McMurtry song, but that was what he heard in his head: *We all must know our place.*

"What she *told* me is she said no and you went ahead and fucked her anyway. What do you outweigh her by? Hunnert pounds? That sounds like rape to me."

"I didn't." Knowing it was probably hopeless.

"You want to go outside, motherfuck, or are you too chicken?"

"Too chicken," Barbie said, and to his surprise, Frankie went away. Barbie decided he'd had enough beer and music for one night and was getting up to go when Frankie returned, this time not with a glass but a pitcher.

"Don't do that," Barbie said, but of course Frankie paid no attention. Splash, in the face. A Bud Light shower. Several people laughed and applauded drunkenly.

"You can come out now and settle this," Frankie said, "or I can wait. Last call's comin, *Baaarbie*."

Barbie went, realizing it was then or later, and believing that if he decked Frankie fast, before a lot of people could see, that would end it. He could even apologize and repeat that he'd never been with Angie. He wouldn't add that Angie had been coming on to him, although he supposed a lot of people knew it (certainly Rose and Anson did). Maybe, with a bloody nose to wake him up, Frankie would see what seemed so obvious to Barbie: this was the little twit's idea of payback.

At first it seemed that it might work out that way. Frankie stood flat-footed on the gravel, his shadow cast two different ways by the glare of the sodium lights at either end of the parking lot, his fists held up like John L. Sullivan. Mean, strong, and stupid: just one more small-town brawler. Used to putting his opponents down with one big blow, then picking them up and hitting them a bunch of little ones until they cried uncle.

He shuffled forward and uncorked his not-so-secret weapon: an uppercut Barbie avoided by the simple expedient of cocking his head slightly to one side. Barbie countered with a straight jab to the solar plexus. Frankie went down with a stunned expression on his face.

"We don't have to—" Barbie began, and that was when Junior Rennie hit him from behind, in the kidneys, probably with his hands laced together to make one big fist. Barbie stumbled forward. Carter Thibodeau was there to meet him, stepping from between two parked cars and throwing a roundhouse. It might have broken Barbie's jaw if it had connected, but Barbie got his arm up in time. That accounted for the worst of his bruises, still an unlovely yellow when he tried to leave town on Dome Day.

He twisted to one side, understanding this had been a planned ambush, knowing he had to get out before someone was really hurt. Not necessarily him. He was willing to run; he wasn't proud. He got three steps before Melvin Searles tripped him up. Barbie sprawled in the gravel on his belly and the kicking started. He covered his head, but a squall of bootleather pounded his legs, ass, and arms. One caught him high in the rib cage just before he managed to knee-scramble behind Stubby Norman's used-furniture panel truck.

His good sense left him then, and he stopped thinking about running away. He got up, faced them, then held out his hands to them, palms up and fingers wiggling. Beckoning. The slot he was standing in was narrow. They'd have to come one by one.

Junior tried first; his enthusiasm was rewarded with a kick in the belly. Barbie was wearing Nikes rather than boots, but it was a hard kick and Junior folded up beside the panel truck, woofing for breath. Frankie scrambled over him and Barbie popped him twice in the face—stinging shots, but not quite hard enough to break anything. Good sense had begun to reassert itself.

Gravel crunched. He turned in time to catch incoming from Thibodeau, who had cut behind him. The blow connected with his temple. Barbie saw stars. ("Or maybe one was a comet," he told Brenda, opening the valve on the new gas canister.) Thibodeau moved in. Barbie pistoned a hard kick to his ankle, and Thibodeau's grin turned to a grimace. He dropped to one knee, looking like a football player holding the ball for a field goal attempt. Except ball-holders usually don't clutch their ankles.

Absurdly, Carter Thibodeau cried: "Fuckin dirty-fighter!"

"Look who's ta—" Barbie got that far before Melvin Searles locked an elbow around his throat. Barbie drove his own elbow back into Searles's midsection and heard the grunt of escaping air. Smelled it, too: beer, cigarettes, Slim Jims. He was turning, knowing that Thibodeau would probably be on him again before he could fight his way entirely clear of the aisle between vehicles into which he had retreated, no longer caring. His face was throbbing, his ribs were throbbing, and he suddenly decided—it seemed quite reasonable—that he was going to put all four of them in the hospital. They could discuss what constituted dirty fighting and what did not as they signed each other's casts.

That was when Chief Perkins—called by either Tommy or Willow Anderson, the roadhouse proprietors—drove into the parking lot with his jackpots lit and his headlights winking back and forth. The combatants were illuminated like actors on a stage.

Perkins hit the siren once; it blipped half a whoop and died. Then he got out, hitching his belt up over his considerable girth.

"Little early in the week for this, isn't it, fellas?"

To which Junior Rennie replied

11

Brenda didn't need Barbie to tell her that; she'd heard it from Howie, and hadn't been surprised. Even as a child, Big Jim's boy had been a fluent confabulator, especially when his self-interest was at stake.

"To which he replied, 'The cook started it.' Am I right?"

"Yep." Barbie pushed the gennie's start button and it roared into life. He smiled at her, although he could feel a flush warming his cheeks. What he'd just told was not his favorite story. Although he supposed he'd pick it over the one of the gym in Fallujah any day. "There you go—lights, camera, action."

"Thank you. How long will it last?"

"Only a couple of days, but this may be over by then."

"Or not. I suppose you know what saved you from a trip to the county lockup that night?"

"Sure," Barbie said. "Your husband saw it happening. Four-on-one. It was kind of hard to miss."

"Any other cop might *not* have seen it, even if it was right in front of his eyes. And it was just luck Howie was on that night; George Frederick was supposed to have the duty, but he called in with stomach flu." She paused. "You might call it providence instead of luck."

"So I might," Barbie agreed.

"Would you like to come inside, Mr. Barbara?"

"Why don't we sit out here? If you don't mind. It's pleasant."

"Fine by me. The weather will turn cold soon enough. Or will it?"

Barbie said he didn't know.

"When Howie got you all to the station, DeLesseps told Howie that you raped Angie McCain. Isn't that how it went?"

"That was his first story. Then he said maybe it wasn't quite rape, but when she got scared and told me to stop, I wouldn't. That would make it rape in the second degree, I guess."

She smiled briefly. "Don't let any feminists hear you say there are degrees of rape."

"I guess I better not. Anyway, your husband put me in the interrogation room—which seems to be a broom closet when it's doing its day job—"

Brenda actually laughed.

"—then hauled Angie in. Sat her where she had to look me in the eye. Hell, we were almost rubbing elbows. It takes mental preparation to lie about something big, especially for a young person. I found that out in the Army. Your husband knew it, too. Told her it would go to court. Explained the penalties for perjury. Long story short, she recanted. Said there'd been no intercourse, let alone rape."

"Howie had a motto: 'Reason before law.' It was the basis for the way he handled things. It will *not* be the way Peter Randolph handles things, partially because he's a foggy thinker but mostly because he won't be able to handle Rennie. My husband could. Howie said that when news of your . . . altercation . . . got back to Mr. Rennie, he insisted that you be tried for *something*. He was furious. Did you know that?"

"No." But he wasn't surprised.

"Howie told Mr. Rennie that if any of it made it into court, he'd see that *all* of it made it into court, including the four-on-one in the parking lot. He added that a good defense attorney might even be able to get some of Frankie and Junior's high school escapades into the record. There were several, although nothing quite like what happened to you."

She shook her head.

"Junior Rennie was never a *great* kid, but he used to be relatively harmless. Over the last year or so, he's changed. Howie saw it, and was troubled by it. I've discovered that Howie knew things about both the son *and* the father . . ." She trailed off. Barbie could see her debating whether or not to go on and deciding not to. She had learned discretion as the wife of a small-town police official, and it was a hard habit to unlearn.

"Howie advised you to leave town before Rennie found some other way to make trouble for you, didn't he? I imagine you got caught by this Dome thing before you could do it."

"Yes to both. Can I have that Diet Coke now, Mrs. Perkins?"

"Call me Brenda. And I'll call you Barbie, if that's what you go by. Please help yourself to a soft drink."

Barbie did.

"You want a key to the fallout shelter so you can get the Geiger counter. I can and will help you there. But it sounded like you were saying Jim Rennie has to know, and with that idea I have trouble. Maybe it's grief clouding my mind, but I don't understand why you'd want to get into any kind of head-butting contest with him. Big Jim freaks out when *anybody* challenges his authority, and you he doesn't like to begin with. Nor does he owe you any favors. If my husband were still Chief, maybe the two of you could go see Rennie together. I would rather have enjoyed that, I think." She leaned forward, looking at him earnestly from her dark-circled eyes. "But Howie's gone and you're apt to wind up in a cell instead of looking around for some mystery generator."

"I know all that, but something new has been added. The Air Force is going to shoot a Cruise missile at the Dome tomorrow at thirteen hundred hours."

"Oh-my-Jesus."

"They've shot other missiles at it, but only to determine how high the barrier goes. Radar doesn't work. Those had dummy warheads. This one will have a very live one. A bunker-buster."

She paled visibly.

"What part of our town are they going to shoot it at?"

"Point of impact will be where the Dome cuts Little Bitch Road. Julia and I were out there just last night. It'll explode about five feet off the ground."

Her mouth dropped open in an unladylike gape. "Not possible!"

"I'm afraid it is. They'll release it from a B-52, and it'll fly a preprogrammed course. I mean *really* programmed. Down to every ridge and dip, once it descends to target height. Those things are *eerie*. If it explodes and doesn't break through, it means everyone in town just gets a bad scare—it's going to sound like Armageddon. If it *does* break through, though—"

Her hand had gone to her throat. "How much damage? Barbie, we have no firetrucks!"

"I'm sure they'll have fire equipment standing by. As to how much damage?" He shrugged. "The whole area will have to be evacuated, that's for sure."

"Is it wise? Is what they're planning wise?"

"It's a moot question, Mrs.—Brenda. They've made their decision. But it gets worse, I'm afraid." And, seeing her expression: "For me, not the town. I've been promoted to Colonel. By Presidential order."

She rolled her eyes. "How nice for you."

"I'm supposed to declare martial law and basically take over Chester's Mill. Won't Jim Rennie enjoy hearing that?"

She surprised him by bursting into laughter. And Barbie surprised himself by joining her.

"You see my problem? The town doesn't have to know about me borrowing an old Geiger counter, but they *do* need to know about the bunker-buster coming their way. Julia Shumway will spread the news if I don't, but the town fathers ought to hear it from me. Because—"

"I know why." Thanks to the reddening sun, Brenda's face had lost its pallor. But she was rubbing her arms absently. "If you're to establish any authority here . . . which is what your superior wants you to do . . ."

"I guess Cox is more like my colleague now," Barbie said.

She sighed. "Andrea Grinnell. We'll take this to her. Then we'll talk to Rennie and Andy Sanders together. At least we'll outnumber them, three to two."

"Rose's sister? Why?"

"You don't know she's the town's Third Selectman?"

And when he shook his head: "Don't look so chagrined. Many don't, although she's held the job for several years. She's usually little more than a rubber-stamp for the two men—which means for Rennie, since Andy Sanders is a rubber-stamp himself—and she has . . . problems . . . but there's a core of toughness there. Or was."

"What problems?"

He thought she might keep that to herself too, but she didn't. "Drug dependency. Pain pills. I don't know how bad it is."

"And I suppose she gets her scrips filled at Sanders's pharmacy."

"Yes. I know it's not a perfect solution, and you'll have to be very careful, but . . . Jim Rennie may be forced by simple expediency to accept your input for a while. Your actual leadership?" She shook her head. "He'll wipe his bottom with any declaration of martial law, whether it's signed by the President or not. I—"

She ceased. Her eyes were looking past him, and widening.

"Mrs. Perkins? Brenda? What is it?"

"Oh," she said. "Oh, my *God.*"

Barbie turned to look, and was stunned to silence himself. The sun was going down red as it often did after warm, fair days unsullied by late showers. But never in his life had he seen a sunset like this one. He had an idea the only people who ever had were those in the vicinity of violent volcanic eruptions.

No, he thought. *Not even them. This is brand new.*

The declining sun wasn't a ball. It was a huge red bowtie shape with a burning circular center. The western sky was smeared as if with a thin film of blood that shaded to orange as it climbed. The horizon was almost invisible through that blurry glare.

"Good Christ, it's like trying to look through a dirty windshield when you're driving into the sun," she said.

And of course that was it, only the Dome was the windshield. It had begun to collect dust and pollen. Pollutants as well. And it would get worse.

We'll have to wash it, he thought, and visualized lines of volunteers with buckets and rags. Absurd. How were they going to wash it forty feet up? Or a hundred and forty? Or a thousand?

"This has to end," she whispered. "Call them and tell them to shoot the biggest missile they can, and damn the consequences. Because this has to end."

Barbie said nothing. Wasn't sure he could have spoken even if he had something to say. That vast, dusty glare had stolen his words. It was like looking through a porthole into hell.

NYUCK-NYUCK-NYUCK

1

Jim Rennie and Andy Sanders watched the weird sunset from the steps of the Bowie Funeral Home. They were due at the Town Hall for another "Emergency Assessment Meeting" at seven o'clock, and Big Jim wanted to be there early to prepare, but for now they stood where they were, watching the day die its strange, smeary death.

"It's like the end of the world." Andy spoke in a low, awestruck voice.

"Bull-pucky!" Big Jim said, and if his voice was harsh— even for him—it was because a similar thought had been going through his own mind. For the first time since the Dome had come down, it had occurred to him that the situation might be beyond their ability to manage—*his* ability to manage—and he rejected the idea furiously. "Do you see Christ the Lord coming down from the sky?"

"No," Andy admitted. What he saw were townspeople he'd known all his life standing in clumps along Main Street, not talking, only watching that strange sunset with their hands shading their eyes.

"Do you see *me*?" Big Jim persisted.

Andy turned to him. "Sure I do," he said. Sounding perplexed. "Sure I do, Big Jim."

"Which means I haven't been Raptured," Big Jim said.

"I gave my heart to Jesus years ago, and if it was End Times, I wouldn't be here. Neither would you, right?"

"Guess not," Andy said, but he felt doubtful. If they were Saved—washed in the Blood of the Lamb—why had they just been talking to Stewart Bowie about shutting down what Big Jim called "our little business"? And how had they gotten into such a business to start with? What did running a meth factory have to do with being Saved?

If he asked Big Jim, Andy knew what the answer would be: the ends sometimes justify the means. The ends in this case had seemed admirable, once upon a time: the new Holy Redeemer Church (the old one had been little more than a clapboard shack with a wooden cross on top); the radio station that had saved only God knew how many souls; the ten percent they tithed—prudently, the contribution checks issued from a bank in the Cayman Islands—to the Lord Jesus Missionary Society, to help what Pastor Coggins liked to call "the little brown brothers."

But looking at that huge blurry sunset that seemed to suggest all human affairs were tiny and unimportant, Andy had to admit those things were no more than justifications. Without the cash income from the meth, his drugstore would have gone under six years ago. The same with the funeral home. The same—probably, although the man beside him would never admit it—with Jim Rennie's Used Cars.

"I know what you're thinking, pal," Big Jim said.

Andy looked up at him timidly. Big Jim was smiling . . . but not the fierce one. This one was gentle, understanding. Andy smiled back, or tried to. He owed Big Jim a lot. Only now things like the drugstore and Claudie's BMW seemed a lot less important. What good was a BMW, even one with self-parking and a voice-activated sound system, to a dead wife?

When this is over and Dodee comes back, I'll give the Beemer to her, Andy decided. *It's what Claudie would have wanted.*

Big Jim raised a blunt-fingered hand to the declining sun that seemed to be spreading across the western sky like a great poisoned egg. "You think all this is our fault, somehow. That God is punishing us for propping up the town when times were hard. That's just not true, pal. This isn't God's work. If you wanted to say getting beat in Vietnam was God's work—God's warning that America was losing her spiritual way—I'd have to agree with you. If you were to say that nine-eleven was the Supreme Being's response to our Supreme Court telling little children they could no longer start their day with a prayer to the God Who made them, I'd have to go along. But God punishing Chester's Mill because we didn't want to end up just another moribund wide spot in the road, like Jay or Millinocket?" He shook his head. "Nosir. No."

"We also put some pretty good change in our own pockets," Andy said timidly.

This was true. They had done more than prop up their own businesses and extend a helping hand to the little brown brothers; Andy had his own account in the Cayman Islands. And for every dollar Andy had—or the Bowies, for that matter—he was willing to bet that Big Jim had put away three. Maybe even four.

" 'The workman is worthy of his hire,' " Big Jim said in a pedantic but kindly tone. "Matthew ten-ten." He neglected to cite the previous verse: *Provide neither gold, nor silver, nor brass in your purses.*

He looked at his watch. "Speaking of work, pal, we better get moving. Got a lot to decide." He started walking. Andy followed, not taking his eyes off the sunset, which was still bright enough to make him think of infected flesh. Then Big Jim stopped again.

"Anyway, you heard Stewart—we're shut down out there. 'All done and buttoned up,' as the little boy said after he made his first wee. He told the Chef himself."

"*That* guy," Andy said dourly.

Big Jim chuckled. "Don't you worry about Phil. We're shut down and we're going to *stay* shut down until the crisis is over. In fact, this might be a sign that we're supposed to close up shop forever. A sign from the Almighty."

"That would be good," Andy said. But he had a depressing insight: if the Dome disappeared, Big Jim would change his mind, and when he did, Andy would go along. Stewart Bowie and his brother Fernald would, too. Eagerly. Partly because the money was so unbelievable—not to mention tax-free—and partly because they were in too deep. He remembered something some long-ago movie star had said: "By the time I discovered I didn't like acting, I was too rich to quit."

"Don't worry so much," Big Jim said. "We'll start moving the propane back into town in a couple of weeks, whether this Dome situation resolves itself or not. We'll use the town sand-trucks. You can drive a standard shift, can't you?"

"Yes," Andy said glumly.

"And"—Big Jim brightened as an idea struck him—"we can use Stewie's hearse! Then we can move some of the canisters even sooner!"

Andy said nothing. He hated the idea that they had appropriated (that was Big Jim's word for it) so much propane from various town sources, but it had seemed the safest way. They were manufacturing on a large scale, and that meant a lot of cooking and a lot of venting the bad gasses. Big Jim had pointed out that buying propane in large amounts could raise questions. Just as buying large amounts of the various over-the-counter drugs that went into the crap might be noticed and cause trouble.

Owning a drugstore had helped with that, although the size of his orders for stuff like Robitussin and Sudafed had made Andy horribly nervous. He'd thought *that* would be their downfall, if their downfall came. He had never considered the huge cache of propane tanks behind the WCIK studio building until now.

"By the way, we'll have plenty of electricity in the Town Hall tonight." Big Jim spoke with the air of one springing a pleasant surprise. "I had Randolph send my boy and his friend Frankie over to the hospital to grab one of their tanks for our gennie."

Andy looked alarmed. "But we already took—"

"I know," Rennie said soothingly. "I know we did. Don't you worry about Cathy Russell, they've got enough for the time being."

"You could have gotten one from the radio station . . . there's so much out there . . ."

"This was closer," Big Jim said. "And safer. Pete Randolph's our guy, but that doesn't mean I want him to know about our little business. Now or ever."

This made Andy even more certain that Big Jim didn't really want to give up the factory.

"Jim, if we start sneaking LP back into town, where will we say it was? Are we going to tell folks the Gas Fairy took it, then changed his mind and gave it back?"

Rennie frowned. "Do you think this is funny, pal?"

"No! I think it's *scary!*"

"I've got a plan. We'll announce a town fuel supply depot, and ration propane from it as needed. Heating oil too, if we can figure out how to use it with the power out. I hate the idea of rationing—it's un-American to the core—but this is like the story of the grasshopper and the ant, you know. There are cotton-pickers in town who'd use up everything in a month, then yell at *us* to take care of em at the first sign of a cold snap!"

"You don't really think this will go on for a *month,* do you?"

"Of course not, but you know what the oldtimers say: hope for the best, prepare for the worst."

Andy thought of pointing out that they'd already used a fair amount of the town's supplies to make crystal meth, but he knew what Big Jim would say: *How could we possibly have known?*

They couldn't have, of course. Who in their right mind would ever have expected this sudden contraction of all resources? You planned for *more than enough.* It was the American way. *Not nearly enough* was an insult to the mind and the spirit.

Andy said, "You're not the only one who won't like the idea of rationing."

"That's why we have a police force. I know we all mourn Howie Perkins's passing, but he's with Jesus now and we've got Pete Randolph. Who's going to be better for the town in this situation. Because he *listens.*" He pointed a finger at Andy. "The people in a town like this—people everywhere, really—aren't much more than children when it comes to their own self-interest. How many times have I said that?"

"Lots," Andy said, and sighed.

"And what do you have to make children do?"

"Eat their vegetables if they want their dessert."

"Yes! And sometimes that means cracking the whip."

"That reminds me of something else," Andy said. "I was talking to Sammy Bushey out at Dinsmore's field— one of Dodee's friends? She said some of the cops were pretty rough out there. *Darn* rough. We might want to talk to Chief Randolph about that."

Jim frowned at him. "What did you expect, pal? Kid gloves? There was darn near a riot out there. We almost had a cotton-picking *riot* right here in Chester's *Mill*!"

"I know, you're right, it's just that—"

"I know the Bushey girl. Knew her whole family. Drug users, car thieves, scofflaws, loan-dodgers and tax-dodgers. What we used to call poor white trash, before it became politically incorrect. Those are the people we have to watch out for right now. *The very people.* They're the ones who'll tear this town apart, given half a chance. Is that what you want?"

"No, course not—"

But Big Jim was in full flight. "Every town has its ants—which is good—and its grasshoppers, which aren't so good but we can live with them because we understand them and can make them do what's in their own best interests, even if we have to squeeze em a little. But every town also has its locusts, just like in the Bible, and that's what people like the Busheys are. On them we've got to bring the hammer down. You might not like it and I might not like it, but personal freedom's going to have to take a hike until this is over. And we'll sacrifice, too. Aren't we going to shut down our little business?"

Andy didn't want to point out that they really had no choice, since they had no way of shipping the stuff out of town anyway, but settled for a simple yes. He didn't want to discuss things any further, and he dreaded the upcoming meeting, which might drag on until midnight. All he wanted was to go home to his empty house and have a stiff drink and then lie down and think about Claudie and cry himself to sleep.

"What matters right now, pal, is keeping things on an

even keel. That means law and order and oversight. *Our* oversight, because we're not grasshoppers. We're ants. *Soldier* ants."

Big Jim considered. When he spoke again, his tone was all business. "I'm rethinking our decision to let Food City continue on a business-as-usual basis. I'm not saying we're going to shut it down—at least not yet—but we'll have to watch it pretty closely over the next couple of days. Like a cotton-picking *hawk*. Same with the Gas and Grocery. And it might not be a bad idea if we were to appropriate some of the more perishable food for our own personal—"

He stopped, squinting at the Town Hall steps. He didn't believe what he saw and raised a hand to block the sunset. It was still there: Brenda Perkins and that gosh-darned troublemaker Dale Barbara. Not side by side, either. Sitting between them, and talking animatedly to Chief Perkins's widow, was Andrea Grinnell, the Third Selectman. They appeared to be passing sheets of paper from hand to hand.

Big Jim did not like this.

At all.

2

He started forward, meaning to put a stop to the conversation no matter the subject. Before he could get half a dozen steps, a kid ran up to him. It was one of the Killian boys. There were about a dozen Killians living on a ramshackle chicken farm out by the Tarker's Mills town line. None of the kids was very bright—which they came by honestly, considering the parents from whose shabby loins they had sprung—but all were members in good standing at Holy Redeemer; all Saved, in other words. This one was

Ronnie . . . at least Rennie thought so, but it was hard to be sure. They all had the same bullet heads, bulging brows, and beaky noses.

The boy was wearing a tattered WCIK tee-shirt and carrying a note. "Hey, Mr. Rennie!" he said. "Gorry, I been lookin all over town for you!"

"I'm afraid I don't have time to talk right now, Ronnie," Big Jim said. He was still looking at the trio sitting on the Town Hall steps. The Three Gosh-Darn Stooges. "Maybe tomor—"

"It's Richie, Mr. Rennie. Ronnie's my brother."

"Richie. Of course. Now if you'll excuse me." Big Jim strode on.

Andy took the note from the boy and caught up to Rennie before he could get to the trio sitting on the steps. "You better look at this."

What Big Jim looked at first was Andy's face, more pinched and worried than ever. Then he took the note.

James—

 I must see you <u>tonight</u>. God has spoken to me. Now I must speak to <u>you</u> before I speak to the town. Please reply. Richie Killian will carry your message to me.
                                        Reverend Lester Coggins

Not Les; not even Lester. No. *Reverend Lester Coggins.* This was not good. Why oh why did everything have to happen at the same time?

The boy was standing in front of the bookstore, looking in his faded shirt and baggy, slipping-down jeans like a gosh-darn orphan. Big Jim beckoned to him. The kid raced forward eagerly. Big Jim took his pen from his pocket (written in gold down the barrel: YOU'LL LUV THE FEELIN' WHEN BIG JIM'S DEALIN') and scribbled a three-word reply: *Midnight. My house.* He folded it over and handed it to the boy.

"Take that back to him. And *don't* read it."

"I won't! No way! God bless you, Mr. Rennie."

"You too, son." He watched the boy speed off.

"What's *that* about?" Andy asked. And before Big Jim could answer: "The factory? Is it the meth—"

"Shut up."

Andy fell back a step, shocked. Big Jim had never told him to shut up before. This could be bad.

"One thing at a time," Big Jim said, and marched forward toward the next problem.

3

Watching Rennie come, Barbie's first thought was *He walks like a man who's sick and doesn't know it.* He also walked like a man who has spent his life kicking ass. He was wearing his most carnivorously sociable smile as he took Brenda's hands and gave them a squeeze. She allowed this with calm good grace.

"Brenda," he said. "My deepest condolences. I would have been over to see you before now . . . and of course I'll be at the funeral . . . but I've been a little busy. We all have."

"I understand," she said.

"We miss Duke so much," Big Jim said.

"That's right," Andy put in, pulling up behind Big Jim: a tugboat in the wake of an ocean liner. "We sure do."

"Thank you both so much."

"And while I'd love to discuss your concerns . . . I can see that you have them. . . ." Big Jim's smile widened, although it did not come within hailing distance of his eyes. "We have a very important meeting. Andrea, I wonder if you'd like to run on ahead and set out those files."

Although pushing fifty, Andrea at that moment looked like a child who has been caught sneaking hot tarts off a windowsill. She started to get up (wincing at the pain in her back as she did so), but Brenda took her arm, and firmly. Andrea sat back down.

Barbie realized that both Grinnell and Sanders looked frightened to death. It wasn't the Dome, at least not at this moment; it was Rennie. Again he thought: *This is not as bad as it gets.*

"I think you'd better make time for us, James," Brenda said pleasantly. "Surely you understand that if this wasn't important—*very*—I'd be at home, mourning my husband."

Big Jim was at a rare loss for words. The people on the street who'd been watching the sunset were now watching this impromptu meeting instead. Perhaps elevating Barbara to an importance he did not deserve simply because he was sitting in close proximity to the town's Third Selectman and the late Police Chief's widow. Passing some piece of paper among themselves as if it were a letter from the Grand High Pope of Rome. Whose idea had this public display been? The Perkins woman's, of course. Andrea wasn't smart enough. Nor brave enough to cross him in such a public way.

"Well, maybe we can spare you a few minutes. Eh, Andy?"

"Sure," Andy said. "Always a few minutes for you, Mrs. Perkins. I'm really sorry about Duke."

"And I'm sorry about your wife," she said gravely.

Their eyes met. It was a genuine Tender Moment, and it made Big Jim feel like tearing his hair out. He knew he wasn't supposed to let such feelings grip him—it was bad for his blood pressure, and what was bad for his blood pressure was bad for his heart—but it was hard, sometimes. Especially when you'd just been handed a note from a fellow who knew far too much and now believed God wanted him to speak to the town. If Big Jim was right about what had gotten into Coggins's head, this current business was piddling by comparison.

Only it might *not* be piddling. Because Brenda Perkins had never liked him, and Brenda Perkins was the widow of a man who was now perceived in town—for absolutely no good reason—as a hero. The first thing he had to do—

"Come on inside," he said. "We'll talk in the conference room." His eyes flicked to Barbie. "Are you a part of this, Mr. Barbara? Because I can't for the life of me understand why."

"This may help," Barbie said, holding out the sheets of paper they'd been passing around. "I used to be in the Army. I was a lieutenant. It seems that I've had my term of service extended. I've also been given a promotion."

Rennie took the sheets, holding them by the corner as if they might be hot. The letter was considerably more elegant than the grubby note Richie Killian had handed him, and from a rather more well-known correspondent. The heading read simply: **FROM THE WHITE HOUSE.** It bore today's date.

Rennie felt the paper. A deep vertical crease had formed between his bushy eyebrows. "This isn't White House stationery."

Of course it is, you silly man, Barbie was tempted to say. *It was delivered an hour ago by a member of the FedEx Elf Squad. Crazy little fucker just teleported through the Dome, no problem.*

"No, it's not." Barbie tried to keep his voice pleasant.

"It came by way of the Internet, as a PDF file. Ms. Shumway downloaded it and printed it out."

Julia Shumway. Another troublemaker.

"Read it, James," Brenda said quietly. "It's important."

Big Jim read it.

4

Benny Drake, Norrie Calvert, and Scarecrow Joe McClatchey stood outside the offices of the Chester's Mill *Democrat*. Each had a flashlight. Benny and Joe held theirs in their hands; Norrie's was tucked into the wide front pocket of her hoodie. They were looking up the street at the Town Hall, where several people—including all three selectmen and the cook from Sweetbriar Rose—appeared to be having a conference.

"I wonder what that's about," Norrie said.

"Grownup shit," Benny said, with a supreme lack of interest, and knocked on the door of the newspaper office. When there was no response, Joe pushed past him and tried the knob. The door opened. He knew at once why Miz Shumway hadn't heard them; her copier was going full blast while she talked with the paper's sports reporter and the guy who had been taking pictures out at the field day.

She saw the kids and waved them in. Single sheets were shooting rapidly in the copier's tray. Pete Freeman and Tony Guay were taking turns pulling them out and stacking them up.

"There you are," Julia said. "I was afraid you kids weren't coming. We're almost ready. If the damn copier doesn't shit the bed, that is."

Joe, Benny, and Norrie received this enchanting bon mot with silent appreciation, each resolving to put it to use as soon as possible.

"Did you get permission from your folks?" Julia asked. "I don't want a bunch of angry parents on my neck."

"Yes, ma'am," Norrie said. "All of us did."

Freeman was tying up a bundle of sheets with twine. Doing a bad job of it, too, Norrie observed. She herself could tie five different knots. Also fishing flies. Her father had shown her. She in turn had shown him how to do nosies on her rail, and when he fell off the first time he'd laughed until tears rolled down his face. She thought she had the best dad in the universe.

"Want me to do that?" Norrie asked.

"If you can do a better job, sure." Pete stood aside.

She started forward, Joe and Benny crowding close behind her. Then she saw the big black headline on the one-sheet extra, and stopped. "Holy shit!"

As soon as the words were out she clapped her hands to her mouth, but Julia only nodded. "It's an authentic holy shit, all right. I hope you all brought bikes, and I hope they all have baskets. You can't haul these around town on skateboards."

"That's what you said, that's what we brought," Joe replied. "Mine doesn't have a basket, but it's got a carrier."

"And I'll tie his load on for him," Norrie said.

Pete Freeman, who was watching with admiration as the girl quickly tied up the bundles (with what looked like a sliding butterfly), said, "I bet you will. Those are good."

"Yeah, I rock," Norrie said matter-of-factly.

"Got flashlights?" Julia asked.

"Yes," they all said together.

"Good. The *Democrat* hasn't used newsboys in thirty years, and I don't want to celebrate the reintroduction of the practice with one of you getting hit on the corner of Main or Prestile."

"That would be a bummer, all right," Joe agreed.

"Every house and business on those two streets gets one, right? Plus Morin and St. Anne Avenue. After that, spread out. Do what you can, but when it gets to be nine o'clock, go on home. Drop any leftover papers on streetcorners. Put a rock on them to hold them down."

Benny looked at the headline again:

CHESTER'S MILL, ATTENTION!
EXPLOSIVES TO BE FIRED AT BARRIER!
CRUISE MISSILE DELIVERY SYSTEM
WESTERN BORDER EVACUATION RECOMMENDED

"I bet this won't work," Joe said darkly, examining the map, obviously hand-drawn, at the bottom of the sheet. The border between Chester's Mill and Tarker's Mills had been highlighted in red. There was a black **X** where Little Bitch Road cut across the town line. The **X** had been labeled **Point of Impact.**

"Bite your tongue, kiddo," Tony Guay said.

5

FROM THE WHITE HOUSE

Greetings and salutations
to the CHESTER'S MILL BOARD OF SELECTMEN:
Andrew Sanders
James P. Rennie
Andrea Grinnell

Dear Sirs and Madam:

First and foremost, I send you greetings, and want to express our nation's deep concern and good wishes. I have designated tomorrow as a national Day of Prayer; across America, churches will be open as people of all faiths pray for you and for those working to understand and reverse what has happened at the borders of your town. Let me assure you that we will not rest until the people of Chester's Mill are freed and those responsible for your imprisonment are punished. That this situation will be resolved—and soon—is my promise to you and to the people of Chester's Mill. I speak with all the solemn weight of my office, as your Commander in Chief.

Second, this letter will introduce Colonel Dale Barbara, of the U.S. Army. Col. Barbara served in Iraq, where he was awarded the Bronze Star, a Merit Service Medal, and two Purple Hearts. He has been recalled to duty and promoted so that he may serve as your conduit to us, and ours to you. I know that, as loyal Americans, you will afford him every assistance. As you aid him, so will we aid you.

My original intent, in accordance with the advice given me by the Joint Chiefs and the Secretaries of Defense and Homeland Security, was to invoke martial law in Chester's Mill and appoint Col. Barbara as interim military governor. Col. Barbara has assured me, however, that this will not be necessary. He tells me he expects full cooperation from Selectmen and local police. He believes his position should be one of "advise and consent." I have agreed to his judgment, subject to review.

Third, I know you are worried about your inability to call friends and loved ones. We understand your concern, but it is imperative that we maintain this "telephonic blackout" to lower the risk of classified information passing into and out of Chester's Mill. You may think this a specious concern; I assure you it is not. It may very well be that someone in Chester's Mill has information regarding the barrier surrounding your town. "In-town" calls should go through.

Fourth, we will continue to maintain a press blackout for the time being, although this matter will remain subject to review. There may come a time when it would be beneficial for town officials and Col. Barbara to hold a press conference, but at present our belief is that a speedy end to this crisis will render such a meeting with the press moot.

My fifth point concerns Internet communications. The Joint Chiefs are strongly in favor of a temporary blackout on e-mail communications, and I was inclined to agree. Col. Barbara, however, has argued strongly in favor of allowing the citizens of Chester's Mill continued Internet access. He points out that e-mail traffic can be legally monitored by the NSA, and as a practical matter such communications can be vetted more easily than cell transmissions. Since he is our "man on the spot," I have agreed to this point, partly on humanitarian grounds. This decision, however, will also be subject to review; changes in policy may occur. Col. Barbara will be a full participant in such reviews, and we look forward to a smooth working relationship between him and all town officials.

Sixth, I offer you the strong possibility that your ordeal may end as early as tomorrow, at 1 PM, EDT. Col. Barbara will explain the military operation that will occur at that time, and he assures me that between the good offices of yourselves and Ms. Julia Shumway, who owns and operates the local newspaper, you will be able to inform the citizens of Chester's Mill what to expect.

And last: you are citizens of the United States of America, and we will never abandon you. Our firmest promise, based on our finest ideals, is simple: No man, woman, or child left behind. Every resource we need to employ in order to end your confinement will be employed. Every dollar we need to spend will be spent. What we expect from you in return is faith and cooperation. Please give us both.

With every prayer and every good wish,
I remain most sincerely yours,

6

Whatever scribble-dee-dee dogsbody might have written it, the bastard had signed it himself, and using all three of his names, including the terrorist one in the middle. Big Jim hadn't voted for him, and at this moment, had he teleported into existence in front of him, Rennie felt he could cheerfully have strangled him.

And Barbara.

Big Jim's fondest wish was that he could whistle up Pete Randolph and have Colonel Fry Cook slammed into a cell. Tell him he could run his gosh-darned martial law command from the basement of the cop-shop with Sam

Verdreaux serving as his aide-de-camp. Maybe Sloppy Sam could even hold the DTs at bay long enough to salute without sticking his thumb in his eye.

But not now. Not yet. Certain phrases from the Blackguard in Chief's letter stood out:

> *As you aid him, so will we aid you.*
> *A smooth working relationship with all town officials.*
> *This decision will be subject to review.*
> *What we expect is faith and cooperation.*

That last one was the most telling. Big Jim was sure the pro-abortion son-of-a-buck knew nothing about faith—to him it was just a buzzword—but when he spoke of cooperation, he knew *exactly* what he was saying, and so did Jim Rennie: *It's a velvet glove, but don't forget the iron fist inside it.*

The President offered sympathy and support (he saw the drug-addled Grinnell woman actually tear up as she read the letter), but if you looked between the lines, you saw the truth. It was a threat letter, pure and simple. Cooperate or you lose your Internet. Cooperate because we'll be making a list of who's naughty and who's nice, and you don't want to be on the naughty side of the ledger when we break through. Because we *will* remember.

Cooperate, pal. Or else.

Rennie thought: *I will never turn my town over to a short-order cook who dared to lay a hand on my son and then dared to challenge my authority. That will never happen, you monkey. Never.*

He also thought: *Softly, calmly.*

Let Colonel Fry Cook explain the military's big plan. If it worked, fine. If it didn't, the U.S. Army's newest colonel was going to discover whole new meanings to the phrase *deep in enemy territory.*

Big Jim smiled and said, "Let's go inside, shall we? Seems we have a lot to talk about."

7

Junior sat in the dark with his girlfriends.

It was strange, even *he* thought so, but it was also soothing.

When he and the other new deputies had gotten back to the police station after the colossal fuckup in Dinsmore's field, Stacey Moggin (still in uniform herself, and looking tired) had told them they could have another four duty-hours if they wanted. There was going to be plenty of overtime on offer, at least for a while, and when it came time for the town to pay, Stacey said, she was sure there'd be bonuses, as well . . . probably provided by a grateful United States government.

Carter, Mel, Georgia Roux, and Frank DeLesseps had all agreed to work the extra hours. It wasn't really the money; they were getting off on the job. Junior was too, but he'd also been hatching another of his headaches. This was depressing after feeling absolutely tip-top all day.

He told Stacey he'd pass, if that was all right. She assured him it was, but reminded him he was scheduled back on duty tomorrow at seven o'clock. "There'll be plenty to do," she said.

On the steps, Frankie hitched up his belt and said, "I think I'll swing by Angie's house. She probably went someplace with Dodee, but I'd hate to think she slipped in the shower—that she's lying there all paralyzed, or something."

Junior felt a throb go through his head. A small white spot began to dance in front of his left eye. It seemed to be jigging and jagging with his heartbeat, which had just speeded up.

"I'll go by, if you want," he told Frankie. "It's on my way."

"Really? You don't mind?"

Junior shook his head. The white spot in front of his eye darted crazily, sickeningly, when he did. Then it settled again.

Frankie lowered his voice. "Sammy Bushey gave me some lip out at the field day."

"*That* hole," Junior said.

"No doubt. She goes, 'What are you going to do, arrest me?' " Frankie raised his voice to a snarky falsetto that scraped Junior's nerves. The dancing white spot actually seemed to turn red, and for a moment he considered putting his hands around his old friend's neck and choking the life out of him so that he, Junior, would never have to be subjected to that falsetto again.

"What I'm thinking," Frankie continued, "is I might go out there after I'm off. Teach her a lesson. You know, Respect Your Local Police."

"She's a skank. Also a lesboreenie."

"That might make it even better." Frankie had paused, looking toward the weird sunset. "This Dome thing could have an upside. We can do pretty much whatever we want. For the time being, anyway. Consider it, chum." Frankie squeezed his crotch.

"Sure," Junior had replied, "but I'm not particularly horny."

Except now he *was*. Well, sort of. It wasn't like he was going to *fuck* them, or anything but—

"But you're still my girlfriends," Junior said in the darkness of the pantry. He'd used a flashlight at first, but then had turned it off. The dark was better. "Aren't you?"

They didn't reply. *If they did,* Junior thought, *I'd have a major miracle to report to my dad and Reverend Coggins.*

He was sitting against a wall lined with shelves of canned goods. He had propped Angie on his right and Dodee on his left. *Menagerie a trios,* as they said in the *Penthouse* Forum. His girls hadn't looked too good with the flashlight on, their swollen faces and bulging eyes only partially obscured by their hanging hair, but once he turned it off . . . hey! They could have been a couple of live chicks!

Except for the smell, that was. A mixture of old shit and decay just starting to happen. But it wasn't too bad, because there were other, more pleasant smells in here: coffee, chocolate, molasses, dried fruit, and—maybe— brown sugar.

Also a faint aroma of perfume. Dodee's? Angie's? He didn't know. What he knew was that his headache was better again and that disturbing white spot had gone away. He slid his hand down and cupped Angie's breast.

"You don't mind me doing that, do you, Ange? I mean, I know you're Frankie's girlfriend, but you guys sort of broke up and hey, it's only copping a feel. Also—I hate to tell you this, but I think he's got cheating on his mind tonight."

He groped with his free hand, found one of Dodee's. It was chilly, but he put it on his crotch anyway. "Oh my, Dodes," he said. "That's pretty bold. But you do what you feel, girl; get down with your bad self."

He'd have to bury them, of course. Soon. The Dome was apt to pop like a soap bubble, or the scientists would find a way to dissolve it. When that happened, the town would be flooded with investigators. And if the Dome stayed in place, there would likely be some sort of food-finding committee going house to house, looking for supplies.

Soon. But not right now. Because this was soothing.

Also sort of exciting. People wouldn't understand, of course, but they wouldn't *have* to understand. Because—

"This is our secret," Junior whispered in the dark. "Isn't it, girls?"

They did not reply (although they would, in time).

Junior sat with his arms around the girls he had murdered, and at some point he drifted off to sleep.

8

When Barbie and Brenda Perkins left the Town Hall at eleven, the meeting was still going on. The two of them walked down Main to Morin without speaking much at first. There was still a small stack of the *Democrat* one-page extras on the corner of Main and Maple. Barbie slid one out from beneath the rock anchoring the pile. Brenda had a Penlite in her purse and shone the beam on the headline.

"Seeing it in print should make it easier to believe, but it doesn't," she said.

"No," he agreed.

"You and Julia collaborated on this to make sure James couldn't cover it up," she said. "Isn't that so?"

Barbie shook his head. "He wouldn't try, because it can't be done. When that missile hits, it's going to make one hell of a bang. Julia just wanted to make sure Rennie doesn't get to spin the news his way, whatever way that might be." He tapped the one-sheet. "To be perfectly blunt, I see this as insurance. Selectman Rennie's got to be thinking, 'If he was ahead of me on this, what other information is he ahead of me on?' "

"James Rennie can be a very dangerous adversary, my

friend." They began walking again. Brenda folded the paper and tucked it under her arm. "My husband was investigating him."

"For what?"

"I don't know how much to tell you," she said. "The choices seem to come down to all or nothing. And Howie had no absolute proof—that's one thing I *do* know. Although he was close."

"This isn't about proof," Barbie said. "It's about me staying out of jail if tomorrow doesn't go well. If what you know might help me with that—"

"If staying out of jail is the only thing you're worried about, I'm disappointed in you."

It wasn't all, and Barbie guessed the widow Perkins knew it. He had listened carefully at the meeting, and although Rennie had taken pains to be at his most ingratiating and sweetly reasonable, Barbie had still been appalled. He thought that, beneath the goshes and gollies and doggone-its, the man was a raptor. He would exert control until it was wrested from him; he would take what he needed until he was stopped. That made him dangerous for everybody, not just for Dale Barbara.

"Mrs. Perkins—"

"Brenda, remember?"

"Brenda, right. Put it this way, Brenda: if the Dome stays in place, this town is going to need help from someone other than a used-car salesman with delusions of grandeur. I can't help anybody if I'm in the calabozo."

"What my husband believed is that Big Jim was helping himself."

"How? To what? And how much?"

She said, "Let's see what happens with the missile. If it doesn't work, I'll tell you everything. If it does, I'll sit down with the County Attorney when the dust settles . . .

and, in the words of Ricky Ricardo, James Rennie will have some 'splainin to do."

"You're not the only one waiting to see what happens with the missile. Tonight, butter wouldn't melt in Rennie's mouth. If the Cruise bounces off instead of punching through, I think we may see his other side."

She snapped off the Penlite and looked up. "See the stars," she said. "So bright. There's the Dipper . . . Cassiopeia . . . the Great Bear. All just the same. I find that comforting. Do you?"

"Yes."

They said nothing for a little while, only looked up at the glimmering sprawl of the Milky Way. "But they always make me feel very small and very . . . very brief." She laughed, then said—rather timidly: "Would you mind if I took your arm, Barbie?"

"Not at all."

She grasped his elbow. He put his hand over hers. Then he walked her home.

9

Big Jim adjourned the meeting at eleven twenty. Peter Randolph bade them all good night and left. He planned to start the evacuation on the west side of town at seven AM sharp, and hoped to have the entire area around Little Bitch Road clear by noon. Andrea followed, walking slowly, with her hands planted in the small of her back. It was a posture with which they had all become familiar.

Although his meeting with Lester Coggins was very much on his mind (and sleep; he wouldn't mind getting a little damned sleep), Big Jim asked her if she could stay behind a moment or two.

She looked at him questioningly. Behind him, Andy Sanders was ostentatiously stacking files and putting them back in the gray steel cabinet.

"And close the door," Big Jim said pleasantly.

Now looking worried, she did as he asked. Andy went on doing the end-of-meeting housework, but his shoulders were hunched, as if against a blow. Whatever it was Jim wanted to talk to her about, Andy knew already. And judging by his posture, it wasn't good.

"What's on your mind, Jim?" she asked.

"Nothing serious." Which meant it was. "But it *did* seem to me, Andrea, that you were getting pretty chummy with that Barbara fellow before the meeting. With Brenda, too, for that matter."

"Brenda? That's just . . ." She started to say *ridiculous,* but that seemed a little strong. "Just silly. I've known Brenda for thirty yea—"

"And Mr. Barbara for three months. If, that is, eating a man's waffles and bacon is a basis for knowing him."

"I think he's Colonel Barbara now."

Big Jim smiled. "Hard to take that seriously when the closest thing he can get to a uniform is a pair of bluejeans and a tee-shirt."

"You saw the President's letter."

"I saw something Julia Shumway could have composed on her own gosh-darn computer. Isn't that right, Andy?"

"Right," Andy said without turning around. He was still filing. And then refiling what he'd already filed, from the look of it.

"And suppose it *was* from the President?" Big Jim said. The smile she hated was spreading on his broad, jowly face. Andrea observed with some fascination that she could see stubble on those jowls, maybe for the first time, and she understood why Jim was always so careful to shave. The stubble gave him a sinister Nixonian look.

"Well . . ." Worry was now edging into fright. She wanted to tell Jim she'd only been being polite, but it had actually been a little more, and she guessed Jim had seen that. He saw a great deal. "Well, he *is* the Commander in Chief, you know."

Big Jim made a *pshaw* gesture. "Do you know what a commander is, Andrea? I'll tell you. Someone who merits loyalty and obedience because he can provide the resources to help those in need. It's supposed to be a fair trade."

"Yes!" she said eagerly. "Resources like that Cruiser missile thing!"

"And if it works, that's all very fine."

"How could it not? He said it might have a thousand-pound warhead!"

"Considering how little we know about the Dome, how can you or any of us be sure? How can we be sure it won't blow the Dome up and leave nothing but a mile-deep crater where Chester's Mill used to be?"

She looked at him in dismay. Hands in the small of her back, rubbing and kneading at the place where the pain lived.

"Well, that's in God's hands," he said. "And you're right, Andrea—it may work. But if it doesn't, we're on our own, and a commander in chief who can't help his citizens isn't worth a squirt of warm pee in a cold chamberpot, as far as I'm concerned. If it doesn't work, and if they don't blow all of us to Glory, somebody is going to have to take hold in this town. Is it going to be some drifter the President taps with his magic wand, or is it going to be the elected officials already in place? Do you see where I'm going with this?"

"Colonel Barbara seemed very capable to me," she whispered.

"Stop calling him that!" Big Jim shouted. Andy dropped a file, and Andrea took a step backward, uttering a squeak of fear as she did so.

Then she straightened, momentarily recovering some of the Yankee steel that had given her the courage to run for Selectman in the first place. "Don't you yell at me, Jim Rennie. I've known you since you were cutting out Sears catalogue pictures in the first grade and pasting them on construction paper, so don't you yell."

"Oh gosh, she's *offended.*" The fierce smile now spread from ear to ear, lifting his upper face into an unsettling mask of jollity. "Isn't that too cotton-picking bad. But it's late and I'm tired and I've handed out about all the sweet syrup I can manage for one day. So you listen to me now, and don't make me repeat myself." He glanced at his watch. "It's eleven thirty-five, and I want to be home by midnight."

"I don't understand what you want of me!"

He rolled his eyes as if he couldn't believe her stupidity. "In a nutshell? I want to know you're going to be on my side—mine and Andy's—if this harebrained missile idea doesn't work. Not with some dishwashing johnny-come-lately."

She squared up her shoulders and let go of her back. She managed to meet his eyes, but her lips were trembling. "And if I think Colonel Barbara—*Mr.* Barbara, if you prefer—is better qualified to manage things in a crisis situation?"

"Well, I have to go with Jiminy Cricket on that one," Big Jim said. "Let your conscience be your guide." His voice had dropped to a murmur that was more frightening than his shout had been. "But there's those pills you take. Those OxyContins."

Andrea felt her skin go cold. "What about them?"

"Andy's got a pretty good supply put aside for you, but if you were to back the wrong horse in this-here race, those pills just might disappear. Isn't that right, Andy?"

Andy had begun washing out the coffeemaker. He looked unhappy and he wouldn't meet Andrea's brimming eyes, but there was no hesitation in his reply. "Yes," he said. "In a case like that, I might have to turn them down the pharmacist's toilet. Dangerous to have drugs like that around with the town cut off and all."

"You can't do that!" she cried. "I have a prescription!"

Big Jim said kindly, "The only prescription you need is sticking with the people who know this town best, Andrea. For the present, it's the only kind of prescription that will do you any good."

"Jim, I need my pills." She heard the whine in her voice—so much like her mother's during the last bad years when she'd been bedridden—and hated it. "I *need* them!"

"I know," Big Jim said. "God has burdened you with a great deal of pain." *Not to mention a big old monkey on your back,* he thought.

"Just do the right thing," Andy said. His dark-circled eyes were sad and earnest. "Jim knows what's best for the town; always has. We don't need some outsider telling us our business."

"If I do, will I keep getting my pain pills?"

Andy's face lit in a smile. "You betcha! I might even take it on myself to up the dosage a little. Say a hundred milligrams more a day? Couldn't you use it? You look awfully uncomfortable."

"I suppose I could use a little more," Andrea said dully. She lowered her head. She hadn't taken a drink, not even a glass of wine, since the night of the Senior Prom when she'd gotten so sick, had never smoked a joint, had never even seen cocaine except on TV. She was a good person. A *very* good person. So how had she gotten into a box like this? By falling while she was going to get the mail? Was that all it took to turn someone into a drug addict? If so, how unfair. How horrible. "But only forty milligrams. Forty more would be enough, I think."

"Are you sure?" Big Jim asked.

She didn't feel sure at all. That was the devil of it.

"Maybe eighty," she said, and wiped the tears from her face. And, in a whisper: "You're blackmailing me."

The whisper was low, but Big Jim heard it. He reached for her. Andrea flinched, but Big Jim only took her hand. Gently.

"No," he said. "That would be a sin. We're helping you. And all we want in return is for you to help us."

10

There was a *thud*.

It brought Sammy wide awake in bed even though she'd smoked half a doob and drunk three of Phil's beers before falling out at ten o'clock. She always kept a couple of sixes in the fridge and still thought of them as "Phil's beers," although he'd been gone since April. She'd heard rumors that he was still in town, but discounted them. Surely if he was still around, she would have seen him *sometime* during the last six months, wouldn't she? It was a small town, just like that song said.

Thud!

That got her bolt upright, and listening for Little Walter's wail. It didn't come and she thought, *Oh God, that damn crib fell apart! And if he can't even cry—*

She threw the covers back and ran for the door. She

smacked into the wall to the left of it, instead. Almost fell down. Damn dark! Damn power company! Damn Phil, going off and leaving her like this, with no one to stick up for her when guys like Frank DeLesseps were mean to her and scared her and—

Thud!

She felt along the top of the dresser and found the flashlight. She turned it on and hurried out the door. She started to turn left, into the bedroom where Little Walter slept, but the thud came again. Not from the left, but from straight ahead, across the cluttered living room. Someone was at the trailer's front door. And now there came muffled laughter. Whoever it was sounded like they had their drink on.

She strode across the room, the tee-shirt she slept in rippling around her chubby thighs (she'd put on a little weight since Phil left, about fifty pounds, but when this Dome shit was over she intended to get on NutriSystem, return to her high school weight) and threw open the door.

Flashlights—four of them, and high-powered—hit her in the face. From behind them came more laughter. One of those laughs was more of a *nyuck-nyuck-nyuck,* like Curly in the Three Stooges. She recognized *that* one, having heard it all through high school: Mel Searles.

"Look at you!" Mel said. "All dressed up and no one to blow."

More laughter. Sammy raised an arm to shield her eyes, but it did no good; the people behind the flashlights were just shapes. But one of the laughers sounded female. That was probably good.

"Turn off those lights before I go blind! And shut up, you'll wake the baby!"

More laughter, louder than ever, but three of the four

lights went out. She trained her own flashlight out the door, and wasn't comforted by what she saw: Frankie DeLesseps and Mel Searles flanking Carter Thibodeau and Georgia Roux. Georgia, the girl who'd put her foot on Sammy's tit that afternoon and called her a dyke. A female, but not a *safe* female.

They were wearing their badges. And they were indeed drunk.

"What do you want? It's late."

"Want some dope," Georgia said. "You sell it, so sell some to us."

"I want to get high as apple pie in a red dirt sky," Mel said, and then laughed: *Nyuck-nyuck-nyuck.*

"I don't have any," Sammy said.

"Bullshit, the place reeks of it," Carter said. "Sell us some. Don't be a bitch."

"Yeah," Georgia said. In the light of Sammy's flash, her eyes had a silvery glitter. "Never mind that we're cops."

They all roared at this. They would wake the baby for sure.

"No!" Sammy tried to shut the door. Thibodeau pushed it open again. He did it with just the flat of his hand—easy as could be—but Sammy went stumbling backward. She tripped over Little Walter's goddam choo-choo and went down on her ass for the second time that day. Her tee-shirt flew up.

"Ooo, pink underwear, are you expecting one of your girlfriends?" Georgia asked, and they all roared again. The flashlights that had gone out now came back on, spotlighting her.

Sammy yanked the tee-shirt down almost hard enough to rip the neck. Then she got unsteadily to her feet, the flashlight beams dancing up and down her body.

"Be a good hostess and invite us in," Frankie said, barging through the door. "Thank you very much." His light flashed around the living room. "What a pigsty."

"Pigsty for a pig!" Georgia bellowed, and they all broke up again. "If I was Phil, I might come back out of the woods just long enough to kick your fuckin ass!" She raised her fist; Carter Thibodeau knuckle-dapped her.

"He still hidin out at the radio station?" Mel asked. "Tweekin the rock? Gettin all paranoid for Jesus?"

"I don't know what you . . ." She wasn't mad anymore, only afraid. This was the disconnected way people talked in the nightmares that came if you smoked weed dusted with PCP. "Phil's gone!"

Her four visitors looked at each other, then laughed. Searles's idiotic *nyuck-nyuck-nyuck* rode above the others.

"Gone! Bugged out!" Frankie crowed.

"Fuckin as *if*!" Carter replied, and then *they* bumped knucks.

Georgia grabbed a bunch of Sammy's paperbacks off the top shelf of the bookcase and looked through them. "Nora Roberts? Sandra Brown? Stephenie Meyer? You read this stuff? Don't you know fuckin Harry Potter rules?" She held the books out, then opened her hands and dropped them on the floor.

The baby still hadn't awakened. It was a miracle. "If I sell you some dope, will you go?" Sammy asked.

"Sure," Frankie said.

"And hurry up," Carter said. "We got an early call tomorrow. Eee-*vack*-u-ation detail. So shag that fat ass of yours."

"Wait here."

She went into the kitchenette and opened the freezer— warm now, everything would be thawed, for some reason that made her feel like crying—and took out one of the gallon Baggies of dope she kept in there. There were three others.

She started to turn around, but someone grabbed her before she could, and someone else plucked the Baggie from her hand. "I want to check out that pink underwear again," Mel said in her ear. "See if you got SUNDAY on your ass." He yanked her shirt up to her waist. "Nope, guess not."

"Stop it! *Quit* it!"

Mel laughed: *Nyuck-nyuck-nyuck.*

A flashlight stabbed her in the eyes, but she recognized the narrow head behind it: Frankie DeLesseps. "You gave me lip today," he said. "Plus, you slapped me and hurt my little hannie. And all I did was this." He reached out and grabbed her breast again.

She tried to jerk away. The beam of light that had been trained on her face tilted momentarily up to the ceiling. Then it came down again, fast. Pain exploded in her head. He had hit her with his flashlight.

"Ow! Ow, that hurts! STOP it!"

"Shit, that didn't hurt. You're just lucky I don't arrest you for pushing dope. Stand still if you don't want another one."

"This dope smells skanky," Mel said in a matter-of-fact voice. He was behind her, still holding up her shirt.

"So does she," Georgia said.

"Gotta confiscate the weed, bee-yatch," Carter said. "Sorry."

Frankie had glommed onto her breast again. "Stand still." He pinched the nipple. "Just stand still." His voice, roughening. His breathing, quickening. She knew where this was going. She closed her eyes. *Just as long as the baby doesn't wake up,* she thought. *And as long as they don't do more. Do worse.*

"Go on," Georgia said. "Show her what she's been missing since Phil left."

Frankie gestured into the living room with his flashlight. "Get on the couch. And spread em."

"Don't you want to read her her rights, first?" Mel asked, and laughed: *Nyuck-nyuck-nyuck.* Sammy thought if she had to hear that laugh one more time, her head would split wide open. But she started for the couch, head down, shoulders slumped.

Carter grabbed her on the way by, turned her, and sprayed the beam of his flashlight up his own face, turning it into a goblin-mask. "Are you going to talk about this, Sammy?"

"N-N-No."

The goblin-mask nodded. "You hold that thought. Because no one would believe you, anyway. Except for us, of course, and then we'd have to come back and *really* fuck you up."

Frankie pushed her onto the couch.

"Do her," Georgia said excitedly, training her light on Sammy. "*Do* that bitch!"

All three of the young men did her. Frankie went first, whispering "You gotta learn to keep your mouth shut except for when you're on your knees" as he pushed into her.

Carter was next. While he was riding her, Little Walter awoke and began to cry.

"Shut up, kid, or I'll hafta readja your rights!" Mel Searles hollered, and then laughed.

Nyuck-nyuck-nyuck.

11

It was almost midnight.

Linda Everett lay fast asleep in her half of the bed; she'd had an exhausting day, she had an early call tomorrow (eee-*vack*-u-ation detail), and not even her worries about Janelle could keep her awake. She didn't snore, exactly, but a soft *queep-queep-queep* sound came from her half of the bed.

Rusty had had an equally exhausting day, but he couldn't sleep, and it wasn't Jan he was worried about. He thought she was going to be all right, at least for a while. He could keep her seizures at bay if they didn't get any worse. If he ran out of Zarontin at the hospital dispensary, he could get more from Sanders Drug.

It was Dr. Haskell he kept thinking about. And Rory Dinsmore, of course. Rusty kept seeing the torn and bloody socket where the boy's eye had been. Kept hearing Ron Haskell telling Ginny, *I'm not death. Deaf, I mean.*

Except he *had* been death.

He rolled over in bed, trying to leave these memories behind, and what came in their place was Rory muttering *It's Halloween.* Overlapping that, his own daughter's voice: *It's the Great Pumpkin's fault! You have to stop the Great Pumpkin!*

His daughter had been having a seizure. The Dinsmore kid had taken a ricochet to the eye and a bullet fragment to the brain. What did that tell him?

It tells me nothing. What did the Scottish guy say on Lost*? "Don't mistake coincidence for fate"?*

Maybe that had been it. Maybe it had. But *Lost* had been a long time ago. The Scottish guy could have said *Don't mistake fate for coincidence.*

He rolled over the other way and this time saw the black headline of that night's *Democrat* one-sheet: **EXPLOSIVES TO BE FIRED AT BARRIER!**

It was hopeless. Sleep was out of the question for now, and the worst thing you could do in a situation like that was try to flog your way into dreamland.

There was half a loaf of Linda's famous cranberry-orange bread downstairs; he'd seen it on the counter when he came in. Rusty decided he'd have a piece of it at the kitchen table and thumb through the latest issue of *American Family Physician*. If an article on whooping cough wouldn't put him to sleep, nothing would.

He got up, a big man dressed in the blue scrubs that were his usual nightwear, and left quietly, so as not to wake Linda.

Halfway to the stairs, he paused and cocked his head.

Audrey was whining, very soft and low. From the girls' room. Rusty went down there and eased the door open. The golden retriever, just a dim shape between the girls' beds, turned to look at him and voiced another of those low whines.

Judy was lying on her side with one hand tucked under her cheek, breathing long and slow. Jannie was a different story. She rolled restlessly from one side to the other, kicking at the bedclothes and muttering. Rusty stepped over the dog and sat down on her bed, under Jannie's latest boy-band poster.

She was dreaming. Not a good dream, by her troubled expression. And that muttering sounded like protests. Rusty tried to make out the words, but before he could, she ceased.

Audrey whined again.

Jan's nightdress was all twisted. Rusty straightened it, pulled up the covers, and brushed Jannie's hair off her forehead. Her eyes were moving rapidly back and forth beneath her closed lids, but he observed no trembling of the limbs, no fluttering fingers, no characteristic smacking of the lips. REM sleep rather than seizure, almost certainly. Which raised an interesting question: could dogs also smell bad dreams?

He bent and kissed Jan's cheek. When he did, her eyes opened, but he wasn't entirely sure she was seeing him. This could have been a petit mal symptom, but Rusty just didn't believe it. Audi would have been barking, he felt sure.

"Go back to sleep, honey," he said.

"He has a golden baseball, Daddy."

"I know he does, honey, go back to sleep."

"It's a *bad* baseball."

"No. It's good. Baseballs are good, especially golden ones."

"Oh," she said.

"Go back to sleep."

"Okay, Daddy." She rolled over and closed her eyes. There was a moment of settling beneath the covers, and then she was still. Audrey, who had been lying on the floor with her head up, watching them, now put her muzzle on her paw and went to sleep herself.

Rusty sat there awhile, listening to his daughters breathe, telling himself there was really nothing to be frightened of, people talked their way in and out of dreams all the time. He told himself that everything was fine—he only had to look at the sleeping dog on the floor if he doubted—but in the middle of the night it was hard to be an optimist. When dawn was still long hours away, bad thoughts took on flesh and began to walk. In the middle of the night thoughts became zombies.

He decided he didn't want the cranberry-orange bread after all. What he wanted was to snuggle against his bedwarm sleeping wife. But before leaving the room, he stroked Audrey's silky head. "Pay attention, girl," he whispered. Audi briefly opened her eyes and looked at him.

He thought, *Golden retriever.* And, following that—the perfect connection: *Golden baseball. A bad baseball.*

That night, despite the girls' newly discovered feminine privacy, Rusty left their door open.

12

Lester Coggins was sitting on Rennie's stoop when Big Jim got back. Coggins was reading his Bible by flashlight. This did not inspire Big Jim with the Reverend's devotion but only worsened a mood that was already bad.

"God bless you, Jim," Coggins said, standing up. When Big Jim offered his hand, Coggins seized it in a fervent fist and pumped it.

"Bless you too," Big Jim said gamely.

Coggins gave his hand a final hard shake and let go. "Jim, I'm here because I've had a revelation. I asked for one last night—yea, for I was sorely troubled—and this afternoon it came. God has spoken to me, both through scripture and through that young boy."

"The Dinsmore kid?"

Coggins kissed his clasped hands with a loud smack and then held them skyward. "The very same. Rory Dinsmore. May God keep him for all eternity."

"He's eating dinner with Jesus right this minute," Big Jim said automatically. He was examining the Reverend in the beam of his own flashlight, and what he was seeing wasn't good. Although the night was cooling rapidly, sweat shone on Coggins's skin. His eyes were wide, showing too much of the whites. His hair stood out in wild curls and bumbershoots. All in all, he looked like a fellow whose gears were slipping and might soon be stripping.

Big Jim thought, *This is not good.*

"Yes," Coggins said, "I'm sure. Eating the great feast . . . wrapped in the everlasting arms . . ."

Big Jim thought it would be hard to do both things at the same time, but kept silent on that score.

"And yet his death was for a purpose, Jim. That's what I've come to tell you."

"Tell me inside," Big Jim said, and before the minister could reply: "Have you seen my son?"

"Junior? No."

"How long have you been here?" Big Jim flicked on the hall light, blessing the generator as he did so.

"An hour. Maybe a little less. Sitting on the steps . . . reading . . . praying . . . meditating."

Rennie wondered if anyone had seen him, but did not ask. Coggins was upset already, and a question like that might upset him more.

"Let's go in my study," he said, and led the way, head down, lumbering slowly along in his big flat strides. Seen from behind, he looked a bit like a bear dressed in human clothes, one who was old and slow but still dangerous.

13

In addition to the picture of the Sermon on the Mount with his safe behind it, there were a great many plaques on the walls of Big Jim's study, commending him for various acts of community service. There was also a framed picture of Big Jim shaking hands with Sarah Palin and another of him shaking with the Big Number 3, Dale Earnhardt, when Earnhardt had done a fundraiser for some children's charity at the annual Oxford Plains Crash-A-Rama. There was even a picture of Big Jim shaking hands with Tiger Woods, who had seemed like a very nice Negro.

The only piece of memorabilia on his desk was a gold-plated baseball in a Lucite cradle. Below it (also in Lucite) was an autograph reading: *To Jim Rennie, with thanks for your help in putting on the Western Maine Charity Softball Tournament of 2007!* It was signed *Bill "Spaceman" Lee.*

As he sat behind his desk in his high-backed chair, Big Jim took the ball from its cradle and began tossing it from hand to hand. It was a fine thing to toss, especially when you were a little upset: nice and heavy, the golden seams smacking comfortably against your palms. Big Jim sometimes wondered what it would be like to have a *solid* gold ball. Perhaps he would look into that when this Dome business was over.

Coggins seated himself on the other side of the desk, in the client's chair. The supplicant's chair. Which was where Big Jim wanted him. The Reverend's eyes went back and forth like the eyes of a man watching a tennis match. Or maybe a hypnotist's crystal.

"Now what's this all about, Lester? Fill me in. But let's keep it short, shall we? I need to get some sleep. Got a lot to do tomorrow."

"Will you pray with me first, Jim?"

Big Jim smiled. It was the fierce one, although not turned up to maximum chill. At least not yet. "Why don't you fill me in before we do that? I like to know what I'm praying about before I get kneebound."

Lester did not keep it short, but Big Jim hardly noticed. He listened with growing dismay that was close to horror. The Reverend's narrative was disjointed and peppered with Biblical quotations, but the gist was clear: he had decided that their little business had displeased the Lord enough for Him to clap a big glass bowl over the whole town. Lester had prayed on what to do about this, scourging himself as he did so (the scourging might have been metaphorical—Big Jim certainly hoped so), and the Lord had led him to some Bible verse about madness, blindness, smiting, etc., etc.

"The Lord said he would shew me a sign, and—"

"Shoe?" Big Jim raised his tufted eyebrows.

Lester ignored him and plunged on, sweating like a man with malaria, his eyes still following the golden ball. Back . . . and forth.

"It was like when I was a teenager and I used to come in my bed."

"Les, that's . . . a little too much information." Tossing the ball from hand to hand.

"God said He would shew me blindness, but not *my* blindness. And this afternoon, out in that field, He did! Didn't he?"

"Well, I guess that's one interpretation—"

"No!" Coggins leaped to his feet. He began to walk in a circle on the rug, his Bible in one hand. With the other he tugged at his hair. "God said that when I saw that sign, I had to tell my congregation exactly what you'd been up to—"

"Just me?" Big Jim asked. He did so in a meditative voice. He was tossing the ball from hand to hand a little faster now. *Smack. Smack. Smack.* Back and forth against palms that were fleshy but still hard.

"No," Lester said in a kind of groan. He paced faster now, no longer looking at the ball. He was waving the Bible with the hand not busy trying to tear his hair out by the roots. He did the same thing in the pulpit sometimes, when he really got going. That stuff was all right in church, but here it was just plain infuriating. "It was you and me and Roger Killian the Bowie brothers and . . ." He lowered his voice. "And that other one. The Chef. I think that man's crazy. If he wasn't when he started last spring, he sure is now."

Look who's talking, little buddy, Big Jim thought.

"We're all involved, but it's you and I who have to confess, Jim. That's what the Lord told me. That's what the boy's blindness meant; it's what he *died* for. We'll confess, and we'll burn that Barn of Satan behind the church. Then God will let us go."

"You'll go, all right, Lester. Straight to Shawshank State Prison."

"I will take the punishment God metes out. And gladly."

"And me? Andy Sanders? The Bowie brothers? And Roger Killian! He's got I think nine kids to support! What if we're not so glad, Lester?"

"I can't help that." Now Lester began to whack himself on the shoulders with his Bible. Back and forth; first one side and then the other. Big Jim found himself synchronizing his tosses of the golden baseball to the preacher's blows. *Whack . . .* and *smack. Whack . . .* and *smack. Whack . . .* and *smack.* "It's sad about the Killian children, of course, but . . . Exodus twenty, verse five: 'For I the Lord thy God am a jealous God, visiting the iniquity of the fathers upon the children unto the third and fourth generation.' We have to bow to that. We have to clean out this chancre however much it may hurt; make right what we have made wrong. That means confession and purification. Purification by fire."

Big Jim raised the hand not currently holding the gold baseball. "Whoa, whoa, *whoa.* Think about what you're saying. This town depends on me—and you, of course—in ordinary times, but in times of crisis, it *needs* us." He stood up, pushing his chair back. This had been a long and terrible day, he was tired, and now this. It made a man angry.

"We have sinned." Coggins spoke stubbornly, still

whacking himself with his Bible. As if he thought treating God's Holy Book like that was perfectly okay.

"What we did, Les, was keep thousands of kids from starving in Africa. We even paid to treat their hellish diseases. We also built you a new church and the most powerful Christian radio station in the northeast."

"And lined our own pockets, don't forget that!" Coggins shrilled. This time he smacked himself full in the face with the Good Book. A thread of blood seeped from one nostril. "Lined em with filthy dope-money!" He smacked himself again. "And Jesus's radio station is being run by a lunatic who cooks the poison that children put into their veins!"

"Actually, I think most of them smoke it."

"Is that supposed to be *funny*?"

Big Jim came around the desk. His temples were throbbing and a bricklike flush was rising in his cheeks. Yet he tried once more, speaking softly, as if to a child doing a tantrum. "Lester, the town needs my leadership. If you go opening your gob, I won't be able to provide that leadership. Not that anyone will believe you—"

"They'll *all* believe!" Coggins cried. "When they see the devil's workshop I've let you run behind my church, they'll *all* believe! And Jim—don't you see—once the sin is out . . . once the sore's been cleansed . . . God will remove His barrier! The crisis will end! They won't *need* your leadership!"

That was when James P. Rennie snapped. *"They'll always need it!"* he roared, and swung the baseball in his closed fist.

It split the skin of Lester's left temple as Lester was turning to face him. Blood poured down the side of Lester's face. His left eye glared out of the gore. He lurched forward with his hands out. The Bible flapped at Big Jim like a blabbery mouth. Blood pattered down onto the carpet. The left shoulder of Lester's sweater was already soaked. *"No, this is not the will of the Lor—"*

"It's *my* will, you troublesome fly." Big Jim swung again, and this time connected with the Reverend's forehead, dead center. Big Jim felt the shock travel all the way up to his shoulder. Yet Lester staggered forward, wagging his Bible. It seemed to be trying to talk.

Big Jim dropped the ball to his side. His shoulder was throbbing. Now blood was *pouring* onto the carpet, and still the son-of-a-buck wouldn't go down; still he came forward, trying to talk and spitting scarlet in a fine spray.

Coggins bumped into the front of the desk—blood splattered across the previously unmarked blotter—and then began to sidle along it. Big Jim tried to raise the ball again and couldn't.

I knew all that high school shotputting would catch up with me someday, he thought.

He switched the ball to his left hand and swung it sideways and upward. It connected with Lester's jaw, knocking his lower face out of true and spraying more blood into the not-quite-steady light of the overhead fixture. A few drops struck the milky glass.

"Guh!" Lester cried. He was still trying to sidle around the desk. Big Jim retreated into the kneehole.

"Dad?"

Junior was standing in the doorway, eyes wide, mouth open.

"Guh!" Lester said, and began to flounder around toward the new voice. He held out the Bible. *"Guh . . . Guh . . . Guh-uh-ODD—"*

"Don't just stand there, help me!" Big Jim roared at his son.

Lester began to stagger toward Junior, flapping the

Bible extravagantly up and down. His sweater was sodden; his pants had turned a muddy maroon; his face was gone, buried in blood.

Junior hurried to meet him. When Lester started to collapse, Junior grabbed him and held him up. "I gotcha, Reverend Coggins—I gotcha, don't worry."

Then Junior clamped his hands around Lester's blood-sticky throat and began to squeeze.

14

Five interminable minutes later.

Big Jim sat in his office chair—*sprawled* in his office chair—with his tie, put on special for the meeting, pulled down and his shirt unbuttoned. He was massaging his hefty left breast. Beneath it, his heart was still galloping and throwing off arrhythmias, but showed no signs of actually going into cardiac arrest.

Junior left. Rennie thought at first he was going to get Randolph, which would have been a mistake, but he was too breathless to call the boy back. Then he came back on his own, carrying the tarp from the back of the camper. He watched Junior shake it out on the floor—oddly businesslike, as if he had done this a thousand times before. *It's all those R-rated movies they watch now,* Big Jim thought. Rubbing the flabby flesh that had once been so firm and so hard.

"I'll . . . help," he wheezed, knowing he could not.

"You'll sit right there and get your breath." His son, on his knees, gave him a dark and unreadable look. There might have been love in it—Big Jim certainly hoped there was—but there were other things, too.

Gotcha now? Was *Gotcha now* part of that look?

Junior rolled Lester onto the tarp. The tarp crackled. Junior studied the body, rolled it a little farther, then flipped the end of the tarp over it. The tarp was green. Big Jim had bought it at Burpee's. Bought it on sale. He remembered Toby Manning saying, *You're getting a heckuva good deal on that one, Mr. Rennie.*

"Bible," Big Jim said. He was still wheezing, but he felt a little better. Heartbeat slowing, thank God. Who knew the climb would get so steep after fifty? He thought: *I have to start working out. Get back in shape. God only gives you one body.*

"Right, yeah, good call," Junior murmured. He grabbed the bloody Bible, wedged it between Coggins's thighs, and began rolling up the body.

"He broke in, Son. He was crazy."

"Sure." Junior did not seem interested in that. What he seemed interested in was rolling the body up . . . just so.

"It was him or me. You'll have to—" Another little taradiddle in his chest. Jim gasped, coughed, pounded his breast. His heart settled again. "You'll have to take him out to Holy Redeemer. When he's found, there's a guy . . . maybe . . ." It was the Chef he was thinking of, but maybe arranging for Chef to carry the can for this was a bad idea. Chef Bushey knew stuff. Of course, he'd probably resist arrest. In which case he might not be taken alive.

"I've got a better place," Junior said. He sounded serene. "And if you're talking about hanging it on someone, I've got a better *idea.*"

"Who?"

"Dale Fucking Barbara."

"You know I don't approve of that language—"

Looking at him over the tarp, eyes glittering, Junior said it again. *"Dale . . . Fucking . . . Barbara."*

"How?"

"I don't know yet. But you better wash off that damn gold ball if you mean to keep it. And get rid of the blotter."

Big Jim got to his feet. He was feeling better now. "You're a good boy to help your old dad this way, Junior."

"If you say so," Junior replied. There was now a big green burrito on the rug. With feet sticking out the end. Junior tucked the tarp over them, but it wouldn't stay. "I'll need some duct tape."

"If you're not going to take him to the church, then where—"

"Never mind," Junior said. "It's safe. The Rev'll keep until we figure out how to put Barbara in the frame."

"Got to see what happens tomorrow before we do anything."

Junior looked at him with an expression of distant contempt Big Jim had never seen before. It came to him that his son now had a great deal of power over him. But surely his own *son* . . .

"We'll have to bury your rug. Thank God it's not the wall-to-wall carpet you used to have in here. And the upside is it caught most of the mess." Then he lifted the big burrito and bore it down the hall. A few minutes later Rennie heard the camper start up.

Big Jim considered the golden baseball. *I should get rid of that, too,* he thought, and knew he wouldn't. It was practically a family heirloom.

And besides, what harm? What harm, if it was clean?

When Junior returned an hour later, the golden baseball was once again gleaming in its Lucite cradle.

**MISSILE STRIKE
IMMINENT**

1

"ATTENTION! THIS IS THE CHESTER'S MILL POLICE! THE AREA IS BEING EVACUATED! IF YOU HEAR ME, COME TO THE SOUND OF MY VOICE! THE AREA IS BEING EVACUATED!"

Thurston Marshall and Carolyn Sturges sat up in bed, listening to this weird blare and looking at each other with wide eyes. They were teachers at Emerson College, in Boston—Thurston a full professor of English (and guest editor for the current issue of *Ploughshares*), Carolyn a graduate assistant in the same department. They had been lovers for the last six months, and the bloom was far from off the rose. They were in Thurston's little cabin on Chester Pond, which lay between Little Bitch Road and Prestile Stream. They had come here for a long "fall foliage" weekend, but most of the foliage they had admired since Friday afternoon had been of the pubic variety. There was no TV in the cabin; Thurston Marshall abominated TV. There was a radio, but they hadn't turned it on. It was eight thirty in the morning on Monday, October twenty-third. Neither of them had any idea anything was wrong until that blaring voice startled them awake.

"ATTENTION! THIS IS THE CHESTER'S MILL POLICE! THE AREA—" Closer. Moving in.

"Thurston! The dope! Where did you leave the dope?"

"Don't worry," he said, but the quaver in his voice suggested he was incapable of taking his own advice. He was a tall, reedy man with a lot of graying hair that he usually tied back in a ponytail. Now it lay loose, almost to his shoulders. He was sixty; Carolyn was twenty-three. "All these little camps are deserted at this time of year, they'll just drive past and back to the Little Bitch R—"

She pounded him on the shoulder—a first. "The car is in the driveway! They'll see the car!"

An *oh shit* look dawned on his face.

"—EVACUATED! IF YOU HEAR ME, COME TO THE SOUND OF MY VOICE! ATTENTION! ATTENTION!" Very close now. Thurston could hear other amplified voices, as well—people using loudhailers, *cops* using loudhailers—but this one was almost on top of them. "THE AREA IS BEING EVAC—" There was a moment of silence. Then: "HELLO, CABIN! COME OUT HERE! MOVE IT!"

Oh, this was a nightmare.

"Where did you leave the dope?" She pounded him again.

The dope was in the other room. In a Baggie that was now half empty, sitting beside a platter of last night's cheese and crackers. If someone came in, it would be the first goddam thing they saw.

"THIS IS THE POLICE! WE ARE NOT SCREW-ING AROUND HERE! THE AREA IS BEING EVACUATED! IF YOU'RE IN THERE, COME OUT BEFORE WE HAVE TO DRAG YOU OUT!"

Pigs, he thought. *Smalltown pigs with smalltown piggy minds.*

Thurston sprang from the bed and ran across the room, hair flying, skinny buttocks flexing.

His grandfather had built the cabin after World

War II, and it had only two rooms: a big bedroom facing the pond and the living room/kitchen. Power was provided by an old Henske generator, which Thurston had turned off before they had retired; its ragged blat was not exactly romantic. The embers of last night's fire—not really necessary, but *très* romantic—still winked sleepily in the fireplace.

Maybe I was wrong, maybe I put the dope back in my attaché—

Unfortunately, no. The dope was there, right next to the remains of the Brie they had gorged on before commencing last night's fuckathon.

He ran to it, and there was a knock on the door. No, a *hammering* on the door.

"Just a minute!" Thurston cried, madly merry. Carolyn was standing in the bedroom doorway, wrapped in a sheet, but he hardly noticed her. Thurston's mind—still suffering residual paranoia from the previous evening's indulgences—tumbled with unconnected thoughts: revoked tenure, *1984* thought-police, revoked tenure, the disgusted reaction of his three children (by two previous wives), and, of course, revoked tenure. "Just a minute, just a sec, let me get dressed—"

But the door burst open, and—in direct violation of about nine different Constitutional guarantees—two young men strode in. One held a bullhorn. Both were dressed in jeans and blue shirts. The jeans were almost comforting, but the shirts bore shoulder-patches and badges.

We don't need no stinkin badges, Thurston thought numbly.

Carolyn shrieked, *"Get out of here!"*

"Check it out, Junes," Frankie DeLesseps said. "It's *When Horny Met Slutty.*"

Thurston snatched up the Baggie, held it behind his back, and dropped it into the sink.

Junior was eyeing the equipment this move revealed. "That's about the longest and skinniest dorkola I've ever seen," he said. He looked tired, and came by the look honestly—he'd had only two hours' sleep—but he was feeling fine, absolutely ripping, old bean. Not a trace of a headache.

This work suited him.

"Get OUT!" Carolyn shouted.

Frankie said, "You want to shut your mouth, sweetheart, and put on some clothes. Everyone on this side of town's being evacuated."

"This is our place! GET THE FUCK OUT!"

Frankie had been smiling. Now he stopped. He strode past the skinny naked man standing by the sink (*quailing* by the sink might have been more accurate) and grabbed Carolyn by the shoulders. He gave her a brisk shake. "Don't give me lip, sweetheart. I'm trying to keep you from getting your ass fried. You and your boyfr—"

"Get your hands off me! You'll go to jail for this! My father's a lawyer!" She tried to slap him. Frankie—not a morning person, never had been—seized her hand and bent it back. Not really hard, but Carolyn screamed. The sheet dropped to the floor.

"Whoa! That's a serious rack," Junior confided to the gaping Thurston Marshall. "Can you keep up with that, old fella?"

"Get your clothes on, both of you," Frankie said. "I don't know how dumb you are, but pretty dumb would be my guess, since you're still here. Don't you know—" He stopped. Looked from the woman's face to the man's. Both equally terrified. Equally mystified.

"Junior!" he said.

"What?"

"Titsy McGee and wrinkle-boy don't know what's going on."

"Don't you dare call me any of your sexist—"

Junior held up his hands. "Ma'am, get dressed. You have to get out of here. The U.S. Air Force is going to fire a Cruise missile at this part of town in"—he looked at his watch—"a little less than five hours."

"ARE YOU INSANE?" Carolyn screamed.

Junior heaved a sigh and then pushed ahead. He guessed he understood the whole cop thing a little better now. It was a great job, but people could be so *stupid.* "If it bounces off, you'd just hear a big bang. Might cause you to shit your pants—if you were wearing any—but it wouldn't hurt you. If it punches through, though, you'd most likely get charbroiled, since it's gonna be really big and you're less than two miles from what they say is gonna be the point of impact."

"Bounces off *what,* you dimwit?" Thurston demanded. With the dope in the sink, he now used one hand to cover his privates . . . or at least tried to; his love-machine was indeed extremely long and skinny.

"The Dome," Frankie said. "And I don't appreciate your mouth." He took a long step forward and punched the current guest editor of *Ploughshares* in the gut. Thurston made a hoarse whoofing sound, doubled over, staggered, almost kept his feet, went to his knees, and vomited up about a teacup's worth of thin white gruel that still smelled of Brie.

Carolyn held her swelling wrist. "You'll go to jail for this," she promised Junior in a low, trembling voice. "Bush and Cheney are long gone. This isn't the United States of North Korea anymore."

"I know that," Junior said, with admirable patience

for one who was thinking he wouldn't mind doing a little more choking; there was a small dark Gila monster in his brain that thought a little more choking would be just the way to start the day off right.

But no. No. He had to do his part in completing the evacuation. He had taken the Oath of Duty, or whatever the fuck it was.

"I *do* know it," he repeated. "But what you two Mass-holes don't get is that you aren't in the United States of *America* anymore, either. You're in the Kingdom of Chester now, and if you don't behave, you're going to end up in the *Dungeons* of Chester. I promise. No phone call, no lawyer, no due process. We're trying to save your lives here. Are you too fuck-dumb to understand that?"

She was staring at him, stunned. Thurston tried to get up, couldn't manage it, and crawled toward her. Frankie helped him along with a boot to the butt. Thurston cried out in shock and pain. "That's for holding us up, Grampa," Frankie said. "I admire your taste in chicks, but we've got a lot to do."

Junior looked at the young woman. Great mouth. Angelina lips. He bet she could, as the saying went, suck the chrome off a trailer hitch. "If he can't get dressed by himself, you help him. We've got four more cabins to check out, and when we get back here, you want to be in that Volvo of yours and on your way into town."

"*I don't understand any of this!*" Carolyn wailed.

"Not surprised," Frankie said, and plucked the Baggie of dope out of the sink. "Didn't you know this stuff makes you stupid?"

She began to cry.

"Don't worry," Frankie said. "I'm confiscating it, and in a couple of days, booya, you'll smarten up all on your own."

"You didn't read us our rights," she wept.

Junior looked astonished. Then he laughed. "You have the right to get the fuck out of here and shut the fuck up, okay? In this situation those are the only rights you have. Do you understand that?"

Frankie was examining the confisticated dope. "Junior," he said, "there's hardly any seeds in this. This is fucking *primo*."

Thurston had reached Carolyn. He got to his feet, farting quite loudly as he did so. Junior and Frankie looked at each other. They tried to hold it in—they were officers of the law, after all—and couldn't. They burst out laughing simultaneously.

"Trombone Charlie is back in town!" Frankie yelled, and they gave each other a high five.

Thurston and Carolyn stood in the bedroom doorway, covering their mutual nakedness in an embrace, staring at the cackling intruders. In the background, like voices in a bad dream, loudhailers continued to announce that the area was being evacuated. Most of the amplified voices were now retreating toward Little Bitch.

"I want that car gone when we get back," Junior said. "Or I *will* fuck you up."

They left. Carolyn dressed herself, then helped Thurston—his stomach hurt too much for him to bend over and put on his own shoes. By the time they were finished, both of them were crying. In the car, on their way back down the camp lane that led to Little Bitch Road, Carolyn tried to reach her father on her cell. She got nothing but silence.

At the intersection of Little Bitch and Route 119, a town police car was pulled across the road. A stocky female cop with red hair pointed at the soft shoulder, then waved at them to use it. Carolyn pulled over instead, and got out. She held up her puffy wrist.

"We were assaulted! By two guys calling themselves cops! One named Junior and one named Frankie! They—"

"Get your ass gone or I'll assault you myself," Georgia Roux said. "I ain't shittin, honeypie."

Carolyn stared at her, stunned. The whole world had turned sideways and slipped into a *Twilight Zone* episode while she was asleep. That had to be it; no other explanation made even marginal sense. They'd hear the Rod Serling voice-over anytime now.

She got back into the Volvo (the sticker on the bumper, faded but still readable: OBAMA '12! YES WE **STILL** CAN) and detoured around the police car. Another, older cop was sitting inside it, going over a checklist on a clipboard. She thought of appealing to him, then thought better of it.

"Try the radio," she said. "Let's find out if something really *is* going on."

Thurston turned it on and got nothing but Elvis Presley and the Jordanaires, trudging through "How Great Thou Art."

Carolyn snapped it off, thought of saying *The nightmare is officially complete,* and didn't. All she wanted was to get out of Weirdsville as soon as possible.

2

On the map, the Chester Pond camp road was a thin hooklike thread, almost not there. After leaving the Marshall cabin, Junior and Frankie sat for a moment in Frankie's car, studying this.

"Can't be anybody else down there," Frankie said. "Not at this time of the year. What do you think? Say fuck it and go back to town?" He cocked a thumb at the cabin.

"They'll be along, and if they're not, who really gives a shit?"

Junior considered it for a moment, then shook his head. They had taken the Oath of Duty. Besides, he wasn't anxious to get back and face his father's pestering about what he'd done with the Reverend's body. Coggins was now keeping his girlfriends company in the McCain pantry, but there was no need for his dad to know that. At least not until the big man figured out how to nail Barbara with it. And Junior believed his father *would* figure it out. If there was one thing Big Jim Rennie was good at, it was nailing people.

Now it doesn't even matter if he finds out I left school, Junior thought, *because I know worse about him. Way worse.*

Not that dropping out seemed very important now; it was chump change compared to what was going on in The Mill. But he'd have to be careful, just the same. Junior wouldn't put it past his father to nail *him,* if the situation seemed to call for it.

"Junior? Earth to Junior."

"I'm here," he said, a little irritated.

"Back to town?"

"Let's check out the other cabins. It's only a quarter of a mile, and if we go back to town, Randolph'll find something else for us to do."

"Wouldn't mind a little chow, though."

"Where? At Sweetbriar? Want some rat poison in your scrambled eggs, courtesy of Dale Barbara?"

"He wouldn't dare."

"You positive?"

"Okay, okay." Frankie started the car and backed down the little stub of driveway. The brightly colored leaves hung moveless on the trees, and the air felt sultry. More like July than October. "But the Massholes better be gone when we come back, or I just might have to introduce Titsy McGee to my helmeted avenger."

"I'll be happy to hold her down," Junior said. "Yippee-ki-yi-yay, motherfucker."

3

The first three cabins were clearly empty; they didn't even bother getting out of the car. By now the camp road was down to a pair of wheelruts with a grassy hump between them. Trees overhung it on both sides, some of the lower branches almost close enough to scrape the roof.

"I think the last one's just around this curve," Frankie said. "The road ends at this shitpot little boat land—"

"Look out!" Junior shouted.

They came out of the blind curve and two kids, a boy and a girl, were standing in the road. They made no effort to get out of the way. Their faces were shocked and blank. If Frankie hadn't been afraid of tearing the Toyota's exhaust system out on the camp road's center hump—if he'd been making any kind of speed at all—he would have hit them. Instead he stood on the brake, and the car stopped two feet short.

"Oh my God, that was close," he said. "I think I'm having a heart attack."

"If my father didn't, you won't," Junior said.

"Huh?"

"Never mind." Junior got out. The kids were still standing there. The girl was taller and older. Maybe nine. The boy looked about five. Their faces were pale and dirty. She was holding his hand. She looked up at Junior, but the boy looked straight ahead, as if examining something of interest in the Toyota's driver's side headlamp.

Junior saw the terror on her face and dropped to one knee in front of her. "Honey, are you okay?"

It was the boy who answered. He spoke while still examining the headlamp. "I want my mother. And I want my breffus."

Frankie joined him. "Are they real?" Speaking in a voice that said *I'm joking, but not really.* He reached out and touched the girl's arm.

She jumped a little, and looked at him. "Mumma didn't come back." She spoke in a low voice.

"What's your name, hon?" Junior asked. "And who's your mommy?"

"I'm Alice Rachel Appleton," she said. "This is Aidan Patrick Appleton. Our mother is Vera Appleton. Our father is Edward Appleton, but he and Mommy got a divorce last year and now he lives in Plano, Texas. We live in Weston, Massachusetts, at Sixteen Oak Way. Our telephone number is—" She recited it with the toneless accuracy of a directory assistance recording.

Junior thought, *Oh boy. More Massholes.* But it made sense; who else would burn expensive gasoline just to watch the fucking leaves fall off the fucking trees?

Frankie was also kneeling now. "Alice," he said, "listen to me, sweetheart. Where is your mother now?"

"Don't know," Tears—big clear globes—began to roll down her cheeks. "We came to see the leaves. Also, we were going to go in the kayak. We like the kayak, don't we, Aide?"

"I'm hungry," Aidan said mournfully, and then he too began to cry.

Seeing them like that made Junior feel like crying himself. He reminded himself he was a cop. Cops didn't cry, at least not on duty. He asked the girl again where her mother was, but it was the little boy who answered.

"She went to get Woops."

"He means Whoopie Pies," Alice said. "But she went to get other stuff, too. Because Mr. Killian didn't caretake the cabin like he was supposed to. Mommy said I could take care of Aidan because I'm a big girl now and she'd be right back, she was only going to Yoder's. She just said don't let Aide go near the pond."

Junior was starting to get the picture. Apparently the woman had expected to find the cabin stocked with food—a few staples, at least—but if she'd known Roger Killian well, she would have known better than to depend on him. The man was a class-A dumbbell, and had passed his less-than-sterling intellect on to his entire brood. Yoder's was a nasty little store just across the Tarker's Mills town line specializing in beer, coffee brandy, and canned spaghetti. Ordinarily it would have been a twenty-minute run there and another twenty back. Only she hadn't come back, and Junior knew why.

"Did she go Saturday morning?" he asked. "She did, didn't she?"

"I *want* her!" Aidan cried. "And I want my *breffus*! My belly hurts!"

"Yes," the girl said. "Saturday morning. We were watching cartoons, only now we can't watch anything, because the electricity's broke."

Junior and Frankie looked at each other. Two nights alone in the dark. The girl maybe nine, the boy about five. Junior didn't like to think about that.

"Did you have anything to eat?" Frankie asked Alice Appleton. "Sweetheart? Anything at all?"

"There was a onion in the vegetable draw," she whispered. "We each had half. With sugar."

"Oh, fuck," Frankie said. Then: "I didn't say that. You didn't hear me say that. Just a second." He went back to the car, opened the passenger door, and began to rummage in the glove compartment.

"Where were you going, Alice?" Junior asked.

"To town. To look for Mommy and to find something to eat. We were going to walk past the next camp and then cut through the woods." She pointed vaguely north. "I thought that would be quicker."

Junior smiled, but he was cold inside. She wasn't pointing toward Chester's Mill; she was pointing in the direction of TR-90. At nothing but miles of tangled second-growth and boggy sumps. Plus the Dome, of course. Out there, Alice and Aidan would almost certainly have died of starvation; Hansel and Gretel minus the happy ending.

And we came so close to turning around. Jesus.

Frankie returned. He had a Milky Way. It looked old and squashed, but it was still in the wrapper. The way the children fixed their eyes on it made Junior think of the kids you saw on the news sometimes. That look on American faces was unreal, horrible.

"It's all I could find," Frankie said, stripping off the wrapper. "We'll get you something better in town."

He broke the Milky Way in two and gave a piece to each child. The candy was gone in five seconds. When he had finished his piece, the boy stuck his fingers knuckle-deep into his mouth. His cheeks hollowed rhythmically in and out as he sucked them.

Like a dog licking grease off a stick, Junior thought.

He turned to Frankie. "Never mind waiting until we get back to town. We're gonna stop at the cabin where the old man and the chick were. And whatever they got, these kids are going to get it."

Frankie nodded and picked up the boy. Junior picked up the little girl. He could smell her sweat, her fear. He stroked her hair as if he could stroke that oily reek away.

"You're all right, honey," he said. "You and your brother both. You're all right. You're safe."

"Do you promise?"

"Yes."

Her arms tightened around his neck. It was one of the best things Junior had ever felt in his life.

4

The western side of Chester's Mill was the least populated part of town, and by quarter of nine that morning it was almost entirely clear. The only police car left on Little Bitch was Unit 2. Jackie Wettington was driving and Linda Everett was riding shotgun. Chief Perkins, a smalltown cop of the old school, would never have sent two women out together, but of course Chief Perkins was no longer in charge, and the women themselves enjoyed the novelty. Men, especially male cops with their endless yee-haw banter, could be tiring.

"Ready to go back?" Jackie asked. "Sweetbriar'll be closed, but we might be able to beg a cup of coffee."

Linda didn't reply. She was thinking about where the Dome cut across Little Bitch. Going out there had been unsettling, and not just because the sentries were still standing with their backs turned, and hadn't budged when she gave them a good morning through the car's roof speaker. It was unsettling because there was now a great big red X spray-painted on the Dome, hanging in midair like a sci-fi hologram. That was the projected point of impact. It seemed impossible that a missile fired from two or three hundred miles away could hit such a small spot, but Rusty had assured her that it could.

"Lin?"

She came back to the here and now. "Sure, I'm ready if you are."

The radio crackled. "Unit Two, Unit Two, do you read, over?"

Linda unracked the mike. "Base, this is Two. We hear you, Stacey, but reception out here isn't very good, over?"

"Everybody says the same," Stacey Moggin replied. "It's worse near the Dome, better as you get closer to town. But you're still on Little Bitch, right? Over."

"Yes," Linda said. "Just checked the Killians and the Bouchers. Both gone. If that missile busts through, Roger Killian's going to have a lot of roast chickens, over."

"We'll have a picnic. Pete wants to talk to you. Chief Randolph, I mean. Over."

Jackie pulled the cruiser to the side of the road. There was a pause with static crackling in it, then Randolph came on. He didn't bother with any *overs,* never had.

"Did you check the church, Unit Two?"

"Holy Redeemer?" Linda asked. "Over."

"That's the only one I know out there, Officer Everett. Unless a Hindu mosque grew overnight."

Linda didn't think Hindus were the ones who worshipped in mosques, but this didn't seem like the right time for corrections. Randolph sounded tired and grouchy. "Holy Redeemer wasn't in our sector," she said. "That one belonged to a couple of the new cops. Thibodeau and Searles, I think. Over."

"Check it again," Randolph said, sounding more irritable than ever. "No one's seen Coggins, and a couple of his parishioners want to canoodle with him, or whatever they call it."

Jackie put a finger to her temple and mimed shooting herself. Linda, who wanted to get back and check on her kids at Marta Edmunds's house, nodded.

"Roger that, Chief," Linda said. "Will do. Over."

"Check the parsonage, too." There was a pause. "Also the radio station. The damn thing keeps bellowing away, so there must be someone there."

"Will do." She started to say *over and out,* then thought of something else. "Chief, is there anything new on the TV? Has the President said anything? Over?"

"I don't have time to listen to every word that guy drops out of his silly mouth. Just go on and hunt up the padre and tell him to get his butt back here. And get your butts back, too. Out."

Linda racked the mike and looked at Jackie.

"Get our butts back there?" Jackie said. "Our *butts?*"

"*He's* a butt," Linda said.

The remark was supposed to be funny, but it fell flat. For a moment they just sat in the idling car, not talking. Then Jackie spoke in a voice that was almost too low to be heard. "This is so bad."

"Randolph instead of Perkins, you mean?"

"That, and the new cops." She gave the last word verbal quotation marks. "Those *kids.* You know what? When I was punching in, Henry Morrison told me Randolph hired two more this morning. They came in off the street with Carter Thibodeau and Pete just signed em up, no questions asked."

Linda knew the sort of guys who hung out with Carter, either at Dipper's or at the Gas & Grocery, where they used the garage to tune up their finance-company motor-cycles. "Two *more? Why?*"

"Pete told Henry we might need em if that missile doesn't work. 'To make sure the situation doesn't get out of hand,' he said. And you know who put *that* idea in his head."

Linda knew, all right. "At least they're not carrying guns."

"A couple are. Not department issue; their personals.

By tomorrow—if this doesn't end today, that is—they all
will be. And as of this morning Pete's letting them ride
together instead of pairing them with real cops. Some
training period, huh? Twenty-four hours, give or take.
Do you realize those kids now outnumber us?"

Linda considered this silently.

"Hitler Youth," Jackie said. "That's what I keep thinking. Probably overreacting, but I hope to God this thing
ends today and I don't have to find out."

"I can't quite see Peter Randolph as Hitler."

"Me, either. I see him more as Hermann Goering. It's
Rennie I think of when I think of Hitler." She put the
cruiser in gear, made a K-turn, and headed them back
toward Christ the Holy Redeemer Church.

5

The church was unlocked and empty, the generator off.
The parsonage was silent, but Reverend Coggins's Chevrolet was parked in the little garage. Peering in, Linda
could read two stickers on the bumper. The one on the
right: IF THE RAPTURE'S TODAY, SOMEBODY
GRAB MY STEERING WHEEL! The one on the left
boasted MY OTHER CAR IS A 10-SPEED.

Linda called the second one to Jackie's attention. "He
does have a bike—I've seen him riding it. But I don't see it
in the garage, so maybe he rode it into town. Saving gas."

"Maybe," Jackie said. "And maybe we ought to check
the house to make sure he didn't slip in the shower and
break his neck."

"Does that mean we might have to look at him naked?"

"No one said police work was pretty," Jackie said.
"Come on."

The house was locked, but in towns where seasonal residents form a large part of the population, the police are adept at gaining entry. They checked the usual places for a spare key. Jackie was the one who found it, hanging on a hook behind a kitchen shutter. It opened the back door.

"Reverend Coggins?" Linda called, sticking her head in. "It's the police, Reverend Coggins, are you here?"

No answer. They went in. The lower floor was neat and orderly, but it gave Linda an uncomfortable feeling. She told herself it was just being in someone else's house. A *religious* person's house, and uninvited.

Jackie went upstairs. "Reverend Coggins? Police. If you're here, please make yourself known."

Linda stood at the foot of the stairs, looking up. The house felt *wrong,* somehow. That made her think of Janelle, shaking in the grip of her seizure. That had been wrong, too. A queer certainty stole into her mind: if Janelle were here right now, she would have another seizure. Yes, and start talking about queer things. Halloween and the Great Pumpkin, maybe.

It was a perfectly ordinary flight of stairs, but she didn't want to go up there, just wanted Jackie to report the place was empty so they could go on to the radio station. But when her partner called for her to come up, Linda did.

6

Jackie was standing in the middle of Coggins's bedroom. There was a plain wooden cross on one wall and a plaque on another. The plaque read HIS EYE IS ON THE SPAR-ROW. The coverlet of the bed was turned back. There were traces of blood on the sheet beneath.

"And this," Jackie said. "Come around here."

Reluctantly, Linda did. Lying on the polished wood floor between the bed and the wall was a knotted length of rope. The knots were bloody.

"Looks like somebody beat him," Jackie said grimly. "Hard enough to knock him out, maybe. Then they laid him on the . . ." She looked at the other woman. "No?"

"I take it you didn't grow up in a religious home," Linda said.

"I did so. We worshipped the Holy Trinity: Santa Claus, the Easter Bunny, and the Tooth Fairy. What about you?"

"Plain old tapwater Baptist, but I heard about things like this. I think he was flagellating himself."

"Yug! People did that for sins, right?"

"Yes. And I don't think it ever went entirely out of style."

"Then this makes sense. Sort of. Go in the bathroom and look on the toilet tank."

Linda made no move to do so. The knotted rope was bad enough, the feel of the house—too empty, somehow—was worse.

"Go on. It's nothing that'll bite you, and I'll bet you a dollar to a dime that you've seen worse."

Linda went into the bathroom. Two magazines were lying on top of the toilet tank. One was a devotional, *The Upper Room*. The other was called *Young Oriental Slits*. Linda doubted if that one was sold in many religious book-shops.

"So," Jackie said. "Are we getting a picture here? He sits on the john, tosses the truffle—"

"Tosses the *truffle*?" Linda giggled in spite of her nerves. Or because of them.

"It's what my mother used to call it," Jackie said. "Anyway, after he's done with that, he opens a medium-sized can of whoop-ass to expiate his sins, then goes to bed and has happy Asian dreams. This morning he gets up, refreshed and sin-free, does his morning devotionals, then rides into town on his bike. Make sense?"

It did. It just didn't explain why the house felt so wrong to her. "Let's check the radio station," she said. "Then we'll head into town ourselves and get coffee. I'm buying."

"Good," Jackie said. "I want mine black. Preferably in a hypo."

7

The low-slung, mostly glass WCIK studio was also locked, but speakers mounted beneath the eaves were playing "Good Night, Sweet Jesus" as interpreted by that noted soul singer Perry Como. Behind the studio the broadcast tower loomed, the flashing red lights at the top barely visible in the strong morning light. Near the tower was a long barnlike structure which Linda assumed must hold the station's generator and whatever other supplies it needed to keep beaming the miracle of God's love to western Maine, eastern New Hampshire, and possibly the inner planets of the solar system.

Jackie knocked, then hammered.

"I don't think anybody's here," Linda said . . . but this place seemed wrong, too. And the air had a funny smell, stale and sallow. It reminded her of the way her mother's kitchen smelled, even after a good airing. Because her mother smoked like a chimney and believed the only things worth eating were those fried in a hot skillet greased with plenty of lard.

Jackie shook her head. "We heard someone, didn't we?"

Linda had no answer for that, because it was true. They had been listening to the station on their drive from the parsonage, and had heard a smooth deejay announcing the next record as "Another message of God's love in song."

This time the hunt for the key was longer, but Jackie finally found it in an envelope taped beneath the mailbox. With it was a scrap of paper on which someone had scrawled 1 6 9 3.

The key was a dupe, and a little sticky, but after some chivvying, it worked. As soon as they were in, they heard the steady beep of the security system. The keypad was on the wall. When Jackie punched in the numbers, the beeping quit. Now there was only the music. Perry Como had given way to something instrumental; Linda thought it sounded suspiciously like the organ solo from "In-A-Gadda-Da-Vida." The speakers in here were a thousand times better than the ones outside and the music was louder, almost like a living thing.

Did people work in this holier-than-thou racket? Linda wondered. *Answer the phones? Do business? How could they?*

There was something wrong in here, too. Linda was sure of it. The place felt more than creepy to her; it felt outright dangerous. When she saw that Jackie had unsnapped the strap on her service automatic, Linda did the same. The feel of the gun-butt under her hand was good. *Thy rod and thy gun-butt, they comfort me,* she thought.

"Hello?" Jackie called. "Reverend Coggins? Anybody?"

There was no answer. The reception desk was empty. To the left of it were two closed doors. Straight ahead was a window running the entire length of the main room. Linda could see blinking lights inside it. The broadcast studio, she assumed.

Jackie pushed the closed doors open with her foot, standing well back. Behind one was an office. Behind the other was a conference room of surprising luxury, dominated by a giant flat-screen TV. It was on, but muted. Anderson Cooper, almost life-sized, looked like he was doing his standup on Castle Rock's Main Street. The buildings were draped with flags and yellow ribbons. Linda saw a sign on the hardware store that read: SET THEM FREE. That made Linda feel even eerier. The super running across the bottom of the screen read DEFENSE DEPARTMENT SOURCES CLAIM MISSILE STRIKE IS IMMINENT.

"Why is the TV on?" Jackie asked.

"Because whoever was minding the store left it that way when—"

A booming voice interrupted her. "That was Raymond Howell's version of 'Christ My Lord and Leader.' "

Both women jumped.

"And this is Norman Drake, reminding you of three important facts: you're listening to the Revival Time Hour on WCIK, God loves you, and He sent his Son to die for you on Calvary's cross. It's nine twenty-five AM, and as we always like to remind you, time is short. Have you given *your* heart to the Lord? Back after this."

Norman Drake gave way to a silver-tongued devil selling the entire Bible on DVDs, and the best thing about it was you could pay in monthly installments and return the whole deal if you weren't just as happy as a pig in shit. Linda and Jackie went to the broadcast studio window and looked in. Neither Norman Drake nor the silver-tongued devil was there, but when the commercial ended and the deejay came back to announce the next song of praise, a green light turned red and a red light turned green. When the music started up, another red light went green.

"It's automated!" Jackie said. "The whole freaking thing!"

"Then why do we feel like someone's here? And don't say you don't."

Jackie didn't. "Because it's weird. The jock even does time-checks. Honey, this setup must have cost a fortune! Talk about the ghost in the machine—how long do you think it will run?"

"Probably till the propane runs out and the generator stops." Linda spotted another closed door and opened it with her foot, as Jackie had . . . only, unlike Jackie, she drew her gun and held it, safety on and muzzle down, beside her leg.

It was a bathroom, and it was empty. There was, however, a picture of a very Caucasian Jesus on the wall.

"I'm not religious," Jackie said, "so you'll have to explain to me why people would want Jesus watching them poop."

Linda shook her head. "Let's get out of here before I lose it," she said. "This place is the Radioland version of the *Mary Celeste.*"

Jackie looked around uneasily. "Well, the vibe is spooky, I'll give you that." She suddenly raised her voice in a harsh shout that made Linda jump. She wanted to tell Jackie not to yell like that. Because someone might hear her and come. Or some*thing.*

"Hey! Yo! Anybody here? Last chance!"

Nothing. No one.

Outside, Linda took a deep breath. "Once, when I was a teenager, some friends and I went to Bar Harbor, and we stopped for a picnic at this scenic turnout. There were half a dozen of us. The day was clear, and you could see practically all the way to Ireland. When we were done eating, I said I wanted to take a picture. My friends were all horsing around and grabassing, and I kept backing up, trying to get everyone in the frame. Then this one girl—Arabella, my best friend back then—stopped trying to give this other girl a wedgie and shouted, 'Stop, Linda, *stop*!' I stopped and looked around. Know what I saw?"

Jackie shook her head.

"The Atlantic Ocean. I'd backed up all the way to the drop-off at the edge of the picnic area. There was a warning sign, but no fence or guardrail. One more step and I would have gone down. And how I felt then is how I felt in there."

"Lin, it was *empty*."

"I don't think so. And I don't think you do, either."

"It was spooky, sure. But we checked the rooms—"

"Not the studio. Plus the TV was on and the music was too loud. You don't think they turn it up that loud ordinarily, do you?"

"How do I know what holy rollers do?" Jackie asked. "Maybe they were expecting the Apocolick."

"*Lypse.*"

"Whatever. Do you want to check the storage barn?"

"Absolutely not," Linda said, and that made Jackie snort laughter.

"Okay. Our report is no sign of the Rev, correct?"

"Correct."

"Then we're off to town. And coffee."

Before getting into Unit Two's shotgun seat, Linda took one more look at the studio building, sitting there wreathed in whitebread audio joy. There was no other sound; she realized she didn't hear a single bird singing, and wondered if they had all killed themselves smashing into the Dome. Surely that wasn't possible. Was it?

Jackie pointed at the mike. "Want me to give the place a shout through the loudspeaker? Say if anyone's hiding in there they should beat feet into town? Because—I just thought of this—maybe they were scared of us."

"What I want is for you to stop screwing around and get out of here."

Jackie didn't argue. She reversed down the short driveway to Little Bitch Road, and turned the cruiser toward The Mill.

8

Time passed. Religious music played. Norman Drake returned and announced that it was nine thirty-four, Eastern Daylight God Loves You Time. This was followed by an ad for Jim Rennie's Used Cars, delivered by the Second Selectman himself. "It's our annual Fall Sales Spectacular, and boy, did we overstock!" Big Jim said in a rueful the-joke's-on-me voice. "We've got Fords, Chevvies, Plymouths! We've got the hard-to-get Dodge Ram and even the harder-to-get Mustang! Folks, I'm sitting on not one or two but *three* Mustangs that are like new, one the famous V6 convertible, and each comes with the famous Jim Rennie Christian Guarantee. We service what we sell, we finance, and we do it all at low low prices. And right now"—he chuckled more ruefully than ever—"we've just *GOT* to clear this *LOT*! So come on down! The coffeepot's always on, neighbor, and you'll love the feelin when Big Jim's dealin!"

A door neither woman had noticed eased open at the back of the studio. Inside were more blinking lights—a galaxy of them. The room was little more than a cubby choked with wires, splitters, routers, and electronic boxes. You would have said there was no room for a man. But The Chef was beyond skinny; he was emaciated. His eyes were only glitters sunk deep in his skull. His skin was pale and blotchy. His lips folded loosely inward over gums that had lost most of their teeth. His shirt and pants were filthy, and his hips were naked wings; Chef's underwear days were now just a memory. It is doubtful that Sammy Bushey would have recognized her missing husband. He had a peanut butter and jelly sandwich in one hand (he could only eat soft things now) and a Glock 9 in the other.

He went to the window overlooking the parking lot, thinking he'd rush out and kill the intruders if they were still there; he had almost done it while they were inside. Only he'd been afraid. Because demons couldn't actually be killed. When their human bodies died, they just flew into another host. When they were between bodies, the demons looked like blackbirds. Chef had seen this in vivid dreams that came on the increasingly rare occasions when he slept.

They were gone, however. His *atman* had been too strong for them.

Rennie had told him he had to shut down out back, and Chef Bushey had, but he might have to start up some of the cookers again, because there had been a big shipment to Boston a week ago and he was almost out of product. He needed smoke. It was what his *atman* fed on these days.

But for now he had enough. He had given up on the blues music that had been so important to him in his Phil Bushey stage of life—B. B. King, Koko and Hound Dog Taylor, Muddy and Howlin' Wolf, even the immortal Little Walter—and he had given up on fucking; he had even pretty much given up on moving his bowels, had been constipated since July. But that was okay. What humiliated the body fed the *atman*.

He checked the parking lot and the road beyond once more to make sure the demons weren't lurking, then tucked the automatic into his belt at the small of his back and headed for the storage shed, which was actually more of a factory these days. A factory that was shut down, but he could and would fix that if necessary.

Chef went to get his pipe.

9

Rusty Everett stood looking into the storage shed behind the hospital. He was using a flashlight, because he and Ginny Tomlinson—now the administrative head of medical services in Chester's Mill, crazy as that was—had decided to kill the power to every part of the plant that didn't absolutely need it. From his left, in its own shed, he could hear the big generator roaring away, eating ever deeper into the current long tank of propane.

Most of the tanks are gone, Twitch had said, and by God, they were. *According to the card on the door, there's supposed to be seven, but there's only two.* On that, Twitch was wrong. There was only one. Rusty ran the beam of his flashlight over the blue **CR HOSP** stenciled on the tank's silver side below the supply company's Dead River logo.

"Told you," Twitch said from behind him, making Rusty jump.

"You told me wrong. There's only one."

"Bullshit!" Twitch stepped into the doorway. Looked while Rusty shone the beam around, highlighting boxes of supplies surrounding a large—and largely empty—center area. Said: "It's *not* bullshit."

"No."

"Fearless leader, someone is stealing our propane."

Rusty didn't want to believe this, but saw no way around it.

Twitch squatted down. "Look here."

Rusty dropped to one knee. The quarter-acre behind

the hospital had been asphalted the previous summer, and without any cold weather to crack or buckle it—not yet, anyway—the area was a smooth black sheet. It made it easy to see the tire tracks in front of the shed's sliding doors.

"That looks like it could have been a town truck," Twitch remarked.

"Or any other big truck."

"Nevertheless, you might want to check the storage shed behind the Town Hall. Twitch no trust-um Big Chief Rennie. Him bad medicine."

"Why would he take our propane? The Selectmen have plenty of their own."

They walked to the door leading into the hospital's laundry—also shut down, at least for the time being. There was a bench beside the door. A sign posted on the bricks read SMOKING HERE WILL BE BANNED AS OF JANUARY 1ST. QUIT NOW AND AVOID THE RUSH!

Twitch took out his Marlboros and offered them to Rusty. Rusty waved them away, then reconsidered and took one. Twitch lit them up. "How do you know?" he asked.

"How do I know what?"

"That they've got plenty of their own. Have you checked?"

"No," Rusty said. "But if they *were* going to poach, why from us? Not only is stealing from the local hospital usually considered bad form by the better class of people, the post office is practically right next door. They must have some."

"Maybe Rennie and his friends already snatched the post office's gas. How much would they have, anyway? One tank? Two? Peanuts."

"I don't understand why they'd need *any*. It makes no sense."

"Nothing about any of this makes sense," Twitch said, and yawned so hugely that Rusty could hear his jaws creak.

"You finished rounds, I take it?" Rusty had a moment to consider the surreal quality of that question. Since Haskell's death, Rusty had become the hospital's head doc, and Twitch—a nurse just three days ago—was now what Rusty had been: a physician's assistant.

"Yep." Twitch sighed. "Mr. Carty isn't going to live out the day."

Rusty had thought the same thing about Ed Carty, who was suffering from end-stage stomach cancer, a week ago, and the man was still hanging in. "Comatose?"

"Roger that, sensei."

Twitch was able to count their other patients off on the digits of one hand—which, Rusty knew, was extraordinarily lucky. He thought he might even have felt lucky, if he hadn't been so tired and worried.

"George Werner I'd call stable."

Werner, an Eastchester resident, sixty years old and obese, had suffered a myocardial infarction on Dome Day. Rusty thought he would pull through . . . this time.

"As for Emily Whitehouse . . ." Twitch shrugged. "It ain't good, sensei."

Emmy Whitehouse, forty years old and not even an ounce overweight, had suffered her own MI an hour or so after Rory Dinsmore's accident. It had been much worse than George Werner's because she'd been an exercise freak and had suffered what Doc Haskell had called "a health-club blowout."

"The Freeman girl is getting better, Jimmy Sirois is holding up, and Nora Coveland is totally cool. Out after lunch. On the whole, not so bad."

"No," Rusty said, "but it'll get worse. I guarantee you.

And . . . if you suffered a catastrophic head injury, would you want me to operate on you?"

"Not really," Twitch said. "I keep hoping Gregory House will show up."

Rusty butted his cigarette in the can and looked at the nearly empty supply shed. Maybe he *should* have a peek into the storage facility behind the Town Hall—what could it hurt?

This time he was the one who yawned.

"How long can you keep this up?" Twitch asked. All the banter had gone out of his voice. "I only ask because right now you're what this town's got."

"As long as I have to. What worries me is getting so tired I screw something up. And of facing stuff that's way beyond my skill set." He thought of Rory Dinsmore . . . and Jimmy Sirois. Thinking of Jimmy was worse, because Rory was now beyond the possibility of medical mistakes. Jimmy, on the other hand . . .

Rusty saw himself back in the operating room, listening to the soft bleep of the equipment. Saw himself looking down at Jimmy's pale bare leg, with a black line drawn on it where the cut would have to be made. Thought of Dougie Twitchell trying out his anesthesiologist skills. Felt Ginny Tomlinson slapping a scalpel into his gloved hand and then looking at him over the top of her mask with her cool blue eyes.

God spare me from that, he thought.

Twitch put a hand on Rusty's arm. "Take it easy," he said. "One day at a time."

"Fuck that, one *hour* at a time," Rusty said, and got up. "I have to go over to the Health Center, see what's shaking there. Thank *Christ* this didn't happen in the summer; we would've had three thousand tourists and seven hundred summer-camp kids on our hands."

"Want me to come?"

Rusty shook his head. "Check on Ed Carty again, why don't you? See if he's still in the land of the living."

Rusty took one more look at the supply shed, then plodded around the corner of the building and on a diagonal toward the Health Center on the far side of Catherine Russell Drive.

10

Ginny was at the hospital, of course; she would give Mrs. Coveland's new bundle of joy a final weigh-in before sending them home. The receptionist on duty at the Health Center was seventeen-year-old Gina Buffalino, who had exactly six weeks' worth of medical experience. As a candy striper. She gave Rusty a deer-in-the-headlights look when he came in that made his heart sink, but the waiting room was empty, and that was a good thing. A *very* good thing.

"Any call-ins?" Rusty asked.

"One. Mrs. Venziano, out on the Black Ridge Road. Her baby got his head caught between the bars of his playpen. She wanted an ambulance. I . . . I told her to grease the kid's head up with olive oil and see if she could get him out that way. It worked."

Rusty grinned. Maybe there was hope for this kid yet. Gina, looking divinely relieved, grinned back.

"Place is empty, at least," Rusty said. "Which is great."

"Not quite. Ms. Grinnell is here—Andrea? I put her in three." Gina hesitated. "She seemed pretty upset."

Rusty's heart, which had begun to rise, sank back down again. Andrea Grinnell. And upset. Which meant she wanted a bump on her OxyContin prescription. Which he, in all good conscience, could not give, even supposing Andy Sanders had enough stock to fill it.

"Okay." He started down the hall to exam room three, then stopped and looked back. "You didn't page me."

Gina flushed. "She asked me specifically not to."

This puzzled Rusty, but only for a second. Andrea might have a pill problem, but she was no dummy. She'd known that if Rusty was over at the hospital, he was probably with Twitch. And Dougie Twitchell happened to be her baby brother, who even at the age of thirty-nine must be protected from the evil facts of life.

Rusty stood at the door with the black **3** decaled on it, trying to gather himself. This was going to be hard. Andrea wasn't one of the defiant boozers he saw who claimed that alcohol formed absolutely no part of their problems; nor was she one of the meth-heads who had been showing up with increasing frequency over the last year or so. Andrea's responsibility for her problem was more difficult to pinpoint, and that complicated the treatment. Certainly she'd been in agony after her fall. Oxy had been the best thing for her, allowing her to cope with the pain so she could sleep and begin therapy. It wasn't her fault that the drug which allowed her to do those things was the one doctors sometimes called hillbilly heroin.

He opened the door and went in, rehearsing his refusal. *Kind but firm,* he told himself. *Kind but firm.*

She was sitting in the corner chair under the cholesterol poster, knees together, head bowed over the purse in her lap. She was a big woman who now looked small. Diminished, somehow. When she raised her head to look at him and he saw how haggard her face was—the lines bracketing her mouth deep, the skin under her eyes almost black—he changed his mind and decided to write the scrip on one of Dr. Haskell's pink pads after all. Maybe after the Dome crisis was over, he'd try to get her into a detox program; threaten to tattle to her brother, if that was what it took. Now, however, he would give her what she needed. Because he had rarely seen need so stark.

"Eric . . . Rusty . . . I'm in trouble."

"I know. I can see it. I'll write you a——"

"No!" She was looking at him with something like horror. "Not even if I beg! I'm a drug addict and I have to get off! I'm just a darn old *junkie*!" Her face folded in on itself. She tried to will it straight again and couldn't. She put her hands over it instead. Big wrenching sobs that were hard to listen to came through her fingers.

Rusty went to her, going down on one knee and putting an arm around her. "Andrea, it's good that you want to stop—excellent—but this might not be the best time—"

She looked at him with streaming, reddened eyes. "You're right about that, it's the *worst* time, but it has to be now! And you mustn't tell Dougie or Rose. Can you help me? Can it even be done? Because I haven't been able to, not on my own. Those hateful pink pills! I put them in the medicine cabinet and say 'No more today,' and an hour later I'm taking them down again! I've never been in a mess like this, not in my whole life."

She dropped her voice as if confiding a great secret.

"I don't think it's my back anymore, I think it's my *brain* telling my back to hurt so I can go on taking those damn pills."

"Why now, Andrea?"

She only shook her head. "Can you help me or not?"

"Yes, but if you're thinking about going cold turkey, don't. For one thing, you're apt to . . ." For a brief moment he saw Jannie, shaking in her bed, muttering about the Great Pumpkin. "You're apt to have seizures."

She either didn't register that or set it aside. "How long?"

"To get past the physical part? Two weeks. Maybe three." *And that's putting you on the fast track,* he thought but didn't say.

She gripped his arm. Her hand was very cold. "Too slow."

An exceedingly unpleasant idea surfaced in Rusty's mind. Probably just transient paranoia brought on by stress, but persuasive. "Andrea, is someone blackmailing you?"

"Are you kidding? Everyone knows I take those pills, it's a small town." Which did not, in Rusty's opinion, actually answer the question. "What's the absolute shortest it can take?"

"With B_{12} shots—plus thiamine and vitamins—you might manage it in ten days. But you'd be miserable. You wouldn't be able to sleep much, and you'll have restless leg syndrome. Not mild, either, they don't call it kicking the habit for nothing. And you'd have to have someone administer the step-down dosage—someone who can hold the pills and won't give them to you when you ask. Because you will."

"Ten days?" She looked hopeful. "And this might be over by then anyway, yes? This Dome thing?"

"Maybe this afternoon. That's what we all hope."

"Ten days," she said.

"Ten days."

And, he thought, *you'll want those goddam things for the rest of your life.* But this he didn't say aloud either.

11

Sweetbriar Rose had been extraordinarily busy for a Monday morning . . . but of course there had never been a Monday morning like this in the town's history. Still, the

patrons had left willingly enough when Rose announced
the grill was closed, and wouldn't reopen until five that
afternoon. "And by then, maybe you can all go over to
Moxie's in Castle Rock and eat there!" she finished. That
had brought spontaneous applause, even though Moxie's
was a famously filthy greasepit.

"No lunch?" Ernie Calvert asked.

Rose looked at Barbie, who raised his hands to his
shoulders. Don't ask me.

"Sandwiches," Rose said. "Until they're gone."

This had brought more applause. People seemed surprisingly upbeat this morning; there had been laughter
and raillery. Perhaps the best sign of the town's improved
mental health was at the rear of the restaurant, where the
bullshit table was back in session.

The TV over the counter—now locked on CNN—
was a big part of the reason. The talking heads had little
more to broadcast than rumors, but most were hopeful.
Several scientists who'd been interviewed said the Cruise
had a good chance of smashing through and ending the
crisis. One estimated the chances of success as "better
than eighty percent." *But of course he's at MIT in Cambridge,*
Barbie thought. *He can afford optimism.*

Now, as he scraped the grill, a knock came at the door.
Barbie looked around and saw Julia Shumway, with three
children clustered around her. They made her look like a
junior high school teacher on a field trip. Barbie went to
the door, wiping his hands on his apron.

"If we let everyone in who wants to eat, we'll be out of
food in no time," Anson said irritably from where he was
swabbing down tables. Rose had gone back to Food City
to try and purchase more meat.

"I don't think she wants to eat," Barbie said, and he
was right about that.

"Good morning, Colonel Barbara," Julia said with her little Mona Lisa smile. "I keep wanting to call you Major Barbara. Like the—"

"The play, I know." Barbie had heard this one a few times before. Like ten thousand. "Is this your posse?"

One of the children was an extremely tall, extremely skinny boy with a mop of dark brown hair; one was a stocky young fellow wearing baggy shorts and a faded 50 Cent tee-shirt; the third was a pretty little girl with a lightning bolt on her cheek. A decal rather than a tattoo, but it still gave her a certain savoir faire. He realized if he told her she looked like the middle-school version of Joan Jett, she wouldn't know who he was talking about.

"Norrie Calvert," Julia said, touching the riot grrl's shoulder. "Benny Drake. And this tall drink of water is Joseph McClatchey. Yesterday's protest demonstration was his idea."

"But I never meant anyone to get hurt," Joe said.

"And it wasn't your fault they did," Barbie told him. "So rest easy on that."

"Are you really the bull goose?" Benny asked, looking him over.

Barbie laughed. "No," he said. "I'm not even going to *try* and be the bull goose unless I absolutely have to."

"But you know the soldiers out there, right?" Norrie asked.

"Well, not personally. For one thing, they're Marines. I was Army."

"You're still Army, according to Colonel Cox," Julia said. She was wearing her cool little smile, but her eyes were dancing with excitement. "Can we talk to you? Young Mr. McClatchey has had an idea, and I think it's brilliant. If it works."

"It'll work," Joe said. "When it comes to computer shi—stuff, *I'm* the bull goose."

"Step into my office," Barbie said, and escorted them toward the counter.

12

It was brilliant, all right, but it was already going on ten thirty, and if they were really going to make this thing happen, they would have to move fast. He turned to Julia. "Do you have your cell ph—"

Julia slapped it smartly into his palm before he could finish. "Cox's number is in memory."

"Great. Now if I knew how to access the memory."

Joe took the phone. "What are you, from the Dark Ages?"

"Yes!" Barbie said. "When knights were bold and ladies fair went without their underwear."

Norrie laughed hard at that, and when she raised her fist, Barbie tapped her small fist with his big one.

Joe pushed a couple of buttons on the minuscule keypad. He listened, then handed the cell to Barbie.

Cox must still have been sitting with one hand on the phone, because he was already on when Barbie put Julia's cell to his ear.

"How's it going, Colonel?" Cox asked.

"We're basically okay."

"And that's a start."

Easy for you to say, Barbie thought. "I imagine things will remain basically okay until the missile either bounces off or punches through and does gross damage to the woods and farms on our side. Which the citizens of Chester's Mill would welcome. What are your guys saying?"

"Not much. No one is making any predictions."

"That's not what we're hearing on the TV."

"I don't have time to keep up with the talking heads." Barbie could hear the shrug in Cox's voice. "We're hopeful. We think we've got a shot. To coin a phrase."

Julia was opening and closing her hands in a *What gives?* gesture.

"Colonel Cox, I'm sitting here with four friends. One of them is a young man named Joe McClatchey, who's had a pretty cool idea. I'm going to put him on the phone with you right now—"

Joe was shaking his head hard enough to make his hair fly. Barbie paid no attention.

"—to explain it."

And he handed Joe the cell. "Talk," he said.

"But—"

"Don't argue with the bull goose, son. Talk."

Joe did so, diffidently at first, with a lot of *ah*s and *erm*s and *y'know*s, but as his idea took hold of him again he sped up, became articulate. Then he listened. After a little while he started to grin. A few moments later he said, "Yessir! Thank you, sir!" and handed the phone back to Barbie. "Check it out, they're gonna try to augment our Wi-Fi before they shoot the missile! Jesus, this is *hot*!" Julia grabbed his arm and Joe said, "I'm sorry, Miz Shumway, I mean *jeepers*."

"Never mind that, can you really work this thing?"

"You kidding? No prob."

"Colonel Cox?" Barbie asked. "Is this true about the Wi-Fi?"

"We can't stop anything you folks want to try to do," Cox said. "I think you were the one who originally pointed that out to me. So we might as well help. You'll have the fastest Internet in the world, at least for today. That's some bright kid you got there, by the way."

"Yes sir, that was my impression," Barbie said, and gave Joe a thumbs-up. The kid was glowing.

Cox said, "If the boy's idea works and you record it, make sure we get a copy. We'll be making our own, of course, but the scientists in charge of this thing will want to see what the hit looks like from your side of the Dome."

"I think we can do better than that," Barbie said. "If Joe here can put this together, I think most of the town will be able to watch it live."

This time Julia raised her fist. Grinning, Barbie bumped it.

13

"Holee shit," Joe said. The awe on his face made him look eight instead of thirteen. The whipcrack confidence was gone from his voice. He and Barbie were standing about thirty yards from where Little Bitch Road ran up against the Dome. It wasn't the soldiers he was looking at, although they had turned around to observe; it was the warning band and the big red **X** sprayed on the Dome that had fascinated him.

"They're moving their bivouac point, or whatever you call it," Julia said. "The tents are gone."

"Sure. In about"—Barbie looked at his watch—"ninety minutes, it's going to get very hot over there. Son, you better get to it." But now that they were actually out here on the deserted road, Barbie began to wonder if Joe could do what he had promised.

"Yeah, but . . . do you see the *trees?*"

Barbie didn't understand at first. He looked at Julia, who shrugged. Then Joe pointed, and he saw. The trees on the Tarker's side of the Dome were dancing in a moderate fall wind, shedding leaves in colorful bursts that fluttered down around the watching Marine sentries. On The Mill side, the branches were barely moving and most of the trees were still fully dressed. Barbie was pretty sure air was coming through the barrier, but not with any force. The Dome was damping the wind. He thought of how he and Paul Gendron, the guy in the Sea Dogs cap, had come to the little stream and had seen the water piling up.

Julia said, "The leaves over here look . . . I don't know . . . *listless,* somehow. Limp."

"It's just because they've got a wind on their side and we've only got a puff of breeze," Barbie said, then wondered if that was really it. Or *all* of it. But what good did it do to speculate about the current air quality in Chester's Mill, when there was nothing they could do about it? "Go on, Joe. Do your thing."

They had swung by the McClatchey house in Julia's Prius to get Joe's PowerBook. (Mrs. McClatchey had made Barbie swear he would keep her son safe, and Barbie had so sworn.) Now Joe pointed at the road. "Here?"

Barbie raised his hands to the sides of his face and sighted at the red **X**. "Little to the left. Can you try it? See how it looks?"

"Yeah." Joe opened the PowerBook and turned it on. The Mac power-up chime sounded as pretty as ever, but Barbie thought he had never seen anything quite so surreal as the silver computer sitting on the patched asphalt of Little Bitch Road with its screen up. It seemed to summarize the last three days perfectly.

"Battery's fresh, so it should run for at least six hours," Joe said.

"Won't it go to sleep?" Julia asked.

Joe gave her an indulgent *Mother, please* look. Then he

turned back to Barbie. "If the missile roasts my Pro, do you promise to buy me another one?"

"Uncle Sam will buy you another one," Barbie promised. "I'll put in the requisition myself."

"Sweet."

Joe bent over the PowerBook. There was a little silver barrel mounted atop the screen. This, Joe had told them, was some current compu-miracle called iSight. He ran his finger over the computer's touchpad, hit ENTER, and suddenly the screen filled with a brilliant image of Little Bitch Road. From ground level, each little bump and irregularity in the tar looked like a mountain. At mid-range, Barbie could see the Marine sentries up to their knees.

"Sir, does he have a picture, sir?" one of them asked.

Barbie looked up. "Let's put it this way, Marine—if I was doing inspection, you'd be doing push-ups with my foot in your ass. There's a scuff on your left boot. Unacceptable on a noncombat assignment."

The Marine looked down at his boot, which was indeed scuffed. Julia laughed. Joe did not. He was absorbed. "It's too low. Miz Shumway, have you got something in the car we can use to—?" He raised his hand about three feet off the road.

"I do," she said.

"And get me my little gym bag, please." He fiddled some more with the PowerBook, then held out his hand. "Cell?"

Barbie handed it to him. Joe hit the tiny buttons with blinding speed. Then: "Benny? Oh, Norrie, okay. You guys there? . . . Good. Never been in a beerjoint before, I bet. You ready? . . . *Excellent.* Stand by." He listened, then grinned. "Are you kidding? Dude, according to what I'm getting, the jack is *awesome.* They're *blasting* the Wi-Fi.

Gotta jet." He snapped the phone closed and handed it back to Barbie.

Julia came back with Joe's gym bag and a carton containing undistributed sheets of the *Democrat*'s Sunday extra edition. Joe set the PowerBook on the carton (the sudden rise in the image from ground level made Barbie a bit dizzy), then checked it and pronounced it totally rad. He rummaged in the gym bag, brought out a black box with an antenna, and plugged it into the computer. The soldiers were clustered on their side of the Dome, watching with interest. *Now I know how a fish feels in an aquarium,* Barbie thought.

"Looks okay," Joe murmured. "I got a green bulb."

"Shouldn't you call your—"

"If it's working, they'll call me," Joe said. Then: "Uh-oh, this could be trouble."

Barbie thought he was referring to the computer, but the boy wasn't even looking at it. Barbie followed his gaze and saw the green Chief of Police car. It wasn't moving fast, but the bubblegums were pulsing. Pete Randolph got out from behind the wheel. Emerging from the passenger side (the cruiser rocked a little when his weight left the springs) came Big Jim Rennie.

"Just what in the heck do you think you're doing?" he asked.

The phone in Barbie's hand buzzed. He handed it to Joe without taking his eyes from the approaching Selectman and Chief of Police.

14

The sign over the door of Dipper's said WELCOME TO THE BIGGEST DANCE FLOOR IN MAINE!, and for the first time in the roadhouse's history, that floor was crowded at eleven forty-five in the morning. Tommy and Willow Anderson greeted people at the door as they arrived, a little like ministers welcoming parishioners to church. In this case, the First Church of Rock Bands Direct from Boston.

At first the audience was quiet, because there was nothing on the big screen but one blue word: WAITING. Benny and Norrie had plugged in their equipment and switched the TV's feed to Input 4. Then, suddenly, Little Bitch Road appeared in living color, complete with brightly colored leaves swirling down around the Marine sentries.

The crowd broke into applause and cheers.

Benny gave Norrie a high five, but that wasn't enough for Norrie; she kissed him on the mouth, and hard. It was the happiest moment of Benny's life, even better than staying vertical while doing a full-pipe roughie.

"Call him!" Norrie demanded.

"Right on," Benny said. His face felt as if it might actually catch fire and burn, but he was grinning. He punched REDIAL and held the phone to his ear. "Dude, we got it! The picture's so radical it—"

Joe cut him off. "Houston, we have a problem."

15

"I don't know what you folks think you're doing," Chief Randolph said, "but I want an explanation, and that thing's shut down until I get one." He pointed at the PowerBook.

"Pardon me, sir," one of the Marines said. He was wearing a second lieutenant's stripes. "That's Colonel

Barbara, and he has official government sanction for this operation."

To this, Big Jim offered his most sarcastic smile. A vein in his neck was throbbing. "This man is a colonel of nothing but troublemakers. He cooks in the local restaurant."

"Sir, my orders—"

Big Jim shook his finger at the second lieutenant. "In Chester's Mill, the only official government we're recognizing right now is our own, soldier, and I am its representative." He turned to Randolph. "Chief, if that kid won't turn it off, pull the plug."

"It has no plug that I can see," Randolph said. He was looking from Barbie to the Marine second lieutenant to Big Jim. He had begun to sweat.

"Then put a boot through the darn screen! Just kill it!"

Randolph stepped forward. Joe, looking scared but determined, stepped in front of the PowerBook on the carton. He still had the cell phone in his hand. "You better not! It's mine, and I'm not breaking any laws!"

"Get back, Chief," Barbie said. "That's an order. If you still recognize the government of the country you live in, you'll obey it."

Randolph looked around. "Jim, maybe—"

"Maybe nothing," Big Jim said. "Right now *this* is the country you live in. *Kill that cotton-picking computer.*"

Julia stepped forward, grabbed the PowerBook, and turned it so that the iSight camera was taking in the new arrivals. Tendrils of hair had escaped her businesslike bun and hung against her pink cheeks. Barbie thought she looked extraordinarily beautiful.

"Ask Norrie if they see!" she told Joe.

Big Jim's smile froze into a grimace. "Woman, put that down!"

"Ask them if they see!"

Joe spoke into the phone. Listened. Then said: "They do. They're seeing Mr. Rennie and Officer Randolph. Norrie says they want to know what's happening."

There was dismay on Randolph's face; fury on Rennie's. "*Who* wants to know?" Randolph asked.

Julia said, "We've set up a live feed to Dipper's—"

"*That* sinpit!" Big Jim said. His hands were clenched. Barbie estimated the man was probably a hundred pounds overweight, and he grimaced when he moved his right arm—as if he'd strained it—but he looked like he could still hit. And right now he looked mad enough to take a swing . . . although whether at him, Julia, or the boy, he didn't know. Maybe Rennie didn't, either.

"People have been gathering there since quarter of eleven," she said. "News travels fast." She smiled with her head cocked to one side. "Would you like to wave to your constituency, Big Jim?"

"It's a bluff," Big Jim said.

"Why would I bluff about something so easy to check?" She turned to Randolph. "Call one of your cops and ask them where the big gathering in town is this morning." Then back to Jim again. "If you shut this down, hundreds of people will know you closed off their view of an event that vitally concerns them. One their lives may depend on, in fact."

"You had no sanction!"

Barbie, ordinarily quite good at controlling himself, felt his temper fraying. It wasn't that the man was stupid; he clearly wasn't. And that was exactly what was making Barbie mad.

"What is your problem, exactly? Do you see any danger here? Because I don't. The idea is to set this thing up, leave it broadcasting, then clear out."

"If the missile doesn't work, it could cause a panic.

Knowing something failed is one thing; actually *seeing* it fail is another. They're apt to do any darn old thing."

"You have a very low opinion of the people you govern, Selectman."

Big Jim opened his mouth to retort—something like *And they have justified it time and again* would have been Barbie's guess—but then remembered that a good portion of the town was watching this confrontation on the big-screen TV. Possibly in HD. "I'd like you to wipe that sarcastic smile off your face, Barbara."

"Are we now policing expressions, too?" Julia asked.

Scarecrow Joe covered his mouth, but not before Randolph and Big Jim saw the kid's grin. And heard the snicker that escaped from between his fingers.

"People," the second lieutenant said, "you had better clear the scene. Time is passing."

"Julia, turn that camera on me," Barbie said.

She did so.

16

Dipper's had never been so packed, not even at the memorable New Year's Eve show in 2009 featuring the Vatican Sex Kittens. And it had never been so silent. Over five hundred people stood shoulder to shoulder and hip to hip, watching as the camera on Joe's PowerBook Pro did a dizzying one-eighty and came to rest on Dale Barbara.

"There's my boy," Rose Twitchell murmured, and smiled.

"Hello there, folks," Barbie said, and the picture was so good that several people *hello*'d back. "I'm Dale Barbara, and I've been recommissioned as a colonel in the United States Army."

A general ripple of surprise greeted this.

"The video deal out here on Little Bitch Road is entirely my responsibility, and as you may have gathered, there has been a difference of opinion between myself and Selectman Rennie about whether or not to continue the feed."

This time the ripple was louder. And not happy.

"We have no time to argue the fine points of command this morning," Barbie continued. "We're going to train the camera on the point where the missile is supposed to hit. Whether or not the broadcast continues is in the hands of your Second Selectman. If he kills the feed, take it up with him. Thanks for your attention."

He walked out of the picture. For a moment the gathering on the dance floor had a view of nothing but woods, then the image rotated again, sank, and settled on the floating **X**. Beyond it, the sentries were packing the last of their gear into two big trucks.

Will Freeman, owner and operator of the local Toyota dealership (and no friend of James Rennie) spoke directly to the TV. "Leave it alone, Jimmy, or there's gonna be a new Selectman in The Mill by the end of the week."

There was a general rumble of agreement. The townspeople stood quietly, watching and waiting to see if the current program—both dull and unbearably exciting—would continue, or if the transmission would end.

17

"What do you want me to do, Big Jim?" Randolph asked. He took a handkerchief from his hip pocket and mopped the back of his neck.

"What do *you* want to do?" Big Jim responded.

For the first time since he'd taken the keys to the green Chief's car, Pete Randolph thought he would be quite willing to turn them over to someone else. He sighed and said, "I want to let this alone."

Big Jim nodded as if to say *Be it on your own head.* Then he smiled—if, that is, a pulling-back of the lips can be so characterized. "Well, you're the Chief." He turned back to Barbie, Julia, and Scarecrow Joe. "We've been outmaneuvered. Haven't we, Mr. Barbara?"

"I assure you that there's no maneuvering going on here, sir," Barbie said.

"Bull . . . *pucky.* This is a bid for power, pure and simple. I've seen plenty in my time. I've seen them succeed . . . and I've seen them fail." He stepped closer to Barbie, still favoring his sore right arm. Up close, Barbie could smell cologne and sweat. Rennie was breathing harshly. He lowered his voice. Perhaps Julia didn't hear what came next. But Barbie did.

"You're all in the pot, sonny. Every cent. If the missile punches through, you win. If it just bounces off . . . *beware me.*" For a moment his eyes—almost buried in their deep folds of flesh, but glinting with cold, clear intelligence—caught Barbie's and held them. Then he turned away. "Come on, Chief Randolph. This situation is complicated enough, thanks to Mr. Barbara and his friends. Let's go back to town. We'll want to get your troops in place in case of a riot."

"That is the most ridiculous thing I've ever heard!" Julia said.

Big Jim flapped a hand at her without turning around.

"Do you want to go to Dipper's, Jim?" Randolph asked. "We've got time."

"I wouldn't set foot in that whore-hole," Big Jim said. He opened the passenger door of the cruiser. "What I want is a nap. But I won't get one, because there's a lot to do. I've got big responsibilities. I didn't ask for them, but I have them."

"Some men are great, and some men have greatness thrust upon them, isn't that so, Jim?" Julia asked. She was smiling her cool smile.

Big Jim turned to her, and the expression of naked hate on his face made her fall back a step. Then Rennie dismissed her. "Come on, Chief."

The cruiser headed back toward The Mill, its lights still flashing in the hazy, oddly summery light.

"Whew," Joe said. "Scary dude."

"My sentiments exactly," Barbie said.

Julia was surveying Barbie, all traces of her smile gone. "You had an enemy," she said. "Now you have a blood-foe."

"I think you do, too."

She nodded. "For both our sakes, I hope this missile thing works."

The second lieutenant said, "Colonel Barbara, we're leaving. I'd feel much more comfortable if I saw you three doing the same."

Barbie nodded and for the first time in years snapped off a salute.

18

A B-52 which had taken off from Carswell Air Force Base in the early hours of that Monday morning had been on-station above Burlington, Vermont, since 1040 hours (the Air Force believes in showing up early for the prom whenever possible). The mission was code-named GRAND ISLE. The pilot-commander was Major Gene

Ray, who had served in both the Gulf and Iraq wars (in private conversations he referred to the latter as "Big Dubya's fuck-a-monkey show"). He had two Fasthawk Cruise missiles in his bomb bay. It was a good stick, the Fasthawk, more reliable and powerful than the old Tomahawk, but it felt very weird to be planning to shoot a live one at an American target.

At 1253, a red light on his control panel turned amber. The COMCOM took control of the plane from Major Ray and began to turn it into position. Below him, Burlington disappeared under the wings.

Ray spoke into his headset. "It's just about show-time, sir."

In Washington, Colonel Cox said: "Roger that, Major. Good luck. Blast the bastard."

"It'll happen," Ray said.

At 1254, the amber light began to pulse. At 1254:55, it turned green. Ray flicked the switch marked 1. There was no sensation and only a faint *whoosh* from below, but he saw the Fasthawk begin its flight on vid. It quickly accelerated to its maximum speed, leaving a jet contrail like a fingernail scratch across the sky.

Gene Ray crossed himself, finishing with a kiss at the base of his thumb. "Go with God, my son," he said.

The Fasthawk's maximum speed was thirty-five hundred miles an hour. Fifty miles from its target—about thirty miles west of Conway, New Hampshire, and now on the east side of the White Mountains—its computer first calculated and then authorized final approach. The missile's speed dropped from thirty-five hundred miles an hour to eighteen hundred and fifty as it descended. It locked on Route 302, which is North Conway's Main Street. Pedestrians looked up uneasily as the Fasthawk passed overhead.

"Isn't that jet way too low?" a woman in the parking

lot of Settlers Green Outlet Village asked her shopping companion, shading her eyes. If the Fasthawk's guidance system could have talked, it might have said, "You ain't seen nothin yet, sweetheart."

It passed over the Maine–New Hampshire border at three thousand feet, trailing a sonic boom that rattled teeth and broke windows. When the guidance system picked up Route 119, it slipped first to a thousand feet, then down to five hundred. By now the computer was in high gear, sampling the guidance system's data and making a thousand course corrections a minute.

In Washington, Colonel James O. Cox said, "Final approach, people. Hang onto your false teeth."

The Fasthawk found Little Bitch Road and dropped almost to ground-level, still blasting at near–Mach 2 speed, reading every hill and turn, its tail burning too brightly to look at, leaving a toxic stench of propellant in its wake. It tore leaves from the trees, even ignited some. It imploded a roadside stand in Tarker's Hollow, sending boards and smashed pumpkins flying into the sky. The boom followed, causing people to fall to the floor with their hands over their heads.

This is going to work, Cox thought. *How can it not?*

19

In Dipper's, there were now eight hundred people crammed together. No one spoke, although Lissa Jamieson's lips moved soundlessly as she prayed to whatever New Age oversoul happened to be currently claiming her attention. She clutched a crystal in one hand; the Reverend Piper Libby was holding her mother's cross against her lips.

Ernie Calvert said, "Here it comes."

"Where?" Marty Arsenault demanded. "I don't see noth—"

"*Listen!*" Brenda Perkins said.

They heard it come: a growing otherworldly hum from the western edge of town, a *mmmm* that rose to *MMMMMM* in a space of seconds. On the big-screen TV they saw almost nothing, until half an hour later, long after the missile had failed. For those still remaining in the roadhouse, Benny Drake was able to slow the recording down until it was advancing frame by frame. They saw the missile come slewing around what was known as Little Bitch Bend. It was no more than four feet off the ground, almost kissing its own blurred shadow. In the next frame the Fasthawk, tipped with a blast-fragmentation warhead designed to explode on contact, was frozen in midair about where the Marines' bivouac had been.

In the next frames, the screen filled with a white so bright it made the watchers shade their eyes. Then, as the white began to fade, they saw the missile fragments—so many black dashes against the diminishing blast—and a huge scorch mark where the red **X** had been. The missile had hit its spot exactly.

After that, the people in Dipper's watched the woods on the Tarker's side of the Dome burst into flame. They watched the asphalt on that side first buckle and then begin to melt.

20

"Fire the other one," Cox said dully, and Gene Ray did. It broke more windows and scared more people in eastern New Hampshire and western Maine.

Otherwise, the result was the same.

IN THE FRAME

IN THE FRAME

1

At 19 Mill Street, home of the McClatchey family, there was a moment of silence when the recording ended. Then Norrie Calvert burst into fresh tears. Benny Drake and Joe McClatchey, after looking at each other over her bowed head with identical *What do I do now* expressions, put their arms around her quaking shoulders and gripped each other's wrists in a kind of soul shake.

"That's *it?*" Claire McClatchey asked unbelievingly. Joe's mother wasn't crying, but she was close; her eyes glistened. She was holding her husband's picture in her hands, had taken it off the wall shortly after Joe and his friends had come in with the DVD. "That's *all?*"

No one answered. Barbie was perched on the arm of the easy chair where Julia was sitting. *I could be in big trouble here,* he thought. But it wasn't his *first* thought; that had been that the town was in big trouble.

Mrs. McClatchey got to her feet. She still held her husband's picture. Sam had gone to the flea market that ran at Oxford Speedway each Saturday until the weather got too cold. His hobby was refinishing furniture, and he often found good stuff at the stalls there. Three days later he was still in Oxford, sharing space at the Raceway Motel with several platoons of reporters and TV people; he and Claire couldn't speak to each other on the phone, but had been able to stay in touch by e-mail. So far.

"What happened to your computer, Joey?" she asked. "Did it blow up?"

Joe, his arm still around Norrie's shoulders, his hand still gripping Benny's wrist, shook his head. "I don't think so," he said. "It probably just melted." He turned to Barbie. "The heat might set the woods on fire out there. Someone ought to do something about that."

"I don't think there are any fire engines in town," Benny said. "Well, maybe one or two old ones."

"Let me see what I can do about that," Julia said. Claire McClatchey towered over her; it was easy enough to see where Joe had gotten his height. "Barbie, it would probably be best if I handled this on my own."

"Why?" Claire looked bewildered. One of her tears finally overspilled and ran down her cheek. "Joe said the government put you in charge, Mr. Barbara—the President himself!"

"I had a disagreement with Mr. Rennie and Chief Randolph about the video feed," Barbie said. "It got a little hot. I doubt if either of them would welcome my advice just now. Julia, I don't think they'd exactly welcome yours, either. At least not yet. If Randolph's halfway competent, he'll send a bunch of deputies out there with whatever's left in the firebarn. At the very least, there'll be hoses and Indian pumps."

Julia considered this, then said: "Would you step outside with me for a minute, Barbie?"

He looked at Joe's mother, but Claire was no longer paying them any attention. She had moved her son aside and was sitting next to Norrie, who pressed her face against Claire's shoulder.

"Dude, the government owes me a computer," Joe said as Barbie and Julia walked toward the front door.

"Noted," Barbie said. "And thank you, Joe. You did well."

"A lot better than their damn missile," Benny muttered.

On the front stoop of the McClatchey home, Barbie and Julia stood silent, looking toward the town common, Prestile Stream, and the Peace Bridge. Then, in a voice that was low-pitched and angry, Julia said: "He's not. That's the thing. That's the goddam thing."

"Who's not what?"

"Peter Randolph is not halfway competent. Not even one-quarter. I went to school with him all the way from kindergarten, where he was a world-champion pants-wetter, to twelfth grade, where he was part of the Bra-Snapping Brigade. He was a C-minus intellect who got B-minus grades because his father was on the school board, and his brainpower has not increased. Our Mr. Rennie has surrounded himself with dullards. Andrea Grinnell is an exception, but she's also a drug addict. OxyContin."

"Back problems," Barbie said. "Rose told me."

Enough of the trees on the common had shed their leaves for Barbie and Julia to be able to see Main Street. It was deserted now—most people would still be at Dipper's, discussing what they had seen—but its sidewalks would soon fill with stunned, disbelieving townsfolk drifting back to their homes. Men and women who would not yet even dare ask each other what came next.

Julia sighed and ran her hands through her hair. "Jim Rennie thinks if he just keeps all the control in his own hands, things will eventually come rightside up. For him and his friends, at least. He's the worst kind of politician—selfish, too egocentric to realize he's way out of his league, and a coward underneath that bluff can-do exterior of his. When things get bad enough, he'll send this town to the devil if he thinks he can save himself by doing so. A cowardly leader is the most dangerous of men. You're the one who should be running this show."

"I appreciate your confidence—"

"But that's not going to happen no matter what your Colonel Cox and the President of the United States may want. It's not going to happen even if fifty thousand people march down Fifth Avenue in New York, waving signs with your face on them. Not with that fucking Dome still over our heads."

"Every time I listen to you, you sound less Republican," Barbie remarked.

She struck him on the bicep with a surprisingly hard fist. "This is not a joke."

"No," Barbie said. "It's not a joke. It's time to call for elections. And I urge you to stand for Second Selectman yourself."

She looked at him pityingly. "Do you think Jim Rennie is going to allow elections as long as the Dome is in place? What world are you living in, my friend?"

"Don't underestimate the will of the town, Julia."

"And don't you underestimate James Rennie. He's been in charge here for donkey's years and people have come to accept him. Also, he's very talented when it comes to finding scapegoats. An out-of-towner—a drifter, in fact—would be perfect in the current situation. Do we know anybody like that?"

"I was expecting an idea from you, not a political analysis."

For a moment he thought she was going to hit him again. Then she drew in a breath, let it out, and smiled.

"You come on all aw-shucks, but you've got some thorns, don't you?"

The Town Hall whistle began to blow a series of short blasts into the warm, still air.

"Someone's called in a fire," Julia said. "I think we know where."

They looked west, where rising smoke smudged the blue. Barbie thought most of it had to be coming from the Tarker's Mills side of the Dome, but the heat would almost certainly have ignited small fires on the Chester side as well.

"You want an idea? Okay, here's one. I'll track down Brenda—she'll either be at home or at Dipper's with everyone else—and suggest she take charge of the fire-fighting operation."

"And if she says no?"

"I'm pretty sure she won't. At least there's no wind to speak of—not on this side of the Dome—so it's probably just grass and brush. She'll tap some guys to pitch in, and she'll know the right ones. They'll be the ones Howie would've picked."

"None of them the new officers, I take it."

"I'll leave that up to her, but I doubt if she'll be calling on Carter Thibodeau or Melvin Searles. Freddy Denton, either. He's been on the cops for five years, but I know from Brenda that Duke was planning to let him go. Freddy plays Santa every year at the elementary school, and the kids love him—he's got a great ho-ho-ho. He's also got a mean streak."

"You'll be going around Rennie again."

"Yes."

"Payback could be a bitch."

"I can be a bitch myself, when I have to be. Brenda too, if she gets her back up."

"Go for it. And make sure she asks that guy Burpee. When it comes to putting out a brushfire, I'd trust him rather than any town firebarn leftovers. He's got everything in that store of his."

She nodded. "That's a damned good idea."

"Sure you don't want me to tag along?"

"You've got other fish to fry. Did Bren give you Duke's key to the fallout shelter?"

"She did."

"Then the fire may be just the distraction you need. Get that Geiger counter." She started for her Prius, then stopped and turned back. "Finding the generator— assuming there is one—is probably the best chance this town has got. Maybe the only one. And Barbie?"

"Right here, ma'am," he said, smiling a little.

She didn't. "Until you've heard Big Jim Rennie's stump speech, don't sell him short. There are reasons he's lasted as long as he has."

"Good at waving the bloody shirt, I take it."

"Yes. And this time the shirt is apt to be yours."

She drove off to find Brenda and Romeo Burpee.

2

Those who had watched the Air Force's failed attempt to punch through the Dome left Dipper's pretty much as Barbie had imagined: slowly, with their heads down, not talking much. Many were walking with their arms about one another; some were crying. Three town police cars were parked across the road from Dipper's, and half a dozen cops stood leaning against them, ready for trouble. But there was no trouble.

The green Chief of Police car was parked farther up, in

the front lot of Brownie's Store (where a hand-lettered sign in the window read CLOSED UNTIL "FREEDOM!" ALLOWS FRESH SUPPLIES). Chief Randolph and Jim Rennie sat inside the car, watching.

"There," Big Jim said with unmistakable satisfaction. "I hope they're happy."

Randolph looked at him curiously. "Didn't you *want* it to work?"

Big Jim grimaced as his sore shoulder twinged. "Of course, but I never thought it would. And that fellow with the girl's name and his new friend Julia managed to get everyone all worked up and hopeful, didn't they? Oh yes, you bet. Do you know she's never endorsed me for office in that rag of hers? Not one single time."

He pointed at the pedestrians streaming back toward town.

"Take a good look, pal—this is what incompetency, false hope, and too much information gets you. They're just unhappy and disappointed now, but when they get over that, they'll be mad. We're going to need more police."

"*More?* We've got eighteen already, counting the part-timers and the new deputies."

"It won't be enough. And we've got—"

The town whistle began to hammer the air with short blasts. They looked west and saw the smoke rising.

"We've got Barbara and Shumway to thank," Big Jim finished.

"Maybe we ought to do something about that fire."

"It's a Tarker's Mills problem. And the U.S. government's, of course. They started a fire with their cotton-picking missile, let them deal with it."

"But if the heat sparked one on this side—"

"Stop being an old woman and drive me back to town. I've got to find Junior. He and I have things to talk about."

3

Brenda Perkins and the Reverend Piper Libby were in Dipper's parking lot, by Piper's Subaru.

"I never thought it would work," Brenda said, "but I'd be a liar if I said I wasn't disappointed."

"Me too," Piper said. "Bitterly. I'd offer you a ride back to town, but I have to check on a parishioner."

"Not out on Little Bitch, I hope," Brenda said. She lifted a thumb at the rising smoke.

"No, the other way. Eastchester. Jack Evans. He lost his wife on Dome Day. A freak accident. Not that all of this isn't freakish."

Brenda nodded. "I saw him out at Dinsmore's field, carrying a sign with his wife's picture on it. Poor, poor man."

Piper went to the open driver's-side window of her car, where Clover was sitting behind the wheel and watching the departing crowd. She rummaged in her pocket, gave him a treat, then said, "Push over, Clove—you know you flunked your last driver's test." To Brenda, she confided: "He can't parallel-park worth a damn."

The shepherd hopped onto the passenger side. Piper opened the car door and looked at the smoke. "I'm sure the woods on the Tarker's Mills side are burning briskly, but that needn't concern us." She gave Brenda a bitter smile. "We have the Dome to protect us."

"Good luck," Brenda said. "Give Jack my sympathy. And my love."

"I'll do that," Piper said, and drove off. Brenda was walking out of the parking lot with her hands in the pockets of her jeans, wondering how she was going to get through the rest of the day, when Julia Shumway drove up and helped her with that.

4

The missiles exploding against the Dome didn't wake Sammy Bushey; it was the clattery wooden crash, followed by Little Walter's screams of pain, that did that.

Carter Thibodeau and his friends had taken all of her fridge-dope when they left, but they hadn't searched the place, so the shoebox with the rough skull-and-crossbones drawn on it was still in the closet. There was also this message, printed in Phil Bushey's scrawly, backslanting letters: MY SHIT! TOUCH IT AND U DIE!

There was no pot inside (Phil had always sneered at pot as a "cocktail-party drug"), and she had no interest in the Baggie of crystal. She was sure the "deputies" would have enjoyed smoking it, but Sammy thought crystal was crazy shit for crazy people—who else would inhale smoke that included the residue of matchbook striker-pads marinated in acetone? There was another, smaller Baggie, however, that contained half a dozen Dreamboats, and when Carter's posse left she had swallowed one of these with warm beer from the bottle stashed under the bed she now slept in alone . . . except for when she took Little Walter in with her, that was. Or Dodee.

She had briefly considered taking all of the Dreamboats and ending her crappy unhappy life once and for all; might even have done it, if not for Little Walter. If she died, who would take care of him? He might even starve to death in his crib, a horrible thought.

Suicide was out, but she had never felt so depressed and sad and hurt in all her life. Dirty, too. She had been degraded before, God knew, sometimes by Phil (who had enjoyed drug-fueled threesomes before losing interest in sex completely), sometimes by others, sometimes by herself—Sammy Bushey had never gotten the concept of being her own best friend.

Certainly she'd had her share of one-night stands, and once, in high school, after the Wildcats basketball team had won the Class D championship, she had taken on four of the starters, one after the other, at a postgame party (the fifth had been passed out in a corner). It had been her own stupid idea. She had also sold what Carter, Mel, and Frankie DeLesseps had taken by force. Most frequently to Freeman Brown, owner of Brownie's Store, where she did most of her shopping because Brownie gave her credit. He was old and didn't smell very good, but he was randy, and that was actually a plus. It made him quick. Six pumps on the mattress in the storeroom was his usual limit, followed by a grunt and a squirt. It was never the highlight of her week, but it was comforting to know that line of credit was there, especially if she came up short at the end of the month and Little Walter needed Pampers.

And Brownie had never hurt her.

What had happened last night was different. De-Lesseps hadn't been so bad, but Carter had hurt her up top and made her bleed down below. Worse had followed; when Mel Searles dropped his pants, he was sporting a tool like the ones she'd sometimes seen in the porno movies Phil had watched before his interest in crystal overtook his interest in sex.

Searles had gone at her hard, and although she tried to remember what she and Dodee had done two days before, it didn't work. She remained as dry as August with no rain. Until, that was, what Carter Thibodeau had only abraded ripped wide open. Then there was lubrication. She had felt it puddling under her, warm and sticky. There had been wetness on her face, too, tears trickling down her cheeks to nestle in the hollows of her ears. During Mel

Searles's endless ride, it came to her that he might actually kill her. If he did, what would happen to Little Walter?

And weaving through it all, the shrill magpie voice of Georgia Roux: *Do her, do her, do that bitch! Make her holler!*

Sammy had hollered, all right. She had hollered plenty, and so had Little Walter, from his crib in the other room.

In the end they had warned her to keep her mouth shut and left her to bleed on the couch, hurt but alive. She'd watched their headlights move across the living room ceiling, then fade as they drove away toward town. Then it was just her and Little Walter. She had walked him back and forth, back and forth, stopping just once to put on a pair of underpants (not the pink ones; she never wanted to wear those again) and stuff the crotch with toilet paper. She had Tampax, but the thought of putting anything up there made her cringe.

Finally Little Walter's head had fallen heavily on her shoulder, and she felt his drool dampening her skin—a reliable sign that he was really and truly out. She had put him back in his crib (praying that he would sleep through the night), and then she had taken the shoebox down from the closet. The Dreamboat—some kind of powerful downer, she didn't know exactly what—had first damped the pain Down There, and then blotted out everything. She had slept for over twelve hours.

Now this.

Little Walter's screams were like a bright light cutting through heavy fog. She lurched out of bed and ran into his bedroom, knowing the goddam crib, which Phil had put together half-stoned, had finally collapsed. Little Walter had been shaking the shit out of it last night when the "deputies" were busy with her. That must have weakened it enough so that this morning, when he began stirring around—

Little Walter was on the floor in the wreckage. He crawled toward her with blood pouring from a cut on his forehead.

"Little Walter!" she screamed, and swept him into her arms. She turned, stumbled over a broken cribslat, went to one knee, got up, and rushed into the bathroom with the baby wailing in her arms. She turned on the water and of course no water came: there was no power to run the well pump. She grabbed a towel and dry-mopped his face, exposing the cut—not deep but long and ragged. It would leave a scar. She pressed the towel against it as hard as she dared, trying to ignore Little Walter's renewed shrieks of pain and outrage. Blood pattered onto her bare feet in dime-sized drops. When she looked down, she saw the blue panties she'd put on after the "deputies" had left were now soaked to a muddy purple. At first she thought it was Little Walter's blood. But her thighs were streaked, too.

5

Somehow she got Little Walter to hold still long enough to plaster three SpongeBob Band-Aids along the gash, and to get him into an undershirt and his one remaining clean overall (on the bib, red stitching proclaimed MOMMY'S LI'L DEVIL). She dressed herself while Little Walter crawled in circles on her bedroom floor, his wild sobbing reduced to lackadaisical sniffles. She started by throwing the blood-soaked underpants into the trash and putting on fresh ones. She padded the crotch with a folded dish-wiper, and took an extra for later. She was still bleeding. Not gushing, but it was a far heavier flow than during her worst periods. And it had gone on all night. The bed was soaked.

She packed Little Walter's go-bag, then picked him up. He was heavy and she felt fresh pain settle in Down There: the sort of throbbing bellyache you got from eating bad food.

"We're going to the Health Center," she said, "and don't you worry, Little Walter, Dr. Haskell will fix us both up. Also, scars don't matter as much to boys. Sometimes girls even think they're sexy. I'll drive as fast as I can, and we'll be there in no time." She opened the door. "Everything's going to be all right."

But her old rustbucket Toyota was far from all right. The "deputies" hadn't bothered with the back tires, but they had punctured both front ones. Sammy looked at the car for a long moment, feeling an even deeper depression settle over her. An idea, fleeting but clear, crossed her mind: she could split the remaining Dreamboats with Little Walter. She could grind his up and put them in one of his Playtex nursers, which he called "boggies." She could disguise the taste with chocolate milk. Little Walter loved chocolate milk. Accompanying the idea came the title of one of Phil's old record albums: *Nothing Matters and What If It Did?*

She pushed the idea away.

"I'm not that kind of mom," she told Little Walter.

He goggled up at her in a way that reminded her of Phil, but in a good way: the expression that only looked like puzzled stupidity on her estranged husband's face was endearingly goofy on her son's. She kissed his nose and he smiled. That was nice, a nice smile, but the Band-Aids on his forehead were turning red. That wasn't so nice.

"Little change of plan," she said, and went back inside. At first she couldn't find the Papoose, but finally spotted it behind what she would from now on think of as the Rape Couch. She finally managed to wriggle Little Walter into it, although lifting him hurt her all over again. The dish-wiper in her underwear was feeling ominously damp, but when she checked the crotch of her sweatpants, there were no spots. That was good.

"Ready for a walk, Little Walter?"

Little Walter only snuggled his cheek into the hollow of her shoulder. Sometimes his paucity of speech bothered her—she had friends whose babies had been babbling whole sentences by sixteen months, and Little Walter only had nine or ten words—but not this morning. This morning she had other things to worry about.

The day felt dismayingly warm for the last full week of October; the sky overhead was its very palest shade of blue and the light was somehow blurry. She felt sweat spring out on her face and neck almost at once, and her crotch was throbbing badly—worse with every step, it seemed, and she had taken only a few. She thought of going back for aspirin, but wasn't it supposed to make bleeding worse? Besides, she wasn't sure she had any.

There was something else, as well, something she hardly dared admit to herself: if she went back into the house, she wasn't sure she'd have the heart to come back out again.

There was a white scrap of paper under the Toyota's left windshield wiper. It had **Just a Note from SAMMY** printed across the top and surrounded by daisies. Torn from her own kitchen pad. The idea caused a certain tired outrage. Scrawled under the daisies was this: *Tell anyone and more than your tires will be flat.* And below, in another hand: *Next time maybe we'll turn you over and play the other side.*

"In your dreams, motherfucker," she said in a wan, tired voice.

She crumpled the note up, dropped it by one flat tire—

poor old Corolla looked almost as tired and sad as she felt—and made her way out to the end of the driveway, pausing to lean against the mailbox for a few seconds. The metal was warm on her skin, the sun hot on her neck. And hardly a breath of breeze. October was supposed to be cool and invigorating. *Maybe it's that global warming stuff,* she thought. She was first to have this idea, but not the last, and the word which eventually stuck was not *global* but *local.*

Motton Road lay before her, deserted and charmless. Starting a mile or so to her left were the nice new homes of Eastchester, to which The Mill's higher-class workadaddies and workamommies came at the end of their days in the shops and offices and banks of Lewiston-Auburn. To her right lay downtown Chester's Mill. And the Health Center.

"Ready, Little Walter?"

Little Walter didn't say if he was or wasn't. He was snoring in the hollow of her shoulder and drooling on her Donna the Buffalo tee-shirt. Sammy took a deep breath, tried to ignore the throb coming from The Land Down Under, hitched up the Papoose, and started toward town.

When the whistle started up on top of the Town Hall, blowing the short blasts that indicated a fire, she first thought it was in her own head, which was feeling decidedly weird. Then she saw the smoke, but it was far to the west. Nothing to concern her and Little Walter . . . unless someone came along who wanted a closer look at the fire, that was. If that happened, they would surely be neighborly enough to drop her off at the Health Center on their way to the excitement.

She began to sing the James McMurtry song that had been popular last summer, got as far as "We roll up the sidewalks at quarter of eight, it's a small town, can't sell you no beer," then quit. Her mouth was too dry to sing. She blinked and saw she was on the edge of falling into the ditch, and not even the one she'd been walking next to when she started out. She'd woven all the way across the road, an excellent way to get hit instead of picked up.

She looked over her shoulder, hoping for traffic. There was none. The road to Eastchester was empty, the tar not quite hot enough to shimmer.

She went back to what she thought of as her side, swaying on her feet now, feeling all jelly-legged. *Drunken sailor,* she thought. *What do you do with a drunken sailor, ear-lye in the morning?* But it wasn't morning, it was afternoon, she had slept the clock around, and when she looked down she saw that the crotch of her sweats had turned purple, just like the underpants she'd been wearing earlier. *That won't come out, and I only have two other pairs of sweats that fit me.* Then she remembered one of those had a big old hole in the seat, and began to cry. The tears felt cool on her hot cheeks.

"It's all right, Little Walter," she said. "Dr. Haskell's going to fix us up. Just fine. Fine as paint. Good as n—"

Then a black rose began to bloom in front of her eyes and the last of her strength left her legs. Sammy felt it go, running out of her muscles like water. She went down, holding onto one final thought: *On your side, on your side, don't squash the baby!*

That much she managed. She lay sprawled on the shoulder of Motton Road, unmoving in the hazy, July-ish sun. Little Walter awoke and began to cry. He tried to struggle out of the Papoose and couldn't; Sammy had snapped him in carefully, and he was pinned. Little Walter began to cry harder. A fly settled on his forehead, sampled the blood oozing through the cartoon images of SpongeBob and Patrick, then flew off. Possibly to report this taste-treat at Fly HQ and summon reinforcements.

Grasshoppers *reeee*'d in the grass.

The town whistle honked.

Little Walter, trapped with his unconscious mother, wailed for a while in the heat, then gave up and lay silent, looking around listlessly as sweat rolled out of his fine hair in large clear drops.

6

Standing beside the Globe Theater's boarded-up box office and under its sagging marquee (the Globe had gone out of business five years before), Barbie had a good view of both the Town Hall and the police station. His good buddy Junior was sitting on the cop-shop steps, massaging his temples as if the rhythmic whoop of the whistle hurt his head.

Al Timmons came out of the Town Hall and jogged down to the street. He was wearing his gray janitor's fatigues, but there was a pair of binoculars hanging from a strap around his neck and an Indian pump on his back— empty of water, from the ease with which he was carrying it. Barbie guessed Al had blown the fire whistle.

Go away, Al, Barbie thought. *How about it?*

Half a dozen trucks rolled up the street. The first two were pickups, the third a panel job. All three lead vehicles were painted a yellow so bright it almost screamed. The pickups had BURPEE'S DEPARTMENT STORE decaled on the doors. The panel truck's box bore the legendary slogan MEET ME FOR SLURPEES AT BURPEES. Romeo himself was in the lead truck. His hair was its usual Daddy Cool marvel of sweeps and spirals. Brenda Perkins was riding shotgun. In the pickup's bed were shovels, hoses, and a brand-new sump pump still plastered with the manufacturer's stickers.

Romeo stopped beside Al Timmons. "Jump in the back, partner," he said, and Al did. Barbie withdrew as far as he could into the shadow of the deserted theater's marquee. He didn't want to be drafted to help fight the fire out on Little Bitch Road; he had business right here in town.

Junior hadn't moved from the PD steps, but he was still rubbing his temples and holding his head. Barbie waited for the trucks to disappear, then hurried across the street. Junior didn't look up, and a moment later he was hidden from Barbie's view by the ivy-covered bulk of the Town Hall.

Barbie went up the steps and paused to read the sign on the message board: TOWN MEETING THURSDAY 7 PM IF CRISIS IS NOT RESOLVED. He thought of Julia saying *Until you've heard Big Jim Rennie's stump speech, don't sell him short.* He might get a chance Thursday night; certainly Rennie would make his pitch to stay in control of the situation.

And for more power, Julia's voice spoke up in his head. *He'll want that, too, of course. For the good of the town.*

The Town Hall had been built of quarried stone a hundred and sixty years before, and the vestibule was cool and dim. The generator was off; no need to run it with no one here.

Except someone was, in the main meeting hall. Barbie heard voices, two of them, belonging to children. The tall oak doors were standing ajar. He looked in and saw a skinny man with a lot of graying hair sitting up front at the selectmen's table. Opposite him was a pretty little girl of about ten. They had a checkerboard between them; the longhair had his chin propped on one hand, studying his next move. Down below, in the aisle between the benches, a young woman was playing leapfrog with a boy of four or five. The checker players were studious; the young woman and the boy were laughing.

Barbie started to withdraw, but too late. The young woman looked up. "Hi? Hello?" She picked up the boy and came toward him. The checker players looked up, too. So much for stealth.

The young woman was holding out the hand she wasn't using to support the little boy's bottom. "I'm Carolyn Sturges. That gentleman is my friend, Thurston Marshall. The little guy is Aidan Appleton. Say hi, Aidan."

"Hi," Aidan said in a small voice, and then plugged his thumb into his mouth. He looked at Barbie with eyes that were round and blue and mildly curious.

The girl ran up the aisle to stand beside Carolyn Sturges. The longhair followed more slowly. He looked tired and shaken. "I'm Alice Rachel Appleton," she said. "Aidan's big sister. Take your thumb out of your mouth, Aide."

Aide didn't.

"Well, it's nice to meet all of you," Barbie said. He didn't tell them his own name. In fact, he sort of wished he were wearing a fake mustache. But this still might be all right. He was almost positive these people were out-of-towners.

"Are you a town official?" Thurston Marshall asked. "If you're a town official, I wish to lodge a complaint."

"I'm just the janitor," Barbie said, then remembered they had almost certainly seen Al Timmons leave. Hell, probably had a conversation with him. "The other janitor. You must have met Al."

"I want my mother," Aidan Appleton said. "I miss her *bad*."

"We met him," Carolyn Sturges said. "He claims the government shot some missiles at whatever is holding us in, and all they did was bounce off and start a fire."

"That's true," Barbie said, and before he could say more, Marshall weighed in again.

"I want to lodge a complaint. In fact, I want to lay a charge. I was assaulted by a so-called police officer. He punched me in the stomach. I had my gall bladder out a few years ago, and I'm afraid I may have internal injuries. Also, Carolyn was verbally abused. She was called a name that degraded her sexually."

Carolyn laid a hand on his arm. "Before we go making any charges, Thurse, you want to remember that we had D-O-P-E."

"Dope!" Alice said at once. "Our mom smokes marijuana sometimes, because it helps when she's having her P-E-R-I-O-D."

"Oh," Carolyn said. "Right." Her smile was wan.

Marshall drew himself up to his full height. "Possession of marijuana is a misdemeanor," he said. "What they did to me was felony assault! And it hurts *terribly*!"

Carolyn gave him a look in which affection was mingled with exasperation. Barbie suddenly understood how it was between them. Sexy May had met Erudite November, and now they were stuck with each other, refugees in the New England version of *No Exit*. "Thurse . . . I'm not sure that misdemeanor idea would fly in court." She smiled apologetically at Barbie. "We had quite a lot. They took it."

"Maybe they'll smoke up the evidence," Barbie said.

She laughed at this. Her graying boyfriend did not. His bushy brows had drawn together. "All the same, I plan to lodge a complaint."

"I'd wait," Barbie said. "The situation here . . . well, let's just say that a punch in the gut isn't going to be considered that big a deal as long as we're still under the Dome."

"*I* consider it a big deal, my young janitor friend."

The young woman now looked more exasperated than affectionate. "Thurse—"

"The good side of that is nobody is going to make a big deal out of some pot, either," Barbie said. "Maybe it's a push, as the gamblers say. How'd you come by the kiddos?"

"The cops we ran into at Thurston's cabin saw us at the restaurant," Carolyn said. "The woman who runs it said they were closed until supper, but she took pity on us when we said we were from Massachusetts. She gave us sandwiches and coffee."

"She gave us *peanut butter and jelly* and coffee," Thurston corrected. "There was no choice, not even tuna fish. I told her peanut butter sticks to my upper plate, but she said they were on rationing. Isn't that about the craziest thing you've ever heard?"

Barbie did think it was crazy, but since it had also been his idea, he said nothing.

"When I saw the cops come in, I was ready for more trouble," Carolyn said, "but Aide and Alice seemed to have mellowed them out."

Thurston snorted. "Not so mellow they apologized. Or did I miss that part?"

Carolyn sighed, then turned back to Barbie. "They said maybe the pastor at the Congregational church could find the four of us an empty house to live in until this is over. I guess we're going to be foster parents, at least for awhile."

She stroked the boy's hair. Thurston Marshall looked less than pleased at the prospect of becoming a foster parent, but he put an arm around the girl's shoulders, and Barbie liked him for that.

"One cop was *Joooo-nyer,*" Alice said. "He's nice. Also a fox. Frankie isn't as good looking, but he was nice, too. He gave us a Milky Way bar. Mom says we're not supposed to take candy from strangers, but—" She shrugged to indicate things had changed, a fact she and Carolyn seemed to understand much more clearly than Thurston.

"They weren't nice before," Thurston said. "They weren't nice when they were punching me in the stomach, Caro."

"You have to take the bitter with the sweet," Alice said philosophically. "That's what my mother says."

Carolyn laughed. Barbie joined in, and after a moment so did Marshall, although he held his stomach while he did it and looked at his young girlfriend with a certain reproach.

"I went up the street and knocked on the church door," Carolyn said. "There was no answer, so I went in—the door was unlocked, but there was nobody there. Do you have any idea when the pastor will be back?"

Barbie shook his head. "I'd take your checkerboard and go on up to the parsonage, if I were you. It's around back. You're looking for a woman named Piper Libby."

"*Cherchez la femme,*" Thurston said.

Barbie shrugged, then nodded. "She's good people, and God knows there are empty houses in The Mill. You could almost have your pick. And you'll probably find supplies in the pantry wherever you go."

This made him think of the fallout shelter again.

Alice, meanwhile, had grabbed the checkers, which she stuffed in her pockets, and the board, which she carried. "Mr. Marshall's beat me every game so far," she told Barbie. "He says it's *pay*-tronizing to let kids win just because they're kids. But I'm getting better, aren't I, Mr. Marshall?"

She smiled up at him. Thurston Marshall smiled back. Barbie thought this unlikely quartet might be okay.

"Youth must be served, Alice my dear," he said. "But not immediately."

"I want Mommy," Aidan said morosely.

"If there was only a way to get in touch with her," Carolyn said. "Alice, you're sure you don't remember her e-mail address?" And to Barbie she said, "Mom left her cell phone at the cabin, so *that's* no good."

"She's a hotmail," Alice said. "That's all I know. Sometimes she says she used to be a hot female, but Daddy took care of that."

Carolyn was looking at her elderly boyfriend. "Blow this pop-shop?"

"Yes. We may as well repair to the parsonage, and hope the lady comes back soon from whatever errand of mercy she happens to be on."

"Parsonage might be unlocked, too," Barbie said. "If it isn't, try under the doormat."

"I wouldn't presume," he said.

"*I* would," Carolyn said, and giggled. The sound made the little boy smile.

"Pre-*zoom*!" Alice Appleton cried, and went flying up the center aisle with her arms outstretched and the checkerboard flapping from one hand. "Pre-*zoom*, pre-*zoom*, come *on*, you guys, let's pre-*zoom*!"

Thurston sighed and started after her. "If you break the checkerboard, Alice, you'll never beat me."

"Yes I will, 'cos *youth* must be *served*!" she called back over her shoulder. "Besides, we could tape it together! Come *on*!"

Aidan wriggled impatiently in Carolyn's arms. She set him down to chase after his sister. Carolyn held out her hand. "Thank you, Mr.——"

"More than welcome," Barbie said, shaking with her. Then he turned to Thurston. The man had the fishbelly grip Barbie associated with guys whose intelligence-to-exercise ratio was out of whack.

They started out after the kids. At the double doors, Thurston Marshall looked back. A shaft of hazy sun from one of the high windows struck across his face, making him look older than he was. Making him look eighty. "I edited the current issue of *Ploughshares*," he said. His voice quivered with indignation and sorrow. "That is a very good literary magazine, one of the best in the country. They had no right to punch me in the stomach, or laugh at me."

"No," Barbie said. "Of course not. Take good care of those kids."

"We will," Carolyn said. She took the man's arm and squeezed it. "Come on, Thurse."

Barbie waited until he heard the outer door close, then went in search of the stairs leading to the Town Hall conference room and kitchen. Julia had said the fallout shelter was half a flight down from there.

7

Piper's first thought was that someone had left a bag of garbage beside the road. Then she got a little closer and saw it was a body.

She pulled over and scrambled out of the car so fast she went to one knee, scraping it. When she got up she saw it wasn't one body but two: a woman and a toddler. The child, at least, was alive, waving its arms feebly.

She ran to them and turned the woman onto her back. She was young, and vaguely familiar, but not a member of Piper's congregation. Her cheek and brow were badly bruised. Piper freed the child from the carrier, and when she held him against her and stroked his sweaty hair, he began to cry hoarsely.

The woman's eyes fluttered open at the sound, and Piper saw that her pants were soaked with blood.

"Li'l Walter," the woman croaked, which Piper misheard.

"Don't worry, there's water in the car. Lie still. I've got your baby, he's okay." Not knowing if he was or not. "I'll take care of him."

"Li'l Walter," the woman in the bloody jeans said again, and closed her eyes.

Piper ran back to her car with her heart beating hard enough for her to feel it in her eyeballs. Her tongue tasted coppery. *God help me,* she prayed, and could think of nothing else, so she thought it again: *God, oh God help me help that woman.*

The Subaru had air-conditioning, but she hadn't been using it in spite of the heat of the day; rarely did. Her understanding was that it wasn't very eco-friendly. But she turned it on now, full blast. She laid the baby on the backseat, rolled up the windows, closed the doors, started back toward the young woman lying in the dust, then was struck by a terrible thought: what if the baby managed to climb over the seat, pushed the wrong button, and locked her out?

God, I'm so stupid. The worst minister in the world when a real crisis comes. Help me not to be so stupid.

She rushed back, opened the driver's door again, looked over the seat, and saw the boy still lying where she had put him, but now sucking his thumb. His eyes went to her briefly, then looked up at the ceiling as if he saw something interesting there. Mental cartoons, maybe.

He had sweated right through the little tee-shirt beneath his overall. Piper twisted the electronic key fob back and forth in her fist until it broke free of the key ring. Then she ran back to the woman, who was trying to sit up.

"Don't," Piper said, kneeling beside her and putting an arm around her. "I don't think you should—"

"Li'l Walter," the woman croaked.

Shit, I forgot the water! God, why did You let me forget the water?

Now the woman was trying to struggle to her feet. Piper didn't like this idea, which ran counter to everything she knew of first aid, but what other option was there? The road was deserted, and she couldn't leave her out in the blaring sun, that would be worse and more of it. So instead of pushing her back down, Piper helped her to stand.

"Slow," she said, now holding the woman around the waist and guiding her staggering steps as best she could. "Slow and easy does it, slow and easy wins the race. It's cool in the car. And there's water."

"Li'l Walter!" The woman swayed, steadied, then tried to move a little faster.

"Water," Piper said. "Right. Then I'm taking you to the hospital."

"Hell . . . Center."

This Piper did understand, and she shook her head firmly. "No way. You're going straight to the hospital. You and your baby both."

"Li'l Walter," the woman whispered. She stood swaying, head down, hair hanging in her face, while Piper opened the passenger door and then eased her inside.

Piper got the bottle of Poland Spring out of the center console and took off the cap. The woman snatched it from her before Piper could offer it, and drank greedily, water overspilling the neck and dripping off her chin to darken the top of her tee-shirt.

"What's your name?" Piper asked.

"Sammy Bushey." And then, even as her stomach cramped from the water, that black rose began to open in front of Sammy's eyes again. The bottle dropped out of her hand and fell to the floormat, gurgling, as she passed out.

Piper drove as fast as she could, which was pretty fast, since Motton Road remained deserted, but when she got to the hospital, she discovered that Dr. Haskell had died the day before and the physician's assistant, Everett, was not there.

Sammy was examined and admitted by that famed medical expert, Dougie Twitchell.

8

While Ginny was trying to stop Sammy Bushey's vaginal bleeding and Twitch was giving the badly dehydrated Little Walter IV fluids, Rusty Everett was sitting quietly on a park bench at the Town Hall edge of the common. The bench was beneath the spreading arms of a tall blue spruce, and he thought he was in shade deep enough to render him effectively invisible. As long as he didn't move around much, that was.

There were interesting things to look at.

He had planned to go directly to the storage building behind the Town Hall (Twitch had called it a shed, but the long wooden building, which also housed The Mill's four snowplows, was actually quite a bit grander than that) and check the propane situation there, but then one of the police cars pulled up, with Frankie DeLesseps at the wheel. Junior Rennie had emerged from the passenger side. The two had spoken for a moment or two, then DeLesseps had driven away.

Junior went up the PD steps, but instead of going in, he sat down there, rubbing his temples as if he had a headache. Rusty decided to wait. He didn't want to be seen checking up on the town's energy supply, especially not by the Second Selectman's son.

At one point Junior took his cell phone out of his pocket, flipped it open, listened, said something, listened some more, said something else, then flipped it closed again. He went back to rubbing his temples. Dr. Haskell had said something about that young man. Migraine headaches, was it? It certainly looked like a migraine. It wasn't just the temple-rubbing; it was the way he was keeping his head down.

Trying to minimize the glare, Rusty thought. *Must have left his Imitrex or Zomig home. Assuming Haskell prescribed it, that is.*

Rusty had half-risen, meaning to cut across Commonwealth Lane to the rear of the Town Hall—Junior clearly not being at his most observant—but then he spotted someone else and sat down again. Dale Barbara, the short-order cook who had reputedly been elevated to the rank of colonel (by the President himself, according to some), was standing beneath the marquee of the Globe, even deeper in the shadows than Rusty was himself. And Barbara also appeared to be keeping an eye on young Mr. Rennie.

Interesting.

Barbara apparently came to the conclusion that Rusty had already drawn: Junior wasn't watching but waiting. Possibly for someone to pick him up. Barbara hustled across the street and—once he was blocked from Junior's potential view by the Town Hall itself—paused to scan the message board out front. Then he went inside.

Rusty decided to sit where he was awhile longer. It was nice under the tree, and he was curious about whom Junior might be waiting for. People were still straggling back from Dipper's (some would have stayed much longer had the booze been flowing). Most of them, like the young man sitting on the steps over yonder, had their heads down. Not in pain, Rusty surmised, but in dejection. Or maybe they were the same. It was certainly a point to ponder.

Now here came a boxy black gas-gobbler Rusty knew well: Big Jim Rennie's Hummer. It honked impatiently at a trio of townsfolk who were walking in the street, shunting them aside like sheep.

The Hummer pulled in at the PD. Junior looked up but didn't stand up. The doors opened. Andy Sanders got out from behind the wheel, Rennie from the passenger side. Rennie, allowing Sanders to drive his beloved black pearl? Sitting on his bench, Rusty raised his eyebrows. He didn't think he'd ever seen anyone but Big Jim himself behind the wheel of that monstrosity. *Maybe he's decided to promote Andy from dogsbody to chauffeur,* he thought, but when he watched Big Jim mount the steps to where his son still sat, he changed his mind.

Like most veteran medicos, Rusty was a pretty fair long-distance diagnostician. He would never have based a course of treatment on it, but you could tell a man who'd had a hip replacement six months ago from one currently suffering with hemorrhoids simply by the way he walked; you could tell a neck strain by the way a woman would turn her whole body instead of just looking back over her shoulder; you could tell a kid who'd picked up a good crop of lice at summer camp by the way he kept scratching his head. Big Jim held his arm against the upper slope of his considerable gut as he went up the steps, the classic body language of a man who has recently suffered either a shoulder strain, an upper arm strain, or both. Not so surprising that Sanders had been delegated to pilot the beast after all.

The three of them talked. Junior didn't get up but Sanders sat down beside him, rummaged in his pocket, and brought out something that twinkled in the hazy afternoon sunlight. Rusty's eyes were good, but he was at least fifty yards too far away to make out what the object might have been. Either glass or metal; that was all he could tell for sure. Junior put it in his pocket, then the three of them talked some more. Rennie gestured to the Hummer—he did it with his good arm—and Junior shook his head. Then Sanders pointed to the Hummer. Junior declined it again, dropped his head, and went back to working his temples. The two men looked at each other, Sanders craning his neck because he was still sitting on the steps. And in Big Jim's shadow, which Rusty thought appropriate. Big Jim shrugged and opened his hands—a *what can you do* gesture. Sanders stood up and the two men went into the PD building, Big Jim pausing long enough to pat his son's shoulder. Junior gave no response to that. He went on sitting where he was, as if he intended to sit out the age. Sanders played doorman for Big Jim, ushering him inside before following.

The two selectmen had no more than left the scene when a quartet came out of the Town Hall: an oldish gent, a young woman, a girl and a boy. The girl was holding the boy's hand and carrying a checkerboard. The boy looked almost as disconsolate as Junior, Rusty thought . . . and damned if he wasn't also rubbing one temple with his free hand. The four of them cut across Comm Lane, then passed directly in front of Rusty's bench.

"Hello," the little girl said brightly. "I'm Alice. This is Aidan."

"We're going to live at the passionage," the little boy named Aidan said dourly. He was still rubbing his temple, and he looked very pale.

"That will be exciting," Rusty said. "Sometimes I wish *I* lived in a passionage."

The man and woman caught up with the kids. They were holding hands. Father and daughter, Rusty surmised.

"Actually, we just want to talk to the Reverend Libby," the woman said. "You wouldn't know if she's back yet, would you?"

"No idea," Rusty said.

"Well, we'll just go over and wait. At the passionage." She smiled up at the older man when she said this. Rusty decided they might not be father and daughter, after all. "That's what the janitor said to do."

"Al Timmons?" Rusty had seen Al hop into the back of a Burpee's Department Store truck.

"No, the other one," the older man said. "He said the Reverend might be able to help us with lodgings."

Rusty nodded. "Was his name Dale?"

"I don't think he actually gave us his name," the woman said.

"Come *on!*" The boy let go of his sister's hand and tugged at the woman's instead. "I want to play that other game you said." But he sounded more querulous than eager. Mild shock, maybe. Or some physical ailment. If the latter, Rusty hoped it was only a cold. The last thing The Mill needed right now was an outbreak of flu.

"They've misplaced their mother, at least temporarily," the woman said in a low voice. "We're taking care of them."

"Good for you," Rusty said, and meant it. "Son, does your head hurt?"

"No."

"Sore throat?"

"No," the boy named Aidan said. His solemn eyes studied Rusty. "Know what? If we don't trick-or-treat this year, I don't even care."

"Aidan *Appleton*!" Alice cried, sounding shocked out of her shoes.

Rusty jerked a little on the bench; he couldn't help it. Then he smiled. "No? Why is that?"

"Because Mommy takes us around and Mommy went for splies."

"He means supplies," the girl named Alice said indulgently.

"She went for Woops," Aidan said. He looked like a little old man—a little old *worried* man. "I'd be ascairt to go Halloweenin without Mommy."

"Come on, Caro," the man said. "We ought to—"

Rusty rose from the bench. "Could I speak to you for a minute, ma'am? Just a step or two over here."

Caro looked puzzled and wary, but stepped with him to the side of the blue spruce.

"Has the boy exhibited any seizure activity?" Rusty asked. "That might include suddenly stopping what he's doing . . . you know, just standing still for a while . . . or a fixed stare . . . smacking of the lips—"

"Nothing like that," the man said, joining them.

"No," Caro agreed, but she looked frightened.

The man saw it and turned an impressive frown on Rusty. "Are you a doctor?"

"Physician's assistant. I thought maybe—"

"Well, I'm sure we appreciate your concern, Mr.—?"

"Eric Everett. Call me Rusty."

"We appreciate your concern, Mr. Everett, but I believe it's misplaced. Bear in mind that these children are without their mother—"

"And they spent two nights alone without much to eat," Caro added. "They were trying to make it to town on their own when those two . . . *officers*"—she wrinkled her nose as if the word had a bad smell—"found them."

Rusty nodded. "That could explain it, I guess. Although the little girl seems fine."

"Children react differently. And we better go. They're getting away from us, Thurse."

Alice and Aidan were running across the park, kicking up colorful bursts of fallen leaves, Alice flapping the checkerboard and yelling, *"Passionage! Passionage!"* at the top of her lungs. The boy was keeping up with her stride for stride and also yelling.

Kid had a momentary fugue, that's all, Rusty thought. *The rest was coincidence. Not even that—what American kid isn't thinking of Halloween during the last half of October?* One thing was sure: if these people were asked later, they would remember exactly where and when they had seen Eric "Rusty" Everett. So much for stealth.

The gray-haired man raised his voice. "Children! Slow down!"

The young woman considered Rusty, then put out her hand. "Thank you for your concern, Mr. Everett. Rusty."

"Probably overconcern. Occupational hazard."

"You're totally forgiven. This has been the craziest weekend in the history of the world. Chalk it up to that."

"You bet. And if you need me, check the hospital or the Health Center." He pointed in the direction of Cathy Russell, which would be visible through the trees once the rest of the leaves fell. *If* they fell.

"Or this bench," she said, still smiling.

"Or this bench, right." Also smiling.

"Caro!" Thurse sounded impatient. "Come *on*!"

She gave Rusty a little wave—no more than a twiddle of the fingertips—then ran after the others. She ran lightly, gracefully. Rusty wondered if Thurse knew that girls who could run lightly and gracefully almost always ran away from their elderly lovers, sooner or later. Maybe he did. Maybe it had happened to him before.

Rusty watched them cut across the common toward the spire of the Congo church. Eventually the trees screened them from sight. When he looked back at the PD building, Junior Rennie was gone.

Rusty sat where he was for a moment or two, drumming his fingers on his thighs. Then he came to a decision and stood up. Checking the town storage shed for the hospital's missing propane tanks could wait. He was more curious about what The Mill's one and only Army officer was doing in the Town Hall.

9

What Barbie was doing as Rusty crossed Comm Lane to the Town Hall was whistling appreciatively through his teeth. The fallout shelter was as long as an Amtrak dining car, and the shelves were fully stocked with canned goods. Most looked pretty fishy: stacks of sardines, ranks of salmon, and a lot of something called Snow's Clam Fry-Ettes, which Barbie sincerely hoped he would never have to sample. There were boxes of dry goods, including many large plastic canisters marked RICE, WHEAT, POW-DERED MILK, and SUGAR. There were stacked flats of bottles labeled DRINKING WATER. He counted ten large cartons of U.S. GOV'T SURPLUS CRACK-

ERS. Two more were labeled U.S. GOV'T SURPLUS CHOCOLATE BARS. On the wall above these was a yellowing sign reading 700 CALORIES A DAY KEEPS HUNGER AT BAY.

"Dream on," Barbie muttered.

There was a door at the far end. He opened it on Stygian blackness, felt around, found a light switch. Another room, not quite so big but still large. It looked old and disused—not dirty, Al Timmons at least must know about it because someone had been dusting the shelves and dry-mopping the floors, but neglected for sure. The stored water was in glass bottles, and he hadn't seen any of those since a brief stint in Saudi.

This second room contained a dozen folded cots plus plain blue blankets and mattresses that had been zipped into clear plastic covers, pending use. There were more supplies, including half a dozen cardboard canisters labeled SANITATION KIT and another dozen marked AIR MASKS. There was a small auxiliary generator that could supply minimal power. It was running; must have started up when he turned on the lights. Flanking the little gennie were two shelves. On one was a radio that looked as if it might have been new around the time C. W. McCall's novelty song "Convoy" had been a hit. On the other shelf were two hotplates and a metal box painted bright yellow. The logo on the side was from the days when CD stood for something other than compact disc. It was what he had come to find.

Barbie picked it up, then almost dropped it—it was heavy. On the front was a gauge labeled COUNTS PER SECOND. When you turned the instrument on and pointed the sensor at something, the needle might stay in the green, rise to the yellow center of the dial . . . or go over into the red. That, Barbie assumed, would not be good.

He turned it on. The little power lamp stayed dark and the needle lay quiet against 0.

"Battery's dead," someone said from behind him. Barbie almost jumped out of his skin. He looked around and saw a tall, heavyset man with blond hair standing in the doorway between the two rooms.

For a moment the name eluded him, although the guy was at the restaurant most Sunday mornings, sometimes with his wife, always with his two little girls. Then it came to him. "Rusty Evers, right?"

"Close; it's Everett." The newcomer held out his hand. A little warily, Barbie walked over and shook it. "Saw you come in. And that"—he nodded to the Geiger counter—"is probably not a bad idea. *Something* must be keeping it in place." He didn't say what he meant by *it* and didn't need to.

"Glad you approve. You almost scared me into a goddam heart attack. But you could take care of that, I guess. You're a doc, right?"

"PA," Rusty said. "That means—"

"I know what it means."

"Okay, you win the waterless cookware." Rusty pointed at the Geiger counter. "That thing probably takes a six-volt dry cell. I'm pretty sure I saw some at Burpee's. Less sure anybody's there right now. So . . . maybe a little more rekkie?"

"What exactly would we be reconning?"

"The supply shed out back."

"And we'd want to do that because?"

"That depends on what we find. If it's what we lost up at the hospital, you and I might exchange a little information."

"Want to share on what you lost?"

"Propane, brother."

Barbie considered this. "What the hell. Let's take a look."

10

Junior stood at the foot of the rickety stairs leading up the side of Sanders Hometown Drug, wondering if he could possibly climb them with his head aching the way it was. Maybe. Probably. On the other hand, he thought he might get halfway up and his skull would pop like a New Year's Eve noisemaker. The spot was back in front of his eye, jigging and jagging with his heartbeat, but it was no longer white. It had turned bright red.

I'd be okay in the dark, he thought. *In the pantry, with my girlfriends.*

If this went right, he could go there. Right now the pantry of the McCain house on Prestile Street seemed like the most desirable place on earth. Of course Coggins was there, too, but so what? Junior could always push *that* gospel-shouting asshole to one side. And Coggins had to stay hidden, at least for the time being. Junior had no interest in protecting his father (and was neither surprised nor dismayed at what his old man had done; Junior had always known Big Jim Rennie had murder in him), but he *did* have an interest in fixing Dale Barbara's little red wagon.

If we handle this right, we can do more than get him out of the way, Big Jim had said that morning. *We can use him to unify the town in the face of this crisis. And that cotton-picking newspaperwoman. I have an idea about her, too.* He had laid a warm and hammy hand on his son's shoulder. *We're a team, son.*

Maybe not forever, but for the time being, they were

pulling the same plow. And they would take care of *Baaarbie*. It had even occurred to Junior that Barbie was responsible for his headaches. If Barbie really had been overseas—Iraq was the rumor—then he might have come home with some weird Middle Eastern souvenirs. Poison, for instance. Junior had eaten in Sweetbriar Rose many times. Barbara could easily have dropped a little sumpin-sumpin in his food. Or his coffee. And if Barbie wasn't working the grill personally, he could have gotten Rose to do it. That cunt was under his spell.

Junior mounted the stairs, walking slowly, pausing every four steps. His head didn't explode, and when he reached the top, he groped in his pocket for the apartment key Andy Sanders had given him. At first he couldn't find it and thought he might have lost it, but at last his fingers came upon it, hiding under some loose change.

He glanced around. A few people were still walking back from Dipper's, but no one looked at him up here on the landing outside Barbie's apartment. The key turned in the lock, and he slipped inside.

He didn't turn on the lights, although Sanders's generator was probably sending juice to the apartment. The dimness made the pulsing spot in front of his eye less visible. He looked around curiously. There were books: shelves and shelves of them. Had *Baaarbie* been planning on leaving them behind when he blew town? Or had he made arrangements—possibly with Petra Searles, who worked downstairs—to ship them someplace? If so, he'd probably made similar arrangements to ship the rug on the living room floor—some camel-jockey-looking arti-fact Barbie had probably picked up in the local bazaar when there were no suspects to waterboard or little boys to bugger.

He hadn't made arrangements to have the stuff

shipped, Junior decided. He hadn't needed to, because he had never planned to leave at all. Once the idea occurred, Junior wondered why he hadn't seen it before. *Baaarbie* liked it here; would never leave of his own free will. He was as happy as a maggot in dog-puke.

Find something he can't talk away, Big Jim had instructed. *Something that can only be his. Do you understand me?*

What do you think I am, Dad, stupid? Junior thought now. *If I'm stupid, how come it was* me *who saved* your *ass last night?*

But his father had a mighty swing on him when he got his mad on, that much was undeniable. He had never slapped or spanked Junior as a child, something Junior had always attributed to his late mother's ameliorating influence. Now he suspected it was because his father understood, deep in his heart, that once he started, he might not be able to stop.

"Like father, like son," Junior said, and giggled. It hurt his head, but he giggled, anyway. What was that old saying about laughter being the best medicine?

He went into Barbie's bedroom, saw the bed was neatly made, and thought briefly of how wonderful it would be to take a big shit right in the middle of it. Yes, and then wipe himself with the pillowcase. *How would you like that,* Baaarbie?

He went to the dresser instead. Three or four pairs of jeans in the top drawer, plus two pairs of khaki shorts. Under the shorts was a cell phone, and for a moment he thought that was what he wanted. But no. It was a discount store special; what the kids at college called a burner or a throw-away. Barbie could always say it wasn't his.

There were half a dozen pairs of skivvies and another four or five pairs of plain white athletic socks in the second drawer. Nothing at all in the third drawer.

He looked under the bed, his head thudding and whamming—not better after all, it seemed. And nothing under there, not even dust-kitties. *Baaarbie* was a neatnik. Junior considered taking the Imitrex in his watch-pocket, but didn't. He'd taken two already, with absolutely no effect except for the metallic aftertaste in the back of his throat. He knew what medicine he needed: the dark pantry on Prestile Street. And the company of his girlfriends.

Meantime, he was here. And there had to be *something*.

"Sumpin," he whispered. "Gotta have a little sumpin-sumpin."

He started back to the living room, wiping water from the corner of his throbbing left eye (not noticing it was tinged with blood), then stopped, struck by an idea. He returned to the dresser, opened the sock-and-underwear drawer again. The socks were balled. When he was in high school, Junior had sometimes hidden a little weed or a couple of uppers in his balled-up socks; once one of Adriette Nedeau's thongs. Socks were a good hiding place. He took out the neatly made bundles one at a time, feeling them up.

He hit paydirt on the third ball, something that felt like a flat piece of metal. No, two of them. He unrolled the socks and shook the heavy one over the top of the dresser.

What fell out were Dale Barbara's dog tags. And in spite of his terrible headache, Junior smiled.

In the frame, Baaarbie, he thought. *You are in the fucking frame.*

11

On the Tarker's Mills side of Little Bitch Road, the fires set by the Fasthawk missiles were still raging, but would be out by dark; fire departments from four towns, augmented by a mixed detachment of Marine and Army grunts, were working on it, and gaining. It would have been out even sooner, Brenda Perkins judged, if the firefighters over there hadn't had a brisk wind to contend with. On The Mill side, they'd had no such problem. It was a blessing today. Later on, it might be a curse. There was no way to know.

Brenda wasn't going to let the question bother her this afternoon, because she felt good. If someone had asked her this morning when she thought she might feel good again, Brenda would have said, *Maybe next year. Maybe never.* And she was wise enough to know this feeling probably wouldn't last. Ninety minutes of hard exercise had a lot to do with it; exercise released endorphins whether the exercise was jogging or pounding out brushfires with the flat of a spade. But this was more than endorphins. It was being in charge of a job that was important, one that she could do.

Other volunteers had come to the smoke. Fourteen men and three women stood on either side of Little Bitch, some still holding the spades and rubber mats they'd been using to put out the creeping flames, some with the Indian pumps they'd been wearing on their backs now unslung and sitting on the unpaved hardpack of the road. Al Timmons, Johnny Carver, and Nell Toomey were coiling hoses and tossing them into the back of the Burpee's truck. Tommy Anderson from Dipper's and Lissa Jamieson—a little New Age-y but also as strong as a horse—were carrying the sump pump they'd used to draw water from Little Bitch Creek to one of the other trucks. Brenda heard laughter, and realized she wasn't the only one currently enjoying an endorphin rush.

The brush on both sides of the road was blackened and

still smoldering, and several trees had gone up, but that was all. The Dome had blocked the wind and had helped them in another way, as well, partially damming the creek and turning the area on this side into a marsh-in-progress. The fire on the other side was a different story. The men fighting it over there were shimmering wraiths seen through the heat and the accumulating soot on the Dome.

Romeo Burpee sauntered up to her. He was holding a soaked broom in one hand and a rubber floormat in the other. The price tag was still clinging to the underside of the mat. The words on it were charred but readable: EVERY DAY IS SALE DAY AT BURPEE'S! He dropped it and stuck out a grimy hand.

Brenda was surprised but willing. She shook firmly. "What's that for, Rommie?"

"For you doin one damn fine job out here," he said.

She laughed, embarrassed but pleased. "Anybody could have done it, given the conditions. It was only a contact fire, and the ground's so squelchy it probably would have put itself out by sunset."

"Maybe," he said, then pointed through the trees to a raggedy clearing with a tumbledown rock wall meandering across it. "Or maybe it would've gotten into that high grass, then the trees on the other side, and then Katy bar the door. It could have burned for a week or a month. Especially with no damn fire department." He turned his head aside and spat. "Even widdout wind, a fire will burn if it gets a foothold. They got mine fires down south that have burned for twenty, thirty years. I read it in *National Geographic*. No wind underground. And how do we know a good wind won't come up? We don't know jack about what that thing does or don't do."

They both looked toward the Dome. The soot and ash had rendered it visible—sort of—to a height of almost a hundred feet. It had also dimmed their view of the Tarker's side, and Brenda didn't like that. It wasn't anything she wanted to consider deeply, not when it might rob some of her good feelings about the afternoon's work, but no—she didn't like it at all. It made her think of last night's weird, smeary sunset.

"Dale Barbara needs to call his friend in Washington," she said. "Tell him when they get the fire out on their side, they have to hose that whatever-it-is off. We can't do it from our side."

"Good idea," Romeo said. But something else was on his mind. "Do you reckonize anything about your crew, ma'am? Because I sure do."

Brenda looked startled. "They're not my crew."

"Oh yes they are," he said. "You were the one givin orders, that makes em your crew. You see any cops?"

She took a look.

"Not a one," Romeo said. "Not Randolph, not Henry Morrison, not Freddy Denton or Rupe Libby, not Georgie Frederick . . . none of the new ones, either. Those kids."

"They're probably busy with . . ." She trailed off.

Romeo nodded. "Right. Busy wit what? You don't know and neither do I. But whatever they're busy wit, I'm not sure I like it. Or think it's wort bein busy wit. There's gonna be a town meeting Thursday night, and if this is still goin on, I think there should be some changes." He paused. "I could be gettin out of my place here, but I think maybe you ought to stand for Chief of Fire n Police."

Brenda considered it, considered the file she had found marked VADER, then shook her head slowly. "It's too soon for anything like that."

"What about just Fire Chief? How bout dat one?" The Lewiston *on parle* coming on stronger in his voice now.

Brenda looked around at the smoldering brush and

charred trashwood trees. Ugly, granted, like something out of a World War I battlefield photo, but no longer dangerous. The people who had shown up here had seen to that. The crew. *Her* crew.

She smiled. "That I might consider."

12

The first time Ginny Tomlinson came down the hospital hallway she was running, responding to a loud beeping that sounded like bad news, and Piper didn't have a chance to speak to her. Didn't even try. She had been in the waiting room long enough to get the picture: three people—two nurses and a teenage candy striper named Gina Buffalino—in charge of an entire hospital. They were coping, but barely. When Ginny came back, she was walking slowly. Her shoulders were slumped. A medical chart dangled from one hand.

"Ginny?" Piper asked. "Okay?"

Piper thought Ginny might snap at her, but she offered a tired smile instead of a snarl. And sat down next to her. "Fine. Just tired." She paused. "Also, Ed Carty just died."

Piper took her hand. "I'm very sorry to hear that."

Ginny squeezed her fingers. "Don't be. You know how women talk about having babies? This one had an easy delivery, this one had it hard?"

Piper nodded.

"Death is like that, too. Mr. Carty was in labor a long time, but now he's delivered."

To Piper the idea seemed beautiful. She thought she could use it in a sermon . . . except she guessed that people wouldn't want to hear a sermon on death this coming Sunday. Not if the Dome was still in place.

They sat for a while, Piper trying to think of the best way to ask what she had to ask. In the end, she didn't have to.

"She was raped," Ginny said. "Probably more than once. I was afraid Twitch was going to have to try his suturing, but I finally got it stopped with a vaginal pack." She paused. "I was crying. Luckily, the girl was too stoned to notice."

"And the baby?"

"Your basic healthy eighteen-month-old, but he gave us a scare. He had a mini-seizure. It was probably exposure to the sun. Plus dehydration . . . hunger . . . and he has a wound of his own." Ginny traced a line across her forehead.

Twitch came down the hall and joined them. He looked light-years from his usual jaunty self.

"Did the men who raped her also hurt the baby?" Piper's voice remained calm, but a thin red fissure was opening in her mind.

"Little Walter? I think he just fell," Twitch said. "Sammy said something about the crib collapsing. It wasn't completely coherent, but I'm pretty sure it was an accident. *That* part, anyway."

Piper was looking at him, bemused. "*That* was what she was saying. I thought it was 'little water.' "

"I'm sure she wanted water," Ginny said, "but Sammy's baby really is Little, first name, Walter, second name. They named him after a blues harmonica player, I believe. She and Phil—" Ginny mimed sucking a joint and holding in the smoke.

"Oh, Phil was a lot more than a smokehound," Twitch said. "When it came to drugs, Phil Bushey was a multi-tasker."

"Is he dead?" Piper asked.

Twitch shrugged. "I haven't seen him around since spring. If he is, good riddance."

Piper looked at him reproachfully.

Twitch ducked his head a little. "Sorry, Rev." He turned to Ginny. "Any sign of Rusty?"

"He needed some time off," she said, "and I told him to go. He'll be back soon, I'm sure."

Piper sat between them, outwardly calm. Inside, the red fissure was widening. There was a sour taste in her mouth. She remembered a night when her father had forbidden her to go out to Skate Scene at the mall because she'd said something smart to her mother (as a teenager, Piper Libby had been an absolute font of smart things to say). She had gone upstairs, called the friend she had expected to meet, and told that friend—in a perfectly pleasant, perfectly even voice—that something had come up and she wouldn't be able to meet her after all. Next weekend? For sure, uh-huh, you bet, have a good time, no, I'm fine, b'bye. Then she had trashed her room. She finished by yanking her beloved Oasis poster off the wall and tearing it up. By then she had been crying hoarsely, not in sorrow but in one of those rages that had blown through her teenage years like force-five hurricanes. Her father came up at some point during the festivities and stood in the doorway, regarding her. When she finally saw him there she stared back defiantly, panting, thinking how much she hated him. How much she hated them both. If they were dead, she could go live with her aunt Ruth in New York. Aunt Ruth knew how to have a good time. Not like some people. He had held his hands out to her, open, extended. It had been a somehow humble gesture, one that had crushed her anger and almost crushed her heart.

If you don't control your temper, your temper will control you, he had said, and then left her, walking down the hallway with his head bent. She hadn't slammed the door behind him. She had closed it, very quietly.

That was the year she had made her often vile temper her number one priority. Killing it completely would be killing part of herself, but she thought if she did not make some fundamental changes, an important part of her would remain fifteen for a long, long time. She had begun working to impose control, and mostly she had succeeded. When she felt that control slipping, she would remember what her father had said, and that open-handed gesture, and his slow walk along the upstairs hall of the house she had grown up in. She had spoken at his funeral service nine years later, saying *My father told me the most important thing I've ever heard.* She hadn't said what that thing was, but her mother had known; she had been sitting in the front pew of the church in which her daughter was now ordained.

For the last twenty years, when she felt the urge to flash out at someone—and often the urge was nearly uncontrollable, because people could be so stupid, so willfully *dumb*—she would summon her father's voice: *If you don't control your temper, your temper will control you.*

But now the red fissure was widening and she felt the old urge to throw things. To scratch skin until the blood came sweating out.

"Did you ask her who did it?"

"Yes, of course," Ginny said. "She won't say. She's scared."

Piper remembered how she'd first thought the mother and baby lying beside the road was a bag of garbage. And that, of course, was what they'd been to whoever did this. She stood up. "I'm going to talk to her."

"That might not be such a good idea right now," Ginny said. "She's had a sedative, and—"

"Let her take a shot," Twitch said. His face was pale. His hands were knotted between his knees. The knuckles cracked repeatedly. "And make it a good one, Rev."

13

Sammy's eyes were at half-mast. They opened slowly when Piper sat down beside her bed. "You . . . were the one who . . ."

"Yes," Piper said, taking her hand. "My name is Piper Libby."

"Thank you," Sammy said. Her eyes began to drift closed again.

"Thank me by telling me the names of the men who raped you."

In the dim room—warm, with the hospital's air-conditioning shut down—Sammy shook her head. "They said they'd hurt me. If I told." She glanced at Piper. It was a cowlike glance, full of dumb resignation. "They might hurt Little Walter, too."

Piper nodded. "I understand you're frightened," she said. "Now tell me who they were. Give me the names."

"Didn't you *hear* me?" Looking away from Piper now. "They said they would hurt—"

Piper had no time for this; the girl would zone out on her. She grasped Sammy's wrist. "I want those names, and you're going to give them to me."

"I don't *dare*." Sammy began to ooze tears.

"You're going to do it because if I hadn't come along, you might be dead now." She paused, then drove the dagger the rest of the way in. She might regret it later, but not now. Right now the girl in the bed was only an obstacle standing between her and what she needed to know. "Not to mention your baby. He might be dead, too. I saved your life, I saved his, and *I want those names.*"

"No." But the girl was weakening now, and part of the Reverend Piper Libby was actually enjoying this. Later she'd be disgusted; later she'd think *You're not that much different from those boys, forcing is forcing.* But now, yes, there was pleasure, just as there had been pleasure in tearing the treasured poster from the wall and ripping it to shreds.

I like it because it is bitter, she thought. *And because it is my heart.*

She leaned over the crying girl. "Dig the wax out of your ears, Sammy, because you need to hear this. What they've done once they'll do again. And when they do, when some other woman shows up here with a bloody snatch and possibly pregnant with a rapist's child, I will come to you, and I will say—"

"No! Stop!"

" 'You were part of it. You were right there, cheering them on.' "

"No!" Sammy cried. *"Not me, that was Georgia! Georgia was the one cheering them on!"*

Piper felt cold disgust. A woman. A woman had been there. In her head, the red fissure opened wider. Soon it would begin to spew lava.

"Give me the names," she said.

And Sammy did.

14

Jackie Wettington and Linda Everett were parked outside Food City. It was closing at five PM instead of eight. Randolph had sent them there thinking the early closing might cause trouble. A ridiculous idea, because the supermarket was almost empty. There were hardly a dozen cars in the parking lot, and the few remaining shoppers were moving in a slow daze, as if sharing the same bad dream. The two officers saw only one cashier, a teenager named Bruce Yardley. The kid was taking currency and writing chits instead of running credit cards. The meat counter was looking depleted, but there was still plenty of chicken and most of the canned and dry-goods shelves were fully stocked.

They were waiting for the last customers to leave when Linda's cell phone rang. She looked at the caller ID and felt a little stab of fear in her stomach. It was Marta Edmunds, who kept Janelle and Judy when Linda and Rusty were both working—as they had been, almost nonstop, since the Dome came down. She hit callback.

"Marta?" she said, praying it was nothing, Marta asking if it was okay for her to take the girls down to the common, something like that. "Everything all right?"

"Well . . . yes. That is, I guess so." Linda hating the worry she heard in Marta's voice. "But . . . you know that seizure thing?"

"Oh God—did she have one?"

"I think so," Marta said, then hurried on: "They're perfectly okay now, in the other room, coloring."

"What happened? Tell me!"

"They were on the swings. I was doing my flowers, getting them ready for winter—"

"Marta, *please*!" Linda said, and Jackie laid a hand on her arm.

"I'm sorry. Audi started to bark, so I turned around. I said, 'Honey, are you all right?' She didn't answer, just got out of the swing and sat down underneath—you know, where there's a little dip from all the feet? She didn't *fall* out or anything, just sat down. She was staring straight ahead and doing that lip-smacking thing you told me to watch for. I ran over . . . kind of shook her . . . and she said . . . let me think . . ."

Here it comes, Linda thought. *Stop Halloween, you have to stop Halloween.*

But no. It was something else entirely.

"She said 'The pink stars are falling. The pink stars are falling in lines.' Then she said, 'It's so dark and everything smells bad.' Then she woke up and now everything's fine."

"Thank God for that," Linda said, and spared a thought for her five-year-old. "Is Judy okay? Did it upset her?"

There was a long pause on the line and then Marta said, "Oh."

"*Oh?* What does that mean, *oh?*"

"It *was* Judy, Linda. Not Janelle. This time it was Judy."

15

I want to play that other game you said, Aidan had told Carolyn Sturges when they had stopped on the common to talk to Rusty. The other game she had in mind was Red Light, although Carolyn had only the slightest recollection of the rules—not surprising, since she hadn't played it since she was six or seven.

But once she was standing against a tree in the commodious backyard of the "passionage," the rules came back to her. And, unexpectedly, to Thurston, who seemed not only willing to play, but eager.

"Remember," he instructed the children (who somehow seemed to have missed the pleasures of Red Light themselves), "she can count to ten as fast as she wants to, and if she catches you moving when she turns around, you have to go all the way back."

"She won't catch *me*," Alice said.

"Me, either," Aidan said stoutly.

"We'll see about that," Carolyn said, and turned her face to the tree: "One, two, three, four . . . five, six, seven . . . eight-nine-ten RED LIGHT!"

She whirled around. Alice was standing with a smile on her mouth and one leg extended in a big old giant step. Thurston, also smiling, had his hands extended in *Phantom of the Opera* claws. She caught the slightest movement from Aidan, but didn't even think about sending him back. He looked happy, and she had no intention of spoiling that.

"Good," she said. "Good little statues. Here comes Round Two." She turned to the tree and counted again, invaded by the old, childishly delicious fear of knowing people were moving in while her back was turned. "Onetwo threefour fivesix seveneightnineten RED-LIGHT!"

She whirled. Alice was now only twenty paces away. Aidan was ten paces or so behind her, trembling on one foot, a scab on his knee very visible. Thurse was behind the boy, one hand on his chest like an orator, smiling. Alice was going to be the one to catch her, but that was all right; in the second game the girl would be "it" and her brother would win. She and Thurse would see to it.

She turned to the tree again. "Onetwothreefo—"

Then Alice screamed.

Carolyn turned and saw Aidan Appleton lying on the ground. At first she thought he was still trying to play the game. One knee—the one with the scab on it—was up, as if he were trying to run on his back. His wide eyes were staring at the sky. His lips were folded into a poochy little **O**. There was a dark spot spreading on his shorts. She rushed to him.

"What's wrong with him?" Alice asked. Carolyn could see all the stress of the terrible weekend crushing in on her face. "Is he all right?"

"Aidan?" Thurse asked. "You okay, big fella?"

Aidan went on trembling, his lips seeming to suck at an invisible straw. His bent leg came down . . . then kicked out. His shoulders twitched.

"He's having some kind of seizure," Carolyn said. "Probably from overexcitement. I think he'll come out of it if we just give him a few m—"

"The pink stars are falling," Aidan said. "They make lines behind them. It's pretty. It's scary. Everyone is watching. No treats, only tricks. Hard to breathe. He calls himself the Chef. It's his fault. He's the one."

Carolyn and Thurston looked at each other. Alice was kneeling by her brother, holding his hand.

"Pink stars," Aidan said. "They fall, they fall, they f—"

"Wake up!" Alice shouted into his face. *"Stop scaring us!"*

Thurston Marshall touched her shoulder gently. "Honey, I don't think that's helping."

Alice paid him no mind. *"Wake up, you . . . you CRAP-HEAD!"*

And Aidan did. He looked at his sister's tear-streaked face, puzzled. Then he looked at Carolyn and smiled—the sweetest goddam smile she had ever seen in her life.

"Did I win?" he asked.

16

The gennie in the Town Hall's supply shed was badly maintained (someone had shoved an old-timey galvanized tin washbasin under it to catch the dripping oil), and, Rusty guessed, about as energy-efficient as Big Jim Rennie's Hummer. But he was more interested in the silver tank attached to it.

Barbie looked briefly at the generator, grimaced at the smell, then moved to the tank. "It isn't as big as I would've expected," he said . . . although it was a hell of a lot bigger than the canisters they used at Sweetbriar, or the one he had changed out for Brenda Perkins.

"It's called 'municipal size,' " Rusty said. "I remember that from the town meeting last year. Sanders and Rennie made a big deal of how the smaller tanks were going to save us yea bucks during 'these times of costly energy.' Each one holds eight hundred gallons."

"Which means a weight of . . . what? Sixty-four hundred pounds?"

Rusty nodded. "Plus the weight of the tank. It's a lot to *lift*—you'd need a forklift or a hydraulic Power Step—but not to move. A Ram pickup is rated for sixty-eight hundred pounds, and it could probably carry more. One of these midsize tanks would fit in the bed, too. Sticking out the end a little bit, is all." Rusty shrugged. "Hang a red flag from it and you're good to go."

"This is the only one here," Barbie said. "When it's gone, the Town Hall lights go out."

"Unless Rennie and Sanders know where there are more," Rusty agreed. "And I'm betting they do."

Barbie ran a hand over the blue stenciling on the tank: **CR HOSP**. "This is what you lost."

"We didn't lose it; it was stolen. That's what I'm thinking. Only there should be five more of our tanks in here, because we're missing a total of six."

Barbie surveyed the long shed. Despite the stored plows and cartons of reserve parts, the place looked empty. Especially around the generator. "Never mind whatever got kited from the hospital; where's the rest of the *town's* tanks?"

"I don't know."

"And what could they be using them for?"

"I don't know," Rusty said, "but I mean to find out."

PINK STARS FALLING

1

Barbie and Rusty stepped outside and breathed deeply of the open air. It had a smoky tang from the recently extinguished fire west of town, but seemed very fresh after the exhaust fumes in the shed. A lackadaisical little breeze cat's-pawed their cheeks. Barbie was carrying the Geiger counter in a brown shopping bag he'd found in the fallout shelter.

"This shit will not stand," Rusty said. His face was set and grim.

"What are you going to do about it?" Barbie asked.

"Now? Nothing. I'm going back to the hospital and do rounds. Tonight, though, I intend to knock on Jim Rennie's door and ask for a goddam explanation. He better have one, and he better have the rest of our propane as well, because we're going to be dead out at the hospital by the day after tomorrow, even with every nonessential shut down."

"This might be over by the day after tomorrow."

"Do you believe it will be?"

Instead of answering the question, Barbie said, "Selectman Rennie could be a dangerous man to press right about now."

"Just now? That tags you for a town newbie like nothing else could. I've been hearing that about Big Jim for the ten thousand or so years he's been running this town. He either tells people to get lost or pleads patience. 'For the good of the town,' he says. That's number one on his hit parade. Town meeting in March is a joke. An article to authorize a new sewer system? Sorry, the town can't afford the taxes. An article to authorize more commercial zoning? Great idea, the town needs the revenue, let's build a Walmart out on 117. The University of Maine Small Town Environmental Study says there's too much graywater in Chester Pond? The selectmen recommend tabling discussion because everybody knows all those scientific studies are run by radical humanist bleeding-heart atheists. But the *hospital* is for the good of the town, wouldn't you say?"

"Yes. I would." Barbie was a little bemused by this outburst.

Rusty stared at the ground with his hands in his back pockets. Then he looked up. "I understand the President tapped you to take over. I think it's high time you did so."

"It's an idea." Barbie smiled. "Except . . . Rennie and Sanders have got their police force; where's mine?"

Before Rusty could reply, his cell phone rang. He flipped it open and looked at the little window. "Linda? What?"

He listened.

"All right, I understand. If you're sure they're both okay *now*. And you're sure it was Judy? Not Janelle?" He listened some more, then said: "I think this is actually good news. I saw two other kids this morning—both with transient seizures that passed off quickly, long before I saw them, and both fine afterward. Had calls on three more. Ginny T. took another one. It could be a side effect of whatever force is powering the Dome."

He listened.

"Because I didn't have a *chance* to," he said. His tone patient, non-confrontational. Barbie could imagine the question which had prompted that: *Kids have been having seizures all day and* now *you tell me?*

"You're picking the kids up?" Rusty asked. He listened. "Okay. That's good. If you sense anything wrong, call me ASAP. I'll come on the run. And make sure Audi stays with them. Yes. Uh-huh. Love you, too." He hooked the phone on his belt and ran both hands through his hair hard enough to make his eyes look briefly Chinese. "Jesus jumped-up Christ."

"Who's Audi?"

"Our golden retriever."

"Tell me about these seizures."

Rusty did so, not omitting what Jannie had said about Halloween and what Judy had said about pink stars.

"The Halloween thing sounds like what the Dinsmore boy was raving about," Barbie said.

"Does, doesn't it?"

"What about the other kids? Any of them talking about Halloween? Or pink stars?"

"The parents I saw today said their kids babbled while the seizure was ongoing, but they were too freaked to pay any attention."

"The kids themselves didn't remember?"

"The kids didn't even know they'd had seizures."

"Is that normal?"

"It's not *ab*normal."

"Any chance your younger daughter was copying the older one? Maybe . . . I don't know . . . vying for attention?"

Rusty hadn't considered this—hadn't had the time, really. Now he did. "Possible, but not likely." He nodded to the old-fashioned yellow Geiger counter in the bag. "You going prospecting with that thing?"

"Not me," Barbie said. "This baby's town property, and the powers that be don't like me much. I wouldn't want to be caught with it." He held the bag out to Rusty.

"Can't. I'm just too busy right now."

"I know," Barbie said, and told Rusty what he wanted him to do. Rusty listened closely, smiling a little.

"Okay," he said. "Works for me. What are you going to be doing while I'm running your errands?"

"Cooking dinner at Sweetbriar. Tonight's special is chicken à la Barbara. Want me to send some up to the hospital?"

"Sweet," Rusty said.

2

On his way back to Cathy Russell, Rusty stopped by the *Democrat*'s office and handed off the Geiger counter to Julia Shumway.

She listened as he relayed Barbie's instructions, smiling faintly. "The man knows how to delegate, I'll say that for him. I'll see to this with pleasure."

Rusty thought of cautioning her to be careful about who saw the town's Geiger counter in her possession, but didn't need to. The bag had disappeared into the kneehole of her desk.

On his way to the hospital, he reached Ginny Tomlinson and asked her about the seizure call she'd taken.

"Little kid named Jimmy Wicker. The grandfather called it in. Bill Wicker?"

Rusty knew him. Bill delivered their mail.

"He was taking care of Jimmy while the boy's mom went to gas up their car. They're almost out of regular at the Gas and Grocery, by the way, and Johnny Carver's had the nerve to jack the price of regular to eleven dollars a gallon. *Eleven!*"

Rusty bore this patiently, thinking he could have had his conversation with Ginny face-to-face. He was almost back to the hospital. When she was done complaining, he asked her if little Jimmy had said anything while he was seizing.

"Yes indeed. Bill said he babbled quite a bit. I think it was something about pink stars. Or Halloween. Or maybe I'm getting it confused with what Rory Dinsmore said after he was shot. People have been talking about that."

Of course they have, Rusty thought grimly. *And they'll be talking about this, too, if they find out. As they probably will.*

"All right," he said. "Thanks, Ginny."

"When you comin back, Red Ryder?"

"Almost there now."

"Good. Because we have a new patient. Sammy Bushey. She was raped."

Rusty groaned.

"It gets better. Piper Libby brought her in. I couldn't get the names of the doers out of the girl, but I think Piper did. She went out of here like her hair was on fire and her ass—" A pause. Ginny yawned loud enough for Rusty to hear. "—her ass was catching."

"Ginny my love—when's the last time you got some sleep?"

"I'm fine."

"Go home,"

"Are you *kidding*?" Sounding aghast.

"No. Go home. Sleep. No setting the alarm, either." Then an idea struck him. "But stop by Sweetbriar Rose on the way, why don't you? They're having chicken. I heard it from a reliable source."

"The Bushey girl—"

"I'll be checking on her in five minutes. What you're going to do is make like a bee and buzz."

He closed his phone before she could protest again.

3

Big Jim Rennie felt remarkably good for a man who had committed murder the night before. This was partially because he did not see it as murder, no more than he had seen the death of his late wife as murder. It was cancer that had taken her. Inoperable. Yes, he had probably given her too many of the pain pills over the last week, and in the end he'd still had to help her with a pillow over her face (but lightly, ever so lightly, slowing her breathing, easing her into the arms of Jesus), but he had done it out of love and kindness. What had happened to Reverend Coggins was a bit more brutal—admittedly—but the man had been so *bullish*. So completely unable to put the town's welfare ahead of his own.

"Well, he's eating dinner with Christ the Lord tonight," Big Jim said. "Roast beef, mashed with gravy, apple crisp for dessert." He himself was eating a large plate of fettuccini alfredo, courtesy of the Stouffer's company. A lot of cholesterol, he supposed, but there was no Dr. Haskell around to nag him about it.

"I outlasted you, you old poop," Big Jim told his empty study, and laughed goodnaturedly. His plate of pasta and a glass filled with milk (Big Jim Rennie did not drink alcohol) were set on his desk blotter. He often ate in the study, and he saw no need to change that simply because Lester Coggins had met his end here. Besides, the room was once more squared away and spandy-clean. Oh, he supposed one of those investigation units like the ones on TV would be able to find plenty of blood-spatter with their luminol and special lights and things, but none of those people was going to be here in the immediate future. As for Pete Randolph doing any sleuthing in the matter . . . the idea was a joke. Randolph was an idiot.

"But," Big Jim told the empty room in a lecturely tone, "he's *my* idiot."

He slurped up the last few strands of pasta, mopped his considerable chin with a napkin, then once more began to jot notes on the yellow legal pad beside the blotter. He had jotted plenty of notes since Saturday; there was so much to do. And if the Dome stayed in place, there would be more still.

Big Jim sort of hoped it *would* remain in place, at least for a while. The Dome offered challenges to which he felt certain he could rise (with God's help, of course). The first order of business was to consolidate his hold on the town. For that he needed more than a scapegoat; he needed a bogeyman. The obvious choice was Barbara, the man the Democrat Party's Commie-in-Chief had tapped to replace James Rennie.

The study door opened. When Big Jim looked up from his notes, his son was standing there. His face was pale and expressionless. There was something not quite right about Junior lately. As busy as he was with the town's affairs (and their other enterprise; that had also kept him busy), Big Jim realized this. But he felt confident in the boy just the same. Even if Junior let him down, Big Jim was sure he could handle it. He'd spent a lifetime making his own luck; that wasn't going to change now.

Besides, the boy had moved the body. That made him part of this. Which was good—the essence of smalltown life, in fact. In a small town, everybody was supposed to be a part of everything. How did that silly song put it? *We all support the team.*

"Son?" he asked. "All right?"

"I'm fine," Junior said. He wasn't, but he was better, the latest poisonous headache finally lifting. Being with his girlfriends had helped, as he'd known it would. The McCain pantry didn't smell so good, but after he'd sat there awhile, holding their hands, he'd gotten used to it. He thought he could even come to like that smell.

"Did you find anything in his apartment?"

"Yes." Junior told him what he had found.

"That's excellent, Son. Really excellent. And are you ready to tell me where you put the . . . where you put him?"

Junior shook his head slowly back and forth, but his eyes stayed in exactly the same place while he did it—pinned on his father's face. It was a little eerie. "You don't need to know. I told you that. It's a safe place, and that's enough."

"So now you're telling *me* what I need to know." But he said it without his usual heat.

"In this case, yes."

Big Jim considered his son carefully. "Are you sure you're all right? You look pale."

"I'm fine. Just a headache. It's going now."

"Why not have something to eat? There are a few more fettuccinis in the freezer, and the microwave does a great job on them." He smiled. "Might as well enjoy them while we can."

The dark, considering eyes dropped for a moment to the puddle of white sauce on Big Jim's plate, then rose again to his father's face. "Not hungry. When should I find the bodies?"

"Bodies?" Big Jim stared. "What do you mean, *bodies?*"

Junior smiled, lips lifting just enough to show the tips of his teeth. "Never mind. It'll help your cred if you're surprised like everyone else. Let's put it this way—once we pull the trigger, this town will be ready to hang *Baaar-bie* from a sour apple tree. When do you want to do it? Tonight? Because that'll work."

Big Jim considered the question. He looked down at his yellow pad. It was crammed with notes (and splattered with alfredo sauce), but only one was circled: *newspaper bitch*.

"Not tonight. We can use him for more than Coggins if we play this right."

"And if the Dome comes down while you're playing it?"

"We'll be fine," Big Jim said. Thinking, *And if Mr. Barbara is somehow able to squirm free of the frame—not likely, but cockroaches have a way of finding cracks when the lights go on—there's always you. You and those other bodies.* "Now get yourself something to eat, even if it's only a salad."

But Junior didn't move. "Don't wait too long, Dad," he said.

"I won't."

Junior considered it, considered *him* with those dark eyes that seemed so strange now, then seemed to lose interest. He yawned. "I'm going up to my room and sleep awhile. I'll eat later."

"Just make sure you do. You're getting too thin."

"Thin is in," his son replied, and offered a hollow smile that was even more disquieting than his eyes. To Big Jim, it looked like a skull's smile. It made him think of the fellow who now just called himself The Chef—as if his previous life as Phil Bushey had been canceled. When Junior left the room, Big Jim breathed a sigh of relief without even being aware of it.

He picked up his pen: so much to do. He would do it, and do it well. It was not impossible that when this thing was over, his picture would be on the cover of *Time* magazine.

4

With her generator still running—although it wouldn't be for much longer unless she could find some more LP canisters—Brenda Perkins was able to fire up her husband's printer and make a hard copy of everything in the VADER file. The incredible list of offenses Howie had compiled—and which he had apparently been about to act on at the time of his death—seemed more real to her on paper than they had on the computer screen. And the more she looked at them, the more they seemed to fit the Jim Rennie she'd known for most of her life. She had always known he was a monster; just not how *big* a monster.

Even the stuff about Coggins's Jesus-jumping church fit . . . although if she was reading this right, it was really not a church at all but a big old holy Maytag that washed money instead of clothes. Money from a drug-manufacturing operation that was, in her husband's words, "maybe one of the biggest in the history of the United States."

But there were problems, which both Police Chief Howie "Duke" Perkins and the State AG had acknowledged. The problems were why the evidence-gathering phase of Operation Vader had gone on as long as it had. Jim Rennie wasn't just a big monster; he was a *smart* monster. That was why he had always been content to remain the Second Selectman. He had Andy Sanders to break trail for him.

And to wear a target—that, too. For a long time, Andy was the only one against whom Howie had had hard evidence. He was the frontman and probably didn't even know it, cheery gladhanding dumbshit that he was. Andy was First Selectman, First Deacon at Holy Redeemer, first in the hearts of the townsfolk, and out front on a trail of corporate documents that finally disappeared into the obfuscatory financial swamps of Nassau and Grand Cayman Island. If Howie and the State Attorney General had moved too soon, he would also have been first to get his picture taken while holding a number. Maybe the only one, should he believe Big Jim's inevitable promises that all would be well if Andy just kept mum. And he probably would. Who was better at dummying up than a dummy?

Last summer, things had begun working toward what Howie had seen as the endgame. That was when Rennie's name had started showing up on some of the paperwork the AG had obtained, most notably that of a Nevada corporation called Town Ventures. The Town Ventures money had disappeared west instead of east, not into the Caribbean but into mainland China, a country where the key ingredients of decongestant drugs could be bought in bulk, with few if any questions.

Why would Rennie allow such exposure? Howie Perkins had been able to think of only one reason: the money had gotten too big too fast for one holy washing machine. Rennie's name had subsequently appeared on papers concerning half a dozen other fundamentalist churches in the northeast. Town Ventures and the other churches (not to mention half a dozen other religious radio stations and AM talkers, none as big as WCIK) were Rennie's first real mistakes. They left dangling strings. Strings could be pulled, and sooner or later—usually sooner—everything unraveled.

You couldn't let go, could you? Brenda thought as she sat behind her husband's desk, studying the papers. *You'd made millions—maybe tens of millions—and the risks were be-*

coming outrageous, but you still couldn't let go. Like a monkey who traps himself because he won't let go of the food. You were sitting on a damn fortune and you just kept on living in that old three-story and selling cars at that pit of yours out on 119. Why?

But she knew. It wasn't the money; it was the town. What he saw as *his* town. Sitting on a beach somewhere in Costa Rica or presiding over a guarded estate in Namibia, Big Jim would become Small Jim. Because a man without a sense of purpose, even one whose bank accounts are stuffed with money, is always a small man.

If she confronted him with what she had, could she make a deal with him? Force him out in return for her silence? She wasn't sure. And she dreaded the confrontation. It would be ugly, possibly dangerous. She would want to have Julia Shumway with her. And Barbie. Only Dale Barbara was now wearing his own target.

Howie's voice, calm but firm, spoke up in her head. *You can afford to wait a little while—I was waiting for a few final items of proof myself—but I wouldn't wait too long, honey. Because the longer this siege goes on, the more dangerous he'll become.*

She thought of Howie starting to back down the driveway, then stopping to put his lips on hers in the sunshine, his mouth almost as well known to her as her own, and certainly as well loved. Caressing the side of her throat as he did it. As if he knew the end was coming, and one last touch would have to pay for all. An easy and romantic conceit for sure, but she almost believed it, and her eyes filled with tears.

Suddenly the papers and all the machinations contained therein seemed less important. Even the Dome didn't seem very important. What mattered was the hole that had appeared so suddenly in her life, sucking out the happiness she had taken for granted. She wondered if poor dumb Andy Sanders felt the same way. She supposed he did.

I'll give it twenty-four hours. If the Dome's still in place tomorrow night, I'll go to Rennie with this stuff—with copies of this stuff—and tell him he has to resign in favor of Dale Barbara. Tell him that if he doesn't, he's going to read all about his drug operation in the paper.

"Tomorrow," she murmured, and closed her eyes. Two minutes later she was asleep in Howie's chair. In Chester's Mill, the supper hour had come. Some meals (including chicken à la king for a hundred or so) were cooked on electric or gas ranges courtesy of the generators in town that were still working, but there were also people who had turned to their woodstoves, either to conserve their gennies or because wood was now all they had. The smoke rose in the still air from hundreds of chimneys.

And spread.

5

After delivering the Geiger counter—the recipient took it willingly, even eagerly, and promised to begin prospecting with it early on Tuesday—Julia headed for Burpee's Department Store with Horace on his leash. Romeo had told her he had a pair of brand-new Kyocera photocopiers in storage, both still in their original shipping cartons. She was welcome to both.

"I also got a little propane tucked away," he said, giving Horace a pat. "I'll see you get what you need—for as long as I can, at least. We gotta keep that newspaper running, am I right? More important than ever, don't you t'ink?"

It was exactly what she t'ought, and Julia had told him so. She had also planted a kiss on his cheek. "I owe you for this, Rommie."

"I'll be expectin a big discount on my weekly advertising circular when this is over." He had then tapped the side of his nose with a forefinger, as if they had a great big secret. Maybe they did.

As she left, her cell phone chirruped. She pulled it out of her pants pocket. "Hello, this is Julia."

"Good evening, Ms. Shumway."

"Oh, Colonel Cox, how wonderful to hear your voice," she said brightly. "You can't imagine how thrilled we country mice are to get out-of-town calls. How's life outside the Dome?"

"Life in general is probably fine," he said. "Where I am, it's on the shabby side. You know about the missiles?"

"Watched them hit. And bounce off. They lit a fine fire on your side—"

"It's not *my*—"

"—and a fairly good one on ours."

"I'm calling for Colonel Barbara," Cox said. "Who should be carrying his own goddam phone by now."

"Goddam right!" she cried, still in her brightest tone. "And people in goddam hell should have goddam icewater!" She stopped in front of the Gas & Grocery, now shut up tight. The hand-lettered sign in the window read **HRS OF OP TOMORROW 11 AM–2 PM <u>GET HERE EARLY!</u>**

"Ms. Shumway—"

"We'll discuss Colonel Barbara in a minute," Julia said. "Right now I want to know two things. First, when is the press going to be allowed at the Dome? Because the people of America deserve more than the government's spin on this, don't you think?"

She expected him to say he did *not* think, that there would be no *New York Times* or CNN at the Dome in the foreseeable future, but Cox surprised her. "Probably by Friday if none of the other tricks up our sleeve work. What's the other thing you want to know, Ms. Shumway? Make it brief, because I'm not a press officer. That's another pay grade."

"You called me, so you're stuck with me. Suck it up, Colonel."

"Ms. Shumway, with all due respect, yours is not the only cell phone in Chester's Mill I can reach out and touch."

"I'm sure that's true, but I don't think Barbie will talk to you if you shine me on. He's not particularly happy with his new position as prospective stockade commandant."

Cox sighed. "What's your question?"

"I want to know the temperature on the south or east side of the Dome—a *true* temperature, meaning away from the fire you guys set."

"Why—"

"Do you have that information or not? I think you do, or can get it. I think you're sitting in front of a computer screen right now, and you have access to everything, probably including my underwear size." She paused. "And if you say sixteen, this call is over."

"Are you exhibiting your sense of humor, Ms. Shumway, or are you always this way?"

"I'm tired and scared. Chalk it up to that."

There was a pause on Cox's end. She thought she heard the click of computer keys. Then he said, "It's forty-seven Fahrenheit in Castle Rock. Will that do?"

"Yes." The disparity wasn't as bad as she had feared, but still considerable. "I'm looking at the thermometer in the window of the Mill Gas and Grocery. It says fifty-eight. That's an eleven-degree difference between locations less than twenty miles apart. Unless there's a hell of a big warm front pushing through western Maine this evening, I'd say something's going on here. Do you agree?"

He didn't answer her question, but what he *did* say took her mind off it. "We're going to try something else. Around nine this evening. It's what I wanted to tell Barbie."

"One hopes Plan B will work better than Plan A. At this moment, I believe the President's appointee is feeding the multitudes at Sweetbriar Rose. Chicken à la king is the rumor." She could see the lights down the street, and her belly rumbled.

"Will you listen and pass on a message?" And she heard what he did not add: *You contentious bitch?*

"Happy to," she said. Smiling. Because she *was* a contentious bitch. When she had to be.

"We're going to try an experimental acid. A hydrofluoric compound, man-made. Nine times as corrosive as the ordinary stuff."

"Living better through chemistry."

"I'm told you could theoretically burn a hole two miles deep in the bedrock with it."

"What highly amusing people you work for, Colonel."

"We're going to try where Motton Road crosses—" There was a rustle of paper. "Where it crosses into Harlow. I expect to be there."

"Then I'll tell Barbie to have someone else wash up."

"Will you also be favoring us with your company, Ms. Shumway?"

She opened her mouth to say *I wouldn't miss it,* and that was when all hell broke loose up the street.

"What's going on there?" Cox asked.

Julia didn't reply. She closed her phone and stuck it in her pocket, already running toward the sound of yelling voices. And something else. Something that sounded like *snarling.*

The gunshot came while she was still half a block away.

6

Piper went back to the parsonage and discovered Carolyn, Thurston, and the Appleton kids waiting there. She was glad to see them, because they took her mind off Sammy Bushey. At least temporarily.

She listened to Carolyn's account of Aidan Appleton's seizure, but the boy seemed fine now—chowing ever deeper into a stack of Fig Newtons. When Carolyn asked if the boy should see a doctor, Piper said, "Unless there's a recurrence, I think you can assume it was brought on by hunger and the excitement of the game."

Thurston smiled ruefully. "We were all excited. Having fun."

When it came to possible lodging, Piper first thought of the McCain house, which was close by. Only she didn't know where their spare key might be hidden.

Alice Appleton was on the floor, feeding Fig Newton crumbs to Clover. The shepherd was doing the old my-muzzle's-on-your-ankle-because-I'm-your-best-friend routine in between offerings. "This is the best dog I've ever seen," she told Piper. "I wish *we* could have a dog."

"I've got a dragon," Aidan offered. He was sitting comfortably on Carolyn's lap.

Alice smiled indulgently. "That's his invisible F-R-E-I-N."

"I see," Piper said. She supposed they could always break a window at the McCain place; needs must when the devil drives.

But as she got up to check on the coffee, a better idea occurred. "The Dumagens'. I should have thought of them right away. They went to Boston for a conference. Coralee Dumagen asked me to water her plants while they're gone."

"I teach in Boston," Thurston said. "At Emerson. I edited the current issue of *Ploughshares*." And sighed.

"The key is under a flowerpot to the left of the door," Piper said. "I don't believe they have a generator, but there's a woodstove in the kitchen." She hesitated, thinking *City people*. "Can you use a woodstove to cook on without setting the house on fire?"

"I grew up in Vermont," Thurston said. "Was in charge of keeping the stoves lit—house *and* barn—until I went off to college. What goes around comes around, doesn't it?" And sighed again.

"There'll be food in the pantry, I'm sure," Piper said.

Carolyn nodded. "That's what the janitor at the Town Hall said."

"Also *Joooon-yer*," Alice put in. "He's a cop. A *foxy* one."

Thurston's mouth turned down. "Alice's foxy cop assaulted me," he said. "Him or the other one. I couldn't tell them apart, myself."

Piper's eyebrows went up.

"Punched Thurse in the stomach," Carolyn said quietly. "Called us Massholes—which, I suppose, we technically are—and laughed at us. For me, that was the worst part, how they laughed at us. They were better once they had the kids with them, but . . ." She shook her head. "They were out of control."

And just like that, Piper was back to Sammy. She felt a pulse beginning to beat in the side of her neck, very slow and hard, but she kept her voice even. "What was the other policeman's name?"

"Frankie," Carolyn said. "Junior called him Frankie D. Do you know these guys? You must, huh?"

"I know them," Piper said.

7

She gave the new, makeshift family directions to the Du-magens'—the house had the advantage of being near to Cathy Russell if the boy had another seizure—and sat awhile at her kitchen table after they were gone, drinking tea. She did it slowly. Took a sip and set the cup down. Took a sip and set it down. Clover whined. He was tuned in to her, and she supposed he could sense her rage.

Maybe it changes my smell. Makes it more acrid or something.

A picture was forming. Not a pretty one. A lot of new cops, very young cops, sworn in less than forty-eight hours ago and already running wild. The sort of license they had exhibited with Sammy Bushey and Thurston Marshall wouldn't spread to veteran cops like Henry Morrison and Jackie Wettington—at least she didn't think so—but to Fred Denton? Toby Whelan? Maybe. *Probably.* With Duke in charge, those guys had been all right. Not great, the kind of guys apt to lip you unnecessarily after a traffic stop, but all right. Certainly the best the town's budget could afford. But her mother had been wont to say, "You buy cheap, you get cheap." And with Peter Randolph in charge—

Something had to be done.

Only she had to control her temper. If she didn't, it would control her.

She took the leash from the peg by the door. Clover was up at once, tail swishing, ears perked, eyes bright.

"Come on, you big lug. We're going to lodge a complaint."

Her shepherd was still licking Fig Newton crumbs from the side of his muzzle as she led him out the door.

8

Walking across the town common with Clover heeling neatly to her right, Piper felt she *did* have her temper under control. She felt that way until she heard the laughter. It came as she and Clove were approaching the police station. She observed the very fellows whose names she had gotten out of Sammy Bushey: DeLesseps, Thibodeau, Searles. Georgia Roux was also present, Georgia who had egged them on, according to Sammy: *Do that bitch*. Freddy Denton was there too. They were sitting at the top of the stone PD steps, drinking sodas, gassing among themselves. Duke Perkins never would have allowed such a thing, and Piper reflected that if he could see them from wherever he was, he'd be rolling in his grave fast enough to set his own remains on fire.

Mel Searles said something and they all broke up again, laughing and backslapping. Thibodeau had his arm around the Roux girl, the tips of his fingers on the sideswell of her breast. She said something, and they all laughed harder.

It came to Piper that they were laughing about the rape—what a goldurn good old time it had been—and after that, her father's advice never had a chance. The Piper who ministered to the poor and the sick, who officiated at marryings and buryings, who preached charity and tolerance on Sundays, was pushed rudely to the back of her mind, where she could only watch as though through a warped and wavery pane of glass. It was the other Piper who took over, the one who had trashed her room at fifteen, crying tears of rage rather than sorrow.

There was a slate-paved square known as War Memorial Plaza between the Town Hall and the newer brick PD building. At its center was a statue of Ernie Calvert's father, Lucien Calvert, who had been awarded a posthumous Silver Star for heroic action in Korea. The names of other Chester's Mill war dead, going all the way back to the Civil War, were engraved on the statue's base. There were also two flagpoles, the Stars and Stripes at the top of one and the state flag, with its farmer, sailor, and moose, at the top of the other. Both hung limp in the reddening light of oncoming sunset. Piper Libby passed between the poles like a woman in a dream, Clover still heeling behind her right knee with his ears up.

The "officers" atop the steps burst into another hearty roar of laughter, and she thought of trolls in one of the fairy stories her dad had sometimes read her. Trolls in a cave, gloating over piles of ill-gotten gold. Then they saw her and quieted.

"Good evenin, Rev'run," Mel Searles said, and got up, giving his belt a self-important little hitch as he did so. *Standing in the presence of a lady,* Piper thought. *Did his mother teach him that? Probably. The fine art of rape he probably learned somewhere else.*

He was still smiling as she reached the steps, but then it faltered and grew tentative, so he must have seen her expression. Just what that expression might be she didn't know. From the inside, her face felt frozen. Immobile.

She saw the biggest of them watching her closely. Thibodeau, his face as immobile as hers felt. *He's like Clover,* she thought. *He smells it on me. The rage.*

"Rev'run?" Mel asked. "Everything okay? There a problem?"

She mounted the steps, not fast, not slow, Clover still heeling neatly behind her right knee. "You *bet* there's a problem," she said, looking up at him.

"What—"

"*You,*" she said. "*You're* the problem."

She pushed him. Mel wasn't expecting it. He was still holding his cup of soda. He went tumbling into Georgia Roux's lap, flailing his arms uselessly for balance, and for a moment the soda was a dark manta ray hanging against the reddening sky. Georgia cried out in surprise as Mel landed on her. She sprawled backward, spilling her own soda. It went running across the wide granite slab in front of the double doors. Piper could smell either whiskey or bourbon. Their Cokes had been spiked with what the rest of the town could no longer buy. No wonder they'd been laughing.

The red fissure inside her head opened wider.

"You can't—" Frankie began, starting to get up himself. She pushed him. In a galaxy far far away, Clover—ordinarily the sweetest of dogs—was growling.

Frankie went on his back, eyes wide and startled, for a moment looking like the Sunday school boy he once might have been.

"*Rape* is the problem!" Piper shouted. "*Rape!*"

"Shut up," Carter said. He was still sitting, and although Georgia was cowering against him, Carter remained calm. The muscles of his arms rippled below his short-sleeved blue shirt. "Shut up and get out of here right now, if you don't want to spend the night in a cell downstai—"

"You're the one who'll be going into a cell," Piper said. "All of you."

"Make her shut up," Georgia said. She wasn't whimpering, but she was close. "Make her shut up, Cart."

"Ma'am—" Freddy Denton. His uniform shirt untucked and bourbon on his breath. Duke would have taken one look and fired his ass. Fired *all* their asses. He started to get up and this time *he* was the one who went sprawling, a look of surprise on his face that would have been comical under other circumstances. It was nice that they had been sitting while she was standing. Made it easier. But oh, how her temples were thudding. She returned her attention to Thibodeau, the most dangerous one. He was still looking at her with maddening calm. As though she were a freak he'd paid a quarter to see in a sideshow tent. But he was looking *up* at her, and that was her advantage.

"But it won't be a cell downstairs," she said, speaking directly to Thibodeau. "It'll be in Shawshank, where they do to little play-yard bullies like you what you did to that girl."

"You stupid bitch," Carter said. He spoke as if remarking on the weather. "We weren't anywhere near her house."

"That's right," Georgia said, sitting up again. There was Coke splattered on one of her cheeks, where a virulent case of teenage acne was fading (but still holding onto a few final outposts). "And besides, everyone knows Sammy Bushey is nothing but a lying lesbo cunt."

Piper's lips stretched in a smile. She turned it on Georgia, who recoiled from the crazy lady who had appeared so suddenly on the steps while they'd been having a nice sunsetter or two. "How did you know the lying lesbo cunt's name? *I* didn't say it."

Georgia's mouth dropped into an O of dismay. And for the first time something flickered beneath Carter Thibodeau's calm. Whether fear or just annoyance, Piper didn't know.

Frank DeLesseps got cautiously to his feet. "You better not go around spreading accusations you can't back up, Reverend Libby."

"Nor assaulting police officers," Freddy Denton said. "I'm willing to let it go this time—everyone's under stress—but you have to cease and desist these accusations right now." He paused, then added lamely: "And the pushing, of course."

Piper's gaze remained fixed on Georgia, her right hand curled so tightly around the black plastic grip of Clover's leash it was throbbing. The dog stood with his forepaws spread and his head lowered, still growling. He sounded like a powerful outboard motor set to idle. The fur on his neck had bushed out enough to hide his collar.

"How'd you know her name, Georgia?"

"I . . . I . . . I just assumed . . ."

Carter gripped her shoulder and squeezed it. "Shut up, babe." And then, to Piper, still not standing (*Because he doesn't want to be pushed back down, the coward*), he said: "I don't know what kind of bee you've got in your Jesus bonnet, but we were all together last night, at Alden Dinsmore's farm. Trying to see if we could get anything out of the soldier-boys stationed on 119, which we couldn't. That's on the other side of town from Busheys'." He looked around at his friends.

"Right," Frankie said.

"Right," Mel chimed in, looking at Piper distrustfully.

"Yeah!" Georgia said. Carter's arm was around her again and her moment of doubt was gone. She looked at Piper defiantly.

"Georgie-girl *assumed* it was Sammy you were yelling about," Carter said with that same infuriating calm. "Because Sammy's the biggest lying scumbucket in this town."

Mel Searles yodeled laughter.

"But you didn't use protection," Piper said. Sammy had told her this, and when she saw Thibodeau's face tighten, she knew it was true. "You didn't use protection and they rape-kitted her." She had no idea if *this* was true, and didn't care. She could see from their widening eyes that they believed it, and their belief was enough. "When they compare your DNA to what they found—"

"That's enough," Carter said. "Shut it."

She turned her furious smile on him. "No, Mr. Thibodeau. We are only getting started, my son."

Freddy Denton reached for her. She pushed him down, then felt her left arm caught and twisted. She turned and looked into Thibodeau's eyes. No calm there now; they were shining with rage.

Hello, my brother, she thought incoherently.

"Fuck you, you fucking bitch," he remarked, and this time she was the one who was pushed.

Piper fell backward down the stairs, trying instinctively to tuck and roll, not wanting to hit her head on one of those stone risers, knowing they could smash her skull in. Kill her or—worse—leave her a vegetable. She struck on her left shoulder instead, and there was a sudden howl of pain there. *Familiar* pain. She had dislocated that one playing high school soccer twenty years ago, and damned if she hadn't just done it again.

Her legs flew over her head and she turned a back somersault, wrenching her neck, coming down on her knees and splitting the skin on both. She finally came to rest on her stomach and breasts. She had tumbled almost all the way to the bottom of the steps. Her cheek was bleeding, her nose was bleeding, her lips were bleeding, her neck hurt, but ah God, her shoulder was the worst, humped up all crooked in a way she remembered well. The last time she'd seen a hump like that, it had been in a red nylon Wildcats jersey. Nevertheless, she struggled to her feet, thanking God she still had the power to command her legs; she could also have been paralyzed.

She'd lost hold of the leash halfway down and Clover jumped at Thibodeau, his teeth snapping at the chest and belly under his shirt, tearing the shirt open, knocking Thibodeau backward, going for the young man's vitals.

"Get him off me!" Carter screamed. Nothing calm about him now. *"He's gonna kill me!"*

And yes, Clover was trying. His front paws were planted on Carter's thighs, going up and down as Carter thrashed. He looked like a German shepherd on a bicycle. He shifted his angle of attack and bit deep into Carter's shoulder, eliciting another scream. Then Clover went for the throat. Carter got his hands on the dog's chest just in time to save his windpipe.

"Make him stop!"

Frank reached for the trailing leash. Clover turned and snapped at his fingers. Frank skittered backward, and Clover returned his attention to the man who had pushed his mistress down the steps. His muzzle opened, revealing a double line of shining white teeth, and he drove at Thibodeau's neck. Carter got his hand up, then shrieked in agony as Clover seized on it and began to shake it like one of his beloved rag toys. Only his rag toys didn't bleed, and Carter's hand did.

Piper came staggering up the steps, holding her left arm across her midriff. Her face was a mask of blood. A tooth clung to the corner of her mouth like a crumb of food.

"GET HIM OFF ME, CHRIST, GET YOUR FUCKIN DOG OFF ME!"

Piper was opening her mouth to tell Clover to stand down when she saw Fred Denton drawing his gun.

"*No!*" she screamed. "*No, I can make him stop!*"

Fred turned to Mel Searles, and pointed at the dog with his free hand. Mel stepped forward and kicked Clover in the haunch. He did it high and hard, as he had once (not so long ago) punted footballs. Clover was whipped sideways, losing his hold on Thibodeau's bleeding, shredded hand, where two fingers now pointed in unusual directions, like crooked signposts.

"*NO!*" Piper screamed again, so loud and so hard the world went gray before her eyes. "*DON'T HURT MY DOG!*"

Fred paid no attention. When Peter Randolph burst out through the double doors, his shirttail out, his pants unzipped, the copy of *Outdoors* he had been reading on the crapper still held in one hand, Fred paid no attention to that, either. He pointed his service automatic at the dog, and fired.

The sound was deafening in the enclosed square. The top of Clover's head lifted off in a spray of blood and bone. He took one step toward his screaming, bleeding mistress—another—then collapsed.

Fred, gun still in hand, strode forward and grabbed Piper by her bad arm. The hump in her shoulder roared a protest. And still she kept her eyes on the corpse of her dog, whom she had raised from a pup.

"You're under arrest, you crazy bitch," Fred said. He pushed his face—pale, sweaty, the eyes seeming ready to pop right out of their sockets—close enough to hers for her to feel the spray of his spittle. "Anything you say can and will be used against your crazy ass."

On the other side of the street, diners were pouring out of Sweetbriar Rose, Barbie among them, still wearing his apron and baseball cap. Julia Shumway arrived first. She took in the scene, not seeing details so much as a gestalt summation: dead dog; clustered cops; bleeding, screaming woman with one shoulder higher than the other; bald cop—Freddy goddam Denton—shaking her by the arm connected to that shoulder; more blood on the steps, suggesting that Piper had fallen down them. Or had been pushed.

Julia did something she had never done before in her life: reached into her handbag, flipped her wallet open, and climbed the steps, holding it out, yelling *"Press! Press! Press!"*

It stopped the shaking, at least.

9

Ten minutes later, in the office that had been Duke Perkins's not so long ago, Carter Thibodeau sat on the sofa under Duke's framed pictures and certificates, with a fresh bandage on his shoulder and paper towels around his hand. Georgia was sitting beside him. Large beads of painsweat stood out on Thibodeau's forehead, but after saying "I don't think nothin's broken," he was silent.

Fred Denton sat in a chair in the corner. His gun was on the Chief's desk. He had surrendered it willingly enough, only saying, "I had to do it—just look at Cart's hand."

Piper sat in the office chair that was now Peter Randolph's. Julia had mopped most of the blood off Piper's face with more paper towels. The woman was shivering with shock and in great pain, but she was as silent about it as Thibodeau. Her eyes were clear.

"Clover only attacked him"—she raised her chin to Carter—"after he pushed me down the stairs. The push caused me to lose hold of the leash. What my dog did was justified. He was protecting me from a criminal assault."

"*She* attacked *us*!" Georgia cried. "Crazy bitch attacked *us*! Came up the steps spouting all this shit—"

"Shut up," Barbie said. "All of you, shut the hell up." He looked at Piper. "This isn't the first time you've dislocated your shoulder, is it?"

"I want you out of here, Mr. Barbara," Randolph said . . . but he spoke with no great conviction.

"I can deal with this," Barbie said. "Can you?"

Randolph made no reply. Mel Searles and Frank De-Lesseps stood outside the door. They looked worried.

Barbie turned back to Piper. "This is a subluxation—a partial separation. Not bad. I can pop it back in before you go to the hospital—"

"*Hospital?*" Fred Denton squawked. "She's under arr—"

"Shut up, Freddy," Randolph said. "Nobody's under arrest. At least not yet."

Barbie held Piper's eyes with his own. "But I have to do it now, before the swelling gets bad. If you wait for Everett to do it at the hospital, they'll have to give you anesthesia." He leaned close to her ear and murmured, "While you're out, they'll be telling their side and you won't be telling yours."

"What are you saying?" Randolph asked sharply.

"That it's going to hurt," Barbie said. "Right, Rev?"

She nodded. "Go on. Coach Gromley did it right on the sidelines, and she was a total dope. Just hurry. And please don't screw it up."

Barbie said: "Julia, grab a sling from the first aid kit, then help me lie her down on her back."

Julia, very pale and feeling ill, did as she was told.

Barbie sat down on the floor to Piper's left, slipped off one shoe, and then grasped her forearm just above her wrist with both hands. "I don't know Coach Gromley's method," he said, "but this is how a medic I knew in Iraq did it. You're going to count to three and then yell wishbone."

"Wishbone," Piper said, bemused in spite of the pain. "Well okay, you're the doctor."

No, Julia thought—Rusty Everett was now the closest thing the town had to a doctor. She'd contacted Linda and gotten his cell phone number, but her call had been immediately shunted to voicemail.

The room was silent. Even Carter Thibodeau was watching. Barbie nodded to Piper. Beads of sweat stood out on her forehead, but she had her game-face on, and Barbie respected the shit out of that. He slipped his sock-foot into her left armpit, snugging it tight. Then, while pulling slowly but steadily on her arm, he applied counter pressure with his foot.

"Okay, here we go. Let's hear you."

"One . . . two . . . three . . . *WISHBONE!*"

When Piper shouted, Barbie pulled. Everyone in the room heard the loud thunk as the joint went back into place. The hump in Piper's blouse magically disappeared. She screamed but didn't pass out. He slipped the sling over her neck and around the arm, immobilizing it as well as he could.

"Better?" he asked.

"Better," she said. "Much, thank God. Still hurts, but not as bad."

"I've got some aspirin in my purse," Julia said.

"Give her the aspirin and then get out," Randolph said. "All of you except for Carter, Freddy, the Reverend, and me."

Julia looked at him unbelievingly. "Are you kidding? The Reverend is going to the hospital. Can you walk, Piper?"

Piper stood up shakily. "I think so. A little way."

"Sit down, Reverend Libby," Randolph said, but Barbie knew she was already gone. He could hear it in Randolph's voice.

"Why don't you make me?" She gingerly lifted her left arm and the sling holding it. The arm trembled, but it was working. "I'm sure you can dislocate it again, very easily. Go on. Show these . . . these *boys* . . . that you're just like them."

"And I'll put it all in the paper!" Julia said brightly. "Circulation will double!"

Barbie said, "Suggest you defer this business until tomorrow, Chief. Allow the lady to get some painkillers stronger than aspirin, and have those knee lacerations checked by Everett. Given the Dome, she's hardly a flight risk."

"Her dog tried to kill me," Carter said. In spite of the pain, he sounded calm again.

"Chief Randolph, DeLesseps, Searles, and Thibodeau are guilty of rape." Piper was swaying now—Julia put an arm around her—but her voice was firm and clear. "Roux is an accessory to rape."

"The hell I am!" Georgia squawked.

"They need to be suspended immediately."

"She's lying," Thibodeau said.

Chief Randolph looked like a man watching a tennis match. He finally settled his gaze on Barbie. "Are you telling me what to do, kiddo?"

"No, sir, just making a suggestion based on my enforcement experience in Iraq. You'll make your own decisions."

Randolph relaxed. "Okay, then. Okay." He looked down, frowning in thought. They all watched him notice his fly was still unzipped and take care of that little problem. Then he looked up again and said, "Julia, take Reverend Piper to the hospital. As for you, Mr. Barbara, I don't care where you go but I want you out of here. I'll take statements from my officers tonight, and from Reverend Libby tomorrow."

"Wait," Thibodeau said. He extended his crooked fingers to Barbie. "Can you do anything about these?"

"I don't know," Barbie said—pleasantly enough, he hoped. The initial ugliness was over, and now came the political aftermath, which he remembered well from dealing with Iraqi cops who were not all that different from the man on the couch and the others crowding the doorway. What it came down to was making nice with people you wished you could spit on. "Can you say *wishbone?*"

10

Rusty had turned his cell phone off before knocking on Big Jim's door. Now Big Jim sat behind his desk, Rusty in the seat before it—the chair of supplicants and applicants.

The study (Rennie probably called it a home office on his tax returns) had a pleasant, piney smell, as if it had recently been given a good scrubbing, but Rusty still didn't like it. It wasn't just the picture of an aggressively Caucasian Jesus delivering the Sermon on the Mount, or the self-congratulatory plaques, or the hardwood floor that really should have had a rug to protect it; it was all those things and something else as well. Rusty Everett had very little use for or belief in the supernatural, but nevertheless, this room felt almost haunted.

It's because he scares you a little, he thought. *That's all it is.*

Hoping that how he felt didn't show in his voice or face, Rusty told Rennie about the hospital's missing propane tanks. About how he had found one of them in the supply shed behind the Town Hall, currently running the Town Hall's generator. And how it was the *only* one.

"So I have two questions," Rusty said. "How did a tank from the hospital supply wander downtown? And where did the rest go?"

Big Jim rocked back in his chair, put his hands behind his neck, and looked up at the ceiling meditatively. Rusty found himself staring at the trophy baseball sitting on Rennie's desk. Propped in front of it was a note from Bill Lee, once of the Boston Red Sox. He could read the note because it was turned outward. Of course it was. It was for guests to see, and marvel over. Like the pictures on the wall, the baseball proclaimed that Big Jim Rennie had rubbed elbows with Famous People: *Look on my autographs, ye mighty, and despair*. To Rusty, the baseball and the note turned outward seemed to sum up his bad feelings about the room he was in. It was window-dressing, a tinny testimonial to smalltown prestige and smalltown power.

"I wasn't aware you had anyone's permission to go poking around in our supply shed," Big Jim remarked to the ceiling. His hammy fingers were still laced together behind his head. "Perhaps you're a town official, and I wasn't aware of it? If so, my mistake—my *bad,* as Junior says. I thought you were basically a nurse with a prescription pad."

Rusty thought this was mostly technique—Rennie trying to piss him off. To divert him.

"I'm not a town official," he said, "but I *am* a hospital employee. And a taxpayer."

"So?"

Rusty could feel blood rushing to his face.

"So those things make it partly *my* supply shed." He waited to see if Big Jim would respond to this, but the man behind the desk remained impassive. "Besides, it was unlocked. Which is all beside the point, isn't it? I saw what I saw, and I'd like an explanation. As a hospital employee."

"And a taxpayer. Don't forget that."

Rusty sat looking at him, not even nodding.

"I can't give you one," Rennie said.

Rusty raised his eyebrows. "Really? I thought you had your fingers on the pulse of this town. Isn't that what you said the last time you ran for Selectman? And now you're telling me you can't explain where the town's propane went? I don't believe it."

For the first time, Rennie looked nettled. "I don't care if you believe it or not. This is news to me." But his eyes darted fractionally to one side as he said it, as if to check that his autographed photo of Tiger Woods was still there; the classic liar's tell.

Rusty said, "The hospital's almost out of LP. Without it, the few of us who are still on the job might as well be working in a Civil War battlefield surgery tent. Our current patients—including a postcoronary and a serious case of diabetes that may warrant amputation—will be in serious trouble if the power goes out. The possible amp is Jimmy Sirois. His car is in the parking lot. It's got a sticker on the bumper that says ELECT BIG JIM."

"I'll investigate," Big Jim said. He spoke with the air of a man conferring a favor. "The town's propane is probably stored in some other town facility. As for yours, I'm sure I can't say."

"*What* other town facilities? There's the FD, and the sand-and-salt pile out on God Creek Road—not even a shed there—but those are the only ones I'm aware of."

"Mr. Everett, I'm a busy man. You'll have to excuse me now."

Rusty stood. His hands wanted to ball into fists, but he wouldn't let them. "I'm going to ask you one more time," he said. "Straight out and straight up. Do you know where those missing tanks are?"

"No." This time it was Dale Earnhardt Rennie's eyes flickered to. "And I'm not going to read any implication into that question, son, because if I did I'd have to resent it. Now why don't you run along and check on Jimmy Sirois? Tell him Big Jim sends his best, and he'll stop by as soon as the nitpickery slows down a little."

Rusty was still battling to hold onto his temper, but this was a fight he was losing. "*Run along?* I think you forgot that you're a public servant, not a private dictator. For the time being I'm this town's chief medical officer, and I want some an—"

Big Jim's cell rang. He snared it. Listened. The lines around his drawn-down mouth grew grimmer. "Gosh*darn* it! Every time I turn my darn *back* . . ." He listened some more, then said: "If you've got people with you in the office, Pete, shut your trap before you open it too wide and fall right the heck in. Call Andy. I'll be right there, and the three of us'll clean this up."

He killed the phone and got to his feet.

"I have to go to the police station. It's either an emergency or more nitpickery, I won't be able to tell which until I get there. And you'll be wanted at either the hospital or the Health Center, I believe. There seems to be a problem with the Reverend Libby."

"Why? What happened to her?"

Big Jim's cold eyes surveyed him from hard little sockets. "I'm sure you'll hear her story. I don't know how true it'll be, but I'm sure you'll hear it. So go do your job, young fella, and let me do mine."

Rusty walked down the front hall and out of the house,

his temples throbbing. In the west, the sunset was a lurid bloodshow. The air was almost completely still, but bore a smoky stench just the same. At the foot of the steps, Rusty raised a finger and pointed it at the public servant waiting for him to leave his property before he, Rennie, left himself. Rennie scowled at the finger, but Rusty did not drop it.

"Nobody needs to tell me to do my job. And I'm going to make looking for that propane part of it. If I find it in the wrong place, someone else is going to be doing *your* job, Selectman Rennie. That's a promise."

Big Jim flapped a contemptuous hand at him. "Get out of here, son. Go to work."

11

During the first fifty-five hours of the Dome's existence, over two dozen children suffered seizures. Some, like those of the Everett girls, were noted. Many more were not, and in the days ahead, the seizure activity would rapidly taper down to nothing. Rusty would compare this to the minor shocks people experienced when they came too close to the Dome. The first time, you got that almost electric *frisson* that stiffened the hair on the back of your neck; after that, most people felt nothing. It was as if they had been inoculated.

"Are you saying the Dome is like chickenpox?" Linda asked him later. "Catch it once and you're set for life?"

Janelle had two seizures, and so did a little kid named Norman Sawyer, but in both cases the second seizure was milder than the first, and not accompanied by any babble. Most of the kids Rusty saw had only the one, and there seemed to be no after-effects.

Only two adults had seizures during those first fifty-five hours. Both came around sunset on Monday evening, and both had easily traceable causes.

With Phil Bushey, aka The Chef, the cause was too much of his own product. Around the time Rusty and Big Jim parted company, Chef Bushey was sitting outside the storage barn behind WCIK, looking dreamily at the sunset (this close to the missile strikes, the scarlet in the sky was further darkened by soot on the Dome), his hitty-pipe clasped loosely in one hand. He was tweeked at least to the ionosphere; maybe a hundred miles beyond. In the few low-lying clouds which floated on that bloody light, he saw the faces of his mother, his father, his grandfather; he saw Sammy and Little Walter as well.

All the cloud-faces were bleeding.

When his right foot began to twitch and then his left foot picked up the beat, he ignored it. Twitchin was part of tweekin, everyone knew that. But then his hands began to tremble and his pipe fell into the long grass (yellow and sere as a result of the factory work that went on out here). A moment later his head began to jerk from side to side.

This is it, he thought with a calm that was partly relief. *I finally overdid it. I'm checking out. Probably for the best.*

But he didn't check out, didn't even *pass* out. He slid slowly sideways, twitching and watching as a black marble rose in the red sky. It expanded to a bowling ball, then an overinflated beachball. It went on growing until it had eaten up the red sky.

The end of the world, he thought. *Probably for the best.*

For a moment he thought he was wrong, because the stars came out. Only they were the wrong color. They were pink. And then, oh God, they began to fall down, leaving long pink trails behind them.

Next came fire. A roaring furnace, as if someone had

opened a hidden trapdoor and loosed Hell itself on Chester's Mill.

"It's our treat," he muttered. His pipe pressed against his arm, making a burn he would see and feel later. He lay twitching in the yellow grass with his eyes turned up to glabrous whites that reflected the lurid sunset. "Our Halloween treat. First the trick . . . then the treat."

The fire was becoming a face, an orange version of the bloody ones he'd been looking at in the clouds just before the fit fell on him. It was the face of Jesus. Jesus was scowling at him.

And talking. Talking to *him*. Telling him that bringing the fire was *his* responsibility. *His.* The fire and the . . . the . . .

"The purity," he muttered as he lay in the grass. "No . . . the *purification*."

Jesus didn't look so mad now. And He was fading. Why? Because The Chef had understood. First came the pink stars; then came the purifying fire; then the trial would end.

The Chef stilled as the seizure passed into the first real sleep he'd had in weeks, perhaps months. When he woke up, it was full dark—every trace of red gone from the sky. He was chilled to the bone, but not damp.

Under the Dome, dew no longer fell.

12

While The Chef was observing the face of Christ in that evening's infected sunset, Third Selectman Andrea Grinnell was sitting on her couch and trying to read. Her generator had quit—or had it ever run at all? She couldn't remember. But she had a gadget called a Mighty Brite light that her sister Rose had tucked into her Christmas stocking last year. She'd never had occasion to use it until now, but it worked just fine. You clamped it to your book and turned it on. Easy-peasy. So light wasn't a problem. The words, unfortunately, were. The words kept squirming around on the page, sometimes even changing places with each other, and Nora Roberts's prose, ordinarily crystal clear, made absolutely no sense. Yet Andrea kept trying, because she could think of nothing else to do.

The house stank, even with the windows open. She was suffering diarrhea and the toilet would no longer flush. She was hungry but couldn't eat. She had tried a sandwich around five PM—just an inoffensive cheese sandwich— and had thrown it up in the kitchen wastebasket minutes after it was down. A shame, because eating that sandwich had been hard work. She was sweating heavily—had already changed her clothes once, probably should change them again, if she could manage to do it—and her feet kept jittering and jerking.

They don't call it kicking the habit for nothing, she thought. *And I'll never make the emergency meeting tonight, if Jim still means to have one.*

Considering how her last conversation with Big Jim and Andy Sanders had gone, maybe that was good; if she showed up, they'd just bully her some more. Make her do things she didn't want to do. Best she stay away until she was clear of this . . . this . . .

"This *shit,*" she said, and brushed her damp hair out of her eyes. "This fucking shit in my system."

Once she was herself again, she would stand up to Jim Rennie. It was long overdue. She would do it in spite of her poor aching back, which was such a misery without her OxyContin (but not the white-hot agony she had expected—that was a welcome surprise). Rusty wanted her to take methadone. *Methadone,* for God's sake! Heroin under an alias!

If you're thinking about going cold turkey, don't, he had told her. *You're apt to have seizures.*

But he'd said it could take ten days his way, and she didn't think she could wait that long. Not with this awful Dome over the town. Best to get it over with. Having come to this conclusion, she had flushed all of her pills— not just the methadone but a few last OxyContin pills she'd found in the back of her nightstand drawer—down the toilet. That had been just two flushes before the toilet gave up the ghost, and now she sat here shivering and trying to convince herself she'd done the right thing.

It was the only thing, she thought. *That kind of takes the right and wrong out of it.*

She tried to turn the page of her book and her stupid hand struck the Mighty Brite gadget. It went tumbling to the floor. The spot of brilliance it threw went up to the ceiling. Andrea looked at it and was suddenly rising out of herself. And fast. It was like riding an invisible express elevator. She had just a moment to look down and see her body still on the couch, twitching helplessly. Foamy drool was slipping down her chin from her mouth. She saw the wetness spreading around the crotch of her jeans and thought, *Yep—I'll have to change again, all right. If I live through this, that is.*

Then she passed through the ceiling, through the bed-room above it, through the attic with its dark stacked boxes and retired lamps, and from there out into the night. The Milky Way sprawled above her, but it was wrong. The Milky Way had turned pink.

And then began to fall.

Somewhere—far, far below her—Andrea heard the body she had left behind. It was screaming.

13

Barbie thought he and Julia would discuss what had happened to Piper Libby on their ride out of town, but they were mostly silent, lost in their own thoughts. Neither of them said they were relieved when the unnatural red sunset finally began to fade, but both of them were.

Julia tried the radio once, found nothing but WCIK booming out "All Prayed Up," and snapped it off again.

Barbie spoke only once, this just after they turned off Route 119 and began to drive west along the narrower blacktop of the Motton Road, where woods bulked up close on either side. "Did I do the right thing?"

In Julia's opinion he had done a great many right things during the confrontation in the Chief's office— including the successful treatment of two patients with dislocations—but she knew what he was talking about.

"Yes. It was the exquisitely wrong time to try asserting command."

He agreed, but felt tired and dispirited and not equal to the job he was beginning to see before him. "I'm sure the enemies of Hitler said pretty much the same thing. They said it in nineteen thirty-four, and they were right. In thirty-six, and they were right. Also in thirty-eight. 'The wrong time to challenge him,' they said. And when they realized the right time had finally come, they were protesting in Auschwitz or Buchenwald."

"This is not the same," she said.

"You think not?"

She made no reply to this, but saw his point. Hitler had been a paperhanger, or so the story went; Jim Rennie was a used car dealer. Six of one, half a dozen of the other.

Up ahead, fingers of brilliance shone through the trees.

They printed an intaglio of shadows on the patched tar of Motton Road.

There were a number of military trucks parked on the other side of the Dome—it was Harlow over there at this edge of town—and thirty or forty soldiers moved hither and yon with a purpose. All had gas masks hooked to their belts. A silver tanker-truck bearing the legend **EXTREME DANGER   KEEP BACK** had been backed up until it almost touched a door-size shape that had been spray-painted on the Dome's surface. A plastic hose was clamped to a valve on the back of tanker. Two men were handling the hose, which ended in a wand no bigger than the barrel of a Bic pen. These men were wearing shiny all-over suits and helmets. There were air tanks on their backs.

On the Chester's Mill side, there was only one spectator. Lissa Jamieson, the town librarian, stood beside an old-fashioned ladies' Schwinn with a milk-box carrier on the rear fender. On the back of the box was a sticker reading WHEN THE POWER OF LOVE IS STRONGER THAN THE LOVE OF POWER, THE WORLD WILL KNOW PEACE—JIMI HENDRIX.

"What are you doing here, Lissa?" Julia asked, getting out of her car. She held up a hand to shield her eyes from the bright lights.

Lissa was nervously fiddling with the ankh she wore around her neck on a silver chain. She looked from Julia to Barbie, then back to Julia again. "I go for a ride on my bike when I'm upset or worried. Sometimes I ride until midnight. It soothes my *pneuma*. I saw the lights and came to the lights." She said this in an incantatory way, and let go of her ankh long enough to trace some kind of complicated symbol in the air. "What are *you* doing out here?"

"Came to watch an experiment," Barbie said. "If it works, you can be the first one to leave Chester's Mill."

Lissa smiled. It looked a little forced, but Barbie liked her for the effort. "If I did that, I'd miss the Tuesday night special at Sweetbriar. Isn't it usually meatloaf?"

"Meatloaf's the plan," he agreed, not adding that if the Dome was still in place the following Tuesday, the *spécialité de la maison* was apt to be zucchini quiche.

"They won't talk," Lissa said. "I tried."

A squat fireplug of a man came out from behind the tanker and into the light. He was dressed in khakis, a poplin jacket, and a hat with the logo of the Maine Black Bears on it. The first thing to strike Barbie was that James O. Cox had put on weight. The second was his heavy jacket, zipped to what was now dangerously close to a double chin. Nobody else—Barbie, Julia, or Lissa—was wearing a jacket. There was no need of them on their side of the Dome.

Cox saluted. Barbie gave it back, and it actually felt pretty good to snap one off.

"Hello, Barbie," Cox said. "How's Ken?"

"Ken's fine," Barbie said. "And I continue to be the bitch that gets all the good shit."

"Not this time, Colonel," Cox said. "This time it appears you got fucked at the drive-thru."

14

"Who's he?" Lissa whispered. She was still working at the ankh. Julia thought she'd snap the chain soon, if she kept at it. "And what are they doing over there?"

"Trying to get us out," Julia said. "And after the rather spectacular failure earlier in the day, I'd have to say they're wise to do it on the quiet." She started forward. "Hello, Colonel Cox—I'm your favorite newspaper editor. Good evening."

Cox's smile was—to his credit, she thought—only slightly sour. "Ms. Shumway. . You're even prettier than I imagined."

"I'll say one thing for you, you're handy with the bullsh—"

Barbie intercepted her three yards from where Cox was standing and took her by the arms.

"What?" she asked.

"The camera." She had almost forgotten she had it around her neck until he pointed to it. "Is it digital?"

"Sure, Pete Freeman's extra." She started to ask why, then got it. "You think the Dome will fry it."

"That'd be the best-case scenario," Barbie said. "Remember what happened to Chief Perkins's pacemaker."

"Shit," she said. "*Shit!* Maybe I've got my old Kodak in the trunk."

Lissa and Cox were looking at each other with what Barbie thought was equal fascination. "What are you going to do?" she asked. "Is there going to be another bang?"

Cox hesitated. Barbie said, "Might as well come clean, Colonel. If you don't tell her, I will."

Cox sighed. "You insist on total transparency, don't you?"

"Why not? If this thing works, the people of Chester's Mill will be singing your praises. The only reason you're playing em close is force of habit."

"No. It's what my superiors have ordered."

"They're in Washington," Barbie said. "And the press is in Castle Rock, most of em probably watching *Girls Gone Wild* on pay-per-view. Out here it's just us chickens."

Cox sighed and pointed to the spray-painted door shape. "That's where the men in the protective suits will apply our experimental compound. If we're lucky, the acid will eat through and we'll then be able to knock that piece of the Dome out the way you can knock a piece of glass out of a window after you've used a glass-cutter."

"And if we're unlucky?" Barbie asked. "If the Dome decomposes, giving off some poison gas that kills us all? Is that what the gas masks are for?"

"Actually," Cox said, "the scientists feel it more likely that the acid might start a chemical reaction that would cause the Dome to catch fire." He saw Lissa's stricken expression and added, "They consider both possibilities very remote."

"They *can,*" Lissa said, twirling her ankh. "They're not the ones who'd get gassed or roasted."

Cox said, "I understand your concern, ma'am—"

"Melissa," Barbie corrected. It suddenly seemed important to him that Cox understand these were *people* under the Dome, not just a few thousand anonymous taxpayers. "Melissa Jamieson. Lissa to her friends. She's the town librarian. She's also the middle-school guidance counselor, and teaches yoga classes, I believe."

"I had to give that up," Lissa said with a fretful smile. "Too many other things to do."

"Very nice to make your acquaintance, Ms. Jamieson," Cox said. "Look—this is a chance worth taking."

"If we felt differently, could we stop you?" she asked.

This Cox did not answer directly. "There's no sign that this thing, whatever it is, is weakening or biodegrading. Unless we're able to breach it, we believe you're in for the long haul."

"Do you have any idea what caused it? Any at all?"

"None," Cox said, but his eyes shifted in a way Rusty Everett would have recognized from his conversation with Big Jim.

Barbie thought, *Why are you lying? Just that knee-jerk*

reaction again? Civilians are like mushrooms, keep them in the dark and feed them shit? Probably that was all it was. But it made him nervous.

"It's strong?" Lissa asked. "Your acid—is it strong?"

"The most corrosive in existence, as far as we know," Cox replied, and Lissa took two large steps back.

Cox turned to the men in the space-suits. "Are you boys about ready?"

They gave him a pair of gloved thumbs-up. Behind them, all activity had stopped. The soldiers stood watching, with their hands on their gas masks.

"Here we go," Cox said. "Barbie, I suggest you escort those two beautiful ladies at least fifty yards back from—"

"Look at the *stars*," Julia said. Her voice was soft, awestruck. Her head was tilted upward, and in her wondering face Barbie saw the child she had been thirty years ago.

He looked up and saw the Big Dipper, the Great Bear, Orion. All where they belonged . . . except they had smeared out of clear focus and turned pink. The Milky Way had turned into a bubblegum spill across the greater dome of the night.

"Cox," he said. "Do you *see* that?"

Cox looked up.

"See what? The stars?"

"What do they look like to you?"

"Well . . . very bright, of course—no light pollution to speak of in these parts—" Then a thought occurred to him, and he snapped his fingers. "What are you seeing? Have they changed color?"

"They're beautiful," Lissa said. Her eyes were wide and shining. "But scary, too."

"They're pink," Julia said. "What's happening?"

"Nothing," Cox said, but he sounded oddly reluctant.

"What?" Barbie asked. "Spill it." And added, without thinking: "Sir."

"We got the meteorological report at nineteen hundred hours," Cox said. "Special emphasis on winds. Just in case . . . well, just in case. Leave it at that. The jet stream's currently coming west as far as Nebraska or Kansas, dipping south, then coming up the Eastern Seaboard. Pretty common pattern for late October."

"What's that got to do with the stars?"

"As it comes north, the jet passes over a lot of cities and manufacturing towns. What it picks up over those locations is collecting on the Dome instead of being whisked north to Canada and the Arctic. There's enough of it now to have created a kind of optical filter. I'm sure it's not dangerous. . . ."

"Not *yet*," Julia said. "What about in a week, or a month? Are you going to hose down our airspace at thirty thousand feet when it starts getting *dark* in here?"

Before Cox could reply, Lissa Jamieson screamed and pointed into the sky. Then she covered her face.

The pink stars were falling, leaving bright contrails behind them.

15

"More dope," Piper said dreamily as Rusty listened to her heartbeat.

Rusty patted Piper's right hand—the left one was badly scraped. "No more dope," he said. "You're officially stoned."

"Jesus wants me to have more dope," she said in that same dreamy voice. "I want to get as high as a mockingbird pie."

"I believe that's 'elephant's eye,' but I'll take it under consideration."

She sat up. Rusty tried to push her back down, but he dared push on only her right shoulder, and that wasn't enough. "Will I be able to get out of here tomorrow? I have to see Chief Randolph. Those boys raped Sammy Bushey."

"And could have killed you," he said. "Dislocation or not, you fell extremely lucky. Let me worry about Sammy."

"Those cops are dangerous." She put her right hand on his wrist. "They can't go on being police. They'll hurt someone else." She licked her lips. "My mouth is so dry."

"I can fix that, but you'll have to lie down."

"Did you take sperm samples from Sammy? Can you match them to the boys? If you can, I'll hound Peter Randolph until he makes them give DNA samples. I'll hound him day and night."

"We're not equipped for DNA matching," Rusty said. *Also, there are no sperm samples. Because Gina Buffalino washed her up, at Sammy's own request.* "I'll get you something to drink. All the fridges except for the ones in the lab are turned off to save juice, but there's an Igloo cooler at the nurses' station."

"Juice," she said, closing her eyes. "Yes, juice would be good. Orange or apple. Not V8. Too salty."

"Apple," he said. "You're on clear liquids tonight."

Piper whispered: "I miss my dog," then turned her head away. Rusty thought she'd probably be out by the time he got back with her juice box.

Halfway down the corridor, Twitch rounded the corner from the nurses' station at a dead run. His eyes were wide and wild. "Come outside, Rusty."

"As soon as I get Reverend Libby a—"

"No, now. You have to see this."

Rusty hurried back to room 29 and peeped in. Piper was snoring in a most unladylike way—not unusual, considering her swelled nose.

He followed Twitch down the corridor, almost running to keep up with the other man's long strides. "What is it?" Meaning, *What now?*

"I can't explain, and you probably wouldn't believe me if I did. You have to see it for yourself." He banged out through the lobby door.

Standing in the driveway beyond the protective canopy where drop-off patients arrived were Ginny Tomlinson, Gina Buffalino, and Harriet Bigelow, a friend whom Gina had recruited to help out at the hospital. The three of them had their arms around each other, as if for comfort, and were staring up into the sky.

It was filled with blazing pink stars, and many appeared to be falling, leaving long, almost fluorescent trails behind them. A shudder worked up Rusty's back.

Judy foresaw this, he thought. *"The pink stars are falling in lines."*

And they were. They were.

It was as if heaven itself was coming down around their ears.

16

Alice and Aidan Appleton were asleep when the pink stars began falling, but Thurston Marshall and Carolyn Sturges weren't. They stood in the backyard of the Dumagen house and watched them come down in brilliant pink lines. Some of the lines crisscrossed each other, and when this happened, pink runes seemed to stand out in the sky before fading.

"Is it the end of the world?" Carolyn asked.

"Not at all," he said. "It's a meteor swarm. They're most commonly observed during autumn here in New England. I think it's too late in the year for the Perseids, so this one's probably a wandering shower—maybe dust and chunks of rock from an asteroid that broke up a trillion years ago. Think of that, Caro!"

She didn't want to. "Are meteor showers always pink?"

"No," he said. "I think it probably looks white on the outside of the Dome, but we're seeing it through a film of dust and particulate matter. Pollution, in other words. It's changed the color."

She thought about that as they watched the silent pink tantrum in the sky. "Thurse, the little boy . . . Aidan . . . when he had that fit or whatever it was, he said . . ."

"I remember what he said. 'The pink stars are falling, they make lines behind them.' "

"How could he know that?"

Thurston only shook his head.

Carolyn hugged him tighter. At times like this (although there had never been a time exactly like this in her life), she was glad Thurston was old enough to be her father. Right now she wished he *was* her father.

"How could he know this was coming? How could he *know*?"

17

Aidan had said something else during his moment of prophecy: *Everyone is watching.* And by nine thirty on that Monday night, when the meteor shower was at its height, that was true.

The news spreads by cell phone and e-mail, but mostly

in the old way: mouth to ear. By quarter of ten, Main Street is full of people watching the silent fireworks display. Most are equally silent. A few are crying. Leo Lamoine, a faithful member of the late Reverend Coggins's Holy Redeemer congregation, shouts it's the Apocalypse, that he sees the Four Horsemen in the sky, that the Rapture will begin soon, et cetera, et cetera. Sloppy Sam Verdreaux—back on the street again since three that afternoon, sober and grumpy—tells Leo that if Leo doesn't shut up about the Acrockashit, he'll be seeing his own stars. Rupe Libby of the CMPD, hand on the butt of his gun, tells them both to shut the hell up and stop scaring people. As if they are not scared already. Willow and Tommy Anderson are in the parking lot of Dipper's, Willow crying with her head on Tommy's shoulder. Rose Twitchell stands beside Anson Wheeler outside Sweetbriar Rose; both are still wearing their aprons and they also have their arms around each other. Norrie Calvert and Benny Drake are with their parents, and when Norrie's hand steals into Benny's, he takes it with a thrill the falling pink stars cannot match. Jack Cale, the current manager of Food City, is in the supermarket parking lot. Jack called Ernie Calvert, the previous manager, late that afternoon and asked if Ernie would help him do a complete inventory of supplies on hand. They were well into this job, hoping to be done by midnight, when the furor on Main Street broke out. Now they stand side by side, watching the pink stars fall. Stewart and Fernald Bowie are outside their funeral parlor, gazing up. Henry Morrison and Jackie Wettington stand across from the funeral parlor with Chaz Bender, who teaches history up to the high school. "It's just a meteor shower seen through a haze of pollution," Chaz tells Jackie and Henry . . . but he still sounds awed.

The fact that accumulating particulate matter has actually changed the color of the stars brings the situation home to people in a new way, and gradually the weeping becomes more widespread. It is a soft sound, almost like rain.

Big Jim is less interested in a bunch of meaningless lights in the sky than he is in how people will *interpret* those lights. Tonight, he expects they'll just go home. Tomorrow, though, things may be different. And the fear he sees on most faces may not be such a bad thing. Fearful people need strong leaders, and if there's one thing Big Jim Rennie knows he can provide, it's strong leadership.

He's outside the police station doors with Chief Randolph and Andy Sanders. Standing below them, crowded together, are his problem children: Thibodeau, Searles, the Roux chippie, and Junior's friend, Frank. Big Jim descends the steps that Libby fell down earlier (*she could have done us all a favor if she'd broken her neck,* he thinks) and taps Frankie on the shoulder. "Enjoying the show, Frankie?"

The boy's big scared eyes make him look twelve instead of twenty-two or whatever he is. "What is it, Mr. Rennie? Do you know?"

"Meteor shower. Just God saying hello to His people." Frank DeLesseps relaxes a little.

"We're going back inside," Big Jim says, jerking his thumb at Randolph and Andy, who are still watching the sky. "We'll talk for a while, then I'll call you four in. I want you all to tell the same cotton-picking story when I do. Have you got that?"

"Yes, Mr. Rennie," Frankie says.

Mel Searles looks at Big Jim, his eyes like saucers and his mouth hanging loose. Big Jim thinks the boy looks like his IQ might reach all the way up to seventy. Not that that's necessarily a bad thing, either. "It looks like the end of the world, Mr. Rennie," he says.

"Nonsense. Are you Saved, son?"

"I guess so," Mel says.

"Then you have nothing to worry about." Big Jim surveys them one by one, ending with Carter Thibodeau. "And the way to salvation tonight, young men, is all of you telling the same story."

Not everyone sees the pink stars. Like the Appleton kids, Rusty Everett's Little Js are fast asleep. So is Piper. So is Andrea Grinnell. So is The Chef, sprawled on the dead grass beside what might be America's biggest methamphetamine lab. Ditto Brenda Perkins, who cried herself to sleep on her couch with the VADER printout scattered on the coffee table before her.

The dead also do not see, unless they look from a brighter place than this darkling plain where ignorant armies clash by night. Myra Evans, Duke Perkins, Chuck Thompson, and Claudette Sanders are tucked away in the Bowie Funeral Home; Dr. Haskell, Mr. Carty, and Rory Dinsmore are in the morgue of Catherine Russell Hospital; Lester Coggins, Dodee Sanders, and Angie McCain are still hanging out in the McCain pantry. So is Junior. He is between Dodee and Angie, holding their hands. His head aches, but only a little. He thinks he might sleep the night here.

On Motton Road, in Eastchester (not far from the place where the attempt to breach the Dome with an experimental acid compound is even then going on beneath the strange pink sky), Jack Evans, husband of the late Myra, is standing in his backyard with a bottle of Jack Daniels in one hand and his home protection weapon of choice, a Ruger SR9, in the other. He drinks and watches the pink stars fall. He knows what they are, and he wishes on every one, and he wishes for death, because without Myra, the bottom has dropped out of his life. He might be able to live without her, and he might be able to live like a rat in a glass cage, but he cannot manage both. When the falling meteors become more intermittent—this is around quarter after ten, about forty-five minutes after the shower began—he swallows the last of the Jack, casts the bottle onto the grass, and blows his brains out. He is The Mill's first official suicide.

He will not be the last.

18

Barbie, Julia, and Lissa Jamieson watched silently as the two space-suited soldiers removed the thin nozzle from the end of the plastic hose. They put it into an opaque plastic bag with a ziplock top, then put the bag into a metal case stenciled with the words **HAZARDOUS MATERIALS**. They locked it with separate keys, then took off their helmets. They looked tired, hot, and out of spirits.

Two older men—too old to be soldiers—wheeled a complicated-looking piece of equipment away from the site of the acid experiment, which had been performed three times. Barbie guessed the older guys, possibly scientists from NSA, had been doing some sort of spectrographic analysis. Or trying to. The gas masks they had been wearing during the testing procedure were now pushed up on top of their heads like weird hats. Barbie could have asked Cox what the tests were supposed to show, and Cox might even have given him a straight answer, but Barbie was also out of spirits.

Overhead, the last few pink meteoroids were zipping down the sky.

Lissa pointed back toward Eastchester. "I heard something that sounded like a gunshot. Did you?"

"Probably a car backfiring or some kid shooting off a bottle rocket," Julia said. She was also tired and drawn. Once, when it became clear that the experiment—the acid test, so to speak—wasn't going to work, Barbie had caught her wiping her eyes. It hadn't stopped her from taking pictures, with her Kodak, though.

Cox walked toward them, his shadow thrown in two different directions by the lights that had been set up. He gestured to the place where the door-shape had been sprayed on the Dome. "I'd guess this little adventure cost the American taxpayer about three-quarters of a million dollars, and that's not counting the R&D expenses that went into developing the acid compound. Which ate the paint we sprayed on there and did absolutely fuck-all else."

"Language, Colonel," Julia said, with a ghost of her old smile.

"Thank you, Madam Editor," Cox said sourly.

"Did you really think this would work?" Barbie asked.

"No, but I didn't think I'd ever live to see a man on Mars, either, but the Russians say they're going to send a crew of four in 2020."

"Oh, I get it," Julia said. "The Martians got wind of it, and they're pissed."

"If so, they retaliated on the wrong country," Cox said . . . and Barbie saw something in his eyes.

"How sure are you, Jim?" he asked softly.

"I beg pardon?"

"That the Dome was put in place by extraterrestrials."

Julia took two steps forward. Her face was pale, her eyes blazing. "Tell us what you know, goddammit!"

Cox raised his hand. "Stop. We don't know *anything*. There is a theory, however. Yes. Marty, come over here."

One of the older gentlemen who had been running

tests approached the Dome. He was holding his gas mask by the strap.

"Your analysis?" Cox asked, and when he saw the older gentleman's hesitation: "Speak freely."

"Well . . ." Marty shrugged. "Trace minerals. Soil and airborne pollutants. Otherwise, nothing. According to spectrographic analysis, that thing isn't there."

"What about the HY-908?" And, to Barbie and the women: "The acid."

"It's gone," Marty said. "The thing that isn't there ate it up."

"Is that possible, according to what you know?"

"No. But the Dome isn't possible, according to what we know."

"And does that lead you to believe that the Dome may be the creation of some life-form with more advanced knowledge of physics, chemistry, biology, whatever?" When Marty hesitated again, Cox repeated what he'd said earlier. "Speak freely."

"It's one possibility. It's also possible that some earthly supervillain set it up. A real-world Lex Luthor. Or it could be the work of a renegade country, like North Korea."

"Who hasn't taken credit for it?" Barbie asked skeptically.

"I lean toward extraterrestrial," Marty said. He knocked on the Dome without wincing; he'd already gotten his little shock from it. "So do most of the scientists working on this right now—if we can be said to be working when we're not actually *doing* anything. It's the Sherlock Rule: When you eliminate the impossible, the answer, no matter how improbable, is what remains."

"Has anyone or anything landed in a flying saucer and demanded to be taken to our leader?" Julia asked.

"No," Cox said.

"Would you know if something had?" Barbie asked, and thought: *Are we having this discussion? Or am I dreaming it?*

"Not necessarily," Cox said, after a brief hesitation.

"It could still be meteorological," Marty said. "Hell, even biological—a living thing. There's a school of thought that this thing is actually some kind of *E. coli* hybrid."

"Colonel Cox," Julia said quietly, "are we something's experiment? Because that's what I feel like."

Lissa Jamieson, meanwhile, was looking back toward the nice houses of the Eastchester burblet. Most of the lights there were out, either because the people who lived there had no generators or were saving them.

"That was a gunshot," she said. "I'm sure that was a gunshot."

FEELING IT

Other than town politics, Big Jim Rennie had only one vice, and that was high school girls' basketball—Lady Wildcats basketball, to be exact. He'd had season tickets ever since 1998, and attended at least a dozen games a year. In 2004, the year the Lady Wildcats won the State Class D championship, he attended all of them. And although the autographs people noticed when they were invited into his home study were inevitably those of Tiger Woods, Dale Earnhardt, and Bill "Spaceman" Lee, the one of which he was proudest—the one he treasured—was Hanna Compton's, the little sophomore point guard who had led the Lady Wildcats to that one and only gold ball.

When you're a season ticket holder, you get to know the other season ticket holders around you, and their reasons for being fans of the game. Many are relatives of the girls who play (and often the sparkplugs of the Booster Club, putting on bake sales and raising money for the increasingly expensive "away" games). Others are basketball purists, who will tell you—with some justification—that the girls' games are just better. Young female players are invested in a team ethic that the boys (who love to run and gun, dunk, and shoot from way downtown) rarely match. The pace is slower, allowing you to see inside the game and enjoy every pick-and-roll or give-and-go. Fans of the girls' game relish the very low scores that boys' basketball fans sneer at, claiming that the girls' game puts a premium on defense and foul shooting, which are the very definition of old-school hoops.

There are also guys who just like to watch long-legged teenage girls run around in short pants.

Big Jim shared all these reasons for enjoying the sport, but his passion sprang from another source entirely, one he never vocalized when discussing the games with his fellow fans. It would not have been politic to do so.

The girls took the sport personally, and that made them better haters.

The boys wanted to win, yes, and sometimes a game could get hot if it was against a traditional rival (in the case of The Mills Wildcats sports teams, the despised Castle Rock Rockets), but mostly with the boys it was about individual accomplishments. Showing off, in other words. And when it was over, it was over.

The girls, on the other hand, loathed losing. They took loss back to the locker room and brooded over it. More importantly, they loathed and hated it as a *team.* Big Jim often saw that hate rear its head; during a loose ball-brawl deep in the second half with the score tied, he could pick up that *No you don't, you little bitch, that ball is MINE* vibe. He picked it up and fed on it.

Before 2004, the Lady Wildcats made the state tournament only once in twenty years, that appearance a one-and-done affair against Buckfield. Then had come Hanna Compton. The greatest hater of all time, in Big Jim's opinion.

As the daughter of Dale Compton, a scrawny pulp-cutter from Tarker's Mills who was usually drunk and always argumentative, Hanna had come by her out-of-my-face 'tude naturally enough. As a freshman she had played JV for most of the season; Coach swung her up to varsity only for the last two games, where she'd outscored everyone and left her opposite number from the Richmond Bobcats writhing on the hardwood after a hard but clean defensive play.

When that game was over, Big Jim had collared Coach Woodhead. "If that girl doesn't start next year, you're crazy," he said.

"I'm not crazy," Coach Woodhead had replied.

Hanna had started hot and finished hotter, blazing a trail that Wildcats fans would still be talking about years later (season average: 27.6 points per game). She could spot up and drop a three-pointer any time she wanted, but what Big Jim liked best was to watch her split the defense and drive for the basket, her pug face set in a sneer of concentration, her bright black eyes daring anyone to get in her way, her short ponytail sticking out behind her like a raised middle finger. The Mill's Second Selectman and premier used car dealer had fallen in love.

In the 2004 championship game, the Lady Wildcats had been leading the Rock Rockets by ten when Hanna fouled out. Luckily for the Cats, there was only a buck-sixteen left to play. They ended up winning by a single point. Of their eighty-six total points, Hanna Compton had scored a brain-freezing *sixty-three*. That spring, her argumentative dad had ended up behind the wheel of a brand-new Cadillac, sold to him at cost-minus-forty-percent by James Rennie, Sr. New cars weren't Big Jim's business, but when he wanted one "off the back of the carrier," he could always get it.

Sitting in Peter Randolph's office, with the last of the pink meteor shower still fading away outside (and his problem children waiting—anxiously, Big Jim hoped—to be summoned and told their fate), Big Jim recalled that fabulous, that outright *mythic,* basketball game; specifically the first eight minutes of the second half, which had begun with the Lady Wildcats down by nine.

Hanna had taken the game over with the single-minded brutality of Joseph Stalin taking over Russia, her black eyes glittering (and seemingly fixed upon some basketball Nirvana beyond the sight of normal mortals), her face locked in that eternal sneer that said, *I'm better than you, I'm the best, get out of my way or I'll run you the fuck down.* Everything she threw up during that eight minutes had gone in, including one absurd half-court shot that she launched when her feet tangled together, getting rid of the rock just to keep from being called for traveling.

There were phrases for that sort of run, the most common being *in the zone.* But the one Big Jim liked was *feeling it,* as in "She's really *feeling it* now." As though the game had some divine texture beyond the reach of ordinary players (although sometimes even ordinary players *felt it,* and were transformed for a brief while into gods and goddesses, every bodily defect seeming to disappear during their transitory divinity), a texture that on special nights could be touched: some rich and marvelous drape such as must adorn the hardwood halls of Valhalla.

Hanna Compton had never played her junior year; the championship game had been her valedictory. That summer, while driving drunk, her father had killed himself, his wife, and all three daughters while driving back to Tarker's Mills from Brownie's, where they had gone for ice cream frappes. The bonus Cadillac had been their coffin.

The multiple-fatality crash had been front-page news in western Maine—Julia Shumway's *Democrat* published an issue with a black border that week—but Big Jim had not been grief-stricken. Hanna never would have played college ball, he suspected; there the girls were bigger, and she might have been reduced to role-player status. She never would have stood for that. Her hate had to be fed by constant action on the floor. Big Jim understood completely. He sympathized completely. It was the main reason he had never even considered leaving The Mill. In the wider world he might have made more money, but wealth was the short beer of existence. Power was champagne.

Running The Mill was good on ordinary days, but in times of crisis it was better than good. In times like that you could fly on the pure wings of intuition, knowing that you couldn't screw up, absolutely *couldn't*. You could read the defense even before the defense had coalesced, and you scored every time you got the ball. You were *feeling it,* and there was no better time for that to happen than in a championship game.

This was *his* championship game, and everything was breaking his way. He had the sense—the total belief—that nothing could go wrong during this magical passage; even things that seemed wrong would become opportunities rather than stumbling blocks, like Hanna's desperation half-court shot that had brought the whole Derry Civic Center to its feet, the Mills fans cheering, the Castle Rockers raving in disbelief.

Feeling it. Which was why he wasn't tired, even though he should have been exhausted. Which was why he wasn't worried about Junior, in spite of Junior's reticence and pale watchfulness. Which was why he wasn't worried about Dale Barbara and Barbara's troublesome coterie of friends, most notably the newspaper bitch. Which was why, when Peter Randolph and Andy Sanders looked at him, dumbfounded, Big Jim only smiled. He could afford to smile. He was *feeling it.*

"Close the supermarket?" Andy asked. "Won't that get a lot of people upset, Big Jim?"

"The supermarket and the Gas and Grocery," Big Jim corrected, still smiling. "Brownie's we don't have to worry about, it's already closed. A good thing, too—it's a dirty little place." *Selling dirty little magazines,* he did not add.

"Jim, there's still plenty of supplies at Food City," Randolph said. "I spoke to Jack Cale about that just this afternoon. Meat's thin, but everything else is holding up."

"I know that," Big Jim said. "I understand inventory, and Cale does, too. He should; he's Jewish, after all."

"Well . . . I'm just saying everything's been orderly so far, because people keep their pantries well stocked." He brightened. "Now, I could see ordering *shorter* hours at Food City. I think Jack could be talked into that. He's probably already thinking ahead to it."

Big Jim shook his head, still smiling. Here was another example of how things broke your way when you were *feeling it.* Duke Perkins would have said it was a mistake to put the town under any extra stress, especially after this night's unsettling celestial event. Duke was dead, however, and that was more than convenient; it was divine.

"Closed up," he repeated. "Both of them. Tight as ticks. And when they reopen, *we'll* be the ones handing out supplies. Stuff will last longer, and the distribution will be fairer. I'll announce a rationing plan at the Thursday meeting." He paused. "If the Dome isn't gone by then, of course."

Andy said hesitantly, "I'm not sure we have the authority to close down businesses, Big Jim."

"In a crisis like this, we not only have the authority, we have the responsibility." He clapped Pete Randolph heartily on the back. The Mill's new Chief wasn't expecting it and gave out a startled squeak.

"What if it starts a panic?" Andy was frowning.

"Well, that's a possibility," Big Jim said. "When you

kick a nest of mice, they're all apt to come running out. We may have to increase the size of our police force quite a bit if this crisis doesn't end soon. Yes, quite a bit."

Randolph looked startled. "We're going on twenty officers now. Including—" He cocked his head toward the door.

"Yep," Big Jim said, "and speaking of those fellers, better bring em in, Chief, so we can finish this and send them home to bed. I think they're going to have a busy day tomorrow."

And if they get roughed up a little, so much the better. They deserve it for not being able to keep their jackhandles in their pants.

2

Frank, Carter, Mel, and Georgia shuffled in like suspects onto a police lineup stage. Their faces were set and defiant, but the defiance was thin; Hanna Compton would have laughed at it. Their eyes were down, studying their shoes. It was clear to Big Jim that they expected to be fired, or worse, and that was just fine with him. Fright was the easiest of emotions to work with.

"Well," he said. "Here are the brave officers."

Georgia Roux muttered something under her breath.

"Speak up, honeybunch." Big Jim cupped a hand to his ear.

"Said we didn't do nothing wrong," she said. Still in that teacher's-being-mean-to-me mumble.

"Then exactly what *did* you do?" And, when Georgia, Frank, and Carter all started to talk at once, he pointed at Frankie. "You." *And make it good, for gosh sake.*

"We *were* out there," Frank said, "but she invited us."

"Right!" Georgia cried, folding her arms below her considerable bosom. *"She—"*

"Shut it." Big Jim pointed a hammy finger at her. "One speaks for all. That's how it works when you're a team. Are you a team?"

Carter Thibodeau saw where this was going. "Yes, sir, Mr. Rennie."

"Glad to hear it." Big Jim nodded for Frank to go on.

"She said she had some beers," Frank said. "That's the only reason we went out. Can't buy it in town, as you know. Anyway, we were sitting around, drinking beers— just a can each, and we were pretty much off-duty—"

"Completely off-duty," the Chief put in. "Isn't that what you meant?"

Frank nodded respectfully. "Yes, sir, that's what I meant to say. We drank our beers and then said we'd better go, but she said she appreciated what we were doing, every one of us, and wanted to say thank you. Then she kind of spread her legs."

"Showing her woofer, you know," Mel clarified with a large and vacant smile.

Big Jim winced and gave silent thanks that Andrea Grinnell wasn't here. Dope addict or not, she could have gone all politically correct in a situation like this.

"She took us in the bedroom one by one," Frankie said. "I know it was a bad decision, and we're all sorry, but it was purely voluntary on her part."

"I'm sure it was," Chief Randolph said. "That girl has quite a reputation. Her husband, too. You didn't see any drugs out there, did you?"

"No sir." A four-part chorus.

"And you didn't hurt her?" Big Jim asked. "I understand she's claiming she was punched around and whatnot."

"Nobody hurt her," Carter said. "Can I say what I think happened?"

Big Jim flapped an assenting hand. He was beginning to think that Mr. Thibodeau had possibilities.

"She probably fell down after we left. Maybe a couple of times. She was pretty drunk. Child Welfare should take that kid away from her before she kills it."

No one picked up on that. In the town's current situation, the Child Welfare office in Castle Rock might as well have been on the moon.

"So basically, you're all clean," Big Jim said.

"As a whistle," Frank replied.

"Well, I think we're satisfied." Big Jim looked around. "Are we satisfied, gentlemen?"

Andy and Randolph nodded, looking relieved.

"Good," Big Jim said. "Now, it's been a long day—an *eventful* day—and we all need some sleep, I'm sure. You young officers especially need it, because you'll report back for duty at seven AM tomorrow. The supermarket and the Gas and Grocery are both going to be closed for the duration of this crisis, and Chief Randolph thought that you'd be just the ones to guard Food City in case the people who show up there don't take kindly to the new order of things. Think you're up to that, Mr. Thibodeau? With your . . . your war wound?"

Carter flexed his arm. "I'm okay. Her dog didn't rip the tendon none."

"We can put Fred Denton with them, too," Chief Randolph said, getting into the spirit of the thing. "Wettington and Morrison at the Gas and Grocery should be enough."

"Jim," Andy said, "maybe we should put the more experienced officers at Food City, and the *less* experienced ones at the smaller—"

"I don't think so," Big Jim said. Smiling. *Feeling it.*

"These young folks are the ones we want at Food City. The very ones. And another thing. A little bird told me that some of you folks have been carrying weapons in your cars, and a couple have even been wearing them on foot patrol."

Silence greeted this.

"You're *probationary* officers," Big Jim said. "If you've got personal handguns, that's your right as Americans. But if I hear that any of you are strapped while standing out in front of Food City tomorrow and dealing with the good folks of this town, your police officer days are over."

"Absolutely right," Randolph said.

Big Jim surveyed Frank, Carter, Mel, and Georgia. "Any problems with that? Any of you?"

They didn't look happy about it. Big Jim hadn't expected that they would be, but they were getting off easy. Thibodeau kept flexing his shoulder and his fingers, testing them.

"What if they weren't loaded?" Frank asked. "What if they were just there, you know, as a warning?"

Big Jim raised a teacherly finger. "I'm going to tell you what my father told me, Frank—there's no such thing as an unloaded gun. We've got a good town here. They'll behave, that's what I'm banking on. If *they* change, *we'll* change. Got it?"

"Yessir, Mr. Rennie." Frank didn't sound happy about it. That was fine with Big Jim.

He rose. Only instead of leading them out, Big Jim extended his hands. He saw their hesitation and nodded, still smiling. "Come on, now. Tomorrow's going to be a big day, and we don't want to let this one go without a word of prayer. So grab on."

They grabbed on. Big Jim closed his eyes and bowed his head. "Dear Lord—"

It went on for some time.

3

Barbie mounted the outside steps to his apartment at a few minutes to midnight, his shoulders sagging with weariness, thinking that the only thing in the world he wanted was six hours of oblivion before answering the alarm and going up to Sweetbriar Rose to cook breakfast.

The weariness left him as soon as he snapped on the lights—which, courtesy of Andy Sanders's generator, still worked.

Someone had been in here.

The sign was so subtle that at first he couldn't isolate it. He closed his eyes, then opened them and let them swing casually about his combination living-room/kitchenette, trying to take in everything. The books he'd been planning to leave behind hadn't been moved around on the shelves; the chairs were where they had been, one under the lamp and the other by the room's only window, with its scenic view of the alley outside; the coffee cup and the toast plate were still in the dish drainer beside the tiny sink.

Then it clicked home, as such things usually did if you didn't push too hard. It was the rug. What he thought of as his Not Lindsay rug.

About five feet long and two wide, Not Lindsay was a repeating diamond pattern in blue, red, white, and brown. He had bought it in Baghdad, but had been assured by an Iraqi policeman he trusted that it was of Kurdish manufacture. "Very old, very beautiful," the policeman had said. His name was Latif abd al-Khaliq Hassan. A good troop. "Look Turkey, but no-no-no." Big grin. White teeth. A week after that day in the marketplace, a sniper's bullet had blown Latif abd al-Khaliq Hassan's brains right out through the back of his head. "Not Turkey, Iraqi!"

The rug-merchant wore a yellow tee-shirt that had said DON'T SHOOT ME, I'M ONLY THE PIANO PLAYER. Latif listened to him, nodding. They laughed together. Then the merchant had made a startlingly American jackoff gesture and they laughed even harder.

"What was that about?" Barbie had asked.

"He says American senator bought five like these. Lindsay Graham. Five rug, five hundred dollar. Five hundred out front, for press. More on the down-low. But all senator rug fake. Yes-yes-yes. This one not fake, this one real. I, Latif Hassan, tell you this, Barbie. Not Lindsay Graham rug."

Latif had raised his hand and Barbie slapped him five. That had been a good day. Hot, but good. He had bought the rug for two hundred dollars American and an all-territories Coby DVD player. Not Lindsay was his one souvenir of Iraq, and he never stepped on it. He always stepped around it. He had planned to leave it behind when he left The Mill—he supposed down deep his idea had been to leave *Iraq* behind when he left The Mill, but fat chance of that. Wherever you went, there you were. The great Zen truth of the age.

He hadn't stepped on it, he was superstitious about that, he always detoured around it, as if to step on it would activate some computer in Washington and he would find himself back in Baghdad or fucking Fallujah. But *somebody* had, because Not Lindsay was mussed. Wrinkled. And a little crooked. It had been perfectly straight when he left this morning, a thousand years ago.

He went into the bedroom. The coverlet was as neat as always, but that sense that someone had been here was equally strong. Was it a lingering smell of sweat? Some psychic vibe? Barbie didn't know and didn't care. He went to his dresser, opened the top drawer, and saw that the pair of extra-faded jeans which had been on top of the pile was now on the bottom. And his khaki shorts, which he'd laid in with the zippers up, were now zippers-down.

He went immediately to the second drawer, and the socks. It took less than five seconds to verify that his dog tags were gone, and he wasn't surprised. No, not surprised at all.

He grabbed the disposable cell he had also been planning to leave behind and went back into the main room. The combined Tarker's-Chester's telephone directory was sitting on a table by the door, a book so skinny it was almost a pamphlet. He looked for the number he wanted, not really expecting it to be there; Chiefs of Police did not make a practice of listing their home phone numbers.

Except, it seemed, in small towns, they did. At least this one had, although the listing was discreet: **H and B Perkins 28 Morin Street.** Even though it was now past midnight, Barbie punched in the number without hesitation. He couldn't afford to wait. He had an idea that time might be extremely short.

4

Her phone was tweeting. Howie, no doubt, calling to tell her he was going to be late, to just lock up the house and go to bed—

Then it came down on her again, like unpleasant presents raining from a poison piñata: the realization that Howie was dead. She didn't know who could be calling her at—she checked her watch—twenty past midnight, but it wasn't Howie.

She winced as she sat up, rubbing her neck, cursing herself for falling asleep on the couch, also cursing who-

ever had wakened her at such an ungodly hour and refreshed her recollection of her strange new singularity.

Then it occurred to her that there could be only one
reason for such a late call: the Dome was either gone or
had been breached. She bumped her leg on the coffee
table hard enough to make the papers there rattle, then
limped to the phone beside Howie's chair (how it hurt her
to look at that empty chair) and snatched it up. "What?
What?"

"It's Dale Barbara."

"Barbie! Has it broken? Has the Dome broken?"

"No. I wish that's why I was calling, but it's not."

"Then *why*? It's almost twelve-thirty in the morning!"

"You said your husband was investigating Jim Rennie."

Brenda paused, getting the sense of this. She had put
her palm against the side of her throat, the place where
Howie had caressed her for the last time. "He was, but I
told you, he had no absolute—"

"I remember what you said," Barbie told her. "You
need to listen to me, Brenda. Can you do that? Are you
awake?"

"I am now."

"Your husband had notes?"

"Yes. On his laptop. I printed them." She was looking
at the VADER file, spread out on the coffee table.

"Good. Tomorrow morning, I want you to put the
printout in an envelope and take it to Julia Shumway. Tell
her to put it in a safe place. An actual safe, if she's got one.
A cash strongbox or a locked file cabinet, if she doesn't.
Tell her she's only to open it if something happens to you
or me or both of us."

"You're scaring me."

"She is *not* to open it otherwise. If you tell her that, will
she do it? My instincts say she will."

"Of course she will, but why not let her look?"

"Because if the editor of the local paper sees what your husband had on Big Jim and Big Jim *knows* she's seen it, most of the leverage we have will be gone. Do you follow that?"

"Ye-es . . ." She found herself wishing desperately that Howie were the one having this post-midnight conversation.

"I said I might be arrested today if the missile strike didn't work. Do you remember me telling you that?"

"Of course."

"Well, I wasn't. That fat sonofabitch knows how to bide his time. But he won't bide it much longer. I'm almost positive it's going to happen tomorrow—later today, I mean. If, that is, you can't put a stop to it by threatening to air whatever dirt your husband dug up."

"What do you think they're going to arrest you for?"

"No idea, but it won't be shoplifting. And once I'm in jail, I think I might have an accident. I saw plenty of accidents like that in Iraq."

"That's crazy." But it had the horrid plausibility she had sometimes experienced in nightmares.

"Think about it, Brenda. Rennie has something to cover up, he needs a scapegoat, and the new Police Chief is in his pocket. The stars are in alignment."

"I was planning to go see him anyway," Brenda said. "And I was going to take Julia with me, for safety's sake."

"Don't take Julia," he said, "but don't go alone."

"You don't actually think he'd—"

"I don't know what he'd do, how far he'd go. Who do you trust besides Julia?"

She flashed back to that afternoon, the fires almost out, standing beside Little Bitch Road, feeling good in spite of her grief because she was flush with endorphins. Romeo Burpee telling her she ought to at least stand for Fire Chief.

"Rommie Burpee," she said.

"Okay, then he's the one."

"Do I tell him what Howie had on—"

"No," Barbie said. "He's just your insurance policy. And here's another one: lock up your husband's laptop."

"Okay . . . but if I lock up the laptop and leave the printout with Julia, what am I going to show Jim? I guess I could print a second copy—"

"No. One of those floating around is enough. For now, at least. Putting the fear of God into him is one thing. Freaking him out would make him too unpredictable. Brenda, do you believe he's dirty?"

She did not hesitate. "With all my heart." *Because Howie believed it—that's good enough for me.*

"And you remember what's in the file?"

"Not the exact figures and the names of all the banks they used, but enough."

"Then he'll believe you," Barbie said. "With or without a second copy of the paperwork, he'll believe you."

5

Brenda put the VADER file in a manila envelope. On the front she printed Julia's name. She put the envelope on the kitchen table, then went into Howie's study and locked his laptop in the safe. The safe was small and she had to turn the Mac on its side, but in the end it just fit. She finished by giving the combination dial not just one but two spins, as per her dead husband's instructions. As she did, the lights went out. For a moment some primitive part of her was certain she had blown them just by giving the dial that extra spin.

Then she realized that the generator out back had died.

6

When Junior came in at five minutes past six on Tuesday morning, his pale cheeks stubbly, his hair standing up in haystacks, Big Jim was sitting at the kitchen table in a white bathrobe the approximate size of a clipper ship's mainsail. He was drinking a Coke.

Junior nodded at it. "A good day starts with a good breakfast."

Big Jim raised the can, took a swallow, and set it down. "There's no coffee. Well, there is, but there's no electricity. The generator's out of LP. Grab yourself a pop, why don't you? They're still fairly cold, and you look like you could use it."

Junior opened the fridge and peered into its dark interior. "Am I supposed to believe you couldn't score some bottled gas anytime you wanted it?"

Big Jim started a little at that, then relaxed. It was a reasonable question, and didn't mean Junior knew anything. *The guilty man flees where none pursueth,* Big Jim reminded himself.

"Let's just say it might not be politic at this point in time."

"Uh-huh."

Junior closed the refrigerator door and sat down on the other side of the table. He looked at his old man with a certain hollow amusement (which Big Jim mistook for affection).

The family that slays together stays together, Junior thought. *At least for the time being. As long as it's . . .*

"Politic," he said.

Big Jim nodded and studied his son, who was supplementing his early-morning beverage with a Big Jerk beefstick.

He did not ask *Where have you been?* He did not ask *What's wrong with you?*, although it was obvious, in the unforgiving first light that flooded the kitchen, that something was. But he *did* have a question.

"There are bodies. Plural. Is that right?"

"Yes." Junior took a big bite of his beefstick and washed it down with Coke. The kitchen was weirdly silent without the hum of the fridge and the burble of the Mr. Coffee.

"And all these bodies can be laid at Mr. Barbara's door?"

"Yes. All." Another chomp. Another swallow. Junior looking at him steadily, rubbing his left temple as he did so.

"Can you plausibly discover those bodies around noon today?"

"No prob."

"And the evidence against our Mr. Barbara, of course."

"Yes." Junior smiled. "It's good evidence."

"Don't report to the police station this morning, son."

"I better," Junior said. "It might look funny if I don't. Besides, I'm not tired. I slept with . . ." He shook his head. "I slept, leave it at that."

Big Jim also did not ask *Who did you sleep with?* He had other concerns than whom his son might be diddling; he was just glad the boy hadn't been among the fellows who'd done their business with that nasty piece of trailer trash out on Motton Road. Doing business with that sort of girl was a good way to catch something and get sick.

He's already sick, a voice in Big Jim's head whispered.

It might have been the fading voice of his wife. *Just look at him.*

That voice was probably right, but this morning he had greater concerns than Junior Rennie's eating disorder, or whatever it was.

"I didn't say go to bed. I want you on motor patrol, and I want you to do a job for me. Just stay away from Food City while you're doing it. There's going to be trouble there, I think."

Junior's eyes livened up. "What kind of trouble?"

Big Jim didn't answer directly. "Can you find Sam Verdreaux?"

"Sure. He'll be in that little shack out on God Creek Road. Ordinarily he'd be sleeping it off, but today he's more apt to be shaking himself awake with the DTs." Junior snickered at this image, then winced and went back to rubbing his temple. "You really think I'm the person to talk to him? He's not my biggest fan right now. He's probably even deleted me from his Facebook page."

"I don't understand."

"It's a joke, Dad. Forget it."

"Do you think he'd warm up to you if you offered him three quarts of whiskey? And more later, if he does a good job?"

"That skanky old bastard would warm up to me if I offered him half a juice glass of Two-Buck Chuck."

"You can get the whiskey from Brownie's," Big Jim said. In addition to cheapass groceries and beaver-books, Brownie's was one of three agency liquor stores in The Mill, and the PD had keys to all three. Big Jim slid the key across the table. "Back door. Don't let anyone see you going in."

"What's Sloppy Sam supposed to do for the booze?"

Big Jim explained. Junior listened impassively . . .

except for his bloodshot eyes, which danced. He had only one more question: Would it work?

Big Jim nodded. "It will. I'm *feeling it.*"

Junior took another chomp on his beefstick and another swallow of his soda. "So'm I, Dad," he said. "So'm I."

7

When Junior was gone, Big Jim went into his study with his robe billowing grandly around him. He took his cell phone from the center drawer of his desk, where he kept it as much as possible. He thought they were Godless things that did nothing but encourage a lot of loose and useless talk—how many man-hours had been lost to useless gabble on these things? And what kind of nasty rays did they shoot into your head while you were gabbling?

Still, they could come in handy. He reckoned that Sam Verdreaux would do as Junior told him, but he also knew it would be foolish not to take out insurance.

He selected a number in the cell phone's "hidden" directory, which could be accessed only via numeric code. The phone rang half a dozen times before it was picked up. *"What?"* the sire of the multitudinous Killian brood barked.

Big Jim winced and held the phone away from his ear for a second. When he put it back, he heard low clucking sounds in the background. "Are you in the chickenhouse, Rog?"

"Uh . . . yessir, Big Jim, I sure am. Chickens got to be fed, come hell or high water." A 180-degree turn from irritation to respect. And Roger Killian *ought* to be respectful; Big Jim had made him a gosh-darn millionaire. If he was wasting what could have been a good life with no financial worries by still getting up at dawn to feed a bunch of chickens, that was God's will. Roger was too dumb to stop. It was his heaven-sent nature, and would no doubt serve Big Jim well today.

And the town, he thought. *It's the town I'm doing this for. The good of the town.*

"Roger, I've got a job for you and your three oldest sons."

"Only got two t'home," Roger said. In his thick Yankee accent, *home* came out *hum.* "Ricky and Randall are here, but Roland was in Oxford buying feed when the Christing Dome came down." He paused and considered what he had just said. In the background, the chickens clucked. "Sorry about the profanity."

"I'm sure God forgives you," Big Jim said. "You and your *two* oldest, then. Can you get them to town by—" Big Jim calculated. It didn't take long. When you were *feeling it,* few decisions did. "Say, nine o'clock, nine fifteen at the latest?"

"I'll have to rouse em, but sure," Roger said. "What are we doin? Bringin in some of the extra propa—"

"No," Big Jim said, "and you hush about that, God love you. Just listen."

Big Jim talked.

Roger Killian, God love him, listened.

In the background roughly eight hundred chickens clucked as they stuffed themselves with steroid-laced feed.

8

"What? *What? Why?*"

Jack Cale was sitting at his desk in the cramped little Food City manager's office. The desk was littered with inventory lists he and Ernie Calvert had finally completed at one in the morning, their hopes of finishing earlier dashed by the meteor shower. Now he swept them up—handwritten on long yellow legal-pad sheets—and shook them at Peter Randolph, who stood in the office doorway. The new Chief had dolled up in full uniform for this visit. "Look at these, Pete, before you do something foolish."

"Sorry, Jack. Market's closed. It'll reopen on Thursday, as a food depot. Share and share alike. We'll keep all the records, Food City Corp won't lose a cent, I promise you—"

"That's not the *point*," Jack nearly groaned. He was a baby-faced thirtysomething with a thatch of wiry red hair he was currently torturing with the hand not holding out the yellow sheets . . . which Peter Randolph showed no signs of taking.

"Here! Here! What in the name of jumped-up Jack Sprat Jesus are you talking about, Peter Randolph?"

Ernie Calvert came barreling up from the basement storage area. He was broad-bellied and red-faced, his gray hair mowed into the crewcut he'd worn all his life. He was wearing a green Food City duster.

"He wants to close the market!" Jack said.

"Why in God's name would you want to do that, when there's still plenty of food?" Ernie asked angrily. "Why would you want to go scaring people like that? They'll be plenty scared in time, if this goes on. Whose dumb idea was this?"

"Selectmen voted," Randolph said. "Any problems you have with the plan, take them up at the special town meeting on Thursday night. If this isn't over by then, of course."

"*What* plan?" Ernie shouted. "Are you telling me Andrea Grinnell was in favor of this? She knows better!"

"I understand she's got the flu," Randolph said. "Flat on her back. So Andy decided. Big Jim seconded the decision." No one had told him to put it this way; no one had to. Randolph knew how Big Jim liked to do business.

"Rationing might make sense at some point," Jack said, "but why now?" He shook the sheets again, his cheeks almost as red as his hair. "Why, when we've still got so *much*?"

"That's the best time to start conserving," Randolph said.

"That's rich, coming from a man with a powerboat on Sebago Lake and a Winnebago Vectra in his dooryard," Jack said.

"Don't forget Big Jim's Hummer," Ernie put in.

"Enough," Randolph said. "The Selectmen decided—"

"Well, *two* of them did," Jack said.

"You mean *one* of them did," Ernie said. "And we know which one."

"—and I carried the message, so there's an end to it. Put a sign in the window. MARKET CLOSED UNTIL FURTHER NOTICE."

"Pete. Look. Be reasonable." Ernie no longer seemed angry; now he seemed almost to be pleading. "That'll scare the dickens out of people. If you're set on this, how about I put CLOSED FOR INVENTORY, WILL RE-OPEN SOON? Maybe add SORRY FOR THE TEMPORARY INCONVENIENCE. Put TEMPORARY in red, or something."

Peter Randolph shook his head slowly and weightily. "Can't let you, Ern. Couldn't let you even if you were still an official employee, like him." He nodded to Jack Cale, who had put down the inventory sheets so he could torture his hair with both hands. "CLOSED UNTIL FURTHER NOTICE. That's what the Selectmen told me, and I carry out their orders. Besides, lies always come back to bite you on the ass."

"Yeah, well, Duke Perkins would have told them to take this particular order and *wipe* their asses with it," Ernie said. "You ought to be ashamed, Pete, carrying that fat shit's water. He says jump, you ask how high."

"You want to shut up right now, if you know what's good for you," Randolph said, pointing at him. The finger shook a little. "If you don't want to spend the rest of the day in jail on a disrespect charge, you just want to close your mouth and follow orders. This is a crisis situation—"

Ernie looked at him unbelievingly. " 'Disrespect charge'? No such animal!"

"There is now. If you don't believe it, go on and try me."

9

Later on—much too late to do any good—Julia Shumway would piece together most of how the Food City riot started, although she never got a chance to print it. Even if she had, she would have done so as a pure news story: the five Ws and the H. If asked to write about the emotional heart of the event, she would have been lost. How to explain that people she'd known all her life—people she respected, people she loved—had turned into a mob? She told herself *I could've gotten a better handle on it if I'd been there from the very beginning and seen how it started,* but that was pure rationalization, a refusal to face the orderless, reasonless beast that can arise when frightened people are provoked. She had seen such beasts on the TV news, usually in foreign countries. She never expected to see one in her own town.

And there was no need for it. This was what she kept coming back to. The town had been cut off for only seventy hours, and it was stuffed with provisions of almost every kind; only propane gas was in mysteriously short supply.

Later she would say, *It was the moment when this town finally realized what was happening.* There was probably truth in the idea, but it didn't satisfy her. All she could say with complete certainty (and she said it only to herself) was that she watched her town lose its mind, and afterward she would never be the same person.

10

The first two people to see the sign are Gina Buffalino and her friend Harriet Bigelow. Both girls are dressed in white nurse's uniforms (this was Ginny Tomlinson's idea; she felt the whites inspired more confidence among the patients than candy-striper pinafores), and they look most seriously cute. They also look tired, in spite of their youthful resiliency. It has been a hard two days, and another is ahead of them, after a night of short sleep. They have come for candy bars—they will get enough for everyone but poor diabetic Jimmy Sirois, that's the plan—and they are talking about the meteor shower. The conversation stops when they see the sign on the door.

"The market *can't* be closed," Gina says unbelievingly. "It's Tuesday morning." She puts her face to the glass with her hands cupped to the sides to cut the glare of the bright morning sun.

While she's so occupied, Anson Wheeler drives up with Rose Twitchell riding shotgun. They have left Barbie back at Sweetbriar, finishing up the breakfast service. Rose is out of the little panel truck with her namesake painted on the side even before Anson has turned off the engine. She has a long list of staples, and wants to get as much as she can, as soon as she can. Then she sees CLOSED UNTIL FURTHER NOTICE posted on the door.

"What the hell? I saw Jack Cale just last night, and he never said a word about this."

She's speaking to Anson, who's chugging along in her wake, but it's Gina Buffalino who answers. "It's still full of stuff, too. All the shelves are stocked."

Other people are pulling in. The market is due to open in five minutes, and Rose isn't the only one who planned to get an early start on her marketing; folks from all over town woke up to find the Dome still in place and decided to stock up on supplies. Asked later to explain this sudden rush of custom, Rose would say: "The same thing happens every winter when the Weather Bureau upgrades a storm warning to a blizzard warning. Sanders and Rennie couldn't have picked a worse day to pull this bullshit."

Among the early arrivals are Units Two and Four of the Chester's Mill PD. Close behind them comes Frank DeLesseps in his Nova (he's ripped off the ASS, GAS, OR GRASS sticker, feeling it hardly becomes an officer of the law). Carter and Georgia are in Two; Mel Searles and Freddy Denton in Four. They have been parked down the street by LeClerc's Maison des Fleurs, by order of Chief Randolph. "No need to get there too soon," he has instructed them. "Wait until there are a dozen or so cars in the parking lot. Hey, maybe they'll just read the sign and go home."

This doesn't happen, of course, just as Big Jim Rennie knew it wouldn't. And the appearance of the officers—especially such young and callow ones, for the most part—acts as an incitement rather than a calmative. Rose is the first to begin haranguing them. She picks on Freddy, showing him her long list of supplies, then pointing through the window, where most of the stuff she wants is ranked neatly on the shelves.

Freddy is polite to begin with, aware that people (not quite a crowd, not yet) are watching, but it's hard to keep his temper with this mouthy little pipsqueak in his face. Doesn't she realize he's only following orders?

"Who do you think is feeding this town, Fred?" Rose asks. Anson puts a hand on her shoulder. Rose shakes it off. She knows Freddy is seeing rage instead of the deep distress she feels, but she can't help it. "Do you think a Sysco truck full of supplies is just going to parachute down from the sky?"

"Ma'am—"

"Oh, can it! Since when am I a ma'am to you? You've been eating blueberry pancakes and that nasty limp bacon you like at my place four and five days a week for twenty years, and calling me Rosie while you did it. But you won't be eating pancakes tomorrow unless I get some *flour* and some *shortening* and some *syrup* and . . ." She breaks off. "Finally! Sense! Thank You, God!"

Jack Cale is opening one of the double doors. Mel and Frank have taken up station in front of it, and he has just room to squeeze between them. The prospective shoppers—there are nearly two dozen now, even though the market's official opening time of nine AM is still a minute away—surge forward, only to stop when Jack selects a key from the bunch on his belt, and locks up again. There's a collective groan.

"Why the hell'd you do that?" Bill Wicker calls out indignantly. "My wife sent me down for aigs!"

"Take it up with the Selectmen and Chief Randolph," Jack responds. His hair is raring every whichway. He throws Frank DeLesseps a black look and fires an even blacker one at Mel Searles, who is trying unsuccessfully to suppress a grin, perhaps even his famous *nyuck-nyuck-nyuck*. "I know *I* will. But for now, I've had enough of this shit. I'm done." He strides off through the crowd with his head down and his cheeks burning even brighter than his hair. Lissa Jamieson, just arriving on her bicycle (everything on her list will fit into the milk box perched on the rear fender; her wants are small-going-on-minuscule), has to swerve to avoid him.

Carter, Georgia, and Freddy are ranged in front of the large plate-glass window, where Jack would have set out wheelbarrows and fertilizer on an ordinary day. Carter's fingers are Band-Aided, and a thicker bandage bulks under his shirt. Freddy has his hand on his gun-butt as Rose Twitchell continues to chew on him, and Carter wishes he could backhand her one. His fingers are okay, but his shoulder aches a bitch. The small cluster of would-be shoppers has become a large cluster, and more cars are turning into the parking lot.

Before Officer Thibodeau can really study the crowd, however, Alden Dinsmore gets into his personal space. Alden looks haggard, and seems to have lost twenty pounds since the death of his son. He's wearing a black mourning band on his left arm and seems dazed.

"Need to go in, son. My wife sent me to stock up on the canned." Alden doesn't say the canned what. Probably the canned everything. Or maybe he just got thinking about the empty bed upstairs, the one that will never be filled again, and the Foo Fighters poster that will never be looked at again, and the model airplane on the desk that will never be finished, and clean forgot.

"Sorry, Mr. Dimmesdale," Carter says. "You can't do that."

"It's Dinsmore," Alden says in a dazed voice. He starts toward the doors. They are locked, no way he can get in, but Carter still gives the farmer a good hearty shove backward. For the first time, Carter has some sympathy for the teachers who used to send him to detention back in high school; it is irritating not to be minded.

Also it's hot and his shoulder aches in spite of the two Percocet his mother gave him. Seventy-five at nine AM is rare in October, and the faded blue color of the sky says it will be hotter by noon, hotter still by three PM.

Alden stumbles backward into Gina Buffalino, and they both would fall if not for Petra Searles—no light-weight she—steadying them. Alden doesn't look angry, only puzzled. "M'wife sent me for the canned," he explains to Petra.

A mutter comes from the gathering people. It's not an angry sound—not quite yet. They came for groceries and the groceries are there but the door is locked. Now a man has been shoved by a high-school dropout who was a car mechanic last week.

Gina is looking at Carter, Mel, and Frank DeLesseps with widening eyes. She points. "Those are the guys that raped her!" she tells her friend Harriet without lowering her voice. "Those are the guys that raped Sammy Bushey!"

The smile disappears from Mel's face; the urge to *nyuck-nyuck* has left him. "Shut up," he says.

At the back of the crowd, Ricky and Randall Killian have arrived in a Chevrolet Canyon pickemup. Sam Ver-dreaux is not far behind, walking, of course; Sam lost his license to drive for good in '07.

Gina takes a step backward, staring at Mel with wide eyes. Beside her, Alden Dinsmore hulks like a farmer-robot with a dead battery. "You guys are supposed to be police? Hel-*lo?*"

"That rape stuff was nothing but a whore lie," Frank says. "And you better quit yelling about it before you get arrested for disturbing the peace."

"Fuckin right," Georgia says. She has moved a little closer to Carter. He ignores her. He is surveying the crowd. And that's what it is now. If fifty people make a crowd, then this is one. More coming, too. Carter wishes he had his gun. He doesn't like the hostility he's seeing.

Velma Winter, who runs Brownie's (or did, before it closed), arrives with Tommy and Willow Anderson. Velma is a big, burly woman who combs her hair like Bobby Darin and looks like she could be the warrior queen of Dyke Nation, but she has buried two husbands and the story you can hear at the bullshit table in Sweetbriar is that she fucked them both to death and is looking for number three at Dipper's on Wednesdays; that's Country Karaoke Night, and draws an older crowd. Now she plants herself in front of Carter, hands on her meaty hips.

"Closed, huh?" she says in a businesslike voice. "Let's see your paperwork."

Carter is confused, and being confused makes him angry. "Back off, bitch. I don't need no paperwork. The Chief sent us down here. The Selectmen ordered it. It's gonna be a food depot."

"Rationing? That what you mean?" She snorts. "Not in *my* town." She shoves between Mel and Frank and starts hammering on the door. "Open up! *Open up in there!*"

"Nobody home," Frank says. "You might as well quit it."

But Ernie Calvert hasn't left. He comes down the pasta-flour-and-sugar aisle. Velma sees him and starts hammering louder. "Open up, Ernie! Open up!"

"Open up!" voices from the crowd agree.

Frank looks at Mel and nods. Together they grab Velma and muscle her two hundred pounds away from the door. Georgia Roux has turned and is waving Ernie back. Ernie doesn't go. Numb fuck just stands there.

"Open up!" Velma bawls. *"Open up! Open up!"*

Tommy and Willow join her. So does Bill Wicker, the postman. So does Lissa, her face shining—all her life she has hoped to be part of a spontaneous demonstration, and here's her chance. She raises a clenched fist and begins to shake it in time—two small shakes on *open* and a big one on *up*. Others imitate her. *Open up* becomes *Oh-pun UP! Oh-pun UP! Oh-pun UP!* Now they are all shaking their fists in that two-plus-one rhythm—maybe seventy people, maybe eighty, and more arriving all the time. The thin blue line in front of the market looks thinner than ever. The four younger cops look toward Freddy Denton for ideas, but Freddy has no ideas.

He does, however, have a gun. *You better fire it into the air pretty soon, Baldy,* Carter thinks, *or these people are gonna run us down.*

Two more cops—Rupert Libby and Toby Whelan—drive down Main Street from the PD (where they've been drinking coffee and watching CNN), blowing past Julia Shumway, who is jogging along with a camera slung over her shoulder.

Jackie Wettington and Henry Morrison also start toward the supermarket, but then the walkie-talkie on Henry's belt crackles. It's Chief Randolph, saying that Henry and Jackie should hold their station at the Gas & Grocery.

"But we hear—" Henry begins.

"Those are your orders," Randolph says, not adding that they are orders he is just passing on—from a higher power, as it were.

"Oh-pun UP! Oh-pun UP! Oh-pun UP!" The crowd shaking fisted power-salutes in the warm air. Still scared, but excited, too. Getting into it. The Chef would have looked

at them and seen a bunch of tyro tweekers, needing only a Grateful Dead tune on the soundtrack to make the picture complete.

The Killian boys and Sam Verdreaux are working their way through the crowd. They chant—not as protective coloration but because that crowd-molting-into-mob vibe is just too strong to resist—but don't bother shaking their fists; they have work to do. No one pays them any particular mind. Later, only a few people will remember seeing them at all.

Nurse Ginny Tomlinson is also working her way through the crowd. She has come to tell the girls they are needed at Cathy Russell; there are new patients, one a serious case. That would be Wanda Crumley from Eastchester. The Crumleys live next to the Evanses, out near the Motton town line. When Wanda went over this morning to check on Jack, she found him dead not twenty feet from where the Dome cut off his wife's hand. Jack was sprawled on his back with a bottle beside him and his brains drying on the grass. Wanda ran back to her house, crying her husband's name, and she had no more than reached him when she was felled by a coronary. Wendell Crumley was lucky not to crash his little Subaru wagon on his way to the hospital—he did eighty most of the way. Rusty is with Wanda now, but Ginny doesn't think Wanda—fifty, overweight, a heavy smoker—is going to make it.

"Girls," she says. "We need you at the hospital."

"Those are the ones, Mrs. Tomlinson!" Gina shouts. She *has* to shout to be heard over the chanting crowd. She's pointing at the cops and beginning to cry—partly from fear and tiredness, mostly from outrage. "Those are the ones who raped her!"

This time Ginny looks beyond the uniforms, and realizes Gina's right. Ginny Tomlinson isn't afflicted with

Piper Libby's admittedly vile temper, but she *has* a temper, and there's an aggravating factor at work here: unlike Piper, Ginny saw the Bushey girl with her pants off. Her vagina lacerated and swelled. Huge bruises on her thighs that couldn't be seen until the blood was washed off. Such a lot of blood.

Ginny forgets about the girls being needed at the hospital. She forgets about getting them out of a dangerous and volatile situation. She even forgets about Wanda Crumley's heart attack. She strides forward, elbowing someone out of her way (it happens to be Bruce Yardley, the cashier-*cum*-bagboy, who is shaking his fist like everyone else), and approaches Mel and Frank. They are both studying the ever more hostile crowd, and they don't see her coming.

Ginny raises both hands, looking for a moment like the bad guy surrendering to the sheriff in a Western. Then she brings both hands around and slaps both young men at the same time. "You *bastards*!" she shouts. "How *could* you? How could you be so *cowardly*? So catdirt *mean*? You'll go to *jail* for this, all of y—"

Mel doesn't think, just reacts. He punches her in the center of her face, breaking her glasses and her nose. She goes stumbling backward, bleeding, crying out. Her old-fashioned RN cap, shocked free of the bobbypins holding it, tumbles from her head. Bruce Yardley, the young cashier, tries to grab her and misses. Ginny hits a line of shopping carts. They go rolling like a little train. She drops to her hands and knees, crying in pain and shock. Bright drops of blood from her nose—not just broken but shattered—begin falling on the big yellow RK of NO PARKING ZONE.

The crowd goes temporarily silent, shocked, as Gina and Harriet rush to where Ginny crouches.

Then Lissa Jamieson's voice rises, a clear perfect soprano: *"YOU PIG BASTARDS!"*

That's when the chunk of rock flies. The first rock-thrower is never identified. It may be the only crime Sloppy Sam Verdreaux ever got away with.

Junior dropped him off at the upper end of town, and Sam, with visions of whiskey dancing in his head, went prospecting on the east bank of Prestile Stream for just the right rock. Had to be big but not too big, or he wouldn't be able to throw it with any accuracy, even though once—a century ago, it seems sometimes; at others it seems very close—he was the starting pitcher for the Mills Wildcats in the first game of the Maine state tourney. He had found it at last, not far from the Peace Bridge: a pound, pound and a half, and as smooth as a goose egg.

One more thing, Junior had said as he dropped Sloppy Sam off. It wasn't Junior's one more thing, but Junior did not tell Sam this any more than Chief Randolph had told Wettington and Morrison, who had ordered them to stay on station. Wouldn't have been politic.

Aim for the chick. That was Junior's final word to Sloppy Sam before leaving him. *She deserves it, so don't miss.*

As Gina and Harriet in their white uniforms kneel beside the sobbing, bleeding RN on her hands and knees (and while everyone else's attention is there too), Sam winds up just as he did on that long-ago day in 1970, lets fly, and throws his first strike in over forty years.

In more ways than one. The twenty-ounce chunk of quartz-shot granite strikes Georgia Roux dead in the mouth, shattering her jaw in five places and all but four of her teeth. She goes reeling back against the plate-glass window, her jaw sagging grotesquely almost to her chest, her yawning mouth pouring blood.

An instant later two more rocks fly, one from Ricky

Killian, one from Randall. Ricky's connects with the back of Bill Allnut's head and knocks the janitor to the pavement, not far from Ginny Tomlinson. *Shit!* Ricky thinks. *I was supposed to hit a fuckin cop!* Not only were those his orders; it's sort of what he has always wanted to do.

Randall's aim is better. He nails Mel Searles square in the forehead. Mel goes down like a bag of mail.

There is a pause, a moment of indrawn breath. Think of a car teetering on two wheels, deciding whether or not to go over. See Rose Twitchell looking around, bewildered and frightened, not sure what's happening, let alone what to do about it. See Anson put his arm around her waist. Listen to Georgia Roux howl through her hanging mouth, her cries weirdly like the sound the wind makes slipping across the waxed string of a tin-can mooseblower. Blood pours over her lacerated tongue as she hollers. See the reinforcements. Toby Whelan and Rupert Libby (he's Piper's cousin, though she doesn't brag on the connection) are first to arrive on the scene. They survey it . . . then hang back. Next comes Linda Everett. She's on foot with another part-time cop, Marty Arsenault, puffing along in her wake. She starts to push through the crowd, but Marty—who didn't even put on his uniform this morning, just rolled out of bed and slipped into an old pair of bluejeans—grabs her by the shoulder. Linda almost breaks away from him, then thinks of her daughters. Ashamed of her own cowardice, she allows Marty to lead her over to where Rupe and Toby are watching developments. Of these four, only Rupe is wearing a gun this morning, and would he shoot? Balls he would; he can see his own wife in that crowd, holding hands with her mother (the mother-in-law Rupe wouldn't have minded shooting). See Julia arrive just behind Linda and Marty, gasping for breath but already grabbing her camera, dropping the lenscap in her hurry to start shooting. See Frank DeLesseps kneel down beside Mel just in time to avoid another rock, which whizzes over his head and shatters a hole in one of the supermarket doors.

Then . . .

Then someone yells. Who will never be known, not even the sex of the shouter will ever be agreed upon, although most think a woman, and Rose will tell Anson later she's almost sure it was Lissa Jamieson.

"GET THEM!"

Someone else bellows *"GROCERIES!"* and the crowd surges forward.

Freddy Denton fires his pistol once, into the air. Then he lowers it, in his panic about to empty it into the crowd. Before he can, someone wrests it from his hand. He goes down, shouting in pain. Then the toe of a big old farmer's boot—Alden Dinsmore's—connects with his temple. The lights don't go completely out for Officer Denton, but they dim considerably, and by the time they come back up to bright, the Great Supermarket Riot is over.

Blood seeps through the bandage on Carter Thibodeau's shoulder and small rosettes are blooming on his blue shirt, but he is—for the time being, at least—unaware of the pain. He makes no attempt to run. He sets his feet and unloads on the first person to come into range. This happens to be Charles "Stubby" Norman, who runs the antique shop on the 117 edge of town. Stubby drops, clutching his spouting mouth.

"Get back, you fucks!" Carter snarls. *"Back, you sons of bitches! No looting! Get back!"*

Marta Edmunds, Rusty's babysitter, tries to help Stubby, and gets a Frank DeLesseps fist to the cheekbone for her pains. She staggers, holding the side of her face and looking unbelievingly at the young man who has just hit her . . . and is then knocked flat, with Stubby beneath her, by a wave of charging would-be shoppers.

Carter and Frank start punching at them, but they land only three blows before they are distracted by a weird, ululating scream. It's the town librarian, her hair hanging around her usually mild face. She's pushing a line of shopping carts, and she might be screaming banzai. Frank leaps out of her way, but the carts take care of Carter, sending him flying. He waves his arms, trying to stay up, and might actually manage to do so, except for Georgia's feet. He trips over them, lands on his back, and is trampled. He rolls over on his stomach, laces his hands over his head, and waits for it to be over.

Julia Shumway clicks and clicks and clicks. Perhaps the pictures will reveal the faces of people she knows, but she sees only strangers in the viewfinder. A mob.

Rupe Libby draws his sidearm and fires four shots into the air. The gunfire rolls off into the warm morning, flat and declamatory, a line of auditory exclamation points. Toby Whelan dives back into the car, bumping his head and knocking off his cap (CHESTER'S MILL DEPUTY on the front in yellow). He snatches the bullhorn off the back seat, puts it to his lips, and shouts: "STOP WHAT YOU'RE DOING! BACK OFF! POLICE! STOP! THAT IS AN ORDER!"

Julia snaps him.

The crowd pays no attention to the gunshots or the bullhorn. They pay no attention to Ernie Calvert when he comes around the side of the building with his green duster churning about his pumping knees. *"Come in the back!"* he yells. *"You don't need to do that, I've opened up the back!"*

The crowd is intent upon breaking and entering. They smash against the doors with their stickers reading IN and OUT and EVERYDAY LOW PRICES. The doors hold at first, then the lock snaps under the crowd's combined weight. The first to arrive are crushed against the doors and suffer injuries: two people with broken ribs, one sprained neck, two broken arms.

Toby Whelan starts to raise the bullhorn again, then just sets it down, with exquisite care, on the hood of the car in which he and Rupe arrived. He picks up his DEPUTY cap, brushes it off, puts it back on. He and Rupe walk toward the store, then stop, helpless. Linda and Marty Arsenault join them. Linda sees Marta and leads her back to the little cluster of cops.

"What happened?" Marta asks, dazed. "Did someone hit me? The side of my face is all hot. Who's watching Judy and Janelle?"

"Your sister took them this morning," Linda says, and hugs her. "Don't worry."

"Cora?"

"Wendy." Cora, Marta's older sister, has been living in Seattle for years. Linda wonders if Marta has suffered a concussion. She thinks that Dr. Haskell should check her, and then remembers that Haskell is either in the hospital morgue or the Bowie Funeral Home. Rusty is on his own now, and today he is going to be very busy.

Carter is half-carrying Georgia toward Unit 2. She is still howling those eerie mooseblower cries. Mel Searles has regained some soupy semblance of consciousness. Frankie leads him toward Linda, Marta, Toby, and the other cops. Mel tries to raise his head, then drops it back to his chest. His split forehead is pouring blood; his shirt is soaked.

People stream into the market. They race along the aisles, pushing shopping carts or grabbing baskets from a stack beside the charcoal briquets display (HAVE YOUR-

SELF A FALL COOKOUT! the sign reads). Manuel Ortega, Alden Dinsmore's hired man, and his good friend Dave Douglas go straight to the checkout cash registers and start punching NO SALE buttons, grabbing money and stuffing it into their pockets, laughing like fools as they do so.

The supermarket is full now; it is sale day. In frozen foods, two women are fighting over the last Pepperidge Farm Lemon Cake. In deli, one man baffs another man with a kielbasa, telling him to leave some of that goddam lunchmeat for other folks. The lunchmeat shopper turns and biffs the kielbasa wielder in the nose. Soon they are rolling on the floor, fists flying.

Other brawls are breaking out. Rance Conroy, proprietor and sole employee of Conroy's Western Maine Electrical Service & Supplies ("Smiles Our Specialty"), punches Brendan Ellerbee, a retired University of Maine science teacher, when Ellerbee beats him to the last large sack of sugar. Ellerbee goes down, but he holds onto the ten-pound bag of Domino's, and when Conroy bends to take it, Ellerbee snarls *"Here, then!"* and smacks him in the face with it. The sugarsack bursts wide open, enveloping Rance Conroy in a white cloud. The electrician falls against one of the shelves, his face as white as a mime's, screaming that he can't see, he's blind. Carla Venziano, with her baby goggling over her shoulder from the carrier on her back, pushes Henrietta Clavard away from the display of Texmati Rice—Baby Steven loves rice, he also loves to play with the empty plastic containers, and Carla means to make sure she has plenty. Henrietta, who was eighty-four in January, goes sprawling on the hard knot of scrawn that used to be her butt. Lissa Jamieson shoves Will Freeman, who owns the local Toyota dealership, out of her way so she can get the last chicken in the coldcase.

Before she can grab it, a teenage girl wearing a PUNK RAGE tee-shirt snatches it, sticks out her pierced tongue at Libby, and hies gaily away.

There's a sound of shattering glass followed by a hearty cheer made up mostly (but not entirely) of men's voices. The beer cooler has been breached. Many shoppers, perhaps planning on HAVING THEMSELVES A FALL COOKOUT, stream in that direction. Instead of *Oh-pun UP,* the chant is now *"Beer! Beer! Beer!"*

Other folks are streaming into the storerooms below and out back. Soon men and women are packing wine out by the jug and the case. Some carry cartons of vino on their heads like native bearers in an old jungle movie.

Julia, her shoes crunching on crumbles of glass, shoots shoots shoots.

Outside, the rest of the town cops are pulling up, including Jackie Wettington and Henry Morrison, who have abandoned their post at the Gas & Grocery by mutual consent. They join the other cops in a huddled worry-cluster off to one side and simply watch. Jackie sees Linda Everett's stricken face and folds Linda into her arms. Ernie Calvert joins them, yelling "So unnecessary! So completely unnecessary!" with tears streaming down his chubby cheeks.

"What do we do now?" Linda asks, her cheek pressed against Jackie's shoulder. Marta stands close beside her, gaping at the market and pressing a palm against the discolored, rapidly swelling bruise on the side of her face. Beyond them, Food City surges with yells, laughter, the occasional cry of pain. Objects are thrown; Linda sees a roll of toilet tissue unspooling like a party streamer as it arcs over the housewares aisle.

"Honey," Jackie says, "I just don't know."

11

Anson snatched Rose's shopping list and went running into the market with it before the lady herself could stop him. Rose hesitated beside the restaurant panel truck, clenching and unclenching her hands, wondering whether or not to go in after him. She had just decided to stay put when an arm slipped around her shoulders. She jumped, then turned her head and saw Barbie. The depth of her relief actually weakened her knees. She clutched his arm— partly for comfort, mostly so she wouldn't faint.

Barbie was smiling, without much humor. "Some fun, huh, kid?"

"I don't know what to do," she said. "Anson's in there . . . *everybody* is . . . and the cops are just *standing around.*"

"Probably don't want to get beat up any worse than they already have been. And I don't blame them. This was well planned and beautifully executed."

"What are you talking about?"

"Never mind. Want to take a shot at stopping it before it gets any worse?"

"How?"

He lifted the bullhorn, plucked from the hood of the car where Toby Whelan left it. When he tried to hand it to her, Rose drew back, holding her hands to her chest. "You do it, Barbie."

"No. You're the one who's been feeding them for years, you're the one they know, you're the one they'll listen to."

She took the bullhorn, although hesitantly. "I don't know what to say. I can't think of a single thing that will make them stop. Toby Whelan already tried. They didn't pay any attention."

"Toby tried to give orders," Barbie said. "Giving orders to a mob is like giving orders to an anthill."

"I still don't know what to—"

"I'm going to tell you." Barbie spoke calmly, and that calmed her. He paused long enough to beckon Linda Everett. She and Jackie came together, their arms around each other's waists.

"Can you get in touch with your husband?" Barbie asked.

"If his cell phone's on."

"Tell him to get down here—with an ambulance, if possible. If he doesn't answer his phone, grab a police car and drive on up to the hospital."

"He's got patients. . . ."

"He's got some patients right here. He just doesn't know it." Barbie pointed to Ginny Tomlinson, now sitting with her back against the cinderblock side of the market and her hands pressed to her bleeding face. Gina and Harriet Bigelow crouched on either side of her, but when Gina tried to stanch the bleeding from Ginny's radically altered nose with a folded handkerchief, Ginny cried out in pain and turned her head away. "Starting with one of his two remaining trained nurses, if I'm not mistaken."

"What are *you* going to do?" Linda asked, taking her cell phone from her belt.

"Rose and I are going to make them stop. Aren't we, Rose?"

12

Rose stopped inside the door, mesmerized by the chaos before her. The eye-watering smell of vinegar was in the air, mingled with the aromas of brine and beer. Mustard and ketchup were splattered like gaudy puke on the linoleum of aisle 3. A cloud of mingled sugar and flour arose from aisle 5. People pushed their loaded shopping carts through it, many coughing and wiping their eyes. Some of the carts slued as they rolled through a drift of spilled dry beans.

"Stay there a sec," Barbie said, although Rose showed no sign of moving; she was hypnotized with the bullhorn clasped between her breasts.

Barbie found Julia shooting pictures of the looted cash registers. "Quit that and come with me," he said.

"No, I have to do this, there's no one else. I don't know where Pete Freeman is, and Tony—"

"You don't have to shoot it, you have to stop it. Before something a lot worse than that happens." He was pointing to Fern Bowie, who was strolling past with a loaded basket in one hand and a beer in the other. His eyebrow was split and blood was dripping down his face, but Fern seemed content enough withal.

"How?"

He led her back to Rose. "Ready, Rose? Showtime."

"I . . . well . . ."

"Remember, *serene*. Don't try to stop them; just try to lower the temperature."

Rose took a deep breath, then raised the bullhorn to her mouth. "HI, EVERYBODY, THIS IS ROSE TWITCHELL, FROM SWEETBRIAR ROSE."

To her everlasting credit, she *did* sound serene. People looked around when they heard her voice—not because it sounded urgent, Barbie knew, but because it didn't. He had seen this in Takrit, Fallujah, Baghdad. Mostly after bombings in crowded public places, when the police and the troop carriers arrived. "PLEASE FINISH YOUR SHOPPING AS QUICKLY AND CALMLY AS POSSIBLE."

A few people chuckled at this, then looked around at each other as if coming to. In aisle 7, Carla Venziano, shamefaced, helped Henrietta Clavard to her feet. *There's plenty of Texmati for both of us,* Carla thought. *What in God's name was I thinking?*

Barbie nodded at Rose to go on, mouthing *Coffee.* In the distance, he could hear the sweet warble of an approaching ambulance.

"WHEN YOU'RE DONE, COME TO SWEET-BRIAR FOR COFFEE. IT'S FRESH AND IT'S ON THE HOUSE."

A few people clapped. Some leatherlungs yelled, *"Who wants coffee? We got BEER!"* Laughter and whoops greeted this sally.

Julia twitched Barbie's sleeve. Her forehead was creased in what Barbie thought was a very Republican frown. "They're not shopping; they're stealing."

"Do you want to editorialize or get them out of here before someone gets killed over a bag of Blue Mountain Dry Roast?" he asked.

She thought it over and nodded, her frown giving way to that inward-turning smile he was coming to like a great deal. "You have a point, Colonel," she said.

Barbie turned to Rose, made a cranking gesture, and she started in again. He began to walk the two women up and down the aisles, starting with the mostly denuded deli and dairy section, on the lookout for anyone who might be cranked up enough to offer interference. There was no one. Rose was gaining confidence, and the market was quieting. People were leaving. Many were pushing carts laden with loot, but Barbie still took it as a good sign. The sooner they were out the better, no matter how much shit they took with them . . . and the key was for them to hear themselves referred to as shoppers rather than stealers. Give a man or woman back his self-respect, and in most cases—not all, but most—you also give back that person's ability to think with at least some clarity.

Anson Wheeler joined them, pushing a shopping cart full of supplies. He looked slightly shamefaced, and his arm was bleeding. "Someone hit me with a jar of olives," he explained. "Now I smell like an Italian sandwich."

Rose handed the bullhorn to Julia, who began broadcasting the same message in the same pleasant voice: Finish up, shoppers, and leave in orderly fashion.

"We can't take that stuff," Rose said, pointing at Anson's cart.

"But we need it, Rosie," he said. He sounded apologetic but firm. "We really do."

"We'll leave some money, then," she said. "If no one's stolen my purse out of the truck, that is."

"Um . . . I don't think that'll work," Anson said. "Some guys were stealing the money out of the registers." He had seen which guys, but didn't want to say. Not with the editor of the local paper walking next to him.

Rose was horrified. "What's happening here? In the name of God, what's *happening*?"

"I don't know," Anson said.

Outside, the ambulance pulled up, the siren dying to a growl. A minute or two later, while Barbie, Rose, and Julia were still canvassing the aisles with the bullhorn (the crowd was thinning out now), someone behind them said, "That's enough. Give me that."

Barbie was not surprised to see acting chief Randolph, tricked out to the nines in his dress uniform. Here he was, a day late and a dollar short. Right on schedule.

Rose was working the bullhorn, extolling the virtues of free coffee at Sweetbriar. Randolph plucked it from her hand and immediately began giving orders and making threats.

"LEAVE NOW! THIS IS CHIEF PETER RANDOLPH, ORDERING YOU TO LEAVE NOW!

DROP WHAT YOU ARE HOLDING AND LEAVE
NOW! IF YOU DROP WHAT YOU'RE HOLDING
AND LEAVE NOW, YOU MAY AVOID CHARGES!"

Rose looked at Barbie, dismayed. He shrugged. It
didn't matter. The spirit of the mob had departed. The
cops who were still ambulatory—even Carter Thibodeau,
staggering but on his feet—started hustling people out.
When the "shoppers" wouldn't drop their loaded baskets, the cops struck several to the ground, and Frank
DeLesseps overturned a loaded shopping cart. His face
was grim and pale and angry.

"Are you going to make those boys stop that?" Julia
asked Randolph.

"No, Ms. Shumway, I am not," Randolph said. "Those
people are looters and they're being treated as such."

"Whose fault is that? Who closed the market?"

"Get out of my way," Randolph said. "I've got work
to do."

"Shame you weren't here when they broke in," Barbie
remarked.

Randolph looked at him. The glance was unfriendly yet
satisfied. Barbie sighed. Somewhere a clock was ticking.
He knew it, and Randolph did, too. Soon the alarm would
ring. If not for the Dome, he could run. But, of course,
if not for the Dome, none of this would be happening.

Down front, Mel Searles tried to take Al Timmons's
loaded shopping basket. When Al wouldn't give it up,
Mel tore it away . . . and then pushed the older man
down. Al cried out in pain and shame and outrage. Chief
Randolph laughed. It was a short, choppy, unamused
sound—*Haw! Haw! Haw!*—and in it Barbie thought
he heard what Chester's Mill might soon become, if the
Dome didn't lift.

"Come on, ladies," he said. "Let's get out of here."

13

Rusty and Twitch were lining up the wounded—about a dozen in all—along the cinderblock side of the market when Barbie, Julia, and Rose came out. Anson was standing by the Sweetbriar panel truck with a paper towel pressed to his bleeding arm.

Rusty's face was grim, but when he saw Barbie, he lightened up a little. "Hey, sport. You're with me this morning. In fact, you're my new RN."

"You wildly overestimate my triage skills," Barbie said, but he walked toward Rusty.

Linda Everett ran past Barbie and threw herself into Rusty's arms. He gave her a brief hug. "Can I help, honey?" she asked. It was Ginny she was looking at, and with horror. Ginny saw the look and wearily closed her eyes.

"No," Rusty said. "You do what you need to. I've got Gina and Harriet, and I've got Nurse Barbara."

"I'll do what I can," Barbie said, and almost added: *Until I'm arrested, that is.*

"You'll be fine," Rusty said. In a lower voice he added, "Gina and Harriet are the most willing helpers in the world, but once they get past giving pills and slapping on Band-Aids, they're pretty much lost."

Linda bent to Ginny. "I'm so sorry," she said.

"I'll be fine," Ginny said, but she did not open her eyes.

Linda gave her husband a kiss and a troubled look, then walked back toward where Jackie Wettington was standing with a pad in her hand, taking Ernie Calvert's statement. Ernie wiped his eyes repeatedly as he talked.

Rusty and Barbie worked side by side for over an hour, while the cops strung yellow police tape in front of the market. At some point, Andy Sanders came down to survey the damage, clucking and shaking his head. Barbie heard him ask someone what the world was coming to, when hometown folks could get up to a thing like this. He also shook Chief Randolph's hand and told him he was doing a hell of a job.

Hell of a job.

14

When you're *feeling it,* lousy breaks disappear. Strife becomes your friend. Bad luck turns hit-the-Megabucks good. You do not accept these things with gratitude (an emotion reserved for wimps and losers, in Big Jim Rennie's opinion) but as your due. *Feeling it* is like riding in a magic swing, and one should (once more in Big Jim's opinion) glide imperiously.

If he had emerged from the big old Rennie manse on Mill Street a little later or a little earlier, he would not have seen what he did, and he might have dealt with Brenda Perkins in an entirely different way. But he came out at exactly the right time. That was how it went when you were *feeling it*; the defense collapsed and you rushed through the magical hole thus created, making the easy layup.

It was the chanted cries of *Oh-pun UP! Oh-pun UP!* that got him out of his study, where he had been making notes for what he planned to call the Disaster Administration . . . of which cheerful, grinning Andy Sanders would be the titular head and Big Jim would be the power behind the throne. *If it ain't broke, don't fix it* was Rule One in Big Jim's political operating manual, and having Andy out front always worked like a charm. Most of Chester's Mill knew he was an idiot, but it didn't matter.

You could run the same game on people over and over, because ninety-eight percent of them were even bigger idiots. And although Big Jim had never planned a political campaign on such a grand scale—it amounted to a municipal dictatorship—he had no doubt it would work.

He hadn't included Brenda Perkins in his list of possible complicating factors, but no matter. When you were *feeling it,* complicating factors had a way of disappearing. This you also accepted as your due.

He walked down the sidewalk to the corner of Mill and Main, a distance of no more than a hundred paces, with his belly swinging placidly before him. The Town Common was directly across the way. A little farther down the hill on the other side of the street were the Town Hall and the PD, with War Memorial Plaza in between.

He couldn't see Food City from the corner, but he could see all of the Main Street business section. And he saw Julia Shumway. She came hurrying out of the *Democrat*'s office, a camera in one hand. She jogged down the street toward the sound of the chanting, trying to sling the camera over her shoulder while on the move. Big Jim watched her. It was funny, really—how anxious she was to get to the latest disaster.

It got funnier. She stopped, turned, jogged back, tried the newspaper office's door, found it open, and locked it. Then she hurried off once more, anxious to watch her friends and neighbors behaving badly.

She is realizing for the first time that once the beast is out of its cage, it could bite anyone, anywhere, Big Jim thought. *But don't worry, Julia—I'll take care of you, just as I always have. You may have to tone down that tiresome rag of yours, but isn't that a small price to pay for safety?*

Of course it was. And if she persisted . . .

"Sometimes stuff happens," Big Jim said. He was

standing on the corner with his hands in his pockets, smiling. And when he heard the first screams . . . the sound of breaking glass . . . the gunshots . . . his smile widened. *Stuff happens* wasn't exactly how Junior put it, but Big Jim reckoned it was close enough for government w—

His smile folded into a frown as he spotted Brenda Perkins. Most of the people on Main Street were heading toward Food City to see what all the ruckus was about, but Brenda was walking *up* Main Street instead of down. Maybe even up to the Rennie house . . . which would mean up to no good.

What could she want with me this morning? What could be so important it trumps a food riot at the local supermarket?

It was entirely possible he was the last thing on Brenda's mind, but his radar was pinging and he watched her closely.

She and Julia passed on opposite sides of the street. Neither noticed the other. Julia was trying to run while managing her camera. Brenda was staring at the red ramshackle bulk of Burpee's Department Store. She had a canvas carrier-bag that swung at her knee.

When she reached Burpee's, Brenda tried the door with no success. Then she stood back and glanced around the way people do when they've hit an unexpected obstacle to their plans and are trying to decide what to do next. She might still have seen Shumway if she'd looked behind her, but she didn't. Brenda looked left, right, then across Main Street, at the offices of the *Democrat*.

After another look at Burpee's, she crossed to the *Democrat* and tried that door. Also locked, of course; Big Jim had watched Julia do it. Brenda tried it again, rattling the knob for good measure. She knocked. Peered in. Then she stood back, hands on hips, carrier-bag dangling. When she once more started up Main Street—trudging, no longer looking around—Big Jim retreated to his house at a brisk pace. He didn't know why he wanted to make sure Brenda didn't see him watching . . . but he didn't *have* to know. You only had to act on your instincts when you were *feeling it*. That was the beauty of the thing.

What he *did* know was that if Brenda knocked on his door, he would be ready for her. No matter what she wanted.

15

Tomorrow morning I want you to take the printout to Julia Shumway, Barbie had told her. But the *Democrat*'s office was locked and dark. Julia was almost certainly at whatever mess was going on at the market. Pete Freeman and Tony Guay probably were, too.

So what was she supposed to do with Howie's VADER file? If there had been a mail slot, she might have slipped the manila envelope in her carrier-bag through it. Only there *was* no mail slot.

Brenda supposed she should either go find Julia at the market or return home to wait until things quieted down and Julia came back to her office. Not being in a particularly logical mood, neither choice appealed. As to the former, it sounded like a full-scale riot was going on at Food City, and Brenda did not want to get sucked in. As to the latter . . .

That was clearly the better choice. The *sensible* choice. Hadn't *All things come to him who waits* been one of Howie's favorite sayings?

But waiting had never been Brenda's forte, and her mother had also had a saying: *Do it and have done with it.* That was what she wanted to do now. Face him, wait out his ranting, his denials, his justifications, and then give him his choice: resign in favor of Dale Barbara or read all about his dirty deeds in the *Democrat*. Confrontation was bitter medicine to her, and the thing to do with bitter medicine was swallow it as fast as you could, then rinse your mouth. She planned to rinse hers with a double bourbon, and she wouldn't wait until noon to do it, either.

Only . . .

Don't go alone. Barbie had said that, too. And when he'd asked who else she trusted, she'd said Romeo Burpee. But Burpee's was closed too. What did that leave?

The question was whether or not Big Jim would actually hurt her, and Brenda thought the answer was no. She believed she was physically safe from Big Jim, no matter what worries Barbie might have—worries that were, no doubt, partly the result of his wartime experiences. This was a dreadful miscalculation on her part, but understandable; she wasn't the only one who clung to the notion that the world was as it had been before the Dome came down.

16

Which still left the problem of the VADER file.

Brenda might be more afraid of Big Jim's tongue than of bodily harm, but she knew it would be mad to show up on his doorstep with the file still in her possession. He might take it from her even if she said it wasn't the only copy. *That* she would not put past him.

Halfway up Town Common Hill, she came to Prestile Street, cutting along the upper edge of the common. The first house belonged to the McCains. The one beyond was Andrea Grinnell's. And although Andrea was almost always overshadowed by her male counterparts on the Board of

Selectmen, Brenda knew she was honest and had no love for Big Jim. Oddly enough, it was Andy Sanders to whom Andrea was more apt to kowtow, although why anyone would take *him* seriously was beyond Brenda's understanding.

Maybe he's got some sort of hold on her, Howie's voice spoke up in her head.

Brenda almost laughed. That was ridiculous. The important thing about Andrea was that she had been a Twitchell before Tommy Grinnell married her, and Twitchells were tough, even the shy ones. Brenda thought she could leave the envelope containing the VADER file with Andrea . . . assuming *her* place wasn't also locked and empty. She didn't think it would be. Hadn't she heard from someone that Andrea was down with the flu?

Brenda crossed Main, rehearsing what she'd say: *Would you hold this for me? I'll be back for it in about half an hour. If I don't come back for it, give it to Julia at the newspaper. Also, make sure Dale Barbara knows.*

And if she was asked what all the mystery was about? Brenda decided she'd be frank. The news that she intended to force Jim Rennie's resignation would probably do Andrea more good than a double dose of Theraflu.

In spite of her desire to get her distasteful errand done, Brenda paused for a moment in front of the McCain house. It looked deserted, but there was nothing strange about that—plenty of families had been out of town when the Dome came down. It was something else. A faint smell, for one thing, as if food were spoiling in there. All at once the day felt hotter, the air closer, and the sounds of whatever was going on at Food City seemed far away. Brenda realized what it came down to: she felt watched. She stood thinking about how much those shaded windows looked like closed eyes. But not completely closed, no. *Peeking* eyes.

Shake it off, woman. You've got things to do.

She walked on to Andrea's house, pausing once to look back over her shoulder. She saw nothing but a house with drawn shades, sitting gloomily in the mild stink of its decaying supplies. Only meat smelled so bad so soon. Henry and LaDonna must have had a lot put by in their freezer, she thought.

17

It was Junior who watched Brenda, Junior on his knees, Junior dressed only in his underpants, his head whamming and slamming. He watched from the living room, peering around the edge of a drawn shade. When she was gone, he went back into the pantry. He would have to give his girlfriends up soon, he knew, but for now he wanted them. And he wanted the dark. He even wanted the stink rising from their blackening skin.

Anything, anything, that would soothe his fiercely aching head.

18

After three twists of the old-fashioned crank doorbell, Brenda resigned herself to going home after all. She was turning away when she heard slow, shuffling steps approaching the door. She arranged a little *Hello, neighbor* smile on her face. It froze there when she saw Andrea—cheeks pale, dark circles under her eyes, hair in disarray, cinching the belt of a bathrobe around her middle, pajamas underneath. And this house smelled, too—not of decaying meat but of vomit.

Andrea's smile was as wan as her cheeks and brow. "I know how I look," she said. The words came out in a croak. "I better not invite you in. I'm on the mend, but I still might be catching."

"Have you seen Dr.—" But no, of course not. Dr. Haskell was dead. "Have you seen Rusty Everett?"

"Indeed I have," Andrea said. "All will soon be well, I'm told."

"You're perspiring."

"Still a little touch of fever, but it's almost gone. Can I help you with something, Bren?"

She almost said no—she didn't want to saddle a woman who was still clearly sick with a responsibility like the one in her carrier-bag—but then Andrea said something that changed her mind. Great events often turn on small wheels.

"I'm so sorry about Howie. I loved that man."

"Thank you, Andrea." *Not just for the sympathy, but for calling him Howie instead of Duke.*

To Brenda he'd always been Howie, her dear Howie, and the VADER file was his last work. Probably his greatest work. Brenda suddenly decided to *put* it to work, and with no further delay. She dipped into the carrier-bag and brought out the manila envelope with Julia's name printed on the front. "Will you hold this for me, dear? Just for a little while? I have an errand to run and I don't want to take it with me."

Brenda would have answered any questions Andrea asked, but Andrea apparently had none. She only took the bulky envelope with a sort of distracted courtesy. And that was all right. It saved time. Also, it would keep Andrea out of the loop, and might spare her political blowback at some later date.

"Happy to," Andrea said. "And now . . . if you'll excuse

me . . . I think I'd better get off my feet. But I'm not going to sleep!" she added, as if Brenda had objected to this plan. "I'll hear you when you come back."

"Thank you," Brenda said. "Are you drinking juices?"

"By the gallon. Take your time, hon—I'll babysit your envelope."

Brenda was going to thank her again, but The Mill's Third Selectman had already closed the door.

19

Toward the end of her conversation with Brenda, Andrea's stomach began to flutter. She fought it, but this was a fight she was going to lose. She blathered something about drinking juice, told Brenda to take her time, then closed the door in the poor woman's face and sprinted for her stinking bathroom, making gutteral *urk-urk* noises deep down in her throat.

There was an end table beside the living room couch, and she tossed the manila envelope at it blindly as she rushed past. The envelope skittered across the polished surface and fell off the other side, into the dark space between the table and the couch.

Andrea made it to the bathroom but not to the toilet . . . which was just as well; it was nearly filled with the stagnant, stinking brew that had been her body's output during the endless night just past. She leaned over the basin instead, retching until it seemed to her that her very esophagus would come loose and land on the splattery porcelain, still warm and pulsing.

That didn't happen, but the world turned gray and teetered away from her on high heels, growing smaller and less tangible as she swayed and tried not to faint. When she felt a little better, she walked slowly down the hall on elastic legs, sliding one hand along the wood to keep her balance. She was shivering and she could hear the jittery clitter of her teeth, a horrible sound she seemed to pick up not with her ears but with the backs of her eyes.

She didn't even consider trying to reach her bedroom upstairs but went out onto the screened-in back porch instead. The porch should have been too cold to be comfortable this late in October, but today the air was sultry. She did not lie down on the old chaise longue so much as collapse into its musty but somehow comforting embrace.

I'll get up in a minute, she told herself. *Get the last bottle of Poland Spring out of the fridge and wash that foul taste out of my mou . . .*

But here her thoughts slipped away. She fell into a deep and profound sleep from which not even the restless twitching of her feet and hands could wake her. She had many dreams. One was of a terrible fire people ran from, coughing and retching, looking for anyplace where they might find air that was still cool and clean. Another was of Brenda Perkins coming to her door and giving her an envelope. When Andrea opened it, a never-ending stream of pink OxyContin pills poured out. By the time she woke up it was evening, and the dreams were forgotten.

So was Brenda Perkins's visit.

20

"Come into my study," Big Jim said cheerfully. "Or would you like something to drink, first? I have Cokes, although I'm afraid they're a little warm. My generator died last night. Out of propane."

"But I imagine you know where you can get more," she said.

He raised his eyebrows questioningly.

"The methamphetamine you're making," she said patiently. "My understanding—based on Howie's notes—is that you've been cooking it in large batches. 'Amounts that boggle the mind' is how he put it. That must take a lot of propane gas."

Now that she was actually into this, she found her jitters had melted away. She even took a certain cold pleasure in watching the color mount in his cheeks and go dashing across his forehead.

"I have no idea what you're talking about. I think your grief . . ." He sighed, spread his blunt-fingered hands. "Come inside. We'll discuss this and I'll set your mind at rest."

She smiled. That she *could* smile was sort of a revelation, and it helped more to imagine Howie watching her—from somewhere. Also telling her to be careful. That was advice she planned to heed.

On the Rennie front lawn, two Adirondack chairs sat amid the fallen leaves. "It's nice enough out here for me," she said.

"I prefer to talk business inside."

"Would you prefer to see your picture on the front page of the *Democrat*? Because I can arrange that."

He winced as if she had struck him, and for just a moment she saw hate in those small, deepset, piggy eyes. "Duke never liked me, and I suppose it's natural that his feelings should have been communicated to—"

"His name was *Howie*!"

Big Jim threw up his hands as if to say there was no reasoning with some women, and led her to the chairs overlooking Mill Street.

Brenda Perkins talked for almost half an hour, growing colder and angrier as she spoke. The meth lab, with Andy Sanders and—almost certainly—Lester Coggins as silent partners. The staggering size of the thing. Its probable location. The mid-level distributors who had been promised immunity in exchange for information. The money trail. How the operation had gotten so big the local pharmacist could no longer safely supply the necessary ingredients, necessitating import from overseas.

"The stuff came into town in trucks marked Gideon Bible Society," Brenda said. "Howie's comment on that was 'too clever by half.' "

Big Jim sat looking out at the silent residential street. She could feel the anger and hate baking off him. It was like heat from a casserole dish.

"You can't prove any of this," he said at last.

"That won't matter if Howie's file turns up in the *Democrat*. It's not due process, but if anyone can understand bypassing a little thing like that, it would be you."

He flapped a hand. "Oh, I'm sure you had a *file*," he said, "but my name is on nothing."

"It's on the Town Ventures paperwork," she said, and Big Jim rocked in his chair as if she had lashed out with her fist and hit him in the temple. "Town Ventures, incorporated in Carson City. And from Nevada, the money trail leads to Chongqing City, the pharma capital of the People's Republic of China." She smiled. "You thought you were smart, didn't you? So smart."

"Where is this file?"

"I left a copy with Julia this morning." Bringing Andrea into it was the last thing she wanted to do. And thinking it was in the newspaper editor's hands would bring him to heel that much quicker. He might feel that he or Andy Sanders could jawbone Andrea.

"There are other copies?"

"What do you think?"

He considered a moment, then said: "I kept it out of the town."

She said nothing.

"It was for the *good* of the town."

"You've done a lot of good for the town, Jim. We've got the same sewer system we had in nineteen sixty, Chester Pond is filthy, the business district is moribund. . . ." She was sitting straight now, gripping the arms of her chair. "You fucking self-righteous turdworm."

"What do you want?" He was staring straight ahead at the empty street. A large vein beat in his temple.

"For you to announce your resignation. Barbie takes over as per the President's—"

"I'll never resign in favor of *that* cotton-picker." He turned to look at her. He was smiling. It was an appalling smile. "You didn't leave anything with Julia, because Julia's at the market, watching the food fight. You might have Duke's file locked away somewhere, but you didn't leave a copy with *anyone*. You tried Rommie, then you tried Julia, then you came here. I saw you walking up Town Common Hill."

"I did," she said. "I did have it." And if she told him where she had left it? Bad luck for Andrea. She started to get up. "You had your chance. Now I'm leaving."

"Your other mistake was thinking you'd be safe outside on the street. An *empty* street." His voice was almost kind, and when he touched her arm, she turned to look at him. He seized her face. And twisted.

Brenda Perkins heard a bitter crack, like the breaking of a branch overloaded with ice, and followed the sound into a great darkness, trying to call her husband's name as she went.

21

Big Jim went inside and got a Jim Rennie's Used Cars gimme cap from the front hall closet. Also some gloves. And a pumpkin from the pantry. Brenda was still in her Adirondack chair, with her chin on her chest. He looked around. No one. The world was his. He put the hat on her head (pulling the brim low), the gloves on her hands, and the pumpkin in her lap. It would serve perfectly well, he thought, until Junior came back and took her to where she could become part of Dale Barbara's butcher's bill. Until then, she was just another stuffed Halloween dummy.

He checked her carrier-bag. It contained her wallet, a comb, and a paperback novel. So *that* was all right. It would be fine down cellar, behind the dead furnace.

He left her with the hat slouched on her head and the pumpkin in her lap and went inside to stash her bag and wait for his son.

IN THE JUG

1

Selectman Rennie's assumption that no one had seen Brenda come to his house that morning was correct. But she *was* seen on her morning travels, not by one person but by three, including one who also lived on Mill Street. If Big Jim had known, would the knowledge have given him pause? Doubtful; by then he was committed to his course and it was too late to turn back. But it might have caused him to reflect (for he *was* a reflective man, in his own way) on murder's similarity to Lay's potato chips: it's hard to stop with just one.

2

Big Jim didn't see the watchers when he came down to the corner of Mill and Main. Neither did Brenda as she walked up Town Common Hill. This was because they didn't want to be seen. They were sheltering just inside the Peace Bridge, which happened to be a condemned structure. But that wasn't the worst of it. If Claire McClatchey had seen the cigarettes, she would have shit a brick. In fact, she might have shit two. And certainly she never would have let Joe chum with Norrie Calvert again, not even if the fate of the town hinged upon their association, because it was Norrie who supplied the smokes—badly bent and croggled Winstons, which she had found on a shelf in the garage. Her father had quit smoking the year before and the pack was covered with a fine scrim of dust, but the cigarettes inside had looked okay to Norrie. There were just three, but three was perfect: one each. Think of it as a good-luck rite, she instructed.

"We'll smoke like Indians praying to the gods for a successful hunt. Then we'll go to work."

"Sounds good," Joe said. He had always been curious about smoking. He couldn't see the attraction, but there must be one, because a lot of people still did it.

"Which gods?" Benny Drake asked.

"The gods of your choice," Norrie answered, looking at him as if he were the dumbest creature in the universe. "*God* god, if that's the one you like." Dressed in faded denim shorts and a pink sleeveless top, her hair for once down and framing her foxy little face instead of scrooped back in its usual sloppin-around-town ponytail, she looked good to both boys. Totally awesome, in fact. "*I* pray to Wonder Woman."

"Wonder Woman is not a goddess," Joe said, taking one of the elderly Winstons and smoothing it straight. "Wonder Woman is a superhero." He considered. "Maybe a superher-*ette*."

"She's a goddess to me," Norrie replied with a grave-eyed sincerity that could not be gainsaid, let alone ridiculed. She was carefully straightening her own cigarette. Benny left his the way it was; he thought a bent cigarette had a certain coolness factor. "I had Wonder Woman Power Bracelets until I was nine, but then I lost them. I think that bitch Yvonne Nedeau stole them."

She lit a match and touched it first to Scarecrow Joe's

cigarette, then to Benny's. When she tried to use it to light her own, Benny blew it out.

"What did you do that for?" she asked.

"Three on a match. Bad luck."

"You *believe* that?"

"Not much," Benny said, "but today we're going to need all the luck we can get." He glanced at the shopping bag in the basket of his bike, then took a pull on his cigarette. He inhaled a little and then coughed the smoke back out, his eyes watering. "This tastes like panther-shit!"

"Smoked a lot of that, have you?" Joe asked. He dragged on his own cigarette. He didn't want to look like a wuss, but he didn't want to start coughing and maybe throw up, either. The smoke burned, but in sort of a good way. Maybe there was something to this, after all. Only he already felt a little woozy.

Go easy on the inhaling part, he thought. *Passing out would be almost as uncool as puking.* Unless, maybe, he passed out in Norrie Calvert's lap. That might be very cool indeed.

Norrie reached into her shorts pocket and brought out the cap of a Verifine juice bottle. "We can use this for an ashtray. I want to do the Indian smoke ritual, but I don't want to catch the Peace Bridge on fire." She then closed her eyes. Her lips began to move. Her cigarette was between her fingers, growing an ash.

Benny looked at Joe, shrugged, then closed his own eyes. "Almighty GI Joe, please hear the prayer of your humble pfc Drake—"

Norrie kicked him without opening her eyes.

Joe got up (a little dizzy, but not too bad; he chanced another drag when he was on his feet) and walked past their parked bikes to the town common end of the covered walkway.

"Where you goin?" Norrie asked without opening her eyes.

"I pray better when I look at nature," Joe said, but he actually just wanted a breath of fresh air. It wasn't the burning tobacco; he sort of liked that. It was the other smells inside the bridge—decaying wood, old booze, and a sour chemical aroma that seemed to be rising up from the Prestile beneath them (that was a smell, The Chef might have told him, that you could come to love).

Even the outside air wasn't that wonderful; it had a slightly *used* quality that made Joe think of the trip he'd made with his parents to New York the previous year. The subways had smelled a little like this, especially late in the day when they were crowded with people headed home.

He tapped ashes into his hand. As he scattered them, he spotted Brenda Perkins making her way up the hill.

A moment later, a hand touched his shoulder. Too light and delicate to be Benny's. "Who's that?" Norrie asked.

"Know the face, not the name," he said.

Benny joined them. "That's Mrs. Perkins. The Sheriff's widow."

Norrie elbowed him. "Police Chief, dummy."

Benny shrugged. "Whatever."

They watched her, mostly because there was no one else to watch. The rest of the town was at the supermarket, apparently having the world's biggest food fight. The three kids had investigated, but from afar; they did not need persuasion to stay away, given the valuable piece of equipment that had been entrusted to their care.

Brenda crossed Main to Prestile, paused outside the McCain house, then went on to Mrs. Grinnell's.

"Let's get going," Benny said.

"We *can't* get going until she's gone," Norrie said.

Benny shrugged. "What's the big deal? If she sees us, we're just some kids goofing around on the town common. And know what? She probably wouldn't see us if she looked right at us. Adults *never* see kids." He considered this. "Unless they're on skateboards."

"Or smoking," Norrie added. They all glanced at their cigarettes.

Joe hooked a thumb at the shopping bag sitting in the carrier attached to the handlebars of Benny's Schwinn High Plains. "They also have a tendency to see kids who are goofing around with expensive town property."

Norrie tucked her cigarette in the corner of her mouth. It made her look wonderfully tough, wonderfully pretty, and wonderfully *adult*.

The boys went back to watching. The Police Chief's widow was now talking to Mrs. Grinnell. It wasn't a long conversation. Mrs. Perkins had taken a big brown envelope from her carrier-bag as she came up the steps, and they watched her hand it to Mrs. Grinnell. A few seconds later, Mrs. Grinnell pretty much slammed the door in her visitor's face.

"Whoa, that was rude," Benny said. "Week's detention."

Joe and Norrie laughed.

Mrs. Perkins stood where she was for a moment, as if perplexed, then went back down the steps. She was now facing the common, and the three children instinctively stepped further into the shadows of the walkway. This caused them to lose sight of her, but Joe found a handy gap in the wooden siding and peered through that.

"Going back to Main," he reported. "Okay, now she's going up the hill . . . now she's crossing over again. . . ."

Benny held an imaginary microphone. "Video at eleven."

Joe ignored this. "Now she's going onto *my* street." He turned to Benny and Norrie. "Do you think she's going to see my mom?"

"Mill Street's four blocks long, dude," Benny said. "What are the chances?"

Joe felt relieved even though he could think of no reason why Mrs. Perkins's going to see his mom would be a bad thing. Except his mother was all worried about Dad being out of town, and Joe would sure hate to see her more upset than she already was. She had almost forbidden him to go on this expedition. Thank God Miz Shumway had talked her out of *that* idea, mostly by telling her that Dale Barbara had mentioned Joe specifically for this job (which Joe—Benny and Norrie, too—preferred to think of as "the mission").

"Mrs. McClatchey," Julia had said, "if anyone can put this gadget to use, Barbie thinks it's probably your son. It could be very important."

That had made Joe feel good, but looking at his mother's face—worried, drawn—made him feel bad. It hadn't even been three days since the Dome had come down, but she'd lost weight. And the way she kept holding his dad's picture, that made him feel bad, too. It was like she thought he'd died instead of just being holed up in a motel somewhere, probably drinking beer and watching HBO.

She had agreed with Miz Shumway, though. "He's a smart boy about gadgets, all right. He always has been." She looked him over from head to foot, and sighed. "When did you get so tall, Son?"

"I don't know," he had replied truthfully.

"If I let you do this, will you be careful?"

"And take your friends with you," Julia said.

"Benny and Norrie? Sure."

"Also," Julia had added, "be a little discreet. Do you know what that means, Joe?"

"Yes, ma'am, I sure do."

It meant don't get caught.

3

Brenda disappeared into the screening trees that lined Mill Street. "Okay," Benny said. "Let's go." He carefully crushed his cigarette in the makeshift ashtray, then lifted the shopping bag out of the bike's wire carrier. Inside the bag was the old-fashioned yellow Geiger counter, which had gone from Barbie to Rusty to Julia . . . and finally to Joe and his posse.

Joe took the juice lid and crushed out his own smoke, thinking he would like to try again when he had more time to concentrate on the experience. On the other hand, it might be better not to. He was addicted to computers, the graphic novels of Brian K. Vaughan, and skateboarding. Maybe that was enough monkeys for one back.

"People are gonna come by," he said to Benny and Norrie. "Probably lots of people, once they get tired of playing in the supermarket. We'll just have to hope they don't pay any attention to us."

In his mind he heard Miz Shumway telling his mom how important this could be to the town. She didn't have to tell *him*; he probably understood it better than they did.

"But if any *cops* come by . . ." Norrie said.

Joe nodded. "Back into the bag it goes. And out comes the Frisbee."

"You really think there's some kind of alien generator buried under the town common?" Benny asked.

"I said there *might* be," Joe replied, more sharply than he had intended. "Anything's possible."

In truth, Joe thought it more than possible; he thought it likely. If the Dome wasn't supernatural in origin, then it was a force field. A force field had to be generated. It looked like a QED situation to him, but he didn't want to get their hopes up too high. Or his own, for that matter.

"Let's start looking," Norrie said. She ducked under the sagging yellow police tape. "I just hope you two prayed enough."

Joe didn't believe in praying for things he could do for himself, but he *had* sent up a brief one on a different subject: that if they found the generator, Norrie Calvert would give him another kiss. A nice long one.

4

Earlier that morning, during their pre-exploration meeting in the McClatchey living room, Scarecrow Joe had taken off his right sneaker, then the white athletic sock beneath.

"Trick or treat, smell my feet, give me something good to eat," Benny said cheerfully.

"Shut up, stupid," Joe replied.

"Don't call your friend stupid," Claire McClatchey said, but she gave Benny a reproachful look.

Norrie added no repartee of her own, only watched with interest as Joe laid the sock on the living room rug and smoothed it out with the flat of his hand.

"This is Chester's Mill," Joe said. "Same shape, right?"

"You are correctamundo," Benny agreed. "It's our fate to live in a town that looks like one of Joe McClatchey's athletic socks."

"Or the old woman's shoe," Norrie put in.

" 'There was an old woman who lived in a shoe,' " Mrs. McClatchey recited. She was sitting on the couch with the picture of her husband in her lap, just as she had been when Miz Shumway came by with the Geiger counter late yesterday afternoon. " 'She had so many children she didn't know what to do.' "

"Good one, Mom," Joe said, trying not to grin. The middle-school version had been revised to *She had so many children her cunt fell off.*

He looked down at the sock again. "So does a sock have a middle?"

Benny and Norrie thought it over. Joe let them. The fact that such a question could interest them was one of the things he dug about them.

"Not like a circle or square has a center," Norrie said at last. "Those are geometric shapes."

Benny said, "I guess a sock is also a geometric shape— technically—but I don't know what you'd call it. A sock-tagon?"

Norrie laughed. Even Claire smiled a little.

"On the map, The Mill's closer to a hexagon," Joe said, "but never mind that. Just use common sense."

Norrie pointed to the place on the sock where the foot-shaped bottom flowed into the tube top. "There. That's the middle."

Joe dotted it with the tip of his pen.

"I'm not sure that'll come out, mister." Claire sighed. "But you need new ones anyway, I suppose." And, before he could ask the next question, she said: "On a map, that would be about where the town common is. Is that where you're going to look?"

"It's where we're going to look *first,*" Joe said, a little deflated at having his explicatory thunder stolen.

"Because if there's a generator," Mrs. McClatchey mused, "you think it should be in the middle of the town-ship. Or as close to it as possible."

Joe nodded.

"Cool, Mrs. McClatchey," Benny said. He raised one hand. "Give me five, mother of my soul-brother."

Smiling wanly, still holding the picture of her husband, Claire McClatchey slapped Benny five. Then she said, "At least the town common's a safe place." She paused to consider that, frowning slightly. "I hope so, anyway, but who really knows?"

"Don't worry," Norrie said. "I'll watch out for them."

"Just promise me that if you *do* find something, you'll let the experts handle things," Claire said.

Mom, Joe thought, *I think maybe* we're *the experts.* But he didn't say it. He knew it would bum her out even more.

"Word up," Benny said, and held his hand up again. "Five more, o mother of my—"

This time she kept both hands on the picture. "I love you, Benny, but sometimes you tire me out."

He smiled sadly. "My mom says the exact same thing."

5

Joe and his friends walked downhill to the bandstand that stood in the center of the common. Behind them, the Prestile murmured. It was lower now, dammed up by the Dome where it crossed into Chester's Mill from the northwest. If the Dome was still in place tomorrow, Joe thought it would be nothing but a mudslick.

"Okay," Benny said. "Enough with the Freddy Fuck-around. Time for the board-bangers to rescue Chester's Mill. Let's fire that baby up."

Carefully (and with real reverence), Joe lifted the Geiger counter out of the shopping bag. The battery that powered it had been a long-dead soldier and the terminals had been thick with gunk, but a little baking soda took care of the corrosion, and Norrie had found not just one but three six-volt dry cells in her father's tool closet. "He's kind of a freak when it comes to batteries," she had confided, "and he's gonna kill himself trying to learn boarding, but I love him."

Joe put his thumb on the power switch, then looked at them grimly. "You know, this thing could read zilch everywhere we take it and there still might be a generator, just not one that emits alpha or beta wa—"

"*Do* it, for God's sakes!" Benny said. "The suspense is killin me."

"He's right," Norrie said. "Do it."

But here was an interesting thing. They had tested the Geiger counter plenty around Joe's house, and it worked fine—when they tried it on an old watch with a radium dial, the needle jerked appreciably. They'd each taken a turn. But now that they were out here—on-site, so to speak—Joe felt frozen. There was sweat on his forehead. He could feel it beading up and getting ready to trickle down.

He might have stood there quite awhile if Norrie hadn't put her hand over his. Then Benny added his. The three of them ended up pushing the slide-switch together. The needle in the COUNTS PER SECOND window immediately jumped to +5, and Norrie clutched Joe's shoulder. Then it settled back to +2, and she relaxed her hold. They had no experience with radiation counters, but they all guessed they were seeing no more than a background count.

Slowly, Joe walked around the bandstand with the Geiger-Müller tube held out on its coiled phone receiver-type cord. The power lamp glowed a bright amber, and the needle jiggled a little bit from time to time, but mostly it stayed close to the zero end of the dial. The little jumps they saw were probably being caused by their own movements. He wasn't surprised—part of him knew it couldn't be so easy—but at the same time, he was bitterly disappointed. It was amazing, really, how well disappointment and lack of surprise complimented each other; they were like the Olsen Twins of emotion.

"Let me," Norrie said. "Maybe I'll have better luck."

He gave it over without protest. Over the next hour or so, they crisscrossed the town common, taking turns with the Geiger counter. They saw a car turn down Mill Street, but didn't notice Junior Rennie—who was feeling better again—behind the wheel. Nor did he notice them. An ambulance sped down Town Common Hill in the direction of Food City with its lights flashing and its siren wailing. This they looked at briefly, but were again absorbed when Junior reappeared shortly after, this time behind the wheel of his father's Hummer.

They never used the Frisbee they had brought as camouflage; they were too preoccupied. Nor did it matter. Few of the townspeople heading back to their homes bothered looking into the Common. A few were hurt. Most were carrying liberated foodstuffs, and some were wheeling loaded shopping carts. Almost all looked ashamed of themselves.

By noon, Joe and his friends were ready to give up. They were also hungry. "Let's go to my house," Joe said. "My mom'll make us something to eat."

"Great," Benny said. "Hope it's chop suey. Your ma's chop suey is tight."

"Can we go through the Peace Bridge and try the other side first?" Norrie asked.

Joe shrugged. "Okay, but there's nothing over there but woods. Also, it's moving away from the center."

"Yes, but . . ." She trailed off.

"But what?"

"Nothing. Just an idea. It's probably stupid."

Joe looked at Benny. Benny shrugged and handed her the Geiger counter.

They went back to the Peace Bridge and ducked under the sagging police tape. The walkway was dim, but not too dim for Joe to look over Norrie's shoulder and see the Geiger counter's needle stir as they passed the half-way point, walking single file so as not to test the rotted boards under their feet too much. When they came out on the other side, a sign informed them YOU ARE NOW LEAVING THE CHESTER'S MILL TOWN COMMON, EST. 1808. A well-worn path led up a slope of oak, ash, and beech. Their fall foliage hung limply, looking sullen rather than gay.

By the time they reached the foot of this path, the needle in the COUNTS PER SECOND window stood between +5 and +10. Beyond +10, the meter's calibration rose steeply to +500 and then to +1000. The top end of the dial was marked in red. The needle was miles below that, but Joe was pretty sure its current position indicated more than just a background count.

Benny was looking at the faintly quivering needle, but Joe was looking at Norrie.

"What were you thinking about?" he asked her. "Don't be afraid to spill it, because it doesn't seem like such a stupid idea, after all."

"No," Benny agreed. He tapped the COUNTS PER SECOND window. The needle jumped, then settled back to +7 or 8.

"I was thinking a generator and a transmitter are practically the same thing," Norrie said. "And a transmitter doesn't have to be in the middle, just high up."

"The CIK tower isn't," Benny said. "Just sits in a clearing, pumpin out the Jesus. I've seen it."

"Yeah, but that thing's, like, super-powerful," Norrie replied. "My Dad said it's a hundred thousand watts, or something. Maybe what we're looking for has a shorter range. So then I thought, 'What's the highest part of the town?' "

"Black Ridge," Joe said.

"Black Ridge," she agreed, and held up a small fist.

Joe bumped her, then pointed. "That way, two miles. Maybe three." He turned the Geiger-Müller tube in that direction and they all watched, fascinated, as the needle rose to +10.

"I'll be fucked," Benny said.

"Maybe when you're forty," Norrie said. Tough as ever . . . but blushing. Just a little.

"There's an old orchard out on the Black Ridge Road," Joe said. "You can see the whole Mill from it—TR-90, too. That's what my dad says, anyway. It could be there. Norrie, you're a genius." He didn't have to wait for her to kiss him, after all. He did the honors, although daring no more than the corner of her mouth.

She looked pleased, but there was still a frown line between her eyes. "It might not mean anything. The needle's not exactly going crazy. Can we go out there on our bikes?"

"Sure!" Joe said.

"After lunch," Benny added. He thought of himself as the practical one.

6

While Joe, Benny, and Norrie were eating lunch at the McClatchey house (it was indeed chop suey) and Rusty

Everett, assisted by Barbie and the two teenage girls, was treating supermarket-riot casualties at Cathy Russell, Big Jim Rennie sat in his study, going over a list and checking off items.

He saw his Hummer roll back up the driveway, and checked off another item: Brenda dropped off with the others. He thought he was ready—as ready as he could be, anyway. And even if the Dome disappeared this afternoon, he thought his butt was covered.

Junior came in and dropped the Hummer's keys on Big Jim's desk. He was pale and needed a shave worse than ever, but he no longer looked like death on a cracker. His left eye was red, but not flaming.

"All set, Son?"

Junior nodded. "Are we going to jail?" He spoke with an almost disinterested curiosity.

"No," Big Jim said. The idea that he might go to jail had never crossed his mind, not even when the Perkins witch had shown up here and started making her accusations. He smiled. "But Dale Barbara is."

"No one's going to believe he killed Brenda Perkins."

Big Jim continued to smile. "They will. They're frightened, and they will. It's how these things work."

"How would you know?"

"Because I'm a student of history. You ought to try it sometime." It was on the tip of his tongue to ask Junior why he had left Bowdoin—had he quit, flunked out, or been asked to leave? But this wasn't the time or the place. Instead he asked his son if he was up to one more errand.

Junior rubbed at his temple. "I guess. In for a penny, in for a pound."

"You'll need help. You could take Frank, I suppose, but I'd prefer the Thibodeau lad, if he's able to move around today. Not Searles, though. A good fellow, but stupid."

Junior said nothing. Big Jim wondered again what was wrong with the boy. But did he really want to know? Perhaps when this crisis was over. In the meantime, he had many pots and skillets on the stove, and dinner would be served soon.

"What do you want me to do?"

"Let me check one thing first." Big Jim picked up his cell. Each time he did this, he expected to find it as useless as tits on a bull, but it was still working. At least for in-town calls, which was all he cared about. He selected PD. It rang three times at the cop-shop before Stacey Moggin picked up. She sounded harried, not at all like her usual businesslike self. Big Jim wasn't surprised by that, given the morning's festivities; he could hear quite an uproar in the background.

"Police," she said. "If this isn't an emergency, please hang up and call back later. We're awfully bus—"

"It's Jim Rennie, hon." He knew that Stacey hated being called *hon*. Which was why he did it. "Put on the Chief. Chop-chop."

"He's trying to break up a fistfight in front of the main desk right now," she said. "Maybe you could call back la—"

"No, I can't call back later," Big Jim said. "Do you think I'd be calling if this wasn't important? Just go over there, hon, and Mace the most aggressive one. Then you send Pete into his office to—"

She didn't let him finish, and she didn't put him on hold, either. The phone hit the desk with a clunk. Big Jim was not put out of countenance; when he was getting under somebody's skin, he liked to know it. In the far distance, he heard someone call someone else a thieving sonofabitch. This made him smile.

A moment later he *was* put on hold; Stacey not bother-

ing to inform him. Big Jim listened to McGruff the Crime
Dog for awhile. Then the phone was picked up. It was
Randolph, sounding out of breath.

"Talk fast, Jim, because this place is a madhouse. The
ones who didn't go to the hospital with broken ribs or
something are mad as hornets. Everybody's blaming everybody else. I'm trying to keep from filling up the cells
downstairs, but it's like half of them *want* to go there."

"Does increasing the size of the police force sound like
a better idea to you today, Chief?"

"Christ, yes. We took a beating. I've got one of the
new officers—that Roux girl—up to the hospital with
the whole lower half of her face broken. She looks like the
Bride of Frankenstein."

Big Jim's smile widened to a grin. Sam Verdreaux had
come through. But of course that was another thing about
feeling it; when you *did* have to pass the ball, on those
infrequent occasions when you couldn't shoot it yourself,
you always passed it to the right person.

"Someone nailed her with a rock. Mel Searles, too. He
was knocked out for a while, but he seems to be all right
now. It's ugly, though. I sent him to the hospital to get
patched up."

"Well, that's a shame," Big Jim said.

"Someone was targeting my officers. More than *one*
someone, I think. Big Jim, can we really get more volunteers?"

"I think you'll find plenty of willing recruits among
the upstanding young people of this town," Big Jim said.
"In fact, I know several from the Holy Redeemer congregation. The Killian boys, for instance."

"Jim, the Killian boys are dumber than Crackerjacks."

"I know, but they're strong and they'll take orders."
He paused. "Also, they can shoot."

"Are we going to arm the new police?" Randolph sounded doubtful and hopeful at the same time.

"After what happened today? Of course. I was thinking ten or a dozen good trustworthy young people to start with. Frank and Junior can help pick them out. And we'll need more if this thing isn't sorted out by next week. Pay em in scrip. Give em first dibs on supplies, when and if rationing starts. Them and their families."

"Okay. Send Junior down, will you? Frank's here, and so's Thibodeau. He got banged around some at the market and he had to get the bandage on his shoulder changed, but he's pretty much good to go." Randolph lowered his voice. "He said Barbara changed the bandage. Did a good job, too."

"That's ducky, but our Mr. Barbara won't be changing bandages for long. And I've got another job for Junior. Officer Thibodeau, too. Send him up here."

"What for?"

"If you needed to know, I'd tell you. Just send him up. Junior and Frank can make a list of possible new recruits later on."

"Well . . . if you say s—"

Randolph was interrupted by a fresh uproar. Something either fell over or was thrown. There was a crash as something else shattered.

"Break that up!" Randolph roared.

Smiling, Big Jim held the phone away from his ear. He could hear perfectly well, just the same.

"Get those two . . . not those two, you idiot, the OTHER two. . . . NO, I don't want em arrested! I want em the hell out of here! On their asses, if they won't go any other way!"

A moment later he was speaking to Big Jim again. "Remind me why I wanted this job, because I'm starting to forget."

"It'll sort itself out," Big Jim soothed. "You'll have five new bodies by tomorrow—fresh young bucks—and another five by Thursday. Another five at least. Now send young Thibodeau up here. And make sure that cell at the far end downstairs is ready for a fresh occupant. Mr. Barbara will be using it as of this afternoon."

"On what charge?"

"How about four counts of murder, plus inciting a riot at the local supermarket? Will that do?"

He hung up before Randolph could reply.

"What do you want me and Carter to do?" Junior asked.

"This afternoon? First, a little reconnaissance and planning. I'll assist with the planning. Then you take part in arresting Barbara. You'll enjoy that, I think."

"Yes I will."

"Once Barbara's in the jug, you and Officer Thibodeau should eat a good supper, because your real job's tonight."

"What?"

"Burning down the *Democrat* office—how does that sound?"

Junior's eyes widened. "Why?"

That his son had to ask was a disappointment. "Because, for the immediate future, having a newspaper is not in the town's best interest. Any objections?"

"Dad—has it ever occurred to you that you might be crazy?"

Big Jim nodded. "Like a fox," he said.

7

"All the times I've been in this room," Ginny Tomlinson said in her new foggy voice, "and I never once imagined myself on the table."

"Even if you had, you probably wouldn't have imagined being worked on by the guy who serves you your morning steak and eggs." Barbie tried to keep it light, but he'd been patching and bandaging since arriving at Cathy Russell on the ambulance's first run, and he was tired. A lot of that, he suspected, was stress: he was scared to death of making someone worse instead of better. He could see the same worry on the faces of Gina Buffalino and Harriet Bigelow, and they didn't have the Jim Rennie clock ticking in their heads to make things worse.

"I think it will be awhile before I'm capable of eating another steak," Ginny said.

Rusty had set her nose before seeing any of the other patients. Barbie had assisted, holding the sides of her head as gently as he could and murmuring encouragement. Rusty plugged her nostrils with gauze soaked in medicinal cocaine. He gave the anesthetic ten minutes to work (using the time to treat a badly sprained wrist and put an elastic bandage on an obese woman's swollen knee), then tweezed out the gauze strips and grabbed a scalpel. The PA was admirably quick. Before Barbie could tell Ginny to say *wishbone*, Rusty had slid the scalpel's handle up the clearer of her nostrils, braced it against her septum, and used it as a lever.

Like a man prying off a hubcap, Barbie had thought, listening to the small but perfectly audible crunch as Ginny's nose came back to something approximating its normal position. She didn't scream, but her fingernails tore holes in the paper covering the examination table, and tears poured down her cheeks.

She was calm now—Rusty had given her a couple of Percocets—but tears were still leaking from her less swollen eye. Her cheeks were a puffy purple. Barbie thought she looked a little like Rocky Balboa after the Apollo Creed fight.

"Look on the bright side," he said.

"Is there one?"

"Definitely. The Roux girl is looking at a month of soup and milkshakes."

"Georgia? I heard she took a hit. How bad?"

"She'll live, but it's going to be a long time before she's pretty."

"That one was never going to be Miss Apple Blossom." And, in a lower voice: "Was it her screaming?"

Barbie nodded. Georgia's yowls had filled the whole hospital, it seemed. "Rusty gave her morphine, but she didn't go down for a long time. She must have the constitution of a horse."

"And the conscience of an alligator," Ginny added in her foggy voice. "I wouldn't wish what happened to her on anybody, but it's still a damned good argument for karmic retribution. How long have I been here? My darn watch is broken."

Barbie glanced at his own. "It's now fourteen thirty. So I guess that puts you about five and a half hours on the road to recovery." He twisted at the hips, heard his back crackle, and felt it loosen up a little. He decided Tom Petty was right: the waiting was the hardest part. He reckoned he would feel easier once he was actually in a cell. Unless he was dead. It had crossed his mind that it might be convenient for him to be killed while resisting arrest.

"What are you smiling about?" she asked.

"Nothing." He held up a set of tweezers. "Now be quiet and let me do this. Soonest begun, soonest done."

"I ought to get up and pitch in."

"If you try it, the only pitching you'll do will be straight down to the floor."

She looked at the tweezers. "Do you know what you're doing with those?"

"You bet. I won a gold medal in Olympic Glass Removal."

"Your bullshit quotient is even higher than my ex-husband's." She was smiling a little. Barbie guessed it hurt her, even with painkillers on board, and he liked her for it.

"You're not going to be one of those tiresome medical people who turns into a tyrant when it's her turn for treatment, are you?" he asked.

"That was Dr. Haskell. He ran a big splinter under his thumbnail once, and when Rusty offered to take it out, The Wiz said he wanted a specialist." She laughed, then winced, then groaned.

"If it makes you feel any better, the cop who punched you took a rock in the head."

"More karma. Is he up and around?"

"Yep." Mel Searles had walked out of the hospital two hours ago with a bandage wrapped around his head.

When Barbie bent toward her with the tweezers, she instinctively turned her head away. He turned it back, pressing his hand—very gently—against the cheek that was less swollen.

"I know you have to," she said. "I'm just a baby about my eyes."

"Given how hard he hit you, you're lucky the glass is around them instead of in them."

"I know. Just don't hurt me, okay?"

"Okay," he said. "You'll be on your feet in no time, Ginny. I'll make this quick."

He wiped his hands to make sure they were dry (he hadn't wanted the gloves, didn't trust his grip in them), then bent closer. There were maybe half a dozen small splinters of broken spectacle-lens peppered in her brows and around her eyes, but the one he was worried about was a tiny dagger just below the corner of her left eye.

Barbie was sure Rusty would have taken it out himself if he'd seen it, but he had been concentrating on her nose.

Do it quick, he thought. *He who hesitates is usually fucked.*

He tweezed the shard out and dropped it into a plastic basin on the counter. A tiny seed-pearl of blood welled up where it had been. He let out his breath. "Okay. Nothing to the rest of these. Smooth sailing."

"From your lips to God's ear," Ginny said.

He had just removed the last of the splinters when Rusty opened the door of the exam room and told Barbie he could use a little help. The PA was holding a tin Sucrets box in one hand.

"Help with what?"

"A hemorrhoid that walks like a man," Rusty said. "This anal sore wants to leave with his ill-gotten gains. Under normal circumstances I'd be delighted to see his miserable backside going out the door, but right now I might be able to use him."

"Ginny?" Barbie asked. "You okay?"

She made a waving gesture at the door. He had reached it, following after Rusty, when she called, "Hey, hand-some." He turned back and she blew him a kiss.

Barbie caught it.

8

There was only one dentist in Chester's Mill. His name was Joe Boxer. His office was at the end of Strout Lane, where his dental suite offered a scenic view of Prestile Stream and the Peace Bridge. Which was nice if you were sitting up. Most visitors to said suite were in the reclin-ing position, with nothing to look at but several dozen pictures of Joe Boxer's Chihuahua pasted on the ceiling.

"In one of them, the goddam dog looks like he's un-loading," Dougie Twitchell told Rusty after one visit. "Maybe it's just the way that kind of dog sits down, but I don't think so. I think I spent half an hour looking at a dishrag with eyes take a shit while The Box dug two wisdom teeth out of my jaw. With a screwdriver, it felt like."

The shingle hung outside Dr. Boxer's office looked like a pair of basketball shorts large enough to fit a fairy-tale giant. They were painted a gaudy green and gold—the colors of the Mills Wildcats. The sign read JOSEPH BOXER, DDS. And, below that: **BOXER IS BRIEF**! And he *was* fairly speedy, everyone agreed, but he rec-ognized no medical plans and accepted only cash. If a pulpcutter walked in with his gums suppurating and his cheeks puffed out like those of a squirrel with a mouthful of nuts and started talking about his dental insurance, Boxer would tell him to get the money from Anthem or Blue Cross or whoever and then come back to see him.

A little competition in town might have forced him to soften these Draconian policies, but the half a dozen who'd tried to make a go of it in The Mill since the early nine-ties had given up. There was speculation that Joe Boxer's good friend Jim Rennie might have had something to do with the paucity of competition, but no proof. Meantime, Boxer might be seen on any given day cruising around in his Porsche, with its bumper sticker reading MY OTHER CAR IS *ALSO* A PORSCHE!

As Rusty came down the hall with Barbie trailing after, Boxer was heading for the main doors. Or trying to; Twitch had him by the arm. Hung from Dr. Boxer's other arm was a basket filled with Eggo waffles. Nothing else; just packages and packages of Eggos. Barbie won-dered—not for the first time—if maybe he was lying in the ditch that ran behind Dipper's parking lot, beaten to a pulp and having a terrible brain-damaged dream.

"I'm *not* staying!" Boxer yapped. "I have to get these home to the freezer! What you're proposing has almost no chance of working, anyway, so take your hands off me."

Barbie observed the butterfly bandage bisecting one of Boxer's eyebrows and the larger bandage on his right forearm. The dentist had fought the good fight for his frozen waffles, it seemed.

"Tell this goon to take his hands off me," he said when he saw Rusty. "I've been treated, and now I'm going home."

"Not just yet," Rusty said. "You were treated gratis, and I expect you to pay that forward."

Boxer was a little guy, no more than five-four, but he drew himself up to his full height and puffed out his chest. "Expect and be damned. I hardly see oral surgery—which the State of Maine hasn't certified me to do, by the way—as a quid pro quo for a couple of bandages. I work for a living, Everett, and I expect to be paid for my work."

"You'll be paid back in heaven," Barbie said. "Isn't that what your friend Rennie would say?"

"He has nothing to do with th—"

Barbie took a step closer and peered into Boxer's green plastic shopping basket. The words **PROPERTY OF FOOD CITY** were printed on the handle. Boxer tried, with no great success, to shield the basket from him.

"Speaking of payment, did you pay for those waffles?"

"Don't be ridiculous. Everybody was taking everything. All *I* took were these." He looked at Barbie defiantly. "I have a very large freezer, and I happen to enjoy waffles."

" 'Everyone was taking everything' won't be much of a defense if you're charged with looting," Barbie said mildly. It was impossible for Boxer to draw himself up any further, and yet somehow he did. His face was so red it was almost purple. "Then take me to court! *What* court? Case closed! Ha!"

He started to turn away again. Barbie reached out and grabbed him, not by the arm but by the basket. "I'll just confiscate this, then, shall I?"

"You can't do that!"

"No? Take me to court, then." Barbie smiled. "Oh, I forgot—*what* court?"

Dr. Boxer glared at him, lips drawn back to show the tips of tiny perfect teeth.

"We'll just toast those old waffles up in the caff," Rusty said. "Yum! Tasty!"

"Yeah, while we've still got some electricity to toast em with," Twitch muttered. "After that we can poke em on forks and cook em over the incinerator out back."

"You can't do this!"

Barbie said, "Let me be perfectly clear: unless you do whatever it is Rusty wants you to do, I have no intention of letting go your Eggos."

Chaz Bender, who had a Band-Aid on the bridge of his nose and another on the side of his neck, laughed. Not very kindly. "Pay up, Doc!" he called. "Isn't that what you always say?"

Boxer turned his glare first on Bender, then on Rusty. "What you want has almost no chance of working. You must know that."

Rusty opened the Sucrets box and held it out. Inside were six teeth. "Torie McDonald picked these up outside the supermarket. She got down on her knees and grubbed through puddles of Georgia Roux's blood to find them. And if you want to have Eggos for breakfast in the near future, Doc, you're going to put them back in Georgia's head."

"And if I just walk away?"

Chaz Bender, the history teacher, took a step forward. His fists were clenched. "In that case, my mercenary friend, I'll beat the shit out of you in the parking lot."

"I'll help," Twitch said.

"I won't help," Barbie said, "but I'll watch."

There was laughter and some applause. Barbie felt simultaneously amused and sick to his stomach.

Boxer's shoulders slumped. All at once he was just a little man caught in a situation too big for him. He took the Sucrets box, then looked at Rusty. "An oral surgeon working under optimum conditions might be able to reimplant these teeth, and they might actually root, although he would be careful to give the patient no guarantees. If I do it, she'll be lucky to get back one or two. She's more likely to pull them down her windpipe and choke on them."

A stocky woman with a lot of flaming red hair shouldered Chaz Bender aside. "I'll sit with her and make sure that doesn't happen. I'm her mother."

Dr. Boxer sighed. "Is she unconscious?"

Before he could get any further, two Chester's Mill police units, one of them the green Chief's car, pulled up in the turnaround. Freddy Denton, Junior Rennie, Frank DeLesseps, and Carter Thibodeau got out of the lead car. Chief Randolph and Jackie Wettington emerged from the Chief's car. Rusty's wife got out of the back. All were armed, and as they approached the main doors of the hospital, they drew their weapons.

The little crowd that had been watching the confrontation with Joe Boxer murmured and drew back, some in its number undoubtedly expecting to be arrested for theft.

Barbie turned to Rusty Everett. "Look at me," he said.

"What do you m—"

"Look at me!" Barbie lifted his arms, turning them to

show both sides. Then he pulled up his tee-shirt, showing first his flat stomach, then turning to exhibit his back. "Do you see marks? Bruises?"

"No—"

"Make sure *they* know that," Barbie said.

It was all he had time for. Randolph led his officers through the door. "Dale Barbara? Step forward."

Before Randolph could lift his gun and point it at him, Barbie did so. Because accidents happen. Sometimes on purpose.

Barbie saw Rusty's puzzlement, and liked him even better for his innocence. He saw Gina Buffalino and Harriet Bigelow, their eyes wide. But most of his attention was reserved for Randolph and his backups. All the faces were stony, but on Thibodeau's and DeLesseps's he saw undeniable satisfaction. For them this was all about payback for that night at Dipper's. And payback was going to be a bitch.

Rusty stepped in front of Barbie, as if to shield him.

"Don't do that," Barbie murmured.

"Rusty, *no!*" Linda cried.

"Peter?" Rusty asked. "What's this about? Barbie's been helping out, and he's been doing a damned good job."

Barbie was afraid to move the big PA aside or even touch him. He raised his arms instead, very slowly, holding his palms out.

When they saw his arms go up, Junior and Freddy Denton came at Barbie, and fast. Junior bumped Randolph on his way by, and the Beretta clutched in the Chief's fist went off. The sound was deafening in the reception area. The bullet went into the floor three inches in front of Randolph's right shoe, making a surprisingly large hole. The smell of gunpowder was immediate and startling.

Gina and Harriet screamed and bolted back down the main corridor, vaulting nimbly over Joe Boxer, who was crawling along with his head tucked and his normally neat hair hanging in his face. Brendan Ellerbee, who had been treated for a mildly dislocated jaw, kicked the dentist in the forearm as he stampeded past. The Sucrets box spun out of Boxer's hand, struck the main desk, and flew open, scattering the teeth Torie McDonald had so carefully picked up.

Junior and Freddy grabbed Rusty, who made no effort to fight them. He looked totally confused. They pushed him aside. Rusty went stumbling across the main lobby, trying to keep his feet. Linda grabbed him, and they sprawled to the floor together.

"What the fuck?" Twitch was roaring. *"What in the fuck?"*

Limping slightly, Carter Thibodeau approached Barbie, who saw what was coming but kept his hands raised. Lowering them could get him killed. And maybe not just him. Now that one gun had been fired, the chance of others going off was that much higher.

"Hello, hoss," Carter said. "Ain't you been a busy boy." He punched Barbie in the stomach.

Barbie had tensed his muscles in anticipation of the blow, but it still doubled him over. The sonofabitch was strong.

"Stop that!" Rusty roared. He still looked bewildered, but now he looked angry, as well. *"Stop that right goddam now!"*

He tried to get up, but Linda put both of her arms around him and held him down. "Don't," she said. "Don't, he's dangerous."

"What?" Rusty turned his head and stared at her with disbelief. "Are you *crazy?*"

Barbie was still holding his hands up, showing them to the cops. Doubled over as he was, it made him look like he was salaaming.

"Thibodeau," Randolph said. "Step back. That's enough."

"Put that gun away, you idiot!" Rusty shouted at Randolph. "You want to kill someone?"

Randolph gave him a brief look of dismissive contempt, then turned to Barbie. "Stand up straight, son."

Barbie did. It hurt, but he managed. He knew that if he hadn't been prepared for Thibodeau's gutpunch, he would have been curled on the floor, gasping for breath. And would Randolph have tried kicking him to his feet? Would the other cops have joined him in spite of the spectators in the hall, some of whom were now creeping back for a better view? Of course, because their blood was up. It was how these things went.

Randolph said, "I'm arresting you for the murders of Angela McCain, Dorothy Sanders, Lester A. Coggins, and Brenda Perkins."

Each name struck Barbie, but the last one hit the hardest. The last one was a fist. That sweet woman. She had forgotten to be careful. Barbie couldn't blame her—she had still been in deep grief for her husband—but he could blame himself for letting her go to Rennie. For encouraging her.

"What happened?" he asked Randolph. "What in God's name did you people do?"

"Like you don't know," Freddy Denton said.

"What kind of psycho are you?" Jackie Wettington asked. Her face was a twisted mask of loathing, her eyes small with rage.

Barbie ignored them both. He was staring into Randolph's face with his hands still raised over his head. All it would take was the smallest excuse and they'd be on him.

Even Jackie, ordinarily the pleasantest of women, might join in, although with her it would take a reason instead of just an excuse. Or perhaps not. Sometimes even good people snapped.

"A better question," he said to Randolph, "is what you let Rennie do. Because this is his mess, and you know it. His fingerprints are all over it."

"Shut up." Randolph turned to Junior. "Cuff him."

Junior reached for Barbie, but before he could so much as touch a raised wrist, Barbie put his hands behind his back and turned around. Rusty and Linda Everett were still on the floor, Linda with her arms wrapped around her husband's chest in a restraining bearhug.

"Remember," Barbie said to Rusty as the plastic cuffs went on . . . and were then tightened until they dug into the scant meat above the heels of his hands.

Rusty stood up. When Linda tried to hold him, he pushed her away and gave her a look she had never seen before. There was sternness in it, and reproach, but there was also pity. "Peter," he said, and when Randolph began to turn away, he raised his voice to a shout. "*I'm talking to you!* You look at me while I do!"

Randolph turned. His face was a stone.

"He knew you were here for him."

"Sure he did," Junior said. "He may be crazy, but he's not stupid."

Rusty took no notice of this. "He showed me his arms, his face, raised his shirt to show me his stomach and back. He's unmarked, unless he raises a bruise where Thibodeau suckerpunched him."

Carter said, "Three women? Three women and a *preacher*? He deserved it."

Rusty didn't shift his gaze from Randolph. "This is a setup."

"All due respect, Eric, not your department," Randolph said. He had holstered his sidearm. Which was a relief.

"That's right," Rusty said. "I'm a patch-em-up guy, not a cop or a lawyer. What I'm telling you is if I have occasion to look him over again while he's in your custody and he's got a lot of cuts and bruises, God help you."

"What are you gonna do, call the Civil Liberties Union?" Frank DeLesseps asked. He was white-lipped with fury. "Your friend there beat four people to death. Brenda Perkins's neck was broken. One of the girls was my fiancée, and she was sexually molested. Probably after she was dead as well as before, is the way it looks."

Most of the crowd that had scattered at the gunshot had crept back to watch, and now a soft and horrified groan arose from it.

"This is the guy you're defending? You ought to be in jail yourself!"

"Frank, shut up!" Linda said.

Rusty looked at Frank DeLesseps, the boy he had treated for chicken pox, measles, head lice picked up at summer camp, a broken wrist suffered sliding into second base, and once, when he was twelve, a particularly malicious case of poison ivy. He saw very little resemblance between that boy and this man. "And if I was locked up? Then what, Frankie? What if your mother has another gallbladder attack, like last year? Do I wait for visiting hours at the jail to treat her?"

Frank stepped forward, raising a hand to either slap or punch. Junior grabbed him. "He'll get his, don't worry. Everyone on Barbara's side will. All in good time."

"Sides?" Rusty sounded honestly bewildered. "What are you talking about, *sides*? This isn't a goddam football game."

Junior smiled as if he knew a secret.

Rusty turned to Linda. "Those are your colleagues talking. Do you like how they sound?"

For a moment she couldn't look at him. Then, with an effort, she did. "They're mad, that's all, and I don't blame them. I am, too. Four people, Eric—didn't you hear? He killed them, and he almost certainly raped at least two of the women. I helped take them out of the hearse at Bowie's. I saw the stains."

Rusty shook his head. "I just spent the morning with him, watching him help people, not hurt them."

"Let it go," Barbie said. "Stand back, big guy. It's not the ti—"

Junior poked him in the ribs. Hard. "You have the right to remain silent, assmunch."

"He did it," Linda said. She stretched out a hand to Rusty, saw he wasn't going to take it, and dropped it to her side. "They found his dog tags in Angie McCain's hand."

Rusty was speechless. He could only watch as Barbie was hustled out to the Chief's car and locked in the backseat with his hands still cuffed behind him. There was one moment when Barbie's eyes found Rusty's. Barbie shook his head. A single shake only, but hard and firm.

Then he was driven away.

There was silence in the lobby. Junior and Frank had gone with Randolph. Carter, Jackie, and Freddy Denton headed out to the other police car. Linda stood looking at her husband with pleading and anger. Then the anger disappeared. She stepped toward him, raising her arms, wanting to be held, if only for a few seconds.

"No," he said.

She stopped. "What's *wrong* with you?"

"What's wrong with *you*? Did you miss what just happened here?"

"Rusty, she was holding his *dog tags*!"

He nodded slowly. "Convenient, wouldn't you say?"

Her face, which had been both hurt and hopeful, now froze. She seemed to notice that her arms were still held out to him, and she lowered them.

"Four people," she said, "three beaten almost beyond recognition. There *are* sides, and you need to think about which one you're on."

"So do you, honey," Rusty said.

From outside, Jackie called, "Linda, come on!"

Rusty was suddenly aware he had an audience, and that many among it had voted for Jim Rennie again and again. "Just think about this, Lin. And think about who Pete Randolph works for."

"Linda!" Jackie called.

Linda Everett left with her head dropped. She didn't look back. Rusty was okay until she got into the car. Then he began to tremble. He thought if he didn't sit down soon, he might fall down.

A hand fell on his shoulder. It was Twitch. "You okay, boss?"

"Yes." As if saying so would make it so. Barbie had been hauled off to jail and he'd had his first real argument with his wife in—what?—four years? More like six. No, he wasn't okay.

"Got a question," Twitch said. "If those people were murdered, why'd they take the bodies to the Bowie Funeral Home instead of bringing them here for postmortem examination? Whose idea was that?"

Before Rusty could reply, the lights went out. The hospital generator had finally run dry.

9

After watching them polish off the last of her chop suey (which had contained the last of her hamburger), Claire motioned the three children to stand in front of her in the kitchen. She looked at them solemnly and they looked back—so young and scarily determined. Then, with a sigh, she handed Joe his backpack. Benny peered inside and saw three PB&Js, three deviled eggs, three bottles of Snapple, and half a dozen oatmeal-raisin cookies. Although still full of lunch, he brightened. "Most excellent, Mrs. McC.! You are a true—"

She paid no heed; all her attention was fixed on Joe. "I understand that this could be important, so I'm going along. I'll even drive you out there if you—"

"Don't have to, Mom," Joe said. "It's an easy ride."

"Safe, too," Norrie added. "Hardly anyone on the roads."

Claire's eyes were locked on her son's in the Mom Death-Stare. "But I need two promises. First, that you'll be home before dark . . . and I don't mean the last gasp of twilight, either, I mean while the sun is still up. Second, if you *do* find something, mark its location and then leave it *utterly* and *completely* alone. I accept that you three might be the best people to look for this whatever-it-might-be, but dealing with it is a job for adults. So do I have your word? Give it to me or I'll have to come with you as your chaperone."

Benny looked doubtful. "I've never been down Black Ridge Road, Mrs. McC., but I've been past it. I don't think your Civic would exactly be, like, up to the task."

"Then promise me or you stay right here, how's that?"

Joe promised. So did the other two. Norrie even crossed herself.

Joe started to shoulder the backpack. Claire slipped in her cell phone. "Don't lose that, mister."

"I won't, Mom." Joe was shifting from foot to foot, anxious to be gone.

"Norrie? Can I trust you to put the brakes on if these two get crazy?"

"Yes, ma'am," Norrie Calvert said, as if she hadn't dared death or disfigurement on her skateboard a thousand times just in the last year. "You sure can."

"I hope so," she said. "I hope so." Claire rubbed at her temples as if she were getting a headache.

"Awesome lunch, Mrs. McC.!" Benny said, and held up his hand. "Slap me five."

"Dear God, what am I doing?" Claire asked. Then she slapped him five.

10

Behind the chest-high front desk in the Police Department lobby, where people came to complain about such troubles as theft, vandalism, and the neighbor's ceaselessly barking dog, was the ready room. It contained desks, lockers, and a coffee station where a grouchy sign announced COFFEE AND DONUTS ARE *NOT* FREE. It was also the booking area. Here Barbie was photographed by Freddy Denton and fingerprinted by Henry Morrison while Peter Randolph and Denton stood close by with their guns drawn.

"Limp, keep em limp!" Henry shouted. This was not the man who had enjoyed talking with Barbie about the Red Sox–Yankees rivalry over lunch at Sweetbriar Rose (always a BLT with a dill pickle spear on the side). This was a fellow who looked like he'd enjoy punching Dale Barbara in the nose. Hard. "You don't roll em, I do, so keep em limp!"

Barbie thought of telling Henry it was hard to relax your hands when you were standing this close to men with guns, especially if you knew the men wouldn't mind using them. He kept his mouth shut instead, and concentrated on relaxing his hands so Henry could roll the prints. And he wasn't bad at it, not at all. Under other circumstances Barbie might have asked Henry why they were bothering, but he held his tongue on this subject, as well.

"All right," Henry said when he judged the prints clear. "Take him downstairs. I want to wash my hands. I feel dirty just touching him."

Jackie and Linda had been standing to one side. Now, as Randolph and Denton holstered their guns and grabbed Barbie's arms, the two women drew their own. They were pointed down but ready.

"I'd puke up everything you ever fed me, if I could," Henry said. "You disgust me."

"I didn't do it," Barbie said. "Think about it, Henry."

Morrison only turned away. *Thinking's in short supply around here today,* Barbie thought. Which, he was sure, was just the way Rennie liked it.

"Linda," he said. "Mrs. Everett."

"Don't talk to me." Her face was paper-pale except for dark purplish crescents beneath her eyes. They looked like bruises.

"Come on, sunshine," Freddy said, and ground a knuckle into the small of Barbie's back, just above the kidney. "Your suite awaits."

11

Joe, Benny, and Norrie rode their bikes north along Route 119. The afternoon was summer-hot, the air hazy and humid. Not a breath of breeze stirred. Crickets sang dozily in the high weeds at the sides of the road. The sky at the horizon had a yellow look that Joe first took for clouds. Then he realized it was a mixture of pollen and pollution on the surface of the Dome. Out here, Prestile Stream ran close beside the highway, and they should have heard it chuckling as it sped southeast toward Castle Rock, eager to join the mighty Androscoggin, but they heard only the crickets and a few crows cawing lackadaisically in the trees.

They passed the Deep Cut Road, and came to the Black Ridge Road about a mile farther on. It was dirt, badly potholed, and marked with two leaning, frost-heaved signs. The one on the left read 4-WHEEL DRIVE REC-OMMENDED. The one on the right added BRIDGE WEIGHT LIMIT 4 TONS LARGE TRUCKS POSTED. Both signs were riddled with bulletholes.

"I like a town where the folks take regular target prac-tice," Benny said. "Makes me feel safe from El Kliyder."

"That's Al Qaeda, nitboy," Joe said.

Benny shook his head, smiling indulgently. "I'm talking about El *Kliyder,* the terrible Mexican bandit who has relocated to western Maine in order to avoid—"

"Let's try the Geiger counter," Norrie said, dismount-ing her bike.

It was back in the carrier of Benny's High Plains Schwinn. They had nested it in a few old towels from Claire's rag-basket. Benny took it out and handed it to Joe, its yellow case the brightest thing in that hazy land-scape. Benny's smile had disappeared. "You do it. I'm too nervous."

Joe considered the Geiger counter, then handed it off to Norrie.

"Chickenshits," she said, not unkindly, and turned it

on. The needle swung immediately to +50. Joe stared at it and felt his heart suddenly bumping in his throat instead of his chest.

"Whoa!" Benny said. "We have liftoff!"

Norrie looked from the needle, which was steady (but still half a dial away from the red), to Joe. "Keep going?"

"Hell, yeah," he said.

12

There was no power shortage at the Police Department—at least not yet. A green-tiled corridor ran the length of the basement beneath fluorescents that cast a depressingly changeless light. Dawn or midnight, it was always the blare of noon down here. Chief Randolph and Freddy Denton escorted (if such a word could be used, considering the fists clamped on his upper arms) Barbie down the steps. The two women officers, guns still drawn, followed behind.

To the left was the file room. To the right were five cells, two on each side and one at the very end. The last was the smallest, with a narrow bunk all but overhanging the seatless steel toilet, and this was the one toward which they frog-marched him.

On orders from Pete Randolph—who had gotten his from Big Jim—even the worst actors in the supermarket riot had been released on their own recognizance (where were they going to go?), and all the cells were supposed to be empty. So it was a surprise when Melvin Searles came bolting from number 4, where he had been lurking. The bandage wound around his head had slipped down and he was wearing sunglasses to mask two gaudily blackening eyes. In one hand he was carrying an athletic sock with something weighting the toe: a homemade blackjack. Barbie's first, blurred impression was that he was about to be attacked by the Invisible Man.

"Bastard!" Mel shouted, and swung his cosh. Barbie ducked. It whizzed over his head, striking Freddy Denton on the shoulder. Freddy bellowed and let go of Barbie. Behind them, the women were shouting.

"Fuckin *murderer*! Who'd you pay to bust my head? Huh?" Mel swung again, and this time connected with the bicep of Barbie's left arm. That arm seemed to fall dead. Not sand in the sock, but a paperweight of some kind. Glass or metal, probably, but at least it was round. If it had had an angle, he would be bleeding.

"You fuckin fucked-up fuck!" Mel roared, and swung the loaded sock again. Chief Randolph ducked backward, also letting go of Barbie. Barbie grabbed the top of the sock, wincing as the weight inside wound the bottom around his wrist. He pulled back hard, and managed to yank Mel Searles's homemade weapon free. At the same time Mel's bandage fell down over his dark glasses like a blindfold.

"Hold it, hold it!" Jackie Wettington cried. "Stop what you're doing, prisoner, this is your only warning!"

Barbie felt a small cold circle form between his shoulder blades. He couldn't see it, but knew without looking that Jackie had drawn her sidearm. *If she shoots me, that's where the bullet will go. And she might, because in a small town where big trouble's almost a complete stranger, even the professionals are amateurs.*

He dropped the sock. Whatever was in it clunked on the lino. Then he raised his hands. "Ma'am, I have dropped it!" he called. "Ma'am, I am unarmed, please lower your weapon!"

Mel brushed the slipping bandage aside. It unrolled

down his back like the tail of a swami's turban. He hit
Barbie twice, once in the solar plexus and once in the pit
of the stomach. This time Barbie wasn't prepared, and the
air exploded out of his lungs with a harsh *PAH* sound. He
doubled over, then went to his knees. Mel hammered a fist
down on the nape of his neck—or maybe it was Freddy;
for all Barbie knew, it could have been the Fearless Leader
himself—and he went sprawling, the world growing thin
and indistinct. Except for a chip in the linoleum. That he
could see very well. With breathtaking clarity, in fact, and
why not? It was less than an inch from his eyes.

"Stop it, stop it, *stop hitting him!*" The voice was coming
from a great distance, but Barbie was pretty sure it belonged to Rusty's wife. *"He's down, don't you see he's down?"*

Feet shuffled around him in a complicated dance.
Someone stepped on his ass, stumbled, cried "Oh *fuck!*"
and then he was kicked in the hip. It was all happening far
away. It might hurt later, but right now it wasn't too bad.

Hands grabbed him and hauled him upright. Barbie
tried to raise his head, but it was easier, on the whole, just
to let it hang. He was propelled down the hall toward the
final cell, the green lino sliding between his feet. What
had Denton said upstairs? *Your suite awaits.*

But I doubt if there's pillow mints or turndown service, Barbie thought. Nor did he care. All he wanted was to be left
alone to lick his wounds.

Outside the cell someone put a shoe in his ass to hurry
him along even more. He flew forward, raising his right
arm to stop himself from crashing face-first into the green
cinderblock wall. He tried to raise his left arm as well,
but it was still dead from the elbow down. He managed
to protect his head, though, and that was good. He rebounded, staggered, then went to his knees again, this
time beside the cot, as if about to say a prayer prior to

turning in. Behind him, the cell door rumbled shut along its track.

Barbie braced his hands on the bunk and pushed himself up, the left arm working a little now. He turned around just in time to see Randolph walking away in a pugnacious strut—fists clenched, head lowered. Beyond him, Denton was unwinding what remained of Searles's bandage while Searles glared (the power of the glare somewhat vitiated by the sunglasses, now sitting askew on his nose). Beyond the male officers, at the foot of the stairs, were the women. They wore identical expressions of dismay and confusion. Linda Everett's face was paler than ever, and Barbie thought he saw the gleam of tears in her lashes.

Barbie summoned all his will and called out to her. "Officer Everett!"

She jumped a little, startled. Had anyone ever called her Officer Everett before? Perhaps schoolchildren, when she pulled crossing-guard duty, which had probably been her heaviest responsibility as a part-time cop. Up until this week.

"Officer Everett! Ma'am! Please, ma'am!"

"Shut up!" Freddy Denton said.

Barbie paid him no mind. He thought he was going to pass out, or at least gray out, but for the time being he held on grimly.

"Tell your husband to examine the bodies! Mrs. Perkins's in particular! Ma'am, he *must* examine the bodies! They won't be at the hospital! Rennie won't allow them to—"

Peter Randolph strode forward. Barbie saw what he had taken off Freddy Denton's belt and tried to raise his arms across his face, but they were just too heavy.

"That's enough out of you, son," Randolph said. He

shoved the Mace dispenser between the bars and squeezed the pistol grip.

13

Halfway over the rust-eaten Black Ridge Bridge, Norrie stopped her bike and stood looking at the far side of the cut.

"We better keep going," Joe said. "Use the daylight while we've got it."

"I know, but look," Norrie said, pointing.

On the other bank, below a steep drop and sprawled on the drying mud where the Prestile had run full before the Dome began to choke its flow, were the bodies of four deer: a buck, two does, and a yearling. All were of good size; it had been a fine summer in The Mill, and they had fed well. Joe could see clouds of flies swarming above the carcasses, could even hear their somnolent buzz. It was a sound that would have been covered by running water on an ordinary day.

"What happened to them?" Benny asked. "Do you think it has anything to do with what we're looking for?"

"If you're talking about radiation," Joe said, "I don't think it works that fast."

"Unless it's really *high* radiation," Norrie said uneasily.

Joe pointed at the Geiger counter's needle. "Maybe, but this still isn't very high. Even if it was all the way in the red, I don't think it would kill animals as big as deer in only three days."

Benny said, "That buck's got a broken leg, you can see it from here."

"I'm pretty sure one of the does has got *two*," Norrie

said. She was shading her eyes. "The front ones. See how they're bent?"

Joe thought the doe looked as if she had died while trying to do some strenuous gymnastic stunt.

"I think they jumped," Norrie said. "Jumped off the bank like those little rat-guys are supposed to."

"Lemons," Benny said.

"Lem-*mings,* birdbrain," Joe said.

"Trying to get away from something?" Norrie asked. "Is that what they were doing?"

Neither boy answered. Both looked younger than they had the week before, like children forced to listen to a campfire story that's much too scary. The three of them stood by their bikes, looking at the dead deer and listening to the somnolent hum of the flies.

"Go on?" Joe asked.

"I think we have to," Norrie said. She swung a leg over the fork of her bike and stood astride it.

"Right," Joe said, and mounted his own bike.

"Ollie," Benny said, "this is another fine mess you've gotten me into."

"Huh?"

"Never mind," Benny said. "Ride, my soul brother, ride."

On the far side of the bridge, they could see that all the deer had broken legs. One of the yearlings also had a crushed skull, probably suffered when it came down on a large boulder that would have been covered by water on an ordinary day.

"Try the Geiger counter again," Joe said.

Norrie turned it on. This time the needle danced just below +75.

14

Pete Randolph exhumed an old cassette recorder from one of Duke Perkins's desk drawers, tested it, and found the batteries still good. When Junior Rennie came in, Randolph pressed REC and set the little Sony on the corner of the desk where the young man could see it.

Junior's latest migraine was down to a dull mutter on the left side of his head, and he felt calm enough; he and his father had been over this, and Junior knew what to say.

"It'll be strictly softball," Big Jim had said. "A formality."

And so it was.

"How'd you find the bodies, son?" Randolph asked, rocking back in the swivel chair behind the desk. He had removed all of Perkins's personal items and put them in a file cabinet on the other side of the room. Now that Brenda was dead, he supposed he could dump them in the trash. Personal effects were no good when there was no next of kin.

"Well," Junior said, "I was coming back from patrol out on 117—I missed the whole supermarket thing—"

"Good luck for you," Randolph said. "That was a total cock-and-balls, if you'll pardon my fran-kays. Coffee?"

"No thanks, sir. I'm subject to migraines, and coffee seems to make them worse."

"Bad habit, anyway. Not as bad as cigarettes, but bad. Did you know I smoked until I was Saved?"

"No, sir, I sure didn't." Junior hoped this idiot would stop blathering and let him tell his story so he could get out of here.

"Yep, by Lester Coggins." Randolph splayed his hands on his chest. "Full-body immersion in the Prestile. Gave my heart to Jesus right then and there. I haven't been as faithful a churchgoer as some, certainly not as faithful as your dad, but Reverend Coggins was a good man." Randolph shook his head. "Dale Barbara's got a lot on his conscience. Always assuming he has one."

"Yes, sir."

"A lot to answer for, too. I gave him a shot of Mace, and that was just a small down payment on what he's got coming. So. You were coming back from patrol and?"

"And I got to thinking that someone told me they'd seen Angie's car in the garage. You know, the McCain garage."

"Who told you that?"

"Frank?" Junior rubbed his temple. "I think maybe it was Frank."

"Go on."

"So anyway, I looked in one of the garage windows, and her car *was* there. I went to the front door and rang the bell, but nobody answered. Then I went around to the back because I was worried. There was . . . a smell."

Randolph nodded sympathetically. "Basically, you just followed your nose. That was good police work, son."

Junior looked at Randolph sharply, wondering if this was a joke or a sly dig, but the Chief's eyes seemed to hold nothing but honest admiration. Junior realized that his father might have found an assistant (the first word actually to occur to him was *accomplice*) who was even dumber than Andy Sanders. He wouldn't have thought that possible.

"Go on, finish up. I know this is painful to you. It's painful to all of us."

"Yes, sir. Basically it's just what you said. The back door was unlocked, and I followed my nose straight to the pantry. I could hardly believe what I found there."

"Did you see the dog tags then?"

"Yes. No. Kind of. I saw Angie had *something* in her

hand . . . on a chain . . . but I couldn't tell what it was, and I didn't want to touch anything." Junior looked down modestly. "I know I'm just a rookie."

"Good call," Randolph said. "*Smart* call. You know, we'd have a whole forensic team from the State Attorney General's office in there under ordinary circumstances—really nail Barbara to the wall—but these aren't ordinary circumstances. Still, we've got enough, I'd say. He was a fool to overlook those dog tags."

"I used my cell phone and called my father. Based on all the radio chatter, I figured you'd be busy down here—"

"Busy?" Randolph rolled his eyes. "Son, you don't know the half of it. You did the right thing calling your dad. He's practically a member of the department."

"Dad grabbed two officers, Fred Denton and Jackie Wettington, and they came on over to the McCains' house. Linda Everett joined us while Freddy was photographing the crime scene. Then Stewart Bowie and his brother showed up with the funeral hack. My dad thought that was best, things being so busy at the hospital with the riot and all."

Randolph nodded. "Just right. Help the living, store the dead. Who found the dog tags?"

"Jackie. She pushed Angie's hand open with a pencil and they fell right out on the floor. Freddy took pictures of everything."

"Helpful at a trial," Randolph said. "Which we'll have to handle ourselves, if this Dome thing doesn't clear up. But we can. You know what the Bible says: With faith, we can move mountains. What time did you find the bodies, son?"

"Around noon." *After I took some time to say goodbye to my girlfriends.*

"And you called your father right away?"

"Not right away." Junior gave Randolph a frank stare. "First I had to go outside and vomit. They were beaten up so bad. I never saw anything like that in my life." He let out a long sigh, being careful to put a small tremble in it. The tape recorder probably wouldn't pick up that tremble, but Randolph would remember it. "When I was done heaving, that was when I called Dad."

"Okay, I think that's all I need." No more questions about the timeline or about his "morning patrol"; not even a request for Junior to write up a report (which was good, since writing inevitably gave him a headache these days). Randolph leaned forward to snap off the tape recorder. "Thank you, Junior. Why don't you take the rest of the day off? Go home and rest. You look beat."

"I'd like to be here when you question him, sir. Barbara."

"Well, you don't have to worry about missing that today. We're going to give him twenty-four hours to stew in his own juices. Your dad's idea, and a good one. We'll question him tomorrow afternoon or tomorrow night, and you'll be there. I give you my word. We're going to question him *vigorously*."

"Yes, sir. Good."

"None of this Miranda stuff."

"No, sir."

"And thanks to the Dome, no turning him over to the County Sheriff, either." Randolph looked at Junior keenly. "Son, this is going to be a true case of what happens in Vegas stays in Vegas."

Junior didn't know whether to say *yes, sir* or *no, sir* to that, because he had no idea what the idiot behind the desk was talking about.

Randolph held him with that keen glance a moment or two longer, as if to assure himself that they understood one another, then clapped his hands together once and stood up. "Go home, Junior. You've got to be shaken up a bit."

"Yes, sir, I am. And I think I will. Rest, that is."

"I had a pack of cigarettes in my pocket when Reverend Coggins dipped me," Randolph said in a tone of fond-hearted reminiscence. He put an arm around Junior's shoulders as they walked to the door. Junior retained his respectful, listening expression, but felt like screaming at the weight of that heavy arm. It was like wearing a meat necktie. "They were ruined, of course. And I never bought another pack. Saved from the devil's weed by the Son of God. How's that for grace?"

"Awesome," Junior managed.

"Brenda and Angie will get most of the attention, of course, and that's normal—prominent town citizen and young girl with her life ahead of her—but Reverend Coggins had his fans, too. Not to mention a large and loving congregation."

Junior could see Randolph's blunt-fingered hand from the corner of his left eye. He wondered what Randolph would do if he suddenly cocked his head around and bit it. Bit one of those fingers right off, maybe, and spat it on the floor.

"Don't forget Dodee." He had no idea why he said it, but it worked. Randolph's hand dropped from his shoulder. The man looked thunderstruck. Junior realized he *had* forgotten Dodee.

"Oh God," Randolph said. "Dodee. Has anyone called Andy and told him?"

"I don't know, sir."

"Your father will have, surely?"

"He's been awfully busy."

That was true. Big Jim was at home in his study, drafting his speech for the town meeting on Thursday night. The one that he'd give just before the townsfolk voted the Selectmen emergency governing powers for the duration of the crisis.

"I better call him," Randolph said. "But maybe I'd better pray on it first. Do you want to get kneebound with me, son?"

Junior would have sooner poured lighter fluid down his pants and set his balls on fire, but didn't say so. "Speak to God on your own, and you'll hear Him answer more clearly. That's what my dad always says."

"All right, son. That's good advice."

Before Randolph could say any more, Junior slipped first out of the office, then out of the police station. He walked home, deep in thought, mourning his lost girlfriends and wondering if he could get another. Maybe more than one.

Under the Dome, all sorts of things might be possible.

15

Pete Randolph *did* try to pray, but there was too much on his mind. Besides, the Lord helped those who helped themselves. He didn't think that was in the Bible, but it was true just the same. He called Andy Sanders's cell from the list of numbers thumbtacked to the bulletin board on the wall. He hoped for no answer, but the guy picked up on the very first ring—wasn't that always the way?

"Hello, Andy. Chief Randolph here. I've got some pretty tough news for you, my friend. Maybe you better sit down."

It was a difficult conversation. Hellacious, actually. When it was finally over, Randolph sat drumming his

fingers on his desk. He thought—again—that if Duke
Perkins were the one sitting behind this desk, he wouldn't
be entirely sorry. Maybe not sorry at all. It had turned out
to be a much harder and dirtier job than he had imagined.
The private office wasn't worth the aggravation. Even the
green Chief's car wasn't; every time he got behind the
wheel and his butt slipped into the hollow Duke's meat-
ier hindquarters had made before him, the same thought
occurred: *You're not up to this.*

Sanders was coming down here. He wanted to confront
Barbara. Randolph had tried to talk him out of it, but
halfway through his suggestion that Andy's time would
be better spent on his knees, praying for the souls of his
wife and daughter—not to mention the strength to bear
his cross—Andy had broken the connection.

Randolph sighed and punched up another number.
After two rings, Big Jim's ill-tempered voice was in his
ear. "What? *What?*"

"It's me, Jim. I know you're working and I hate to in-
terrupt you, but could you come down here? I need help."

16

The three children stood in the somehow depthless afternoon light, under a sky that now had a decided yellowish
tinge, and looked at the dead bear at the foot of the telephone pole. The pole was leaning crookedly. Four feet
up from its base, the creosoted wood was splintered and
splashed with blood. Other stuff, too. White stuff that
Joe supposed was fragments of bone. And grayish mealy
stuff that had to be brai—

He turned around, trying to control his gorge. He almost had it, too, but then Benny threw up—a big wet

yurp sound—and Norrie followed suit. Joe gave in and joined the club.

When they were under control again, Joe unslung his backpack, took out the bottles of Snapple, and handed them around. He used the first mouthful to rinse with, and spat it out. Norrie and Benny did the same. Then they drank. The sweet tea was warm, but it still felt like heaven on Joe's raw throat.

Norrie took two cautious steps toward the black, fly-buzzing heap at the foot of the phone pole. "Like the deer," she said. "Poor guy didn't have any riverbank to jump over, so he beat his brains out on a phone-pole."

"Maybe it had rabies," Benny said in a thin voice. "Maybe the deer did, too."

Joe guessed that was a technical possibility, but he didn't believe it. "I've been thinking about this suicide thing." He hated the tremble he heard in his voice, but couldn't seem to do anything about it. "Whales and dolphins do it—they beach themselves, I've seen it on TV. And my dad says octopuses do it."

"Pi," Norrie said. "Octopi."

"Whatever. My dad said when their environment gets polluted, they eat off their own tentacles."

"Dude, do you want me to throw up again?" Benny asked. He sounded querulous and tired.

"Is that what's going on here?" Norrie asked. "The environment's polluted?"

Joe glanced up at the yellowish sky. Then he pointed southwest, where a hanging black residue from the fire started by the missile strike discolored the air. The smutch looked to be two or three hundred feet high and a mile across. Maybe more.

"Yes," she said, "but that's different. Isn't it?"

Joe shrugged.

"If we're gonna feel a sudden urge to kill ourselves, maybe we should go back," Benny said. "I got a lot to live for. I still haven't been able to beat *Warhammer*."

"Try the Geiger counter on the bear," Norrie said.

Joe held the sensor tube out toward the bear's carcass. The needle didn't drop, but it didn't rise, either.

Norrie pointed east. Ahead of them, the road emerged from the thick band of black oak that gave the ridge its name. Once they were out of the trees, Joe thought they'd be able to see the apple orchard at the top.

"Let's at least keep going until we're out of the trees," she said. "We'll take a reading from there, and if it's still going up, we'll head back to town and tell Dr. Everett or that guy Barbara or both of them. Let them figure it out."

Benny looked doubtful. "I don't know."

"If we feel anything weird, we'll turn back right away," Joe said.

"If it might help, we should do it," Norrie said. "I want to get out of The Mill before I go completely stir-crazy."

She smiled to show this was a joke, but it didn't *sound* like a joke, and Joe didn't take it as one. Lots of people kidded about what a small burg The Mill was—it was probably why the James McMurtry song had been so popular—and it was, intellectually speaking, he supposed. Demographically, too. He could think of only one Asian American—Pamela Chen, who sometimes helped Lissa Jamieson out at the library—and there were no black people at all since the Laverty family had moved to Auburn. There was no McDonald's, let alone a Starbucks, and the movie theater was closed down. But until now it had always felt geographically big to him, with plenty of room to roam. It was amazing how much it shrank in his mind once he realized that he and his mom and dad couldn't just pile into the family car and drive to

Lewiston for fried clams and ice cream at Yoder's. Also, the town had plenty of resources, but they wouldn't last forever.

"You're right," he said. "It's important. Worth the risk. At least I think so. You can stay here if you want to, Benny. This part of the mission is strictly volunteer."

"No, I'm in," Benny said. "If I let you guys go without me, you'd rank me to the dogs and back."

"You're already there!" Joe and Norrie yelled in unison, then looked at each other and laughed.

17

"That's right, *cry*!"

The voice was coming from far away. Barbie struggled toward it, but it was hard to open his burning eyes.

"You've got a lot to cry *about*!"

The person making these declarations sounded like he was crying himself. And the voice was familiar. Barbie tried to see, but his lids felt swollen and heavy. The eyes beneath were pulsing with his heartbeat. His sinuses were so full his ears crackled when he swallowed.

"Why did you kill her? Why did you kill my baby?"

Some sonofabitch Maced me. Denton? No, Randolph.

Barbie managed to open his eyes by placing the heels of his hands over his eyebrows and shoving upward. He saw Andy Sanders standing outside the cell with tears rolling down his cheeks. And what was Sanders seeing? A guy in a cell, and a guy in a cell always looked guilty.

Sanders screamed, *"She was all I had!"*

Randolph stood behind him, looking embarrassed and shuffling like a kid twenty minutes overdue for a bathroom pass. Even with his eyes burning and his sinuses pounding, Barbie wasn't surprised that Randolph had let Sanders come down here. Not because Sanders was the town's First Selectman, but because Peter Randolph found it almost impossible to say no.

"Now, Andy," Randolph said. "That's enough. You wanted to see him and I let you, even though it was against my better judgment. He's jugged good and proper, and he'll pay the price for what he did. So now come on upstairs and I'll pour you a cup of—"

Andy grabbed the front of Randolph's uniform. He was four inches shorter, but Randolph still looked scared. Barbie didn't blame him. He was viewing the world through a deep red film, but he could see Andy Sanders's fury clearly enough.

"Give me your gun! A trial's too good for him! He's apt to get off, anyway! He's got friends in high places, Jim says so! I want some satisfaction! I *deserve* some satisfaction, *so give me your gun!*"

Barbie didn't think Randolph's desire to please would go so far as handing over his weapon so that Andy could shoot him in this cell like a rat in a rainbarrel, but he wasn't entirely sure; there might be a reason other than the craven need to please that had caused Randolph to bring Sanders down here, and to bring him down alone.

He struggled to his feet. "Mr. Sanders." Some of the Mace had gotten into his mouth. His tongue and throat were swollen, his voice an unconvincing nasal croak. "I did not kill your daughter, sir. I did not kill anyone. If you think about this you'll see that your friend Rennie needs a scapegoat and I'm the most convenient—"

But Andy was in no shape to think about anything. He dropped his hands to Randolph's holster and began clawing at the Glock there. Alarmed, Randolph struggled to keep it where it was.

At that moment, a large-bellied figure descended the stairs, moving gracefully despite his bulk.

"Andy!" Big Jim boomed. "Andy, pal—come here!"

He opened his arms. Andy stopped struggling for the gun and rushed to him like a weeping child to the arms of his father. And Big Jim enfolded him.

"I want a gun!" Andy babbled, lifting his tear-streaked, snot-creamy face to Big Jim's. "Get me a gun, Jim! Now! Right now! I want to shoot him for what he did! It's my right as a father! He killed my baby girl!"

"Maybe not just her," Big Jim said. "Maybe not just Angie, Lester, and poor Brenda, either."

This halted the verbal flood. Andy stared up into Big Jim's slab of a face, dumbfounded. Fascinated.

"Maybe your wife, too. Duke. Myra Evans. All the others."

"Wha . . ."

"Somebody's responsible for the Dome, pal—am I right?"

"Ye . . ." Andy was capable of no more, but Big Jim nodded benignly.

"And it seems to me that the people who did it had to have at least one inside man. Someone to stir the pot. And who's better at pot-stirring than a short-order cook?" He put an arm around Andy's shoulder and led him to Chief Randolph. Big Jim glanced back at Barbie's red and swollen face as if looking at some species of bug. "We'll find proof. I have no doubt of it. He's already demonstrated he's not smart enough to cover his tracks."

Barbie fixed his attention on Randolph. "This is a setup," he said in his nasal foghorning voice. "It might have started just because Rennie needed to cover his ass, but now it's just a naked power-grab. You may not be expendable yet, Chief, but when you are, you'll go, too."

"Shut up," Randolph said.

Rennie was stroking Andy's hair. Barbie thought of his mother and how she used to stroke their cocker spaniel, Missy, when Missy got old and stupid and incontinent. "He'll pay the price, Andy—you have my word on that. But first we're going to get all the details: the what, the when, the why, and who else was involved. Because he's not in it alone, you can bet your rooty-toot on that. He's got accomplices. He'll pay the price, but first we're going to wring him dry of information."

"What price?" Andy asked. He was looking up at Big Jim almost rapturously now. "What price will he pay?"

"Well, if he knows how to lift the Dome—and I wouldn't put it past him—I guess we'll have to be satisfied with seeing him in Shawshank. Life without parole."

"Not good enough," Andy whispered.

Rennie was still stroking Andy's head. "If the Dome doesn't let go?" He smiled. "In that case, we'll have to try him ourselves. And when we find him guilty, we'll execute him. Do you like that better?"

"Much," Andy whispered.

"So do I, pal."

Stroking. Stroking.

"So do I."

18

They came out of the woods three abreast and stopped, looking up at the orchard.

"There's something up there!" Benny said. "I see it!" His voice sounded excited, but to Joe it also sounded strangely far away.

"So do I," Norrie said. "It looks like a . . . a . . ." *Radio beacon* were the words she wanted to say, but she never got them out. She managed only an *rrr-rrr-rrr* sound, like a toddler playing trucks in a sandpile. Then she fell off her bike and lay on the road with her arms and legs jerking.

"Norrie?" Joe looked down at her—more with bemusement than alarm—then up at Benny. Their eyes met for just a moment and then Benny also toppled, pulling his bike over on top of him. He began to thrash, kicking the High Plains off to one side. The Geiger counter flew into the ditch dial-side down.

Joe tottered toward it and reached out an arm that seemed to stretch like rubber. He turned the yellow box over. The needle had jumped to +200, just below the red danger zone. He saw this, then fell into a black hole full of orange flames. He thought they were coming from a huge heap of pumpkins—a funeral pyre of blazing jack-o-lanterns. Somewhere voices were calling: lost and terrified. Then the darkness swallowed him.

19

When Julia came into the *Democrat* office after leaving the supermarket, Tony Guay, the former sports reporter who was now the entire news department, was typing on his laptop. She handed him the camera and said, "Stop what you're doing and print these."

She sat down at her computer to write her story. She'd been holding the open in her head all the way up Main Street: *Ernie Calvert, the former manager of Food City, called for people to come in the back. He said he had opened the doors for them. But by then it was too late. The riot was on.* It was a good lead. The problem was, she couldn't write it. She kept hitting all the wrong keys.

"Go upstairs and lie down," Tony said.

"No, I have to write—"

"You're not going to write anything like you are. You're shaking like a leaf. It's shock. Lie down for an hour. I'll print the pictures and send them to your computer desktop. Transcribe your notes, too. Go on up."

She didn't like what he was saying, but recognized the wisdom of it. Only it turned out to be more than an hour. She hadn't slept well since Friday night, which seemed a century ago, and she had no more than put her head on the pillow before she fell into a deep sleep.

When she woke up, she saw with panic that the shadows in her bedroom had grown long. It was late afternoon. And Horace! He would've wet in some corner and would give her his most shamefaced look, as though it were his fault instead of hers.

She slipped on her sneakers, hurried into the kitchen, and found her Corgi not by the door, whining to go out, but peacefully asleep on his blanket bed between the stove and the refrigerator. There was a note on the kitchen table, propped up against the salt and pepper shakers.

3 PM

Julia—

Pete F. and I collaborated on the supermarket story. It ain't great, but will be when you put your stamp on it. The pix you got aren't bad, either. Rommie Burpee came by & says he still has plenty of paper, so we're OK on that score. Also says you need to write an editorial about what happened. "Totally unnecessary," he said. "And totally incompetent. Unless they <u>wanted</u> it to happen. I wouldn't put it past that guy, and I don't mean Randolph." Pete and I agree that there should be an editorial, but we need to watch our step until all the facts are known. We also

agreed that you needed some sleep in order to write it the
way it needs to be written. Those were suitcases under your
eyes, boss! I'm going home to spend some time with my wife
& kids. Pete's gone to the PD. Says "something big" has
happened, and he wants to find out what.

Tony G.

PS! I walked Horace. He did all his business.

Julia, not wanting Horace to forget she was a part of
his life, woke him up long enough for him to gobble half
a Beggin' Strip, then went downstairs to punch up the
news story and write the editorial Tony and Pete were
suggesting. Just as she was starting, her cell rang.

"Shumway, *Democrat*."

"Julia!" It was Pete Freeman. "I think you better get
down here. Marty Arsenault's on the desk and he won't
let me in. Told me to wait out-goddam-side! He's no cop,
just a dumb pulp-jockey who picks up a little side-money
directing traffic in the summertime, but now he's acting
like Chief Big Dick of Horny Mountain."

"Pete, I've got a ton of stuff to do here, so unless—"

"Brenda Perkins is dead. So are Angie McCain, Dodee
Sanders—"

"What?" She stood up so suddenly her chair tipped
over.

"—and Lester Coggins. They were killed. And get
this—Dale Barbara's been arrested for the murders. He's
in jail downstairs."

"I'll be right there."

"Ahh, fuck," Pete said. "Here comes Andy Sanders,
and he's cryin his goddam eyes out. Should I try for a
comment, or—"

"Not if the man lost his daughter three days after losing his wife. We're not the *New York Post*. I'll be right there."

She broke the connection without waiting for a reply. Initially she felt calm enough; she even remembered to lock up the office. But once she was on the sidewalk, in the heat and under that tobacco-stained sky, her calm broke and she began to run.

20

Joe, Norrie, and Benny lay twitching on the Black Ridge Road in sunlight that was too diffuse. Heat that was too hot blared down on them. A crow, not in the least suicidal, landed on a telephone wire and gazed at them with bright, intelligent eyes. It cawed once, then flapped away through the strange afternoon air.

"Halloween," Joe muttered.

"Make them stop *screaming,*" Benny groaned.

"No sun," Norrie said. Her hands groped at the air. She was crying. "No sun, oh my God, there's no more sun."

At the top of Black Ridge, in the apple orchard that overlooked all of Chester's Mill, a brilliant mauve light flashed.

Every fifteen seconds, it flashed again.

21

Julia hurried up the police station steps, her face still puffy from sleep, her hair standing up in back. When Pete made to fall in beside her, she shook her head. "Better stay here. I may call you in when I get the interview."

"Love the positive thinking, but don't hold your

breath," Pete said. "Not long after Andy showed up, guess who?" He pointed at the Hummer parked in front of a fire hydrant. Linda Everett and Jackie Wettington were standing near it, deep in conversation. Both women looked seriously freaked out.

Inside the station, Julia was first struck by how warm it was—the air-conditioning had been turned off, presumably to save juice. Next, by the number of young men who were sitting around, including two of the God-knew-how-many Killian brothers—there was no mistaking those long beaks and bullet heads. The young men all seemed to be filling out forms. "What if you didn't *have* no last place of employment?" one asked another.

There was tearful shouting from downstairs: Andy Sanders.

Julia headed toward the ready room, where she had been a frequent visitor over the years, even a contributor to the coffee-and-donuts fund (a wicker basket). She had never been stopped before, but this time Marty Arsenault said, "You can't go back there, Miz Shumway. Orders." He spoke in an apologetic, conciliatory voice he probably had not used with Pete Freeman.

Just then Big Jim Rennie and Andy Sanders came up the stairs from what Mill PD officers called the Chicken Coop. Andy was crying. Big Jim had an arm around him and was speaking soothingly. Peter Randolph came behind them. Randolph's uniform was resplendent, but the face above it was that of a man who has barely escaped a bomb-blast.

"Jim! Pete!" Julia called. "I want to talk to you, for the *Democrat*!"

Big Jim turned around long enough to give her a glance that said people in hell wanted icewater, too. Then he began leading Andy toward the Chief's office. Rennie was talking about praying.

Julia tried to bolt past the desk. Still looking apologetic, Marty grabbed her arm.

She said, "When you asked me to keep that little altercation with your wife last year out of the paper, Marty, I did. Because you would have lost your job otherwise. So if you've got an ounce of gratitude in you, *let me go.*"

Marty let her go. "I tried to stop you but you wouldn't listen," he muttered. "Remember that."

Julia trotted across the ready room. "Just a damn minute," she said to Big Jim. "You and Chief Randolph are town officials, and you're going to talk to me."

This time the look Big Jim gave her was angry as well as contemptuous. "No. We're not. You have no business back here."

"But he does?" she asked, and nodded to Andy Sanders. "If what I'm hearing about Dodee is right, he's the *last* person who should have been allowed downstairs."

"That sonofabitch killed my precious girl!" Andy bawled.

Big Jim jabbed a finger at Julia. "You'll get the story when we're ready to give it out. Not before."

"I want to see Barbara."

"He's under arrest for four murders. Are you insane?"

"If the father of one of his supposed victims can get downstairs to see him, why not me?"

"Because you're neither a victim nor a next of kin," Big Jim said. His upper lip rose, exposing his teeth.

"Does he have a lawyer?"

"I'm done talking to you, wom—"

"He doesn't need a lawyer, he needs to be hung! HE KILLED MY PRECIOUS GIRL!"

"Come on, pal," Big Jim said. "We'll take it to the Lord in prayer."

"What kind of evidence do you have? Has he confessed? If he hasn't, what kind of alibi has he offered?

How does it match up with the times of death? Do you even know the times of death? If the bodies were just discovered, how can you? Were they shot, or stabbed, or—"

"Pete, get rid of this rhymes-with-witch," Big Jim said without turning around. "If she won't go on her own, throw her out. And tell whoever's on the desk that he's fired."

Marty Arsenault winced and passed a hand over his eyes. Big Jim escorted Andy into the Chief's office and closed the door.

"Is he charged?" Julia asked Randolph. "You can't charge him without a lawyer, you know. It isn't legal."

And although he still didn't look dangerous, only stunned, Pete Randolph said something that chilled her heart. "Until the Dome goes away, Julia, I guess legal is whatever we decide it is."

"When were they killed? Tell me that much, anyhow."

"Well, it looks like the two girls were fir—"

The office door opened, and she had no doubt at all that Big Jim had been standing on the other side, listening. Andy was sitting behind what was now Randolph's desk with his face in his hands.

"Get her *out*!" Big Jim snarled. "I don't want to have to tell you again."

"You can't hold him incommunicado, and you can't deny information to the people of this town!" Julia shouted.

"You're wrong on both counts," Big Jim said. "Have you ever heard that saying, 'If you're not part of the solution, you're part of the problem'? Well, you're not solving anything by being here. You're a tiresome noseyparker. You always were. And if you don't leave, you're going to be arrested. Fair warning."

"Fine! Arrest me! Stick me in a cell downstairs!" She

held out her hands with the wrists together, as if for hand-cuffs.

For one moment, she thought Jim Rennie was going to hit her. The desire to do so was clear on his face. Instead, he spoke to Pete Randolph. "For the last time, get this noseyparker out of here. If she resists, *throw* her out." And he slammed the door.

Not meeting her eyes and with his cheeks the color of freshly fired brick, Randolph took her arm. This time, Julia went. As she passed the duty desk, Marty Arsenault said—more in disconsolation than anger—"Now look. I lost my job to one of *these* thuds, who don't know their asses from their elbows."

"You won't lose your job, Marts," Randolph said. "I can talk him around."

A moment later, she was outside, blinking in the sun-light.

"So," Pete Freeman said. "How'd *that* go?"

22

Benny was the first to come out of it. And aside from being hot—his shirt was stuck to his less-than-heroic chest—he felt okay. He crawled to Norrie and shook her. She opened her eyes and looked at him, dazed. Her hair was clumped to her sweaty cheeks.

"What happened?" she asked. "I must have fallen asleep. I had a dream, only I can't remember what it was. It was bad, though. I know that."

Joe McClatchey rolled over and pushed himself to his knees.

"Jo-Jo?" Benny asked. He hadn't called his friend Jo-Jo since fourth grade. "You okay?"

"Yeah. The pumpkins were on fire."

"*What* pumpkins?"

Joe shook his head. He couldn't remember. All he knew was that he wanted to grab some shade and drink the rest of his Snapple. Then he thought of the Geiger counter. He fished it out of the ditch and saw with relief that it was still working—they'd built things tough in the twentieth century, it seemed.

He showed Benny the +200 reading, and tried to show Norrie, but she was looking up the slope of Black Ridge to the orchard at the top.

"What's that?" she asked, and pointed.

Joe initially saw nothing. Then a bright purple light flashed out. It was almost too bright to look at. Shortly thereafter, it flashed again. He looked down at his watch, wanting to time the flashes, but his watch had stopped at 4:02.

"I think it's what we were looking for," he said, getting to his feet. He expected his legs to feel rubbery, but they didn't. Except for being too hot, he felt pretty much okay. "Now let's get the hell out of here before it makes us sterile, or something."

"Dude," Benny said. "Who wants kids? They might turn out like me." Nevertheless, he mounted his bike.

They rode back the way they came, not stopping to rest and drink until they were over the bridge and back to Route 119.